VIA Folios 150

Fake Italian

·FAKE· ITALIAN

AN 83% TRUE AUTOBIOGRAPHY WITH PSEUDONYMS AND SOME TALL TALES

Marc DiPaolo

BORDIGHERA PRESS

Library of Congress Cataloging-in-Publication Data

Names: Di Paolo, Marc, author.
Title: *Fake Italian: an 83% true autobiography with pseudonyms and some tall tales* / Marc DiPaolo.
Description: New York, NY : Bordighera Press, 2021. | Series: VIA folios; 150 | Summary: "New York, 1987: In a city torn apart by racial tension, Damien Cavalieri is an adolescent without a tribe. His mother-who pines for the 1950s Brooklyn Italian community she grew up in-fears he lacks commitment to his heritage. Damien's fellow Staten Islanders agree, dubbing him a "fake Italian" and bullying him for being artistic. Complicating matters, his efforts to make friends and date girls outside of the Italian community are thwarted time and again by circumstances beyond his control. When a tragic accident shakes Damien to his core, he begins a journey of self-discovery that will lead him to Italy, where he will learn, once and for all, who he really is"-- Provided by publisher.

Identifiers: LCCN 2020050102 | ISBN 9781599541617 (trade paperback)
Subjects: LCSH: Italian Americans--Fiction. | New York (N.Y.)--Fiction. | GSAFD: Autobiographical fiction.
Classification: LCC PS3604.I1166 F35 2021 | DDC 813/.6--dc23
LC record available at https://lccn.loc.gov/2020050102

Printed in the United States.

Published by
BORDIGHERA PRESS
John D. Calandra Italian American Institute
25 W. 43rd Street, 17th Floor
New York, NY 10036

TABLE OF CONTENTS

For Lynda Barry,
who empathized with me when I told her I saw myself as a "fake" ethnic
American and encouraged me to turn that pain into art . . .

for Elena Ferrante, Ralph Ellison, and Jane Austen,
who wrote the coming-of-age stories that moved and inspired me the most . . .

. . . and for all the family and friends who have
laughed with me, cried for me,
and made my life worth living.

Why is it that I want to write? . . . [P]erhaps I'll actually experience some relief from the process of writing it all down. Today, for example, I'm particularly oppressed by an old memory from my distant past. It came to me vividly several days ago, and since then it's stayed with me, like an annoying musical motif that doesn't want to leave you alone. And yet you must get rid of it. I have hundreds of such memories; but at times a single one emerges from those hundreds and oppresses me. For some reason I believe if I write it down I can get rid of it. Why not try?

FYODOR DOSTOEVSKY

If you want to tell people the truth,
you'd better make them laugh or they'll kill you.

GEORGE BERNARD SHAW

Please do not understand me too quickly.

ANDRÉ GIDE

PREFACE

Even though it is based on actual events in my life, this biomythography and pseudo-picaresque novel should be read as a constructed reality populated by invented characters. And yet, I am telling *a* truth in these pages about my Italian American cultural experience growing up in the 1980s and 1990s. Also, it would be wise for me to advise those who prefer reading about moral exemplar protagonists operating in a world better than our own to turn back now. This book accurately portrays hate speech; reactionary political and religious beliefs, and physical, sexual, and psychological violence. That I leaven the book with humor might well make it an even less palatable read for some, because one person's insightful political satire is another's exercise in poor taste. All this begs the question: Why would I linger upon depictions of evil, when it has been the effort of so many of the heroes of our time to redress all that is reprehensible in our culture? Hopefully, in depicting certain forms of evil, I have not inadvertently romanticized or advocated for everything that I am trying to oppose in the writing of this book. I am forever frustrated that Oliver Stone wanted to bury Gordon Gekko, not praise him, and yet *Wall Street* is the favorite film of many business majors *for all the wrong reasons*. Ultimately, I believe in wisdom, compassion, and rebirth, all of which are impossible to strive for without a willingness to face reality and wrestle with difficult truths.

I began work on this project because I have come upon middle age during a trying period in American history. Indeed, I write these words quarantined in my house during the Covid-19 outbreak and the George Floyd protests of the summer of 2020. Had I written it in under different circumstances, this may have been a very different book. I feel as if America has reached a crossroads, as has my own life. I do not pretend to have any answers, but I am in a reflective mood, looking back on my personal history, struggling to understand myself and my country.

As one of my favorite authors wrote:

Midway along the journey of our life

I woke to find myself in a dark wood,
for I had wandered off from the straight path.

How hard it is to tell what it was like,
this wood of wilderness, savage and stubborn
(the thought of it brings back all my old fears),

a bitter place! Death could scarce be bitterer.
But if I would show the good that came of it
I must talk about things other than the good.

MARC DiPAOLO
July 4, 2020

PART I: SEPARATION ANXIETY

CHAPTER ONE
Two Kinds of Italians

Staten Island, September 8, 1987.

7:12 a.m.

"Yo, Damien Cavalieri!" Tony yelled. "What are you doin'? Reading a fuckin' book?"

It was the first day of sixth grade. Tony Nocerino and I were making our maiden voyage to a new institution — Intermediate School 420: The Robert Loggia School — on a classic yellow school bus. Standing in the aisle, Tony leaned against the pine green seat in front of me, staring disdainfully down at my copy of Peter Benchley's *Jaws*. Seated, I looked up at him with irritation, wondering if I could telepathically command him to go away. My fellow eleven-year-old, olive-skinned southern Italian could easily have been my cousin, and yet, the conspicuous difference between our outfits overshadowed our shared ethnicity. I was a nerdy pre-teen in inexpensive dress clothes: a gray, pin-striped suit, purple dress shirt, purple tie, and black leather shoes. Tony was a neighborhood jock in designer athletic wear: a black-and-white tank top, black Z. Cavaricci pants, white Reebok high-tops, and a gold necklace with a Christ head pendant. Mom had paid less for my entire dress ensemble than what Tony's electrician dad had laid out for his sneakers alone. Having grown up poor in a Brooklyn tenement, Mom lived well below her means even after educating herself into the lower-middle-class and becoming a tenured college composition instructor. Only my cousin's wedding prodded Mom to buy me a nice suit from London Fog instead of contenting herself with getting something from one of her usual haunts: K-Mart or Ross Dress for Less. The nicest clothes I owned, this suit was definitely the perfect outfit to wear on my first day at a new school. Or so I thought.

When I had boarded the school bus at seven a.m., I quietly chose a seat in a middle row. Tony and his crew of eight raucous Italian American boys sauntered in last, whooping, hollering, and slapping each other five. They filled out the back seats and immediately started blasting Andrew Dice Clay's dirty nursery rhyme "Hickory Dickory Dock" from a silver boom box, guffawing at every filthy punchline.

When Tony caught my eye and waved at me to join his posse, I demurred. "Thanks, man," I said. "I'm good here." That was rude, but I couldn't help it. My unreliable, ambivert temperament leaned heavily towards introverted today. Crass and operatically misogynist, the Andrew Dice Clay cassette wasn't encouraging me to join Tony's group, either. Also, these nine neighborhood toughs who lived one block over from me had always made me uncomfortable. Though we were all eleven, they had moved on to covering the neighborhood in shaving cream and eggs on Halloween three years ago. I remained a guileless trick-or-treater. Two of our memorable interactions involved them covering my body with welts by bombarding me with a tightly packed balls of snow and slush three winters back, and their snatching the Decepticon Soundwave out of my hands and fleeing for the hills eighteen months ago. Since these unkind goofballs were the only Italians I knew who were not blood relations, they made me feel alienated from my own people. I wanted to feel ethnic solidarity with them but did not on any level. Ultimately, we were connected only by a mutual love of cold cuts and shared attraction to fellow Staten Islander Alyssa Milano from *Who's the Boss?*

I closed my *Jaws* paperback and looked up. Tony was madder than ever at me for twice failing to join his band of Merry Men. *How do I placate him? Aha!* "I dig sitting up here with the cute Thai girls, Tony." I glimpsed Tuesday Phapant scowling in her seat across the aisle out of the corner of my eye. She turned her red beret and green wool pea coat on me, clutching her black schoolbag to her chest. The bag had a volleyball-sized Donnie Wahlberg pin stuck to it.

Tony snorted at my attempt to change the subject. "Every time I bike past your block, you're readin' outside. Was it some girl book last week?"

"*Anne of Avonlea.*"

"Yeah! That's it! How faggy are you, readin' that?"

"I saw the *WonderWorks* TV show and wanted to pump Megan Follows, so I thought I'd read the book." This was my lame attempt to speak the language of the Staten Island philistine.

Tony was unmoved. "Buy her *Playboy* instead of readin' a book wit' no pictures!"

Dammit. I had taken liberties with Megan Follows by discussing her in gutter terms and betrayed my cousin Gabriel, who I suspected was gay, by being quick to deny "effeminacy." Even if Gabriel were not gay, I had betrayed my favorite singer, Elton John. Since Tony was still glowering at me, I had thrown Megan and Elton under the yellow school bus for nothing. "But if I ever meet her in person, I can tell her I read her book and sweep her off her feet!" I smiled crookedly, hoping to come off "evil" to Tony. Did my curly hair and arched, satanic eyebrows give me a "Joker" appearance? No. I flatter myself. My head is too round and mouth too small for me to resemble the pointy-chinned, grotesquely grinning Batman villain. Still, I remained hopeful my gray suit and purple shirt were at least Joker-esque.

Tony shook his head at today's book. "Now you're into *Jaws*? Just watch da movie!"

"That movie is *the most awesome movie ever*, so I'm reading the book." I owned the movie on video disk, the soundtrack on vinyl, an "Amity Means Friendship" t-shirt, a set of trading cards, and an official game where the object was to hook human bones and other detritus out of a plastic Great White's mouth before it snapped shut on you. Thanks to my love of the shark, the film, Roy Scheider's heroic Police Chief Martin Brody, and Richard Dreyfus' marine biologist Matt Hooper, I wanted to grow up to be a marine biologist. At nine, I informed my parents of my intention to spend my life in a shark cage observing my favorite animals: manta rays, seahorses, and hammerhead sharks. My backup career plan involving riding Aquaman's giant seahorse across the world's oceans, because how cool was that dang seahorse? I had been a mere seven-years-old when I wandered away from my parents in the department store Korvettes. Since I couldn't find them, I strode up to the front entrance customer service desk and told a woman nursing a migraine I was lost. My parents were relieved and confused when, a few frantic minutes after misplacing me, they heard her voice over the intercom: "Will the parents of a Chief Martin Brody come to customer service?" Relieved, not angry, my parents retrieved me. They waited until we got to the car to ask why I hadn't told the lady my real name. "That's boring!" I declared. "*Anyone else* would do that. Besides, *Chief Brody is awesome!"* I did not tell Tony this Korvettes story. He was unworthy of this long-cherished family anecdote.

"Readin' is for homework!" Tony yelled. "Who reads for fun?"

"It isn't like I'm reading a calculus textbook to unwind," I groused. "*Jaws* is about *a shark that eats people!* The book is very different. First off, Mayor Vaughn owes the Mafia a ton of money he borrowed to develop Amity real estate. If he closes the beaches, he goes bankrupt. They'll shoot him. He flees town at the end. Might not make it. And Mrs. Brody and Hooper have crazy sex. Didja know vaginas can get wet, open, and soak car passenger seats? I didn't!"

"Just watch the film!"

"Unless you're seeing a version I haven't, there's no wet vaginas in the movie! Okay, sure, the shark is barely in the book, and that makes it boring sometimes. Still, the real villains are Mayor Vaughn, the local business owners, the Mafia, and something called 'the economy.' According to 'the economy,' you gotta leave the beaches open, no matter what — even if the shark eats lots of women and children. God orders the shark to keep killing tourists, and not go away like Hooper expects, to punish the townspeople for worshipping money. And you know the 'bigger boat' scene? In the book, the shark could have taken Brody's head off when it popped up out of the water. Instead, it floats there, grinning at him, like, 'You can't win! I work for God.' Also, the shark 'knows' that Brody wants to close the beaches, so it spares him. Wild."

Tony made his hands imitate me talking. "You talk too much. Yap, yap, yap."

I waved Tony away. "I give up. If Mrs. Brody's wet, open vagina didn't interest you, I don't know why I wasted my time telling you the shark works for God."

The Italians in the back flipped the cassette over in their tape deck and hit play on the ghetto blaster for a second dose of the Diceman's nursery rhymes. One guy with spiked blonde Billy Idol hair met my eyes and flicked his chin at me. Changing subjects with the flipped cassette, Tony pointed at my brass Timex wristwatch, complete with imitation leather band and Roman numerals on its face. "What's with that watch? Why ain't it digital?"

"Digital is ugly, man," I scoffed. "I like pretty shit." *If this watch annoys him, I hope he never sees my brass pocket watch with the 19th-century train engraved on the casing.*

Tony shuffled from one foot to the other, embarrassed. "You know how to read hands?"

I stared up at him, incredulous. "You don't?"

"'Course not! I only use digital. What's with the hands?"

"It's James Bond stylin', man. Chicks sure dig guys who wear Timex watches." *Unreal. He thinks my formal clothes are more expensive than his, but he's wearing the high-end brands.*

No longer cowed, Tony puffed up his chest again. "You're stylin'? Is that why you're wearin' a fuckin' suit today? With your fancy watch?"

This would be the moment where my friend Mitchell Sherry would suggest I challenge Tony to a fistfight. Mitchell would want me to say, "You wanna fight, Tony? We can do it right here, right now!" Throw a gauntlet and scare the enemy away. The big problem would be, what if Tony called my bluff and I'd have to fight? Then I would have escalated a verbal brawl to a physical one. A red belt in Tae Kwon Do, I took martial arts for the meditation, exercise, and the beautiful-and-deadly Master Yumi Park, who I had a hard-to-make-heads-or-tails-of attraction to. Master Park might not approve of my using Tae Kwon Do against Tony, since it was intended for defensive use only. Also, I had sparred in the dojo often but had never been in a street fight. Instead of escalating the argument, I appealed to Tony's better angels. "I didn't wear this suit just to piss you off. I didn't know I was gonna be the only idiot dressed up."

"You're such a faggot, Damien Cavalieri, with your gray suit and purple shirt. And your watch and your book. Ain't that just like a Jew? Sittin' readin' with his Jew nose in a book?"

Tony amused and irritated me by not realizing I was Italian. Unfortunately, I focused on that when I should have been appalled by his blatant anti-Semitism. "You think I'm Jewish?"

Tony held up his index finger, a gentleman detective in tea cozy mystery novel declaring he knows the murder's identity. "With that nose of yours? What else could you be but Jewish?"

I placed a self-conscious finger on the tip of my nose. Even pre-pubescent and round-faced, I had strong features giving me a distinctive, ethnic appearance: brown eyes, arched eyebrows, a prominent nose, big ears that did not stick out, and puffed up, dark brown 1980s hair. No wonder Tony couldn't determine my ethnicity. I resembled two screen icons — the Neapolitan American actor Ralph Macchio, who played Daniel LaRusso in *The Karate Kid*, and the Jewish comedian Harold Ramis, who played Egon Spengler in *Ghostbusters*. (I would later learn that I kinda looked like Michael Imperioli as well, but he had yet to achieve fame as Christopher Moltisanti on *The Sopranos* when I was a kid.) The Macchio and Ramis resemblances were oddly appropriate. I had Daniel LaRusso's East Coast accent, feckless charm, angry temperament, and budding interest in girls and martial arts. I had Egon Spengler's bookishness, introversion, over-seriousness, and tendency to monologue at length about arcane interests to a disengaged audience. With slight adjustments to my wardrobe, I could emphasize my resemblance to either actor. If I wore my glasses and a lab coat and held a Twinkie aloft, I could make a mean Egon Spengler on Halloween. If I put in my contact lenses, wore my white Tae Kwon Do uniform, and emphasized my light Brooklyn accent, I could get a big reaction as Daniel LaRusso at another Halloween party. Like Macchio, I was Neapolitan American. Even though I was not Jewish, like Ramis, I grew up living on an Orthodox Jewish neighborhood in Staten Island and was educated alongside Reformed Jewish students in gifted classrooms in the Willowbrook and New Springville public schools of "the forgotten borough" of New York City. I also immersed myself in Jewish popular culture. I adored the comic books of Will Eisner, Jack Kirby, and Stan Lee, the comedy of Neil Simon, the Marx Brothers, and Henny Youngman, and a broad array of Jewish American movies and literary works. Thanks to this extended cultural engagement, I picked up Jewish speech patterns, mannerisms, and clothing styles, and developed an ersatz Jewish sense of humor. I was "half-Italian" by nature and "half-Jewish" by nurture.

The defining problem of my life — my "fake Italian" background and confused cultural identity — was the natural and unintentional consequence of my childhood not resembling my mother's in any respect. Mom was raised an Italian Catholic in a WWII and post-war era Italian American enclave in Brooklyn. She grew up saturated in the cultural mores of the home country, though her attending public schools meant she was not sheltered from exposure to children from other ethnic groups. Knowing I would not grow up in an Italian enclave, Mom made a point of raising me as an Italian who was proud of my heritage. She fostered in me an appreciation of Italian food, religion, culture, and history. Irony of ironies, despite growing up a proud Italian American, I cultivated close relationships with *absolutely no Italian Americans. Zero. Nada. Zilch.* One would think that growing up in Staten Island — allegedly the place in the world with the highest concentration of Italians outside of Italy itself — would make it inevitable that I would have dozens of Italian friends and acquaintances throughout the borough. Nope. For whatever reason, I was either not placed in the same classes as other Italians or, if I did come across another Italian, we would either be indifferent or hostile to each other. Instead of knowing Italian kids at school, I knew Jewish kids, Irish kids, and Greek kids. My best friend in kindergarten, first, and second grade was the one Black boy in my class: Doug Brooks. Doug shared my love of LEGO brick medieval castle construction sets and hoped to grow up to be an architect.

Meeting no other Italians my age for my earliest school years, I had no model for how to act like an Italian kid. During my formative years, I "acted Italian" at home and "acted Jewish" when I went to school. At school, I showcased a vaudeville sense of humor influenced by all the Jewish comedians I adored from old radio shows, films, stand-up specials, and Saturday Night Live. I used Jewish exclamations like "Oy vey!", sang the lyrics to "Hava Nagila" when I was nervous, and dressed in khakis, button-down shirts, and loafers — outfits caricatured as "Jewish."

Of course, my unconscious talent for mimicry and longing to feel a part of something larger than myself meant that I also picked up interests, tastes, and mannerisms from kids from other ethnic backgrounds as well. Thanks to my Black, Greek, and Irish friends, I learned to become fascinated by Black Power movements and Sidney Poitier films, gyros, Greek history and philosophy, Irish drinking songs, and peace and justice efforts in Northern Ireland. The natural consequence of my soaking up these cultural influences in pre-school, kindergarten, and grades one through five is that, by time I wound up in the same classes as other Italians in sixth grade, they had no idea what in God's name my ethnicity was. I signaled all sorts of incompatible political, religious, and ethnic affiliations. The harrowing bus conversation on the first day of sixth grade would be the first of many awkward moments when I would greet Italian kids by saying "L'Chaim," "word up!" or "wassup, my nigga?" and they'd look at me and say, "You sure you're Italian? You talk like a Black or a Jew. Fucking fugazi Italian."

The bus struck a pothole and almost bowled Tony over. After he recovered, I said, "First off, don't say stuff like that about Jews. That ain't right. Secondly, I'm Italian." I tensed as Tony's entourage abandoned Andrew Dice Clay to stand beside him.

Tony massaged his jaw. "You shittin' me? You're Italian?"

"My name ends in a vowel!" I didn't roll my eyes. My tone did that for me. "Names that end in a vowel are Italian!"

"Billy Idol" added, in a Brooklyn-professor voice, "Except for '-ski,' which is Polish."

A Sicilian kid with brown hair entered the discussion sounding like a soft-spoken NPR commentator. "What's confusing is 'Shapiro' ends in a vowel, and that one is Jewish."

"Exception that proves the rule," I declared. "My last name is fucking Italian! *Cavalieri.*"

Tony couldn't have looked more astonished if he were a cave man who had just discovered the secret of making fire. "Yeah? You can tell what someone is by their last name?"

I waved my arms about, agitated, as I talked. Many Italians literally *conduct* their conversations, but I do it even more than most. "You think Baroness Paula von Gunther is a German? Mr. Patrick O'Donnell is Irish? And what about Hector Ramirez? Where's he from?"

"Billy Idol" belly laughed. "Kathmandu! Tony, everyone knows this shit!"

"I never heard any of this in my life," Tony said defensively. Then he looked at me with fresh, approving eyes. "Wow! You're a paisan! What parta Italy you from?"

"I ain't telling you, stunad! 'Cuz if I wuz Jewish, you wouldn't like me." When I got angry, the Brooklyn undercurrent of my accent got stronger and I sounded more like the Thing in *The Fantastic Four* — the world's coolest Brooklyn Jewish superhero.

"Aw, come on, man." Tony punched me on the shoulder. "Don't be like that."

I wished I had stood up earlier in the conversation. I was still sitting, like a mook. "I'm Italian and alla sudden we're friends now? Begone. Leave me with *Jaws* and Tuesday Phapant!"

Across the aisle, Tuesday snorted.

Tony slapped himself on the chest, Tarzan introducing himself to Jane. "I'm Sicilian."

"Congratulations." This was the perfect opportunity for me to test-drive an insult I'd heard my grandfather once toss at my pugnacious Aunt Beatrice. "You know what they say, Tony. There's two kinds of Italians: Italians and Sicilians." *(I swear, I had nothing against Sicilians. I just wasn't gonna leave that insult holstered.)*

Tony's smile disappeared. "Where are you from, then? Naples?"

"Good guess."

"Fuck you, ya Neapolitan piece of shit."

I waved him away. "Ah, get outta here, *cafone*."

Tony slapped his hand on a bus seat in frustration. "I don't get you, Damien. You're one of us, yet you make fun of Sicilians, and you're sitting here in a suit readin' like a mameluke."

"You don't read, and I do and *I'm* the mameluke?"

"Not for nuthin', but real men don't read. If you're readin', you're either a fag or a Jew."

Billy Idol sucked his teeth. "Hey, man, my mom is Jewish. Lay off with that, willya?"

Tony gaped. "No way! Does that mean 'Bobby Mammolito' is a Jewish name?"

"No, you idiot. Mammolito is an Italian last name. My dad's name. My mom's maiden name is Ashkenazi. That's Jewish. I'm a pizza bagel." Bobby put his arm around Tony, leading him and the others away.

"Shana Tova!" I yelled. I glanced at Tuesday and smirked. "I think we're alone now."

"Great," she muttered.

Man, she has a real attitude problem! What turned her against me? The ethnic slurs? Sexist remarks? Cursing? Homophobia? I may have postponed my first fistfight of the year, but Tuesday's disapproval was the price I paid for my daring escape. "Must be your lucky day."

Tuesday whirled on me. "Is that a crack about my name?"

Dammit. "I didn't mean anything by it. I couldn't. It's not Tuesday. It's Monday."

Huffy, Tuesday slouched and crossed her arms against her chest. "Are you going to read me the *Jaws* scene about Mrs. Body's wet vagina?"

I paused. "You don't *really* want me to do that, right?"

She sighed again. "I can't believe you're sitting next to me."

I supposed she had reason to lack sympathy for me, given my crack about cute Thai girls, but she carried her annoyance a bit far, given the verbal beating I'd taken in front of her. Could I say something to mollify her? "May I ask how you got your name?"

"How else? I was born on a Tuesday, jackass!"

"But that's not an answer!" I shot back. "I'm not named 'Thursday.' My uncle's middle name isn't 'Boxing Day'!"

"Oh, do be quiet! Your incessant nonsense talk makes my eardrums hurt."

"Well, I'm sorry!" Now it was my turn to slouch in my chair, cross my arms against my chest, and look huffy. "I guess this just isn't your day."

CHAPTER TWO
They Thought I Was Spicoli

September 9, 1987.

Staring at the popcorn ceiling in my bedroom, I was wide awake at two a.m. struggling to drive away gyroscopic negative thoughts. Thanks to my mild hyperthymesia, I had an extraordinary ability to recall verbatim lengthy verbal exchanges from the most emotionally turbulent times in my life. On top of that, select images — setting, clothing, facial expressions, and where people stood or sat in relation to me — were burned in my mind. These memories of often traumatic events were not omnipresent but came back unbidden when triggered by a fresh event reminiscent of the past. Worst of all, the hyperthymesia descended upon me when I tried to sleep. It manifested as an audio track of the most awful moments I'd experienced played on endless, Satanic CD repeat that drowned out all other thoughts. Today's loathsome verbal duel on the bus loomed large in tonight's playlist of dreadful conversations. I looked for something besides my popcorn ceiling to focus on to help me silence the relentless, discordant voices.

Visible from the soft light of my bedside lamp was my newly framed poster of Christina Applegate as Kelly Bundy from the sitcom *Married . . . with Children.* Hugging herself, Kelly wore an enormous black cross over a low-cut black belly shirt with a red rose on it. Denim cutoffs, and black leggings completed the sexy outfit. I focused on Kelly's face, taking in her big, teased blonde hair, luminous hazel eyes, and huge, gold-hoop earrings. Everything about her was gorgeous, but it was her striking eyes that I turned up my table light to see more clearly.

I'm a mess, Kelly. Can you keep me company? I didn't *really* expect Kelly to spring to life and emerge from the poster on my bedroom wall. Still, it was a real bummer when she didn't. In the recent Woody Allen picture Mom had rented, *The Purple Rose of Cairo,* a fictional hero in a Hollywood film stepped out of a movie, walked up the theater aisle, and took a lonely, star-struck fan into his arms. Be cool if something like that happened to me this evening. Still, as welcome as the Pygmalion fantasy was, it didn't address my actual need: a time machine.

I had made an enormous mistake at the end of last term, during my final days at Public School 12: The Alfred Dreyfus School. I had found out I would not be allowed into the Intellectually Gifted Children program in junior high and did not lift a finger to fight this "expulsion." I should not be too hard on myself for being so cowed. Both the revelation and the justification shocked and dumbfounded me, leaving me ill-equipped to offer a well-reasoned defense of my educational rights and needs. It was all so odd. I was told that the Robert Loggia School required its sixth grade accelerated students to study Spanish, in effect forbidding the study of Italian. Not knowing this in advance, I had informed the administration that I wanted to study the language of my mother country. I did not think I was functionally asking to remove myself from gifted classes at my new school. And yet, thanks to this decision, I was automatically slated to join a mainstream class. My reaction to this news was, essentially, *Oh, yeah? Fuck you, too.* I convinced myself that what was not my choice was, in fact, my call. I pretended to be a leather-jacket-wearing rebel with a switchblade comb, like Fonzie, lifting a middle finger to the gifted class gods. *You jerks are telling me which language I must study, eh? Well, down with you and your snooty program! I abjure you! Ha ha ha ha!* Using this misguided line of thinking, I cut off my schnoz to spite my face. I should have fought back. I didn't. And so, I sacrificed a first-rate, public-school education, knowledge of America's most important second language, and denied myself access to a class of intellectual peers.

Was I fighting back against "the Man" by walking away from a gifted program? No. It would be easy to condemn this gifted program as elitist and racially exclusive. It was also terrifyingly competitive: Second- and third-graders never stopped measuring themselves against their peers, desperate to prove themselves the absolute smartest person in the class. Despite these flaws, the program was the best way public school kids could get a private-school-level education. In allowing myself to be crowbarred out of the sanctuary of the gifted program, I embraced exile to an environment where being smart was an enormous liability. As my dreadful first day of mainstream classes in the sixth grade had just confirmed, I'd thrown myself to the wolves by exposing myself to bullying for the first time. And I would be bullied by *my people*.

In practical terms, I also lost my best friend, Mitchell. Mitchell was not foolish or masochistic enough to follow me into hell by joining the mainstream class in the Robert Loggia intermediate school. Last spring, he confronted me in the schoolyard during the final recess of fifth grade, brushing an agitated hand through his sandy hair. "You had to take Italian, huh? You couldn't take Spanish?"

I kicked at the monkey bars, grumbling, "Everyone I know is Irish, Italian, Jewish, or Black. Are there any other ethnicities? I never met even one Mexican. Not one."

"Such a New Yorker. Try heading to Tombstone, Arizona, where everyone is Mormon, Latino, or Native American."

I'd only seen people from those backgrounds in Westerns, so I laughed in disbelief. "Sounds like a different country!"

"It kinda is. America is a big place. And demographics are changing, too."

"I dunno. Mom tells me once you leave New York City, everyone is a Protestant who calls people like us Papists. Better we stay here where it's safe."

"Have it your way." Even when I disappointed Mitchell by acting stubborn, arrogant, and prejudiced, he had faith I'd dig my heart out from under all that detritus one day.

Why *was* studying Italian so important to me? I was Italian and proud, but I sometimes felt like a phony. I worried I was not the genuine article. After all, Mom grew up among Italian friends and family. I hadn't. Instead of raising my brother and me in her old neighborhood in Brooklyn, Mom moved us to Willowbrook on Staten Island because the neighborhood public school was one of the best in the borough, boasting an innovative gifted program for the young. My parents had hoped I'd join this program in first grade, but I didn't make the cut. In kindergarten, a multiple-choice exam testing predominantly STEM (Science, Technology, Engineering, and Mathematics) and grammar aptitude vetted prospective gifted students. Those subjects were not my strong suit. Despite my enthusiastic childhood talk of wanting to be a marine biologist, I had always been an artist and a humanist first and foremost. I believed in science, and was fascinated and impressed by science, but I was not a scientist at heart. What I loved about Great Whites was their majesty, not their biology. By the second grade, I showed advanced spoken and written language skills and an aptitude for art and history. My teacher arranged for me to be tested by an education specialist trained to work with youthful artistic temperaments that rebelled against the regimentation of institutional schooling. That specialist determined that, of the many types of intelligence, I was gifted in linguistic, intrapersonal, interpersonal, and existential areas. He concluded that I had unrealized potential in developing my naturalist and musical abilities, but I was on the poorer side when it came to logical, mathematical, and spatial intelligence. He had me admitted into the Advanced Learners Early Childhood program in the third grade. (At the time, Staten Island parents and teachers referred to the program as ALEC, but I dislike referring to it as ALEC now, since *my* ALEC has since been defunded and shut down by Staten Island Republicans, and one of the world's most evil organizations uses that same acronym these days.) The one student who welcomed me with open arms to the ALEC class was another artist with a slight attention-deficit-disorder: a big-hearted, blonde Irish hippie child name Mitchell Sherry. Mitchell was the one who first taught me about the vital importance of being a champion of social justice, when such concerns were far from my mind as a kid. He was also my hero for introducing me to John Byrne's *Fantastic Four* and Wendy and Richard Pini's *Elfquest* comic books. We drew together, took walks, went swimming at his grandparents' pool club, and had classic movie watch parties. After Mitchell and I became friends, we were inseparable during the school day. Until I chose not to take Spanish.

My brain CD of unpleasant audio memories would not stop playing . . .

Public School 12: The Alfred Dreyfus School
Advanced Learners Early Childhood Program, 3rd grade class
Staten Island, NY, 1984

Fall, 1984

Ari: You've joined the gifted program *now*? Why weren't you in our class since first grade like the rest of us, Damien?

Me: I didn't pass the test in kindergarten. I'm not good at math.

Ari: So, you're in here and you didn't pass? Are your parents in the Mafia?

Me: No, Ari. I'm great at English. I took a new test that wasn't all math questions.

Ari: So, what are your parent's jobs? My dad is a corporate lawyer, and my mother is a plastic surgeon. They make piles of money. I'm going to grow up to be a neurosurgeon. This is my personal jingle: "A neurosurgeon I will be, I'll fix you up for a great big fee!"

Me: My dad makes horror movies on Super 8. My mom teaches college composition classes. They have *real* jobs, not *fake* ones like your parents. And if you become a neurosurgeon, you shouldn't charge a lot of money. Everyone has a right to get treatment they can afford.

Winter, 1984

Ari: I'm scared about this history test, Damien. I don't think I'm going to get a 100. My parents always ground me and beat me with a belt when I don't get a hundred.

Me: We have a history test today? Oh, no!

Ari: We do.

Me: Wait a minute. What's wrong with your parents? Are they crazy, or something?

Spring, 1985

Mr. Aaronovitch: Damien, what was the name of the first human being to land on the moon?

Me: Alice Kramden.

Mr. Aaronovitch: That's funny. Who was it really?

Me: The 'small step for man' dude. Buzz Aldrin.

Mr. Aaronovitch: Buzz was the second man on the lunar surface. You just quoted his mission commander. Who was that?

Me: John Glenn.

Mr. Aaronovitch: He's the first man to orbit the Earth. Name the first man to walk on the moon.

Me: The first moonwalker was Michael Jackson.

Public School 12: The Alfred Dreyfus School
   Advanced Learners Early Childhood Program, 4th grade class
   Staten Island, NY, 1985

Miss Becker: Everyone who didn't do the homework, stand up. Admit it now. You get in more trouble if I find out later. Ah. Damien. And Mitchell. Again. Why didn't you do it today?

Mitchell: I forgot.

Me: Me too. [BRAP!]

Miss Becker: Was that fart real or fake, Damien?

Me: Do I get in more trouble if it was real, or if it was fake?

Miss Becker: Tell your parents to stop packing mozzarella sticks in your lunch. You may be lactose intolerant.

Me: What's lactose intolerant?

Public School 12: The Alfred Dreyfus School
   Advanced Learners Early Childhood Program, 5th grade class
   Staten Island, NY, 1986

Mr. Altman: Damien, let me see the back cover of the book you did your report on.

Me: Okay. Here it is, Mr. Altman.

Mr. Altman: Did you like the book?

Me: Mom loves Agatha Christie. She knew I'd like *Ten Little Indians*. I didn't figure it out. I was fooled into thinking the real bad guy died earlier in the book. He faked his death.

Mr. Altman: Your book report wording is different from the back cover of the book.

Me: Shouldn't it be?

Mr. Altman: Your writing is good. I'm sorry we didn't do more English work this year.

Me: There was a lot of math and science. People kept thinking I was stupid because I couldn't remember 12 times 12 was 144, no matter how hard I tried. Took me all year to remember it. I was better at science. I really liked learning about the transpiration pull.

Mr. Altman: I'm partial to the transpiration pull myself.

Public School 12: The Alfred Dreyfus School
Advanced Learners Early Childhood Program,
5th grade graduation week
Staten Island, NY, Spring 1987

Mr. Altman: Damien, I figured out why you aren't in the accelerated program in middle school. You chose Italian as your foreign language instead of Spanish.

Me: Why does that matter, Mr. Altman?

Mr. Altman: The others picked Spanish because that's the language all Americans will need to know. By picking Italian, you self-selected out of gifted classes and chose mainstream.

Me: Why can't I be in all the same gifted classes as the rest of these folks, except I go to a mainstream Italian class?

Mr. Altman: The school doesn't want you ever leaving your homeroom class to link up with other students. They want the same students together all the time.

Me: That's stupid.

Mr. Altman: It is a safety thing. They're worried about losing students in the shuffle. And it is more paperwork for them if they make these concessions.

Me: So, if I leave the gifted program, I get to take Italian and be with Italian students, and if I stay in the gifted program, I take Spanish and there won't be other Italians in the class?

Mr. Altman: Maybe not many. You were the only Italian in this class. But you don't want to sacrifice the quality of your education, do you?

Me: I'm tired of being the only Italian boy in my class. And I want to take Italian. They're being stupid about my choice, but if that's the way it has to be . . . whatever, I guess.

The memory of me saying this to Altman snapped me awake from my half-slumber. The CD in my head skipped:

I'm tired of being the only Italian boy in my class. And I want to take Italian. They're being stupid about my choice, but if that's the way it has to be . . . whatever, I guess.

My words repeated and repeated and repeated and repeated and repeated.

I wanted to scream audibly, but could not, so I screamed inside my head.

CHAPTER THREE
Sharped-Dressed Man

September 8, 1987

7:44 a.m.

Yup. I'm the only idiot in a gray pinstriped suit and purple shirt.

Stepping off the yellow school bus onto the grounds of the Robert Loggia School in New Springville, I scanned the several dozen students milling about outside the institutional, unremarkable three-story building. These sixth, seventh, and eighth graders were not sporting suits. In fact, they weren't dressed in anything like what I'd pictured a modern-day tween or teen wearing. When I'd imagined Staten Island kids in Rockabilly clothes, prohibition wear, or Catholic school uniforms, I couldn't have landed farther outside the zeitgeist if I had planned. These were not "movie" or "TV show" kids from a nostalgic yarn about a modern-day filmmaker's glory days, which took place before Buddy Holly, Ritchie Valens, and "The Big Bopper" got on that plane. This was a school of students who had all chosen to dress according to a small handful of mainstream and counterculture "types." In the fall of 1987, the most popular clothes among Staten Island Italian boys between eleven and fifteen were Reebok or Nike high-top sneakers and either track suits, parachute pants, or Z. Cavariccis. Almost all these boys had "Billy Idol" spiked hair, wore gold chains and Christ heads around their necks, and strutted instead of walked. In contrast, heavy metal fans wore big, permed hair, black pants, silver chains, and band T-shirts featuring Eddie the Head or Dr. Feelgood. A small handful of Jewish honor students wandered around in single-color polo shirts and beige slacks. They stuck out like sore thumbs but were not as ridiculous as I was in my suit.

A few exceptions notwithstanding, the eleven-year-old girls tended to have massive, teased hairstyles — high, wide, and curly — and wore huge hoop earrings, ripped jeans, and washed denim jackets over airbrushed t-shirts. A few metal head girls also wore the Eddie the Head t-shirts. A jaw-dropping number of young women wore tennis-to-soccer-ball-sized *New Kids on the Block* badges. If you listened in on their exchanges, the girls spent a ton of time engaged in friendly debate over which *New Kid* was the "cutest" or "hottest."

Naturally, I had no idea who in hell *The New Kids on the Block* were, and I felt like a horse's ass. In fact, I had never heard of *any* of the bands or soloists featured on any of the clothing items and accessories worn by the other students. I certainly didn't know a single one of their songs. My parents were both of the opinion that popular music stopped being worth listening to when the Beatles arrived, brought the rest of the uncouth, drug-addled bands of the British Invasion with them, and drove all the Italian Do Wop performers of the 1950s into hiding. Mom listened exclusively to early 1950s rock, especially Dion DiMucci, Fabian Forte, Bobby Darin, Frankie Valli, and the Platters. Dad preferred old country music (think "Mule Train" and "Ghost Riders in the Sky"), big band music (Glenn Miller and Benny Goodman), and Irish drinking songs by the Clancy Brothers and Tommy Makem. With only the smallest handful of exceptions — Elton John, Madonna, Willie Nelson, John Denver, Blondie, Simon and Garfunkel, and Lionel Richie — my parents never listened to any song produced after 1961. Since I listened to what they listened to, I had heard virtually no music, popular or underground, produced between 1961 and 1987. I had never heard of Pink Floyd or listened to "The Wall." I hadn't heard of the Beastie Boys and didn't know this "Paul Revere" song students kept rapping. Nor had I heard of Aerosmith, Billy Joel, the Carpenters, the Doors, ELO, Europe, the Grateful Dead, Led Zeppelin, Ozzy Osbourne, the Police, Queen, Rush, Toto, Velvet Underground, the Who, or any of the Woodstock performers. Only Michael Jackson was famous enough for me to have heard of, and I knew exactly two songs: "Thriller" and "Beat It." From a music history perspective, I arrived in sixth grade a freshly thawed Captain America, awakened after spending the decades since World War II frozen in ice. Like Steve Rogers, I would be forced to ask my new friends about the music I missed out on while I was asleep, and jot down their favorites into a spiral notebook for future reference. (Note: Mitchell says I'll love "Boris the Spider," "Sunday Morning" (1967), "The Trees," and "On the Turning Away." UPDATE: HE WAS RIGHT!)

Overcoming my terror of the other students and their mysterious rock band t-shirts, I stepped away from the bus and onto the curb, heading towards the brick building. I found it a challenge not to fixate on the five letters missing from the words "In er ediate Sc ool 420: T e Robert Loggia Sch ol" written in plain black letters on the façade. In my mind's eye, I saw the sign welcoming new souls to hell in Dante's *Inferno* displayed over the front entrance. Flaming letters scorched into white marble read:

> I am the way into the city of woe,
> I am the way into eternal pain,
> I am the way to go among the lost . . .

> Abandon all hope you who enter here.

I navigated a vast crowd of mostly Italian American tweens and teens blocking the concrete path to the main doors, loitering on the surrounding lawn, talking, smoking, and skateboarding. (Wait. I'm remembering it wrong. Nobody was skateboarding. Bloody "Mandela effect" false memory inspired by *Clueless*!) I strove to avoid eye-contact with each individual Guido and Guidette and put some daylight between me and the southern Italian collective. Unfortunately, these folks were not as interested in living and let live as I was. Each student noticed my gray pinstriped suit and purple dress shirt as I passed. Some burst out into raucous laughter, others launched gum, paper airplanes, and wadded up balls of paper in my direction. Most of the projectiles missed me, but some ricocheted off my head and back. These projectiles didn't come all at once, like in a 1980s teen sex comedy scene, but regularly, throughout the day, in the hallways, in the classrooms, in the lunchroom, on the bus, and pretty much anywhere my feet took me, beginning on my long walk to the front entrance. A steady stream of jeers, taunts, and catcalls burned themselves onto my bad memory CD, ready to be played the minute I tucked myself into bed. These Catskills-worthy insults included: "Queer!" "Snapperhead!" "Sissy!" "Weirdo!" "Faggot!" "Pasty-faced piece of shit." "Geek!" "Strunz!" "Nerd!" "Pansy!" "Gay-ass motherfucker!" "Pillow-biter!" "Fudgepacker!" Borscht Belt-level material, right? I kept my head down and kept moving.

These damned kids seemed to really hate my suit, which confused me, because Giorgio Armani was an Italian, and Italians liked to look good. My outfit was intended as an ethnic solidarity signal flare: my people would know me from my flashy clothes, just as I would know them from theirs. Never in a million years did I expect track suits to be the staple outfit of a stylish tribe known for designing the Maserati and clothes with bold colors and cool accessories like scarves and sunglasses. I had worn this pinstriped suit at Cousin Concetta Basile's wedding a month before. It had been my first-ever wedding. It was also the evening I learned how to dance. At the start of the reception, Mom taught me to do both slow and "disco" dancing. Less than half an hour later, I found myself dancing with First-Cousin-Once-Removed Baby Bianca Natali. We danced to Billy Idol's "Mony Mony," Kylie Minogue's "Locomotion," and Belinda Carlisle's "Mad About You." In the weeks following the wedding, I made several attempts to listen to radio stations that played cool recent songs like those. Dad invariably came in the room, complained the music was loud and uncouth, and demanded I turn it off.

I wish I'd gone to Catholic school instead of public school, I thought as I passed through the front doors of the Robert Loggia school for the first time, finding a sea of the same kind of students awaiting me. *Those kids wear suits, right? Nuns beat the shit out of them if they step out of line?* I followed a series of paper arrows taped up on walls at the most confusing intersections, pointing me to the auditorium. Us newbies herded inside looking for seats in a three-row, multiple aisle seating arrangement with a two-hundred-and-fifty-person capacity. Not yet sure how to sort into classes, the students who had arrived before me had opted for an "ethnic identity" seating theme. Serene Jewish students collected themselves in the front of the auditorium. Fidgeting Irish kids sat in the rows behind them. Then followed a sea of whooping, paper-airplane-tossing Italian kids, followed by a hodgepodge of Spanish, Greek, and Thai kids towards the back rows. These poor kids were outnumbered and looked hunched and haunted.

This ethnic seating arrangement troubled me. If birds of a feather flock together, then why do the feathers have to be "racial" feathers or "ethnic" feathers? Couldn't they be "taste in music" feathers or "my favorite class is . . . " feathers, or "I prefer tapioca to brownies" feathers? In the end, weren't we all more similar than different? That was when I looked behind me and finally noticed the Black students gathered in the extreme rear of the auditorium. They stood against the brick wall, loitered in the aisles, or sat perched on the backs of the chairs, with their feet planted on the seats. Trying not to look as if they were bracing themselves for trouble, they murmured amongst themselves, darting wary glances at the caffeinated, horny, and sleep-deprived white kids in the room. They looked even more worried than I felt. *Wait a minute. Why are the Black kids in the back? Didn't Rosa Parks put an end to that sort of thing? Are we going backwards as a society and returning to segregation?* Wasn't this New York City, the great Melting Pot? Wasn't this the city that stood for the multicultural, pacifist values of Norman Lear, *Sesame Street, Mr. Rogers, Wonder Woman, The Muppet Show,* and *Star Trek* — all the hippie, utopian television shows I had been weaned on though syndication (since I'd been born in 1976, too late to see most of their premieres)? Or was that all baloney after all? Upbeat propaganda? A wish for a better future? No, I wasn't living on *Sesame Street.* Instead, I was living in the New York that Jesse Jackson had dubbed "Hymie-town." The New York that had murdered Michael Griffith in Howard Beach and celebrated the vigilantism of Bernhard Goetz. I was living in *Shitty* New York — the New York Snake Plissken had to escape from — not *Mr. Rogers'* New York. If Staten Island had been part of Mr. Rogers' neighborhood, I could have sat anywhere in that auditorium. Instead, I could sit nowhere. If my suspicions were correct, I was too Italian for the Jews and too Jewish for the Italians. I had to shoehorn my way into another ethnic group's section, or I was up shit's creek.

What the students all seemed to have in common, no matter their ethnicity, was they were scary. I'll admit, I had the warped perception of a terrified new freshman, but the other students seemed to take being combative and carnal to levels I had yet to dream of attempting. At five-feet tall and eighty pounds, I was tall and slender for an eleven-year-old but had a little boy's cheeks and brown doe-eyes. My height drew attention to me, making it harder for me to shrink into the background, but it did not make me appear formidable. Now that

I'd made the mistake of drawing attention to myself with a formal, gaudy, and effeminate outfit, could I begin radiating a menacing air to prevent that attention from settling permanently into relentless bullying? I wasn't sure. The first order of business was to pick the least terrifying group of students to sit with. I considered sitting with the Black students, and looking for my old friend Doug once I got back there, but I was too emotionally flattened by my awful experiences so far to have the energy to attempt to cross the color line. Instead, I chose to sit in the most racially mixed part of the auditorium, among the assortment of Greek, Thai, and Hispanic students. I would join the reluctant, ad hoc chapter of Jessie Jackson's rainbow coalition! When I arrived, a lone Italian, I was less politically powerful than they. The motley crew of students saw a unique opportunity to make themselves feel better by punching down at me instead of up at bullies. I nodded hello at a tall-for-his-age Greek and sat in front of him. He jackhammer-kicked the back of my chair, yelling with each strike, "Why you wearin' a suit?" over and over again.

I leaped up, whirled on him, and used one of my mom's quaint insults, "Hey! Why don't you go take a flying leap?" Then I went to find another seat, behind a pre-pubescent girl with gray eyes, shoulder-length blonde hair, and red lipstick. Glammed up, she wasn't instantly recognizable as Debbie Cohen, a once frumpy malcontent in the mainstream classes in our last school. Ari once described her as "a self-hating Jew." She *did* use anti-Semitic slurs casually and frequently. Debbie Cohen turned around, looking blankly at my cherubic face.

"Heeeeey, how's it going?" I asked, offering up a smile.

"Fag boy! You're such a fag boy! Fag boy!" She regarded my dumbfounded expression with contempt and returned her eyes to the front of the room.

Principal Poliseno appeared on stage to address the masses. Tiny and confrontational, Mr. Poliseno was Super Mario in a black suit, black tie, and black glasses, flanked on either side by a delegation of teachers and administrators, and the American and New York State flags. Three security guards stood in a row below him, guarding the front of the stage with their arms crossed before them in a power pose. "Quiet!" Mr. Poliseno bellowed, showing off his bullhorn throat. He won instant silence, roaring that none of us were babies anymore, so we'd better behave ourselves or the teachers would break their feet off in our asses!

Oooh! Even the teachers are violent. Fantastic.

As Poliseno shouted away for what would be half an hour, Debbie Cohen turned around once every five minutes to inform me — just loud enough for me to hear, but not loud enough for anyone else — that I was a "fag boy." I thought about how much I liked Charles Laughton, Roddy McDowall, Stephen Fry, and other actors and singers who (I had heard somewhere) were gay. I wasn't sure "fag boy" should stand as an insult. Still, her relentless hissing, contemptuous expression, and evident desire to wound whittled away at my patience. I placed my hand over my heart, smiling serenely. "I get to be gay like Capote? Wicked awesome!"

"You're a fag who likes other fags. You're a fag who likes other fags. Fag boy, fag boy. Who's a little fag boy? Fag boy!"

It dawned upon me that I knew few swear words and racial slurs to toss about, while all these other eleven-year-olds seem to know longshoreman terminology for every possible sexual position and undesirable immigrant population. My mom cursed a little, keeping to the words "fuck" and "shit" when she was in a lather about my dad looking a waitress up and down or not doing enough housework. Dad had a dirty mind, loved showing softcore lesbian vampire movies to me, and was not the most racially sensitive person in the world. Still, my half-Italian, half-German American dad had a German-aristocrat sensibility that prevented him from saying anything "rude." He would refer to "farts" as "making a flower" and refrain from referencing the most uncouth bodily functions. He was not square enough to use terms like "cheese and crackers" instead of cursing, but he was not far from being that sort of person. I had an awareness of the "n" word and knew the racial slurs thrown at Italians — dago, WOP, and guinea — from Brian DePalma's *Untouchables* movie. My parents themselves *never* used ethnic slurs. Ever. I overheard charming terms like "kike" and "gook" for the first time on the first day of sixth grade. Also, the wide variety of terrible things to call women, such as "split tail" or "cunt" were both new to me in junior high and jarring to hear. I was not comfortable using any of those terms and never did try very hard to get comfortable using them. Did I ever blurt out oaths? Sure. When I was upset. What words did I use? I'd learned "sonofabitch," "Jesus Christ!" and "God damn it!" from my childhood horror and science fiction heroes, Chief Brody, Ellen Ripley, and Doctor Leonard H. McCoy, so those were my go-to profanities. While the people of the Bible belt might find Ripley's blasphemy worse than the more graphic curses I'd been hearing all morning, it was clear "God damn it" wasn't going to scare anyone in the Robert Loggia School. As David Mamet would observe, confining myself to the PG-13 oaths of my movie heroes was like bringing a knife to a gunfight. Since I had no idea what to say to these people when they insulted me, I felt muzzled. Of course, the more muzzled I felt, the more likely I would resort to physical violence to protect myself when relentlessly nibbled at by a bloodthirsty school of eleven-year-old piranhas. All this preamble is to explain — not excuse — the fact that I eventually wound up striking Debbie. I had lost count of how many times she chanted "fag boy" at me before I snapped and gave her a sharp slap across the face. Mute, frozen, and wide-eyed, she stared at me. I suspect my own expression was similar. I had not intended to hit her. I'd lost total control of my arm. It shot out at her of its own accord. *Did I just slap a Jewish girl? Do I have a Nazi arm I can't control, like Dr. Strangelove? Yeah, she was taunting me, but gentlemen don't hit women! Non-Nazis don't attack Jews! What have I done?*

Debbie gaped at me. "You slapped me? You slapped a *girl!* Why would you do that?"

I stared down at my hand, which had assumed a claw shape. *What? Is it a claw now?*

Debbie kept staring, dumbstruck. "You're a *bad person.*"

"Hey! Turn around!" Mr. Poliseno shouted at Debbie.

Debbie mouthed "You're a bad person" at me and turned around to face front. For the following three years, Debbie Cohen said not one more word to me. Moments after Debbie put her back to me, a piece of gum landed on my head. Plucking it out before it glued itself to my hair, I grimaced and flicked it onto the dirty, gray, tiled floor. Sticking my tongue out and making "eeeew" sounds, I wiped my saliva-covered hands off on my pants. The Aryan-looking kid next to me said, "You probably have AIDS now."

"The AIDS virus dies with contact with the air," I said testily.

"Nah," the Aryan boy said. "You totally have AIDS now."

I shot him a withering look. "Next piece of gum flies my way? I'm making you eat it."

Assholes. I'm surrounded by total assholes. Fucking multi-ethnic Planet of the Apes *around here. Except . . . no. That's racist and insulting to Cornelius and Zira and Dr. Zaius.*

I was never going to enjoy this first day of school, but my life had been made infinitely harder by just how badly this morning had been organized. With "ethnic-centric" thinking foremost in my mind, I wondered if this horror-show had been orchestrated by Mr. Poliseno. *Such incompetence. Never put an Italian in charge of anything.* I thought of an ethnic humor T-shirt my German grandmother Antje once wore, much to my father's chagrin, since he morally disapproved of ethnic humor. It said:

> *Heaven is where the cooks are French, the police are British, the mechanics are German, the lovers are Italian, and everything is organized by the Swiss.*
>
> *Hell is where the cooks are British, the police are German, the mechanics are French, the lovers are Swiss, and everything is organized by the Italians.*

As problematic as ethnic humor was, the t-shirt seemed apt and true to me, as I found myself trapped in a hell overseen by an Italian organizer: Mr. Poliseno. After Mr. Poliseno finished threatening the students — scaring me and seemingly no one else — he ordered the homeroom teachers to collect their students, line them up, and march them to their respective classrooms. This dumbass process took forever. The morons in charge should have labeled each row in the auditorium with a homeroom teacher's name in the first place, so the kids sat down pre-sorted. My auditorium experience might have been less colorful had they done this. Instead, these "organizers" had left the seating up to us, thereby sacrificing me to leaderless, chaotic, and libertarian forces. Still, maybe homeroom would suck less than this sixth-grade pre-game show.

Homeroom was a rough-and-tumble assemblage of mostly Italian kids looking respectively bored, furious, sleepy, lobotomized, and arrogant. Our homeroom teacher was a hundred-and-thirty-seven-year old man in baggy golf clothing who was either too broke to retire or hated his wife and did not enjoy fishing. Tired of staring at my shoes and apologizing to the world for living, I presented myself to my new homies as a wild and crazy guy. I leapt through the doorway, spread my arms dramatically, and sang out, "Warriors! Come out to play! Wa-riorrrrrrrrrs, come out to plaaaaay-aaaaaaay!" I gleefully quoted the 1979 cult film *The Warriors,* gambling some of the students would recognize the dialogue, not be offended that I was comparing them to members of near-future dystopian New York street gangs, and introduce themselves to me as fellow cult film aficionados. Instead, the bewildered students stopped, stared, and returned to whatever the fuck it was they were doing.

Since there were, once again, no assigned seats, I chose a temporary spot next to a quiet, stone-faced Thai girl I didn't know. She wore a black leather jacket over a blue dress with white polka dots. It was exactly the kind of Rockabilly look I had been hoping to see on someone today. "I'm finding all this a bit overwhelming," I said to her. "How are you holding up?"

The Thai girl continued staring into what I suppose would be called the middle-distance.

I added, "Look, I swear to you, I'm not that bad a guy. You can talk to me."

The Thai girl remained quiet. *Jezuz Key-rist! It's like tawkin' to a fuckin' brick wall ova heah.* I was so upset, even my thoughts were getting an angry New Yawk accent. I tried again, and said, calmly and all-friendly like: "Nice polka dots."

The Thai girl remained quiet.

I laughed bitterly. "Lemme give you some advice. If you're gonna succeed here, you gotta stop being a blabbermouth. Nobody likes folks who talk their ears off."

The Thai girl remained quiet.

My eyes watered. I lowered my head on the table, hiding my face behind folded arms.

"Hey, yo!" A girl in the back of the room yelled while chewing gum (which seemed dangerous). "That kid in the suit is fucking crying, man! He's fucking crying! Check out the kid in the suit! He's wearing a fucking suit and he's fucking crying!" The response to this outcry was some giggling, followed by a return to regarding me as invisible. At least nobody threw gum at me. With my face buried, I didn't see Arwen Undómiel Pokatny approach. Arwen was an Irish and Polish girl with a round face, half-moon eyeglasses, and raven-black hair in a pull-through ponytail. She wore a black MA-1 flight jacket covered in left-wing political pins and badges, a black "Iggy and the Stooges T-shirt," black shorts, black tights, and black Doc Martens. She placed a reassuring hand on my arm, but I was too ashamed of my tears to look up at her. I kept my head hidden in my arms.

Without changing her inflection, Arwen said in a deep, smooth, and whispery voice, "Don't take it so hard, my friend. This place can't be as bad as it seems."

I spoke into my arms. "Leave me alone."

"I'm as at sea as you are," Arwen added. "I suspect we are not alone. Everyone else is at least a little scared. Some are more frightened than others, I'll grant you."

"Thank you," I said into my arms, my eyes closed. She sounded nice, but she also sounded pretty. *Funny that people can sound pretty.* I didn't want a pretty girl to see me crying.

I looked up a minute later. Nobody stood near me anymore. Glancing about the room, I couldn't tell which girl had been kind to me.

CHAPTER FOUR
The Empty Set

I will now tell you about some of the best things that happened to me during my first day of school, so that this account isn't uniformly negative. In gym, the sixth graders faced off against the eighth graders in what was supposed to be touch football. The eighth graders tackled us while a gym teacher who looked like Red Buttons made phone calls to his bookie. I have hated football with a burning passion ever since that day. In shop, I asked the bald, emaciated teacher if I *had* to cut a Playboy-bunny-shaped Plexiglas clock when I'd prefer to make a TARDIS-shaped clock. "Yes," he said, laconically. In math, Mr. Preponte — a mullet-wearing insult comedian disguised as a teacher — taught us about sets of numbers, drawing in yellow chalk on the forest green chalkboard. He first wrote up a set of all the even numbers between 2 and 10 {2, 4, 6, 8, 10} and followed up with an "empty set" that had no numbers in it, represented by either {} or Ø. Mr. Preponte pointed at the {}. "An empty set has nothing in it. Think of it as the set of all the girls in this room who find Damien Cavalieri sexually attractive." Somehow, everyone knew my name already. They turned as one, took in my mortified face, and bust a gut laughing. The math teacher rushed to add, "That was *so* wrong of me. I'm *so sorry*! I meant the number of girls *worldwide* who find Damien sexually attractive! Ha!" I would like to tell you I responded by sarcastically praising his mullet, but I only stared back at him with bloodshot eyes. Twenty minutes into the first lesson, I wanted to murder my math teacher. What a change from a year ago, when the kind and brilliant Mrs. Schuler taught me about the seven bridges of Königsberg, the wheat and chessboard problem, and the prisoner's dilemma.

After a handful of mind-bogglingly poor classes, my brightest hope became history. I had a soft spot for the subject because of the historical films and television shows my parents watched, the military strategy tabletop games dad played with me (like Risk, Stratego, and Axis and Allies), and the summers my family spent visiting battlefields, historic homes, and open-air living history museums in Colonial Williamsburg, Richmondtown, and Gettysburg. Last year, my fifth-grade honors history teacher, the stiff and conservatively dressed Mr. Dugan, completed the established curriculum quickly enough to leave time at the end of the school year to present an unpacking of the Iran-Contra scandal that was so even-handed the students could not determine Mr. Dugan's political affiliation. Unlike Mr. Dugan, this year's teacher, Mr. Orlov, was a radical Republican who never stopped bashing Democrats. He was also a batshit crazy Korean War veteran with a tablespoon's worth of knowledge of history. He taught by leafing through our textbook in the middle of the class as we sat waiting, trying to cobble together some points on the spot by consulting the photo captions and boldfaced key terms scattered about the chapter. Orlov was just the sort of funny, pathetic, and banal evil older white man who Dabney Coleman or Gene Hackman could play in a film, only senile, charisma-free, and prone to hallucinations. Orlov had a mass of pure white curls on his head and a bushy, dazzling white mustache. Watery gray eyes alternated between haunted, confused, provoked, and flirtatious. On the first day, as with each subsequent, he began the class period by wandering over to the window, standing with his legs spread wide, and his arms up before the classroom window. "All hail, the Sun God, Ra!" Each day, he'd follow up this sunworshipper ritual with a round of attendance, during which he eyeballed the eleven-year-old girls. "Puberty starts earlier every year," he nodded sagely. "I'm seeing some sensational secondary sex characteristics flowering amongst you young ladies." Remarkably, the students of both sexes were so thunderstruck by his words they complained neither to him nor anyone else in authority. Orlov had no remarks to make about the poetic beauty of the pimples breaking out across the faces of the boys, or the melodious qualities of their cracking voices. At no point was Orlov able to recall our names, but he overcame this amnesia by calling every boy "Chief," "Bub," "Cochise," or "Hiawatha" and every girl "honey," "sweetie," "princess," and "sugar." Orlov began the first lesson by asking for the answer to the "Do Now": "Define 'BARBARIAN.'" Naturally, he pointed to yours truly, the boy in the suit. For the umpteenth time, I kicked myself for wearing it. I slouched under his gaze, "Muscular warriors who went around pillaging ancient villages for food, gold, and women."

Orlov glowered at me. "Okay, what's your name?"

"Damien Cavalieri."

His voice rose in a crescendo of rage. "You want to get up here and teach this class, Damien? You think you're smarter than me? Because I knew smart guys in Korea! Guess where they are today? They're dead! That's what happens to smart guys! Where'd you learn this stuff so young that you think you're smarter than me?"

I sat back up. "*Conan the Barbarian* with Arnold Schwarzenegger. But the barbarians were good guys. They fought James Earl Jones' serpent cult."

Somewhere in the back, Arwen Undómiel Pokatny giggled. Her voice rang out, "Damien! 'What is good in life?'"

I turned around to face her and started mimicking Arnold's thick Austrian accent. "'To crush your enemies, see them driven before you, and hear the lamentations of their women!'"

Orlov waved an impatient hand to silence us. His eyes were losing focus as his memories of the Korean War flooded over him. "Think you're hot shit now, Damian? Well, one of these days, your prostate is gonna swell to the size of a watermelon. A watermelon, I say!"

Now my eyes glazed over. Good memories of past ALEC classes washed over me. In the fifth-grade ALEC science class, they taught us about evolution, and we discussed the greenhouse effect. In my ALEC civics class, we debated the pros and cons of the death penalty and immigration, and learned how Altamont, the murder of Sharon Tate, and the election of Richard Nixon laid the groundwork for the Reagan Revolution. I missed my ALEC psychology class, where we studied the bystander effect by learning about the Queens stabbing murder of Kitty Genovese, who could have been rescued by any one of thirty-eight witnesses, only none intervened. During this heartbreaking lesson, I became certain that, had I been outside of her apartment building on March 13, 1964, I would have been just as big a coward as those thirty-eight. Her blood would have been on my hands as well. I hoped that, should I ever encounter a new Kitty Genovese, I would be man enough to intervene, instead of do nothing.

"Are you with me?" Orlov barked. "Pay attention!"

"Can I have the bathroom pass?" I asked. "I'm feeling under the weather."

The class cracked up. Several students mimicked me, delighted by my use of such quaint terminology. "'Under the weather' he said! 'Under the weather!'"

Mitchell and I entered the pale-blue-tiled lavatory at almost precisely the same time, both holding a vinyl-record-sized hunk of wood with "HALL PASS" written on it in navy blue magic marker. We stood by the sinks as someone in the middle of three lavatory stalls moaned in agony over the world's worst case of constipation. Mitchell asked the boy if he needed the nurse and the boy replied he was fine. Mitchell seemed pleased by our chance meeting. "How's it going?"

My shoulders slumped. I somehow managed to avoid bursting into tears. "Awful."

Mitchell nodded. "The gifted class isn't what it used to be. I had to put two bullies in their place when they started mocking the quirkier kids."

Mitchell was a hero, just like his late father, who had died tragically in a freak accident a few years back. A "Central Park Horse and Carriage Ride" horse had broken free of its harness and trotted into multiple lanes of fast-moving car traffic. Mitchell's father, an uninvolved bystander, had intervened to lead the horse back to the safety of the sidewalk. When he reached out to grab the horse's bridle, it got spooked, reared up, and kicked him in the head, killing him. Since his father's passing, Mitchell had been raised by his young, widowed mother, a feminist nurse, with an assist from his older sister and active, gregarious grandparents. Mitchell, like the other surviving members of his family, had chosen to honor his fallen father by living life according to the same code: do good whenever you can, even if you place yourself in danger in the process. Personally, I worried when Mitchell would place himself in harm's way for others, especially given what happened to his father. After all, my mother's go-to advice was *keep your head down and stay neutral.* "You sticking your nose in where it doesn't belong again?" I teased. "My momma told me if it didn't concern me or the family directly, don't get involved."

"I had to chase away some idiot named Dietrich Krebs from bothering Tsvi-Mayer."

"Tsvi-Mayer? He's cool! He has a stutter? So what? Damn. What's wrong with people?"

Mitchell shrugged. "I don't know. Maybe he's bitter his name is Dietrich Krebs?"

"What's so hard about being nice? Do people get up in the morning and say to themselves, 'I'm gonna be the asshole at school today!' How is that their ambition in life?"

There was a tiny splash. The boy in the middle stall whooped with joy. "Yes!"

"Congratulations, man," I said to the unseen porcelain punisher. "Mitchell, how is this school like this? The students and teachers are in a competition to see who's the stupidest, meanest, and most violent. We need a permanent S.W.A.T. team here, or something."

Mitchell shook his head. "Do me a favor. Never read a book by Ayn Rand. Putting armed guards in this school would just add to the total number of bullies in the building and hand heavy ordinance to the most aggressive ones. What are cops but people like Dietrich Krebs all grown up? They'd turn this place into a concentration camp. The school is shit because the politicians don't pay teachers enough. Reagan hasn't socialized medicine, passed the Equal Rights Amendment, or protected the power of unions. In fact, he's done the opposite, and is flushing our whole society down the toilet. The working-classes are feeling the kick in the pants first."

"Yeah, but at least Reagan freed the hostages." I didn't understand anything Mitchell was saying, but I wasn't willing to dismiss it out of hand, no matter how full of non sequiturs his speech appeared to be. "Wait. This school sucks cuz we don't have Canadian health coverage?"

"If the broader society is cruel and Darwinian, schools are going to be cruel and Darwinian." Mitchell made a Möbius strip in the air with his finger. "Everything is connected."

That was the first thing he said that I agreed with instinctively. "Yeah, that tracks."

The boy in the middle stall was back to grunting as he gave birth to a new piece of poo.

Mitchell said, "Get this: Our history teacher, Dave Orange, may be certifiably insane! During attendance, Dietrich Krebs yelled out, 'I'm here, Agent Orange.' Turns out Mr. Orange was a Vietnam veteran with vivid memories of Agent Orange attacks. He flipped out at being called that, pushed his desk over on its side, and ran up to Krebs like he was gonna throttle the kid. (Frankly, I would've supported him if he had.) Mr. Orange raved for three minutes about how none of us would ever understand Vietnam. Then he started crying and ran away."

"Yikes!"

"Five minutes after he'd gone, we were all sitting there in the classroom, waiting for him to come back, feeling sad and confused. Principal Poliseno walked by, realized no class was going on, and asked us all where 'Dave' was: Dave Orange. Imitating Cheech and Chong, a couple of kids called out, 'Dave's not here, man.' (I have to admit, that was pretty funny.) We told him what happened. Poliseno chewed out Krebs and then ran off to find Dave to make sure he wasn't trying to hang himself in a utility closet somewhere."

"Jesus Christ!"

"I know!"

I put both my hands in my pockets and sighed. "I've got an unstable military vet for a history teacher, too. Mr. Orlov."

"No!" Mitchell's face blanched. "Not Orlov! He was in my grandfather's unit in Korea!"

"No way!"

"Grandpa said he was an asshole in 1951, and still is. They go to the same church now."

"Whoa. Imagine knowing *that* guy for thirty-five frickin' years."

"Grandpa thinks of Orlov like a poltergeist who follows him around the world, haunting him with endless assholery."

I couldn't help myself and chuckled.

"No, it isn't funny. Orlov drives my grandfather nuts. Now *you* have to deal with him?"

"Me and Mr. Orlov are gonna be fast friends." I intertwined my fingers. "Like this."

Mitchell shook his head and muttered something I didn't hear under his breath.

After all this terrible preamble, I just knew my Italian class was going to be the greatest class I had ever taken, or ever would take. Naturally, I walked into a spitball firing, paper airplane flying classroom from hell. The class was a free-for-all. I had to shut down a little, emotionally, to shield myself from sensory overload. Foot tapping impatiently, a teacher with crystal blue frog eyes and lustrous, shoulder-length blonde hair stood with her arms across her chest. As she waited for the chaos to die down, Stefano Manganiello — a tiny, baby-faced boy with spiked black hair — scurried about the room, grabbing the hands of the male students, placing them over his crotch, and yelling at the top of his lungs, "Caught! Caught trying to grab my balls! Caught!" For the sake of variety, Stefano would sometimes run up to a random boy, ask, "What's the capital of Thailand?" and punch in the groin anyone dumb enough to reply "Bangkok." The blonde teacher bellowed a demand for him to stop. He responded by leaping upon his desk and singing "Gloria" by Laura Branigan.

"What's all this *mishegoss*?" I breathed. Since I like to comfort myself in moments of stress by mentally evoking a movie, I chose to imagine myself trapped in the insanity of Dorry's Tavern in *Gremlins* — a pub overwhelmed by evil, rampaging Muppets. Yes, the Italian kids were the Gremlins. Meanwhile, the six non-Italian kids were as befuddled and frightened as I was, hoping and praying the tornado would pass. *They* were here to learn, but *not the Italians*. I was shocked and confused. I couldn't fathom why *Italians* would manically derail *Italian class*. Didn't they have even a trace of ethnic pride? I wondered how many trailblazing Italian American educators had to infiltrate the New York City Board of Education years ago to forge intermediate school Italian language education in the five boroughs. Was this how their efforts were repaid? *My mother wouldn't behave like this if she were here. She would be sitting quietly, keen to learn the language her parents had jettisoned in the name of becoming real Americans.* I felt the same. What accounted for the gulf between our attitudes? Thinking back on the class as I write these words, I believe I have the solution to the mystery that perplexed me at the time: the incremental cultural assimilation of my parents and their parents. My maternal great-grandparents had emigrated to America from Naples late in life and had a difficult time adjusting culturally and learning English. They raised their children to speak English. My mother grew up speaking English exclusively. The story was much the same for my dad's family. As a fourth-generation immigrant, I came to this class with as little knowledge of Italian as my great-grandparents had of English. In contrast, most of *these* Italian kids grew up with both English and Italian in their Staten Island homes and spoke both languages, because it was their parents or grandparents who had emigrated. *I* needed this class. *They* didn't.

Complicating matters further, many of these kids were Sicilian, spoke a Sicilian dialect, and resented the fact that this class would be about learning Toscano: a nationally standardized dialect indebted to the writings of Dante, Petrarch, Boccaccio, Machiavelli, and Manzoni. These Staten Island kids were here to learn a language from scratch that they had grown up with and "already knew." The only reason they were here, then, was to hear, "Speak Toscano, not Sicilian!" from the teacher time and again. Of course, the inference would be that Sicily was "nothing" next to Florence. All they needed to see was the word "Toscano" on the blackboard the first day, and they knew what the rest of the year held in store: the teacher would harangue them endlessly for reverting to colloquialisms they had picked up at home, instead of speaking textbook Italian. To prevent the teacher from making them experience both relentless region-based-humiliation and mind-numbing boredom being drilled on all the Italian they already knew — "Today we will learn the months of the year, class!" (*Yawn*) — they began acting out two seconds into the first lesson. It was a brilliant plan. After all, if the teacher couldn't get a word in edgewise, she couldn't bore them to tears or make them feel bad about their dialect.

Meanwhile, I was here, a Neapolitan American, to learn Toscano because I knew *no* form of Italian: not Sicilian, not Toscano, not anything. I was happy to do it. I had come here, by choice, to rediscover a lost heritage. Once again, my attitude placed me in an "establishment position" where I was eager to embrace "upper class" Italian mores and a learning environment that cast the other Italian kids in the role of peasants. No wonder they hated me and my suit. I remain largely ignorant of the history of this conflict, but I assume I was — unintentionally and indirectly — taking the sides of Italian fascists with a record of striving to eradicate all the regional languages of Italy using Toscano as their main weapon. Not only was this not my intention, I was today years old when I realized that such a view of my intentions was even possible. And yet, square as I can be at times, I have never considered myself "establishment." Then and now, I saw myself as culturally inferior to these kids, who spoke at least a dialect of Italian, even if it wasn't "proper" Italian. I was in awe of their bilingual superpowers. When I overheard the girls speaking Sicilian to one another, I found myself as erotically thrilled as Jamie Lee Curtis when Kevin Kline and John Cleese spoke Italian to her in *A Fish Called Wanda*. In my mind, these Sicilian American kids were not the peasants. I was the peasant trying to claw my way up to their plane from the bottom of my monolingual pit. I was the fake Italian hoping to become a real one.

What was the upshot of all this? On that first day, I concluded that I would probably learn nothing this year because of all the screaming, singing, and carrying on. How could I possibly learn to speak Italian under these circumstances? *This* was the class I gave up ALEC for?

Two tiny, steely eyed music teachers stood before an astonishingly quiet and attentive gathering of forty sixth graders assembled in the auditorium. Mrs. Vitali, a stocky woman with short, spiked, gray hair, spoke first. "You are here because you want a music minor. Those with experience playing an instrument will audition here. Anyone interested in chorus will audition with Mrs. Laird in her classroom." Mrs. Laird, a slim woman with a jet-black bowl cut, nodded. I raised my hand and asked Mrs. Vitali if anyone who had never played an instrument could audition. She replied, "I prefer students with experience. What instrument are you interested in?"

"Flute, guitar, or piano." I picked them because they struck me as best for solo playing.

"We don't need anyone else on keyboard." Mrs. Vitali walked to the auditorium's elevated stage, poked through the array of instruments she had laid out, and produced a flute and acoustic guitar. As she handed me the flute, I forced the extrovert side of my personality to the forefront and slipped into a chatty mode. "I like my dad's Christmas album with James Galway. It has 'I Saw Three Ships.' And his Jethro Tull vinyl, *Aqualung*." This piece of trivia intended to foster intimacy bored Mrs. Vitali. I looked furtively at the other students, who were either equally disinterested or watching attentively, hoping the boy in the gray pinstripe suit would humiliate himself. I placed my lips around the mouth hole and blew. Silence.

"Pretend you're blowing into a soda bottle." Mrs. Vitali's voice was a model of practiced patience. I tried again. Nothing. I tried three more times. I made spitting sounds.

"Damien blows!" one student yelled. I didn't get it.

"Okay, that's more than enough of that." Mrs. Vitali took the flute from me and handed me the guitar. As my fingers curled around the big-hipped, big-bosomed wooden body, I couldn't shake the feeling that the guitar was a curvaceous woman. All thumbs, I couldn't get a proper grip on Galatea, play her, and avoid taking liberties. Palms sweaty and terrified of dropping it, I searched for a less suggestive handhold. *Pardon me, ma'am. I know we've only just met. Please excuse me for strumming your strings.* Mrs. Vitali let out an impatient sigh and swiped the guitar from my grasp. "I don't know what you were doing there, but you don't seem comfortable. Instrument playing just isn't in your blood. You should audition for chorus."

"Singing?" I liked to sing along to my parents' collection of vintage music records as I danced around the turntable in our family basement but singing with others in public performance was an alien and disturbing notion. "Girls sing. Boys don't sing." Thanks to what I had heard of rock, folk, country, and hair metal, I was under the impression that women sang songs and men either spoke their way through songs, like Johnny Cash, or screamed their way through songs, like Axl Rose. Bob Dylan, Rod Stewart, and other male singers annoyed me.

"I need more altos," Mrs. Laird said. "You come with me." Mrs. Laird looked over my shoulder at the others. "Everyone interested in chorus, come with me."

Two other boys and twenty girls followed Mrs. Laird and me out of the room and down the hallway. *I'm surrounded by girls? Where are all the boys? What in hell am I supposed to talk to girls about? I bet none of them like dimetrodons!*

We filed into Mrs. Laird's music room, a long affair with three rows of seats. At the front of the room was Mrs. Laird's upright piano and a black chalkboard with a grand staff painted onto it, with a treble clef painted on the upper staff and bass clef on the lower. An overhead projector on a dolly cast the lyrics to "The Cat Came Back" on the side wall. The facing wall had windows with a captivating view of the faculty parking lot seen through open venetian blinds.

The auditions commenced. Each prospective chorus member took turns trying to match with their voices the notes Mrs. Laird played on her saloon piano. Dry-throated, tentative, and quivering, I sang off-key throughout my first effort. My (undiagnosed) asthmatic breathing was odd to boot. Mrs. Laird's expression revealed a determination to wring better from me. "Try again." I took a breath. She played more notes. I matched them perfectly. Mrs. Laird looked at me with relief. "As I suspected. You choke when you're nervous, but you're good when you hit your stride. Don't be nervous."

It was hard not to be nervous being one of only three boys in the class. The first two rows held sopranos. The three altos were sent to the third row, in back of the room. Since no one's voice was deeper than an alto level yet, that was the extent of the sorting. My fellow altos were Viola Costa and Aurora Robertazzi. They had been left back twice, were two years older than the rest of us, and well into puberty. Their world-weary air was one giveaway that they did not belong among us. Their enormous boobs provided additional evidence. They were so curvaceous they made the rest of the girls in chorus look like Charlie Brown. Viola wore Daisy-Duke shorts and an unbuttoned white blouse over a white bustier. Blue-glitter eyeshadow, blood-red lipstick, and blood-red fingernails contributed to an over-made-up look. Her partner-in-crime, Aurora, wore jeans and a turtle-neck sweater, both two sizes too small, and too much make-up. After whispering conspiratorially to one another, Viola and Aurora sat on either side of me. I felt keenly aware of being eleven years old, five-feet tall, and gawky. These girls were fourteen, five-four, voluptuous, bathed in perfume, and terrifying. They were the predators. I was the prey.

"Nice suit," Viola whispered in my left ear. "So hot."

My brain knew enough to be insulted and humiliated, but my crotch didn't get the memo.

"Does anyone have a stapler?" Mrs. Laird called out to the class. She fiddled with music at her piano. I reached into my backpack, produced a stapler, and brought it to her. She used it and handed it right back. I returned to my seat and slid the stapler into my canvas messenger bag.

"What else you got in there?" Aurora asked, mocking me for being too-well-prepared.

"Deck of cards if you want to play Spades later."

Digging her red nails into my thigh, Aurora spoke into my ear in a breathy voice. "I want to play with your cock later." At my other side, Viola coordinated her attack with Aurora's, pursing her lips and blowing into my other ear. I flushed beat red and looked down at my shoes. *They're making fun.* Of course, like an idiot, I was in danger of becoming aroused by flirtatious bullying. I hated myself for it. I tried to make my voice firm, but it quivered. "Knock it off."

"'Knock it off,'" the girls said to each other, perfectly imitating my shaky tone.

I tried to focus on Mrs. Laird, who explained we would be singing "The Cat Came Back" today. Viola continued the tag-team verbal teasing by directing her next thoughts to Aurora. "Why wait? Why not give him a blowjob right here, right now, in the back of the room?"

Incredible as it might seem in this day and age, I had grown up without cable television in the era before the invention of the internet, so I had managed to reach the sixth grade without ever finding out what a blowjob was. My mind raced as I struggled to use context clues to figure out what it was. *What are they offering me? I take my dick out and they blow on it like they blow in my ear? Tickle it and make it get bigger? No. That can't be right. Wait. The movie* Parenthood. *Mary Steenburgen unzipped Steve Martin when he was driving, started sucking on his dick, and they got into a car accident. If that's it, shouldn't it be a "suck" job? Man, with all the stupid vampire sex movies Dad showed me growing up* — Santo vs. the Vampire Women, Lust for a Vampire, The Vampire Lovers — *nobody ever used the term "blowjob" for nuthin!*

"Whip it out," Aurora whispered. "I want to see it."

I forced a smile. "You two are funny. You're too much."

Aurora turned "Whip it out" into a whispered mantra. She was remarkably adept at making her yearning sound as genuine as possible.

Little joke between friends. If I'm gonna be teased relentlessly, this is much better than getting tripped, gum spat in my hair, or called "fag" every minute of every day. This is almost nice in comparison, right? Two older chicks with big boobs flirting with me. No problem here. I mean, hey, isn't one of them wearing lingerie instead of a shirt, for God's sake? That's cool! Daisy Duke shorts? Bonus. This is a win-win. Too bad they're kinda destroying me with this crap. Making me feel like total shit. My stomach was starting to churn. "Okay, that's enough."

Aurora rubbed my shoulder, feeling the material of my suit. "This suit is making me wet. My pussy is crying out for you."

Okay, at least I have some idea of what she's talking about now because of Jaws. My penis was beginning to wake up in my pants. I attempted to use telepathy to will it back into its usual state of limp submission. *No, no! You go back to sleep, moron. It's a con.*

Viola traced her blood red fingernails up and down my thigh. She dug her nails deep into my pant leg, as if trying to puncture the skin underneath. "Whip it out. Fuck my mouth."

Guess confirmed. Now I know what a blowjob is. Thanks for the assist, Parenthood.

Aurora joined in. "Cum inside my mouth. I wanna swallow it. Suck you dry."

Oh, great. Sex bullying in stereo. Even more graphic. What happened to the guy who just slapped Debbie Cohen? Where's he when I need him? The problem was, I was so ashamed of myself for hitting a girl, I promised myself never to raise a hand to a woman again. How could I fight back if I had banished Dr. Strangelove for good? "Cut it out, or I'm gonna hit you," I lied.

"Oooooh!" cooed Aurora. "Are you gonna spank us? With a paddle with holes in it?"

"What are you gonna do?" asked Viola.

I had nothing. No idea. *Wouldn't threatening to go to the teacher just sound stupid? What would I say to Mrs. Laird: "Please, make the girls stop flirting with me?"* I crossed my arms in front of my chest, scowled, and looked at my shoes. "This is getting a bit mean, you know."

Viola pretended to be getting more excited by the moment. Her breathing turned ragged. Her chest heaved up and down in her bustier. "But we need you, little boy. We need you inside us. We want to eat your tiny hairless dick."

The blood pounded in my ears. I could barely hear anything Mrs. Laird was saying. Nobody else was in the room but us. I was consumed by rage, shame, fear, and volcanic sexual arousal. "Please stop it."

Viola pretended to be shocked and offended. "You think we don't mean it? Can't you see how much we love you? You're the boy we've been waiting for all our lives. We *love* you."

"That's so not cool. Don't ever say you love someone if you don't mean it." They were about to ruin the word "love" for me for good. Now I understood how Cordelia felt in *King Lear*.

Viola looked past me at Aurora. "He can't know how wet I am right now."

"I need to know," Aurora whispered. "Do you have hair on your dick yet?"

"He hasn't hit puberty," Viola giggled. "I bet he's got nothing down there."

No, I didn't have pubic hair yet. No, I had never once ejaculated.

"He's so tiny and innocent," Viola smirked.

"In his cute little suit, like a little businessman," Aurora said. "Wanna play boss and secretary, little boy?"

I lowered my head between my legs, folding myself into a seated fetal position.

"Are you alright back there?" Mrs. Laird called out, finally noticing something odd.

I looked up. "Stomachache. Can I go to the bathroom?"

"Are you going to throw up?" Mrs. Laird asked. "If you aren't, wait 'til after class. And there's been a lot of talking in that back row. Keep it down." I nodded and said nothing. Mrs. Laird resumed her lecture about what the coming year would entail.

"Thanks for not ratting us out," Aurora whispered.

I exhaled through my nose. "Please tell me you aren't going to do this to me every lesson. If this is about the suit, I promise I'll wear better clothes tomorrow."

Viola whispered, "As soon as I get home from school, I'm gonna strip naked in my living room. I'm gonna spread out across the couch, and I'm gonna finger-fuck myself until I cum hard. And I'm gonna do it imagining I'm getting pounded by your adorable little hairless cock. And I'm gonna scream out your name when I cum."

I held my head in my hands like I was massaging a migraine out of my temple. I tried to conceal as much of my face as I could. I had no idea what kind of expression I wore. It must have been grotesque in the extreme: I couldn't have been more aroused, humiliated, enraged, and nauseated all at once.

CHAPTER FIVE
How Was Your Day?

Hyperventilating and drenched in perspiration, I barged into the outer chamber of Principal Poliseno's office. The beige, non-descript waiting room had a dark ash finished secretary's desk with a faux Fiddle Leaf Tree in a pot beside it. Poliseno's secretary, Ms. Pac-Man, asked what I wanted. Gasping for air, I requested an audience with the man himself. His Super-Mario-like presence filled his office doorway, the logo of the New York City Board of Education hanging just overhead. "Yes?" He made no gesture to invite me in.

I huffed, holding my side when I felt a mystery twinge of pain. "I turned down a spot in the gifted program here. It was a mistake. I've changed my mind. I want in."

"I don't understand," Poliseno said. "The rosters were triple-checked for accuracy."

I dragged the back of my hand across my forehead to wipe away some of the sweat. "I wanted to take Italian, but there's a policy that people in gifted classes can't take Italian here, so I was placed in a mainstream class. I want to be in the gifted program and take Italian. Or be in honors and take Spanish. Whichever you allow."

Mr. Poliseno frowned. "There's no such policy."

I continued to struggle to control my ragged breathing. I was an asthmatic and didn't know it. I wouldn't be diagnosed for another thirteen years. I was also mildly bipolar and wouldn't be prescribed Bupropion until I was forty (on November 9, 2016, for obvious reasons). "Why was my fifth-grade teacher told about that policy when he called to ask about me?"

Mr. Poliseno shook his head. "We don't have that policy."

"Great. I'll take Italian and the gifted class, then."

Mr. Poliseno shook his head. "Listen, I don't know who you think you are barging in and making demands, but if you were placed in a mainstream class, then that's where you belong, especially since this policy you are referring to is a total fiction."

I pulled myself up to my full height. "*I am Damien Cavalieri!*"

"'I am Damien Cavalieri!' Like that's supposed to mean something to me."

"I'm a gifted student. I deserve to be in the gifted class."

"Oh, yeah? Where's your proof?"

A prideful Klingon, I pounded my fist against my chest. "In the pudding! Talk to me for five minutes. You'll see I'm brilliant! Head and shoulders above any other sixth grader."

"You seem to think highly of yourself!"

"I do! I give myself four stars . . . *out of four!*"

Mr. Poliseno waved me away dismissively, "Yeah, yeah. Tell your story walkin'." He stepped back into his office and closed the door.

The yellow school bus dropped me off in the same place it had picked me up a lifetime ago that morning, on Willowbrook Road across the street from a ditch with a stream running from the backyards of the neighborhood houses into a pond in nearby Willowbrook Park. Surprisingly, Tony Nocerino and his band of Merry Men split up and went home after spending the bus ride flipping me off at regular intervals. Normally, they spent every afternoon frolicking beside the stream, listening to Guns N' Roses, and throwing rocks at the cardinals in the White Oak trees. I was eager to flee enemy occupied territory for the safety of my home, but I didn't trust myself not to disintegrate into tears in front of my parents the second I walked through the door. The relief of being home would be too much for me. Would some exposure to nature give me some small sense of calm before I stepped over the threshold, into our living room? I also wasn't sure how much information I wanted to dump on my parents about my day. So much of it had been filled with abject misery. Compounding the problem, there wasn't much I imagined they could do to solve my problems, except send me to Catholic school, where I wasn't sure I wanted to go. I crossed the street. Slipping on the slickness of the grass but gaining surer footing as I made my way downhill into the ditch, I reached the rocky bottom at the edge of the small stream. From where I stood, I could see the sky, the trees, and the stream, but my view of the street above and the houses across it was obscured by the slope I had just descended. The area was dotted with White Oak trees. I saw one cardinal. This little waterway was a delightful secret in the middle of such suburban sprawl. No wonder Tony came here every day. I counted myself lucky I would have this one chance to enjoy it. I didn't want to stay long because, with my luck, the jackasses would be here any second. As afraid as I was of discovery, I needed this. I was grateful to have it. The gentle sounds the stream made as it flowed past my feet were already having a medicating effect on me. I smiled, remembering the absurd Mr. Orlov and that maniac in Italian running around yelling "Bangkok!" and punching people in the balls. Then, even those colorful characters left my thoughts. The stream washed the day from my mind. I loved nature. The best part of Staten Island was the Greenbelt Conservancy. I lived in the Borough of Parks.

Drifting on the wind, caressing my ears, the dulcet tones of Axl Rose moved closer. Someone was playing "Welcome to the Jungle" on a boombox. The song was now directly above me. Tony stopped at the top of the ditch, looking down on me. The Merry Men were behind him. "Yo! Cavalieri! That's our creek! Step off!"

"I like it," I called back up. "I kinda wanna keep it for myself!"

Tony bent over and scooped up a round, smooth, palm-sized rock. The others picked up rocks of their own. "You had your chance to join us this morning. You read *Jaws* instead."

Ten rocks flew towards me. One connected with my stomach. Another my right temple. A third my left knee. Mercifully, the others missed. I toppled over backwards, sinking my well-dressed butt into the muddy creek bank and banging the back of my head on the wet rocks. The group of boys skidded down the grass to join me beside the water. I sat up, looking frantically for an escape route. I struggled to my feet. Three more rocks struck me in my back. One bounced off the top of my head. I lost consciousness and fell face forward into the grass.

I didn't know where I was when I woke up and rolled over onto my back. Looking to my side, I saw the Merry Men sitting, sharing a bag of Twizzlers, listening to a new song that seemed to be about dancing in a brownstone. I propped myself up on my elbows. There was something obscuring my vision on my left eyeglass lens. Drying blood. Bruised and wet, I wasn't sure if my damp clothes had soaked up more water or blood.

The Billy-Idol haired Bobby Mammolito nodded at me. "You okay over there?" I gave Bobby a dumbfounded look. Bobby pressed on. "Lemme ax you something. If you wake up in a tent, and your pants are unzipped, and your underwears are sticky, and your asshole hurt, but you didn't see anybody around, would you tell anyone?"

"I don't know." I grimaced. "I guess not."

Bobby brightened. "Great! Wanna come camping with me?"

Half of the others burst out laughing. The rest flinched at the joke. Tony eyed Bobby warily. "What's with the gay shit?"

"Chill out, man." Bobby hocked a loogie into the stream. "It's just a joke."

Tony pointed an angry finger at me. "None of us fucked yur ass when you wuz asleep, just soz ya know!"

"Jolly decent of you, Tony," I said in an ineptly recreated "Received Pronunciation" British accent. I glanced about for an escape route, but had trouble focusing my eyes or attention. I had a distracting sense of déjà vu. There was something "Stephen King" about this tableau. Was this real life, or had I wandered into *Stand by Me?* Or that phonebook-sized novel with the demon clown that Mitchell was telling me about? Which one had rocks and bullies by a lake?

"All right, you little bastards! Get the fuck away from my son!"

All of us looked up to see my mother standing on the high ground in her ice gray polo coat, staring down upon us. She held aloft a massive rock and a small plastic grocery bag filled to bursting with other huge rocks she had gathered along the roadside above. The petite forty-three-year-old with a round face and curly, shoulder-length black hair was Italy's answer to Shirley Temple, Betty Boop, and the Utz potato chips girl. Adorable as she was usually, she was now far less cute and far more red-faced with rage. She looked ready to murder.

"What're you gonna do, bitch?" Tony shot back, "Throw rocks at us?"

A rock the size of a volleyball hurtled towards Tony, striking him in the collarbone. He dropped to the ground. Faced with the options of racing uphill towards the madwoman and her rock arsenal or sprinting off the other way into the backyards of the suburban homes flanking the stream, the others chose retreat. Bobby Mammolito led the retreat, winking at me before he headed off. I wasn't sure what the wink meant. An apology for the rock assault? An olive branch? An acknowledgement that my mom was cool? A promise to lead the others away from Mom when the Merry Men were itching for a rumble? Who knew? I was too tired to care.

Tony hurled a curse at my mom, scrambled to his feet, and ran off after the others, wondering why they were running when they should have been able to beat her in a fight.

I stood up and looked at Mom, who watched the retreating figures until they disappeared. She said to me out of the corner of her mouth, "Can't you walk three blocks home without something like this happening? I can't let you out of my sight for a minute!"

"I know, Mom." I lumbered up the grassy slope and stood beside her. "I feel the same."

Our blue Oldsmobile Cutlass Ciera was half on the grass, half on the street, with the passenger door open. I got in. Mom slipped into the driver's seat. We drove three blocks home.

I sat at the circular oak kitchen table, underneath the tan rotary phone mounted on our hot orange kitchen wall. The rest of the wall was decorated with two of Mom's wooden-framed crewel embroidery scenes — one of an old mill and another of a 19th-century general store interior. Mom had set me up at the kitchen table with a hot cup of tea and three Stella D'oro S-shaped Italian breakfast treats. The tea and cookies had helped, but I still stared sullenly at my snacks, holding my bandaged forehead.

My dad crept into the room, eager to check up on me. With his 1970s pornstache, blue checkered shirt, cotton dockers, and brown penny loafers, my eccentric and loveably reactionary dad looked like Nicolas Cage in *Moonstruck* and used Bruce Dern's most unusual facial expressions and mannerisms. If Dad hadn't looked like a prominent Italian American actor, few would peg him as Italian. Admittedly, he loved eating Italian food as often as possible and had affection for Mario Lanza. He was familiar with his Italian roots, knowing his Italian-speaking grandparents were natives of Naples and Salerno. His father had been bi-lingual, but dad spoke only English and knew of no living relatives in Italy. Despite these Italian connections and how little he knew about his German relatives and ancestry, he took greater pride in his German bloodline. He fancied himself a German aristocrat and assumed many upper-class mannerisms (when he wasn't behaving like a lecherous Benny Hill comedy sketch character). When asked what part of Italy he came from, he would say, "North. Far north. Munich." Dad was a character.

Dad took a seat next to me, pretending he hadn't heard about my misadventures through Mom. "So, how was your day?"

"Swell." I burst out laughing, provoking dad to chortle. Dad hadn't been sure I would recognize his *Jaws* movie quote until I had responded with the correct follow-up line. In the film, Chief Brody was wrongfully blamed for the death of a little boy who was eaten by the shark, when it had been Mayor Vaughn's fault little Alex Kintner had died. The Chief is brooding at his dining room table when Matt Hooper arrives, sits beside him and asks, "How was your day?" They laugh at the graveyard humor and share a drink. (Hooper is *way* nicer in the movie.)

When dad and I recovered our laughing fit, I nodded approvingly at him. "You know exactly who you're dealing with."

Dad had a broader grin, a more prominent chin, and bigger eyes than me. I tried not to be jealous that he would make the better Joker. "Tell you what," Dad said softly, "if the kids at school are jerks, to hell with them. Have your tea. Have your cookies. To hell with them. Put them right out of your mind. Read a comic book. Watch a movie. Do something you like to do. Don't do homework. When you're sad, always do something you enjoy to get out of it."

I took another bite of the Stella D'Oro cookie. "Good advice."

Lying in bed that night, I remembered every insult. Every disdainful face. Every bruise and cut and piece of wet gum landing in my hair. I hadn't the first idea how to stop obsessing over these things. I'd heard rumors about masturbation being fun and stress relieving, but I hadn't really tried touching myself before. I knew I wasn't supposed to, as a

Roman Catholic, but I was also at a loss how to get through the night if I couldn't sleep. Looking up into Kelly Bundy's hazel eyes, I reached under the elastic waist of my pajama pants and massaged my penis. I closed my eyes and tried to imagine Kelly going down on me, but Aurora and Viola drove her out of my mind, invading my thoughts. Their mocking faces wouldn't go away when I wished them gone. Since I was stuck with them, I tried to imagine them saying the same words to me in my bedroom they whispered in class. This time, they spoke every piece of pornographic dialogue with total conviction. (No. Who was I kidding? When they offered me head, even in the privacy of my room, in my imagination, they were only kidding. Only teasing. Only bullying. The soul-flaying mockery was back in their voices.) After five minutes of frustration and humiliation, I gave up fantasizing about the girls from Chorus. My effort to warp grim reality into something more acceptable hadn't work for an instant. I knew it was a lie. I couldn't begin to make myself aroused.

Those two found the prospect of sex with me endlessly hysterical. Maybe the idea of sex with me is fundamentally funny. I am eleven, after all. I'm just a kid. Or maybe all *women will* always *feel that way about me, no matter how much my body matures? If these two babes thought the very idea of sex with me was absurd, wouldn't every other girl? The number of women worldwide who are attracted to me is an empty set.*

CHAPTER SIX
O Fortuna!

Three years earlier . . .
    November 9, 1984
    Staten Island
    "Before I got married, I used to be a fun and interesting person."
    Mom sat on the overstuffed green couch in the living room of our semi-attached house, flipping through several photo albums chronicling her multiple 1960s excursions to Europe. She had used funds left over from her full-tuition college scholarships to see England, Italy, Greece, Spain, and France. She traveled in the company of childhood and college friends, none of whom she had seen since marrying my father, Vincent Cavalieri junior. Coiffed like Jackie Kennedy, Mom wore then-trendy fashions in the faded color photographs: canary yellow women's pantsuits, electric blue matching blouse and skirt sets, and lots of plaid. The Gianna Basile in these photos was twenty years younger than Gianna Cavalieri but had the same "Betty Boop"-look. I fancied we strongly resembled each other. I was in third grade, the youngest and tallest boy in ALEC, with brown hair parted on the side, a slightly crooked nose, large-but-pinned-back ears, and arched eyebrows. I wore oversized brown plastic glasses, brown corduroy pants, and a "space age" turquoise and white pullover. I touched my eight-year-old finger to a ginger-bread cottage snapshot. "Is this Asterix the Gaul's house?"
    Pointed roof cottages, well-manicured lawns and gardens, and low stone walls filled four pages of photos, placing Mom and her besties in a fairy tale England come alive. "That's the Cotswolds," Mom sighed. "Of course, it would be too expensive for us to go now." She reached for the table lamp beside her and turned it on. Night was falling. We could see the sun setting through the sliding doors that led out to our backyard deck and above-ground pool. We lived in a semi-attached home with a railroad apartment feel on the main level. The wood-paneling and soft blue, plush carpeted combined earth tones with cool colors to give our family room a womb-like effect. Across the room, a painting of Ichabod Crane racing across the Pocantico River Bridge

to escape the Headless Horseman hung over our TV and VHS stand.

As Mom flipped through the album, I saw Polaroids of buildings built of stone and marble during Ancient Rome, the Middle Ages, and the Renaissance. These glorious edifices, centuries old, stood in majestic rebuke of the family homes of Staten Island, made of anything but Roman marble. Nobly designed for the working-classes and the lower-middle-classes — that is to say, people exactly like us — the homes of Staten Island had a cookie-cutter feel. I was grateful for the affordable housing, but disappointed that "affordable housing" meant, by necessity, "uninspired housing," since street after street of Staten Island looked exactly the same, like Privet Drive in Little Whinging, Surrey. Imagine if the architects of the Cotswolds or San Gimignano had designed the stretches of Staten Island intended for the upwardly mobile urban poor? Sadly, American architecture is Puritanical: functional and cheap, not useful and beautiful.

I felt trapped in Staten Island. I wanted to see Italy, but the European countries featured in Mom's photo albums seemed as far away to me as Mars and as fictional as Oz. In fact, given Mom's grousing about money and marriage, I was now convinced I would never see Europe. Her rhetoric had been too fatalistic and too effective by half. Oz was now far more real and attainable than the Cotswolds. If wanted to travel, I would have to travel in my imagination, via science fiction, fantasy, and horror popular fiction. I could travel in the TARDIS with the Doctor by watching *Doctor Who* or on the Starship Enterprise with Kirk, Spock, and McCoy by watching *Star Trek*. Any time I wanted New York to be more welcoming or whimsical than it was, I could read about the alternate reality New York of Marvel Comics, where Doctor Strange lived in Greenwich Village, Spider-Man in Queens, and the Fantastic Four and Avengers in Manhattan. Conversely, if I wanted to confront everything I hated about New York and modern America, I could read serious, respectable literature about it, or watch Spike Lee and Martin Scorsese films. There was plenty of time to read bleak novels and watch depressing arthouse movies when I got older. Back then, I preferred Marvel's New York to the moral ambiguities of the *real* New York and its artistic representations. Mom's taste was the reverse. She wanted to see her life reflected in art. She had no time for "the stuff you and your dad like with robots and mummies in it."

Mom reached her photos of Greece. "When you go to college, you must study abroad."

"Yes, Mom. I want to." *How?*

To my amusement and discomfort, Mom stumbled upon some photos of her college boyfriends: Three Persian men studying at Long Island University on student visas, all of whom were part of a resistance movement against the Shah. Mom pointed at a swarthy, fit man in sunglasses. "That's Kamran. When I first met him, I told him the emerald ring he wore was lovely. He just took it off and handed it to me! He told me that Persian custom demanded you offer a possession as a gift to a person who expresses admiration for it. I had to accept it from him or risk insulting him." Kamran seemed like a nice enough fellow, though it was a blurry and grainy photo of him. I blinked several times to make it out better. No, it wasn't my eyesight.

"You should have told him you liked his car," I joked.

If Mom had married Kamran instead of Vincent Cavalieri, Jr., would I even exist? Good thing this handsome fellow hadn't won Mom over for more than a brief romantic interlude. And yet, dad's approval rating was tanking these days, while Kamran's was on the rise, if for no other reason than nostalgia. As Mom switched albums to photos from three decades earlier, when she was a baby and a young girl, my brother Leo came into the room. At five, he was three years younger than me and had a full-on-adorable-male-Betty-Boop-face. I enjoyed hugging and kissing him far too much, but he was so dang cute. Leo arrived in time to glimpse pictures of Mom looking more like Shirley Temple than ever in black-and-white. We also saw Uncle Carmine at eighteen, a slim, Italian Elvis Presley, instead of the chubbier, Paul-Sorvino-meets-Ralph-Kramden figure of today. Then there were the photos of my grandparents, and Bianca and Baby Bianca, of toddler "Alexa Hente" and his twin, Gabriel. As Mom looked at the youthful faces, playing in parks in Brooklyn, sunbathing on the roofs of tenements, and swimming in Lake Hopatcong, she mourned the past and cried freely. She pointed to a bald man I didn't recognize who had his shirt off and wore a gold crucifix about his neck. "That's one of my uncles. He died when I was ten. He had something curable, but he never went to the doctor in his life. He waited too long to get treatment, and it killed him. Almost my entire family is dead."

Leo leaned in and frowned at the photos. "These are all the dead Italians who matter so much more to you than we do?" It was a surprisingly bitter and psychologically insightful question from a five-year-old, but Leo had been well-prepped to ask it, given how regularly Mom had gone through this photo album ritual over the past year. She had done it *a lot*. Thanks to her tone deafness and a dying hearing aid battery, Mom didn't hear Leo's question. He shook his head in sad, angry confusion and walked away. Unfortunately, Leo was right to feel neglected. Recently, Mom had grown so mired in the past that she no longer occupied the present day as completely as we did. It was understandable. She had just suffered the devastating loss of her father, Angelo. Mom had worshipped the man. Even though I'd only known him as a frail, irascible figure, I had some sense of why. I have many memories of Grandpa Angelo sitting in the backyard on a folding chair, his shirt off in the summer heat, watching me run around the sloping grass, throwing a football in the air to myself and failing to catch it on the way back down. He would also sit in front of the house on the same folding chair as I'd shoot basketball hoops by myself. As I played, he would work on the newspaper crossword puzzle of the day, wearing his glasses on a chain around his neck, but using them only when he couldn't make out a line of small newsprint. If Tony Nocerino and the Merry Men from Buchanan Avenue would wander into our Orthodox Jewish neighborhood on Kell Avenue and give me a hard time, Grandpa would get up out of his chair, wave his fist at them and yell, "Get away from him, you dumb sons of bitches!" Then they'd scurry off.

When Grandpa had the chance to, he'd make spaghetti and meatballs using an old recipe for gravy that involved tomato paste, garlic, olive oil, Italian seasonings, a dash of red wine, and two cans of peeled tomatoes. (Apologies to Peter Clemenza and Mario Batali: Grandpa did not use any sugar.) He enjoyed buying fresh food imported from Italy that was a little higher end than Mom's consistent repertoire of spaghetti, rigatoni, fusilli, fettucine, and ravioli. His menu included calamari, mussels, egg creams, and wine. Mom liked to live under her means and never met a credit card statement she didn't pay off instantly. Her father was poorer, but slightly more extravagant. During Easter 1983, Grandpa found two giant chocolate bunnies for my brother and I. Mom balked at her father spending so much on chocolate. Grandpa looked first at the bunnies, then Leo's cherubic face, then mine. "I like to see how happy they look when they each eat their own bunny." Mom felt like a killjoy, but also boundless love for her father.

To hear Mom tell it, her relationship with Grandpa was so untroubled, they only had one disagreement. Mom was the first member of her family to go to college, which was why Grandpa was not prepared when she broached the subject of enrolling in Long Island University in 1960. "College!" he exclaimed. "What for? It's a breeding ground for degenerates." However, Mom told him firmly she wanted to go. He backed down once he understood how serious she was. Mom loved literature and wanted to study it but didn't want to move away from her family to get the degree. She won a full scholarship to LIU, a school reachable from their 64th street apartment in Brooklyn via public transportation. Mom studied there from 1961 to 1965. Between the full scholarship and an additional Regents College Scholarship, she was provided more than enough money to earn her bachelor's and master's, travel to Europe, and come within striking distance of a doctorate in English. As fulfilling as these experiences were, they were tainted by tragedy. Mom's mother, Francesca Basile, died suddenly on Aug 11, 1963, radically undercutting Mom's baseline capacity for happiness.

At Francesca's wake, Mom's maternal grandmother and aunt seemed to blame LIU for killing Francesca. Maybe they blamed Mom herself for Francesca's death.

"If only you hadn't won that scholarship..." Her portly, black-veil-wearing grandmother let the unfinished sentence hang in the air.

Mom's portly, black-veil wearing aunt nodded in sad agreement. Mom was too stunned to reply.

The inference was clear. Mom had accidentally murdered her own mother by winning a college scholarship. She was being condemned by a fatalistic Southern Italian superstition — there is a finite amount of good luck in the world, so be careful not to use up your family's portion too soon. Will the jealous place an evil eye upon the family? Will the Wheel of Fortune turn again and crush us all? Good news often felt much the same as bad news to those with this mindset.

Thankfully, Mom's cousin, Emily Basile-Scrosciare, overheard the grandmother and aunt, and swooped in to offer a more scientific view of Francesca's passing. Young Emily was the newly minted Wall Street stockbroker of the family. She would eventually retire at forty-one by making a killing in investments and not blowing it all on hedonistic partying as many of her male colleagues did. To my knowledge, no one ever accused Emily of bringing misfortune down upon the family by doing so well in her career. Of course, she did have to deal with her share of jealousy from the rest of the family and was sometimes viewed as standoffish. For my part, I'll always be grateful to her for trying to save my mother from being burdened by supernatural guilt. On the night of the wake, Emily reassured Mom that a college scholarship had not murdered Francesca. In fact, Grandma Francesca was a chain-smoker and compulsive cleaner who used harsh chemicals and cleaning agents to wash and wax the floor of her 64th street apartment every day. "I saw Francesca scrubbing the floor on her hands and knees day in and day out," Emily explained. "Coughing, breathing in poisonous fumes, and smoking. I said to her, 'You're gonna poison yourself breathing all that stuff in every day!' Francesca said back, 'If it kills me, it kills me. I want a clean house.' Watching her do that made me vow never to become a housewife. I'm not dying for a clean house. And I'd never be a smoker, either." After hearing Emily's story, Mom's brain understood that Emily was right. Grandma Francesca's lung cancer probably came from both her smoking and the cleaning agents, not an evil curse brought down from on high because Mom had dared go to college. Mom's heart, however, rejected Emily's theory and embraced the supernatural explanation that placed the blame squarely upon her head.

I wouldn't get to know Emily until years later, when I was eight and she was nearing retirement. Even at eight, Emily's poise, expensive clothes, expertly applied make-up, perfect teeth, and slender figure impressed me. She is one of the few centered, happy, and successful people I have ever met. Thinking of her now, I wonder: Who in their right mind would pick Francesca's life path instead of Emily's? Die from breathing noxious fumes during housework or retire wealthy and gorgeous at forty? Was that, essentially, the choice that awaited all women? Throughout my childhood, Mom strove to be an uncomfortable combination of the two: career woman, housewife, and mother all in one. Nineteen-eighty-three was the year the effort to walk the toughest path of all began to break my mother.

Mom's graduate school and career plans hadn't panned out as she expected. Within a few years of graduating college and going to graduate school at New York University, Mom had reached the stage when she had finished all of her courses and it was time for her to read several hundred books to prepare for her various subject area comprehensive exams. Of course, she was eager to begin her teaching career and make some money and had recently landed a job teaching writing courses at Fordham University as an adjunct. She went to the chair of the English Department at NYU and asked for a leave of absence, during which she could gradually read all the books on her reading list and still teach on the side. She was, as it happens, exhausting herself keeping up with both adjunct teaching and fulfilling her obligations as a graduate student. The chair of the department said soberly, "You can rest when you are dead." Mom replied, "I'm not that tired," and withdrew from the program. She never completed her doctorate in English.

Fortunately for Mom, she found full-time employment at a city university which, after a large shakeup that included a merger and the institution of the revolutionary multicultural policy of open enrollment, became New York City Technical College. She wound up teaching composition, remedial writing, and first-year literature courses there for twenty-five years. All in all, Mom's career as both a student and teacher in the New York higher education system was shaped by the changing fortunes of the humanities majors from the sixties through the eighties. Thanks to the Cold War and fears that the Russians were gaining ground on the United States technologically and via the overall strength of its intelligentsia, the American government subsidized higher education to an astonishing degree. Humanities majors like my mother reaped the benefit from the initiative as much as scientists-in-training.

Unfortunately, by the time she finished her time in graduate school and began looking for a teaching career, the bottom fell out of English departments in higher education, especially in the City University of New York. Open enrollment meant colleges were made available to everyone, including those who were new immigrants who didn't speak English well, those who had gotten their GEDs and hadn't been in a classroom in years, and those who had been purposefully cursed with dreadful grade school education by the evils of institutional racism. The democratization of college and the end to elitism were noble goals, but those, effectively, led to the watering-down of the literature curriculum at Mom's college and many others. For one thing, the pragmatism of first-generation college students compelled many of them to look to vocational-school-type majors first and discouraged some from even considering majoring in a humanities or liberal arts field. For another, the degree of remediation required to *try* to teach these legions of new students basic writing skills to make up for what they hadn't learned in grade school was considerable. They had so much catching up to do just to be able to survive life in a two-year-professionally-oriented-college. Life in a four-year-liberal-arts-college would be even more challenging to prepare for. How could students with no discernable ability to read or write in English be expected to understand the works of Nathaniel Hawthorne or Herman Melville? Mom only managed to teach "Bartleby the Scrivener" and "Young Goodman Brown" for the first couple of years of her career. Soon after, her courses changed. She taught basic grammar and the four-paragraph essay to remedial writing students at New York City Technical College her whole career. "Being a college teacher is a good job, overall," she told me. "Still, if you can find a way to teach more literature courses than remedial writing, I'd recommend it. If it were up to me, I'd teach a lot more American Romanticism. This whole teaching primarily remedial writing thing I have to do? 'I would prefer not to.'" She would shake her head at students who would describe the sex they had last night in their essays instead of answering the writing prompts; scrunch her eyes at illegible handwriting, awful grammar, and terrible spelling, as well as wonder why she would have to fail the same student four times before they disappeared when school policy demanded they could only take remedial writing twice before being expelled. Mom had trouble making her way through these papers. To boost her morale, she blasted her Charles Aznavour albums as she graded. Thankfully, I didn't mind the music, or the volume Mom needed to play it at to hear it. While she graded, I stole her blank blue examination books and wrote and drew my own "Little Golden Books," often involving a kaiju attacking New York, or hands coming up from open manhole covers and dragging innocent pedestrians into the sewers.

Since Mom never read for her doctoral-level comprehensive exams and rarely taught great literature, she missed the hardcore literature she had read as a graduate student. She remembered the comprehensives reading list she had never completed. While she had no intention of finishing her doctorate, she hit the classics again, reading seventy-five books in a summer. This feat amazed her brother. At a family reunion the summer following Mom's great classics-reading-list tear, Uncle Carmine took to bragging about Mom's great accomplishment to his Wall Street cousins, Emily Basile-Scrosciare and her husband, Matt Scrosciare.

"You know who the smartest person I ever met is?" Uncle Carmine asked. "My sister! Gianna is so smart. She read eighty books in a summer. Eighty! I can't get over it. My dad read two books in his life: *The Godfather* and the Bible. I've read one book: *The Conscience of a Conservative* by Barry Goldwater. I couldn't read eighty books in a lifetime. I couldn't even read to the end of the list of eighty books she made. I read the first ten books, didn't recognize the titles, and stopped reading. Compare that with my sister!"

Matt cut in, huffily, "Emily and I read a book a week. We're retired and we have the time to do it. Gianna isn't the only brain in the family."

Emily chuckled. "Matt hates that I read the last chapter of a book I'm reading first and then go to the beginning. Sometimes, when I bring a book home from Barnes and Noble, I lay it on the table and go to the bathroom. When I come out, Matt has already stapled the pages of the final chapter together to keep me from reading it first!"

"And I hide the staple remover until I know she's reached the end," Matt grinned.

A judge delivering a verdict, Uncle Carmine proclaimed, "Yeah, you two aren't as smart as my sister. I bet you four thousand dollars Gianna reads higher quality books."

In fact, Mom read both serious literature and bestsellers. Her reading habits taught me it was easy to blur the line between "homework" and "fun" and "serious literature" and "potboilers." The adaptations for all the above kinds of books eventually found their way to PBS anyway. When Mom was in an Agatha Christie zone, she read at least one novel a week, singing the praises of Miss Marple. I wanted to join her and be a reader, too, but wasn't sure what books would work for me. I wasn't sold on mysteries. "Serious" science fiction seemed to have too many soldiers and androids in it. The earliest books I dared to read were the ones I was assigned in school: *The Secret of NIMH*, *Little House on the Prairie*, and *Ramona the Brave*. When the teacher asked us to pick out books to read on our own during free period, most of the boys in my class opted for *The Hitchhiker's Guide to the Galaxy* and the girls gravitated towards *A Wrinkle in Time* or books in *The Baby-Sitters Club* and *Sweet Valley High* sets. Personally, I was most eager to read *Jane Eyre*, *Great Expectations*, *Dracula*, and *Frankenstein*, because those were the narratives that I had seen gripping black-and-white adaptations of, thanks to PBS and both parents' taste in all things Gothic. Unfortunately, I had to read watered-down *Classics Illustrated* versions first to lay the groundwork for understanding the *real* novels in high school and college.

It was in the fifth grade that I finally settled into the habit of reading in the overstuffed armchair next to the plush couch my mother laid down on when she read. We would read together for several hours. I enjoyed equally the act of reading and the sense of bonding I felt sharing in my mother's love of books. I had finally settled upon a boxed set to hack my way through: L. Frank Baum's *Oz* novels. I was one of the few who had gone to Radio City Music Hall to see the premiere of the delightfully terrifying 1985 Disney film *Return to Oz*, an infamous box office bomb that triggered the reprinting of the original fourteen books, all of which I bought. Several supplemental *Oz* books by Ruth Plumly Thompson also appeared on bookshelves, but they were $6 instead of $3 and not in my price range, so I didn't buy them. I read and enjoyed the first eight of the fourteen Baum books before I burnt out. It was when I found these books to be far superior to the films inspired by them that I became "a reader." To my mind, the best scene from *The Wizard of Oz* never made it into the 1939 classic. Dorothy and company encounter the Dainty China Country — a town made of porcelain filled with living porcelain people — built across the yellow brick road. Our heroes couldn't make their way across the town without accidentally destroying buildings and putting cracks into people. It was a powerful and imaginative segment, well beyond the special effects available to '30s Hollywood. Reading it, I knew no adaptation would ever match the books for sheer imaginative power, no matter how respected the MGM film with the way-too-old Dorothy was. Even more remarkable, there was no scene in either of the two main Oz films like the one at the end of *The Emerald City of Oz,* when Dorothy discovered Toto could talk, just like every other animal in Oz. *What a revelation! Toto can talk!* No one who stuck to the films knew that! I did. I had secret knowledge lost to the rest of humanity because I was a *reader.* Mom didn't like the same kinds of books I did, and it sometimes bothered me that I didn't read hers and she didn't read mine, but I loved that we shared an appreciation of narrative, and often did our reading together.

Since we were both Italian, emotional, loved literature, and had similar features, I thought of myself as functionally Mom as a boy. However, she was far more logical and pragmatic than I was. In the early years of the Internet, we took two online personality tests that were comically revealing. The first was: "How left-brained and how right-brained are you?" Leo and I both got thirty percent left-brain (organized and systematic) and seventy percent right-brained (creative and intuitive). Mom, in contrast, registered as 94% organized and systematic and 6% creative and intuitive. The second internet personality test was "Which Jane Austen heroine are you?" Mom was Elinor Dashwood. I got Marianne Dashwood. If you don't know your Jane Austen, all you need to know is these results match the left/right brain results. I also loved science fiction, horror, and fantasy, and Mom loved realistic fiction. Given her urban worldview and indifference to NASA, I sometimes giggled imagining her reciting Gil Scott-Heron's "Whitey on the Moon."

During our early years as kids, Mom drove to work every day on the Brooklyn-Queens-Expressway. During the next two decades, the commute grew gradually worse as the traffic grew more congested and the Verrazano-Narrows Bridge toll skyrocketed. In addition to detesting the commute to what she referred to as "glorious downtown Brooklyn," Mom found the actual teaching work tiresome. As a full-time teacher without a PhD, Mom was expected to teach more classes than professors with PhDs. She was also asked to serve on more committees. She was not expected to publish scholarship or attend academic conferences. Despite her relatively short number of hours in the classroom compared to the number of hours punch-clock employees spent doing nine-to-five jobs with two weeks of vacation per year, she clearly worked like a mule grading and regrading a dozen essay assignments granted to upwards of two-hundred students a semester. Also, after Mom returned home from work, exhausted, she found herself numbed by the prospect of having to cook dinner and do housework every night. Her husband worked nights on the weekdays, so he wasn't around to help much. Even when he was home on weekends, he had a tendency towards indolence that left most household chores up to her. Essentially, Dad took out the garbage regularly, tended to the rasboras in his fish tank, planned family trips, did most of the driving, and occasionally cooked Chipped Beef on Toast for breakfast or Chicken a la King for dinner. Mom did the rest of the work. She would test his laziness by leaving laundry pointedly undone, a lawn unmowed, or a kitchen sink dripping, waiting to see how long it would take for him to notice. When he wouldn't address the issue for a week, Mom would ask him, politely, to take care of it. After another week passed, Mom flew into a rage and did it herself, screaming, "Fine! Leave it for the maid! Let the maid do it!" The most memorable of these incidents happened when I was in high school. I woke at three a.m. to the sounds of extreme labor coming from the hallway bathroom outside my bedroom. Wiping the sleep from my eyes, I stumbled up to the bathroom in my striped blue-and-white pajamas and looked inside. Breathing irregularly and sweating profusely, Mom stood on a step ladder using a roller to apply adobe brown paint to the bathroom walls; an open can of paint balanced precariously on the yellow sink. "Your father took too long." She failed at sounding casual.

"Can't you do this in the morning?" I asked.

Mom kept painting.

I sighed. "This is pretty weird, Mom."

She ignored me. If her mother could keep a small apartment gorgeous and sparkling clean every day, she would do the same for our three-level house, even if it killed her.

"Crom!" I exclaimed. "I'll do it tomorrow."

Mom kept painting.

"By the Hoary Hosts of Hoggoth!" I cried, now going to the well with as many super-hero-related spells and curses I could recall. "Nothing I say is gonna stop you, is it?"

Mom dipped the roller into the paint and slapped some more adobe brown on the wall.

Wiping sleep from his eyes, Leo emerged from his room. "Is Mom doing her martyr thing? Performing the Stations of the Cross?" He peered through the bathroom door at Mom, who would keep painting until the job was done. "Yup."

I nodded. "'Mom paints the bathroom of Pontius Pilate.' 'Mom falls the first time.'"

Leo added, "'Mom washes the Temple of Jerusalem's *opus sectile* floor on hands and knees using Pine-Sol.' 'Mom falls the second time.' Yeah, she's not stopping any time soon."

"Sweet Christmas! Let's go back to sleep."

CHAPTER SEVEN
The Smallest Ass at the Family Reunion

After Grandma Francesca died, Grandpa Angelo never even looked at another woman — except for Heather Locklear on *T.J. Hooker*. As Grandpa explained, it was okay for him to watch the show religiously to gaze upon Heather, because she looked exactly like Grandma did when they first met. Ever the romantic, Grandpa's son Carmine chuckled, "Let's be serious, Dad. I loved Mom, but she was never as pretty as Heather Locklear." Uncle Carmine was nine years older than his baby sister, my mother. He and Grandpa had spent Mom's childhood working together at the Bon Soir night club in Greenwich Village.

Grandpa was the service bartender at the Bon Soir, responsible for making the drinks in the back for waiters to pick up and bring to the patrons. Since Grandpa worked near the performers while they waited backstage, he had plenty of time to chat with Kaye Ballard, Phyllis Diller, Carolyn ("Morticia Addams") Jones, and a pre-famous Barbra Streisand and her boyfriend Elliott Gould. In addition to getting to meet performers, Grandpa and Uncle Carmine rubbed elbows with some famous customers, including Abbott and Costello, Max Baer, and "Slapsie" Maxie Rosenbloom, all of whom autographed the same hardcover scrapbook.

Grandpa's work in the bar encouraged him to drink a little too much, but he was supposedly a harmless and funny drunk. According to Mom, one night, Grandpa came home buzzed to find his family watching *The Millionaire* on television, and dinner plates and Chinese take-out boxes still on the table. Too drunk to realize he picked an already eaten spare rib off a plate of discarded bones to gnaw on, he started cursing, "Jesus Christ. There's no fucking meat on these fucking spare ribs!" Mom, Carmine, and Francesca laughed uproariously at this mistake, pointing out the five untouched spare ribs they left for him in the take-out bag on the table. Mom always laughed when she told this story, but Uncle Carmine never found it funny.

"Dad drank way too much." Carmine's words carried enormous weight. Using his natural, "Edward G. Robinson" voice, Carmine spoke his version of the unvarnished truth in simple, declarative, conversation-ending sentences. I was uncomfortable that Carmine's version of the truth rarely matched Mom's. Still, Mom's mythology was kinder and more romantic. Also, I found Carmine an unreliable narrator, especially when he would grumble highly controversial sentiments out of the side of his mouth like, "All boys should have mandatory military service before they're twenty," expecting us to agree wholeheartedly without pause. A larger-than-life figure, my Mom's brother had a big heart, was easy to mimic, and difficult to talk to.

Carmine was also remarkable in being a "self-made man." Throughout his youth, he scrimped, saved, and schemed to class jump his way out of his parents' three-room Brooklyn apartment. He concocted elaborate business plans and hit up relatives for investment capital to buy a Burger King franchise, gas station, or restaurant. While Mom was too risk-averse to give him any of her money, he raised the cash he needed somehow, eventually purchasing a string of businesses that made him one of the few wealthy members of our extended family outside of Cousin Emily. Carmine's money bought him a three-story home and Olympic pool in Marlboro, New Jersey — a palatial spread compared to our family's modest semi-attached house, let alone the tiny Brooklyn and Greenwich Village apartments the older Basiles had lived in all their lives. There were the usual jealousies directed at him, as well as expressions of profound respect.

Mom voiced disapproval of his ostentatious displays of wealth more often than she praised his business acumen, but her disapproval was not borne out of jealousy. Instead, she was troubled by his drive to succeed because she viewed it as a repudiation of their second-generation immigrant upbringing. Mom was not wrong. As much as she loved her childhood, Carmine did not share her enthusiasm for the bygone era. Mom felt nostalgia for a Brooklyn Italian community he could not wait to escape from at the time and did not enjoy recalling now. Neither one could understand the other's perspective. Their conversations made me wonder if there were such a thing as a coherent family history. In the end, did each person write their own life story? What of "history" itself? Was history not so much a reliable account of past events, but just another form of folklore? Were *all* histories and biographies *fictional?* Was "non-fiction" even real? On one of Carmine's visits to our Staten Island home, Mom showed her brother her collection of non-fiction books about Italian American history, spearheaded by *La Storia: Five Centuries of the Italian American Experience* by Jerre Mangione. Intuiting what her newfound interest in ethnic history and anthropology was about, Carmine slouched in his chair and looked sideways at Mom. "All our relatives were a bit nuts, Gianna. I'm not saying don't love 'em. If you can't forgive your family members for being stupid idiots, who can you forgive? I'm saying you need to admit they were nuts and not pretend they were angels."

Mom wasn't sure if he was mocking their relatives or praising them. "I still don't think Dad's drinking was a big deal."

I watched their exchange with interest and tension: I wasn't sure where it was headed. I sat with them, Dad, and Leo at the dining room table on a Sunday afternoon, drinking tea and eating Napoleons. Carmine swallowed the ends of his sentences, making him extra special hard for my tone-deaf mother to hear, but he made a valiant attempt to speak to her. "Gianna, you don't see people as they are. You see them as you want to see them. Everyone has some flaw."

"I loved our family growing up. The big Sunday dinners after church. Making fresh ravioli with the flour and water and eggs. I miss that so much."

Uncle Carmine shook his head sadly. "I couldn't wait to get away."

"Remember Cousin Aldo? Wasn't he great? Coming over in his police uniform to taste the fresh ravioli made by the grandmothers?"

"Aldo? The corrupt cop on the take? I hated that sonofabitch."

Mom's hearing aid stopped working as he said this. She took the hearing aid out and fiddled with it, trying to figure out if the battery was dead or if ear wax had plugged up the tubing. "And how about the grace that Uncle Chicky would say every time before dinner?"

Uncle Carmine laughed. "'Potatoes and meat? Christ, let's eat!' That's a legitimately good memory. Uncle Chicky was a cool cat."

I laughed loudly. "I like that grace!" I finally found the perfect place for me to shoehorn myself into a conversation I had been shut out of. Meanwhile, Dad and Leo remained on the sidelines, looking unsure what to do with their hands.

"Yeah, that grace was funny." Carmine shrugged and resumed speaking in a clipped tone. "I still got out of there as soon as I could."

Mom nodded. "I know what you mean. I miss them all too. So many died so young."

Uncle Carmine glanced at Dad. "I guess it's just as well she can't hear a word I say. She talks so much about 'the good old days.' I don't get it."

Leo nodded. "I don't get it, either."

Dad sighed. "She can't hear anything."

Encouraged by Leo's taking his side, Carmine said to him, "I bet her nostalgia is only because Staten Island sucks. You all should move to Jersey." Carmine didn't like the fact that our house was semi-attached and felt we could buy a better place for the same money closer to his home. When he named his home state, he didn't say "Joysie" instead of "Jersey" — that's a Joe Piscopo *Saturday Night Live* comedy sketch exaggeration of how people from Jersey talk — but I still loved the way Carmine said "Jersey."

"Staten Island is kinda the same as Jersey," Dad replied. It was funny when Dad, who didn't have a kind word to say about Staten Island, would get his back up whenever Carmine would talk smack about our borough.

"Staten Island is shitty New Jersey," Carmine declared.

I piped in. "My teacher says there's no such place as New Jersey. He says 'There's suburbs of New York City and suburbs of Philadelphia, but New Jersey itself doesn't exist.'"

"Well, I don't like your teacher," Uncle Carmine declared. To him, that ended the argument. He was right about my teacher. He was right about Staten Island. He was right about Chicky, the corrupt cop, and Grandpa's drinking, and he was right about mandatory military service for high-school-age boys. It was cool to be right about absolutely everything. I hoped one day I would grow up to be as right as Uncle Carmine.

While Dad and Uncle Carmine weren't above a bit of verbal sparring, the real animosity in our extended family was between my dad and Carmine's wife, Beatrice. A heavyset Sicilian housewife with spiked, white hair, Aunt Beatrice cursed, smoked, drank ten cups of coffee a day, and watched soap operas all afternoon as she cooked and did the laundry. The first time I saw the Walt Disney film *The Little Mermaid* in 1989, I couldn't stop laughing at how much the villain, Ursula the Sea Witch, reminded me of Aunt Beatrice. The throaty voice! The imperious air! They were twins! I didn't feel guilty making this mental association between a family member and an over-the-top cartoon villain because Beatrice always struck me as mean-spirited. My aunt was a strict mother, and sent her children — eldest child, Concetta, and the twins, Gabriel and Lorenzo — to bed every night at seven p.m. whether the sun was up or not. And yet, her kids adored her. Clearly, they knew firsthand a softer side of her that I never saw. Whenever the subject of Beatrice was brought up, Mom said the same thing, almost verbatim, "I never cursed, drank coffee, or watched soaps until my brother married her." Dad would always offer back the same retort: "So the sweetheart was a wonderful influence on you? Taught you how to be *uncouth*!" Dad was the sort of person who would overlook Hannibal Lecter's cannibalism because Lecter had good manners but loathe the Beatles for cursing and challenging authority. Dad was fixated on manners to a borderline absurdist degree. Still, in the case of Beatrice, I was with him. Beatrice was a significant figure in our family history because she relentlessly opposed my mom marrying my dad.

"Carmine feels the same way!" Beatrice informed Mom on the phone shortly after the engagement announcement. She was brave, but not brave enough to talk with Mom in person.

"Then let *him* talk to me! Not that it's any of his business, either."

In the end, everyone attended my parents' wedding. The surprise boycott came later. At the very last second, Beatrice adamantly refused to get into the car with Carmine and Grandpa when they were about to pull out of their driveway and head to the church for my baptism. Mom was sad and shocked when Carmine arrived with his three children and Grandpa, but not Beatrice. Grandpa stalked back and forth in the church foyer swearing under his breath, "That Black bitch. That nigger. Stupid, angry, busybody Sicilian. Can't come to meet a fucking newborn baby and attend a fucking baptism. Goddamn Sicilians! Always starting trouble!" Grandpa didn't stand for Beatrice's behavior and demanded she attend every family function from then on, even if my dad were involved. Beatrice complied with ill grace, vowing to call Dad "Shithead" instead of by his name. The first time I was there to hear her casually call Dad "Shithead" in the middle of a conversation without blinking, I was so startled I burst out laughing. Dad was humiliated in front of his own son.

On August 16, 1984, our family of four attended what would be the first-of-three annual Basile family reunions at Carmine and Beatrice's Jersey estate. We found about sixty of Mom's cousins, second cousins, aunts, uncles, and other relatives gathered around Carmine's outdoor pool, drinking beer and cocktails, and eating barbeque hot dogs, hamburgers, and chicken, along with some spaghetti and Caprese salad skewers. Everyone, including us, wore their nicest 1980s short-sleeve summer outfits. Looking more like Ursula the Sea Witch than ever, wearing red lipstick, pale blue eyeshadow, a purple tank top, and purple shorts, Beatrice saw us first, and approached. She made a point of greeting Mom, Leo, and me warmly. Then she placed a fake smile on her lips and said to Dad, "How are you, Shithead? How's your crappy job?" She couldn't remember which crappy job Dad had at the moment, or she would have tailored the insult for maximum effect. Dad was not usually around during the evenings on weekdays because he worked nights, first as a mail clerk at the law office Fried Frank, then as a salesman who worked on commission for Tops Appliance City. Dad stared daggers at Beatrice, who gave no fucks about his rage. She thought him lazy in general, but particularly resented his good fortune getting an astronomically high Vietnam War draft lottery number when she lost a younger brother his age to the Tet Offensive.

Walking away from Beatrice and the three of us, Dad found himself a beer by an open cooler placed strategically by the front gate and sat down at an empty deck table. Emotionally shut down already, he was no longer eager to be social to anyone. Mom only half heard what Beatrice had said, but could guess what happened. Not willing to allow the whole reunion to go up in smoke less than three minutes in, she continued to greet the family with Leo beside her.

I sat beside Dad. Fortunately, Grandpa had seen the exchange from afar and joined us at the table. Grandpa looked gaunt and pale. The lung cancer was taking its toll.

"Where were you the night of the murder?" I asked Grandpa, producing a small pad and a golf pencil, ready to take his statement.

Grandpa looked at Dad for an explanation, and Dad provided one: "He loves Columbo."

Grandpa smiled and said to me, "I was closing up at the Bon Soir. Got home late."

I nodded at him. "That alibi checks out. We already have corroboration."

Grandpa looked at Dad. "Howya doin', Vincent?"

Dad sat slouching in his vinyl chair. The sun on his shoulders and shade provided by the yellow umbrella had yet to restore his mellow good cheer. "Ah, you know."

Grandpa pursed his lips. It was the mannerism we mimicked most when doing affectionate impressions of him. "You working on any new horror movies with your friends?"

Dad brightened and sat upright. "We're hoping to do one soon. Remember Joe Boland? The great bear of an Irishman with jet black hair all over his body — giant black beard, shaggy hair, hairy palms — who played our Rasputin and Dracula? He's back on board. I've got most of my old crew back together, but we have a few key people we need to replace. The script is almost done. I'm hoping we can start shooting soon. It's called *The Pod People Take Staten Island*!" His enthusiasm for movies and filmmaking was infectious, and horror movies were his greatest passion of all. In the 1970s, Dad majored in theater at LIU Brooklyn, building a ragtag troupe of actors and film crew members with dreams of making their own horror movies on a shoe-string budget, a la *Night of the Living Dead*. Without the resources required to complete a ninety-minute sound feature film, they settled on the less-ambitious goal of shooting silent, color horror shorts on Super 8 film stock. Even though Dad's favorite Hammer films were European period pieces, he built upon the model of *Dracula A.D. 1972* by transplanting the villains of Victorian Gothic horror literature to the present day. Essentially, Dad and his friends made a silent, color, *Rasputin A.D. 1973* and *Dracula A.D. 1974: When Co-op City Dripped Blood.* To this day, the gritty realism of the silent, "home movie" footage, shot in the box-cars-and-plaid-clothing Bronx of the 1970s make the films a compelling time capsule. The comparatively short running time, action-packed plot, hammy acting, absent sound, and gonzo practical effects make the films surprisingly watchable — especially when a female vampire in a black nightgown summons a tarantula out of thin air and orders it to eat the face off of a drunken, sleeping physician. Growing up watching my Dad's films was a blast. They were all super cool, but my favorite was *Twilight of the Living Dead*, because Mom was the star and spent most of the film fleeing and fighting off a trio of zombies. While Mom and Dad had been shooting the film, a heroic and confused passerby ran into the shot to help rescue Mom from the shambling flesh-eaters. The fellow didn't understand a movie was being made and had been worried Mom was in genuine trouble. He was so nice, he wound up with a cameo in the film.

In retrospect, it was a shame Dad had no idea how to parley these personal projects into a full-fledged career in filmmaking. Like Ed Wood, Dad learned to do everything because he didn't have a large crew to work with. He became a competent hand at directing, acting, screenwriting, lighting, photography, editing, and special effects, but was not comfortable working with sound and had no idea how to even attempt to find distribution for his films. Even with a portfolio of five films under his belt that were longer than shorts but shorter than feature films, he made no substantial connections in the industry and never connected with the cult film overlords he needed to: Roger Corman, Milton Subotsky, and Max Rosenberg. The greatest success to come out of his amateur troupe was their youngest cameraman, teenage Tommy Dolan, who went on to shoot live sports coverage for CBS. Still, listening to Dad talk with such passion about his filmmaking craft by the Olympic pool, Grandpa could see what his daughter saw in my father, and was disappointed Carmine and Beatrice could not.

"I want you to show me that *Rasputin* film." Grandpa barely had the sentence out of his mouth when he winced in pain. He reached over his shoulder to massage the area above the bandaged, open wound in his back. Dad moved to offer help, but Grandpa waved him off.

I piped up. "I was in a vampire movie."

"Yeah?" Grandpa asked. "He's in this next one?"

"No," Dad replied. "I made a fun little five-minute vampire movie with him and Leo. I put some plastic fangs in Damien's mouth and dabbed some theater blood on his lips and had him chase Leo around the backyard. It came out cute."

"I got to be the vampire!"

Grandpa gave me an encouraging smile through another wave of pain.

"You have another doctor's appointment soon?" Dad asked him.

"Too soon. Not soon enough."

When it looked like Dad and Grandpa were going to start talking about medical treatments and hospital visits, I knew the conversation would turn boring, sad, and technical, so I left to find Mom and Leo. I had only gotten a yard or two away when a trio of women I had never met before stopped me by the side of the pool. The leader, "Wall Street" Emily, tried to explain the difference between second cousins and first cousins once removed. One of them was a second cousin to me and one was a first cousin once removed. I didn't understand a word Emily said and couldn't grasp if she was one of those categories or her two pals were. The more frightened and confused I became, the more times Emily tried to unpack the terms for me.

"You do understand now, right?" Emily asked.

I was still at a loss, so I changed the subject. "Where were you the night of the murder?"

The other women were totally floored by my question. Emily was game and answered immediately. "In Monte Carlo on my yacht, entertaining Habib Bourguiba of Tunisia."

I consulted my spiral notebook. "Then why were you seen at the Staten Island OTB?"

"I only place my bets in person, at the track. I never go to OTB."

I poked the underside of my jaw with my pencil eraser. "Interesting."

Meanwhile, Mom's Aunt Bianca, a sweet, elderly lady in bright red lipstick, a yellow dress, broad-brimmed yellow hat, and sunglasses, was walking about the pool party sprinkling holy water on everyone with her fingers. "Yesterday was the Feast of the Assumption. The priests blessed the ocean waters. I'm sprinkling holy ocean water on you to bring you God's blessing." A couple of bald men, sitting by the pool in folding chairs smoking cigars, nodded in appreciation at Bianca. The one who looked the most like a cast member from *Barney Miller* said, "I can use all the blessings I can get. I'm getting too old and too fat."

Bianca sprinkled one of the younger relatives: an athletic, thirty-five-year-old woman in a black leather skirt and form-flattering top. The sexy woman yelped, "Hey, with throwin' water!"

"It is a pool party, Nicole," laughed the same bald man who spoke before.

Still standing beside me, Emily Basile-Scrosciare called over to her leather-skirt-wearing younger sister. "Come talk to Damien, Nicole. He's adorable."

"They're all adorable," Nicole grumbled. "Then they hit puberty and turn into sharks."

Not understanding, I pumped my little fist in the air. "Sharks! Like in *Jaws*!"

"Oooookay, then, Nicole." Emily sighed. "My sister. Jeezum Crow."

Holding an empty serving plate, my cousin Gabriel walked by me on the way to his mother, Beatrice, who was cooking up another batch of hamburgers for him to distribute. Gabriel was easily one of my favorite relatives, for partly selfish reasons: he gave me fun presents for my birthday, like *Masters of the Universe* action figures and Bon Jovi records instead of socks and fresh undershirts, like my aunt always got me. As he passed me, he asked if I wanted a burger. I nodded. He said, "I love that Nicole to death, but she's such a little bitch, isn't she?" He patted me on the head and continued walking towards the barbeque.

Meanwhile, Nicole continued to fret over her wet leather skirt, gesturing wildly at the empty pool. "Nobody is swimming! None of us wants to get wet! We like being dry!"

I raised my hand. "I wanna swim." I never missed an opportunity to swim. I also didn't know how to talk to adults without raising my hand to be called on.

Nicole clapped her hands in my direction, silently and sarcastically. "Good for you."

Mom's Aunt Bianca sprinkled some ocean water on me. "And a blessing for the birthday boy. Your birthday was two weeks ago, wasn't it?"

"August 1," I proclaimed.

"Remember that God and your Great Aunt Bianca love you." This was my first encounter with Aunt Bianca, the most adorable human being of all time.

"Where were you the night of the murder?" I asked Aunt Bianca.

Aunt Bianca laughed heartily. "At church, playing Bingo with the other old fogies."

Carmine offered Bianca a hamburger on a paper plate. "Burger, Aunt Bianca?"

"Oh, I'm fine." Bianca smiled and sprinkled some sea water on Uncle Carmine.

"Blessed water?" Carmine asked. "Make sure you get everybody. Especially my wife!" He laughed. (I assumed Beatrice would take even less kindly to getting damp than Nicole.)

"I will!" Bianca promised.

Carmine looked thoughtful. "Hey, Aunt Bianca, lemme ax you a question. When are you gonna move out of dat apartment you're in?" *Whoa. Did Carmine's accent just get stronger?*

"Oh, I love it there! It is the best apartment building anyone could live in. We all love it." The "we" included her sweet, shy, sanitation-worker husband — now nursing a beer as he wandered alone about the outskirts of Carmine's property — and their daughter, Baby Bianca.

"I thought all the Italians left!" Carmine exclaimed.

"There are still Italians in the building."

"But you got all these Blacks and Hispanics and Asians in there now, too, right?"

Bianca beamed. "And they are all wonderful! I've had everyone from every apartment over for dinner at one time or another. And I've thrown parties and invited everyone!"

"You had them *all* over?"

"Why, yes! We are all God's children," she twittered.

"I tell you what, Bianca, when they made you, they broke the mold!"

"'We are all God's children,'" I repeated to myself. "I like that."

"And some of God's children are a pain in my ass." Carmine leaned in conspiratorially. "Hey, I gotta joke for you, Bianca. 'What's the definition of mass confusion?'"

Aunt Bianca shrugged.

"'Father's Day in Harlem!'"

Aunt Bianca frowned and caressed his cheek. "Oh, my dear, dear Carmine. God loves you even though you just told a mean-spirited joke that isn't funny at all."

Carmine was uncharacteristically chastened. He glanced over Bianca's shoulder at his athletic but lethargic teenage son, Lorenzo. Sleepy-eyed and dressed down in gym shorts and a Phil Simms football jersey, Lorenzo had just rolled out of bed, having slept through all the party preparations. He was the spitting image of Carmine at a slim twenty. Lorenzo, his twin brother Gabriel, Carmine, and Grandpa all had essentially the same face, though they were very different ages and weights. Carmine laughed openly at his lazy son. "Here he is. Alexa Hente! The Demanding One. You decided to grace us with your presence? Is it noon already?"

Yawning, Lorenzo pointed at me. "Where's his dad?"

"Sitting with your grandfather near the gate. Why?"

"He's the only one here who doesn't give me shit."

Carmine laughed again. "Because he's lazier than you are!"

"Where were you the night of the murder?" I asked Lorenzo.

Lorenzo scratched an itch under his right buttock. "I ain't got no alibi because I'm the one that did it."

"You better come with me!" I yelled.

"You'll never take me alive, copper."

"I'll see you behind bars, if it is the last thing I do, Alexa Hente!" I cried, my first in the air. Lorenzo yawned and moved away, done with the conversation. Aunt Bianca sprinkled some ocean water on Lorenzo as he stumbled past.

Mom was talking to her father's brother Skippy, who was another gentle soul like Bianca. I couldn't imagine the chubby, ruddy-faced old man saying an unkind word or committing a selfish act. Astoundingly or wisely, Mom had chosen him to complain to about approaching middle age and going deaf, when he had her problems to the power of ten. Still, they probably could have had a lot of meaningful things to say to one another — if they weren't both too deaf to hear each other. In an effort to avoid saying only, "Can you repeat that?" and "Excuse me?" each one guessed the appropriate follow-up to the last thing that was said. The result was a string of non sequiturs that would have made Monty Python and Laurence Sterne proud. My invisible cuteness detector was registering off-the-charts levels of cuteness. I moved in closer for a cleaner reading. Of course, moving in close increased the risk of death by cuteness overload. Now, it might seem cruel, insensitive, and impolitic to consider two people with hearing disabilities in conversation adorable, but when you consider one looked like Betty Boop and the other looked like Ernest Borgnine from *Marty*, and both parties were trying valiantly to conceal how little they were hearing (and failing utterly), then you might begin to see where the conversation was captivating to watch. (No, that still sounds like a jerky and ableist thing to say. I have enough verbal irony as I write this to realize that. Still, please remember, it was 1983, and I was eight.) Anyway, I ran up to both Mom and Uncle Skippy and showered them with kisses on their cheeks. "T.C.F.W.! Too Cute for Words! I can't take it! I can't!"

Mom laughed and lightly pushed me away. "Get outta here! Silly."

I pounded my chest with both fists, King Kong celebrating tearing open a Tyrannosaurus Rex's mouth. "I have succeeded in bestowing a fuss upon those worthy of many kisses! Boom!"

Leo had been sitting there quietly the whole time, watching the conversation in enormous suspense, wondering what unexpected turn it would take next. I struck up a conversation with him about the Muppets and our stuffed animals while Mom and Uncle Skippy talked about folks from the old neighborhood in Brooklyn they both knew who had died recently.

"Remember Nina? With the clubbed foot? Her father was local bocce champion?"

"No," Mom said.

"Her sister fell off the Cyclone Roller Coaster in Coney Island?"

"Oh, yeah! I remember her."

"She just died."

"Oh, no!"

Mom and Skippy had this same conversation ten more times about ten more people, with the names and a few key details changed. After the tenth such exchange, Leo and I were beside ourselves with laughter, tears flowing down our cheeks. Both Mom and Skippy thought we were laughing at something else, but it was the parade of dead friends and relatives we had never met that was the funniest graveyard comedy routine of all time. Right around the time Mom and Skippy had verbally buried half of Brooklyn, Baby Bianca, my Great-Aunt-Bianca's twenty-year-old daughter, appeared from somewhere inside Uncle Carmine's house. Baby Bianca was dressed in a one-piece yellow bathing suit and a pair of yellow flip-flops, with a large brown beach towel draped over her shoulder. With high cheekbones and long, straight black hair, she could have been Shannen Doherty's stunt double. Baby Bianca walked up to me and said, "I hear you're the only one going in with me? Would you believe nobody else brought their bathing suits! With this gorgeous pool? Davvero?"

The funny bald man must have overheard her because he piped up, "Everyone else here is fat!" *I love that guy! Who is he? I need an introduction.*

"Then what's the pool for if nobody is gonna swim in it?" Baby Bianca called back to the mystery bald man.

Alexa Hente's twin brother Gabriel walked past holding a freshly replenished plate of hamburgers. "Keeping up with the Joneses," he observed saucily, while handing me a burger on a small disposable plate. Considering he grew up in a wealthy family, Gabriel liked to cast aspersions upon his parents for being nouveau riche. "What's the point in being rich if you aren't happy? Am I right, little man?"

"Yeah! Buy a pool, swim in the pool!" I bit into my burger.

When Bianca dove into the pool, I ran up to Mom, clutching the burger. "Hey, Mom! Can I go swimming?" I was still wearing my clothes: tan cargo shorts and a paisley, button-down, short-sleeve shirt. Mom had brought all our swimsuits, expecting us to change inside after we had eaten lunch. While lunch did look good, I was eager to get swimming. After touring the hotel swimming pools and beaches of Wildwood, New Jersey, each summer, I discovered that swimming was my very favorite pastime. "Mom, I want to swim with Baby Bianca. Can I go in now?" Mom couldn't hear me. She and Skippy were still communicating about as effectively as ambassadors from two different alien races tasked with making First Contact. If I waited too long to change into my suit, Bianca would come out just as I was going in and I'd have to swim all alone. Without a buddy! I found this situation totally unacceptable. I wolfed down my burger so quickly I nearly gagged on it.

Meanwhile, Dad was checking in with Lorenzo ("Alexa Hente") Basile's sex life. They were sitting with Grandpa at the same round deck table with the large umbrella. "You're, what? Twenty? Going with any sexy ladies these days?"

A young athlete as a study in inertia, Lorenzo looked like a dead fish that someone had tossed carelessly onto a deck chair to dry out in the sun. "Women. Who needs 'em?"

Grandpa spoke directly to Dad. "Don't let him fool you. His heart's broken." He searched for Lorenzo's eyes and found them. "My heart broke when my wife died. I know what that looks like. I know when my grandson is in pain."

"What the hell happened?" Dad asked Lorenzo.

"He dated a Jewish girl," Grandpa explained. "There was some opposition on both sides. Things didn't work out. I thought they were gonna get married."

"Me too." Lorenzo sighed.

"The opposition was that great?" Dad asked.

"It would have been easier if everyone drew a line in the sand," Lorenzo said. "It was all passive aggressive shit. Everyone was a little too polite. A little too unenthusiastic. That was hard to fight. All the slights were so small, they seemed not worth fighting over. They chipped away at us, and we didn't notice they were doing it." Lorenzo's voice trailed off as his attention was drawn over Dad's shoulder. "Wait a minute. What's your son doing?" Lorenzo watched as I placed my socks and shoes on the floor next to Dad and took a running jump into the swimming pool, landing in the water in my clothing. Lorenzo chuckled. "What the hell is he doing?"

Nonchalant, Dad glanced in my direction to see me walking on my hands in the shallow end of the pool. "He jumped in after a girl, so I'm okay with it."

Shuffling away from the barbeque, Aunt Beatrice rushed out onto the deck of the pool, still grasping her giant barbeque tongs. She brandished the tongs with her right hand, placing her other hand angrily on her left hip. "What the hell are you doing? Put on a bathing suit, retard!"

I surfaced. When the water emptied out of my ears, I asked Beatrice what she wanted.

"I axed you a question!" she yelled. "Are you a special needs child?"

I jumped up and down in the water, punching the air with both fists. "I am the dominatrix! I rule all I survey!"

Laughing, Baby Bianca swam up to me. "No, dummy. You are 'the dominator.'"

"I am the domi—what? Dominator? Isn't that what I said?"

"You're behaving very strangely!" Aunt Beatrice yelled.

I swam up to the edge of the pool and looked up at her furious face. "You're behaving pretty strangely yourself. Where were you the night of the murder, toots?"

Aunt Beatrice's jaw dropped open at being called "toots." She was not used to being on the receiving end of an offensive soubriquet. She could dish it out but couldn't take it.

My Mom pulled herself away from Skippy and walked up to Beatrice by the pool. Beatrice shot her a dirty look. "Is your son a retard, or what?"

"I'm a retard!" I called out gleefully. "And you're a retard! And we are all retards!"

Mom crossed her arms in front of her chest and glared at her sister-in-law. "Listen, if you keep calling my son 'retarded' and my husband 'shithead,' I'm gonna make you eat those tongs."

Beatrice looked my Mom in the eyes for several seconds before returning to the grill. Once Beatrice was gone, Mom frowned down at me. "What's with you?"

I raised a Black Power fist in the air. "I am the dominatrix! I'm a retarded kid from Staten Island! I bring love to all God's children in New Jersey!"

On the drive home, I sat in the back seat reading *Island of the Blue Dolphins* by Scott O'Dell. I was wearing my bathing suit since it was dry and unused. My wet clothes were wrapped up in the towel I'd used to dry off and tossed into the trunk. Everyone else had gone into the pool in their actual bathing suits, so they could wear regular clothes home and not be cold in the air-conditioned car.

The first person to speak was Dad, who made the following pronouncement: "That's it for me. I need a break from your family for at least six months."

Mom looked about the car. "Did any of you have any good conversations? Because I can't hear too well, and I didn't get to talk to everyone."

"You didn't miss nothing," Dad said. "These people are as boring as that Stanley Kubrick movie with the Neanderthals and the obelisk."

"I loved the pool!" I yelled.

"I loved the food," Leo offered. "The braciole. Both the beef and the pork. That was amazing. I never had that before."

"Yeah," Dad enthused. "That was great! We should have that at home. Hey, Gianna, why do you cook the same crap all the time? Why not make some braciole?"

"I can make some braciole." Mercifully, Mom had not heard Dad's entire statement.

"I wish someone would tell me what that chicken was caught on," I said. "Something blue? What's blue?"

Leo smacked me on the shoulder. "It's called 'Chicken cordon bleu.' It's French."

"I liked it," I declared. "It was tasty and looked healthy. Bet it's high in beta-carotene."

"The food was good," Dad observed. "Too bad the company wasn't."

"I know what you mean," Mom smiled. "It's great to see everyone in one place." She enthused about how wonderful it was to see everyone at a reunion instead of a funeral. Oddly, a good dozen of the single relatives were getting suspiciously old without tying the knot, making happier occasions such as weddings and baptisms a rarity. This trend exacerbated Mom's perception that her family was going extinct.

"I don't know how many of them I like outside of your father and the Biancas," Dad said.

"Oh, I like them all," Mom said.

"If I rated them as a family, I'd give them two-and-a-half stars *at best*," Dad declared.

"The one person who always rubs me the wrong way is Emily," Mom said.

"Um, excuse me! You mean, Emily Basile-Scrosciare," Dad corrected.

A strange exasperation crept into Mom's voice. "I can't relate to any woman who chooses not to have children, but then shows people photos of her cats, and tells stories about her cats like they're her children. It's really weird."

"I'm allergic to them," I said, "but I can see where some people would like cats. I just don't like when Emily tries to explain the family tree to me. And who is Habib of Tunisia?"

"Can she even have children?" Leo asked. "We don't know. Maybe she's lonely and loves her cats. Besides, kids are a pain in the neck. You see them screaming, running around, and throwing food at their parents at Denny's every time we go." He sounded twenty instead of five.

"I'll say one thing for Emily," Dad added, "she dresses very chick."

"*What?*" Mom asked.

"Emily!"

"What *about* Emily?"

"She's very *chick*."

"She's *what?*"

"Chick!" Dad yelled.

Leo intervened. "Dad means *chic*, Mom. Dad thinks Emily dresses *chic*."

"Oh, *chic!*" Mom giggled. "My hearing is *terrible*. I thought your dad kept calling her a *chick*."

I laughed and clapped. "He *did*, Mom! You heard him right the first time!"

"What the hell is *chic?*" Dad asked. "I'm saying she's chick!"

"You really mean *chic*, Dad," I said.

"Well, I *never* heard 'chick' pronounced that way," Dad sulked.

"Of course, a lot of the single women are getting older and don't know how to do it gracefully," Mom observed prudishly. "As much as Emily likes to doll herself up, at least she looks classy. That sister of hers always comes off *trashy*. I hate it when Nicole wears sexy clothing. She's getting a little long in the tooth for a leather skirt."

"I don't care how old you are," Dad replied. "You can wear a leather skirt your whole life if you have the ass to pull it off. You got a nice, round ass and some great legs? Wear a leather skirt at seventy! I'll be there to appreciate it. But that woman has no ass whatsoever."

"Sure, she has an ass. It just isn't huge, is all."

Dad shook his head violently. "No! There's her back. You look down. There's her legs. No ass in-between. Back. Legs. Back. Legs. No ass in sight. People with no asses shouldn't wear sexy bottoms. They should wear baggy bottoms and put all their efforts on their tops. Wear something low-cut with a necklace to draw the eyes."

"I have enough ass for the both of us," Mom grumbled. "She can have half of mine."

"No, no. Don't wish your ass away. Bad enough Nicole doesn't have enough ass. I don't want you losing too much of yours, too. Where would that leave me, I ask you? With no asses to look at during these boring family reunions."

"Why does it matter if she doesn't have an ass?" I asked. "If I could get rid of my ass, I would. Asses fart." I was angry at my own ass because I was lactose intolerant and didn't know it, so I couldn't understand why I spent so much time after lunch and in the early evening farting continuously and running to the bathroom. Also, I was genuinely confused and upset on Nicole's behalf. It wasn't just Nicole they took apart after each visit. A good number of relatives got the Friar's Club Roast treatment in the aftermath of a given family gathering, and I was never into it. After all, I'd just had a nice time talking with everyone. I didn't ever see the justification. However, since I had no ear for passive-aggressive jibes, I didn't understand that Mom and Dad often had plenty to vent about following a visit I had deemed an unqualified success mainly because it involved me and Leo playing pool and air hockey in an unfamiliar basement. In hindsight, Nicole probably said something to piss them both off. Meanwhile, I viewed Nicole as a put-upon, lonely woman who was sad all the time. I didn't feel right saying anything negative about Nicole, even though she wasn't the sort of person I was usually interested in spending time with. (*I mean, for God's sake, when I mentioned the Starship Enterprise to her, she had no idea what it was! You don't need to be a* Star Trek *fan to have heard of the damn Enterprise! Still, I was willing to let that slide since she seemed so gosh darn sad.*)

"I guess she's on the prowl again," Mom wondered aloud.

"You think?"

"Nobody with a belly full of fish uses that much bait."

"Isn't she with that guy with the walrus mustache?" Dad asked.

"They got divorced."

Dad was genuinely surprised while not being invested in the news. Mom explained that they had broken up a few months after the last family wedding, during which I ate as many cocktail shrimp and deviled eggs as I could while they made a spectacle of themselves arguing over the most effective way to lose twenty pounds. I intuited right away that Walrus Mustache was not just a bully, but a total knob. I was at the same table as the couple, watching Walrus Mustache rebuking, humiliating, and sniping at Nicole, making her cry all evening. The fighting built to a crescendo, ending with screaming in the hotel lobby at one a.m., after most of the guests had gone home. All night, I had no idea how to intervene and I desperately wanted to.

"I hated him," I announced. I understood that, as a boy, I was supposed to side with boys when they argued with girls, but I could tell, even that young, that Walrus Mustache was evil.

"Was he in the Mafia?" Dad asked. He added as an aside to me, "I hated him, too." I gave Dad a thumbs up.

"There was a rumor about that," Mom mused, "but I think he was just an asshole. Nobody in the family is in the Mafia. My brother was a bartender, so he knew some gangsters through work. He tried to stay out of their way. They never tipped or even paid their bills."

Dad laughed to himself. "Buncha losers. And *The Godfather* makes them look so cool. Ha! Back to the other jackass. I heard a rumor that Walrus Mustache beat Nicole's ass like an animal on a regular basis."

"Oh, no!" I gasped. *That poor woman! Who cares if she wears a miniskirt or not?* I raised my hand in the back seat like I was at school. "I have a question about Nicole's ass."

Dad glanced at me in the rear-view mirror. "You don't have to raise your hand."

Mom murmured, "I suppose we shouldn't be discussing Nicole's bum with the children."

"If she doesn't have an ass," I began, and then got too embarrassed to finish.

Mom and Dad exchanged glances, barely suppressing laughter.

Leo knew where I was going and finished the question for me, "How can Walrus Mustache beat it on a regular basis?"

Mom burst out laughing. "Of course, she has an ass!"

I pointed an accusing finger at Dad. "But he just said she didn't!"

October 2, 1984

Grandpa Angelo died less than two months after the family reunion. Mom and Carmine were so devastated that it fell to Dad to work with Aunt Beatrice to make most of the wake and funeral arrangements together. If anyone had predicted Dad and Beatrice would engage in tacky bickering during this period, they were proven wrong by what did happen. In their interactions with the funeral director, Beatrice found herself struck by Dad's sensitive and thoughtful questions. Throughout the planning stage and the packing up of Grandpa's possessions, a man she had thought of as a gadabout had demonstrated decisiveness, maturity, and intelligence. She never called him "Shithead" again.

Mom, Dad, Carmine, and Beatrice had been together the first time they unlocked Angelo's apartment after he died. Everywhere were signs of a life on pause that Angelo had expected to return to after a routine specialist's visit. Angelo's glasses still lay open on top of a newspaper on the kitchen table. The crossword puzzle was half done. Uncle Carmine picked up his father's glasses and held them close to his chest. "He's not coming back for these. Or finishing that crossword."

Mom slid sunglasses over her eyes to hide her freshly gathering tears.

CHAPTER EIGHT
I'm Not One of You

September 8, 1987

6:00 pm

Chris Wolffe, a beefy blonde dude in an American-flag-covered martial arts gi, sat sullenly at the dojo reception desk in a chair that was too small for either his body or ego. A painted mural of the Park family dominated the wall beside him. In the mural stood Master Yumi Park — arms crossed, ironic eyebrow raised — sandwiched between her mischievous, grinning brothers, Lorne and Pernell. Towering above the three siblings in white martial arts uniforms was their father, the black-clad, imperious Grandmaster Min-Jun Park. The school logo and slogan painted across the top read: "The Richmond County Institute of Martial Arts: Where the *Real* Karate Kids Train." I had just arrived, dressed in my white gi and red belt, carrying a change of clothes in the black RCIMA duffel bag slung over my shoulder. "Master Park?"

Chris looked dully at me. "She's in her office. Just knock."

The sounds of a stapler clipping stacks of pages together came through the birch veneer door. My knock was so soft it was barely audible.

"Knock with authority!" Master Park's voice replied brightly through the door. "I don't respond to feeble tapping noises." As she said this, I heard a stapler strike go wrong somehow. The soprano voice of a woman I'd seen put her fist through ten stacked cinderblocks called out, "Owie! Owie, owie, owie, owie!" Had I distracted her and caused her to staple her own hand? If only I hadn't chosen that exact moment to knock!

Her voice rang out again. "I can feel the Catholic guilt through the door. I bet twenty dollars that's Damien! Knock with authority!"

I put some force into my next three knocks and the door opened. A woman roughly my height, with full, curly, shoulder-length, black 1980s hair emerged wearing the same martial arts uniform she had on in the mural. She regarded me sympathetically while sucking on her own index finger. "Did you staple yourself?" I asked quietly.

She took her finger out of her mouth and stared at it as it bled anew. Since the question was too stupid to answer, she said instead, "You need to be more assertive. It is a wonderful thing, you being a gentleman, and all. Wonderful. But if you go through life knocking on doors like that, you're gonna get eaten alive." As she licked some more blood off her wound, she noticed my black-and-blue face for the first time and started. "What the fuck happened to you?"

"I played by a stream some other kids see as their private spot. They threw rocks at me."

Master Park pinched her thumb and index finger together to stop the bleeding. She lifted my head by the chin with her uninjured hand, peering at my face. "Strangers?"

"They live a block over. I know them. Kinda."

"Bunch of jackasses?"

I shrugged. "I invaded their territory."

"That's a riot that you're defending their right to stone you to death. You always defend the motives of people who attack you? What kind of terrible person would throw rocks at you?"

"I dunno."

"You are a fundamentally likeable person. Anyone who would dislike you or mistreat you has to be a total jackass. End of story."

I blushed. "Thank you, sir."

Since I was not much of an athlete, I had four equally important reasons for taking Tae Kwon Do. The first was to hang out with Mitchell. The second was to lose the baby fat around my stomach. The third was the movie *The Karate Kid*. The fourth was because I had an enormous crush on Master Yumi Park. Yumi was the Valkyrie who leapt through rings of fire and fought off six men at once during free martial arts demonstrations in the courtyard of the Staten Island Mall. Her father, the Tenth Dan Black Belt Grandmaster, owned three schools and taught at the flagship location in Eltingville. Her brothers, Lorne and Pernell, handled the other satellite school in St. George, while Yumi, a Third Dan Black Belt, oversaw the Manor Road location within walking distance of Mitchell's home near the Staten Island Armory. Mitchell had been part of the same weekend mall demonstration and invited me to cheer on his green-belt prowess. He had been trying to stoke my interest in joining for a month and was glad I was there to watch. He calculated that, as much as I would enjoy seeing his moves, Yumi's awe-inspiring presence would motivate me to sign up immediately. Sharp guy.

"These injuries look fresh," she murmured. "When did this happen?"

"Three hours ago."

Chris Wolffe, the hulking fellow in the American flag uniform piped in, "Get some brass knuckles. Go Cobra Kai on their asses."

Master Park kept her eyes on my injuries. "Cobra Kai? That's not our brand. We're the good guys. Tae Kwon Do is for defense only."

Chris laughed. "Defense with a good pair of brass knuckles."

"Get an ice pack from next door, will you?" Master Park ordered, keeping her eyes on my injuries. Chris assumed an "I don't clean the latrine with a toothbrush — do you even know who my father is?" air but thought better of voicing a complaint. "Yes, sir."

"Wait. Do you want candy or ice cream, Nabi?" She sometimes called me Nabi without telling me what it meant. I've heard conflicting reports it means "butterfly" or "cute little kitten." The first time I heard what it meant, I turned into Rudolph the Red Nosed-Reindeer, leaping through the air, yelling, "She thinks I'm a cute little kitten! Or a butterfly!" I wasn't expecting her candy question but had a ready-made answer: Rocky road. She repeated my request to Chris, who bowed at her and strutted out the door.

"He didn't have to go to any trouble, sir," I said.

"Oh, yes he did. Come with me, Mr. Cavalieri." She led me into the dojo, a gymnasium with a basketball-court-like floor and the dance-studio mirror-wall feature. Against the wall facing the mirror were folded-and-stacked gymnastic mats, throwing star targets, and hanging scrolls covered in Korean writing. "While we're waiting for dessert, let's try some meditation."

"Okay." I sat cross-legged on the floor in front of her and closed my eyes.

"'Yes, sir,'" she reminded me, still standing.

Blast. "Yes, sir."

"Sijak."

Meditation required clearing one's mind and striving to attain a semblance of inner peace. Considering my usual cacophony of thoughts, inner peace was nearly impossible for me to achieve. Here again, I tried again to meditate, but the Satanic CD started up instantly, replaying the worst conversations of the last two days, accompanied by images of rocks flying at my face, girls in chorus teasing me, and mullet man pointing to the "empty set" symbol on the blackboard.

"Uh-oh! The wheels are turning in your head again!" Master Park observed teasingly.

I cleared my throat. "I'll make myself stop thinking."

"You can't *force* yourself to feel *peaceful*, stupid-head. You'll just wind up constipated."

"I'm trying."

"Have you heard the story of the man who *tried* to pick up the pencil from the floor?"

"No."

"Guess what? He picked up the pencil off the floor! Don't *try* to meditate. Just *meditate*."

I smirked. "Know who you sound like?"

"If you say Yoda, I'm going to kick you."

"Never mind." I relaxed and took the lid off my thoughts. Instead of clearing my head, calming myself, focusing, and finding my center, I tried to drive away terrible memories by thinking about one of the newest *Doctor Who* serials. It was a bloodbath called "The Caves of Androzani," in which the entire ensemble cast was slaughtered during an outer-space drug cartel war. The only two survivors were women: the innocent American botany student, Peri, and Timmon, the savvy secretary of an evil corporate mogul who exposes her boss's white-collar crimes and takes over his empire. Even the Doctor died! He heroically sacrificed one of his thirteen lives to save Peri. After mulling over "Caves of Androzani," I mentally tinkered with my half-finished fanfiction novel: *Bringer of Darkness*. What if the Daleks killed the Doctor and conquered his home planet? What if Peri had to pilot the TARDIS by herself, go back in time, and try to prevent his death? (In broad strokes, my manuscript's plot predicted the later adventures *Day of the Doctor*, *The Genocide Machine* and *Divided Loyalties*.)

Master Park threw a punch at my face, stopping it one inch from my nose. I didn't move. I couldn't see her, but imagined her face growing more satisfied with me. She followed up by kicking the air next to both my ears. Then something whizzed past my shoulder. It embedded in the wall behind me with an alarming *thunk*. "Was that a throwing star?" I asked.

"Shush! Keep your eyes closed."

I hadn't opened them. I felt oddly comfortable sitting cross-legged on a hardwood floor. Then I felt even more odd as Master Park climbed up on my crossed legs, planting her bare feet on my thighs. I smirked, but knew I wasn't supposed to ask what she was doing. "While you're not concentrating *anyway*," she said breezily. She noticed some give in my legs and began bouncing lightly up and down on them, testing out her new trampoline. "You're flexible. Interesting. Thin guy, big-boned, and flexible. Surprisingly flexible. This is kinda fun. Wheeee! I could do this all afternoon."

Feel free. I wasn't sure what she was up to, but I was sure of one thing: if I wasn't meditating before, I *certainly* couldn't now. I heard Master Yumi Park speak my thoughts aloud, archly, "'How am I supposed to meditate with this crazy, tiny Korean lady bouncing on my legs? Is she gonna climb up on my shoulders next?'"

I couldn't stop myself from chuckling.

She jumped off my legs, landing softly on the hardwood floor in front of me. "You need to meditate. They're gonna keep coming at you. Wearing you down."

"Tony and his gang?"

"*Everyone*. You're a nice person, so everyone is going to try to destroy you. You can't let them, because the biggest tragedy of all will be if you let them beat the kindness out of you."

"Yeah."

"You have a big heart. Don't let them hit it with a flame-thrower and turn it to ashes."

"Okay. How do I protect myself?"

"You need to block them out. Find peace inside yourself. Remember when I punched the air in front of you and you ignored it? Kicked next to your ears? Threw the star? You only registered all that enough to be aware of elevated threats! Exactly how I wanted you to react. Ignore the endless stream of shit that comes your way, day in and day out, like you ignored me."

"Okay."

"You have a sense of humor, right? You smiled when I jumped on you?"

"Yeah."

"Use that. Something horrible happens, make a joke out of it. Be unflappable."

"Like Bill Murray in *Ghostbusters*?"

"Exactly! Besides, does anyone ever say anything of substance to you? Or is it all them pontificating? Bragging? Dragging you down into their own depression and egomania?"

"I guess I hear a lot of outrageous nonsense from people."

"Don't close yourself off to life or numb your emotions. Be ready to respond to a real person with something genuine to offer. Be there to help someone in need. Tune the rest of the horseshit out. Laugh at it. Ignore it. Meditate. If you don't tune out the jackasses, they will break you. And if they break you, you will not be ready to open your heart to decent human beings when they finally make themselves known to you."

I nodded. "Yes, sir."

"You have a big heart, a big brain, and a big sense of humor. Use them."

September 9, 1987

On the second day of sixth grade, I did not wear a blue blazer. Instead, I wore beige cargo shorts and blue Hawaiian shirt, an outfit that gave my sexual harassers in chorus no end of amusement. I had hoped that it being less formal would have been a bonus, but no such luck.

"Never wear shorts again! Nobody wants to see your pasty legs!"

"And your short-sleeve shirt! Look at those wimpy arms!"

I promised myself I would never wear shorts again. I didn't exactly keep that promise, but I pretty much only wear shorts when the temperature goes well over one-hundred degrees.

*

On day three of sixth grade, I wore a pair of jeans and a T-shirt with the TARDIS on it. Since nobody in the school had heard of *Doctor Who*, this outfit was another damp squib. These days, the average teenager can recognize the TARDIS or a Funko Pop figure of a Dalek in Hot Topic and "fan girls" are a source of embarrassment to male chauvinist geeks. In the mid-eighties, I would have killed for a cute girl in 6th grade to have recognized the time machine on my shirt and gushed over it. I would *not* have given her a *Doctor Who* quiz to determine whether her fandom was "authentic." That would have made me mean, stupid, and self-destructive.

"Why do you have a phone booth on your t-shirt?" one Italian girl asked during homeroom. She had not introduced herself, but she might have been named Michelle. She approached me as I made my own fun playing fake hopscotch on the tiled floor at the back of our homeroom. The rest of the students were milling around and talking, waiting for the first period bell to ring before heading off to classes. I tried to be casual as I stopped playing solo hopscotch. "Guess you don't watch PBS."

"PBS? Are you kidding?"

"Only channel worth watching! First of all, there's nudity and cursing and violence on PBS! And no commercials! You ever see the naked African tribes? The insane male bonding scene in *A Room with a View*? You don't get that on other channels! They're *mad boring!*"

"PBS is an education channel."

"And it is very educational! You get to see penises waving in the air! You'll love it!"

"Gross."

Why does this tactic never, ever work? I try to convince people education is sexy and they never bite. Or they think I'm a pervert. But education is mad sexy!

Michelle-maybe chewed her gum thoughtfully as she looked me up and down. "Are you working hard to look bad? You need to spike your hair and swap out Velcro sneakers for Reebok high tops. And get yourself some Cavariccis and a leather jacket and change your glasses for contact lenses. Then you would be okay-looking."

"I don't want spiked hair. I like Billy Idol. I don't want his hair."

Michelle-maybe threw her hands up in the air theatrically. "Jesus! I'm just trying to help you here, snappahead! You don't want to spike your hair, throw some gel in it. Comb it back."

"Comb it back? What's that?"

"You take some fucking gel and put it in your fucking hair and then you take a fucking comb and you use it to comb your fucking hair back."

I held my hands up defensively. "Alright, alright, alright!"

"I know you're supposed to be Italian, but you look like a comic store nerd the way you dress. If you clean up okay, maybe I'll try making out with you. I gotta see what you look like after a makeover. Right now, you might be good-looking, but you dress like shit."

I sneered at her. "Don't do me no favors."

"Fine! Be that way." Michelle-maybe flipped me off before joining a circle of her friends a few yards away.

I shouldn't have said that. She looks like she'd be fun to make out with. Me and my damn pride. I tried to cheer myself up by resuming my game on the imaginary hopscotch court.

"Mr. Cavalieri!" my homeroom teacher, Mr. Figliozzi, called out unexpectedly, surprising me into stopping. "There's a fine line between genius and insanity. A fine line."

I smiled crookedly. "Thanks for the warning."

On the following morning, I showered and attempted to comb my hair back with gel. I had to admit, it looked better. Michelle-maybe was probably also right about the Velcro sneakers and the general badness of yesterday's outfit. I was a little scared of getting contacts. Putting stuff right on my eyes sounded gross. I'd probably do it wrong and blind myself. And for what? A school chock of people who yell "fag" at me? They weren't worth it. Still, I was willing to make a few concessions as long as I could stay my essential self. I just wanted to avoid morphing into a carbon copy of every other Staten Island teenager. I stood in front of my bedroom closet, at a total loss for what kind of outfit to put on. *Wow, I have no clue. How do I look Italian without looking like I'm doing an* impersonation *of an Italian? Or like an extra in* Saturday Night Fever? *There's more to Italian men than gangsters and pizza Guidos. So, how do I prove that? Is there a different kind of Italian I can dress like?*

Two weeks later, inspiration struck. I asked Mom to take me clothes shopping. It was a cruel thing to do, asking a woman who grew up in extreme poverty in a Brooklyn immigrant community to drop the kind of coin I was asking her to drop, but we needed to go at least a little upscale. Mom was flexible, but only so flexible; she was willing to buy two outfits that would get the Michelle-maybe seal of approval, but no more than two, since those two sets of shirts and pants cost what six complete K-Mart outfits would have. Also, the one new pair of high-top sneakers cost the same amount as three sets of K-Mart shoes. At the beginning of the trip, I was worried I'd sold out my principles by even listening to Michelle. By the end, I was so happy with the clothes I got that I wasn't mad at myself or Michelle anymore. She had been trying to help me. That was obvious, now. The Monday following our fateful shopping trip, I returned to school with my hair combed back, wearing John Lennon glasses; black Cavariccis; a white, buttoned down, long-sleeve shirt; white Reebok hightop sneakers; and a rumpled gray raincoat like the one worn by Lieutenant Columbo on television.

I am Columbo! And who is Columbo? As Peter Falk said, "a guy with a mind like Einstein who sounds like the box boy at Food Giant!" That's me, world! Worship me or get out of my way! The students glanced at me with tired half-interest, determining that enough of the ensemble was inoffensive that they would overlook the raincoat. The first time I wore this ensemble in homeroom, I caught Michelle-maybe's attention. She nodded at me and offered me a sober thumbs up. I replied with two thumbs up. The good news was I was far less frequently accosted in the hallways thanks to my new "Italian American Man" superhero costume. The bad news was that this outfit did little to discourage the broads who flanked me in chorus from snickering constantly while imagining out loud what my penis looked like.

"That raincoat is hot," Viola whispered in his ear. "You can button it up and I can slip under it. I can suck you off underneath it. Nobody would know what was going on."

To me, raincoats meant Columbo, not pervert or pedophile or nut with a sawed-off shotgun, but these two wasted no time educating me on the various shady connotations of the clothing article. The images Viola conjured in my head had a certain appeal, but she was still laughing out of the side of her face. No matter how much fleeting enjoyment some of her dirty talk afforded me, it was only a matter of seconds before shame struck me down. I was sick of this teasing but had no clue how to stop it. Three months into the term, they were still mocking me. I asked them to "please stop." My voice squeaked. Aurora and Viola opened their mouths wide, miming a silent, booming laugh. (Mrs. Laird had been telling them to shush a lot lately, so they didn't want to be too loud.) "Somebody's hitting *puberty*," Aurora cooed.

"If you get hair on your dick, show us," Viola purred into my ear.

"Yeah, yeah, yeah," I grumbled. "Whatever."

"No, please. If you don't show me, I'll *die of disappointment*." Viola feigned wilting like a flower starved of sunlight. "I need your cock like a plant needs the sun!"

The next day, Mitchell found me in the hallway between classes and asked me about rumors he'd heard that I was being sexually harassed in chorus. I turned redder than marinara sauce. "Why would anyone object to two pretty girls flirting with them? Be serious."

"What's that? A Watergate-era non-denial denial? I hear they're mocking you non-stop."

"It's all in good fun." Why should Mitchell have to get involved? If I couldn't make it clear that I was not enjoying this treatment, I was probably culpable.

"Let me know if you need help," Mitchell said. "I'm here when you want to talk." He changed the subject when he saw I was about to cry but not about to talk. "Hey, listen: K-Rock did a countdown of the hundred best rock songs of all time. Guess what number one was?"

I leaned against the hallway wall, watching steams of students who had been ignoring or bullying me flow past. Hated him. Hated her. Didn't know him. Didn't know her. Those five guys? Wanted them dropped in boiling acid. Anyway, I tried to figure it out. "'Runaround Sue'?"

"Think more edgy and 1970s," Mitchell suggested sympathetically. "Remember, this is K-Rock, not 101.1 CBS-FM."

"'Why Don't We Do It in the Road'? 'Another Brick in the Wall'?"

"No and no."

"'People are Strange'? 'I Can't Get No Satisfaction'?" I was running out of 1970s songs famous enough to have been included on the soundtrack of a movie I knew.

"Want to hear the answer?"

I sighed. "Let's have it."

"'Stairway to Heaven.'"

My jaw dropped. *What a stupid choice!* "That's crazy!"

Mitchell was surprised by how aghast I was. "Don't you like the song?"

I laughed. "I like Neil Sedaka as much as the next guy, but picking *that* as the best song?"

Mitchell had never heard of Neil Sedaka. "Who? What song are you talking about?"

"'I'll build a stairway to heaven, 'Cause heaven is where you are,'" I sang.

Mitchell smirked. "Yeah, that's not the same song. You've heard the Neil Sedaka song 'Stairway to Heaven,' but not Led Zeppelin's?"

"Is Led Zeppelin the band that sings 'Love Bites'?"

"You don't know the difference between Led Zeppelin and Def Leppard?"

"Um . . . "

January 12, 1988

"Whip it out." Viola's tongue flickered on my earlobe.

My wet earlobe was the inducement I needed to act. "Okay." I unzipped my pants. The blue of my boxer shorts was visible through the open fly. One strand of pubic hair peaked out through the fly hole. My penis couldn't figure out if it was excited enough by the ear lick to emerge from hiding or invested enough in its own self-preservation to stay tucked in its foxhole. It trembled in place, fixed at its current height, awaiting further instructions.

Viola recoiled. "What the fuck are you doing?"

"How about you put your money where your mouth is?" I tried to talk and sneer like Clint Eastwood, but my face wore an "I've just tasted castor oil" expression instead.

Viola's pretense of friendliness and flirtation vanished. "Fuck off and die, kid."

Darting a glance at her friend, Aurora, I gestured invitingly at my crotch. "How about it?"

Aurora's eyes narrowed. "I don't suck Tic-Tacs."

"Suit yourself." I zipped back up and feigned interest in the lesson.

"Are you gonna just pretend you didn't do that?" Viola whispered to me. "Because we ain't ever gonna forget."

I nodded. "Good. I was hoping you'd get the message."

Teachers and security guards are never around when you need them. At 2:40, I hurried out of the school building, sprinting towards the yellow school bus parked by the playground, running right into the waiting arms of my favorite people: Tony Nocerino, his Merry Men, and the loves of my life, Viola and Aurora. I belted out a grotesquely cheery, "Hello! I believe you're here to kill me?" and mimicked Arsenio Hall's "Woof! Woof! Woof!" welcome chant and circular fist pump. My enemies responded by circling me. I was an important supporting character at the end of a George A. Romero zombie film, about to be given the gift of an extended, uber-violent death. In moments, the zombies would tear open my stomach, unfurl my intestines, and bite into them as my eyes rolled back up into my head. Well, it wasn't as bad as that. They didn't feast upon my flesh but contented themselves with kicking the shit out of me.

I don't know who punched me first, but a powerful blow landed at the base of my skull. I dropped to the ground. Then Tony Nocerino and the Merry Men (minus Bobby Mammolito) rained punches and kicks down upon me. I wondered stupidly where Bobby was as Tony screamed: "Fuckin' Jew flasher! That's so disgusting! A flasher! Don't you dare expose yourself to these nice Italian girls! Don't you even *look* at an Italian girl! Dirty! Fuckin'! Jew!" Tony kicked me to emphasize each word. He finished up by stomping down hard on my left wrist.

I either felt something crack or imagined I did.

Viola's cigarette-smoking face appeared over mine. Her newly lit cigarette burned brightly. She blew smoke in my face, stinging my eyes. As I tried to blink the burning sensation away, she plucked the cigarette out of her mouth and put it out on my chest, burning a hole through my shirt, scorching the flesh above my heart. I screamed.

Bobby Mammolito leaned against the brick façade of the school building and consulted his watch. He whistled. "We're gonna miss the bus, assholes!" The beating continued another twenty seconds. His second whistle was ear-piercing. "Dunno if it matters, but he's Neapolitan!"

Wincing from the whistle, Tony stopped punching me. "No way! He's Italian?"

Bobby's eyes widened. "What are you, Mr. Burns?"

"Vaffanculo!" I yelled.

Tony massaged his chin, thoughtfully. "I forgot he's Italian. I keep forgetting that."

"That doesn't matter!" Viola yelled. "He unzipped his pants in front of me!"

"So what?" Tony asked. "*I* unzipped my pants in fronta you. If he ain't a Jew, it's okay."

"Oh, fuck you, Tony!" Viola yelled.

"A guy's gotta try, amirite?" Bobby called out.

"And fuck you, too, Bobby!" Viola yelled.

"I'm just sayin' I don't think he's done anything to warrant this beatdown, you know?" Bobby yelled again. "Weren't the girls the ones messing with him for, like . . . months and shit?"

The Merry Men looked down on my bleeding figure. I looked dumbly back up at them. I was numb and in shock. Naturally, as soon as I got home, laid down in bed, and my heartrate abated, I would feel the full force of every punch, kick, and cigarette burn. For now, though, I imagined I had a comical and confused look on my face, underneath the blood, snot, spit, sweat, and heavy bruising. My vision was blurry, adding to my overall sense of confusion. I didn't know where my glasses were. On the concrete path somewhere? On a nearby patch of grass? These morons thought "Never hit a man with glasses" meant it was okay to punch a nearsighted kid if you swatted his glasses off first. One of the blurry Italians leaned closer to me. His features almost became discernable as he asked, apologetically, "Are you really one of us?"

I propped myself up on my elbows. A trickle of blood slid down the corner of my mouth and dripped onto my Columbo raincoat. "I . . . am . . . NOT . . . one . . . of . . . YOU!!!"

Tony chuckled and shook his head. "This is the piece of shit you want to defend, Bobby? He don't got no pride in being Italian!" More kicks followed, striking me up and down my body. I didn't know what part of me to defend.

Bobby whistled again. "The bus is gonna fucking leave! I'm going now, because I don't wanna miss it. To hell with you lunatics." And yet, Bobby kept rubbernecking.

Tony kicked me in the solar plexus, sending a shockwave of pain through my body. I hadn't seen it coming and was too slow to curl up into a ball and blunt the force of the blow. Tony walked off to the idling bus. Viola spat in my face and followed him. Aurora looked down on me with tears in her eyes. She mouthed the words "I'm sorry" and left with the others. Bobby lingered, looked down at me, and shook his head. "They worked you over worse than I expected." He waited for me to acknowledge the half-apology, but I couldn't move a muscle.

"You okay?" Bobby asked.

"Suffering Sappho," I muttered, plagiarizing Wonder Woman's oddest exclamation.

"Ah, you're okay. Good to know." Bobby left me, a bleeding heap on the sidewalk. I could hear him humming "The Best is Yet to Come" as he disappeared into the bus. The door closed behind him and the bus pulled away.

I lost consciousness, slipping into a fever dream.

I was a werewolf with dark brown fur, sprinting on four legs through the Bavarian forest, desperate to escape my pursuing kinsmen. They ran after me on their hind legs, upright; their gorgeous, silver fur glowed in the light of the full moon. There were ten of them and one of me, and they were gaining. In a moment, they would be upon me. I would not survive the battle. These were *The Howling* werewolves, tall and menacing, eager to hunt me down and kill me for my lack of blood purity. I was the less human, less decorous werewolf: the doglike breed from *An American Werewolf in London*. I was a mangy mutt. I deserved to die.

Dr. Stephanie Greenberg turned my purple wrist gently over in her hand. "Believe it or not, the swelling will go down faster if you fractured it. I'll order an x-ray. What happened?"

"Some Pizza Guido stomped on it." I was in the examination room of a convenient care clinic in Heartland Village in Staten Island, which we went to every time I was sick or injured. I didn't have a general practitioner and saw a different doctor or nurse each time we came here. There was also, invariably, a four-hour wait whenever I came to this office, even if no one else was in the waiting room. During these trips to the doctor, I got to see some entertaining shows I didn't watch normally, like *The Price is Right*, *Love Connection*, and syndicated reruns of *Match Game* and *Hill Street Blues*. Thankfully, after today's epic wait in an empty waiting room, I was being examined by yet another doctor I had never seen before. This young doctor wore her black hair up in a bun, the standard white doctor's coat, and a stethoscope around her neck. I tried not to notice her full lips and nut-brown eyes. Of course, Dad was going to say something inappropriate in five . . . four . . . three . . . two . . .

Dad leaned conspiratorially forward, whispering to Dr. Greenberg. "My son flirted with the wrong girl. You ever flirt with the wrong person, doctor?"

Dr. Greenberg continued to examine my injuries. "Luckily, a lot of these injuries look worse than they are. Still, you are going to want to wash the cigarette burn regularly. Keep it covered in ointment until it heals."

"You ever hear that you're too pretty to be a doctor?" Dad asked.

Dr. Greenberg looked me in the eyes without acknowledging Dad with her peripheral vision. "You've been through a traumatic experience. I'm writing down a name and number for you. A counselor who specializes in teenagers." She jotted down the information on the back of one of her business cards for me. "I'm going to arrange for that x-ray now." Dr. Greenberg left.

I whirled on Dad. "What the heck was that? She's a doctor, Dad! She's been to medical school! She's a serious woman!"

"With some serious breasts. Did you get a load of them? Hot damn."

I dropped my head in my hands.

Dad looked at me, puzzled. "What?"

CHAPTER NINE
Wonder Woman, the Brides of Dracula, and Dad

September 14, 1983

When I was seven, I was allowed to go out and play on Kell Avenue in suburban Staten Island under one condition: when Mom looked out the front door up and down the long, nearly traffic-free, residential block, she would catch sight of me somewhere. One day, I went farther than I had before, and found myself tempted to go farther still. I stood at the corner of Kell and Westwood Avenue, daunted by the width of the street I'd have to cross, fearing my mother's psychic powers. Up until last week, Mom had a musical jewelry box in her bedroom, a souvenir from one of her 1960s Italy excursions. I was not supposed to touch it. Ever. The problem was, I liked the song a lot, even though I couldn't identify it. Last week, I went into the bedroom to open the music box. I was extra gentle with it because I didn't want her to know I'd touched it. As I lifted the lid, it came off in my hand as if it were meant to. It lifted so easily that I had to take notice of the snapped hinges to realize that — yes — it was broken. I was responsible. I returned the music box to where it had been, gently replaced the lid, and sprinted out of the bedroom, hoping Mom wouldn't blame me for the broken hinge. This was a hope in vain. While I was not sure what the hell had happened, Mom was convinced that I had done something rough with the hinges to break them. I was convinced it would have come off as easily in her hand if she had opened it first. And yet, in retrospect, I wonder if I hadn't just snapped the lid off with my little monkey hands, not knowing my own strength. After all, in 2013, I snapped the spoiler off the trunk of my friend Jim's car by slamming the trunk shut too hard. (*Ape man can't be trusted with anything nice.*) The music box incident forced me to conclude that I should *not disobey any more rules at any time for any reason.* This moral was reinforced by the overly didactic gothic horror stories for children that I grew up with: *Pinocchio* and *Charlie and the Chocolate Factory.* Break a rule? Get turned into a donkey or gruesomely disposed of to the musical accompaniment of Oompa Loompas! Be nice and a fundamentally decent person? Inherit a chocolate factory.

I really wanted to inherit a chocolate factory.

Why wouldn't Mom let me travel beyond the boundaries of our one residential block? Was it a fear of me getting hit by a car? Falling in a ditch in one of the few remaining undeveloped stretches of grassland? Or did she fear my running into a crazy-person kidnapper or child-killer? We *did* move to Staten Island during "the Summer of Sam," when I was one, and the 1983 made-for-TV movie *Adam* about the abduction and murder of six-year-old Adam Walsh put the fear of God into many parents during the Reagan Revolution. Over the course of my childhood, the number of kids participating in Halloween in our neighborhood dropped sharply thanks to fears of apples concealing razor blades and cocaine-laced candy corn. There were also, during the retrograde 1980s, a plethora of rumors about Staten Island being hagridden with Satanic cults, though it wasn't clear if there really were Satanists in Richmond County or if parents were merely spooked their children listened to Black Sabbath and Judas Priest. As a kid, I couldn't understand why Mom was so afraid of our neighbors. They seemed like reasonably nice people when I caught a glimpse of them sprinting back and forth between their car and front door. On the other hand, one neighbor in particular — a silent, angry-looking middle-aged woman named Mrs. Grass — *never* waved hello to me, no matter how many times I waved to her. One time, I made Maria-Bamford-like pterodactyl screeches at her to see if I could frighten her into acknowledging my existence. She continued ignoring me and let herself into her home. I was impressed and upset that my pterodactyl screech did not rattle her. I stepped into my living room and saw my parents watching. Dad said, "Don't make dinosaur sounds at the neighbors."

Mom added, "Mrs. Grass needs a good lay. I don't think her husband is up to the job."

So, yes, the mostly working-class Staten Islanders hid in their semi-attached homes and only ventured outside to play basketball in the hoop mounted over their garage doors or swim in their above-ground pools in their backyards. They only spoke to their neighbors during street-wide blackouts. This was why, whenever the police and reporters would ask any given Islander, "What was your neighbor like *before* he killed thirty-seven Russian women and buried them in his basement?" the response would always be, "He was so normal! What was his name again?"

Anyway, here I was at the intersection, afraid to cross the bloody street. I was a Hobbit at the edge of the Shire, terrified to take my first step into a larger world. Two local kids whizzed by on bicycles, then looped around back and passed me again. Back then, people on my block still rode bicycles: a rare sight in recent years, since all those who used to cycle had either got old enough to buy cars or moved off Staten Island. I had blown my one chance at a bike of my own when Mom saw me almost plow into a moving car on my first day of riding. It was irritating yet understandable that Mom was taking few chances with her young son's life, but she tore the bicycle out of my hands and never let me ride it again.

One of the bicycle boys saw me standing by the street corner, staring impotently across the block, and skidded up beside me. The boy, Ilan Schulman, was part of the local Orthodox Jewish community. He wore a green Camp Morasha T-shirt and a yarmulke over curly black hair. Laughing genially after I told him my problem, Ilan lowered his bike onto the curb and walked back and forth across the street. "It's easy," he said. "See? Your Mom will never know you did it." That was true. Unless Mom chose that second to look for me, there would be no forensic evidence of the transgression. Evidence was a big problem, not just for me, but every kid on the block. Kell Avenue was so inordinately dull that the kids next door, the Birnbaums, entertained themselves by walking along the roof of their family car. Every so often, their mom would appear in the doorway, yell at them for walking on the car, and then head back inside when they slid down the hood to the ground. This saga played itself out time and again, but the kids were so small at that age that it took them a full year to put a truly significant dent in the car's body. Once that happened, I never saw the kids prancing on their Mom's Impala again. They had left *evidence*, just as I had left evidence when I broke Mom's music box. Evidence was the enemy of fun, but I wouldn't be leaving any such evidence just by crossing a darn street. I ran across Westwood. I looked at the world on the other side. I ran back home. I was so nervous that I didn't enjoy the experience at all.

I'll be the first to admit that most people find me a bit strange. They often wonder how I wound up turning out the way that I did. My family members have competing theories involving a traumatic head injury or developmental disability that either occurred in the womb or shortly after I was born. In late December of 1975, my honeymooning parents took a ride on Space Mountain in Walt Disney World, not knowing Mom was pregnant with me. End of first theory. On August 1, 1976, I was born one month premature, the size of half of a loaf of bread, earning me the nickname "half a loaf." A full-sized kid a year later, I graduated to "loaf" and "Captain loaf," respectively. On October 9, 1976, Dad was amusing himself by tickling me and rolling me around on the Queen-sized bed in the master bedroom of their roach-infested apartment in Sheepshead Bay, Brooklyn. Tragically, I rolled past his receiving right hand, dropping right off the bed and slamming my head against the hardwood. The three events combined constitute "The Origin of 'Italian American Man,' Staten Island's First Guido Superhero!"

Just kidding. These were not big head injuries. Other factors were, of course, more important in setting my personality in stone early on. I was born into "The Oregon Trail" Generation, situated in the No Man's Land between Generation X and the Millennial Generation. That generational identity played a role in shaping my cognitive and emotional development, as did my astrological sign of Leo and my being born in "The Year of the Dragon." Even more revealing is my Myers-Briggs Type Indicator personality inventory INFP (introversion, intuition, feeling, perception), which casts me as a "mediator" and "idealist" in the mode of real-life figures John Lennon, Tom Hiddleston, and J.R.R. Tolkien, and the fictional characters Amélie Poulain, Anne of Green Gables, Frodo Baggins, and Peeta Mellark.

All these forces of culture, biology and mysticism conspired to make me more than a little odd, but one of the most significant events in my cognitive development was my early exposure to the *Wonder Woman* television show starring Lynda Carter. The show had broadcast new episodes when I was in my infancy, so I saw most of them when I was five- or six-years-old during afternoon repeats broadcast on one or another of New York City's three syndicated television stations: WPIX,

WNYW, or WWOR. I loved that Wonder Woman used her metal bracelets to deflect bullets and a lasso to subdue villains. This practice was a big, welcome departure from killing the bad guys, like cowboys in Westerns did. Also, the round-faced, black-haired actress Lynda Carter had a Mexican mother, subconsciously reminding me of my round-faced, black-haired Italian American mother, Gianna Cavalieri. On some level, I've always viewed Mom and Wonder Woman as one and the same person. That has been an occasion for much confusion and consternation when men see my Wonder Woman comics and merchandise and say things to me like, "Yeah, baby! She can tie me up anytime! I know that's why you like her, too! Hubba, hubba!" When pressed on the issue, I'd sometimes manage to say something like, "I was so little when I first saw her show, I didn't even know what being attracted to a woman was. I just thought Diana of Paradise Island was cool." *Wanting* Wonder Woman always struck me as inappropriate, much like having the hots for Audrey Hepburn. Who *lusts after* Audrey Hepburn? *And that's Mom they're talking about!*

My father was one of those people who thought Lynda Carter was hot, so he didn't mind watching the show with me. He didn't mind when Mom bought me a tin Wonder Woman lunchbox and an invisible jet toy. He also shrugged off the purchase of a vinyl Wonder Woman placemat. The arrival of the Wonder Woman Barbie, however, made him reach for the TUMS. When he pressed Mom on the purchase, she explained that the Amazon princess was my best buddy. Dad balked at that terminology. "If we're going to do this, she's his imaginary girlfriend. If we call her his *buddy*, we'll wind up with a son who becomes *friends* with women, like Gabriel, who has all those fat women friends he isn't sleeping with."

"There's nothing wrong with raising our son to be *friends* with women. And don't say bad things about my nephew, Gabriel!"

Dad crossed his arms over his chest. "No straight man on earth wants to 'just be friends' with Lynda Carter. Let's be serious. No straight man can be 'just friends' with any woman. It isn't possible. The sexual tension is always impossible to ignore."

"I don't know that that's true."

"I do. Let's not lead our son up the garden path thinking he can be 'just friends' with women. And let's not make him gay, either." Dad lost the argument and did not make his displeasure known to me. For more than a year, I took my Wonder Woman Barbie and placemat everywhere my parents, younger brother, and I went: church, family reunions, trips to the park, and to pre-school and first-grade class. Each time I tucked the placemat under my arm and clutched the Barbie in my hands, Dad gritted his teeth and grumbled under his breath. After witnessing six months of my co-dependent relationship with the superhero, he resolved to confront me about the creepiness of my attachment to her. As he was mulling over potential approaches, he wandered in on me — then seven-years-old — sitting on the brown shag living room floor carpet, undressing the Wonder Woman Barbie. Once I slipped the clothes off, I inspected its smooth, anatomically incorrect nude body.

"No nipples or labia, huh? She doesn't look real at all."

I started at the sound of Dad's voice. Hastily, I dressed the doll again. I felt like I had been caught doing something wrong and began perspiring. Even as I dressed her, I considered that Dad was right. It didn't look like the women I'd caught fleeting glimpses of in the showers and dressing room at the YMCA when Mom took me swimming. I knew what nipples were, but that other word he used was beyond me. "Yes. The labia is the most important part," I said, pretending to know what it was.

Dad decided then and there that the last thing I needed was an anatomically incorrect doll to undress. That night, when I fell asleep, Dad snuck quietly into the bedroom I shared with my brother and gathered up all my Wonder Woman merchandise. He put his electric blue windbreaker on, tiptoed past Mom, who was still awake grading freshman composition papers in the kitchen, and slipped out the side door. He walked up to the two garbage cans he had placed out in the front of the house in time for morning sanitation pickup, plucked the lid off the nearest can, and dropped my Barbie, placemat, lunchbox, and plastic invisible jet inside. By the time I woke up the next morning, the sanitation crew had made their collection. Our empty garbage cans lay on their sides in the middle of the street, rolling one yard back and forth in the wind. No evidence remained that I had ever owned a single stitch of Wonder Woman memorabilia.

Dad was unnerved by how long I cried and screamed over the loss.

A week later, Dad found me hidden in the wood-paneled basement, sitting at a long oak table in the toy room filled with shelf after shelf of *Star Wars, Masters of the Universe,* and *Transformers* toys, trying and failing to copy John Buscema's pencil art for *The Savage Sword of Conan* comic. Each time I made a mistake drawing Conan decapitating someone, I crumpled up the page and tossed it on the floor next to the other discarded Buscema copies. "I'm terrible. I must be better. I want to go to LaGuardia or the School of Visual Arts when I grow up."

"High school and college are both a long way away." Dad eyeballed some of my Transformers and began buttering me up. "I think these toys are very impressive. I really like Shockwave and Optometrist Prime."

"*Optimus* Prime," I said, severely.

Dad laughed at himself. "Of course! I have to remember that." Dad looked with less favor upon the rows of *Star Wars* action figures, saving his most sour facial expression for Luke, Leia, Han, Yoda, and Lando. "I can't shake the terrible feeling these people are all liberals."

I blinked a few times, not knowing what he meant. "You have to like Lando, at least. He's my favorite. He got put in a tight spot, poor guy. Vader made him betray his friend."

"Hey, guess what? I have something for you." Dad sat beside me, producing the oversized military history coffee table book he had been hiding behind his back. "Ta-da! I bought a biography of *Rommel, the Desert Fox*!" When I gave Dad a quizzical look, he elaborated. "One of the things I don't like about Wonder Woman is she fights Germans. We're Germans. Remember, World War II soldiers weren't all Nazis. The Wehrmacht were apolitical."

"Mom says we're Italian."

"You're three-quarters Italian and one-quarter German. Never forget the German part! We can claim Mozart, Oktoberfest, and the Desert Fox! Rommel was a tank commander in North Africa in World War II. He was such a brilliant tactician that even the Allied commanders respected him. He launched offensives without orders, would win, and not get court-martialed!"

I started to show grudging interest. "Wow."

"Nothing succeeds like success. You bend the rules. You break the rules. If you succeed, you will be beloved. Captain Kirk proves the same point."

"That's true. Is he still alive?"

Dad looked at me suspiciously. "Captain Kirk is a fictional character."

"I know, Dad! I mean is Rommel still alive?"

"Oh!" Dad frowned. "No. He died because of a stupid failed attempt to assassinate Hitler. That idiot von Stauffenberg put a bomb in a suitcase under a thick table. The table shielded Hitler from the full brunt of the blast. So stupid. If you're gonna kill someone, don't mess around with a bomb! A Mafia hitman would have just walked right up to Hitler and shot him in the head. Unfortunately, von Stauffenberg wanted to replace Hitler with Rommel as head of Germany. When Hitler found out, he ordered Rommel to shoot himself. Remember: don't be too charismatic or jealous people will take you out."

I thought I needed to be charismatic so I could get away with breaking rules?

Dad placed the book on the table next to me. I regarded my father's hero. Based on the cover photo alone, Rommel was a humorless man with a severely short haircut, cold eyes, a deeply cleft chin, and oversized ears. He wore a giant cross of iron over a gray tank commander's uniform. This man was nowhere near as adorable as Diana, Princess of Themyscira. Where Diana was soft, Rommel was flinty. Where Diana exuded compassion, Rommel radiated rigidity. "Rommel is an appropriate hero for a man," Dad concluded. "Feel free to fantasize about feeling up Wonder Woman, but if you're looking for a hero, here's your man."

No. Rommel is just not cute enough. He'll never replace Wonder Woman in my heart.

Dad's concern about my exposure to Wonder Woman was a bit ironic, since he had no compunction about showing me a number of lesbian vampire movies with softcore porn seasoning — especially Hammer studios' Karnstein Quadrilogy: *Vampire Lovers, Lust for a Vampire, Twins of Evil,* and *Captain Kronos: Vampire Hunter*. In the

1980s, many fortunate young boys grew up with access to a cable channel or two, such as HBO or MTV, or stumbled across their father's dirty magazine collection by accident. Often that was the extent of pre-internet-era sex education. In my own case, we didn't have cable, and I never found my Dad's dirty magazines, so my sex education came largely from my father's nearly limitless supply of vampire movies from around the world, made between the Bela Lugosi *Dracula* (1931) and the original *Fright Night* (1985). I also learned a little bit about the broad concept of sex from the two 1981 sex comedies Dad dragged me to the theater to watch when I was five, the Bill Murray military romp *Stripes* (co-starring my man Harold Ramis) and a sleezy comedy with Peter Falk about female mud wrestlers called ...*All the Marbles*. As a kid, I didn't mind the sex comedies so much. It was the horror films that occasionally branded gory images on my semi-photographic memory. For example, Dad treated me to the Stephen King portmanteau horror film *Creepshow* in 1982, when I was six. It gave me lifelong roach and zombie phobias. Not every movie Dad took me to see was a hard R, but they were mostly cult and genre films. There were notable trips with Dad to see *Godzilla 1985, Invaders from Mars,* and *Aliens.* The whole family went together to see *Gremlins, Ghostbusters, Little Shop of Horrors,* and each new *Star Trek* film. Any more mainstream fare was off the menu (so I still haven't seen *The Big Chill,* for example).

In 1988, when I was twelve, Dad took me to see *The Unholy,* an *Exorcist*-style "Catholic horror movie" about a priest-murdering demon disguised as nubile redhead. Every year on Good Friday, the demon Desiderius dressed in a see-through black nightgown and approached priests as they knelt before the altar. She tempted them by brushing her breasts against their faces. If, in a moment of weakness, the men reached up with trembling hands to caress her breasts, she slashed their throats open with long red fingernails. That film left an indelible impression upon me, shaping my views of both sex and religion for life. The AIDS-era lesson was clear: *No touchy boobie! No touchy! Touchy boobie? Get throat cut!*

The Unholy notwithstanding, Dad left the wildest film viewings of all for home, when he managed to acquire on home video all the cult Grindhouse films he had watched during his formative years.

They had shaped his youth. He couldn't wait to show them to me and shape my youth with them as well. I remember Dad proudly unpacking his first Panasonic VHS player in 1983. As he pulled the bubble-wrap off the cutting-edge technology, he proudly explained to Mom how he was going to build his personal movie collection. "Now that I have this Panasonic, I can get all my movies on VHS!" He saw this machine as an upgrade from our video disk player, and entertained hopes that a far deeper library of films would be available to him than the Disney cartoons and epic movies he'd been getting on disk the last several years.

"The horror movies we saw on dates in those XXX theaters in Manhattan?" Mom asked.

"The Grindhouse theaters!" Dad shouted, unnecessarily loudly. He liked to shout when discussing his favorite movies. He had had noticeably more *joie de vivre* when the topic of movies came up than he did when discussing *any other topic*. "Especially the Hammer and Amicus movies we saw, but I also want to get the old Universal and RKO horror movies." Mom perused dad's handwritten wish list, vaguely remembering being dragged to see half of them over the past eight years: "*Werewolf in a Girl's Dormitory, Them!, The Uninvited, Invisible Man, Curse of the Demon, Bedlam, The Innocents, Bride of Frankenstein, Island of Lost Souls, Death Takes a Holiday, Invasion of the Body Snatchers* (both), and *The Louisiana Hussy.*"

Dad beamed. "I had a great thing happen. The video rental guy doesn't carry these movies. The catalog he orders from charges $70 for customers. He'll order all these movies for me *at cost*! Forty dollars each! All I have to do is let him unwrap them, dub himself a copy on a blank VHS of his own, and he'll give me the once-viewed movie *at cost!*" Unsurprisingly, twenty years later, that video store owner was arrested for violating federal copyright law by duplicating several thousand movies. Dad and I will always be grateful for the man's unparalleled selection of cult and arthouse films. Such fare was not found in mainstream Blockbuster Video outlets, which stocked thirty copies of new releases like *Rambo: First Blood Part II* instead. I was younger than Quentin Tarantino, but VHS rentals were my film school, too.

"Forty dollars is still a lot for a movie," Mom demurred. "And this is a long list."

"That's the first of many such lists!" Dad declared. As an avid film collector, Dad had several genres and periods he favored: Pre-Hays Code sex romps of 1930s Hollywood, 1940s film noir, 1950s science fiction, 1960s Euro horror, 1970s westerns, and 1980s action movies. All told, his taste in films was impeccable. For example, one time he proclaimed: "All the Westerns people talk about being so great? *The Searchers, Fistful of Dollars, High Noon, Rio Bravo*? They're two-and-a-half starts *at best*! The best Westerns are *Valdez is Coming, Hired Hand, Fastest Gun Alive, Day of the Outlaw, Requiescant, Appaloosa*, and *The Long Riders*." The opinion was so heretical, I didn't believe it. Then I watched all the films he name-dropped and determined he was correct: The more obscure films were far superior to the lionized ones.

Leo enjoyed watching these movies just as much as Dad and me. Still, he had a more ironic sensibility than we did, and could see the ridiculousness in our collective movie-watching obsession. He used a pink Pekingese plush toy named Amanda Wingfield (after the poor-but-genteel mother from Tennessee Williams' *Glass Menagerie*) to needle us. Affecting a stricken, ashamed female voice, Leo spoke through the Amanda plushie: "'Nobody goes to the movies night after night. Nobody in their right mind goes to the movies as often as you!'"

"My sons are talking over my head again." Dad didn't get the reference, but I laughed with Leo because Mom had taken us to see a Wagner College theater production of the play.

For a guy who adored cult and camp films, Dad was surprisingly into deconstructing films and finding plot loopholes instead of being forgiving of their low-budget, gonzo daring. At first, I liked the critical thinking skills Dad taught me when he demonstrated the flaws in every film we screened. Later, I just wanted to see what was good about a film and became allergic to focusing on what was bad. Each time Dad raised a complaint, I provided apologetic readings: "I bet that happened between scenes, Dad! They just didn't show it for pacing reasons." (Years later, the "Deleted Scenes" included on DVDs would retroactively prove me right often.) Annoyed, Dad wondered why I would side with the movie over him 99 percent of the time. I wasn't trying to be a jerk. I was just way more into "feeling" a story and judging it on its own terms than I was into picking at its seams. I had the most fun watching films with Dad when he gave himself over to a movie and just enjoyed it with me. There were moments when he would allow himself to laugh uproariously at a joke, fully feeling the emotion of the film. He'd do this most often when watching Marx Brothers mayhem or when Claude Rains or Gene Hackman said something arch or misogynist in one of their edgy, Oscar-worthy supporting roles. I was also tickled that Dad and Mom reminded me of both Groucho Marx and his eternal foil, Margaret Dumont, not just in their physical appearance, but in their relationship. When Groucho's roving eye would fixate on a pretty flapper, Dumont would give him the cold shoulder, reminding him she was the one with the money. Then Groucho would say, "Can't you see what I'm trying to tell you? I love you!" and break the fourth wall by wagging his painted-on eyebrows at the movie audience. During each scene with this flavor, Dad would laugh and say, "He sounds cynical, but in his heart of hearts, I know he loves Margaret Dumont." I found Dad's projecting on Groucho both alarming and reassuring. *Groucho is a cad who truly loves the woman he cheats on? Dad relates to Groucho? Uh-oh. Are Groucho and Dumont my parents!?!*

Other topics of conversations during film viewings included Dad's fun facts ("I tried out for the role of the kid genie in *The 7th Voyage of Sinbad*, but didn't get the part") and character-actor identification exercises ("I can't believe you didn't recognize Michael Ripper! He's in all these Hammer movies. He's the constable in *Plague of the Zombies*, the barkeep in *Scars of Dracula*, the drunk Irishman in *The Mummy*, and the drunk Irishman in *Curse of the Werewolf*.") Sometimes questions seemed innocent that were not, including, "What is your favorite Hammer movie?" My first mistake in instances like these was to offer my honest opinion: "Dunno. *The Devil Rides Out, Cash on Demand*, or *The Mummy*?" Dad shook his head. "You should have picked *Horror of Dracula, Brides of Dracula*, or *Kiss of the Vampire*."

Joking and needling my father aside, we had a lot of fun watching films together over the years and did it as often as we could. I found that watching movies with Dad made me happier than doing just about anything else. Since vampire movies were Dad's favorite films, they became my favorite films. Over the course of ten years — from 1983 to 1993 — I saw every possible adaptation of Bram Stoker's novel *Dracula* with Dad at my side. No matter the adaptation, Dad's favorite scene was the one in which Dracula's female consorts tried to seduce and murder his guest, Jonathan Harker, while he slept on the couch in the parlor. Dad really got into these moments: "Dracula's three brides are descending upon Jonathan! A blonde, a brunette, and a redhead. If you gotta go, that's the way you should go! Killed by three hot vampire women!"

I found it a reasonable assertion when I considered how unappealing other kinds of deaths seemed in comparison. Still, I wished Dad would stop talking about death by sex. Once we discovered a praying mantis while poking around in the rough, uncultivated land at the end of our suburban street and dad fed it. He caught a cricket, placed it on the ground a foot away from the mantis, and watched it pounce and bite the cricket's head off. "Zeus!" he yelled.

I was mesmerized by the sight of the mantis chomping away at the struggling cricket.

"Praying mantises do this to the males right after they mate, not unlike human women!" Dad joked, nudging me with his elbow.

At seven, I was never quite sure how to respond when Dad asked me to identify the sexiest vampire woman in the movies we watched. He'd press me, "Come on, now! Don't be shy. Who would you most like to bite you in the neck and drink your blood?"

I hid behind my bag of cheddar cheese Doritos and remained silent.

"You have to have some preference! I'll give you a hint, son. Not an ice queen blonde. Always go for the sultry, dark-haired woman. I can't abide Eva Marie Saint types. Horrible."

On the TV screen, one of Dracula's brides whispered, "I want to suck on Jonathan."

"Me, first!" another bride declared.

"They're fighting for the right to suck on him!" Dad cried, pointing at the TV. "Yes!"

I scrunched my eyebrows together. "I can see how that's cool." (No, I couldn't.)

"We should stay up late tonight," Dad declared. "*Lust for a Vampire* is up next."

I took a closer look at the actresses hovering about Harker. "I think all three are pretty."

"You have no standards!" Dad declared. "You're like a socialist."

I hid behind the Dorito bag again. "Nobody is *unattractive*."

"The blonde is unattractive. This blonde is as washed-out as every other blonde."

"I think the redhead is my favorite." The redhead reminded me of Spider-Man's girlfriend, Mary Jane Watson, in the comic books I read. Mary Jane was probably partly responsible for my blossoming affection for hazel-eyed redheads, as was the redheaded girl in my class, Claudia Occhiogrosso, a child model who starred in a Wendy's commercial.

"Redheads are two-and-a-half stars, but they're better than blondes. I only know two hot blondes: Nan Peterson from *The Hideous Sun Demon* and Nan Grey from *Dracula's Daughter*."

"I like Nan Grey," Leo chimed in unexpectedly.

Dad nodded. "She's so sexy, I can almost forgive her for being blonde."

All joking about the ridiculousness of "scream queens" and the sexism of horror movies aside, they have their good parts, or I wouldn't still embrace them as an adult. Horror movies and gothic novels might be dismissed as sadistic and nihilistic, but many of the gentlest and most oppressed people I've known have found comfort and catharsis in the only genre that understands their pain. Horror shows what it is like to be bullied, stalked, and sexually harassed, and it addresses the inevitability of death unflinchingly, while many other popular genres would prefer to pretend their protagonists live happily forever after. Indeed, as absurd as the supernatural elements of his stories are, Stephen King may well understand the dark underbelly of the American dream better than many more respected and naturalistic storytellers. King is adept at dramatizing the pains of childhood, the small-mindedness of small towns, and the existential angst of the introverted intellectual. King's readers see themselves in his characters, and that identification helps them understand themselves and stop feeling alone in the world. At least, that is the effect his writing has on me. *Stephen King gets it. I'm not crazy after all.*

King's worldview is not my father's. Dad finds King's gritty depictions of working-class life uncouth, so King does not provide Dad the comfort he provides me. Still, Dad's love of horror stories in general seems to be therapeutic, as mine is. Though not much of a reader, Dad found film noir and horror screenings comforting. Instead of providing fuel for fresh nightmares, they gave him a brief reprieve from the bad memories and nightmares of an unhappy childhood. Next to whatever appalling things happened to him in real life before I was born, Hammer's sexy vampire women were fun fairy tale creatures, imaginary girlfriends, and old buddies who kept him company, not anything truly "horrific." While I was grateful to Stephen King for placing before me unflinching reflections of the sixth-grade bullies who scarred me for life — both realistically in the form of Carrie's tormentors and allegorically in the shape of Pennywise the Dancing Clown — Dad did not want to confront his pain *quite* as directly. He preferred wish-fulfillment horror films as far removed from his Bronx childhood as he could imagine. Dad loved nineteenth-century European settings, polished villains, and happy endings in which a gentleman adventurer, often played by Peter Cushing, saved the women and children, and vanquished the evil. Peter Cushing even looked remarkably like my grandfather, Vincent senior. I'm sure that influenced Dad's affection for Cushing.

Unfortunately, horror movies were not very effective at keeping Dad's bad dreams away. Sweating and gasping for air, Dad often woke in the middle of the night. He had flashbacks to his childhood he couldn't shake. What would he dream about? I wasn't sure. Maybe he'd remember working a paper route for two years, saving for his future as a writer-director, only to find his stash emptied out one morning after his parents raided it for rent money. What lesson had they taught him? Don't work hard, because someone will just come along and rob you blind after you wasted years of your life working and saving. Dad could also be dreaming of his dog, a Golden Retriever he named Polyphemus in honor of the cyclops from *The Odyssey* and *The 7th Voyage of Sinbad*. He was eight years old when his parents announced that they would be moving to a new apartment in Co-op City tomorrow; it was smaller, cheaper, and did not allow pets. What lesson had his parents taught him when they dropped this bombshell? Don't allow yourself to love anyone, pet or human, because they will only be taken from you. These were the bad memories he had told me about. There were others so painful he referred to them elliptically or kept them to himself. He once mentioned "getting mugged by a Puerto Rican kid with a switchblade for my paper route money" as justification for blocking me from getting a paper route of my own. He cited "being made to walk on broken glass down an alley by some redheaded Irish thug" for why he didn't let me wander more than a few yards from our house. "Sniffing glue and boosting cars with my friends, and then crashing the car into the side of the road" was the provocative reason he never let me attend any sleepover parties. Dad had lived too much as a youth and didn't want me exposed to any of the dangerous elements that had almost landed him in jail or killed him. Mom, meanwhile, had been so pure of heart, she had done nothing illegal her whole life, and lived through the entire 1960s without even trying pot. Dad laughed at her over this. "I've had it. Nothing, really. You could have tried it, Gianna!"

Between Dad's wild childhood and mom's sheltered one, neither of them was going to let me off my short leash, that was for damn sure. Dad sought to protect me from having his childhood all over again, just as he continued to run as far from it as he could. That is why, as frustrated as he was that he and Mom had accidentally purchased a home in the wrong ethnic enclave, he was glad to raise his children in a nearly crime-free neighborhood. Still, feeling isolated by being one of the few Christian households on Kell Avenue, Dad would get bored with the silence and inactivity of Shabbos and pine for a weekend jaunt to Pennsylvania. When he could con my mother into agreeing, he would take solo trips to ski at Camelback Mountain Resort and gamble at Mount Airy Casino and Resort, sometimes meeting up with his great bear of a friend, Joe Boland. More frequently, he would bring us all along on day trips to the Poconos to fish for largemouth and striped bass at Brown Fish and Pay Lakes, dine at the Great Wall Chinese restaurant, browse wax waterfall sculptures at Pocono Candle in East

Stroudsburg, or pick up "Pocono Crunch" dessert at Callie's Candy Kitchen. Once a year, we ventured deeper into Pennsylvania to visit the Amish Communities of Lancaster. Over time, I developed a fascination with the Amish, and a respect for their stubborn refusal to participate in modern life. I felt a certain kind of jealousy for the Amish. As much as I might be tempted to criticize my father for being motivated by a "white flight" syndrome in his yearning for rural Pennsylvania, he did instill in me something sorely lacking in both suburbanites and city dwellers alike: an appreciation of nature. Thanks to Dad, I grew up a staunch environmentalist. Ironically, I was an environmentalist who happened to be deathly allergic to Nature. All my life, I have sneezed up a storm and developed allergic shiners — looking like I had two black eyes — upon the minutest exposure to birch, grass, oak, ragweed, and cedar pollen, as well as mold, pet dander, cigarette smoke, and whatever the fuck is in most barns. Additional symptoms included mysterious irritability, fatigue, and constant low-level sinus pressure that spiked into an agonizing migraine at four a.m. after causing a blood-curdling nightmare. These symptoms also appeared three hours after any visit I made to the house of a person with one cat, or two seconds standing in the doorway of a home with three cats. Unfortunately, Dad's favorite relatives — Aunt Irene and Uncle Cesar — owned a cat. We could never visit their house without my getting badly sick.

Instead of professional allergy treatment, I armed myself with Dimetapp to pull off going outside. Dimetapp was better at sedating me than blunting my symptoms. Dad finally took me to an allergist, who exposed me to forty allergens by pinpricking me up and down both arms and all over my back. He left the examination room for fifteen minutes to give the samples I was allergic to time to flare up. Upon his return, he found my entire back and both arms covered in bumps. "Good lord!" he cried. "You are an allergic person! You may need to become the next *Boy in the Plastic Bubble!*" May you never fascinate the specialist with your condition.

Dad and I were the biggest fans of Pennsylvania in the family. Leo could take it or leave it. He liked everything Dad and I liked about the area, but was more acutely aware of the rural poverty, gun clubs, and

Confederate flags, as well as what they signified. Meanwhile, Mom was never at ease in the Poconos or Lancaster county for more than an afternoon. Thanks to her upbringing, going outside into the great outdoors meant playing stickball in front of her Brooklyn apartment, watching old Italian men who owned their own homes play bocce on their stamp-sized front lawns, or sunbathing on the roof of the apartment building in a lawn chair. Spending time in a rural area that was miles from the nearest hospital, grocery store, firehouse, or police station terrified Mom. On one of the few occasions Dad successfully coaxed her into staying overnight in a cabin in the woods, Mom stayed awake all night, staring up at the ceiling, panicked by the possibility of an enormous grizzly bear bursting through the front door and eating us all alive. Dad slept his first restful night beside her, comforted by the number of miles he had placed between himself and the Puerto Rican kid who had mugged him and the Irish thug who had forced him to walk on broken glass.

Since Dad had only worked wage-slave jobs that ranged from minimum wage to payment on commission, he did not make enough money to buy the Pennsylvania weekend home he longed for. Mom was the one with the living wage, as well as the family member least enamored of Pennsylvania. Periodically, Dad would coax Mom into agreeing to look at model homes in Pocono housing communities that catered to the New York weekender crowd. When he'd find a house that looked good to him, he'd flash Bambi eyes at Mom, asking wordlessly, "Can you buy this for me? I can't afford it on my own." Mom would refuse. Wasn't the area too quiet to stomach? Where were the honking car horns? The furious arguments of neighbors heard through paper mâché walls? The drunk staggering home from the pub, peeing on the alley wall? No, she couldn't buy a house. During one of these fruitless model-viewings, the unfortunate salesman had the misguided impression my parents might have serious interest in closing a deal that day. The salesman made two additional, wildly incorrect assumptions: first, that Dad was the breadwinner, and second, that Dad could be goaded into putting the money down if he were teased about being whipped. In front of Mom, the salesman said to Dad, "You don't need your wife's approval here, right?"

Mom heard that one. I'll never forget how crimson Mom's face turned. "You've got some nerve talking about me like I'm not sitting right here! Like I'm the enemy of fun!"

Dad jerked a thumb in Mom's direction. "She's the one with the money."

"Who in the hell needs to own two houses two hours apart?" Mom shouted. "Let's keep the one house and drive out on weekends like we've been doing and save our money."

They were now talking like they were alone, and not right next to me, Leo, and the salesman. Leo thought now was a good time to tune everyone out. He sat on the grass near our car and resumed reading his Carl Barks *Uncle Scrooge* comic.

Mom added, "Everywhere we go is only ninety minutes away, the way you drive, Mad Max. And what about Damien's allergies? Can he live in a rural area for an *entire weekend*, when *a few hours* are a stretch for him?"

Dad winced. "Not without his head exploding, like in *Scanners*." Dad looked back at the salesman. "I guess that's a 'no.'"

The salesman had figured this out and was already halfway to his jeep.

Under my fascinated gaze, my parents morphed into doubles of Groucho Marx and Margaret Dumont. Margaret Dumont tapped her foot impatiently at Groucho. He wagged his eyebrows and held up a picture of Kamron, her college boyfriend. "You mean a woman of your culture and money and beauty and money and wealth and money would marry this fellow instead of me?"

CHAPTER TEN
Hulk Lonely, Hulk Want Friend

January 12, 1988

On the drive home from our embarrassing appointment with Dr. Greenberg, Dad redeemed himself by offering a feasible plan to improve my daily commute. "If we break it down: you have trouble on the bus ride, in the hallways, during lunchtime, in chorus, in gym, and in the mainstream classes. Those are a lot of danger points during any given day. Altogether, it is very overwhelming. If we take each problem in isolation, we can come up with solutions to at least some. It seems to me you can try again to get moved back into the gifted program, since you belong there. I'm not sure why you're getting resistance. The easiest problem to solve is the bus. A completely different school bus makes two stops near our house: one in front of Young Israel and one near St. Luke's on Bradley Avenue. Try that second bus. If the kids on it are any less belligerent, take it every day, and say goodbye to Tony and the Merry Men."

"How do I know those kids aren't worse?" I asked glumly.

Dad shrugged. "I drove past them this morning to scope them out. There seemed to be a bunch of calm kids with yarmulkes, a couple of quiet Japanese boys, and a few Saudis and Indians from India. Heck of a change from the goofballs you've been dealing with."

I smirked. "I can switch to the bus with the 'model immigrants.'"

Dad cocked his head to the side. "What's a 'model immigrant?'"

"Left-handed compliment. Doesn't matter. I'll try it."

Astonishingly, Dad wound up being correct. The people on that bus were either harmless or nice to me. As a wacky bonus, they constituted exactly the interesting racial and ethnic mix of students I had been hungering for. It was Mr. Rogers' Yellow School Bus. Dad's simple suggestion lowered my overall blood pressure and decreased the total number of bad experiences I had for the remainder of junior high. I still had the rest of the school day to contend with, but my commute was painless from then on. As Chief Brody would say, "Thank Christ."

When Dad and I got home from Dr. Greenberg's, I filled my mother in on my sprained wrist and the doctor's suggestion I get counseling. I conveniently forgot to mention Dad's obnoxious flirtation. The three of us stood by the stove in the orange kitchen as Mom boiled water for ravioli. "You don't need a psychiatrist or a counselor," Mom concluded. "Just go to Confession. I'm thinking of talking to Monsignor Tobin about helping you spend more time around the church. You can take sanctuary in the rectory and do part-time work there."

I stared dubiously at her. Church was dull. "I'd rather take shelter in a comic store."

"We should all go to church more. There's a really good new Jesuit."

I sucked my teeth. "Anybody is better than Monsignor Tobin. Forty-minute homilies on *Footprints in the Sand*? Twenty-minute prologues to his homilies about how the homily he is about to give won't go on for too long this time! Insisting that, even if he is a little long-winded, we shouldn't time him. Then, two minutes into his homily about the day's reading, he segues into a fifteen-minute golf story and a brief aside about how attractive a young Elizabeth Taylor was in *The Courage of Lassie*. And how does he work golf *and* Elizabeth Taylor into *every* homily? I swear to God, if I become a priest, I won't talk about *Jaws* or *Doctor Who* every week! I don't even have fun timing this guy, because Leo is better at guessing how long he'll waffle on for. Each time I think I got it, Leo adds another three minutes to my guess and wins the bet!"

"I'm half deaf, so I can't hear him," Mom said. "I only know he's talking too long."

"Be thankful you're deaf. He's worse than a Vogon poet."

"The church is near Dad's new bus stop, if you need a place to hide from any Irish kids."

I frowned. "What Irish kids?"

Mom was confused that I was confused. "The bullies. I assumed they were Irish."

"Where'd you get that idea? I never said they were Irish. They were Italian."

Dad thought it improper to discuss race and ethnicity. Anxious, he left the kitchen, lingering in the hall, pacing and grumbling as Mom and I trafficked in ethnic stereotypes. Mom didn't notice Dad's performance. I ignored it because I found it hypocritical. He often said outrageous and culturally insensitive things. Of course, Dad knew he didn't *mean* the prejudiced things he said, but when he heard others say similar things, he worried they were *serious*. Frankly, all three of us needed to bone up on our Critical Race Theory. If only Chimamanda Ngozi Adichie's TED talk "The Danger of a Single Story" had been available to us at the time.

Mom shook her head. "No way. Italians would never act this way. They must have been Irish. The Irish are all drunk racists who like to start fights."

"Mom, they were Italian kids right out of central casting for *Grease 3*. The only kids who have treated me like a human being have been four Irish boys, three Jewish boys, and one Black boy. That's it. Nobody else has been nice to me. Unfortunately, they told me in fifth grade that one of my main skills is pattern recognition, so I'm convincing myself to stick close to those ethnic groups and give the others a wide berth. Not very healthy behavior, I'll admit, but I'm a whipped dog these days."

"Pretty soon you'll find a nice Italian girl to date and everything will be fine."

"Not with whatever pheromone I'm giving off. I make Italian girls retch. Near as I can tell, all Italian girls are as tough as nails and don't respect weak men. They need to be with hardcore alphas, like Gary Cooper or Robert DeNiro. None of them have anything but disdain for a marshmallow peep like me, and I don't blame them. Half of them are, legitimately, too tough for me, and I *like* tough women. Realistically, I'm gonna wind up dating an Irish or a Jewish girl. You know why I think this? Precedent! Pattern recognition."

Dad's voice came from the hall. "The whole 'no group is a monolithic entity' thing doesn't register with you two?"

"Who mugged you again?" I asked. "Puerto Ricans? You never forget that detail."

Mom scowled. "I don't know how I'd react if you dated an Irish girl. The Italians and the Irish were born enemies. Irish cops, nuns, and priests treated my family badly all the time."

"I don't understand why that would be the case. We're all Catholic immigrants here. It should be us all standing united against the Klan, right?"

Mom sighed. "As bad as the Irish treat Italians, they treat the Blacks even worse."

I began to object and stopped. "Well, yeah. *Actually, they do.* They've turned treating Blacks like shit into an art form."

Mom placed a reassuring hand on my shoulder and looked me in the eyes. "One day, you'll meet a wonderful Italian girl who loves you."

I threw my arms up in the air. "When? *2010: The Year We Make Contact?*"

"Wouldn't you love to have an Italian girlfriend?"

"Sure! I would also love to ride Pegasus."

"Oh, don't be melodramatic."

"I'm going by verifiable empirical evidence. I'm gonna end up a sixty-year-old bachelor hermit beekeeper, like Sherlock Holmes." I pressed an index finger against my temple. "I can see it in my mind as if it has already happened."

Dad stuck his head back in the kitchen. "Is our son being melodramatic again? Showering the kitchen with hyperbole?"

I threw my hands in the air for the second time in under a minute. "Just don't get too attached to the idea I'm gonna wind up with an Italian girl. I asked my Magic 8-Ball about it fifty times, and each time I got 'Outlook not so good.'"

"Listen," Dad said calmly, "don't go looking for an Italian girl. Find a level-headed, overly organized German girl who can do your taxes for you."

"A German?"

"Yeah. A German."

I smirked. "Speaking of ethnic stereotyping, I have a joke for you, Dad."

"Uh-oh," Dad said.

"How many Germans does it take to screw in a lightbulb?"

Dad frowned. "I have no idea."

"One!"

Dad was left waiting for the punchline. "I don't get it."

"They're efficient and not very funny."

After midnight, I laid in bed, staring at the popcorn ceiling, listening to the radio on my headphones. I stumbled upon an honors student my age telling a radio therapist about her mother beating and blaming her for being molested by her father. She still lived at home with both parents, maintained her A-average, and moonlighted as a high-priced call girl to earn enough money to move out. It was the kind of story you might find in an exploitation film like *Angel* ("High School Honor Student by Day, Hollywood Hooker by Night: Her Two Worlds Are About to Collide!"), only this was real life. The young woman on the phone used elevated vocabulary, was deeply self-aware, and had a mordant sense of humor. I felt sympathy pains for her, wished I could be her friend, and tried to tramp down any stirrings of romantic feelings because almost all her suffering was rooted in male sexual desire and violence. I also berated myself for being so taken with her eloquence, as if she would not have been worthy of my sympathy had she been less articulate. When the next three callers were women with equally bleak stories, I became too upset to listen to any more nighttime confessions. As much as I had suffered so far in sixth grade, this evening's listening had opened my eyes. My pain was *nothing* compared to the agonies that these radio callers had experienced.

Things could be worse; I could be a woman. Who knew the mountains of shit they have to climb every day? Jesus H. Christ.

Knowing other people had things worse than me made me more sympathetic to them, because I knew if I felt this bad, how fucking awful did they feel dealing with much worse trauma? Crikey. On the other hand, knowing that others had it worse didn't make me feel any better about my own problems. Dealing with the other students in junior high still sucked, even if it didn't suck as bad as the problems faced by the night callers.

I scrolled through some more stations, stumbling across a mournful country music song called "Fancy" about a dirt-poor teenage girl who had to sell herself into a relationship with a rich man so she could class-jump and become a famous country music star. I had been told by my classmates for years that it wasn't cool for a New Yorker to like country music, but I had grown up with John Denver, Johnny Cash, Dolly Paton, Willie Nelson, and Kenny Rogers, so I wasn't opposed to the genre at all. I had just fallen out of touch with it. Who was singing now? And who knew that a twangy song about a woman's impoverished childhood would become an instant favorite? I wasn't a woman. I wasn't poor. I felt a connection to Fancy. I didn't know why. *Sing to me about being a chick in dire poverty, Fancy! Make me appreciate my charmed life!* Real and fictional, the women on the radio put my pain in perspective, but I still was sad for them all, especially the honors student I had no way to help. When the song ended, the disk jockey explained that I had just been listening to Bobbie Gentry.

Bobbie Gentry. Wild. Never heard of her. I need to go to Tape World in the mall and get myself a Bobbie Gentry cassette at my earliest opportunity.

This course of action decided, I finally drifted to sleep.

January 13, 1988

I stood tenth in line for the lunch counter, but the queue was moving steadily. The sour-faced lunch lady and her mouth-watering assortment of processed meat came into view. Shortly before I reached the counter, four Black male students ambled into view and slotted themselves into the line right in front of me. The "Great Cut" was a daily cafeteria occurrence: These four students inserted themselves halfway up the line, leaving the other students they had just cut fuming in impotent silence. Rather than stand there, staring angrily at their backs, letting racist thoughts fester, I lanced the boil of my own bitterness and cut them right back. The tallest of the four men couldn't believe the worm had turned. He stared at me.

"Good afternoon," I chirped.

The four circled me. The tallest stared me down. "You startin' somethin', motherfucker?"

I stared up at the tall man and smiled, wearily. "Nah. Just hungry."

Another voice called out from a yard away, "Hey, Tyrone! What's going on here?" A fifth Black student appeared and cut the line in the same place as the other four. I recognized him right away. It was Doug Brooks, my best friend from kindergarten. We had once been inseparable, playing endless hours of LEGO together. Then we were placed into two different classes and never saw each other in any meaningful capacity again. Doug held up his hand to slap me five and — somehow — I managed to pull it off without missing, like a spaz. Thankfully, Doug learned his lesson from the last time we bumped into each other, in fifth grade. He had tried the dap with me then, and I got exactly zero steps of the handshake right. We had a good laugh over it. "How are you doin', my brother?"

"How you doin', Doug?" I asked, sadly.

Tyrone jerked a finger in my direction. "He's not your brother! He's 'mayonnaise made with olive oil,' and he's startin' trouble, homey."

Doug shrugged. "He don't wanna eat your shit. That don't make him racist."

No, allowing our friendship to end makes me racist, Doug.

"I don't like the way he cut us. Like he's makin' a point of puttin' us back in our place!"

"Damien don't take kindly to bein' disrespected. He's got a lot of pride." Doug indicated my obvious injuries. "He fights back. I seen him having trouble with the goombahs around here, just like us. You think he's inna mood for you after he's been through serious shit with them?"

Tyrone sucked his teeth. "He's just like the rest of them."

"I'm tellin' you he ain't one of them," Doug added. "I want you to cut him some slack."

"Next!" the lunch lady yelled, staring at nobody.

It was Tyrone's turn. Tyrone bowed at me while gesturing theatrically at the impatient woman. "Oh, please, *do* go on ahead!"

I froze, not sure what to do. Doug patted me on the shoulder. "You get your lunch."

I cleared my throat nervously and walked up to the counter. As I passed Tyrone, I said, "Thanks, Tyrone. I appreciate it." Tyrone rolled his eyes at me. After securing a terrible, processed chicken lunch, I sat at the nearest empty table, harboring some small hope that Doug and his friends would join me. I looked in their direction, planning to wave them over, but they headed to the back of the cafeteria to sit with the other Black students, not even noticing I was watching them. *I should have stayed near Doug, not sat down like an idiot. Sure, I'm not making a love connection with Tyrone, but I just missed an opportunity.*

I swallowed a sporkful of flavorless processed chicken as two of Tony Nocerino's main lieutenants — Rocco Tentori and Bobby Mammolito — led a handful of C-list Merry Men to sit at the other end of my chrome cafeteria bench table. *Shit. I'm not on their bus anymore, but we still cross paths in the lunchroom. Don't make eye contact. Just eat.* Rolling down the table, an apple struck my gray, cardboard lunch tray. My tiny carton of milk tipped over, drenching my processed chicken and green beans. "What the flying–?"

"Yo! Why are yous playing grab-ass with the eggplants?" the pale, gaunt Rocco yelled.

"I like eggplant!" I yelled back. "Besides, we're eggplant parmesan!"

"The hell we are!" some random Merry Man piped in. Bobby Mammolito sat silent.

"What are you, runnin' with the porch monkeys, now?" Rocco added.

"Fuck you, Skeletor!" I picked the apple up and beaned it off Rocco's New-York-Mets-baseball-cap-wearing head. "Don't you talk about Doug!" Not used to nerds fighting back, Rocco rubbed his forehead and shut up. Bobby leaped to his feet, laughing and pointing at me. "I love this fuckin' guy! Yo, Egon! You're fuckin' hilarious when you get angry!"

Bobby's mirth and enthusiasm might have had a cooling effect on my rage had Mrs. Hall not swooped onto the scene. The slender Black woman grabbed me under my arm, pulled me up from my seat, and dragged me towards the cafeteria exit. "Throwing food, eh? If you can't eat like a gentleman, you are no longer welcome in this cafeteria." She nudged me through the red, swinging double doors into the hallway.

Incredulous and exasperated, I spoke in a whiny voice that squeaked: "They were bullying me." I stood in the hall, my arms spread helplessly, hoping to look credible.

Shaking her head, Mrs. Hall tapped her foot impatiently. "I saw you curse and throw an apple at the head of a kid who was minding his own business."

"They rolled the apple first, Mrs. Hall!"

"Sure, sure." Mrs. Hall closed the cafeteria door in my face.

I stared at the closed red doors in mute surprise and confusion.

Wait a minute. Am I banned from the cafeteria just for today, or permanently?

January 13, 1988

5:00 pm

"You sure that's the move you wanna make?"

Withering under Dad's gaze, I lifted my hand off the white queen.

"You've got the blood of two chess Grandmasters in you," Dad reminded me. "Your father and grandfather. You need to focus and be more aggressive."

He was right. I should have won this game already. Dad was down both knights, one rook, and a bishop. I was down a rook, knight, and three pawns. I was well-positioned to checkmate his king. I suspected I was within three moves of victory, but every time I thought I had Dad pinned down, he slipped free. He got out of my last "checkmate" by using his remaining bishop to take the rook I'd cornered his king with. I was getting frustrated.

"You do this every time. You're not a closer. You don't know how to end a game."

"I know."

"You could see moves before. You're psyching yourself out in the endgame. You know, it's okay if you defeat me." Dad certainly didn't hold back the way I did. He defeated me nine out of ten games that day alone. I looked up at him. "I guess I really *don't* want to win if it means beating you. Can I play one-man chess? I want to play against myself."

Dad slumped back in his chair. "You have *one* move left. Can't you at least identify it?"

I looked at the pieces again.

January 14, 1988

Hence from Verona art thou banished.

I should have met with Mrs. Hall, protested my innocence, and clarified the terms of my lunchroom expulsion. Instead, I made a point of not doing this. My "permanent exile" became my justification for never returning to a cafeteria I loathed. During the first day of my banishment, I ventured outside to the empty playground to eat my bagged lunch. (*Thanks, Mom.*) The January air was biting, but my gray raincoat and matching fedora kept me serviceably warm over a brick-red, button-down shirt and blue jeans. I sat cross-legged against the chain link fence, with my back to the school. I faced the residential neighborhood across the street, watching as the occasional car sped by too quickly for a school zone. *They're gonna get a ticket.* It took me all of five minutes to consume the peanut-butter-and-jelly sandwich, apple juice, and mozzarella string cheese. My lactose intolerance would act up not long after I polished off the string cheese, but nobody would be around to smell it after I dealt it. Solitude had its advantages. As a rare bonus, Mom packed me a single Pokatny Confections cupcake for dessert. She didn't usually pack dessert, and I loved Pokatny cupcakes. Amusingly, as I unwrapped the cupcake, a silver and red Pokatny Confections delivery truck trundled by. "Wild. Today's Pokatny Day." I ate it too quickly to appreciate it. I wondered if I'd ever learn to eat slowly, instead of inhale food. *Slow down, dude. Slow down. This food is delicious and nutritious. High in beta-carotene.*

Anticipating the need to entertain myself for the rest of my solitary lunch hour, I had filled my crossbody messenger bag with *Secret Wars, X-Men, Avengers,* and *Aquaman* comic books. I removed *Secret Wars* #6 from the bag, eager to revisit the adorable subplot in which Janet Van Dyne befriended the wounded supervillain, the Lizard, and domesticated him with her affection. *Is there a cuter plot template than Beauty and the Beast, I ask you?* Certainly, it was more morally uplifting and emotionally satisfying than "St. George killing the dragon." *Make love, not war.* I sat on my heels, crouching, and reading.

The shadow of a seven-foot-tall eighth grader fell over me. Backlit by the sun, the eighth grader was an imposing, spike-haired silhouette wearing a red jacket with a popped collar and a black onyx signet initial ring with a bold "F" on it. Did the "F" stand for "Fuckhead?" He spoke in an authentic, high-pitched General Patton voice: "So, we got a nerd all alone, huh?"

"Want to join me? I've got comics to share. We can read together."
I made this unusual offer because it was exactly the sort of idealistic,
tactically brilliant move Wonder Woman would make to disarm her
enemies. After all, her Amazon code of military ethics went: "Don't
kill if you can wound. Don't wound if you can subdue. Don't subdue
if you can pacify. Don't raise your hand at all until you've first extended
it." She was my go-to hero to mimic when I was feeling generous.
If my Wonder Woman overture failed, I had other heroes I could
emulate in times of conflict that employed less pleasant approaches
to conflict resolution.

"If you give me one of them, I'll rip it to pieces," Fuckhead replied.

"God bless you. Arrivaderci."

"I know you. You're the dick cheese Tony beat up."

"If you call twelve-on-one a fair fight then, yeah, I guess you can
say he beat me up. And what the heck is dick cheese? Dicks don't
have cheese!"

"How about you and me go a round?"

"What are you, twice my size? I'm five-foot-four."

"I'm *six*-foot-four," Fuckhead said proudly.

I grinned. "Taking me on makes you a real hero, then."

"I don't like what you did to Viola. You need to remember that
the guy doesn't unzip himself in front of the girl. He waits for the girl
to unzip *him*. You remember that, pervert!"

Fascinating. "I like that rule and am going to adopt it. Seriously."

Fuckhead's tone grew more threatening. "You ain't gonna live to
adopt it!"

"Listen, I like that you're defending your friend, but we're wandering
into some seriously morally gray territory here. I'm less totally guilty
than you think I am. I'm borderline innocent."

"Get up."

I glanced down at my satchel bag laden with dozens of comics.
If I used the shoulder strap to swing it like a weapon, the satchel bag
would make a perfect mace in a sling. It might even feel like swinging
Thor's hammer, Mjolnir, from the leather strap. *Mjolnir. Awesome.* I
lowered my voice to a baritone level for the first time as I quoted the

Mighty Thor, hero of the Marvel Comics Universe: "When life doth seem too much to bear — 'tis not the time to renounce the struggle. The ostrich hides. The jackal flees. BUT *MAN* — AND GOD — *DO PERSEVERE!*" I gathered the shoulder strap in my fist.

"What?" Fuckhead's silhouette acted confused.

"How dare thee threaten, Thor, son of Odin? Get thee back to Jotunheim, frost giant, or prepare to taste the might of Mjolnir!" I rose to my feet.

"What the hell are you-"

In one, swift, smooth motion, I arced Mjolnir through the air, crashing it against the side of Fuckhead's face. He dropped, rolled on his back, clutched his face, and howled in pain.

"Are we done, here?" I asked.

"No!" He looked up at me, holding his crimson face, tears streaming from his eyes. He'd be back on his feet, attacking me in another moment.

"Okay, then." I raised the saddle bag over my head and brought it down with all my strength on the tall, crying boy's head.

Then I smashed my bag against him again.

And again and again and again.

One half hour later, Fuckhead and I stood before Mrs. Hall in her office. I stared at my shoes, hiding the thin smile on my face. Crying, Fuckhead clutched his bleeding face. "He hit me with his bag. A lot. Like gettin' slammed by Cassius Clay!"

"Muhammad Ali," Mrs. Hall corrected. "Tell me, are you a full foot taller than Damien?"

Fuckhead cried silently, knowing what was coming.

"Guess he wasn't the easy pickings you expected him to be, huh?" asked Mrs. Hall. "That's what you get for picking a fight with somebody not knowing how tough he is."

I stopped concealing my smile.

The next day, I tried once again to read my comic in peace.

"SSS-Swamp iss mine!" the Lizard hissed, trying to look menacing as it bled out through an arm injury. The Wasp, who was more of a camp, *Absolutely Fabulous* character than your usual super heroine, realized he was as frightened of her as she was of him. She attempted to defuse the situation with humor, "Right! Your swamp! I was just passing by on my way to the Plaza so I thought I'd stop in! Charming muck! Tres chic!" I laughed. Female superheroes were the best. Their powers were less impressive, so they had to use their brains. I wondered if any male comic book fan alive liked Janet Van Dyne as much as I did. I doubted it.

My enjoyment of *Secret Wars* #6 ended abruptly when the diminutive Phil McCracken appeared, wearing his trademark all-white track suit, blonde spiked hair, and the massive chip on his shoulder. "I heard what you did to my man Flavio yesterday! Hit him with your school bag! How's that fighting fair? I hear one sleazy story about you after the next!"

"Flavio"? Fuckhead's real name is Flavio. Wild. I was outside again during lunch hour, my back against the chain-link fence, being confronted by some lunkhead with an enflamed amygdala for the second day running. On a lark, I replied to Phil McCracken in the Incredible Hulk's growling, echoing, Louis Armstrong voice: "Hulk want to be left alone. Hulk hates stupid Phil McCracken."

Phil strutted over, stopping just short of shoving his groin in my face. "Talk regular."

I stared at Phil's crotch. "Phil McCracken tiny. No honor in Hulk swatting fly."

"Are you making fun of my height now, bitch?"

I climbed to my feet. I was twice Phil's size. "Phil McCracken is so angry and so little! Like a baby Hulk! So cute and cuddly!"

Phil thrust his chest against mine, glaring up into my eyes. "I'm not cute! I'm one dangerous bastard. You better not fuck with me."

I threw my arms around Phil, crushing the teeny-tiny bully in a vice-like hug. "Hulk want to adopt Phil McCracken! Hulk loves Phil McCracken!"

"Get off me, you gay motherfucker! Quit hugging me!"

"Hulk wants to kiss Phil McCracken's smooth baby cheeks!" I planted a big, wet smooch on Phil's cheek.

Phil broke free, lurched backwards, and nearly tripped over himself. "You kissed me? Are you out of your mind! You kissed me! Are you gay, or something?"

"No. Hulk love Betty Ross."

Phil shook his fist at me. "You *are* gay, aren't you?"

I faked wide, sad eyes, and spoke in Hulkish melancholy. "Hulk lonely. Hulk want friend. Will Phil McCracken be Hulk's friend?" In my head, the sad piano theme to the old *Incredible Hulk* television show played.

"Fuck that!" Phil sprinted away. It would be the last I ever saw of him.

"Homophobe!" I tossed my head back and belly-laughed like a drunk Viking. Then I sat down and checked in on Wasp and Lizard. *I wonder if I'm ever gonna finish this fucking scene?*

Ten minutes later, Michelle-maybe appeared with an expression that somehow blended glee, mischief, and homophobia. "You kissed Phil? No way!"

"Yes, way." Since Michelle was attractive, I gave my Hulk voice the rest of the day off.

"Why?" she asked.

I shrugged. "Why not? I'm a big fan of Phil's. I loved him in *Of Mice and Men*."

"Why would you kiss him? Are you gay?"

"You got me, I am. Wait . . . Psych! I *ain't*."

"You're not gay, but you kissed a man?"

I talked with my hands, gesticulating wildly. "He's so tiny *and so violent*! I knew he must be extra special anti-gay. So, I did the worst thing to him I possibly could have. Kissed him! Now he's terrified I'll fill his crack in!"

"I've never seen you with a girl," Michelle-maybe said.

"I'm very, very uncomfortable with being single. It keeps me up at night. But I'm very comfortable with being straight."

"I can't believe you kissed Phil."

"I don't see what the big deal is. No skin off my nose. And I have a big fucking nose."

Michelle-maybe eyeballed me warily. "I think you might be insane."

"Don't be *silly*. I'm *definitely* insane."

The next day at lunch, nobody bothered me. I was able to eat in peace against the fence. I finally made it up to *Secret Wars* #7. Took bloody long enough!

A week later, Bobby Mammolito joined five Italian girls and boys I'd never met before in standing in a crescent around me. I sat on the playground floor, my back against the chain-link fence, eating a roll filled with prosciutto, fresh mozzarella, red peppers, and oil and vinegar. I wore beige slacks and a black T-shirt with a picture of the Bates Motel on it that read "I Love Mother." I had forgotten my coat and hat and was freezing my balls off.

"There's a rumor going around that you're a cugine, not a Jew," said the lead girl, who I pretended was named Concetta, because "why the fuck not?"

Chewing slowly, savoring the taste, I was determined to enjoy this amazing ciabatta sandwich. I swallowed the bite and offered Concetta-maybe my attention. "And you are?"

"Don't you know me? Everyone knows me!" said Concetta-maybe.

I took another bite of my sandwich and took my time chewing. I added, "It is so weird how everyone knows me, but I don't know anybody else. I'm keeping a low profile, too."

"Being loud and weird and wearing suits and kissing Phil?" asked Concetta-maybe.

I smiled crookedly. "Isn't that how you keep a low profile?"

"I axed you a question. Are you Italian or not?"

I reached down my Bates Motel t-shirt and withdrew Grandpa Angelo's miraculous medal. Keeping it around my neck, I held it up for all to see.

"No way!" Concetta-maybe said. "Where's your family from?"

"Naples. With some Salerno and Armento seasoning."

"Gnarly," said Concetta-maybe.

"Bombdiggity!" I agreed.

"What's your name again?" Concetta-maybe asked. "We can't agree. We all know you as 'the Jew in the raincoat with the bag of comic books who showed Viola his dick and kissed Phil McCraken.' I guess you gotta have a name, right?"

"I told them your name was Egon Spengler," Bobby Mammolito said.

I brightened. "Bobby! How goes it?"

"Nuttin'. Same shit, different day."

"Ain't that the truth!"

Concetta-maybe waved Bobby silent and looked at me. "So, what is your name?"

"Orin Scrivello, D.D.S." I placed the last bite of my amazing ciabatta into my mouth and smiled as I swallowed it.

Concetta-maybe looked confused. "Who?"

Before Concetta-maybe knew what was happening, I leapt to my feet and began singing "Dentist" — one of the most famous songs from the off-Broadway musical and recent film adaptation *Little Shop of Horrors* — in my newly minted baritone. I sang about how, when I was a child, I tormented neighborhood puppies and killed family pet guppies. Realizing I was a sadist, my mother suggested I grow up to be a dentist, so I could cause pain every day and get paid for it. Concetta-maybe took several steps back and held her hands up for protection as I serenaded her, "No, no, no. This ain't going down. This ain't going down." I backed off Concetta-maybe and gave the group a wide berth as I danced and continuing to sing.

Laughing and clapping, Bobby Mammolito exclaimed, "This fucking guy! This fucking guy right over here! Right over here! Lookit 'em! Egon Spengler in da house!"

When I reached a "call and response" part of the song, I paused and gestured to Bobby, who joined in to provide the response, much to everyone else's shock and amusement.

"Awesome," I said. "Good man."

Bobby smiled shyly. "That's Steve Martin's song, man. Couldn't leave ya hangin'!"

Then I launched into the main chorus. I was in full Steve Martin impersonation mode when I pirouetted and found myself face-to-face with Mrs. Hall. She had probably been there for the entire song. "Are you on something, kid?" Mrs. Hall asked.

I struck a forced casual pose. "High on life, Mrs. Hall. As Harry Harrison likes to say on 101 CBS FM, 'Every brand-new day should be opened like a precious gift.'"

"And every brand-new day I have another wild story about you to tell my husband over dinner," Mrs. Hall replied.

"That's what I'm here for!" Chuckling, I bent down to gather my stuff. Unable to resist, I sang the do-wop style radio station jingle to myself: "One-oh-one, CBS FM, one-oh-one, CBS FM. We play your favorite oldies, CBS FM! Neeeeeew Yoooooork."

"Hold up!" Mrs. Hall raised a finger. "Why are you here instead of in the cafeteria?" I reminded her of the apple-throwing incident. She flinched at my stupidity. "That was for the rest of that period, knucklehead! You were supposed to come back the next day!"

"Oh," I said, inspiring the other kids to crack up.

Mrs. Hall stared daggers at them. "That will be all, thank you." When they grudgingly dispersed, she returned her attention to me. "You've been wandering the school grounds every lunch period with nowhere to go? That's not only ridiculous and against the rules, but it's also dangerous. You can't get into all these fistfights and do these song-and-dance routines because you're out here playing vagabond. You need to return to the lunchroom. If you don't want to, you need to find a place to be during lunch: the music room, gym, or working as a teacher's assistant. Personally, I want you back in the lunchroom ASAP."

"Where are all the Black students?" I asked Assistant Principle John Thomas Pecker.

A lanky man with flushed pink skin, Mr. Pecker had a sandy blonde bowl cut and wore a tan suit. His undecorated tan office included a tan desk, tan wastepaper basket, and tan coat rack with a tan coat hanging on it. I sat across from him in a tan swivel chair, my left foot resting atop my right knee. Dumbfounded, Mr. Pecker repeated my question back to me.

"Yes. Where do they go?" I asked. "I see them at assemblies and lunch. Then I walk the hallways between classes, and I see zero Black students. Zippo. Nada. Zilch. Where are they?"

"If you must know, the Black students tend to self-select for special education classes in the basement. They're down there with the students with cognitive and physical disabilities . . . "

My eyes widened theatrically. "And with Freddy Krueger in the boiler room?"

Mr. Pecker shook his head in disapproval. "That's a prejudiced attitude to take."

"*I'm* not the one who shoved all the Black kids into the basement." I spoke quickly to prevent Pecker from objecting to that outrageous sentence. "Anyway, let me get this straight: The honors program has all your 'model immigrants' in it: Asians, Jews, the Irish, a couple of guys from Pakistan, and some Greeks. Mainstream classes have Italians, a handful of Hispanics, and two American Indians. Then the basement has special ed classes with people who have actual disabilities, plus Black kids, who are treated like they have disabilities when they don't?"

Mr. Pecker laced his fingers behind his head. "I'm not sure we have paperwork available to the public identifying student demographics and sorting them."

"Makes sense," I said. "If this place is organized the way I think it is, this isn't a school, but some kind of weird eugenics experiment run by Baroness von Gunther."

Mr. Pecker adopted an artificial air of extreme patience and self-control that suggested the opposite was going on in his head. "You're the one who's got issues with race. I don't look at people and see their race or ethnicity, so I haven't noticed this 'sorting.' If you're noticing this, you have an unhealthy obsession. You need to stop labeling people, or you'll become racist."

I waved away Mr. Pecker's response with an impatient wrist flap. "First of all, this is New York. *All anyone talks about* is race. *I've had it up to here with race and ethnicity.* Second of all, you mean to tell me there's not one Black dude or one Hispanic chick in the gifted classes? Not one? Nobody with dark skin has read *Candide* and kinda got a kick out of it?"

Mr. Pecker slapped his palm down on his desk. "There's a Black girl in the gifted class!"

If I was supposed to be impressed and mollified, I wasn't. "*One?* Stop the presses!"

"One is one," declared Pecker.

"*One* Black person is *worse* than *no black people*. No Black people at all would be an obvious injustice. *One Black person* is a 'token Black' and can be accused of being put in there to fill a 'quota.' You get a buncha white yahoos crying 'reverse racism' because a 'token Black' is there. They can't do that when there are *no* Black people or *more than one token*. You need a good handful of Black people in there, or the whole situation reeks of injustice."

Pecker calmed himself. "You sound like an ACORN activist."

A what? "Look, I've been miserable here. As my people say, 'the fish rots from the head down.' So, here's the thing. I was denied entry into the gifted program twice, basically because I'm Italian. Now, if I was shut out for being Italian, I guarantee you whatever metric you're using to assess Black people is off. You need a new rubric, and you should put me and Doug Brooks into the gifted class. Doug is a gifted architect. You should see him make a LEGO castle. It will blow your damn mind. And I bet he wasn't even vetted for the gifted program because of his skin color. All this time I was worried I was fighting with Black students and Italian students and Jewish students, I thought *I was racist*. But, you know, I'm starting to think the real problem is the school. Somehow, *the school itself* is racist. I think we all need to sit down and figure out how to fix it. Step one is putting me and Doug into the gifted program. You feel me?"

Mr. Pecker noticed there was a security guard milling about in the hallway. He called the guard into the room and had me physically carried from the office.

CHAPTER ELEVEN
Christmas with the Addams Family

November 11, 1984

Dad was planted in an overstuffed orange armchair before a small analog television in our finished basement, playing *Advanced Dungeons & Dragons: Treasure of Tarmin* on the Intellivision video game console. Leo and I sat cross-legged on either side of him, watching as he made his way through a first-person adventure game in a state-of-the-art 3-D environment (that would seem like a boxy, pixelated mess nest to the PS4 *Spider-Man* game I'm playing these days during quarantine). Dad's hero character navigated a green maze, opening a series of blue doors, hoping to find treasure, weapons, and monsters he could vanquish with a spear, sword, or magic fireball. "This is fun, right boys?" Dad asked, suddenly aware he was playing a one-player game and we were just watching. "The three good guys are hiding together in the basement." Dad had spent yesterday in Atlantic City with his buddies, the Bollands, gambling and acting like a carefree single fellow, while Mom stayed home to run the household and watch us kids. When Dad returned home early this morning at 4 a.m., instead of at the agreed upon 11:30 p.m. last night, he had music to face. Dad opted to hide with us rather than face it.

"Intellivision. That's Intelligent Television," Leo observed. "Cute." He was five and I was eight. We were both pretty wee in 1984. Leo was proud of himself for figuring out what the game console's name signified, and disappointed when I took the conversation in another direction: "If we're the three good guys, is Mom the bad guy?"

"She's kinda scary now, isn't she?" Dad asked.

She was. Mom worked hard enough on a day-to-day basis that, whenever Dad did something unusually fun without her, she resented it. If he went skiing with friends at Camelback Ski Mountain, or took me to see Tom Seaver pitch at a Mets game, or brought Leo and I fishing for porgies, sea bass, and fluke on Sheepshead Bay, he would return home to an unusually angry Gianna Cavalieri. He would rather battle fictional pixel monsters in a video game than face his real-world, non-analog wife. On the television screen, Dad's hero avatar opened a blue door and a giant ant greeted him. Dad pressed some buttons on his controller, hurled a spear at the ant, and it vanished in an amusing puff of pixel smoke. As Dad slayed his digital opponent, we could all hear Mom shouting, cursing, and stalking around on the floor above our heads. Sometimes she would stop and pound her fist upon the kitchen table, kick the wall, or throw a chair across the room. She had swallowed weeks of complaints against Dad, not speaking up when he annoyed her. She was silent no longer.

"She's always concerned with how *right* she is," Dad sighed. "Such a martyr."

"Maybe she wanted to go on the trip with you," I suggested.

"She doesn't like the stuff I like to do. She used to be game. When we were dating. Now, nothing interests her." On the television screen, Dad's hero went down a blue ladder to the next subterranean level, in search of more enemies to fight and booty to discover.

"Why is she so mad?" I asked.

Leo cocked an ear to listen to more of Mom's outbursts. "She's pretty clear about that. Nobody does chores. Nobody talks to her. We sleep too late on weekends. We don't notice when things break and need fixing. We don't get her presents on Mother's Day and Valentine's Day."

Dad snorted. "Who cares about Mother's Day? I *never* celebrated that growing up. Is that even a proper holiday? That and Valentine's Day are scams to sell chocolates and greeting cards."

I was finding it difficult to agree. Mom was more correct than he was, but terrifying.

"It isn't what she's upset about, really," Dad said. "Those complaints. They don't normally bother her. They aren't real complaints."

"They're fake complaints?" I asked. "Who would make fake complaints?"

"She goes *out of her mind* when she gets her period."

I scratched my head. "When she gets her *what*?"

"Women get weird once a month according to a cycle of the moon. It's a thing they do."

"Like a werewolf?" I asked. *Was Mom a werewolf? How did I not know this?*

"*Exactly* like a werewolf." Dad sounded like he was joking, but his face was grave.

"Does the full moon make her honest about what's bothering her?" Leo asked.

"It sounds like a bunch of baloney to me," Dad rejoined.

"But we do all the things she's complaining about," Leo insisted. "She's right."

Dad looked down at Leo. "So, what's your point?"

Leo said, "You can do some of the things she's asking you to do."

Dad waved his suggestion away. "There's no pleasing her. Nothing I do is enough."

"You should at least try," I said, supporting Leo.

"When she's this mad? No way."

We heard a thunderous crash overhead. *What was that?*

Leo cocked his ear, listening. "Dad's right. We should wait until she cools off."

"Isn't now the *best* time to talk to her?" I asked. "Why hide down here for two days? Let's face the problem head on and solve it right now!"

"The psychiatrists call what I'm doing 'avoidance behavior,'" said Dad. "My favorite way of dealing with problems. I recommend it. Remember that phrase: avoidance behavior."

I slap my knee decisively. "I've got it! *I'll* go talk to her. And you can come, too, Leo."

"I will," Leo said. "But later."

"Don't do it," Dad warned.

"We'll do it together when she's calmer," Leo said.

"There's no time like the present!" I got up and walked towards the steps.

"Nice knowing you," Dad muttered, and continuing playing his game.

I had been expecting to wander into a war zone, thanks to the mysterious banging and crashing bleeding through the basement ceiling over the past several hours. Instead, I found Mom sitting with a cup of coffee, brooding in an impeccably clean kitchen. Both Felix Unger and her late mother would have been proud: the tile floor sparkled, countertops were pristine, and the oven had been freshly scrubbed. The contrast between Mom in full rant-and-rave mode and the current, noiseless tableau was equally startling. I asked myself what was worse: When Mom threw violent tantrums or when she sat, fuming, for hours in silence? Easy call. The silence was worse. I always knew what she was thinking, anyway. I heard her noiselessly screamed thoughts in my head, and breathed air around her heavy with the humidity of deferred dreams.

What plagued her? Only everything. This tiny, iron-willed, Italian lady with the adorable face was miserable. She was inconsolable over her father's death, eternally worried about money, disappointed in her wannabe filmmaker husband's shortcomings, bitter about the arc of her career as a college English professor, fearful of her own mortality as she drifted into middle-age, and eternally frustrated with her hearing loss, allergies, dizzy spells, collapsed arches, the size of her hips and thighs, and the general condition of her body. I would have given anything to take all her problems away from her. If I could be granted three wishes, the first would be to make her happy. Without a genie, I was powerless to help her. In fact, I was part of the problem. I was a burden. She was responsible for my well-being. Even the love I felt for her, and the need I had for her attention, was just one more weight upon her shoulders that crushed her will to live. If she could flee from everything about her life and go anywhere else, she would. Of course, fleeing wasn't in her character, but she fantasized about it, anyway. Sometimes, I wished she would run away to parts unknown, both for her sake and for all our sakes.

What could I do to help Mom help herself? Beg her to work less hard? As if that were possible for her. Suggest she see a counselor or take a Valium? Out of the question. Urge her to reinvent her whole life from top to bottom? She lacked the energy, vision, means, and will to do that. The best I could do to help her was make her tea, give her a hug, tell her a joke or two, buy her astonishingly insightful gifts for her birthday and Christmas, make a small gesture to help her out around the house, and listen to her vent and rage. That was all I could offer her. It wasn't enough. I wanted to share her burden. To carry it for her. Failing that, maybe if I ran away, when she couldn't, I could be one less thing for her to worry about. I had no idea. Not the first clue.

"Hi, Mom," I whispered.

Mom took another sip of her coffee.

I tried to think of what adult small talk sounded like. "What's doin'?"

Mom kept staring past me. I really, really hated talking to walls. It happened to me a lot.

I tried one last time. "I came to see if I can help."

"It's too late," Mom said quietly.

I magically produced a small yellow pad and a golf pencil from my back jeans pocket. "I can take notes! What are your demands?"

"Did your father send you to butter me up?"

"I sent myself!" I proudly punched my own chest like a Klingon. "Qapla'!"

"Tell him that's pretty low, sending you." Mom sipped her coffee again. "Just go back downstairs. Be 'the three good guys.'"

I blinked several times. "You know that's what Dad calls us? Pretty funny, right?"

Mom turned slowly and looked at me. "*Hilarious.*"

Three days later, Dad made his first overture to establish détente. Leo and I were playing a game with our stuffed animals not far from Mom, who was doing a crossword puzzle. Dad cheerfully announced he was taking us all out to dinner. Mom stared dubiously at him. "You haven't bought a meal for me since our second date. What's the catch?"

Dad produced two coupons from his pocket. "Buy one dinner and get 75% off the second dinner. Also, free sodas!"

"Coupons," Mom said flatly. "I should have known."

I ran up to Dad. "Are we going to Jade Island?" It was my favorite restaurant: a Tiki culture classic that served Polynesian and Chinese American food, and made the best shrimp and lobster sauce, egg foo young, Happy Family, and pu-pu platter I've eaten anywhere in America.

"Killmeyer's Old Bavaria Inn!" Dad grinned. "Traditional German food! I've never been there, and it is high time I went. It is on the whole other side of the island, so we should leave soon if we don't want to eat too late."

I craned my neck to look at the coupons. "There's such a thing as German food?"

Dad was offended. "Of course! Sauerkraut, sausages, potato dumplings, goulash, Jello."

I clutched at my own throat and gagged. "That sounds *awful*! I didn't think *anything* could *possibly* be worse than Tex-Mex! I was wrong! German food found a way to be *worse*!"

Mom looked dubiously at Dad. "Do they serve anything edible?"

Dad paused dramatically, and then delivered what he thought would be the perfect suggestion. "Cranberry Pork Loin! The menu describes it as 'boneless pork medallions sautéed in a sauce of Amaretto and cranberries. Served with sweet potato fries and fresh vegetables.' I memorized the one thing on the menu you and Damien would order."

"Oooooh!" I said. "Cranberry is the best!"

"Actually, that sounds great," Mom said. "I'm fucking starving." She stood up. "I'm going to change. I'll be ready in fifteen minutes."

"I'll put on my Nightcrawler T-shirt!" I announced. "He's German Catholic, a flirty swashbuckler like Errol Flynn, and he's in the X-Men! I love Nightcrawler!"

Mom paused. "Here's the thing, though. I want the basement vacuumed before we go. Get it done right now, or you're still in the doghouse."

Dad sighed with relief. Détente at last. "It will be taken care it. Promise."

"Good." Mom hurried upstairs to change. Dad shot me a commanding look. "Do me a favor. I'm gonna need you to vacuum the basement before we leave. Can you handle it?"

My armpits began to perspire. I hadn't ever vacuumed anything before. "Um . . . "

"Glad to hear it. You go get it done ASAP, or we're never getting out of here."

December 23, 1983

A Mormon Tabernacle Choir Christmas vinyl played on a turntable as Mom greeted her in-laws, helping them shed their winter coats when they stepped inside her living room. Because it had been eighteen months since their last visit, the in-laws took a second to register the plush carpeting, cool colors, and artificial, "snow"-covered Christmas tree that stood in front of the bay windows looking out onto the suburban street. Mom reflected, bitterly, that her actual parents had both died and abandoned her to this grotesque mockery of an extended family. Of course, her brother and his wife and three children were all still alive, but Carmine and Beatrice and their kids were celebrating Christmas together in New Jersey without her. Carmine was furious with Mom for not lending him the money he needed to keep his restaurant afloat. He hadn't spoken to her since having to close its doors last month. Beatrice was acting as go-between, working through Dad to repair the rift, but their joint efforts had yet to bear fruit. Now, Mom was stuck celebrating Christmas with her in-laws, the Addams family.

Playing the role of the Cavalieri family patriarch was Vincent senior, a hawk-nosed, sallow-cheeked, and taciturn chess Grandmaster who looked like Peter Cushing. Mom was never sure what his actual job was before he retired. The importer of record for some company? Vincent senior came as a matched set with the chain-smoking Antje, a ditzy, gossipy, and relentlessly passive-aggressive housewife and former telephone operator with curly, chestnut hair. Vincent and Antje had brought with them their nervous-energy younger son, Garth — a traveling medical supply salesperson — and his needy, punk-rock girlfriend, Sheena — a traveling beauty product salesperson. Dad, Leo, and I joined the new arrivals in the living room and distributed a round of welcome hugs and kisses.

Grandma Antje looked me up and down. "Okay, I know it is winter, but you, young man, look like a ghost. Have you seen the sun even once in the past six months?"

"I look like a *ghost*?" I smiled. "Awesome!"

"No," said Antje. "Not awesome."

"Oh, put a sock in it, Antje," Aunt Irene said, reminding Mom that at least one tolerable relative was on hand. Vincent senior's strawberry blonde sister, Aunt Irene, was a firecracker who looked like a sixty-year-old Joan Blondell. She was brilliant and had the soul of an artist but had chosen family over career. She greeted me with a big hug and kiss.

The Bronx wing of the Cavalieri family had arrived at the semi-attached home of the Staten Island Cavalieris in two cars. Garth and Sheena drove Antje and Vincent senior in a box-shaped, turquoise car that they had successfully parked on our driveway. Meanwhile, Aunt Irene's husband and daughter were still circling the block to find a second parking spot to place their boxy maroon car. There was never much parking on our block on Shabbos. Dad gathered their four winter coats in his arms and trotted them upstairs to throw on the master bedroom bed, since the closet beside the front door was filled to bursting. Mom stood, flanked by Leo and me, helping them get settled.

Without a separate foyer or mud room, the living room served multiple functions, operating as a foyer, study, dining room, and living room. The area by the door held the Christmas tree, framed by a loveseat and sofa placed around a rectangular wood-and-glass coffee table. Against the wall opposite the sofa was a set of mahogany shelves filled with American pre-Civil War literature, British literature of the long 19th century, Russian masterpieces, and complete collections of Agatha Christie mysteries, Sherlock Holmes stories, and P.G. Wodehouse's adventures of Jeeves and Wooster. Amongst these works could be found a broad sampling of more contemporary books, including *Bury My Heart at Wounded Knee*, Gore Vidal's *Burr*, *The Autobiography of Malcolm X*, *The Accidental Tourist*, and a selection of books by Italian and Italian American authors, including Dante, Giuseppe Tomasi di Lampedusa, John Fante, Helen Barolini, Tina De Rosa, Pietro di Donato, Diane di Prima, and Gregory Corso. Grandpa Vincent ran his disapproving eyes over the selection. "You have nothing to read."

Flabbergasted, Mom gestured expansively at the collection. "Excuse me?"

"It's all fiction and historical gossip," he tutted. "Where's the science? Only in science and mathematics can we find truth. The rest is fever dreams and propaganda."

"These books are about what it means to be *human*," Mom glared back.

Aunt Irene burst out laughing. "My brother doesn't know what it means to be human!"

"I know I'm right," Grandpa Vincent insisted.

"Remember when you were a kid, you loved reading all those Sax Rohmer *Fu Manchu* books?" Irene asked her brother archly.

Vincent senior didn't reply.

"How would you describe those books?" Irene asked.

"Potboilers. Trash literature." Vincent shot his sister an annoyed look. "I was a kid."

"You liked fiction *then*," Mom added. *Racist, imperialist fiction,* she thought, *but* fiction.

Vincent pointed his chin up at his daughter-in-law. "I'm older and wiser now."

"You're certainly older!" Irene slapped him affectionately on the shoulder. He blinked.

Perusing the library herself, Grandma noticed the one Christmas knickknack placed eye-level amongst the books: a ceramic statue scene of Santa Claus smoking a pipe and reading the Bible in an armchair beside a roaring fire. "That's cute."

Mom couldn't believe that Grandma had said something nice and braced herself for a snide comment. The snide comment came, but not from Grandma. Irene elbowed Mom in the side. "Hey! Any more religious kitsch around? Statues of Mary stepping on a snake? Vials of Dead Sea 'holy water' that *really* came from Cardinal O'Connor's toilet? Ha! Disney Studios and George Lucas think they know how to merchandise! They're pikers next to the Church!"

I blushed. Irene's good opinion was important to me, and I understood she was making fun of us, even though I didn't grasp her meaning. I'd never heard the word "kitsch" before.

"Look around for yourself," Mom said to Irene. "Go on a kitsch artifact hunt."

Grandma walked past the circle of couches into the dining room portion of the living room, which included a flip-top mahogany desk decorated with Mom's collection of ceramic houses from a Charles Dickens style Christmas village, and a bowed fish tank filled with guppies positioned under the stairway leading upstairs. Across from the fish tank stood a grandfather clock and mahogany dining room table. Dad's Lionel toy train set looped around the table, passing diminutive homes and town square buildings, villagers, and miniature trees and mailboxes. Garth and Sheena crept up to the dining room table, watching the Lionel train circle the tracks. Garth gave Sheena a nervous smile. "My brother loves stuff like this."

A gentle soul uncomfortable in his own skin, Uncle Garth would say complimentary things, then look about the room expectantly for approval. If he found the approval he sought, he'd flash a half-second smile, giggle, and grin toothily. Just as quickly as it appeared, the grin would vanish. Then Garth would look about warily, worried the approval he'd just won would be capriciously withdrawn. If, under different circumstances, Garth said something calculated to garner approval and didn't get the instant validation he sought, he would shrink back, chastened. Desperate for love, if he felt affection was being withheld from him for too long, his good-natured giggling would curdle and turn into a volcanic rant — a litany of insults and grievances directed at all and sundry, twice as vicious and long-reaching in historical scope as the worst of Mom's periodic meltdowns. As a child, I found Uncle Garth's mood swings impossible to fathom. By the time I was a teenager, I understood him perfectly, seeing in the Jekyll-and-Hyde monster he had become a probable fate for me if I went feeling unloved for too many years.

Garth's girlfriend, Sheena, wore too much of everything: mascara, eyeshadow, hairspray, and perfume. A Cyndi Lauper wannabe, she wore a billowy, blue-sleeved blouse, skin-tight leopard spotted pants, and black leather pixie boots. While Sheena spent an ungodly amount of time a day putting on make-up and striving to look like an MTV video jockey, Garth owned his regular guy looks, not bothering to wear contact lenses or comb over his prematurely thinning hair. Nor did he wear anything more fashionable than a powder blue polo shirt with a little polo player breast emblem on it. They were like one of those improbable sitcom couples where the woman was at least twice as attractive as the man. However, in this case, it was clear why they were together: Both Garth and Sheena were deeply insecure people who fed off each other's neurotic tendencies, augmenting them in one another instead of mitigating them.

Uncle Garth mussed my hair affectionately. "You know Sheena, right? She's gonna be your aunt, sometime. When we figure out what we're doing with our lives, and stuff."

Sheena blew me a kiss from two feet away. Then she spoke in her thick, "Harley Quinn," New Yawk accent: "Yeah, we met befaw, rite, Damien? Hey, lemme ax yew somethin', Damien, becauz we wur tawkin about it in the caw."

Garth's eyes bulged. "Don't bother the kid about this. That was a private talk."

Sheena placed her hand over her heart. "How old do ya think I yam?"

My body temperature jumped, and palms went clammy. "I'm no good at guessing age."

"Kids always tell da truth. I'll trust what ya say! I won't get mad, I sweah!"

"I don't know anyone's age. I only know I'm eight."

Sheena beckoned, her six brass bracelets jangling. "Come awn, come awn."

I made little fists, clamping my eyes shut until I saw a red haze. "Forty?" I guessed, meekly. I opened my eyes. Sheena couldn't have looked more shocked and surprised if I had drawn a gun from a holster and shot her through the heart. "Fawty! You tink I look fawty!"

Garth put a reassuring hand on her shoulder. "He's just a kid. He doesn't know."

"I can't beweeve he tinks I look fawty!"

"But my mom is forty, and she's beautiful," I offered, helplessly. "I don't know how old people are. I assume everyone is my age or forty. Or old, like Merlin."

Garth shot Sheena an amused glance and offered her a nervous giggle. Sheena pursed her lips in annoyed thought. Aunt Irene appeared behind Garth and Sheena. "That's what you get for asking an eight-year-old."

"I figured he'd be awnest."

Grandma placed a loving hand upon Sheena's shoulder. "You're gorgeous, Sheena! Look how marvelously your pants show off your curves! You have a taut, finely sculpted posterior!"

"I try." Sheena wiggled her ass, appreciatively.

"Adults sure like showing each other their culi," Leo whispered to me. "'Here's my culi.' 'Oh, yeah? Here's *my* culi!' That's every adult conversation."

I felt too sad, nervous, and guilty to laugh. "Is all this because I got her age wrong?"

Leo looked thoughtful. "I think it is every kid conversation, too: 'Culis to you.'"

Grandma continued her catalogue of Sheena's mouthwatering lady parts. "You have pert breasts, a swan neck, and a straight nose. And look how your eyeshadow brings out your crystal blue eyes. I luxuriate in the lingering scent of your perfume as you glide through the room."

Irene whispered to Garth. "Your mom better cool it before she gets around to complimenting Sheena's alluring cameltoe."

Garth stopped himself from laughing, but the effort turned his balding head crimson.

"Sheena, you are what every man wants!" Grandma cried. "What every woman fears! You are the ultimate, modern-day woman, in your formidable, indominable prime!"

Irene crossed her eyes to make me laugh when she saw me looking her way.

"Awwwwwww, shucks, Mom." Sheena was already calling Grandma "Mom," while my mom never called the old woman "Mom." Mom was incapable of betraying Grandma Francesca's memory by referring to Grandma Antje as "Mom." Sheena's expression of fealty was one of many reasons Grandma Antje preferred Sheena to my mom. The other was that Grandma was not an intellectual and neither was Sheena — both were in over their heads around my mother, Irene, and the Vincents. Grandma turned to Mom, who stood beside the bookshelves, staring at the titles, trying to figure out what was so awful about her collection. Grandma presented Mom to Sheena as if Mom were a museum exhibit. "Now, Sheena, let's compare you to Gianna. Gianna has put on more than a few pounds sitting around reading all those books. Sheena, no one would mistake your twenty-four years with Gianna's forty. You have nothing to worry about. Don't take Damien's age guess to heart."

"Antje!" Irene gasped. "What an unforgivable way to talk about Gianna! Are you nuts?"

Grandma sniffed. "I speak my mind. It is my cardinal virtue."

Thanks to her poor hearing, Mom only understood about ten percent of Grandma's speech, but ten percent was enough to make her flush in silent rage. Unfortunately, Grandma wasn't finished: "Don't worry, Gianna. All hope is not lost. As with most housewives, you are a mere thirty pounds away from a rosier pair of cheeks and less saggy hindquarters." Grandma produced a Weight Watchers brochure from her purse and offered it to Mom. When Mom refused to take it from her, Grandma placed it gently on the coffee table. Then Grandma put her arm around mine and led me away. "Have you heard the story of Fatty Arbuckle?"

As Sheena, Garth, Grandma, and I disappeared into the kitchen, Mom was left alone with Irene. Irene took Mom's hands in hers. "I know. I've hated her my entire life, Gianna."

Mom gritted her teeth. "She's been here *maybe* ten minutes?"

"I'll testify that you killed her in self-defense."

Noticing more than hearing that the Mormon Tabernacle Choir album had come to an end, Mom put on Johnny Mathis' "Give Me Your Love for Christmas" before following the other guests into the adjoining room. Irene lingered by the train set alone. She turned in time to see Dad come back downstairs and noticed his expression sour. "Not Johnny Mathis again!"

Irene shook her head at him. "Where were you? You just threw your wife to the wolves."

Dad looked helplessly at his aunt. "I was only gone a minute! There's been a fight?" Dad felt like cursing and did it so infrequently, he had to summon the expletive from his diaphragm. "That's . . . fucking . . . great. It's Christmas and I think I hate everyone except you."

"No, you don't," Irene reassured him. "You only hate your mom and Sheena."

Dad considered this. "That may be true."

Irene gave Dad the short version of what had transpired. His anger moved from being free-floating to settling squarely on Grandma and Sheena on behalf of my mother and me. "We're dealing with a real meatball squad, here."

"Exactly," confirmed Irene.

When Dad entered the kitchen, he found his mother praising the scent of Sheena's perfume as having been brought down to the Earth from Mt. Olympus itself. "Don't you just love Sheena's new perfume, Gianna?" Grandma gushed. "The name is darling! Love's Baby Soft!"

"It is *truly* magnificent," Mom managed to say.

Pretending he didn't hear a word of that last exchange, Dad called out to the crowd, "Can any of you smell that? What is it? It's horrible! Burning my nose! Does anyone know what it is?"

Mom nodded in approval. Sheena looked sheepish. Garth was outraged. Grandma looked confused. "I don't smell anything."

"It's cold out, but I'm opening a few windows until whatever that is disperses." Dad proceeded to throw every window on the main level open, giving us all instant goosebumps.

Mom really loved Dad at that moment. It was a helluva performance.

Meanwhile, an oblivious Grandpa Vincent Cavalieri senior sat on our living room couch, staring off into space, daydreaming about the legions of prostitutes he had bought sex from during his salad days. My father, Vincent Cavalieri Jr., once referred to his father, Vincent senior, as "the world's greatest intellectual sex maniac." It was an odd title to bestow upon a reclusive, hawk-nosed logician in black, plastic spectacles. And yet, Grandpa spent every Friday night of his adult life shooting pool, drinking, smoking, and picking up prostitutes. This revelation shocked me since, growing up, I regarded Grandpa as, essentially, a Vulcan from *Star Trek*. Vulcan he may have been, but he also went into Vulcan heat *every weekend* (#PonFarrFridays). In actuality, Grandpa was more like horny iconoclast comix creator Robert Crumb — with some "Fast Eddie" Felson seasoning — than either the Mr. Spock or Mycroft Holmes figures I'd pigeonholed him as. Prostitutes aside, the billiards element of Grandpa's weekend ritual fit his nerd profile perfectly. His geometry and physics knowledge dovetailed to make him the Bronx's undefeated pool shark answer to *Rain Man*. Sadly, over time, word got out that challenging Grandpa to a billiards match was an exercise in masochism, as was betting against him.

Despite being a pool shark, chess Grandmaster, and left-brained chemistry prodigy, Grandpa suffered from an immobilizing lack of ambition and abundance of jangled nerves. Brilliant as he was, these flaws prevented himself from taking any risks in life. Sometime during Dad's 1950s childhood, Grandpa became obsessed with a radio show riddle that would have awarded five hundred dollars to the first listener to solve it. Grandpa worked several hours at his desk finding the indisputably correct answer, but was too painfully shy to call it in. Grandpa's lame excuse to young Dad was, "Someone's probably solved it already, anyway." It took two more days for someone else to win the five hundred dollars. Dad never forgave Grandpa for missing this rare opportunity to monetize his brilliance. To Dad, the obvious moral of this story was, "Always try to win, even when defeat seems certain. Even if you think you're wrong, you *might* be right. Even if you expect a 'no,' ask anyway. Go for the 'No!' Force them to say 'no.' You may get a 'yes' you weren't expecting." Dad imparted this lesson to me frequently.

Yes, Grandpa *was* more of a mouse than a man. He was so cautious, his motto was, "It only has to happen once," as in: "You only need to lose an eye one time." Clearly, he did not believe a mistake could ever be rectified. He would rather make no choices at all than make mistakes. It took World War II to bring Grandpa some of the most noteworthy, non-whore-related excitement of his life. During the war years, he was the oldest enlisted member of the Flying Tigers, the First American Volunteer Group of the Chinese Air Force. Later, he wrote a war memoir that he was too skittish to publish: *Ding How: The Misadventures of a G.I. in China.* I read the manuscript at sixteen and was impressed by Grandpa's Douglas-Adams-meets-Samuel-Fuller narrative voice: a dry, self-effacing sense of humor and philosophical outlook on life, laced with colorful language and good-old-boy talk that his own son would find "uncouth." Until I read this memoir, I never knew grandfather was almost killed when the Japanese bombed the air strip control tower he worked as radio operator in. It was also a surprise when I discovered he had barely escaped from the MP's jeep searchlight one night when he'd snuck into a Chinese brothel. Of course, most people who knew grandfather well didn't really know anything about him at all, because he virtually never spoke. He let his chatterbox wife do all his speaking for him. The ever-silent man had constructed an emotional wall about himself that made him less endearing in the flesh than he was on the printed page. Sadly, Grandpa's coldness damaged the psychological and emotional health of his wife and children. These two Grandpas — the fundamentally loveable author of unpublished nonfiction and the cowardly recluse who was too cold to Grandma, Dad, and Uncle Garth — made it impossible for me to love or hate the man. He was a well-rounded Hemingway character to contemplate with detached fascination, and not my Grandpa. When he died, I mourned an author I enjoyed reading, not a relative.

Shortly after the curious incident of Sheena's stinky perfume, Leo sat beside Grandpa and attempted to get him to talk. "How are you, Grandpa?" Leo asked, sweetly, showing Grandpa his stuffed animal lion, also named Leo. "This is Leo. He's my avatar. Part me, part Edmund Blackadder. He wants to say 'hi.'" In a ventriloquist act unconcerned with the concealing of moving lips, human Leo made cuddly toy Leo say in falsetto, "'Merry Christmas!'"

Grandpa placed his palm down on the couch and made it slither across the cushion towards my brother's leg. "Rattlesnake," Grandpa whispered.

"What?" human Leo asked.

"The snake," Grandpa whispered. "Beware the snake." He moved his hand another inch closer, touching the tip of his middle finger against Leo's right leg. "The snake."

Leaping off the couch, Leo scampered to my side. "Grandpa's doing the 'snake' again."

"That's your thing you do, right?" I asked.

"It's *all he says* to me!"

I snorted. "He doesn't say *anything* to me. Anyway, you two mutes need to be more outgoing. You *both* make me nervous. I *always* have to do *all* the talking!"

Justifiably annoyed at my reaction, Leo moved away from me and walked over to Sheena, who was standing in the kitchen corner, between the sink and the refrigerator. Rocking herself lightly, with her arms crossed over her chest, Sheena grasped her own elbows so tightly her knuckles turned white. Leo noticed her long, red, Lee Press On

Nails first. Then he saw the intersecting white and red scratch marks tracked on the backs of her hands. Sheena's head snapped around as he approached. She let out a strangled cry, shrank away from him, and hid her hands behind her back. "Are you staring at my hands? Don't stare at my hands! *Don't!*"

Leo stopped short, holding his stuffed animal lion aloft. "I was coming over to say 'hi.'"

"You're here to stare, complain about my perfume, and tell me I look fawty!"

Mom hastened over to Leo and Sheena. "Is everything okay?"

Garth appeared between Mom and Sheena as if he'd teleported there, smiling unnaturally broadly at Leo. "Sheena is sensitive about her hands. It's no big deal, Leo."

Leo stared at Garth and blinked repeatedly. Garth replied with a nervous, high-pitched laugh reminiscent of Tom Hulce's from *Amadeus*. Eager to cut through the tension, I leaped into the midst of the crowd and struck a dramatic pose. "I heard a fantastic song at school! 'Ask Me No Question' by Yellowman!" I dove headfirst into serenading my family, not grasping that a song full to bursting with double-entendres was not appropriate for Christmas.

Grandma silenced my singing by declaring, "Sheena has no reason to feel self-conscious. She is a goddess among mere mortals." Grandma Antje Cavalieri shared her husband's hawk nose but not his intellect. The German American with the curly, chestnut hair chain-smoked and monologued ceaselessly during all conversations, resenting it whenever anyone else tried to get a few words in edgewise. Grandma's gossipy tendencies were at their most destructive when she worked as a telephone operator during World War II. She listened in on her neighbors' phone conversations, collecting dirt on them. Her fellow phone operator and future sister-in-law Irene Cavalieri silenced her whenever she tried to spill the tea about all the adultery being committed in their building: "These are people's lives, you idiot!" A love of gossip drew Grandma into an obsessive interest in Hollywood scandal sheet news. She never tired of telling young Dad the story of how Fatty Arbuckle accidentally killed Virginia Rappe during sex by crushing her to death under his enormous girth. Grandma also informed Dad about the deep, dark secrets of his favorite actors: *You like Claude Rains? He's so egotistical! Charles Laughton? A closeted gay man in a sham marriage with Elsa Lanchester! Chico Marx? Compulsive gambler and sex-addict. And Jewish!* Grandma went to the movies religiously, taking my father to see everything under the sun, from Westerns to heritage films to screwball comedies. While she preferred glamorous MGM extravaganzas to all other films, she was not above taking Dad to more grotesque fare when he was still in knee-high socks. Grandma didn't like science fiction, but a movie was a movie, so she was simultaneously bored and entertained by *The Beast from 20,000 Fathoms* in 1953.

Roaring and moving on all fours down the streets of New York City, a gargantuan, reptilian monster bit the heads off the police officers who dared shoot at him. The Beast stomped parked cars flat, lumbering relentlessly towards the auditorium where Dad and Grandma sat, ready to burst forth from the silver screen into the real world. Screaming, Dad fled from the theater. Grandma caught up with him outside by the parking meters, scolded him for embarrassing her in public, and dragged him back into the theater to finish the film she had paid $1.02 for two tickets to see. A reasonable parent might have learned from this experience not to take her son to see terrifying atom-age movies, but Grandma continued to take him to see every movie released in her neighborhood. She was a bored housewife who hated being cooped up at home and had no one handy willing to watch her son for her. In 1958, grandma took her son to see *Horror of Dracula*, exposing him for the first time to a gorgeous vampire woman who tried to "kiss" small children and drink their blood. Lucy, "the Bloofer Lady" character played by Carol Marsh, was so terrifying and *so sexy* to a Vincent Cavalieri junior on the cusp of puberty that he developed a life-long fetish for vampire women. Starting when he was old enough to go to the movies under his own steam, Dad spent the rest of his life watching every vampire film he could find to recreate the thrill he felt as a young boy watching Carol Marsh sexily attempt to murder a little girl.

Why was Grandma so bored and unhappy in her marriage that she had to resort to spending most of her spare time in a movie theater, taking her son to see deeply inappropriate pictures? In 1941, Antje had been seventeen when she met the twenty-seven-year-old Vincent senior. Vincent's stunningly beautiful and razor-sharp younger sister Irene had made the mistake of inviting Antje to her family's apartment for a bite during a lunch break from their telephone operator job. Naturally, the moment Irene left Antje alone in the family room with Vincent, Antje draped herself over the cold intellectual and began nibbling his ear. By the time Irene had returned to the family room with the demitasse, her brother and least favorite co-worker were an item. Horrified at her accidental matchmaking, Irene campaigned against her brother taking Antje out on even a single date. In December 1941, Antje and Vincent married outside an air force base before he left for China. At the ceremony, Irene admitted to herself that she had failed to scuttle the romance.

Antje's main motivation in seducing and marrying her coworker's brother was getting herself out of the fire-trap apartment she shared with abusive parents and six siblings. Antje had escaped this unhappy childhood home into an unhappy union with an introvert who believed in open marriages. Since Antje was an extrovert of below-average intellect who did not believe in open marriages, she had exchanged a physically abusive home for an emotionally abusive one without realizing it. A couple of years before Garth's birth, when Dad was seven, the crisis came to a boiling point. Antje suffered a nervous breakdown. She was placed into a mental institution for the better part of a year. Her emotional collapse almost triggered a sympathetic meltdown from her husband. While he wasn't placed in the room next to his wife, Vincent senior's fragile emotional state meant he couldn't handle raising my dad.

Enter Aunt Irene, who took my father in. Living with Aunt Irene gave my dad the happiest ten months of his life. At twenty-six, Irene was not yet married, and had raised questions as to whether she would ever marry. Still, she started dating her future husband, a gruff-but-funny veteran of the North African campaign named Cesar Kowalski, five months into Dad's time living with her. The vet came by for weekly dates with the eternally busy Irene. Irene's impassive, Italian-speaking mother would babysit Dad during their nights out. While

Cesar waited in the living room for Irene to get ready, he regaled Dad with stories of facing off against legendary panzer division commander Erwin Rommel. The war stories enraptured Dad, who spent the next day in the local library researching German tiger tanks and the life and career of the Desert Fox. Despite seeing some signs of what we would later discover was Cesar's less-than-admirable treatment of Irene, Dad generally found Irene and Cesar to be fascinating couple who stood in stark contrast with his cold, dull, incompetent parents. When Dad's extended stay with Irene ended, he returned home to find a recovered-but-permanently damaged mother and an even-more-withdrawn-than-usual father. The grim homecoming made Dad wish he could turn around and go immediately back to Irene.

"That was the only time in my childhood I felt like I'd been given real love," Dad told me wistfully, when I was ten. "I didn't know how to process it." Then, embarrassed at his emotional vulnerability, he added, evilly. "Because I couldn't process it, I wound up wanting to zonk my own aunt! Ha! *I'm a terrible person.*"

That Christmas brought Irene and her family to our home. Our front door opened, and the two remaining Christmas guests, Irene's husband, Cesar Kowalski, and their daughter, Carmella, entered. They removed their winter coats, scarves, and hats. Red-faced, square-jawed, prematurely gray, and smelling of bourbon, Cesar had entered our home in mid-tirade: "And fuck the Major Deegan Expressway! And fuck the Cross Bronx Excrapway! And I musta circled this block fifty times looking for parking, and all I saw was three hundred Orthodox Jews walking to synagogue in the middle of the street, not using the sidewalks. Buncha lemmings! I got a new invention! It's called fucking sidewalks!"

Emerging form her winter outwear looking fetching in *Charlie's Angels*-style red bell-bottoms and a filly white blouse, Carmella was a vivacious, long-haired teenage artist, psychic, and Tarot Card reader. She smiled brightly at us and shrugged to indicate there was nothing she could do to get her father into the spirit of the occasion. Standing in the kitchen, watching the scene unfold from a safe distance, Dad chuckled and said to Irene, "Your husband's funny."

"In small doses." Dad didn't notice that Irene's face blanched at the sound of Cesar's yelling voice, or that she had shrunk in her clothes. He didn't know her long sleeves and pants concealed fresh, purple bruises. Dad headed into the living room to greet the new arrivals.

"You okay, Aunt Irene?" I asked.

"When you get married, be nice to your wife, okay?"

"Of course!" I whispered back. "Why wouldn't I be?"

"Kids, take me to the basement and show me your toys."

Delighted, Leo sprinted wordlessly out of the kitchen, into the hallway, and thundered his way down the staircase to the basement. Irene slunk after him with the stealth of someone sneaking past a machine-gun nest mounted atop the Berlin Wall. I followed, leisurely. We escaped Cesar's notice, but Carmella spotted us and loped after us.

Irene, Carmella, Leo, and I congregated in the back room of the shag-carpeted, wooden-paneled, finished basement. The room had little sense of feng shui, since none of us were sure what its main function was. There was an exercise bike; TV and VHS combo; record player and vinyl collection; a gecko in a plastic terrarium; a long oak table covered in LEGO, drawing paper, and colored pencils, and a set of display shelves filled with He-Man, Transformers, Star Wars, Gremlins, Aliens, and Real Ghostbusters toys. Hanging on the walls were my parents' diplomas and a Sacred Heart of Jesus print. Delighted and annoyed, Irene smirked at Jesus.

"Want to hear the *Chariots of Fire* theme?" I asked. "I fake conduct to Vangelis! We also have movie soundtracks by John Barry, John Williams, John Carpenter, and Jerry Goldsmith."

"This is your little escape area, huh?" Aunt Irene looked about for the best place to sit. Her options included the exercise bike and a wooden chair by the art table.

"Had your fill of Dad already?" Carmella asked her Mom, watching as Leo fed a cricket to his pet gecko, Harry Sullivan.

"That was a loooooooooong drive," Irene said.

"I like this plan of hiding in the basement with the children," Carmella replied.

"HEY!" Cesar's voice thundered down the basement stairwell from the main floor landing. "Where is everyone? How dare you all leave me up here with Garth and Sheena?"

Irene flinched and closed her eyes. "Never get married." She slouched towards the stairs and my brother followed.

I was too lackadaisical to go right back up, so I stayed. Staying with me, Carmella fished a pack of cigarettes and lighter out of her skintight red bell-bottoms and lit herself a cigarette.

"My Mom's not going to like the smell of the cigarettes," I warned.

Carmella shrugged and puffed away.

I raised my hand like I was at school. "Miss! Can I ask you something?"

"You don't have to raise your hand."

I lowered it. "Dad says you can tell the future and read minds and stuff."

Carmella chuckled. "Not exactly."

"Oh." I'd just found out that there was no such thing as Santa.

Carmella walked up to me, sat on her heels, leaned her elbows on her knees and stared searchingly at my face. Deciding to trust me, she started talking with her cigarette dangling perilously from her mouth. "I bet I seem listless to you, right? Know why? It's hard enough dealing with everyone's feelings when you hear what they say and see what they do. When you can feel directly what they're feeling, too? That's a little much. So, I like to hide in basements at Christmas parties with inquisitive little boys and answer their questions about my superpowers."

"I feel like I always know what everyone else is feeling," I said. "And I can guess a lot of what they're thinking. But I don't understand it all, because sometimes it's about the stock market or cancer. But I can figure out a lot, and it gets to me. People say weird things to each other, and I don't know how I feel about what they say. When I go to bed, it all comes back."

"Fellow empath. Whadda ya know?" Carmella took the cigarette out of her mouth. "Want to try a puff of this?" She placed the lipstick-covered end of the cigarette in my mouth. I took in a shallow breath of smoke. My eyes watered. I coughed. Nodding, Carmella took the cigarette back. "You've had the CPI: The Cigarette Puff Initiation into the Secret Society of Empaths."

"Is that real?" I asked, hopefully.

"Nope. Wouldn't it be great if it were?" Carmella's lower back hurt, so she stood.

"Can you read my future in a tarot deck?"

Carmella mimed patting her pockets in search of a deck she knew she didn't have. "Not on me right now." She held up an inspired finger. "How do you feel about a palm reading?"

"Yes, please, Cousin Carmella!"

"First Cousin Once Removed Carmella."

"I don't understand."

"Fuhgeddaboudit." Carmella dropped herself onto the wooden chair beside the art table. The table was littered with LEGO bricks and my crumpled, failed attempts at drawing Conan, Psi-Judge Anderson, Spider-Man, and the Thing. Keeping her cigarette dangling from the corner of her mouth, Carmella held out her hands and took mine. "First of all, you give off a blue aura, which means you are quiet, sensitive, and intuitive. You avoid confrontation. You can't accept it when relationships you value come to an end."

"Blue? Cool."

"Now for the palm." Carmella read my love line first, which confused and annoyed me, because I suspected it was about kissing. The line was split at the end, suggesting the people I loved tended to hurt me.

I was confused. "The people who I love are always good to me."

"When you start dating, you will be the kind of guy who never believes it when a girl says she loves you. You'd prefer it if she never said it but spent time with you instead. Actions speak louder than words. In general, you don't believe people when they say things to you."

I was legitimately confused. "I kinda believe everything people tell me."

"You don't, though. You don't trust anyone at all. Not in matters of love, anyway." Carmella coughed, and the cigarette almost fell out of her mouth. She maneuvered it around with her lips, felt it tuck back into the corner of her mouth, and stared down at my palm.

"I trust you," I said. "You're cool and have magic powers."

Carmella noticed small "sensitivity bumps" on the tips of my fingers. "You are an old soul, remarkably mature for your age. This means you will have absolutely nothing in common with boys your age. You will even be more mature than girls your age. Your ideal friends and girlfriends are women one to ten years older. Male friends need to be ten years older than you and have an intellectual job, like librarian or professor."

I frowned. "These older people will see me as a little kid, though."

"No, they'll recognize a kindred spirit in you. After they do a double-take over your age."

I was getting impatient. "We can stop talking about girls now, right? Will I ever own every issue of *Amazing Spider-Man*?"

"I'd like to remind you he's eight," Aunt Irene's voice rang out. She had returned to find out why we had not followed her upstairs. "I see you two would rather hide down here flirting than come upstairs and protect me from Cesar?"

I blushed. "We're *not* flirting!" (I thought the word "flirting" meant "kissing.")

"I'd like to remind you he's eight." Carmella smiled behind a cloud of cigarette smoke. She re-checked my palm. On the area of my hand where my fingers met my palm, there were a series of small, raised areas. "These are usually found on emotional people. You have two sides to your personality: your sensitive side and your masculine side. You haven't figured out a way to balance them, but you are in touch with both." She turned my hand around. "You bite your nails. That's not a psychic insight. That's an observation. It means you're eating at yourself. You shouldn't do that. You should get your feelings off your chest. If people are being jerks, tell them they're jerks. It's not your fault they're jerks, so don't bite your nails."

"Okay."

"As an older and wiser psychic, can I help you in any other way before we wrap this up?"

I nodded. "I've always wanted to know one thing and I'm too young to know."

"Okay, shoot."

"Who is Kotter, and what is he coming back to?"

Aunt Irene laughed. "I guess he *is* young, isn't he? 'Who is Kotter?' Ha!"

Carmella patted me on the head. "You're Kotter! Or, you will be . . . in a few years."

We heard the approach of soft footsteps and turned as one to see Garth creeping into the room like Gollum. "Can I join you down here? It's getting tense upstairs. Mom's telling Leo the Fatty Arbuckle story. Gianna tried to cut her off a couple of times, but she's soldiering on. Then Gianna got mad and started yelling at Mom. Vincent hauled Gianna out of the kitchen. And then Mom kept telling Leo about Fatty Arbuckle. So, I came down here."

As if on cue, Sheena crept into the room. "Can I come down here, too? I've heard dat Fatty Arbuckle story eight times today. And dat's just today!"

"The more the merrier," Irene said.

I looked over the motley crew. Deeply unsympathetic, yet deeply sympathetic. Totally uncharismatic, yet oddly charismatic. I liked these people, but I didn't know them. They were family, but I didn't love them. Just then, I had an accurate premonition. I would never see any of them again. Indeed, I would be saying my farewells to virtually all of them over the course of the next two years. One year from then, during a weekend trip to an Atlantic City resort, Grandpa would experience severe chest pains, but refuse Grandma's exhortations to call an ambulance. He would be dead by sunrise. Dad never forgive his mother for failing to call 911. The interesting parent had died first, leaving the boring one unjustly alive. After Grandpa's death, Garth and Sheena married. Only Grandma had been invited to the secret wedding ceremony at the city clerk's office in lower Manhattan, mere hours before the couple moved to Baltimore.

Cesar died less than a year after Garth and Sheena went away to Maryland. My father was upset by Cesar's passing, but Irene felt emancipated from her decades-long prison sentence of a marriage. She was happy! Reborn! Ready for a new life! Until Grandma darkened her door.

Irene's evil sister-in-law had arrived without calling first. Antje laid out her scheme for them to live together. "It will be like *The Golden Girls*!" Antje effused.

Aunt Irene felt a chill. Would she exchange one jailer for another? Cesar for Antje?

Antje surveyed Irene's home, sniffing with disapproval. "If I'm going to live here, we're going to need to make some serious changes in the décor. We should gut this place. Start over."

"'Gut it'?" Irene's eyes flashed. "You want to 'gut' my house?"

Antje puffed away at her filtered cigarette. "It *is* tacky, isn't it? Don't you think?"

"No! No, it isn't *tacky*."

"If you say so." Antje toured each level of the house and the grounds around it, remodeling it from top-to-bottom in her head.

Irene called after her, "I never invited you to move in! You're being presumptuous!"

Antje called back, "You know you'll get a bang out of having me around all the time!"

Three months later, Irene appeared without warning on our doorstep. She visited with us for an hour while Carmella circled our block endlessly, unable to find a parking spot. Dad was heartbroken. He'd lost his father, Cesar, and now Irene. Irene was simultaneously apologetic and unapologetic. "I've spent my life surrounded by people I hate. I refuse to do it a moment more."

"Where are you moving?" Dad asked, plaintively.

"I can't tell you. If I tell you, Antje will find a way to ferret my new address out of you."

"We won't tell her," Leo and I chorused.

Irene set her jaw firmly. "You all never figured out just how awful and underhanded Antje really is. She's an implacable enemy. I have to be free of her. I need to be, functionally, in witness protection to escape her clutches. This is my last chance to live."

Carmella pulled up in her large, broken-down station wagon, double-parking it in front of our house. Dad, Leo, and I walked Irene to the car. Mom watched from the open door, standing inside the living room. Irene gave my father a long hug. Carmella stepped out of the car, leaving the engine running. Today's skin-tight bell-bottoms were canary yellow. She still wore a frilly white blouse. Puffing at a cigarette, Carmella looked at me over the rim of her sunglasses. "We're gonna disappear into the mist for parts unknown."

"Don't go!" I exclaimed. "We're supposed to get married!"

Carmella's jaw dropped. Irene laughed and slapped herself in the thigh.

"I'm supposed to be with older girls! You said it yourself!" I'd been cheated. God was taking First Cousin Once Removed Carmella from me! What had I done to deserve that? And I had known Carmella's mother far better, so Irene's departure was twice as painful.

Carmella mussed my hair. "That's very sweet of you."

Aunt Irene laughed again. "Vincent, your son is a card. I love him."

Remembering something, Carmella snapped her fingers. She opened the rear driver's side door and leaned inside, fishing around some bags. She emerged holding a bedroom pillow and brought it over to me. "I got this for you as a goodbye present. It protects people from curses and bad dreams while they sleep. I filled a white mojo bag to the brim with anise seeds and sewed it inside this pillow. It is a medieval witch's spell. Keeps the evil eye and bad dreams away."

"Cool!" My fingers closed around the pillow with reverence. "This is the greatest present in human history! A gift for the ages!"

"If you believe it will work, it will," she said. "That's how these charms work. They bring out the power inside you. They don't have power in and of themselves. Really, it's just a pillow and some seeds." I got a nice cousin hug from Carmella and aunt hug from Irene.

Before I knew it, their car was pulling away from our home, driving towards the Staten Island Expressway. Would they head north towards the Verrazano and Brooklyn or south towards the Outerbridge Crossing and New Jersey? None of us knew. Their departure had effectively brought an end to our extended family. Only Grandma would be around to visit with now, and Dad tried to see her only once every two years, making a time-lapse story of her mental deterioration at the hands of Alzheimer's Disease even more dramatic. Our extended family would be just our Staten Island nuclear family now: Vincent junior. Gianna. Leo. Damien. Us against the world. Everyone else was just a stranger.

The last Christmas season visit three generations of Cavalieris made together was confined to four hours. No presents were exchanged, no Christmas carols sung, and no alcohol consumed. Mom had prepared bruschetta, spaghetti with muscles in tomato sauce, tartufo, and coffee. No one helped Mom either serve or clear off any of the three courses. Sheena, Garth, and Irene were the only ones to compliment her cooking. Since the Cavalieris virtually never slept over each other's homes or bought one another gifts, the guests were ready to leave once dessert was gobbled down. They retrieved their coats, offered us farewell hugs, and went outside. Irene and Carmella began the long walk with Cesar around the block to find where they had last seen their car. Garth and Sheena helped Antje and Vincent senior into the back seat of their car. Then they waved goodbye to us, got in the front, and drove away.

The moment they were gone, Dad asked Leo and me if we wanted to take a drive to Electronics Boutique in the mall to look up the answer to a puzzle he was stuck on in the new Sierra Entertainment graphic adventure game, *King's Quest*. The store wouldn't be open for much longer. Still, Dad really wanted to get out of the house as soon as possible. I refused the offer, but Leo accepted. Dad furtively looked at my silent mother, who was still tidying up, unassisted. "You sure you don't wanna come?" After I expressed a wish to stay home and read comic books, Dad and Leo got in Dad's car and headed off.

Needing time alone to recover from all the socializing, I grabbed a small stack of Roger Stern *Spider-Man* and John Byrne *Fantastic Four* comics that Mitchell had introduced me to and headed to the basement to read. After thirty minutes, I was becoming sure that Roderick Kingsley was, indeed, Spider-Man's mysterious new archenemy, Hobgoblin. My one reservation was a scene when Roderick and Hobgoblin were both in the same room at the same time. *I think it may be Kingsley. Mom has no idea who the Hobgoblin is, but I must tell her I may have solved this great comic book mystery!*

I emerged from the basement to find that, in the time it took for me to read a handful of comic books, most of the Christmas decorations had disappeared. Mom had returned her Dickens Christmas village houses and religious Santa sculpture to the original boxes that she stored them in during off-season. The wreath was torn from the front door and tossed to the side like a sweaty gym sock. Miraculously, Dad's Lionel train set remained intact, but no longer running. Mom must have been fearful of breaking an expensive adult toy she didn't understand how to disassemble. Worst of all were the bare and dusty bookshelves. Mom had packed up all her works of literature into small cardboard boxes and taped them shut.

I found Mom glaring at the Christmas tree with her hands on her hips. A huge cardboard box stood open on the floor beside her, ready to receive the tree. First, Mom had to remove all the ornaments and place them carefully back into the five boxes she left open on the sofa. Mom removed the red and gold ball ornaments, placing them back in their respective boxes. She then unwound the tinsel from the tree. I walked up beside Mom, curious as to why she was doing this Grinch impression. It was the evening of the 23rd, yet she was stripping the house bare of its Christmas decorations.

"I've been a terrible mother," she said in a voice so controlled that it alarmed me. "Here we are, celebrating Christmas when there's no such thing as God or Jesus or Heaven. Or Santa or Rudolph or the Little Drummer Boy."

"I like the Little Drummer Boy," I said.

"And there's no telling the difference between Aunt Bianca's holy water and toilet water. Toilet water! How repulsive!" I was surprised that Mom's rage was directed at Aunt Irene, who had leapt to her defense when the others had teased her about her books and weight. Then Mom made it clear. "If your Dad's wonderful, hilarious, and brilliant Aunt Irene thinks all this is a waste of time, who am I to argue? She thinks I'm raising you to be superstitious fools! Sorry!"

"I don't think Aunt Irene meant for you to do that," I said, tentatively.

"And I'm sorry for poisoning your mind with literature. Why should I have you read books that aren't true? Only science books for us from now on. No literature. None!"

"I like literature, Mom! Keep the books for me!"

"I like literature, too." Mom threw her hands in the air. "But what do I know? I'm just a Southern Italian immigrant! All your father's family are oh, so sophisticated! You'd never know they also came from the same dirty peasant stock as me. They've done so much better evolving and educating themselves. They're not superstitious like me. They're smart. Never mind that I teach college and they're housewives, clerks, and traveling salesmen!"

Mom plucked the angel off the top of the tree and pitched it into an open box. She pulled my tiny, framed baby picture ornament out of the tree, with the year 1976 written over it. Leo's baby picture ornament, 1979, came out of the tree next. Then she tore Rudolph and Jack Frost and several faux-crystal snowflakes away from the tree and chucked them into the box. "On the one hand, I might be a little sad my mom and dad are dead, and there's no heaven. I might feel lonely that I'm on Staten Island with all my surviving relatives living hours away."

I waved at her. "I'm right here, Mom!"

"I grew up in an Italian neighborhood. Now, I live among Orthodox Jews who can't eat in my home because I don't have separate dishes and silverware for meat and dairy products!"

"I'm Italian, Mom! We can be Italian together!" I moved to tap her on her arm to remind her that I was there.

"But I am not alone," Mom yelled. "I have more family and friends than I know what to do with! I have a husband who tells our children that he's the good guy and I'm the bad guy! I have a mother-in-law so *concerned* for the state of my health that she ever so *helpfully* has made me aware of the existence of Weight Watchers! Let's not forget Sheena, who bathes in the worst-smelling perfume ever, scratches the skin off her own hands, and scares the living shit out of my children. Small waist and even smaller brain! If only I had a waist that small, since my larger brain doesn't garner me any respect from my 'chess Grandmaster' father-in-law." Mom used her fingers to put scare quotes around "chess Grandmaster." "What good is a large brain if it is packed full of literature and not scientific fun factoids and memorized Bobby Fischer games?"

I felt scared and sad, but I understood why she was upset. "They're gone now, Mom."

Mom's furious energy fizzled. Her body sagged. The fire in her eyes dimmed. Her clenched fists went limp. All that remained was fatigue and defeat. "I'm too tired to take down this whole damn tree." Mom stared down at the floor, her arms hanging slack by her sides. "I didn't know when I was well-off. I miss being a teenager. I miss my parents being alive. I miss bouncing around Europe. I miss dating the Persians. Miss my one date with Fabian."

My eyes bulged. "Fabian? The 'Turn Me Loose' Fabian?"

"Everyone in my family is dying off, one by one. I'm forty. I'm never going to Italy again. And I'm going to spend every Christmas with my in-laws discussing Fatty Arbuckle. Why in hell are those freaks alive when my parents are dead? Mutes! Cynics! Psychics! Gossips! Bullies! That's my family now! The fucking Addams Family!" She straightened, reached up with her arms, grasped the tip of the Christmas tree, and pulled it off balance, towards her. The tree collapsed in a heap onto the floor between us. Then Mom marched into the kitchen.

I dropped to my knees next to the tree, scooping the tip up in my arms and standing to lift it. I got it a foot or so off the ground, but was too small to push it all the way back up into a standing position. A Styrofoam Christmas tree ball beaned off my head.

"Leave it!"

When I lowered the tree to the floor and sat beside it, mom retreated into the kitchen.

For an instant, Mom seemed as if she might settle down at the kitchen table and let her rage ebb. Then she noticed our rotary phone fixed to the wall, and felt her anger reach a new height. She tore the phone from its mounting and began wrapping it up in its own cords as if she were hogtying a pig. "Our phone is out of date, is it? We need a touchtone! What did everyone's favorite Aunt Irene ask? 'Does that phone dial Nixon direct?' Ha, ha, ha! Very funny!" I missed that exchange. I wondered if Mom was right to be mad, or if she didn't have a sense of humor.

I heard a key in the front door lock. The boys walked in, with Leo brandishing a walkthrough guide to *King's Quest*. Dad exhaled sharply through his nose when he saw what the Tasmanian devil had done to the family room. "I knew this was coming." He looked down at me. "Bet you wish you'd come with us to Electronics Boutique."

"Boy, oh boy, oh boy," Leo said.

"Welcome home," Mom's sarcastic voice called out. She stood on the threshold between kitchen and living room, watching the "Three Good Guys" reunite beside the fallen tree.

Dad's voice sounded tired and neutral. "Honey, I love what you've done with the place."

"*Very* funny," mom glowered.

Dad's voice grew louder, building to a crescendo. "So, what now? I lock you in the bedroom? Hire Grace Poole to bring your meals to you? Because you've gone barking mad!"

"Oh, leave me alone," Mom whimpered, bursting into tears.

"Leave *you* alone? Who took the house apart? You're a Goddamn maniac!"

"Merry Christmas." Walking like she was half-dead, Mom proceeded up the stairs to go to bed. She closed and locked the bedroom door behind her.

Leo put a hand on my shoulder. "Are you okay?"

Dad scoffed. "'Course he's ain't okay." He walked over to the wine cabinet built into the now-empty bookshelf and opened it fearfully. Luckily for him, the wine, liqueurs, and cocktail mixes had survived Mom's tidying. "I need a Brandy Alexander desperately." He glanced at Leo and me. "I'm making three."

CHAPTER TWELVE
Marina Dazzo

January 19, 1988

"Heart and Soul," the Hoagy Carmichael and Frank Loesser song from the giant keyboard scene in *Big*, bled through the lime green band room door. Chattering voices, girls giggling, and guys making mock grunting, farting, and roaring sounds also came to my ears throughout the lunch period, along with snatches of marching band music, hair metal covers, and big band tunes. Yes, the band kids were having a grand-old time eating lunch and playing their instruments behind the green door, far from the cafeteria's horrors. *It would be more fun for me if they'd let me in, too.* Still, I wouldn't be accosted by nitwits while I ate here. Band members alone had reason to be in an isolated hallway that housed only the auditorium and music room. I sat cross-legged on the hall floor, reading *Garfield* and *Far Side* comics, eating a salami and provolone sandwich. I wiped sandwich crumbs off my Reba McEntire T-shirt, relieved no mayonnaise or bits of salami had stained it.

The green door opened. An Amazon emerged. Tall, buxom, and big-hipped, she wore a safety orange blazer over a low-cut black t-shirt, black dress pants, and black dress shoes. She had a prominent Roman nose, brown eyes, bushy eyebrows, and an uncombable mass of shoulder-length brown curls. She smiled down at me and spoke in perfect English with a light Italian accent, making me wonder just how "fresh off the boat" she was. "It *is* you. I hear you've been having a terrible year in chorus. And everywhere else, really."

I scrunched my eyebrows together. Now I was as aware of my own bushy eyebrows as I was hers. "Who told you about all that?"

"Kyle Ahearne heard it all when it was happening. He told Salty Margaritas. Salty told us just now. We were all just talking about you in there because we couldn't figure out what you were doing sitting on the floor in this hallway . . . *like a weirdo!*"

Embarrassed, I cleared my throat. "I didn't mean to alarm anybody." I made a mental note that I should find Kyle Ahearne and introduce myself. He was one of the few boys in chorus, but so quiet that I hadn't given him any serious thought.

"Why don't you finish your lunch in here? Vitali is gone for the rest of the period, so you probably won't get thrown out on your ear. Unless you like sitting out here on the floor . . . *like a weirdo* . . . losing all the circulation in your legs." Smiling more broadly at my reluctance to stand, she waved me up off the ground. "Annamu!"

Tiny bee-sting prickles moved up and down my legs, warning me that my legs had, indeed, fallen asleep. I pulled myself up, massaging my legs to improve circulation. "Thanks." When I straightened, I realized that Marina was a full head taller than me. "Whoa. You're tall!"

The girl feigned shock. "Am I? Nobody's ever told me that before!"

I looked around for a mouse hole in the wall I could crawl into. "Sorry."

She chuckled. "I get it. Italians usually come in three sizes: small, smaller, and smallest! But I'm a Redwood! Crazy, huh? And I see you've got some height on you, yourself."

"Do I?" I was hoping I'd wind up tall. "I haven't hit a growth spurt in a while, but I'm a quarter German and all the Germans in my family are tall as André the Giant."

"You've got Danny DeVito beat. Oh! I'm Marina Dazzo." Marina extended her hand.

I accepted it. "Damien Cavalieri."

"After Saint Damien of Hawaii?"

"Actually, my dad named me after Damien Thorn."

Marina shook her head. "Okay, I'll bite. Who's Damien Thorn?"

"A horror movie villain from *The Omen* trilogy. Sam Neill played him in *The Final Conflict*. As cool as Sam Neill is, I'd have preferred it if Dad had named me after a *Dark Shadows* character, like Barnabas or Quentin."

"I bet all of that would be really interesting if I had any idea what the fuck you were talking about." Marina waved me inside. "Hey, everyone. This is my little Damien-poo. He's this lost little lamb wandering the halls, frightened of wolves. I think we should adopt him." She gestured towards each band member individually, introducing them in turn. Among the group was Eric Indelicato, a steroid-enhanced Italian boy in a black muscle shirt who played electric guitar. There were three other

Italian girls who appeared eternally stationed at Marina's side: Ludovica Saviano, Jennifer Raffone, and Julia Puglia. Ludovica took an instant liking to me for no discernable reason, Jennifer looked like she wanted to throttle me at first sight, and Julia was radically committed to being indifferent to my presence. The non-Italians in the room included my old bus-route buddy Tuesday Phapant on keyboard, a slim Black girl with a Jheri Curl permanent wave hairstyle named Alisha Clark on clarinet, and a Greek named Salty Margaritas, who was in the back of the room reading a biography of John F. Kennedy, sporting a *Michael Dukakis 1988* t-shirt, and eating a gyro he had brought from home.

"Thanks for telling them my sad story, Salty," I called over to him.

Salty farted in reply and kept reading his JFK biography. A Greek nationalist, Salty was an observant member of the Greek Orthodox Church and famous in school for drinking three full bottles of ouzo every evening after dinner. His birth certificate read Demosthenes Margaritis, but everyone called him Salty Margaritas. Hence, the tattoo of a salty margarita on his left shoulder that he paid for at nine-years-old without telling his parents. The barrel-chested Greek had also shaved his head so he could look like Mr. Clean. He was an interesting and provocative dude.

Marina placed a hand on my shoulder. "My fellow Sicilians are treating you like dirt!"

"Pretty much. Though I guess Bobby Mammolito has his moments."

"I'm glad. He's my boyfriend. And he told me a bit about you, too. Are you a Sicilian?"

"Actually, I'm Neapolitan." I offered her an apologetic look. *Ha! When I'm dealing with assholes, I'm proud I'm not Sicilian, but when I meet a gorgeous giantess, you're goddamn right I'm sad I'm not Sicilian! Wait. Bobby Mammolito is her boyfriend? I'm having trouble with that.*

Marina gave a theatrical tut and sad shake of her head. "Ah! Too bad! Too bad. But nobody's perfect." She grinned.

I made a show of looking her up and down. "I dunno. You're looking pretty perfect from where I'm standing."

"Aw, shucks." Marina gave a little hip wiggle of joy. "Thank you, ya big flirt."

Tuesday Phapant rolled her eyes and grunted in exaggerated disgust. "*Un*-believable."

"She's a whole lotta woman!" Salty roared. "Built like a brick shithouse! Makes Samantha Fox look like a tiny, starving Ethiopian!"

Marina showed her open palm to Salty. "Talk to the hand, Salty."

Tuesday moaned and dropped her head in her hands.

"Not your day?" I asked her.

"Fuck you," said Tuesday.

Marina smiled. "Anyhoo, *you* need a taste of some *Italian solidarity!*"

"It would make a nice change of pace," I agreed.

"Group hug!" Marina's shout was a pre-arranged signal to Ludovica, Jennifer, and Julia to circle and embrace me in an extended, perfume-scented hug. Jennifer participated in the group hug with enormous reluctance, Julia hugged away with ironic detachment, and Ludovica and Marina showered me with genuine affection and sympathy. When the hug ended, I was feeling warm and safe. "I needed that," I blushed. "Thank you."

"Getting group hugged by a buncha girls with big boobies is the best feeling in the world," Salty declared from the back corner of the room. "It is the only reason I enjoy going to church sometimes. The kiss of peace. 'Christ is in our midst!' 'He is and always shall be!' You get lotsa kisses and hugs from girls with big boobies. In *sweaters*! Hubba, hubba, hubba."

Marina beaned Salty off the head with a magically produced rolled-up ball of paper.

"Come on, man," I called back at Salty. "Don't spoil it."

Salty laughed. "He's worried I decreased his odds of getting another Sweater Girl hug."

Marina held up her flute. "We're about to have a little contest. See who can play the opening bars of Europe's 'The Final Countdown' the best. Since you'll be an impartial judge, Damien, you get to decide who the winner is."

Salty put his JFK book down. "How's *he* gonna be impartial? You just smooshed your huge knockers against his chest! If he doesn't crown you the winner, I'll eat my flat hat."

"Stop talking about my boobs!" Marina yelled. "God! All day every day everybody's talkin' 'bout my boobs!"

"They're the hugest fun bags I've ever seen," Salty replied. "And what else is worth talking about in life, besides boobs? Pretty much nothing."

"Hey!" I called back to him. "Go back to reading about that idiot JFK."

Salty, who spent most of his time trying to offend others, was himself affronted. "'That idiot JFK?' He saved the world during the Cuban Missile Crisis!"

I waved Salty away dismissively. "JFK caused the Cuban Missile Crisis in the first place! You don't get credit for solving a problem that you create yourself. And he and his brothers murdered Marilyn Monroe and that chick in Chappaquiddick. The only good thing JFK ever did was rescue some crewman when P.T. Boat 109 sank. I couldn't care less about JFK, son of Joe Kennedy, the Prohibition-era bootlegger! Give me President Al Capone junior, instead. At least he'd be an Italian gangster president, not an Irish gangster president."

Salty placed his hand upon his heart and looked grave. "Wow. I had no idea you were so Republican. Maybe we should kick your ass back out into that hallway again. You Italians. You're like the Irish. You forget your immigrant past. Not like us Greek Americans. We remember. We haven't sold our souls to the GOP yet. We began leftist. We *remain* leftist."

"Ah, I don't give two fucks about politics," Marina said. "I try to vote pro-life if I can, but I don't really understand the issues." She added in a low whisper, "Good deflection."

Tuesday Phapant cut off any further debate by playing the opening keyboard riff of "The Final Countdown" on her Yamaha. I'd never heard the song before, or of the Swedish rock band that wrote it. I was surprised how much I adored the riff. "This song is badass."

"My turn." The muscular Eric Indelicato played the same riff on his electric guitar.

"Your playing is incredible," I marveled.

"I have to go *after* keyboard and electric guitar? That doesn't seem fair." Marina lifted her flute to her lips and played a gentle-but-up-tempo rendition. When she finished, she said diffidently. "Not a keyboard, I know."

"I loved it," I said.

"He's gonna pick Marina," Salty said loudly to Eric Indelicato. "Just so you know."

Tuesday stared daggers at me, daring me to pick Marina. "So, who's the winner?"

"I can't figure this guy out," Alisha Clark said to Tuesday. "Is he a bit smarmy?"

"I don't know if that's the right word," Tuesday replied, "but you're getting warm."

I chose to ignore that last exchange and focus on answering Tuesday's question. "Why do I have to pick a winner? You were *all* great. I'm half a communist, so I don't like competitions. I kinda think everyone should win."

"You're a half-communist Republican?" Salty asked, completely incredulous. "That's the stupidest thing I've ever heard. Who are you, and why are you so strange?"

"The original riff is a keyboard riff," Eric said firmly. "Tuesday should win, because she played it well on the right instrument."

"I wouldn't know," I said to Eric. "I haven't heard the original."

"*Boobs*, Eric," Tuesday decided. "He's gonna vote for the *boobs*."

Marina arched her eyebrow at me. "You've never heard it?"

"My parents don't like it when I listen to music that came out after the British Invasion. They think everything louder than Frankie Valli is too loud."

Salty chuckled. "Does that explain the horrendous Reba McEntire t-shirt you're wearing? You're a New Yorker and you're listening to a country music singer from Oklahoma?"

I gestured at Marina. "I gotta say, considering you were playing against some flashy instruments, your classic sound came off great. You might have been my favorite, by a hair."

"I'm shocked! Shocked!" Salty cried out, imitating Claude Rains from *Casablanca*.

I wagged a contradicting finger at him. "You predicted I'd choose Marina. That made me want to pick *anyone* but her, but I legitimately think she did the best. I'm not letting you use reverse psychology to scare me away from picking the right winner. I refuse."

Salty massaged his chin as he stared at me. "You're telling the truth. At least, you think you are." He returned to reading. "And yet, you have no credibility whatsoever, because you're desperate to suckle her. And put where you pee where she pees."

I scowled. "What's this crap about me not having credibility? I'm the most honest person I know! I tell the truth, and I've got no poker face!"

"Ah, your mother," Salty shot back.

I had no idea what "your mother" meant, so I replied, "Yeah? Your grandmother!"

"Don't you talk about my grandmother!" Salty yelled back.

Am I talking about his grandmother? I don't even know what the hell I'm saying!

"Never mind Salty." Marina hugged me. "Thanks for picking me."

"There you go," Salty muttered to himself. "That's what he was after. Another press against the sweater pies. And I don't blame him one bit."

I was about to get very angry. Then Mrs. Vitali walked in. "Oh! We have an interloper!"

I waved to her and gave her my crooked smile. "Greetings, Mrs. Vitali! How are you this fine afternoon?"

"You are not in band, Mr. Cavalieri, so you do not belong here. Vamoose."

Interesting that she knows my name. I wonder how? "I hear you," I replied.

Salty gestured to the door. "Get thee to Oklahoma, foul Reba McEntire fan!"

Marina smiled sadly at me. "Sorry you have to go. I can't change the rules, though."

"You sheltered me as long as you could, and I really appreciate finally getting some Italian solidarity." I started to leave, but then stopped. "Marina, I want to tell you a line from one of my favorite movies: 'Beauty fades eventually, but a kind soul remains forever.'"

"Oh, that is nice. I like that."

I threw a dirty glance at Salty. "Don't listen to Salty. Your flute playing is beautiful, and you're beautiful, but your big heart may be the most beautiful thing about you of all."

Salty moaned. "Oh, my God! I'm gonna hurl."

I waited for the heckling to end and continued. "Don't let Salty tease you for being gorgeous. Don't let him reduce you to your lovely figure. You're beautiful through and through." Marina blushed. Tuesday clutched at her own throat with one hand and held her nose with another. Mrs. Vitali cleared her throat loudly. "Okay, that's enough of that. Begone, Romeo."

I scooped up my saddle bag of comic books and ambled into the hallway.

"Yo, Damien!" Eric Indelicato called out.

I turned back. "What?"

"What movie was that line from?"

"*Captain Kronos: Vampire Hunter.*"

Mrs. Vitali shut the heavy green door in my face.

That night, Marina and I made love in an outdoor hot tub surrounded by redwood trees.

I awoke covered in my own semen. *Oh, no!*

I'd never ejaculated before. *God damn it!*

The sticky, cold mess in my lap glued my pajamas to skin. *Gross, gross, gross.*

It had a nostril-scorching stench that made me want to retch. I ran to the bathroom and scrubbed myself down with a damp, soapy washcloth. Even after I dried myself off with a second washcloth, I felt clammy and soiled. I took as hot a shower as I could bear, hoping the sound of it wouldn't wake anyone. After the shower, I put on a fresh pair of pajamas. *What the fuck do I do with my other pair of pajamas and the used towel and washcloths?* The crotch was soiled. So was the bottom portion of that pajama top. My semen sure traveled. I took the gooey laundry downstairs, hurling it directly into the washing machine. I worried about the possibility of someone in the family accidentally brushing their fingers over cum-damp clothes, so I draped a few additional pieces of dirty clothing over them. Starting the wash up would be the safest thing to do. Too bad I had never done a laundry. How come neither parent had ever showed me how to do a fucking wash? Was this secret knowledge, reserved only for Freemasons? I considered giving it a try, but the first bottle I picked up said "bleach" on it, and that was enough to frighten me away. I dithered and cursed myself for another five minutes, before deciding there was nothing more to do. I sprinted back up to my bathroom, hoping the carpet would muffle the sounds of my middle-of-the-night footfalls. I stared at myself in the bathroom mirror. "You moron! She clearly likes you as a friend. She's not *remotely* interested."

I pulled the elastic waistband of my fresh pajama pants out with my thumb and stared down at my limp, satisfied penis. "What's with you?" I whisper-yelled at it. "Taking liberties like that! I didn't give you permission to think about her in that way! Neither did she! I'm so disgusted with you!" I sat on the area rug, staring glumly at the toilet bowl. *Does this mean I'm in love? Is that the sign? The night pants thing? Because that is so not good. Let's not punish her for being kind. She doesn't need some pimply, half-blind, allergy-ridden, comic geek having weird ass dreams about her just because she was a little nice to him. No, I can't be in love. This is just a crush. I should be able to nip it in the bud.* I pressed my eyes tight together and chanted to myself. *You are not in love. This is just a passing fancy. You'll be yourself in the morning.*

After ten minutes of chanting and staring at the toilet, I had the sinking, crushing realization that I had fallen in the love for the first time.

"That is so fucking stupid," I whispered aloud to myself. "You talked to her for a handful of minutes, tops! No time at all. This better not be how I feel from now on." I stared back down at my crotch. "If you're sticking me with a Marina Dazzo obsession for the foreseeable future, I'm not getting you anything for Christmas."

My penis failed to respond.

"So, Salty was right, huh? Those were some fantastic boobs, weren't they?"

My penis stirred.

Yeah, yeah. You're no help at all, are you? And there's no way on God's green earth she fell in love with me after two hugs and a musical interlude. No way in the world. So, I'm not saying nothing. I am not telling her how I feel. I'm keeping this our secret.

Friday, February 12, 1988

Marina found a single red rose taped to her locker, with an unsigned note attached that read: "Happy Valentine's Day, Marina. And thank you.

CHAPTER THIRTEEN
She May Be a Nazi, But She's Hot

September 24, 1987

Without the benefit of PornHub, I pieced my sex education together from a variety of unreliable sources, ranging from my father's anecdotes and sly asides, the *Truly Tasteless Jokes* book series, locker room talk before and after gym class, '80s and '90s sex thrillers written by Joe Eszterhas and Scott Turow, and religious instruction at Saint Luke's Roman Catholic Church. Each Thursday night, Catholic public-school kids attended three hours of after-dinner religious instruction in preparation for receiving the Sacrament of Confirmation and becoming "Soldiers of Christ." Kids who attended the church's K-12 private school got all the theological drilling they needed during regular school hours. They were ready. Us heathens needed remedial religion before we could stand before the bishop and be anointed with oil of Chrism.

Miss O'Sullivan, the petite, twenty-one-year-old religious instruction teacher, had short, curly blonde hair, sparkling blue eyes, and perfect white teeth. She wore the same outfit each week like a uniform: a figure-flattering ankle-length gray skirt over black high-heeled shoes, a frilly white blouse buttoned up to her neck, and a plain gold cross hanging just above her bosom. She appeared serene, but her aura of tranquility flickered each time she expressed a terrifyingly doctrinaire religious belief or was challenged by a saucy student. Our first lesson with Miss O'Sullivan fell three days after I discovered the joys of being tortured by students, teachers, and administrators alike on day one of sixth grade. After taking this shocking abuse, I was primed to be Miss O'Sullivan's perfect victim. All she needed to do was smile, and I would be hers.

Ten minutes into the first lesson, the luminous reactionary produced a pristine white handkerchief from her purse and held it open for the students to examine. "I don't agree with the modern Catholic Church's decision to downplay the existence of hell. I don't approve of hints that salvation may not just go to Christians. In fact, one of our own parish's priests, a certain Jesuit who shall remain nameless, comes dangerously close to espousing Origen's heresy of Apocatastasis. They call it 'Universalism.' I believe in real Catholicism, which teaches that your soul must be as pristine as this handkerchief the moment of death, or you will burn forever."

"This bitch can burn forever," Christina Gelormino whispered to Nancy Boyle.

Nancy nodded her massive head of dark brown teased hair. "She's a real asshole."

"A whole ass." The duo sat behind me in matching gray over-the-shoulder sweatshirts.

Like Fr. Charles Coughlin speaking through *Sesame Street*'s Elmo, Miss O'Sullivan was a sexy woman giving a cute fire-and-brimstone sermon — the spoonful of sugar needed to make the Inquisition palatable again in the twentieth century. "The moment you commit a mortal sin, you must repent. Run to confession. Unburden yourself. Do your penance. Sandblast the stain off your soul. If you do not return your soul to a lily-white state, you will *definitely* go to hell."

I'm doomed. My handkerchief must be covered in all kinds of boogers by now. I know exactly what my specially tailored room in hell will look like: me chained to a chair — forever immobile — forced to watch impossibly fit women doing yoga.

"Asshole." Nancy confirmed.

"Whole ass," Christina repeated.

Even Miss O'Sullivan's stern, disapproving looks were charming. "In our increasingly permissive society, we practice 'free love.' 'Free love.' What an absurd term. Love isn't free. There's always a price to be paid. It is all fun and games until we get AIDS. Or we become pregnant and are tempted to abort the baby to avoid reaping what we sow. We, as a society, are taking the bullet train to Hades. Someone needs to hold the line on morality. It won't be anyone in the secularist and morally bankrupt Democratic Party, that's for sure. For some hope for our collective future, we need to look to the Republicans as our guiding light. Only the wisest within our church have come to this inescapable conclusion. It is a small number, but it is growing. Make no mistake: on Election Day, any *real* Roman Catholic will *always* cast a ballot for the pro-life candidate. Anyone who votes for the pro-choice candidate votes for a Culture of Death." Somehow, she could make us *hear* the capital letters she spoke. Feigning a casual air, she passed a glossy photo around the classroom without describing it first. I started when it fell on my desk.

"What you see before you," Miss O'Sullivan continued, "are the bloody remains of aborted babies, small enough to hold in the palm of your hand, but definitely human and definitely murdered. Recall these images every Election Day. And on prom night."

I passed the photo backwards. Christina Gelormino took the world's briefest look at the photo and came close to gagging on her watermelon gum. "What the fuck?" she said between chews. She turned the photo face down and passed it to Nancy. "If I were you, I wouldn't look."

"I shouldn't, right?" Nancy's teased hair shivered.

Christina's hooped earrings shook back and forth.

"Everything all right back there, Miss Gelormino? Miss Boyle?" asked O'Sullivan.

"Peachy keen," Nancy grinned.

Christina raised her hand enthusiastically. "Miss O'Sullivan! I have a question."

Miss O'Sullivan looked dubious. "What is it?"

"Is it considered a mortal sin if I have an aborted third-trimester fetus pickled in brine in a mason jar on my nightstand?"

Miss O'Sullivan paled. "What did you just say?!?!"

Christina blew a tiny bubble and burst it with her teeth, making it pop loud as a gunshot.

"No chewing gum in class," Miss O'Sullivan admonished. "Throw that away, now."

Christina gulped the gum down. "It's gone."

"No more gum chewing."

"Aye, aye, Cap'n," she saluted. By high school, Christina would need surgery to remove from her stomach all the gum she swallowed over the years to dodge teacher anger.

The three-hour marathon class continued, and the heckling girls remained silent for most of it. Still, the ears of all thirteen students rang with Miss O'Sullivan's hyperbolic and reactionary rhetoric. Her most bizarre yarn concerned François Chanceux, a virginal, nineteenth-century Frenchman dragged to a brothel by his debauched friend, Auguste Connard. Feeling guilty for caving to peer pressure, François prayed a decade on his rosary before having sex with the prostitute. Then he paid his tally, lost his purity, and slipped into a satisfying, post-coital sleep. Unbeknownst to the slumbering François, Auguste said no prayers on his rosary before fornicating with two prostitutes at once. At midnight, Auguste wandered out into the street, raging drunk, and got himself run over by an out-of-control horse-drawn carriage. Three hours later, a knock at the bedroom door awakened François. The former virgin stumbled out of bed, barely able to see in the pitch darkness. He opened the door, finding himself face-to-face with the mangled, blood-spattered Auguste. The gory apparition prodded François' shoulder with a bony finger. "It is a good thing you prayed your rosary, François. We were *both* meant to die in the accident that claimed my life. Our Lady cast a sleep spell over you, saving you from my grisly fate." From that day, François never visited another brothel or went anywhere without a rosary.

Christina raised her hand. "I don't get it. The moral of the story is we need to pray the rosary before we commit a sin, or we'll become a zombie?"

"I've never wanted to go to a whorehouse," Nancy said thoughtfully. "I guess if I go, I need to be sure to bring my rosary, amirite?"

Miss O'Sullivan flashed an insincere smile at the hecklers. "I think the moral is obvious."

The girls made me more aware of the absurdities of the story than I would have in their absence. Still, I gave credence to it. I had grown up learning to trust people who stood in front of a classroom. The fable also had the advantage of being the kind of cool horror story I always enjoyed, with echoes of *Tales from the Crypt* and "The Adventure of the German Student" by Washington Irving. Dad's Aunt Irene would laugh at me for believing any of it, but I couldn't help myself. I was gullible enough to buy Miss O'Sullivan's complete line of bullshit.

Brothel-goer or not, I gotta get me a rosary. Knowing what a screw-up I am, I'm sure I'll need a "Get Out of Jail Free" card sooner rather than later.

"I am such a goof!" Christina called out. "I was expecting a zombie-free lesson. I should have guessed you'd tell us a haunted cathouse story! I want to put in a request for a story about Scilla and Cariddi next week. They're sea monsters who live off the coast of Sicily."

Miss O'Sullivan smiled beatifically at the two girls, but her eyes told a different story.

Nancy called out, "Yo! Tell Miss O'Sullivan the story you just told me about your dad!"

Christina feigned reluctance, though her eyes shone with mirth. "Oh, I couldn't!"

"You should!" exclaimed Nancy.

Miss O'Sullivan knew it was unwise to be interested but couldn't help it. "What story?"

Christina said, "Last night at dinner, my dad let out this enormous fart. My mom waved the air away from her nose and said 'pew.' But my dad is Italian, and in Italian, the word 'piu' means 'more.' So, Dad farted *again*!" Christina laughed infectiously. I joined in.

"Thank you for sharing that with us," Miss O'Sullivan said.

Nancy smacked Christina in the arm. "Not that story, waistoid! The other one."

"Oh! I know the one!"

Miss O'Sullivan held both hands up. "No, please. One story is enough."

"My dad made a toast at a formal dinner welcoming some Japanese businessman to America and he ended by saying 'cin cin,' which is Italian for 'cheers.' The problem is, the word means something different in Japan, and they thought he was saying 'penis penis.'"

"Okay, that was vulgar," Miss O'Sullivan protested.

"It was *cultural*!" Christina insisted.

"That's enough out of you two!" Miss O'Sullivan yelled.

When O'Sullivan wasn't looking, I whispered, "Both stories were cool."

"Aha! You aren't a total loss after all, Damien," Christina declared. "Good!"

After class, when the other students had gone, I lingered to speak privately with Miss O'Sullivan. I couldn't stop myself from tearing up. "Sorry. That was a disturbing photo."

Miss O'Sullivan placed her hand gently on my chest, feeling my heartbeat through the fabric of my Spider-Man t-shirt. "You have a beautiful soul. You bleed for the world."

I blinked away my tears. "I don't understand why things are the way they are. Everyone is so mean and selfish. I try not to harm anyone."

Miss O'Sullivan's touch felt warm. She left her hand in place. "Remember, women are as much a victim of this horrifying Nazi ideology as the children they are coerced into killing."

I frowned. "I'm part German. I don't want to be tricked into becoming a Nazi like past generations of Germans were. It is a thing with me."

"Yes. Oppose fascism, even if it cloaks itself in calls to protect women's rights. You need to change the world. Make it a kinder place." Her hand remained on my chest, over my heart.

"That's what I've always supported. A kinder world."

Miss O'Sullivan's ice blue eyes shimmered. "You will become a saint one day, Damien."

I gave her an aw-shucks smile. "Oh, well, that can't possibly be true, Miss O'Sullivan. And you can't know that when we've only just met."

She smiled radiantly. "That is *exactly* what a saint would say. I can see into you, through your eyes. Keep being yourself. Be kind. Fight fascism. Make no compromises."

Tired and grumpy, Dad walked in. "Every car but mine left already, but we're still here?"

Flushing, Miss O'Sullivan removed her hand from my chest. "Good night to you both."

"Night, Miss," Dad said. His mood must have softened when he got a better look at Miss O'Sullivan and saw her hand on me. I picked up my raincoat and fedora and followed Dad outside. As we got into our blue Cutlass Ciera, Dad asks slyly, "What was *that* all about?"

I shrugged. "She was being nice to me."

"Did you notice that she's not wearing a wedding ring? I think you can make it work."

"Dad, I'm eleven. She's gotta be . . . twenty-four? That might not even be legal!"

Dad shrugged. "Wait five years and ask her out."

I cleared my throat. "I don't know how I feel about this conversation."

"Maybe I'll ask her out," Dad said to himself.

I shot my father a dark look.

"I knew you wanted to slip her one!" Dad laughed. "I was baiting you."

I pulled a face. "Very clever."

CHAPTER FOURTEEN
Behind the Green Door

January 22, 1988

Wearing a t-shirt, vest, black pants, and scrunched down hat, I sat across from Mitchell in his Drama classroom. We were doing a dress-rehearsal reading of the *Honeymooners* skit script we put together. I played an outraged Ed Norton, sick of eating the same bagged lunch every day at work. "All I get is peanut butter sandwiches, peanut butter sandwiches, and more peanut butter sandwiches! I'm telling you, I'm tired of it, Ralph!"

Wearing a makeshift blue bus driver uniform, Mitchell slipped ably into the Ralph Kramden role. "Why don't you complain to Trixie?"

I threw my hand in the air. "What for? I make my own sandwiches!"

On loan from Shop, I was happy to get away from that class, happier still to be doing a *Honeymooners* bit, and completely delighted to be spending time with Mitchell. The pregnant drama teacher, Mrs. Navarro, moved about the room, offering personalized attention to the various groups of rehearsing students. "We're ready for her to hear us do a run through," I said.

Mitchell changed the subject abruptly. "What's this I'm hearing about you and Marina?"

I toyed with denying the rumor, but was tired of not being honest with Mitchell: "I like her. She's not into me. It's the worst thing I've ever felt. I want to make it stop."

"I'm sorry," said Mitchell.

"These aren't even real feelings I'm having," I complained. "They're just hormones, but they're making me think about Marina *all the time*! She's become my idée fixe."

"Emotions are real. If you're feeling it, it's real. Are you sure she doesn't like you back?"

I rolled my eyes. "Yeah. She pines for me day and night."

"Have you even tried talking to her?" Mitchell asked.

I took my Norton hat off and played with it absently. "I wouldn't know what to say."

"The thing about girls is they get up in the morning and put their pants on, just like us."

"I know that!" (Actually, I didn't.)

"I'm lucky," Mitchell said. "I live with my older sister and my mother." Mitchell's mother was a diminutive nurse young enough to be mistaken for his older sister. During my visits, I sometimes found her collapsed in a heap on the living room couch, recovering from an all-night shift in the emergency room. Mitchell's sister was around less often but had an urbane air. Once, she fed carrots to her fat white rabbit as I watched. "He's an asshole," she explained, "or I'd let you feed him. He'd bite your finger off." Living with those two women would be an education, for sure. I had the impression they were intensely cool. Mitchell continued, "Women are just people, you know? Knowing that means I can talk to anyone. Too bad you haven't known many girls. If you'd grown up with a sister, you'd be dangerous."

"Yeah, a regular Casanova."

Mrs. Navarro came by to see how we were doing. Mitchell pretended to read the script. "'Why don't you complain to Trixie?'"

I caught on. "'What for? I make my own sandwiches!'"

Mrs. Navarro smiled at us. "*Honeymooners*? That should be fun. I'm looking forward to that." She moved away.

"Is it possible to fall out of love with someone?" I asked. "Because I'm not buying the idea that it is 'better to have loved and lost than never to have loved at all.'"

"Pick her apart. Where are her flaws? Does she have gnarled toes? She snaggle-toothed?"

I squirmed. "That's hardly gentlemanly behavior. I like this girl as a person. I don't just lust after her, you know. She's big-hearted. So, if she has flaws, I choose not to see them."

"I'm trying to help you, here. Stop being obstinate. Listen, take Lucy Ghiaccio over there in the corner. You see her?" When I didn't turn around to look, he continued talking. "She's got her back to us right now. She's got an ass you can bounce quarters off of, but she's dumb as a post. That's *not* sexy. Focus on Marina's flaws if you want to disenchant yourself."

I shrugged. "I guess. That's a little mean for my taste, you know."

"Check Lucy out now," Mitchell urged. "Her jeans fit just right."

"She didn't put those jeans on for me."

"This is for your own good. We're helping you fall out of love with Marina."

"That ass isn't for me. Besides, I'm more of a breast man."

"Would you just look at Lucy, please?" Mitchell growled.

Slow, stiff, and unnatural, I signaled to half the class that I was turning around to gape openly at a girl's undercarriage. Unfortunately for me, Lucy's homicidal brother, Armand, was also visiting today to rehearse *Glengarry Glen Ross* with one of Mitchell's classmates. The mad-eyed, werewolf-hairy man leapt across the room, seized me by my t-shirt, and raised an open switchblade to my right eye. Armand's breath was hot on my face. "Are you starin' at my sister's ass? Huh? Are you? Huh? Are you?"

My prop hat fell off my head to the gray tiled floor.

No lookie heinie. Lookie heinie, get eye poked out with switchblade.

"Hey, get away from him!" Mitchell yelled.

Time had slowed. It was as if someone else were being attacked.

Inching towards us with her hands up, Mrs. Navarro tried to intervene without getting me killed. "Dear God, what is happening over here?"

I wasn't really here. I was swimming underwater.

Snarling like a rabid dog, the black-haired Frank-Zappa-lookalike bared his clenched teeth at Mitchell and Mrs. Navarro. "He was starin' at my sister's ass."

Mrs. Navarro cleared her throat. "Damian was just looking at the clock, Armand."

I felt warm and weird. I examined my pants to see if I had urinated over myself. No.

The color drained from her face, Lucy appeared at our side. "Armand, stop doing this!"

Fancy that. She looks just *like Paulette Goddard in* Modern Times. *And I'm going to die.*

"Papà said I gotta look out for you, Lucy!" The sweat from Armand's hands seeped into my Ed Norton t-shirt. "Papà says you're too young to date. You got the body of a woman, but you're still his little girl. We gotta protect you from slime balls, like this guy!"

Lucy kept her voice steady. "I'm not dating!"

"All eyes are on you, all the time. I can't rest for a second!"

"I know!" Lucy yelled. "I walk into a room and everyone is staring at me! It always feels like I have ants crawling all over my body. That's all the eyes in the room roving all over me!"

"Exactly!" Armand waved the point of his switchblade around in front of my pupil. "What about this ant? I should poke his fuckin' eye out!"

Lucy gave me a despairing look. "No! Leave him alone."

"Are you sure?"

"Yes!" Lucy yelled.

Armand released his grip and shoved me away in one quick motion of his arm. "Fine! But you gotta stop wearing those 'fuck me' jeans. They're way too damn tight."

Lucy glared at her brother. "I'll wear whatever I want to wear, Armand."

"You're just askin' to get stared at, dressin' like that," Armand groused.

I'm not sure what possessed me to speak, but I wanted to help the girl who had just helped me. "It ain't her clothes, man. She's gorgeous. Guys'll stare if she's in a burlap sack."

Mrs. Navarro looked like she was about to wail in horror when I said this, but Armand seemed to hear what I was saying. "She'd still be a beautiful in a burlap sack, wouldn't she?"

Mrs. Navarro cut in. "Can we all return to our seats now?"

Lucy grabbed Armand by the wrist and dragged him out into the hallway to give him a piece of her mind.

Mrs. Navarro looked me over, trying to see if I had any cuts of me. When I seemed fine, but only shaken, she asked me to sit down. She left to pour me a glass of water from her sink.

Mitchell put a protective hand on my shoulder. "Are you okay?"

"'If your right eye causes you to sin,'" I croaked, "'gouge it out and throw it away.'"

"That was all my fault." Mitchell seemed twice as shaken as I was.

As usual, I was numb. The horror wouldn't settle on me until later, when I tried to go to sleep.

I forced a smile to reassure him. "Think about it. I'm lonely and heartsick. She's ripe. Armand's a maniac. That encounter was inevitable."

"Yeah, but I brought you here and made you look."

"Listen, you're absolutely right about her having some Serious Badonk able to pass the Quarter Test. The real irony is that Armand sees me as this enormous threat to his sister's chastity, when I don't know the first thing about sex."

"You know, there's not that much to know about sex. It's just people squelching, really."

"'Squelching'?" I stuck my tongue out like I'd licked a toad. "Dude. That's mad gross." A thought struck me and I laughed. "Hey, guess what? I'm not sure Lucy's dumb."

Mitchell joined me, laughing. "I was wrong about that, too!"

"That was pretty hot when she defended me," I said. "You think I should ask her out?"

"Don't you dare!" Mitchell punched me in the shoulder.

My crooked smile was back. "So, let me see if I understand your line of thinking here: You wanted to teach me how to forget wanting Marina. Your strategy was to point out a second hot Italian bitch I'm not allowed to have? So's I can obsess over her, too? I'm not sure that improves my situation! And how's ogling a perfect ten supposed to teach me to pick girls apart?"

Mitchell ran a hand through his hair. "I thought Lucy would show that there are better looking girls than Marina. And that we could also find something wrong with Lucy, too."

"I'm not sure there's *anything* wrong with Lucy."

"Okay, so I didn't pick the best example for my lesson."

I sighed. "That bit when she was talking about the ants on her? I felt awful for her."

"It's true for all attractive girls. That's how us guys make them feel. It must be something walking into a room knowing everyone in it wants to fuck you."

"And she's stuck with that brother of hers!"

Mitchell frowned. "Yeah."

I felt myself getting angry again. "I bet real money that guy's Sicilian."

Mitchell smashed his fist down on the table in frustration, startling me. "I hate this fucking school!"

January 22, 1988

That same day, in chorus, Mrs. Laird reshuffled the positions of the singers based on our rapidly changing voices. The sopranos were now in the front row. The altos were in the middle, and tenors and baritones in the back. Now a baritone, I remained in the back row. My two shoulder-pad-wearing tormentors moved up a row to join the altos. Funny how the smallest change could resolve one of the biggest problems. A terrible chapter in my life had ended with a wave of the teacher's magic wand and no fanfare at all.

Kyle Ahearne joined me in the back. He'd dropped from soprano to tenor overnight. Sandy haired, with a strong chin, and crystal eyes, Kyle reassured me with his "young Franco Nero" presence. *If I find a genie in a lamp, one of my three wishes will be to look like Franco Nero in his prime in* Django *or* Camelot. A tennis instructor in training from an extended family of police officers and nurses, Kyle harbored a lot of secret anger and pain that he released through wise-cracking, teasing, and unexpected outbursts. He didn't tell me much about his life other than that his mom divorced his father for gambling and drinking too much and replaced him with a man who was a hundred times more abusive. Kyle's favorite book was *This Boy's Life* by Tobias Wolff, because he said it was essentially his life story. Other than those tidbits of information, and his angry references to his stepfather as "Mr. Personality," Kyle was guarded and his home life mysterious. Whatever demons Kyle had to deal with in secret, he was unusually kind to me. While most others found my perspective irritating or unfathomable, Kyle was perceptive about my thoughts and feelings even when I left them unexpressed.

Reseated, it was time for us to take the first exam of the spring semester. "Damien will be singing the song 'The Green Door,'" Mrs.

Laird announced. "It was written by Bob Davie and Marvin Moore, and most famously sung by Jim Lowe in 1956."

I stood and made my way to the front of the room, hoping that the lyrics wouldn't give away why I picked the song. The students weren't all watching me, but enough had their eyes on me to make me self-conscious. My performance anxiety flared up, causing ghost nausea and a dread of making eye-contact with my audience. Mrs. Laird played the intro and I started to sing. "The Green Door" is a song about an insomniac finding himself wandering the city at night, coming across a green speakeasy entrance. Not sure if it is a bar, jazz club, brothel, or something even cooler, the insomniac knocks on the door. It opens a crack, but his attempt to guess the password fails and the door slams shut in his face. He stays outside the green door, listening to the sounds of laughter and an old piano playing up-tempo, sensual music, wondering what secrets the closed door is keeping from him. I did a respectable job singing, starting tentatively, but getting better as I went along. By the time I reached the line, "All I want to do is join the happy crowd behind the green door," I sang it with a melancholy so profound I surprised myself. When I finished, every instinct urged me to sprint to the back of the room and hide my head under my seat. Smiling through gritted teeth, I willed myself to stay in place.

Jumping to his feet, clapping his meaty hands together, Kyle Ahearne of the blue eyes and blonde five-o'clock shadow yelled, "Go, Cavalieri, go! That was the bomb!" This fellow who had been so quiet all year that I hadn't known who he was when Marina mentioned him was now whooping it up on my behalf. Kyle wasn't clapping just because he felt bad for me, and the other students weren't clapping sarcastically. I had done well! My weak sauce opening hadn't spoiled the performance after all. I didn't want the spell to break, so I remained stock still. Since I couldn't express my gratitude through a stone face, I imagined Sally Field in my head, feeling the right emotion on my behalf, crying and beaming, "I've wanted more than anything to have your respect . . . and . . . right now, you like me!"

Only one fellow seated in the front row wasn't entertained: Eddie Squillante of the bushy unibrow. After the clapping subsided, Eddie started sawing his index finger back and forth in the air over his thumb.

"This is the world's smallest violin playing just for you."

My temper flared. "And it's being played by the kid with the world's smallest penis."

Kyle Ahearne guffawed.

Mrs. Laird held up a hand to silence us. "Okay, enough." She regarded me thoughtfully. "You've developed a nice baritone."

"Thank you, Mrs. Laird."

"For our next concert, we're doing music from *Phantom of the Opera.*"

She had my attention. "Oh? I like that one! I listen to that CD every day."

Alto Arwen Undómiel Pokatny looked aghast. "Really? That musical is so trivial. One simple song played on repeat for three hours. And Sarah Brightman can't even sing!"

She can't? I think her voice is sexy. And there's lots of songs!

Mrs. Laird nodded at Arwen. "I know what you mean, but it is still a fun piece of popular music for us to perform." She looked at me. "We are performing three songs as an ensemble, but we need a soloist to play the Phantom during 'Music of the Night' and the title duet."

I didn't hear a shoe hit the floor. "Are you asking me?"

"Yes," said Mrs. Laird.

"Why him?" complained Eddie Squillante. "He gets too nervous!"

Assuming a measured voice, Arwen Undómiel Pokatny chimed in to help me. "With the right coaching, Damien could excel. He has a tinge of the romantic hero about him that we can play up for effect. Yes, he gets self-conscious and goes off the rails sometimes. Still, if he takes the time he needs to warm up before the performance, he'll be wonderful."

Mrs. Laird inclined her head at me. "You'll just have to work extra hard to channel the spirit of the Phantom. You're at your best when you stop mimicking other people's styles and make a piece of music your own. You'll need to infuse these songs with genuine emotion."

I regarded my bitten-down fingernails. "I don't think channeling him will be a problem for me."

*

January 25, 1988

Mrs. Hall sat at her desk, scanning my fifth-grade report card. She noted a steady arc of improvement from the array of "U"s for "Unsatisfactory" during the first quarter period that built gradually to all "E"s for "Excellent" in the fourth quarter. She also held a letter by Mr. Altman, who voiced his confusion over my placement in mainstream and vouched for my belonging in the gifted program at the Robert Loggia School based on my performance in his ALEC class. Mitchell and I sat across from her as she perused these materials.

"Mr. Altman makes a strong case for Damien, right?" Mitchell asked.

Mrs. Hall regarded Mitchell with amused interest. "Are you his lawyer?"

"I'm the Sherry in Sherry, Bennett, Robbins, Oppenheim, and Taft."

Mrs. Hall chuckled and kept reading.

Nervous, I looked about the room. I decided that I liked Mrs. Hall's office. It was far more tastefully decorated than the other administrative offices I knew, and I'd never been thrown out of it. She had real plants instead of plastic ones, original framed art instead of the usual mall prints, and bookshelves filled with books worth reading. A song I'd never heard before, "Swing to Bop" by Charlie Christian, played from speakers mounted in the ceiling corners.

"I'm not sure how I wound up separated from the other ALEC students," I interjected. "A clerical error, maybe? We were hoping you could correct it."

Mrs. Hall looked from the package of evidence we had assembled to her internal dossier on me. "Isn't it a bit late to be dealing with all this? Your GPA is perfect, so you'll wind up in honors next year, anyway. If you move now, your freshman year will be disrupted."

"He'd prefer to switch now," Mitchell said.

"If the classes aren't all full," Mrs. Hall said.

"There'll be an opening," Mitchell reassured her. "Today is my last day. I'm transferring to a Jesuit school in Manhattan tomorrow." I couldn't have been more ambivalent about Mitchell's decision to leave, since his departure created an opening for me in the gifted class.

Mrs. Hall said, "I'll fix your schedule today, Damien. You will go to your new classes tomorrow." She paused. "Oh, wait a minute! I don't think there's a gifted section of Italian."

Looking "shocked," I placed my hand to my lips. "Really? No honors Italian class?"

Mitchell was even better at feigning surprise. "Wow. That's . . . news to us."

"Such a shame," I sighed. "Still, if it is possible to stay in my current Italian class and chorus elective and change all the other classes into honors sections, then that would be the most elegant and effective possible arrangement for my purposes."

Mitchell gestured deferentially to Mrs. Hall. "If it isn't too much trouble, of course."

Mrs. Hall frowned. "Why would it be too much trouble? I'll have this fixed for you five minutes after you leave this office."

"Magnificent," I said.

"I'm sorry this has happened to you," she said. "Such a strange clerical error."

"Isn't it?" Mitchell asked.

"Very strange," I agreed. "So, so odd."

It took some restraint not celebrating the second Mitchell and I made it out into the corridor. We walked several yards down the windowless, tiled, gray hallway before I felt safe to whisper, "You're such a mensch! I think you just saved me from a total nervous breakdown."

"You're welcome," said Mitchell. "Though there were a few moments there when you were so nervous, we almost snatched defeat from the jaws of victory."

"Are you kidding? I was so suave and polished in there!" I declared, laughing at myself.

"You didn't like lying, so you were 'confessing' by acting guilty. Only, you don't need to feel bad. She knew we were up to something and didn't care because she saw your great grades. And she likes us. Basically, she put you in honors because she's nice, fair, and competent."

"Isn't 'competent administrator' an oxymoron?" I joked.

"Here's the thing about navigating bureaucracy: the right hand doesn't know what the left is doing. If the right hand says, 'no,' ask the left. The left will probably say 'yes' and hand you the right paperwork. I had a feeling Mrs. Hall was the most reasonable administrator."

"More reasonable than John Thomas Pecker? How is that possible?"

"That guy!" Mitchell laughed. "He blows dead moose!"

"I love the 'clerical error' angle you came up with. It makes it all just an easily fixable mistake instead of me asking for special treatment or accusing them of being anti-Italian."

As we walked, Mitchell fished a massive, hardcover copy of Stephen King's *It* out of his backpack. "This is really good, by the way. It is pretty much the story of our year here. I think Dietrich Krebs is Pennywise." Based on the position of his bookmark, he was two-thirds done.

I laughed. "Look at that thing! It's huge! I can't take all that in!"

Mitchell laughed, too. "That's what *she* said!"

I paused. "Mrs. Hall agrees that Stephen King needs a more aggressive editor?"

Mitchell considered explaining his joke to me but decided against it. "Never mind. Seriously, you should get Mrs. Hall a gift to thank her. Something like a Whitman's Sampler."

"I'd rather buy myself a Whitman's Sampler," I groused.

"Don't be a cheapskate! She just saved your bacon."

"I come from a long line of cheapskates!"

"Come on."

"Okay, I'll get her a damn Whitman's Sampler. But I really don't like buying gifts for other people. It cuts into my comic-book-buying budget."

"Where's your gratitude? You've heard of karma, right? Get some good karma. Put some good energy out there by buying her a box of chocolates. Then the good energy will come back."

"Boy, do I love distributing bad energy and buying myself comic books!"

Mitchell gave me a friendly warning look. "Just remember, Mrs. Hall can always change her mind and put your ass right back where she found it."

I frowned. "Why are you always tryin' to cheer me up?"

"I'm just trying to get you all set up here before I leave for my new school."

"You've done so much for me, Mitchell. You're kind of incredible. It makes me wonder." I lowered my voice to an awed whisper. "Are you Jesus?"

"Nah! I don't know if Jesus would go for all my charcoal drawings of nude women. Not that I was drooling when I did them. They're art, after all. And I'm not like that. But I still can't imagine Jesus drawing as many nude women as I do."

"You'd be surprised," I said. "I've seen Jesus' sketchbook. Our Lord and Savior loves drawing Varga-Girl-style pinups. He specializes in plump, rosy-cheeked innocents getting their skirts blown up by a gust of wind or their panties pulled off by a mischievous cocker spaniel."

"That's a pretty strange comedy monologue, even for you."

I smacked Mitchell across the top of his shoulder. "And what's with this transferring shit? I'm going to be in the gifted class now. You should stick around!"

To his credit, Mitchell mulled this over for a full minute. "I can't stay here. And I can't handle being in the same class as Dietrich Krebs anymore. He's relentless with the bullying."

"I'm surprised you'd allow yourself to be chased off by anyone."

Mitchell stopped walking abruptly, forcing me to come to a stop, too. "Listen," he said, "tomorrow is your first day in the same class with that guy. What you need to do is establish your alpha male status right away. Krebs is going to come right up to you to mess with you. You need to scare the living shit out of him right away, or he will never leave you alone."

I exhaled sharply through my nose. "That's not my style."

"I know that! I don't care! You have to do it!"

"I don't think I have it in me to just up and attack someone at first sight."

"You don't have to have it in you. Just convince him you do. Remember what Sun Tzu wrote: 'Appear strong when you are weak and weak when you are strong.'"

I offered Mitchell my crooked smile. "I have a different motto: 'Appear weak when you are weak and weak when you are strong.'"

Mitchell snickered. "You're impossible. Remind me why I like you again?"

Continuing to act as my guardian angel for the day, Mitchell introduced me to the school's only librarian, Anita Duchamps, a genial, low-key woman too nice to work at this ridiculous school. After completing the introductions, Mitchell turned to say farewell. "We can still hang after school, but this feels like a big goodbye."

To prevent myself from breaking down right there, I extended my index finger towards Mitchell's forehead and said in my best, croaky E.T. voice, "Beeeeeee gooooooood."

Mitchell hugged me. It was a real hug, not a half hug, or one that came with a painful back slap to seem more masculine. "Keep in touch."

"I will," I said.

I thought I was telling the truth.

Mrs. Duchamps led me into an office behind the check-out desk. Two students sat across from each another, eating bagged lunches and reading books in a small office filled with a square, white table too large for it. Tall, slender, and all in black, the girl was *The Rocky and Bullwinkle Show's* Natasha Fatale come to life. Her co-worker, the tiny blonde-boy, perused a dog-eared copy of Frank Herbert's *Dune* while finishing a Capri Sun and egg-salad sandwich.

"We have a refugee," Mrs. Duchamps informed the other library monitors. "He's a bit shell-shocked, but willing to work." She introduced the others to me as David Litvinov and Miriam Pokatny, then left us together. I decided to stay standing until invited to sit. "Greetings."

David took another sip of his Capri Sun. "If you're named after the kid from *The Omen* with the three sixes under his hair, then your parents like horror movies way too much."

"I kinda like being the Antichrist." I gestured towards the *Dune* book. "Is it any good? I had a feeling it would be too serious for me since it's all about Middle Eastern politics."

David melodramatically laughed in Miriam's face. "You see? I told you! If you really want to join the Mossad, you should read this first. Best book ever on the Arab-Israeli conflict."

Miriam waved an angry finger in David's face. "I'm not reading any book recommended to me by a PLO sympathizer! You and your 'two-state solution based on pre-1967 borders.'"

"All the cool Jews are on my side," David said primly. "Harvey Pekar, Leonard Nimoy, Wallace Shawn, and a bunch more! Who's on your side? Jewish Republicans? Barf." David whispered to me, "She'll never forgive the Muslims for the Munich Olympics."

"I see." I didn't. *Did they use steroids to beat the Israelis at figure skating, or something?*

David jerked a thumb in my direction. "He doesn't seem too bad for an Italian."

"There's a low bar, right there," Miriam said. "Anti-Semites and homophobes to a man."

"You're so *militant!*" David looked at me and mouthed: "She's *so* militant!"

Miriam stared David down. "You'd be militant, too, if your grandfather had a concentration camp identification number tattoo on his arm."

"You think mine didn't?" David gestured to the seat next to him. "Please sit, Mr. Antichrist. You're making me nervous standing there like one of the Queen's Guard."

I took a seat at the third side of the square table, between the others, but didn't uncoil.

"You're a book-reader, then?" David asked me. "I have this question I ask all readers: 'If you had to live inside one work of literature forever, what would it be?'"

I relaxed. *I love that question.* "I've thought about this a lot. I have three answers to that. My first instinct is to say *The Hobbit*, because I relate strongly to Bilbo and love reading the story, but I think living in the book wouldn't be much fun, because I'd be terrified of giant spiders and the dragon all the time. My serious answer is Christine De Pizan's *City of Ladies*, because it'd mean living out my life in a utopia populated by kind, wise, and brilliant women. Unfortunately, they'd never actually let me live there, so there goes that choice, on a practical level. My wise-ass answer, in total poor taste, is *The Decameron*: Ninth Day, Sixth Story, 'Pinuccio and Adriano,' but only if I get to be Pinuccio."

"I don't know it," said David. "Is there a lot of sex in that story?"

"Maybe," I said.

David laughed and glanced at Miriam. "He's funny, right?"

Miriam blew a raspberry. "A man making a sex joke? How unheard of."

"For a dick joke, it was pretty literary," David remarked.

"Okay, just kidding," I said. "I want to be in *A Cold Wind in August* by Burton Wohl."

"Is that another dick joke?" asked Miriam.

"I refuse to answer on the ground that I may incriminate myself," I said.

Miriam feigned some interest in me. "Okay. Let's have it. What's your story?"

I slipped my raincoat off and draped it over the back of my chair. It was long enough that the bottom splayed out on the floor behind me. "I'm on the lookout for new friends. Been going through resumes and cover letters but haven't seen many promising candidates."

"It is so hard to hire good friends these days," David joked.

"Any way you can send me a one-page CV? Nobody ever reads page two. If the hiring committee isn't gripped by the end of the first paragraph, it gets placed in the circular file."

David adopted an expression of mock terror. "Ah! File 13! Don't want to end up there. I'll polish my resume and cover letter and print them both up on the ol' dot matrix."

Miriam propped her chin up on her fist and looked from one of us to the other. "I see you two will be getting along like a house on fire."

"Booyah!" I yelled.

Miriam slid back in her chair and was silent for a full minute. When she spoke next, the ambient temperature plummeted, and David looked intimidated. "David, I *still* want that name."

I perked up. "Whose name?"

David looked suspiciously apologetic. "We were talking about something before you arrived. She wants to know who her stepsister likes. 'Like' as in '*like* like,' not just 'like.'"

"You have a stepsister?" I asked.

"Arwen. We have the same last name: Pokatny." Miriam looked me up and down, reluctant to tell me more. "Do you know her?"

"I'm terrible with names," I said. "I might know her by sight. When I get introduced to people, I get so nervous, I instantly forget their names."

Miriam nodded. "I'm Miriam and he's David."

David waved. "Howdy."

"Hi," I said.

David looked at me sideways. "Seriously? You don't know Arwen? At all?"

"No. Who is she?"

"You'll get to meet her soon," Miriam said. "She's the fourth library monitor. That reminds me, we better wrap this up before she gets back. I want that name, David."

"Why does it matter who she likes?" I asked.

"Her parents don't want her dating anyone who isn't Jewish," David explained.

"Intermarriage is killing the Jewish faith," Miriam pronounced.

"And yet Jerry Stiller and Anne Meara seem so happy," David replied sarcastically. "Why do you all care so much who Arwen fucks? What business is it of yours?"

"It is all about business," Miriam replied. "If she wants to inherit her share of Pokatny Confections, she better not let any gentiles in her pants, or she's out of the will."

I perked up. "Pokatny Confections! Wild! Y'all make the best cupcakes!"

Miriam talked over me. "You'd think being warned a thousand times to date inside the faith would be enough, but nooooooo! Now I'm hearing she's sniffing around some shegetz."

"A boy who isn't Jewish, or a Jewish boy who isn't Jewish enough," David explained.

"Ah," I said. "Gotcha."

"Thankfully," Miriam continued, "I hear he may not like her back."

"Do tell," said David.

"I heard she's been watching him from afar, and he doesn't even know who she is. That she wants to introduce herself to him any day now, but she's afraid to. Why? He isn't into tomboys and may have the hots for someone else. I've heard *a lot*. I have not heard his name."

"Gee, I wonder why," David muttered.

"Miriam, you can't control who you fall for," I said. "I've fallen head-over-heels for someone in band who isn't *remotely* interested in me. And I was kinda smitten with my dad's cousin a while back. I've got a crush on my martial arts instructor at the moment. That's not going anywhere. I even like my religion teacher. In fact, I'm getting scared that I'm only ever gonna be hot for unattainable women. Anyway, I'm glad I'm not going to risk losing my inheritance over who I fantasize about, especially if I can't have them anyway. Imagine getting in trouble for having feelings and not acting on them! You shouldn't be so hard on her, Miriam."

The office door opened, and Arwen walked in. She had a round face but a strong, dimpled chin, wore half-moon eyeglasses and black hair in a pull-through ponytail. She wore a black MA-1 flight jacket covered in left-wing political badges, a black Alien Sex Fiend T-shirt, and black stretch twill pants. She saw me and stopped short. Recovering an instant later, she slid her backpack under the table as she sat across from me. "Welcome to the eye of the storm. We have all our classes together, but I keep to myself, so you may not recognize me. I am Arwen."

"Obviously, her parents like *Lord of the Rings*," David joked. "Ironically, they didn't think her name through. They really should have picked Éowyn instead."

"Oh, of course! It took me a second, but I know you." I wondered why I didn't already know the name of the person who vouched for me becoming the phantom of the opera and who joked around with me about Conan while Orlov tried to cut me down to size. "I'm not good with faces and names. I look at my shoes a lot to avoid making eye contact with people."

A look of pain flitted across Arwen's face. "I have seen the pressure others have placed upon you and I am not surprised."

Miriam cut in. "I was just asking David if he had any idea who your secret crush is."

Arwen spun in her seat and stared back into her stepsister's eyes. "I think, perhaps, you relish your role as father's spy a little too much?"

Miriam smiled sweetly. "If it isn't a gentile, you have nothing to worry about."

Arwen glanced at David. "Catch me up. Have any suspects' names been bandied about?"

David shook his head. "Nope."

"What is he, Catholic?" Miriam asked. "Lutheran? Episcopalian?"

Arwen feigned innocence. "I haven't admitted to being attracted to anyone."

"I overheard you tell David he's a bit like an American John Lennon," said Miriam.

"John Lennon!" I tutted. "That arrogant son of a bitch?"

Arwen could not have looked more confused. "You of all people dislike John Lennon?"

I placed my hand over my heart. "Personally, I'm not into all this Beatles worship crap. And I don't just automatically like something because I'm told I'm supposed to. I'm sorry, *Gone with the Wind* and *Macbeth,* you both bore and annoy me. Besides, John Lennon doesn't need me to like him. He's more popular than Jesus."

Arwen was still astonished. "What about 'Imagine'? That song speaks to most people."

"I hate that song most of all. Lennon wants to achieve world peace by obliterating all cultural differences and making us into hive-minded drones. I don't want my religion or ethnicity bleached out of me. Besides, the song is emotionally dishonest. It is obviously filled with rage but is presented as a syrupy sweet ballad. If there's one thing I can't stand, it's a phony."

Arwen's expression went from surprised to amused and relieved. "Ironically, I think Lennon would respect you for having this opinion."

I was intrigued, despite my obstinacy. "Oh?"

Arwen explained: "In 1971, Paul McCartney made the mistake of telling *Melody Maker* magazine he preferred the idealistic, apolitical Lennon who wrote 'Imagine' to the enraged and preachy Lennon who wrote 'Working-Class Hero.' When Lennon read this, he mocked McCartney in an open letter response that said, 'So you think "Imagine" ain't political? It's "Working Class Hero" with sugar on it for conservatives like yourself!'"

I chuckled. "Man, he hated McCartney by the end! I didn't know it got that bad."

Arwen looked thoughtful. "He never liked the imposter McCartney much. I think he had genuine affection for the original before he died."

"Wait. What?" I scratched my head. "Isn't John the only dead Beatle?"

"A story for another time," Arwen said.

"'The walrus was Paul,'" Miriam said sadly. "'Paul is dead.'"

"Good lord," David muttered. "You two girls and that ridiculous conspiracy theory!"

"I have another question," I said. "What's 'Working-Class Hero?'"

Arwen said, "I'll wager it will become your new favorite song when you finally hear it."

"What makes you so sure?" I asked.

"Would you happen to know your Myers-Briggs Type Indicator personality category?"

I shrugged. "I don't know what that is."

"I'm certain that you are an INFP: Introversion, Intuition, Feeling, Perception. The mediator and idealist. If you are an INFP, that places you in the same category as Mr. Rogers, J.R.R. Tolkien, A. A. Milne, George Orwell, and John Lennon. That would make you the opposite of the ESTJ: the supervisor: Andrew Jackson, Eliot Ness, and Jerry Falwell."

"'Supervisor?' I don't gel with businessmen or soldiers, so that makes sense," I admitted. "As to INFP, I'm proud to be lumped in with Tolkien and Mr. Rogers. Shame about John Lennon."

Arwen smirked. "You dope! You *are* John Lennon."

"Bah!" I snorted. "Bah, I say! I just got here and already I'm being insulted."

Miriam cleared her throat loudly. Arwen, David, and I turned as one to look at her. She pointed an angry finger in my direction while glaring at her stepsister. "I don't know what you think you're playing at, Arwen, but there's no way in hell you'll be allowed to date this guy."

"Um . . . what?" I asked.

Arwen did yeoman work looking innocent. "Whatever do you mean, Miriam?"

Miriam turned her furious eyes on me. "What are your intentions with my sister?"

I assumed a defensive posture, holding up both hands. "Whoa! What are you talking about? I don't want any trouble here. I just want to work as a library monitor in peace."

"If you're the one she's been mooning over, you'll get no peace," Miriam warned.

Poised, polished, and angry, Arwen gave her stepsister her most withering Lauren Bacall look. "I have not been mooning over Damien."

Miriam glared at me. "What about you? Have you been mooning over Arwen?"

I lowered my hands onto my lap and tried to look calm. "You don't have to worry about the fate of Pokatny Confections. I'm not a threat. I'm in . . . deep '*like* like' with Marina Dazzo."

Arwen nodded vigorously. "That's true. He is madly in love with her. Everyone knows."

I winced. *Madly in love? Everyone knows? Gadzooks!* "Arwen is not one-hundred-percent my type, anyway, but I'd like us to be friends, if she'll stop comparing me to Lennon."

Miriam looked back and forth between Arwen and me. "You two better behave yourselves, or I'm telling Father." She rose, shook her head in disgust, and walked out.

David exhaled the breath he had been holding in for three minutes. "I saw my whole life flash before my eyes when you walked in, Damien. You've strolled right into a minefield here."

I looked at Arwen pleadingly. "Did I? Look, I just want a safe place to go where I can eat lunch and not get into a fistfight. I don't want to cause a calamity."

Arwen's tone and facial expressions were startlingly devoid of obvious emotion. "My father's parents disowned him when he married an Irish Catholic girl. She died of leukemia not long after giving birth to me. Dad felt like he'd lost everything. Then he married again: A Jewish widow with one daughter. She was healthy and wouldn't die on him. Dad's parents took him back. These days, he thinks marrying my mom was the biggest mistake of his life. He's trying to protect me from experiencing the agony he went through, so he's barring me from

even associating with non-Jews, let alone dating or marrying them."
Arwen took a John Lennon CD from her bag and gave it to me. "Do
me a favor. Listen to 'Working-Class Hero.'"

I glanced at the CD, dubiously. "Okay, fine, but what's with your
Willy Wonka empire? You're not in danger of losing it because of me?
That's a hell of a burden to put on me."

Arwen's voice caught for the first time. "If I were you, I would
not worry about it. After all, I am not one-hundred-percent your type
and you are in love with Marina Dazzo."

CHAPTER FIFTEEN
The Volcano People of Vesuvius

January 26, 1988

I wore my grey pinstripe suit with a purple dress shirt to my first day of gifted program classes at Robert Loggia Intermediate School. I strode confidently into a standard public-school classroom decorated with Shakespeare, Jane Austen, and Mark Twain portrait-and-aphorism posters. The teacher wasn't there yet, but six of my old ALEC classmates flocked to greet me. Expressions of relief at my being back and outrage at my having been refused entry into the program in the first place felt validating. Grateful to be reunited with Ari Zuckerman and the others, I surprised myself by having to suppress tears. The problem, of course, was that Mitchell was gone. Had I chosen to study Spanish, I would have been placed in this class with Mitchell on day one. We could have stood side-by-side against bullies like Dietrich Krebs, protecting ourselves and Tsvi-Mayer together. Since I was not here to support Mitchell, Dietrich had driven him away. Now, Mitchell was gone, I was here without him, and it was only a matter of time before I had my first encounter with Dietrich.

"What's with the fucking suit?" asked a lazy, nasal voice coming from behind me.

I whipped around to face a square-headed, blonde-haired, blue-eyed jerk in a white sweater and acid washed jeans. "Dietrich Krebs! How are you? How's the wife and kids?"

"Do I know you?" Dietrich glanced about for evidence he was on *Candid Camera.*

"Of course! I'm the Joker!" I produced a number two lead pencil from my pocket and pointed it like a rapier at Dietrich's chest.

Dietrich eyed the pencil point hovering over him. "Watch where you're pointing that."

"I'm the patron saint of nerd rage, misunderstood artists, and failed comedians. I'm smart, funny, and purple!"

"Never heard of you," scoffed Dietrich. "And those clothes aren't in style! What kinda loser wears a suit to school?"

"I wear what I want to wear when I want to wear it. And I do what I want to do when I want to do it." I sprang upon Dietrich, snatched him by the throat, and slammed him up against the wall. Adrenaline, fear, and fury consumed me. I felt only the throbbing pulse in my temple. It was someone else speaking when I placed my lips near his ear and hissed, "Don't fuck with me. If you fuck with me, or any other student in this room, I swear to God, I will end you. You won't know when, or where, but I will come for you, and I will end you. Do you hear me?"

Dietrich was so shocked he had been attacked that he offered no resistance. I had expected him to punch, kick, or spit at me. He just stared. That's when it sank in. Dietrich didn't know me. He didn't know I was gentle at heart. He didn't know I was terrified of him. He didn't even get my comic-book-villain inside joke. All he knew was I was an insane stranger attacking him with a pencil. *Appear strong when you are weak and weak when you are strong. Sun Tzu.*

After five seconds of eternity, Dietrich went limp. "I'll be cool. I promise."

I let him go and backed away, keeping the pencil up, my eyes fixed on his. I took my seat just in time for the English teacher to walk in holding enough copies of *The Bell Jar* for everyone in the class. Realizing he was the last student left standing, Dietrich sat down. That's when I caught Tsvi-Mayer giving me two enthusiastic thumbs up from the front of the room. I smiled and mirrored the two thumbs up. It hadn't even noticed that David Litvinov was sitting behind me until I heard him say, "I have to admit, I'm impressed."

"That was cool when I committed assault and battery," I tried and failed to whisper.

"It kinda was, actually," said David. "That was a rock-solid Richard Widmark, too."

I grinned. "I'm so pleased you noticed."

David grabbed my shoulders in approval and admiration. "You really are the G.O.A.T.!"

I arched my right eyebrow in confusion. "I'm a *goat*? How am I a goat?"

Dietrich's tinny voice rang out. "Miss Katz! The new kid just attacked me with a pencil."

Miss Katz gave him a "Boy that Cried Wolf" look over the rim of her glasses. "Damien? That doesn't sound like him."

How does Miss Katz know me? Why does everyone know me already before I meet them?

"Ask anyone!" Dietrich yelled.

Miss Katz began distributing the copies of *The Bell Jar*. "Ari, did you see anything?"

"Nothing at all," Ari lied.

Miss Katz cast her eyes around the rest of the class. "Anyone see anything?"

All the students shook their heads back and forth.

I'm home, I thought.

January 27, 1988

Sitting on the living room couch, Mom graded remedial writing assignments while keeping the daytime soap opera *One Life to Live* on in the background. Conventional on the surface, the soap improbably embraced science fiction storytelling during my junior high school years and had me hooked. From 1987 to 1990, I was wowed by storylines in which Clint Buchanan traveled back in time to the Old West and had a gunfight at high noon with his own great-grandfather, the evil Patrick had extensive plastic surgery to look just like Bo Buchanan and took over Bo's life, and Victoria Lord's high school reunion unearthed repressed memories of teenage years she'd spent living in the subterranean city Eterna — before her villainous father kidnapped and mindwiped her. It helped that the actresses were charismatic and their characters likable. Also, I had a man crush on the funny adventurer Max Holden, played by Italian American actor James DePaiva. On today's suspenseful episode, Victoria asked her sister Tina, "Who do you really love: Max or Cord?" The camera zoomed in on Tina's conflicted face. Cue dramatic music. Fade to black.

"Pick Max!" I yelled at the television.

"I prefer Cord," Mom said.

The first commercial of the set showed an older woman and her fully grown daughter walking along the beach together. "Mom," the young woman began, "do you douche?"

"Every day," the mother replied. "But only with Massengill Vinegar and Water."

I've seen this commercial five hundred times and I'm still not sure what the hell a douche is. Is Massengill used to rise out the inside of a vagina? It must be, right? What else could it be?

"Mom?"

"Yes?" Mom asked absently, not looking up from the paper she was grading.

I wasn't comfortable asking about the douche, but there was another thing I was also tired of not understanding. "This guy at school named Salty told me a math joke I don't understand. I was hoping I could tell you it and you could explain it to me."

"Okay." Mom used her red pen to correct a misspelling of the word "believe."

"'What goes into thirteen twice?'"

"I don't know. What?"

"'Roman Polanski.'"

Mom kept her eyes down on the paper. "Oh, that's *disgusting.*"

"I can't figure out why the answer isn't 'six-point-five.' Can you figure it out?"

"It isn't a math joke. Don't go around repeating it to people."

"Who's Roman Polanski?"

"*Never mind* who he is."

God damn it, Salty.

February 19, 1988

Dad discovered me in the basement, laying on my back on the black-and-tan shag carpet, listening to "Teenager in Love" for the hundredth time on the first vinyl album Mom purchased: 1959's *Presenting Dion and the Belmonts.* "Put on some different music, will ya?" he asked.

"'There is love in me the likes of which you've never seen. There is rage in me the likes of which should never escape. If I am not satisfied in one, I shall indulge the other.'"

"Good *Frankenstein* quote," Dad said. "I'm still tired of that album. Change it." He left.

I rose from the floor like a somnambulist. I put on the 1987 Broadway cast recording of *Les Misérables*. I dropped the needle on Frances Ruffelle's "On My Own" fifteen times.

Dad reappeared on the sixteenth run-through. "What the hell is wrong with you?"

"'The world is full of happiness that I have never known.'"

"Put on some happier music, will ya? You're depressing me." Dad left.

Listlessly, I switched to Dad's new acquisition, the single "Make Me Lose Control" by Eric Carmen. The song lifted my spirits. I sang along as I lay on the carpet. Then I spun "Obsession" by Animotion. Risking censure, I played both "What Becomes of the Broken Hearted" by Jimmy Ruffin and "Tennessee Waltz" by Patti Page three times.

Dad appeared again as night fell. "I don't want you eating dinner with this face on. When you're upset, you make your mother upset. When she's upset, she disturbs my peace."

I forced a smile. "How's this?"

"Ghastly. Your mood is a decision. If you decide you are happy, then you fake it for a moment and then you become happy. Stop indulging in whatever you're indulging in."

"Would you like to know why I'm upset?"

"We've got spaghetti carbonara tonight. I want to enjoy it in silence."

Dad and I joined Mom and Leo at the round, walnut-wood kitchen table. Dad poured the Diet Coke, filling each of our glasses up to one inch below the rim. "Thank God you finally got Diet Coke again, after subjecting us to all that Cream Soda."

"I like Cream Soda," Mom replied. "If you don't like it, you can buy the groceries."

"I'm thanking you for doing shopping smarter."

"I don't mind the Cream Soda, Mom," I said.

"Meathead," Dad muttered.

We ate in silence for several minutes.

"This carbonara is great," Dad said. "Never prepare it this way again."

What? Leo and I exchanged shocked and amused glances.

Mom adjusted her hearing aid to hear him better. It emitted a piercing whistle.

"That damn thing is going off again," Dad barked.

Mom fidgeted with her earpiece again. The electronic shriek ended. "What was that?"

"The carbonara is great," Dad said. "Use a different recipe next time."

"It was noticeably better last time," Leo agreed.

Mom looked crestfallen. "My carbonara isn't good?"

"What did you do to it?" Dad asked.

"Nothing," Mom said. "I used the same recipe."

Dad sighed. "You definitely did something different."

"I like it," I cut in. "I don't taste a big difference."

"I wish there were more girls in this house." Mom shook her head and looked down at her plate. "I work a full-time job. I come home and I have another full-time job cooking and cleaning this house from top-to-bottom. I guess I have the feminist movement to thank for that."

"You have us to thank," I said. "We don't pull our weight around here."

"I do plenty," Dad said. "I take out the garbage. Did you see me? I did it just now."

"What else do you do?" asked Leo.

Dad pretended not to hear the question.

"Dad and I can go shopping for you, Mom," I offered.

"You speak for yourself," Dad said.

"Oh, no," said Mom. "You'd both spend twice what I do on groceries. That time you two went, you didn't use coupons or buy generic brands. And you get strange, expensive things like gourmet salted caramel ice cream and cocktail shrimp. I don't need that kind of help."

Dad pointed at me. "That's mostly his fault."

"Let us try again," I said.

Mom refused.

"We should do the shopping," Dad said. "We wouldn't buy cream soda."

"What was that?" Mom asked.

Dad waved an irritated hand at Mom. "And that's another thing! She used to be Johnny on the spot with the Cheez Doodles, but she hasn't bought me any the last three shopping trips!"

"When did you decide you like Cheez Doodles?" I asked.

"I discovered them last year. I need my Cheez Doodles, and your mother won't buy them for me. How am I supposed to get my Cheez Doodles if she won't get them for me?"

Cheswick wants his cigarettes. "They're not scarce. You don't have to go to a speakeasy near St. Mark's Place in the Village, give them a secret password, and they hand you a bag of Cheez Doodles. Go to any CVS or corner grocery and get your own Cheez Doodles."

"I want her to get them for me!"

"Damn punk music!" I said to Leo. "Ever since Dad started listening to the Clash, gave himself a pink mohawk, and put safety pins on his clothes, it's like I don't know him anymore."

Dad gave Leo a helpless glance. "What's your brother talking about?"

Leo chuckled. "He's talking trash to rile you up."

"Dad, I fear your mohawk and everything it stands for."

"I wouldn't describe my hairstyle as particularly mohawk-like," Dad complained.

Fortunately, Mom's hearing aid had fizzed out three minutes before, so she missed the tail end of the carbonara conversation and the entirety of both the Cheez Doodles and mohawk exchanges. Since she had lost the thread of the conversation, her next remark was a complete non sequitur. "Have you made friends with any Italian kids yet, Damien?"

Leo scoffed. "*Italians?* Who needs *Italians?* Every time I read a letter to the editor in the *New York Post* about global warming being a hoax or there being no such thing as racism any more except Black people being against white people, guess what? As sure as night follows day, the moron who wrote it was an Italian. 'I hate science and Black people. Love, Tony Simplicio.'"

Mom heard none of that, so I just responded to her question. "I *finally* met someone nice. Marina Dazzo, the flute player in the band. She's one of the few kids who has been kind to me."

"Do you think she'd be a good friend?" Mom asked.

"She would, if I were in band. She's with that crowd. Life is full of cliques. I haven't found mine. And I keep looking for a kindred spirit on the order of Mitchell, but I haven't found anyone else who walks alone along the boulevard of broken dreams who isn't a sociopath."

Dad sighed. It was his warning for me not to wander into maudlin territory, or I'd risk spoiling his already compromised spaghetti carbonara dinner. "This talk is getting pretty heavy."

"And you haven't had to sit through his thoughts on the problem of evil," Leo joked.

Mom didn't hear Dad and kept talking to me. "I don't see why you can't just hang out with her when she's not in band."

"It isn't done," I said. "You hang with people in your hallway. Nobody further afield."

"What if you were dating?" Dad asked. "Could she find the time to see you then?"

"I left her a rose. Marina was touched on some level, but she was more frightened by how much I cared for her. She looked worried that she had my Chinese rice paper heart in her hand and she was accidentally going to crumple it. I've steered clear of her ever since."

Dad poked me in the shoulder. "Snap her bra! Classic way to show a girl you like her."

"No, Dad."

Dad grinned evilly. "If you want to know if a girl likes you, grab her tit. If she likes you, she'll kiss you. If she doesn't, she'll slap you. Ninety-nine out of a hundred women will slap you but keep trying until you find the one that won't. If you have to go through all ninety-nine women, and get ninety-nine slaps before you find the one who will let you grab her tit, it is worth all the slaps you had to take to get that welcomed tit squeeze in there."

"Dad, that seems like extraordinarily bad advice. If I don't wind up traumatizing ninety-nine women at a clip, I'll wind up in a straight jacket after getting slapped ninety-nine times in one evening. That kind of machine-gun rejection is not for me. No, thank you." I glanced over at my brother. "See? Dad's gotten so punk rock! Sid Vicious in da house!"

Trying to regain entry into the discussion after failing to lip-read the last several sentences, Mom said, "I'm glad you found a nice Italian girl. There will be more coming."

"Don't hold your breath," I said.

"Excellent!" Mom smiled.

Dad fell mute as he recalled the hundred-tit-grabs-a-night of his glory days.

Leo gave me a sympathetic look. "One can't hear and the other won't hear."

"Yeah."

"If you'd have played things differently, would Marina have gone out with you?"

"I can't imagine any scenario in which we wind up together, even as friends. I don't think snapping her bra would have garnered me a better result."

"And doing that wouldn't have been very 'on-brand' for you." Leo stared at me through his Buddy Holly glasses. "I hate to see you suffer like this. Dad does, too, but he expresses concern by grumping about you listening to music on repeat. His way of asking you if you are okay is telling you to change the record."

"That sounds right." I glanced at Dad, who was probably dreaming of Lucy the vampire.

Leo brightened. "I know what we should do. Fun brother stuff to take your mind off school crap! I say we get all our stuffed animals together and play with them for a while."

It was an excellent idea. Growing up watching Jim Henson Muppet films and television programs had left an indelible mark on our imaginations. Over the years, we had worked together to grant the stuffed animals in our joint collection complete personalities, personal histories, and comedy voices precisely because they were blank slates and not based on licensed properties. These were the plush, imaginatively designed Soft Classics, Cuddle Wit, and Beanie Baby brand stuffed animals that we had purchased in Toys R Us or won playing Skee-Ball on the boardwalk of Wildwood, NJ. In addition to playing casual stuffed animal games, we would get more ambitious by using Dad's film equipment to make stop-motion shorts featuring our stuffed animals. We would also use our tape decks to make fake radio shows using our character voices. One was a rockumentary about the band *Wee Claude and Mooch* and their life-changing 1978 single, "Eat My Poo Pellets." Another was a 1991 memorial to the 1,400-pound Walter Hudson, the World's Fattest Man, who had to be lowered by forklift into his grave when he died at 46.

"Then," Leo continued, "we make ourselves some peanut butter and jelly sandwiches and watch lots of *Doctor Who*. I say 'Aztecs,' 'Mind Robber,' 'Time Warrior,' and 'Sunmakers.'"

"'I love this plan'!" I yelled, directly quoting Bill Murray from *Ghostbusters*. "'I'm excited to be a part of it! Let's do it!'"

Our mother smiled, not quite knowing what was happening. Dad scowled and said into his plate, "Can you keep it down? I'm trying to eat this terrible carbonara!"

March 9, 1988

Salty and I sat in the dugout by our school baseball diamond, waiting for our next turn at bat. I kicked at the dirt floor with the front of my high-top sneakers. "I'm hitting foul balls like they're going out of style."

The Greek American was pleasantly surprised I had blasted ball after ball an amazing height into the air and forgave them for landing on the wrong side of the foul line each time. "I'm impressed you connected with the ball at all."

I slipped a baseball out of the pocket of my blue New York Mets windbreaker and rolled it around in my hands. Four years ago, at Shea Stadium, second baseman Wally Backman hit a popup that slammed into my right shoulder, bounced off it, and rolled down a flight of stairs. The fan who recovered it saw me wailing, felt sorry for me, and surrendered the ball to me as a gift. There were scuff marks on the ball, blurring the words printed on it where it had bounced off a railing just before slamming into me.

Salty punched me in the same shoulder Wally Backman had struck. "You're a Mets fan?"

"Dad took me to see a couple of games. I got really attached to Tom Seaver as pitcher. Then we go see another game, and Herm Winningham is pitching. Herm seemed cool and all, but . . . they traded Tom Seaver! Bastards. So, I decided I didn't like sports."

"You were not the only Met fan heartbroken by the team losing Tom Terrific. Twice."

"These baseball trades suck! You get to like someone, and he vanishes!"

Salty nodded. "That's the human condition. You love someone and they leave you."

"I get enough of that from real life! I don't need that shit from sports, too. I'm out."

"Well, while we're discussing terrible news and people disappearing in a puff of smoke, I've got some bad news I have to tell you about Marina Dazzo."

"Oh, no! What?" I put the baseball back in my pocket and gave him my full attention.

Salty eyed me warily. "Promise me you won't freak out. And you won't tell anybody it was me who told you."

"*What happened?*"

"There's a rumor she went down on Bobby during a movie and swallowed."

My stomach churned. "Charming story. Should I nominate her for a Purple Heart?"

Salty nodded. "I've known her forever. We were in band together in our last school, too. I feel like she's my sister, or something. And I *never* feel that way about girls. Usually I just wanna fuck all of them. Anyway, she just started dating this guy. He's her first boyfriend. I can't imagine anyone getting any action out of her before they dated at least three years. Heck, she's more Catholic than you are! This is just too soon. So, I'm sure that Bobby is . . . "

" . . . spreading calumny?" I asked.

"*Exactly*. Spreading calumny."

I started digging a hole in the dirt with the tip of my shoe. "Even if it's true, it was a romantic moment he spoiled by telling everybody in the world. Turning her into a spectacle."

"Personally, I think he tried something on her at the movies, she balked and dumped him, and he's getting even with her with this rumor. She's been absent for a few days."

"What are you gonna do now?" I asked.

Salty shrugged. "She won't take my calls. Wait until she comes back and talk to her."

"That's no good! What if, in the meantime, dude keeps talking smack about her?"

"The damage may be done. People believe it because she hit puberty before most of the rest of us, and her boobs are so big."

I stood up. "I'm gonna do something."

"What . . . *now*? I think it's better if you bide your time. Haven't you ever heard the Klingon proverb, 'Revenge is a dish best served cold?' I learned that from Ricardo Montalbán."

"It's actually an Italian proverb, but I prefer 'Strike while the iron is hot.'"

"Don't tell me you're gonna coldcock him! Are you even capable of violence?"

I pounded my chest. "I'm Neapolitan! One of the Volcano People of Vesuvius!"

"Don't get me wrong, I want you to beat up the douchebag."

I was about to run back to the locker room but stopped. "Lemme ask you a question."

"What?"

I sat down next to him. "Is *Massengill Vinegar and Water* used to rise out the interior of a vagina? And is the soiled water collected into a bag that is called a 'douchebag?' So, calling Bobby a douchebag suggests he is as worthless as the contents of a plastic receptacle that holds wastewater left over from a vaginal sanitary rinse? I suppose it is possible that the water in the douchebag is clean, but that would be a less effective insult than if the water were dirty, right?"

Salty grinned. "I've always wondered what it would be like to be friends with Lieutenant Commander Data, and now I know. It is every bit as hilarious as I expected."

Smoking a cigarette and standing in the schoolyard at lunchtime, Bobby Mammolito was in a lather about Marina dumping him. All he did was reach under her shirt in the movie theater! She dropped him like a hot potato. He wasn't going to let that treatment go unanswered. He told half the people he knew what "really" went down on that date and would soon tell the other half.

Bobby didn't hear or see anyone racing towards him. All he knew was that one moment he was standing, smoking and scowling, and the next he had the wind knocked out of him from behind. He was dragged down to the asphalt, his left arm pinned behind his back at the wrist.

"Ciao, Bobby. Come stai?" I growled into his ear.

"Egon? What the hell, man?"

I planted my knee in his back to keep him down. "How could you say those things about Marina, you *Massengill Vinegar and Water douchebag?*"

Bobby coughed out a surprised laugh. "What are you, Zorro? What's it to you?"

I wrenched at Bobby's arm. It felt on the point of breaking. Bobby bit back a squeal of pain. I placed my lips against Bobby's ear and hissed. "Take it all back and shut the fuck up about Marina or I'll break your arm. *Capisci?*"

"*Capisco.*"

Bobby felt his wrist released. My weight disappeared from his back. He clambered to his feet and whirled around to confront me. I stood there with my hands in my trench coat pockets, staring at Bobby indifferently. He raised his fists and pranced around me.

I regarded him like an ant not worth stepping on. "Man, am I disappointed in you. I thought you were cooler than this. You can dish out sneak attacks but you can't take 'em?"

Bobby lowered his fists. "She rejected me."

"Join the club. You don't see me making up stupid rumors about her."

"I bet you were mad at her, too, when she thought everyone else in the world left her the anonymous rose except you. It didn't even occur to her it was you 'til I figured it out for her."

I pointed a commanding finger at Bobby and punctuated each sentence by poking the air with it. "Put out this fire you started. This time next week, I don't even wanna see embers of this rumor glowing. And I *do not* want us to have to have another conversation."

Bobby smiled, despite himself.

"Now what?!"

"You're a funny guy, Egon. You never cease to amaze me."

March 11, 1988

I soon discovered what it was like to be ambushed from behind. Every day, I took an unjustifiable detour down the band hallway "on the way to" the library, in the hopes of catching a glimpse of Marina to find out if she was okay. As I walked past the lime green door, the muscular Eric Indelicato opened it and sprinted out. He wrapped his massive arms around me in a reverse bear hug, clutching his hands together by the wrists and lifting me bodily from the floor. He carried me like a rag doll into the band room, where Salty, Tuesday, Alisha Clark, and Julia Puglia stood in a circle around a weeping Marina Dazzo. Keeping me trapped in his arms, Eric walked me up to Marina and held me aloft mere inches from her face. "This guy will make you feel loved, Marina. His heart beats for you alone. Right, Damien?"

Marina avoided my eyes and looked downcast, making me struggle against Eric with renewed ferocity. "Let me go!"

"Oh, no!" Eric yelled. "Now's your chance to tell her to her face how you really feel."

Alisha stood and rushed to my defense. "You crazy, Eric? Leave him be! Put him down!"

I looked helplessly at Salty, who mouthed "Not I, Lord" while pointing at Eric. Reading a science textbook, Tuesday pretended to be oblivious to the proceedings. The normally disinterested Julia Puglia watched me with open fascination. I stopped flailing and dared to look directly at Marina. Our eyes met.

"I'm sorry," I said.

Marina was confused about exactly what I was apologizing for, but said, "That's okay."

"We got your main squeeze right here, Damien," Eric joked. "Enjoying the proximity?"

I harrumphed. "Um . . . not really, no."

"Tell her it was you who got her the rose!" Julia burst out.

"I already know it was him," Marina said.

"He never told you to your face that he loves you," Eric said. "I want to hear him say it."

"I ain't saying nothin' in front of Salty and Tuesday," I hissed.

"Hey!" both Salty and Tuesday called out, affronted.

"This is your chance, man," Eric urged. "This is my present to you, cuz I like you."

Should I tell Marina I love her? The arguments for and against swirled in my head. I remembered Dad's condemning his father for being too timid to call in the answer to the radio contest riddle: "Always try to win, even when defeat seems certain." Then I heard Aurora and Viola in my head, so insincere: "You're the boy we've been waiting for all our lives. We *love* you." Finally, I remembered Mr. Preponte pointing at the empty set. No. I would not be revealing my feelings to Marina, either in private or in front of all these strangers in the band room. "I already told her face-to-face how I felt about her."

"When?" asked Eric. "*I* didn't hear it!"

Jesus! How was I still stuck in Eric's reverse bear-hug? Didn't he get tired? "Sure, you did! I gave her the cool *Captain Kronos* compliment. That said it all."

"You chicken! Tell her in your own words! Don't quote vampire movies."

"Am I being expelled?" I asked Eric. "Dying? Moving to Paraguay? If not, it can wait."

Eric laughed. "It would be too late to tell her you love her if you're dying! Tell her now."

"If a meteor were about to hit," Marina said, "he needn't worry about my reaction."

"Is that it?" Eric asked me. "Has she figured you out?"

"I hate how my life is basically a Neil Simon play," I groused.

I had been hanging limp for several minutes. Suddenly, I bucked wildly and broke free of Eric's grasp. "Okay," I said. "I'm gonna bust outta here."

Eric seemed strangely sad. Why was he so invested in my coming clean? What was at stake for him? "There's nothing harder than saying 'I love you' to someone."

"I'll admit it. I'm in love. I'm in a satisfying, one-sided relationship with the lady in the red foxhunting jacket and black pencil skirt in last month's *Frederick's of Hollywood* catalogue."

Salty raised his hand as if he were in class. "Hey, Damien. You should know, I told her you're the reason Bobby stopped with the rumor-mongering."

I sighed. "Why would you tell–"

Marina talked over me. "Thank you. That meant a lot."

"She dumped Bobby," Eric interjected.

"I deserve better." Marina stared at me, her eyes glinting with . . . what? Curiosity? Empathy? Fear? Embarrassment? Was it possible for eyes to show so many emotions all at once? Yes. Hers did. She made no motion to come closer. Nothing in her body language invited me to approach her. There was *no way in hell* Marina wanted me to confess my love to her. It would put her on the spot and humiliate me. In fact, I doubted I would ever tell *any woman* I loved her, *ever*. I never wanted to see that look of fear and pity in a woman's eyes again. I headed to the door. Eric blocked my way like Dante's leopard. "Tell Marina how you feel."

"Okay, okay, okay." I put my hands in my pockets, spun on my heels, and looked at Marina. "Marina, I think you're the cat's pajamas."

"Yeah?" Marina blushed. I hadn't the first fucking clue what the blush meant. "Well, I think you're the bee's knees."

I gave her a small bow of thanks. "Now, I really am gonna jet." I gave Marina one final wave and said, "Peace out, home skillet." I walked out the door with as steady a step as I could muster, though I probably still looked like I was fleeing a crime scene.

"Don't trip, money grip!" Marina called after me.

CHAPTER SIXTEEN
The Awesome Blossom

March 11, 1988

Minutes after my heart-warming encounter with Eric and Marina, I found Arwen in the interior room of the library eating lunch alone while reading *Confess, Fletch* by Gregory Mcdonald. I stopped at the threshold, worried I would be invading her sanctuary if I entered.

"Are you a vampire waiting for me to invite you in?" Arwen beckoned me inside. I walked in with my head down and sat across from her, placing my hands flat on the table.

She kept her eyes on the book, making a show of reading and speaking to me at the same time. "David and Miriam are at the science fair. They did a project together about steps that vineyards can take to adapt to global warming." When I allowed myself to look at her, I realized she had given herself a minor makeover. With her glasses off, her silver eyes were in full view. The ponytail was gone, and her black hair fell in long, wavy strands about her shoulders. Her black jacket was off, draped over the back of her chair. Instead of one of her usual, oversized indie band t-shirts, she wore a form-fitting red satin blouse with a plunging v-neckline. A 14-karat gold chai pendant charm dangled just above her cleavage. Between the blouse, necklace, and surprising size and shapeliness of the breasts she had been hiding under her jacket, I found myself gaping openly down her shirt. All the other times I'd seen her, she had been intent on deemphasized her femininity — covering herself in layers of boyish clothes, restraining her hair, and speaking academic-sounding sentences in a flat voice. Now, she was flaunting her plumage.

My God, she needs a concealed-carry permit for those big guns.

"How are you doing today?" she asked.

I almost leapt out of my skin. "Good, good," I stammered, forcing my eyes back down on my hands. "How are you? How's the. . . um. . . . *Fletch*?"

"It is a lightly comic neo-noir. Like Douglas Adams, Mcdonald drives his story with witty banter and does not waste time describing setting or granting his characters interiority."

"Silly writing style," I observed. *Don't look at her boobs. Don't look at her boobs. Don't look at her boobs. Don't look at her boobs. Don't look at her boobs. Don't look at her boobs.*

The admonishing chant playing on repeat in my head fizzled out. I snuck another look at Arwen's cleavage. It was a sight to behold. The part of my brain not focused on following the curve of her red shirt around the underside of her beasts realized she was reading a book I had gotten in trouble for buying several years ago. Dad had thought a paperback about a beautiful, nude corpse dumped in Fletch's borrowed apartment was too risqué for me. He forced me to return it to Waldenbooks in exchange for the more toffee-nosed *Paradise Lost*. At the time, I was outraged that Dad had turned Puritan on me after taking me to see *Stripes* in the theater. That was then. Now I was sitting at a table with a surprisingly sexy girl who was 'secretly' attracted to me, reading a book I had been barred from reading, and I was not allowed to so much as reach out to touch her hand, because her parents had declared interfaith romance forbidden. I imagined being trapped inside an unknown Edward Hopper painting: "The Library at Lunch." Art history scholars could write exhaustingly about how Hopper rendered illicit romance — and the emotional isolation of the male — in stark, understated terms and in the most prosaic of institutional settings.

"You like my shirt?" Arwen asked, still not looking up from her book.

Caught! Pretending I hadn't heard the question, I looked back down at my hands. It was difficult to project a casual air with huge beads of sweat collecting on my forehead. *You're god damn right, I like your shirt. And I like your boobs. And I especially like your boobs in that shirt. And now I really want to see your boobs out of that shirt. Like . . . now. I want to tackle you and kiss you all over your body. Do you want me to?*

Arwen finally looked up and gingerly placed her book upon the table. She leaned back in her chair, deliberately giving me an even clearer view of her chest. It was all I could do not to lean forward, reach across the table, and caress her right then and there. *She's messing with me! What's she trying to pull?* Mischievously, recklessly, Arwen had decided to push all my buttons just to see what would happen.

Of course, I lit up and went into overdrive like some great big . . . lighting up and going into overdrive thing. I was furious with myself. One half hour ago, I had not been remotely attracted to this girl. One strategically worn red shirt later, I was a goner.

Am I that *easy to manipulate? I* can't *be!*

"You can wear that shirt any time you want to," I said, pretending to be confident.

Arwen assumed an expression of feigned surprise. "Are you suggesting you like today's look better than my usual, 'tomboy' attire?"

"Marginally."

"You and every guy! I dress down most days, so I'm not felt up by strangers in public."

She'd sounded a discordant note I could not let pass. "Oh, *no! Really?* I'm sorry." Of course. "Every guy" followed my dad's rule of 100: Grab her tit and if she likes you, she won't smack you. That was the go-to strategy for all guys, all the time, right? So, that meant girls like Arwen were felt up non-stop by armies of strangers every day if they showed off their goods. Why had I not been able to imagine that sooner? The ramifications of the realization shook me to my core, even as I found myself caught up in an overpowering urge to jump on top of Arwen and tear her clothes off. The two conflicting impulses, both equally strong, short-circuited me.

"I am a bit surprised that you are shocked, but let's let that pass." Her expression brightened. "Today's a special occasion! Our chaperones are gone, so I wore this for you."

This last remark was encouraging enough that I dared to look Arwen in the eyes. Could they be flirtatious, earnest, wary, and sad all at once? "Why?" I asked, stupidly.

Arwen mimed casting a fishing line out, hooking me by the mouth, and reeling me in.

Her jokey pantomime reminded me that I hated being toyed with. Now I was mentally lumping Arwen in with Viola and Aurora. *These women sure love fucking with me, don't they? I'm so much fun to tease, huh?* "What about your candy empire? Aren't you playing with fire?"

Arwen let out a long sigh, like a deflating balloon.

I spread my arms wide. "Well?"

Arwen's eyes flashed lightning. "Are you *serious*? Why would you bring that up *now*?"

When would there be a better time to bring it up? "I dunno. Are we allowed to date, then? Can we go out somewhere this weekend?"

Arwen was about to shout but grew concerned that the librarian might hear us arguing. At the height of her frustration with me, she lowered her voice as much as she could muster. "Of course not, you fucking idiot."

I gestured towards her revealing red blouse. "Then what's all this in aid of?"

Arwen crossed her arms and glared at me. "You can't *possibly* be this stupid. No one is *this* stupid. Why are you sabotaging yourself?"

"Because you're not being serious! You're playing with my head. This isn't real, what you're doing, and it's not cool."

Arwen was beyond confused. "What? I don't–. What are you talking about? What's not real? You don't think these are silicone, do you? Because they are *so* not silicone!"

"No, no, no. I feel like you're playing a prank on me to get even with me for saying you're 'not-one-hundred-percent my type.' And, you know something? You're right. It was a crappy thing to say. I just was trying to navigate a tricky situation with your stepsister, and I could have done a better job. I'm sorry. I blew it. Please forgive me."

Arwen stared at me, unblinking, for ten seconds. "I ran this conversation in my head fifty times, and never once did it go . . . like *this*."

"How did you want it to go?" I asked.

I became very aware of the sound of the clock's second hand as it ticked five seconds.

"Okay, *okay*. I'll put my knockers back into storage." Arwen slipped her coat back on and zipped it up. She put her glasses back on and returned the scrunchie to her hair to recreate the ponytail. Sexy chick Superman was gone, and dowdy chick Clark Kent was back. "Just pretend they aren't there and don't let them bother you."

"You want me to sit here across from you every day, with you dressed like a mummy, and I'm supposed to pretend I don't know you've got world-class tits?"

Arwen shot me a disappointed look. "Are you a toddler? Just be a gentleman. If you can't do that, be professional in the library. And, if you can't do that, jerk off in the mornings before coming to school. Get it all out of your system before you see me."

"I do that every day anyway. It's the only way I can function."

"Whatever," Arwen growled. "Do what you have to do to treat me like a human being."

"Holy tonal whiplash, Batman," I muttered.

"What was that?" Arwen asked. "I didn't hear you."

I looked down at my feet and realized I hadn't unpacked my lunch from my schoolbag. That was as good an excuse as any to leave now. This library monitor gig was already proving to be a disaster. Talk about "Out of the frying pan, into the fire!" I should find my old spot by the wire fence and eat alone outside. I'd just have to hope that Mrs. Hall wouldn't know I was back there, and Fuckhead Flavio wouldn't spot me. *Oh, shit, Arwen is looking at me like she expects me to say something.* I cleared my throat. "You shouldn't feel like you have to dress like a nun to get me to behave myself. And you shouldn't dress sexy just to get a rise out of me when there's no way in hell we can ever be together. All that shit's bogus. Look, I just came from one insanely stressful conversation. Now I'm in another insane conversation that I should have seen coming but didn't. I gotta be honest, here. I'm about to totally freak out. I'm on the verge of a total nervous breakdown. I really can't take this school anymore."

I hadn't even started to stand up, but my tone had given me away. Arwen flipped from angry to fearful. "Aw, come on, Damien. Don't run away. Stay."

"This whole library monitor thing was a big mistake."

"Please?" Arwen gestured for me to stay seated. "I am sorry if you think I'm just messing with you. I swear I'm not. But you're right. I shouldn't have done it for a whole bunch of reasons. I just like you. And I had an impulse. And . . . I shouldn't have followed it."

"I don't understand what you want from me, at all," I said. "I haven't the first clue!"

Arwen's eyes narrowed. "You're a weird guy. I gotta say. I just showed you my boobs and you got mad at me? What guy gets mad at a pair of boobs flashed at him?"

"Ha! That's fair. That's more than fair. The problem is . . . " I began.

The ticking of the clock made an encore performance for another six seconds.

"Yes?" asked Arwen.

"The problem is . . . it's taking all my willpower not to jump across this table and kiss you, right now. I'm having a really hard time controlling myself, you know?"

Arwen used her innocent voice again. "Why control yourself?"

All my fears were gone. I'd never kissed anyone. I wasn't sure if I knew how, but that didn't matter. I didn't know if I was going to lose my heart to yet another girl I couldn't have. That didn't matter either. I wasn't sure if the librarian would barge in on us. So what? All I needed to do was walk around the table, take her by the hand, stand her up, and kiss her. I rose.

The library door swung open and Miriam strode up to the table. Hands on her hips, she looked back and forth between us. Flushed and flustered, Arwen sank back in her chair. "Hi."

I dropped back into my seat and saluted Miriam as if she were my superior officer in the U.S. Navy. "If it isn't the fantabulous Miriam! How the fuck are you?"

"David and I left you two unchaperoned." Miriam sounded like the villain of Walt Disney animated musical fairy tale: arch and terrifying. She focused her suspicion on Arwen's flight jacket. "Aren't you warm, all zipped up indoors?"

"Oddly enough, I'm cold."

"What's today's band t-shirt?"

"They Might Be Giants."

Arwen is an impressive liar. She must have lots of practice. "They *Might* Be Giants," I joked. "But They Could Also Be Dwarves."

Miriam flicked at Arwen's jacket. "If you've got your red shirt on, I'm gonna wig out."

"Which red shirt would that be?"

"You know damn well which red shirt I'm talking about! The awesome blossom!"

With that exchange, I understood — way too late — what Arwen was trying to achieve by flirting with me. Her main goal wasn't to mess with my head. Not everything was about me. She was defying Miriam. She wanted to feel some measure of control over her life, so she was willing to make out with me in secret a time or two to metaphorically flip off Miriam. She was not daring enough to outright defy her parents by dating me long term in secret. That was why Arwen was so upset with me for killing the mood and asking for a "permission slip to make out" signed by her parents before I felt man enough to kiss her. ("I'll kiss you, if I am certain I have your dad's blessing." Barf me out.) By being afraid and affronted, I spoiled a forbidden moment we would have both enjoyed and derailed a wicked fun "fuck you" to Miriam. I was deluding myself thinking more was at stake than really was. A make-out session or two with a Catholic boy would not have been a big enough infraction for her parents to cut her out of any will. I should have kissed her when I had the chance. Arwen was right. I was really fucking stupid. But Miriam would have caught us for sure. Had Arwen *wanted* Miriam to catch us?

Arwen poked her finger at Miriam's crotch. "How about you unzip yourself and show us your panties? One look at you with your pants pulled down and Damien would pitch a tent!"

Miriam stepped back as Arwen's fingers brushed the denim over her upper pelvis. "Knock it off. You know why I'm here." She regarded me again. "Why do you wear purple shirts so damn often?"

"Purple is my favorite." I went into motor-mouth mode to distract Miriam from interrogating her stepsister. "You know, purple is a rare, pretty, and underrated color! The color of aristocrats, mystics, geniuses, artists . . . and the perennially over-the-top!"

Miriam nodded. "Don't forget the color of sexual frustration."

"Well, that's news to me." I snorted. "I appreciate you bringing that up. Thanks for that." I decided it was time to start ignoring her and fish my lunch out of my backpack.

Just then, the library door opened again and a guy who wasn't David eased his way inside. Tight blue jeans, a crisp white t-shirt, and fingerless black leather motorcycle gloves gave the stranger a "1980s Fonzie" look. He kissed Arwen on the cheek. "Howya doin, honey?"

"Good, Rolf," she said sweetly, avoiding looking at me directly because she knew Miriam and I were watching.

Rolf? I thought. *There's a boyfriend? Named Rolf? Rolf is my sixth favorite Muppet. Miss Piggy, then Kermit, then Fozzie, then Statler and Waldorf, then Rolf.*

"Just wanted you to know I hadn't forgotten you here, all alone in the library," Rolf said, flashing his perfect white teeth first at her, then at me.

"I do have Damien to keep me company," Arwen observed airily.

Rolf nodded in my direction. "You taking good care of my girlfriend?"

I raised my eyebrows innocently. "Sure. We're having fun."

"Yeah? Don't have too much fun, now." Rolf winked threateningly at me.

"Keep an eye on this one, Rolf," Miriam said. "He's angling to be your replacement."

"'Replacement?' For God's sake, I just met Rolf *two seconds ago*."

"Okay," Arwen grumbled. "You two stop threatening my friend and go away."

Rolf rankled. "We just got here and you're chasing us out?"

"Just don't be a dick to Damien, alright?" Arwen warned.

Rolf Kaminsky and Miriam stayed another ten minutes, talking about nothing much but keeping an eye on my reactions to everything they said. If they expected Arwen to do something suspicious in front of them, they went away disappointed. Rolf got Arwen to agree to come over his place later, then headed away with Miriam, who shot me a triumphant smile as they left.

Once the door closed behind them, Arwen picked up her book and resumed reading it.

"I should have known there'd be a boyfriend running around loose," I said.

Arwen chuckled. "Of course!"

"I assume he's Jewish?" I asked.

"He's Polish, so Miriam and my parents think he is," Arwen said smugly.

"So, he's Catholic, but your family thinks he's Jewish. How marvelous for you. Is it too late for me to pretend to be Jewish, too?"

Arwen continued to talk to me through her book. "The word is out on you, my Italian Catholic Republican friend."

"How does everyone know me and everything about me?" I asked myself, out loud.

"Everyone knows all about you because you have the world's biggest mouth."

"I don't know anyone's name, or anything about them. It's because I'm loud and wear a raincoat, isn't it? Am I that fascinating? Wish I weren't. Damn, shit, and fuck-a-doodle-doo."

"I understand how you feel."

"Am I wildly off base here, or does the sudden appearance of a secret Catholic boyfriend make my position in your little universe even harder to fathom?"

Arwen lowered the book and offered me a pained look. "I know. I'm sorry."

I gestured towards her jacket. "I tell you what: How about you give me another look at them perfect titties and I'll consider forgiving you?"

Arwen smirked, showed me her middle finger, and went back to her book.

The sound of the second-hand of the clock returned with a vengeance.

"Why did his name have to be Rolf?" I asked rhetorically.

CHAPTER SEVENTEEN
The Good Jesuit

April 3, 1988

On Sunday, Mom woke me up in time to attend the 10 am mass, so I could finally see the cool new Jesuit. If she hadn't, I would have slept until 10:30. "I can't go because I'm deaf and heat sensitive," she said. "That church gives me a woozy head every time. But you need to go."

"By myself?" The odds of Dad and Leo accompanying me were slim to none.

"Put on some nice clothes."

I dressed in beige cargo shorts and a red Hawaiian shirt and walked the mile to church. Walking at a steady clip, I approached the no-frills, Protestant-looking church with the red-brick, Bauhaus architecture on the corner of Bradley Avenue and Willowbrook Road. I went through the row of glass front doors and entered the dimly lit interior. A twelve-foot-tall crucifix dominated the brick wall behind the altar. Nailed to the cross was a loincloth-covered Caucasian Christ, bleeding from an open wound in his stomach. His head was arced up in agony, his eyes misted over, his mouth slack. I sat in the cherry wood pew just in front of the altar. My Dad was a front-and-center seat guy, and I inherited his preference. I had poor vision — even with my glasses on — and liked to see what the heck was going on. Also, the very front row was the one place in the church I was guaranteed to not have to sit next to anyone. I had arrived with only a few minutes to go before mass started. The church was about two-thirds filled, mostly by Asian and elderly white parishioners, plus two or three young Irish and Italian women in their late teens. There were surprisingly few children or middle-aged parishioners. In a few months, word would get out about this charismatic, loveable Jesuit, and this mass would be filled to bursting with children and a surprisingly racially diverse crowd of adults. Proto-Pope Francis had arrived.

My first look at the new Jesuit came when the entrance procession led him to the altar, and he turned around to greet the parishioners. Father Jack Stańczyk had a weather-beaten, all-American, John-Boy-from-*The-Waltons* look: blonde hair, blue eyes, and silver, wire-rimmed glasses. An experienced innocent, this fellow had been through the mill and somehow managed to come out the other side of repeated tragedies a decent human being. During the first few minutes of the mass, Father Jack gave no hint that he was about to play the trickster. Mass-as-usual played out much as one might expect. However, when homily time arrived, a mad gleam reached his eyes, and he shouted, "And now for something completely different!"

Father Jack scurried up to the oak-colored lectern. "I have good news, my brothers and sisters: Monsignor Tobin has gone golfing at Baltusrol in Springfield, New Jersey! He's left me unsupervised! This means I can give you the kind of homily I've always wanted to!"

Unnerved, the congregation stirred.

Oh, this is gonna be good.

Father Jack assumed a temperate, well-mannered air. "As a college cinema studies professor, I've always loved film soundtracks."

Ooooooh!

He continued, "I've always found it captivating watching film characters going through their lives unaware that their actions are accompanied by non-diegetic music scored by the likes of Max Steiner, Bernard Herrmann, and Rachel Portman. When I have funny thoughts like that, it never takes me long to wonder what kind of theme song I would like for my life." John Williams' theme to Christopher Reeve's *Superman* started playing from every speaker in church. Hilarity, confusion, disapproval, and joy spread amongst the parishioners. The theme trailed off.

"I know, I know," Father Jack beamed. "I'm a legend in my own mind. Still, a healthy self-image is a good thing if you don't take it too far." He pointed at us as a collective. "I invite you to do the same. Cultivate a healthy self-image. I'd like you all to ask yourself this question: if a movie were made about your life story, what would your theme song be?"

Ennio Morricone's Days of Heaven *suite,* I thought. *Or all Ennio's scores together.* (In more recent years, I've toyed with "Chevaliers de Sangreal/503" by Hans Zimmer, plus the pop songs "Hombre Religioso (Religious Man)" by Mister Loco and "The Mighty" by Sting.)

Seeing the parishioners exchange confused, bemused, and shy glances, Fr. Jack held up a finger. "Remember, your choice of main theme doesn't have to smack of Wagnerian heroism. You could go for carnivalesque, comic, or sentimental, like the Nino Rota score to a Fellini film." On cue, the theme to *Le Notti Di Cabiria* piped into the church, then faded. "We drift through life, tired and beleaguered, putting no thought or feeling into our actions. But what if we imagined the music we might make every moment of every day with each of our interactions?"

I wasn't sure where all this was going, but the man had my attention. Fr. Jack continued, "When we feel out of control of our own lives and its music score, here's one thing to consider: whatever may be going on, God only writes beautiful, loving music for us. He doesn't write theme songs for us that suggest we are the villains of our lives, or that we are fundamentally unlovable. God does not write Darth Vader's *Imperial March* for any of us." The iconic villain theme from the *Empire Strikes Back* lasted long enough to be recognizable before going away.

Fr. Jack's tone became serious. "It is fashionable in modern American Christianity for priests and reverends, both Protestant and Catholic, to emphasize all the 'very good, very practical' reasons why certain people should be expelled from the Church. They harp on why so many of us are damnable creatures, unworthy of God's love. Why? Usually because they've violated some form of sexual taboo, or because they are a member of the wrong faith community. Who does God slam the Great Green Door of Heaven on? We hear much on EWTN and the 700 Club about all those whom God has abjured. God does not love people who are gay, or who have been divorced, or had abortions. God does not love those who are Jewish or Moslem or — Heaven help us all — Democrats! God hates all sinners."

Wow, that took a grim turn. We've traveled a long way from the Superman *theme.*

Fr. Jack paused for effect, waiting to see how many of the parishioners expected him to either validate fundamentalist Catholicism or politically hang himself challenging it too vociferously. "This is just my humble opinion, but it seems to me that anyone who suggests that God turns his back on any of us is not speaking for God. Our

God is the God of love. His only son, Jesus Christ, is the Prince of Peace. Jesus of Nazareth was the gentle carpenter who gave up his life out of love for all of humanity. This Jesus, the Word of God made flesh, commands us to 'love the Lord your God with all your heart, and with all your soul, and with all your mind.' He commands us to love ourselves, our neighbors, and our enemies, equally, with all our hearts, minds, and souls. Jesus demands that we leave no room for hate in our hearts and minds: no room for hating God, ourselves, our neighbors, or our enemies. For Catholics, hatred is verboten.

"If you ever hear a voice telling you to hate others, silence that voice. If you ever hear a voice telling you that *you* are worthy of hate, silence that voice. Tell it to get behind you, the way Jesus told Satan to get behind him. If you hear that voice coming at you from the radio from a so-called fire-and-brimstone preacher, turn that radio off. Get that voice behind you. If you hear a voice of hatred from a politician, get that Satanic voice behind you. In fact, please offer serious consideration to voting against it, because that voice doesn't deserve political power to reinforce its bad intentions. Under no circumstances is a voice of hatred the true voice of God. Remember, God loves you just as He loves your neighbor. God is not about hate. Anyone who claims to be speaking on God's behalf when speaking hate is a fraud!"

Amen. This homily is starting to get to me. I was not used to feeling emotions in church. I was not used to feeling anything but boredom, guilt, and shame. I had felt much the same way throughout my Thursday night training for Confirmation. Yes, Miss O'Sullivan was pretty and liked me, but her main goal was to make us all feel self-loathing for every time we stepped wrong. She also goaded us into feeling self-righteous fury whenever we observed another step wrong. Fr. Jack's words stirred in me emotions that I had not felt when Miss O'Sullivan spoke, felt in any mass before, or felt *anywhere* before. He was using the language of hope, love, forgiveness, charity, and peace. These were not the dominant ideals or emotions of the 1980s in general, nor were they the dominant ideals or emotions of 1980s Roman Catholicism. Fr. Jack had approached me with a giant hacksaw, ready to free my heart and brain from the invisible iron maidens they had been imprisoned in. I looked about the room for signs of Miss

O'Sullivan, wondering if my newfound love for Fr. Jack represented some form of infidelity. And yet, as the song went, if loving Fr. Jack and his message was wrong, I did not want to be right.

Fr. Jack continued. "We are all the heroes of our own lives. None of us is the antagonist. We may make mistakes. We may fail. We may even deliberately harm ourselves and others. And yet, we are not evil, in our hearts. Even when we commit one of the seven deadly sins — or, more accurately, succumb to one of the seven deadly tendencies — God is never far away. God is always rooting for us, hoping for us to rediscover their opposite numbers: the seven virtues. Think of the times when we find ourselves depressed and unloved. We indulge in gluttony, and try to fill the lonely, painful void within ourselves with endless amounts of food. In the process, we poison ourselves with sugar and fat. During those moments, God urges us to love ourselves, take better care of ourselves, and eat with temperance. When we fall into obsessive, possessive, violent lust, God cheers us on to help us discover a more chaste love: one that recognizes the full humanity of the person we feel drawn to. When we hoard and indulge in solitary acts of greed, God reminds us of the joys of charity. God reminds us the connections we make with others through selflessness, generosity, and loving human interaction. When we fall into sloth, God reminds us that diligence is what saves us from losing the burning spark of passion and inspiration within. When we find ourselves consumed with wrath, God liberates us from the debilitating, self-destructive fury by helping forgiveness descend upon us. When we learn to hate others out of envy, God urges us to count our blessings instead. When we take too much pride in our self, God reminds us that being prideful is the first step towards alienating yourself from everyone else in life. Humility is the first step towards mending broken relationships."

I leaned forward in rapt attention. *Is this homily as good as I think it is?*

"Don't confuse God's voice with the voice of the devil," Fr. Jack said. "They can sometimes sound the same. Here's how you can tell the difference: The devil's main goal is to convince us all that we are fundamentally unlovable, and that all of humanity is one great big pile of manure. Anyone who tries to influence you on behalf of the devil will speak in those terms. They'll try to convince you that you are pond scum, as is everyone else. Do not internalize this voice. Reject it. 'If the devil taunts you with your past, remind him of his future.'"

Fr. Jack paused for the light laughter. "But how are we to recognize God's authentic voice? If he sounds like a caregiver instead of a warrior. If he grants forgiveness for the unforgivable instead of acts like a hanging judge in a Western. God is a healer. God is a teacher. God is there to inspire us to be better people and get the most out of being alive. God is not here to smite us, mercilessly, for every flaw, real or imagined. God will never turn his back on you just because you made one mistake, or have one small, blemish on the white handkerchief of your soul. God loves us, despite our imperfections. On some level, God loves us because of our imperfections. There's something lovable about losers. Let's face it: We're all losers. All of us. But we are adorable losers. Sometimes, we may be tempted to think, 'God cannot love me because I'm too fat. God loved me when I was thin, but I gained five pounds, and that's four pounds too many, so I've fallen from grace. Nobody could love a fatso like me! Not even God.' Let's imagine the same train of thought attached to gaining fifty pounds, or a hundred, or three-hundred pounds. The result is the same. When we think in those terms, we feel our heart break. As we dwell on these thoughts, we allow ourselves to be mired in a quicksand of self-destructive thinking. God loved you five pounds ago. God will love you five thousand pounds from now. To quote the bard, Sir Mix-a-Lot, '*Cosmo* thinks your fat, but God ain't down with that.'"

The parishioners who knew the song "Baby Got Back" chortled. The other parishioners had lost the thread of the homily too long ago to be concerned about missing this one joke.

"God loves you. And if you think, 'God won't love me because I'm gay,' remember that Jerry Falwell may not love you because you're gay, but Jerry Falwell is not God. God loves you. God loves soldiers who have killed others in war, married people who have had affairs, and women who have had abortions. We are all ugly sometimes. We all do ugly things sometimes. But God loves us. God loves everything about us."

I frowned. *I don't know about that one. That may be going too far.*

God loves everything *about Phil McCracken? Mr. Orlov? Tony Nocerino? The mullet math guy? I hope not.*

Fr. Jack paused one final time, ready to begin his summation. "And that is the most important point I want to make, my brothers and sisters. If there's just one thing you take away from this homily, I'm hoping that it is not that I played the *Superman* theme when the Monsignor was away playing golf. (Though I will admit that I did that to get your attention.) What I'm hoping you remember is: God loves *everything* about you and is cheering you on with inspiring John Williams music. God hears the joyous strains of the *Superman* theme whenever He thinks of you." The priest gestured expansively. "Do you know what God loves about all of you?"

Silence.

Father Jack sighed. "You're supposed to yell, 'Everything!'" Embarrassed, he cleared his throat. "Okay, okay. I know this is a Catholic Church and we don't like to make a sound." Some self-conscious laughs came back to him. "Yell 'Everything!' like we're in a charismatic Protestant Church where they know how to make some noise. *What does God love about you?*"

"Everything!" roughly half of the parishioners yelled back. One quarter of the remainder spoke the words without yelling them. The rest remained obstinately silent.

"And do you know what God loves about your friends and family?" Fr. Jack asked.

"Everything!" slightly fewer parishioners replied.

Fr. Jack wagged an admonishing finger at the crowd. "I think I'm losing some of you, but we are going to go with the hardest one to admit: What does God love about your enemies?"

Reluctantly, a handful of parishioners yelled back, "Everything."

"Nothing!" One heckler roared. "God does not love my enemies!"

"But God loves you, sir, for yelling that just now," Fr. Jack called back, inspiring more scattered laughter. "God loves your enemies, too. And He expects you to treat your enemies like the brothers and sisters that they are. We are all children of God. We need to remember this, especially when we are mired in bitter feuds. Do you feel justified in hating yourself because you are 'too sinful' to be in God's good graces?

You are wrong. Do you feel justified in condemning others because they don't 'deserve' a place at God's table? You are wrong. Do you feel that you can hurt other human beings because their sinfulness makes them not fully human? That's your anger talking. That's your pain. That's not reality. You may not love your enemies, but God certainly does, and you are not in charge. God is. God has the final say in who is worthy of love, not you. When you wake up in the morning and look yourself in the mirror, there are times when the voice of the devil will tell you that you are worthless. You may hear the same thing from angry political voices on the radio. These voices of propaganda either accuse you of being evil or invite you to scapegoat others as evil. Blame *them* for all your problems. No matter where or when or how you hear a demonic voice tell you that all people are unlovable, do not listen to it. Whether it is a priest or politician, your own manic depression or over-inflated superego, or the very devil himself, say to yourself, 'God loves everything about me, and everything about us all.'

"Every day that you interact with another human being, whether you feel like kissing them or punching them or just steering clear of them, remember that they, too, are children of the Lord. If any of them look like they are suffering, that they are hating themselves right now, then you need to do everything in your power to say to them, directly or indirectly, 'God loves you. God loves everything about you.' Show them that love. Be an instrument of God's love. Make the world a brighter place. For when you love yourself, and love God, and love your neighbor — including your enemy — you are making beautiful music. It may be a non-diegetic soundtrack, but it is a glorious one. Far, far more beautiful than any film score the great Ennio Morricone could compose. That is why I say to you all: 'Go forth and make beautiful music in the name of God!'"

Wow. Father Jack, I want to be just like you when I grow up.

CHAPTER EIGHTEEN
Sweep the Leg

One year later . . .

The Richmond County Institute of Martial Arts

April 3, 1989

Tony Nocerino charged.

I whipped my leg straight up and down in an ax kick, accidentally brushing his cheek.

Tony stopped short and howled. A baby tooth popped out of his mouth. The tiny molar bounced onto the dojo's polished, hardwood floor. Eyes wide, Tony clutched a shaking hand to his bloody lips. He scampered off to the bathroom, tears in his eyes.

What have I done? I whipped myself up into a state of total panic.

Ten minutes later, Master Yumi Park reassured me it was not a permanent tooth.

Oh, thank God. But how does he still have baby teeth to lose?

This thirty-second sparring match was six months ago. The consequences of those thirty seconds were more lasting than I could have expected. Tony never forgot his humiliation. My fear of hurting an opponent became so overpowering that I rarely won another Tae Kwon Do sparring match. Worst of all, the day I went up for my black belt, I put in a remarkably inept performance in front of my parents, Mitchell, Uncle Carmine, Aunt Beatrice, and Cousin Gabriel. I held back so much during my sparring match with Nan Gibson — a college sophomore also going up for black belt — I would have performed better if I'd stayed home. Ironically, I had no reason to hold back, since Nan could outfight me with two broken legs and a 104-degree fever. I earned the black belt anyway but felt I didn't deserve the new rank.

And yet, here I was, acting as ranking student, leading the basic warm-up exercises. After I completed the twenty-minute set, Master Yumi Park emerged from her office and transitioned the class from calisthenics to sparring practice. "First match!" Yumi declared. The thirty intermediate-school-age students scrambled and sat themselves cross-legged in a circle around the sparring mat. Yumi pointed to the mat. "Cavalieri and Nocerino. Best two out of three."

As Tony got up to join me, one of his idiot friends yelled out, "Sweep the leg!"

Another Merry Man yelled, "Put him in a body bag!"

Yumi cleared her throat loudly, silencing them. "The next person to quote *Karate Kid* gets a front-snap kick to the face."

"You mean a Crane Kick?" the first wise guy called out.

"Okay, that's a *Karate Kid* reference. Ten push-ups on your palms."

The fellow wanted to complain but didn't and complied, doing the pushups hastily and without bending his elbows enough.

"Those are some sloppy push-ups," Yumi observed. "Five more. Good ones."

"Yes, sir!" Fortunately for him, Yumi didn't hear him humming a pop song from the first *Karate Kid*: Joe Esposito's "You're the Best."

"That's more like it." Yumi walked next to me and whispered. "You've had problems with Nocerino for years, am I right?"

"He's having difficulty seeing me as a Black Belt."

"Paint him a picture. No holding back like you've been doing lately, or you answer to me." Yumi threw an annoyed glance at the increasingly talkative class. "Hey! With the talking." They shut up quick. Yumi stepped back to watch from the sidelines. "Fighting stance!"

Tony and I bellowed deep "Ki-Hap!" cries. I snapped into the stance: knees bent lightly, toes up, balled fists held up, guarding my midsection. I was braced for a fight, yet limber. Broadcasting overconfidence, Tony lazily assumed a loose fighting stance. He let his arms flop around by his sides instead of keeping them up in defensive posture, leaving himself vulnerable.

Okay, now I'm gonna destroy this arrogant piece of shit.

"Sijak!"

I expected Tony to attack with a stepping side kick. He did. I dodged the telegraphed move. Tony threw a reverse-punch. I blocked it with my forearm. I followed up with a short jab to the chest. "Ki-hap!"

Tony stepped back, surprised by the contact.

Boom, baby!

"Point, Damien!" Yumi called. "Continue!"

I attacked Tony with a combination of kicks and punches, keeping him reeling under the pressure. Tony sensed he was being forced out of the ring. He ducked under my last kick, running around me to the center of the mat. As Tony ran past me, he aimed a reverse punch at my ribs. I twisted out of the way, avoiding the full brunt of the blow. Tony's fist grazed my side. Both of us drew apart, pausing to see if the punch was point-worthy.

"Almost, Tony, almost," Yumi said. "You needed a follow-up punch there."

Out of the corner of my eye, I caught sight of Nan Gibson, who had arrived early for the next lesson. She stood by the dojo entrance in her civvies, glowering at me for sparring with Tony with greater ferocity than I had demonstrated during our black belt trials.

Tony's leg smacked hard against my stomach. It hurt like a mo-fo.

"Point!" Yumi shouted. "Tie. Next point wins."

I walked in a small circle outside the ring, cursing myself for being distracted. Piecing my confidence back together as I returned to the ring took some effort. "Wake up, Mr. Cavalieri," Yumi commanded.

Tony and I bowed to each other for the third and final time, and slid back into fighting stance. Tony's stance wasn't slack any more. Seeing Yumi drop her arm, we walked with sideward steps around the edge of the ring, watching one another for weaknesses.

I threw a roundhouse kick, which Tony blocked. Tony tried a left-hand jab, but I side-stepped it. He pulled back and resumed circling me. Now he was intent on dancing around me, waiting for me to get impatient, attack recklessly, and run straight into his kicks and punches. I joined Tony in the circling, also biding my time.

Yumi yawned theatrically. "Boring! The whole class is falling asleep." At her gesture, everyone began making loud snoring sounds.

"Y'all need sleep apnea machines," I called out.

Tony lunged, screaming a Korean battle cry. He raised his leg to his chest, preparing to lash out with another roundhouse kick.

I was faster. My right leg whipped straight up, slicing the air right in front of Tony's face. It was another ax-kick. The same kick that had cost him a baby tooth.

Tony couldn't help himself. He paled. He flinched. He stepped backward awkwardly. His hands dropped to his side, leaving his chest unprotected.

I fired off a front-snap kick. The kick slammed against Tony's chest.

Tony fell over backwards. He lay on his back, staring at the ceiling, dumbfounded.

"Point two," Yumi said.

My classmates offered me a smattering of applause, which felt surreal. This was the fellow who had ordered his friends to throw rocks at my head by the creek a few years ago. There were no applauding witnesses to that indignity. And let's not forget the ambush outside the school bus with the cigarette burn. This time, during a pseudo-rematch, my winning was accompanied by nearly cinematic applause. I smiled and bowed in thanks to my fellow students, which included several clapping Merry Men. As I bowed, I noticed that my black belt had loosened, and hung to the floor. I turned around to face the back of the Dojo as a sign of respect and adjusted the uniform, smoothing out its creases and pulling the belt taught.

"That last kick was a *Karate Kid* reference!" the fellow who had done the pushups before complained. "Crane kick! You should make Damien do pushups, too!"

"'Not yet,'" Yumi replied, imitating Mr. Miyagi for the first time. "Mr. Cavalieri, you and Mr. Nocerino shake hands. It was a good match."

I was satisfied with the win, so I had no trouble stretching out my hand to Tony. Tony stared dumbly at the outstretched hand for a split second before offering his hand grudgingly in return. His handshake was loose, and he looked away as we shook. There was an unspoken promise that I wouldn't spread the word about his loss so long as he never gave me grief again.

"Seven concrete blocks?" I eyed the seven pavers that spanned two vertical cinder blocks, spaced apart at half-inch intervals by wooden shims. I'd punched through three before. Still!

"Don't worry," Yumi reassured me. "They've been pre-broken. You'd only be breaking apart glued halves. Just remember to follow through."

Phew. Naturally, it was far easier to break pre-broken and glued pieces of wood and concrete than unbroken ones. Her advice was also key. If I imagined the side of my knife hand coming to a stop as it struck the concrete, then that would happen. If I imagined my open hand passing through all seven concrete blocks, sweeping down past my leg in one fluid arc, then *that* would happen. After a couple of practice, mimed chops, I made my requisite yell and struck the stack of blocks. My hand passed through one, then all seven of the concrete blocks, facing more resistance than I expected. I wasn't breaking glue. I was putting my open hand through seven unbroken concrete blocks. I stepped back, looking back and forth between my raw, red hand and the broken, collapsed stack of concrete. *Did she just lie to me?*

Yumi smiled. "If I told you they were unbroken, you would have psyched yourself out."

"You should have warned me," I breathed.

"If I'd warned you, you wouldn't have succeeded. I know who I'm dealing with." Yumi clasped her hands behind her back and absently rocked back and forth on her heels.

I frowned. "I suppose so." *Yeah, she's telling falsehoods now.* I was annoyed, so I didn't notice right away that Yumi was rocking back and forth for a long time. "Are you okay, sir?"

She frowned. "I may have some disappointing news."

I braced myself without having any idea what I was bracing myself for. "Oh?"

She tried to sound nonchalant. "It is possible this will be my last night of teaching."

"Oh?" Would I never see her again? If this were true, it would be the worst news since being separated from Mitchell, Irene, and Carmella all within a two-year period. Yumi was a high school senior and could well be preparing to go off to college next fall, but I didn't think that was what was going on. I suspected there were problems in the Park family. I didn't know the Park men, of course. Yumi's school was in walking distance from my home, so I never attended classes at the Eltingville flagship school, where Grandmaster Min-Jun Park taught, or the St. George satellite, where her brothers, Lorne and Pernell, taught. I also wasn't privy to any gossip about any of them. However, two weeks ago, I saw a quarter-page Sunday newspaper ad for a newly minted Tae Kwon Do school operated by Lorne and Pernell called *Next Generation Tae Kwon Do*. The different branding signaled the school was unaffiliated with their father's franchise, and the possible consequence of a family feud over money issues. Had the sons grown old enough to ask the Grandmaster for autonomous control of a branch school, and he refused them? Perhaps they felt he was underpaying and infantilizing them, and they had earned the gift through their labor teaching at his schools. For his part, the Grandmaster probably saw them as grasping at his purse or demanding a share of their inheritance before he was dead. This was what I imagined their perspectives to be. One week ago, a full-page Sunday newspaper advertisement appeared for Grandmaster Min-Jun Park's *Richmond County Institute of Tae Kwon Do*. It read: "Ignore the pretenders. Take *real* Tae Kwon Do lessons from a *real* Grandmaster." The Grandmaster was accusing two of his boys of being *fake* martial arts instructors. Daddy was *angry*. After seeing this ad, I became afraid for Yumi. The feud seemed to be escalating. How trapped between her father and her brothers did she feel? Yumi had yet to defect to *Next Generation Tae Kwon Do* and remained teaching at the *Richmond County Institute of Martial Arts*. Still, I suspected she was doing her best to play a neutral Sweden, working to broker peace while neither openly defying her father nor condemning her brothers. If the peace took too long to come, sooner or later, both her father and brothers would demand that she choose a side unequivocally. Of course, I knew none of this for certain. All I knew was that I'd seen two provocative advertisements in two Sunday papers. The rest was speculation and fancy. Still, the stress registering on Yumi's face seemed to validate my theory.

"The main pain in life is impermanence," Yumi said.

"I didn't know that."

"I wanted to say 'goodbye' to you just in case this is my last day."

I felt a lump in my throat. "Is it *Next Generation Tae Kwon Do*?"

"The Grandmaster is coming to speak with me." She consulted the digital watch she wore under her uniform. "He's always exactly on time."

"That sounds intense," I said. *Interesting that she didn't call him "Dad" or "Father."*

Yumi smiled sadly, "I'm a disappointment to him in many ways. The fact that I'm a Democrat is just icing on the cake."

"I'm sorry to hear that," I said. "I can't see how anyone could be disappointed in you."

Grandmaster Min-Jun Park's silent, imposing figure filled the front entrance of the dojo. He stood there in a silver sharkskin suit, waiting.

Yumi gave me a final smile.

It'll be "cool" when she's not here tomorrow.

April 4, 1989

I practically ran back to the dojo the next day and found Chris Wolffe, the beefy blonde dude in an American flag karate uniform, alone inside Yumi's office.

"Yumi around?" I hoped she would surprise us by emerging from a shadowy alcove.

"Master Park will not be teaching here anymore," Chris said flatly. "I'm in charge."

"Is she okay?"

"Why wouldn't she be okay?" Chris looked annoyed that I was more concerned about my past teacher than delighted by the news of him being appointed the new teacher.

I shifted my weight from one foot to the other. "It just seems like something's going on."

"You're *worried* about Yumi?"

I paraphrased C.S. Lewis: "I was up all night, crying until I had no tears left in me."

"She's fine," Chris said. "If she wasn't, it wouldn't be any of your business anyway."

"Okay. Fair enough."

Chris sat down in the swivel chair behind Yumi's old desk. "You should know, I don't play favorites like she does. You're not gonna be treated different from any other student."

"I wasn't expecting any special treatment."

"Weren't you?" Chris folded his hands in front of him on the desk. "I know you think you're better than the rest of us. I'm sure you're thinking of quitting just because Yumi is gone. And you have your black belt and can say you're done. Hooray. But only quitters quit. If you're a real martial arts student, you study Tae Kwon Do for life. It doesn't matter who your teacher is. If you stop now, just because your favorite sensei is gone, then you were never serious in the first place, and you're gonna get very soft and very fat, very quickly."

I placed a hand over my heart. "Well, I appreciate you saying that, Chris."

I considered Chris' exhibitionist American flag uniform. I had no problem with Spider-Man, Wonder Woman, Captain America, and Superman wearing the colors of the American flag on their costumes. Those superheroes symbolized the best of Western democratic values. They were fictional characters written and drawn by antifascist Jewish, Italian, and Latino comic book creators. Chris, meanwhile, looked like he was brandishing the American flag like an alpha male weapon against "girly men" like me. His martial arts uniform was WWF-reminiscent, "Hans and Franz" bullshit. He wasn't a real patriot or a real teacher. He was a bully and an opportunist who fell into a job he didn't deserve because he was in the right place at the right time. No doubt his classes would contain almost no meditation or general fitness. There would be aggressive attack moves, weapons study, and macho posturing aplenty. More "Cobra Kai," less "Miyagi." Yumi should be sitting at that desk, not this jackass.

Since Chris expected me to react to his "pep talk," I settled on quoting one of my favorite *Doctor Who* serials, "The Enemy of the World": "'People spend all their time making nice things and then other people come along and break them.'"

Chris scrunched his eyebrows together. "What?"

"This will be my final day. I take my leave of you, kind sir." I ended my martial arts education with Tolkien: "'I will not say, "Do not weep;" for not all tears are an evil.'"

"What?" asked Chris.

I gave him a Queen Elizabeth II pageant wave and walked out of the dojo.

As twilight fell, I walked the one-and-a-half miles down North Gannon Avenue towards home, passing suburban homes on my right and the Staten Island Expressway on my left. Master Yumi Park would no longer be my teacher. I felt numb. Had I been a character in a movie, I might have fallen to my knees in slow motion, raised my fists heavenwards, tossed my head back, and screamed, "Noooooooooo!" Or I could have assumed a stoic look as a single tear slid from my eye. Or I could have pounded a table with both fists and hissed, "She has been taken from me!" As amusing as these images might have been, they didn't make me laugh. Nor did I entertain doing those ridiculous things. Great news. Apocalyptic news. Both left me equally unmoved. Had my emotions been sandblasted out of my heart? When had this happened? Was there any one cause, or was the process so incremental — and brought about by so many small insults and minor tragedies — that I didn't realize I was the proverbial frog in boiling water?

"What the fuck is wrong with you?" I muttered to myself.

A stop-off at Saint Luke's Roman Catholic Church was in order. It was only a block or so out of my way. It should have occurred to me that the church would be locked during the evenings for security reasons, but the chains on the handles seemed like overkill and sent the wrong message. Normally, I would have been too shy to present myself at the adjacent rectory building, but I was just annoyed enough by the chains that I went there. Peering through an eye-level glass window set inside the oak door, I saw a brightly lit waiting room with a red carpet, dark brown wood-paneled walls, a desk, and high-school girl receptionist I knew by sight. The receptionist saw my face framed in the window, somehow avoided being startled by it, and opened the door for me to step into the foyer. "Can I help you?"

I kicked my baritone up an octave or three to appear less threatening. "Father Jack Stańczyk in?"

"He only comes in on weekends to say a mass or two. He doesn't live here."

"Oh." That explained why I had so few opportunities to see him outside of mass during my year of increased church engagement. I suspected this was the case but was still disappointed. "I don't suppose Miss O'Sullivan works here?"

"She moved to New Jersey. Would you like to speak with Monsignor Tobin?"

Years of Tobin's dreadful homilies came to mind. "Okay. I'm Damien Cavalieri."

"No, you're not." The bald, bearded Monsignor Steve Tobin appeared behind the receptionist. Off-duty and relaxing after dinner, Tobin had unbuttoned the top of his black dress shirt. Half his starched white collar hung out in midair. "That's not how you pronounce your name. You're saying 'Cavalerry?' You're butchering and Americanizing it. You should say it the way they do in Italy. Pronounce it 'Kah-val-year-ee.' Have some ethnic pride. Be a real Italian!"

I arched my right eyebrow. "Is that how we're supposed to say it?" The irony of a priest named Tobin lecturing me on proper Italian pronunciation was not lost on me. I considered his point. He was right, of course. My pronunciation was off. According to the rules I had somehow managed to learn in two years of raucous Italian classes, Mom and Dad had encouraged me to say our family name incorrectly all along. Cavalerry was at best simplified and Americanized, at worst completely inaccurate. "But the salesmen who call us can't even pronounce our name the watered-down way. They say 'Cave-a-liar-eye.' How can I hope anyone could say it correctly?"

"You're not going to let courtesy callers decide your surname for you, are you? Of course not! Say your name right. Anyway, I've seen you around sometimes. What can I do for you?"

I wasn't sure what I was going to say before I said it. "I want to be a Jesuit, maybe."

The Monsignor was not expecting me to go there. He assumed a less casual stance. "Why jump right to Jesuit? That is, if you think you might have a calling?"

"Father Jack Stańczyk. I'd like to be a similar sort of priest."

Tobin placed his hands in his pockets and chose his words carefully. "I'm glad to hear you are interested in joining the priesthood. I'm slightly concerned about your choice of role model. If you had said you wanted to follow my example, or those provided by the religious instruction teachers I've been hiring, like Miss O'Sullivan, who you mentioned, I'd feel better. She and I understand that there are two kinds of Catholics. There's the real Catholics and the buffet Catholics. Real Catholics believe in the Magisterium, the Catechism of the Catholic

Church, and the authority of the Congregation for the Doctrine of the Faith. We believe that the reforms imposed upon the Church during the Second Vatican Council were a mistake that need reversing. Fake Catholics are another story. They reject all these bedrock beliefs."

"You're not saying that Father Jack isn't a real Catholic, are you?"

Tobin must have seen how stricken I looked. He held his hands up, as if I were a potential suicide threatening to jump off a ledge. "I do have reservations about the liberation theology that creeps into his homilies. Jack weaves in too much Dorothy Day and too little Opus Dei."

Tobin might as well have been speaking Latin. "Fr. Jack just seems like a nice man."

"I can offer you a sympathetic ear if you want to talk."

Father Jack was the person I really needed, but he wasn't there. I also needed Master Park. I needed Mitchell. I needed my small handful of cool relatives: Gabriel, the Biancas, or that interesting rich lady with the batty sister in the miniskirt. I needed someone. Tobin might be boring, confusing, and bald, but he was here. "I'd like that."

"Excellent. Would you like some tea or some coffee while we talk?"

"Tea sounds good."

Tobin started off to get me some tea, remembered something, and turned back to me. "Stop me if you heard this one. A mother tells her parish priest that her son is very interested in joining a seminary. She asked what would be involved in becoming a priest. He explained to her, 'If your son wants to be a diocesan priest, he'll have to study for eight years. If he wants to become a Franciscan, he'll have to study for ten years. If he wants to become a Jesuit, he'll have to study for fourteen years.' The mother considered all this and decided, 'He better become a Jesuit. He's a little slow!'"

I was legitimately confused. "That would be funnier if Jesuits were stupid in real life, but they aren't. Like, jokes have to be true to be funny . . . "

The Monsignor shrugged. "I guess you can't please everybody. That one usually kills it."

PART II: ANUPTAPHOBIA

CHAPTER NINETEEN
The Kindness of Strangers

Four years later . . .

September 6, 1993

"By 2007, seventy-five percent of all Americans will have AIDS," beer-bellied health teacher Dirk Sabato intoned. "There are twenty-five students here. Look to your left. Look to your right. Three out of four of you will get AIDS before you die."

"My parents went to Woodstock," Arwen whispered to me. "What a difference twenty years makes!" We sat together in the back of the classroom, talking and flirting every day during health. This practice was made possible by Dirk Sabato not minding students jawing nonstop and Arwen's damn boyfriend Rolf not being in this class with us. In one lesson, Dirk slipped a condom onto a banana, and Arwen asked me if I wanted her to do that to me. When Dirk produced a female pelvis anatomical model with removable organs, I asked Arwen if that's what hers looked like. We said those kinds of subtle, deep things to one another all the time.

"Imagine having an outdoor rock orgy these days!" I said. "Shit. Our parents' generation gets sex, drugs, and 'All Along the Watchtower.' We get AIDS, 'Just Say No,' and 'Sussudio!'"

"Yeah, but you're the only one I know who actually *listened* to Nancy Reagan and SPECDA. Everyone else said 'yes' to drugs. And 'yes.' And 'YES!'"

School Program to Educate and Control Drug Abuse. I listened credulously to their rep because he stood in front of a blackboard. I listen to everyone who stands before a blackboard.

"I hear you," I said. "But drugs killed John Belushi and half the Woodstock performers. I can't help being not too pumped about drugs after that."

"Don't knock drugs until you tried them."

I shook my head. "I've seen *French Connection II* too many times."

Arwen rolled her eyes. "You are no fun. What can I do to convince you to try cocaine?"

"I dunno. Can I snort some off your breasts?"

Arwen ran her tongue over her upper teeth and smiled. "Maybe."

I arched an eyebrow. "Yeah? Cocaine is sounding better already."

Arwen leaned in closer to me and placed her hand on my shoulder. "It's better with two."

Dirk Sabato inclined his head to see us in the back. "Okay, that's enough! Stop talking! Every day with you two. Give it a rest."

Sure. Now he interrupts. Good timing, buddy.

Goddamn motherfucker.

In my senior year at Grace Coolidge High School, I may have been a little lame, but I was far cooler than I had been during my first year of middle school. I had fewer pimples, wore contact lenses, had gotten better at using gel to keep my thick, curly hair under control, and had grown a goatee with a slightly reddish tint that didn't quite match my dark brown hair. I'd also taken to dressing more like the Italian comic book hero Dylan Dog: blue jeans, a red dress shirt, and black jacket. Still, there was a limit to my coolness. I'll admit, it is difficult to be modish when tooling around in your mother's borrowed blue Oldsmobile Cutlass Ciera. However, I had near constant access to the car from lunchtime to ten p.m. since Mom always woke at five a.m. and was done driving for the day by noon. To make the car seem more badass than it was, I referred to it as "Starscream," but that name only worked if I didn't look too closely at it.

I drove around Staten Island at nine p.m. a couple of nights each school week, when surprisingly few people were on the road. Pretending I was driving the Batmobile or K.I.T.T., I rolled down the windows and blasted my idea of awesome driving music: Danny Elfman's *Batman* theme, Bryan Adams' "Summer of '69," Van Halen's "Hot for Teacher," and Aerosmith's "Rag Doll." My personal favorite moment came when I pulled up to a stop light with the windows rolled down, blasting John Carpenter's love theme to *Starman* at 10 p.m. I was thinking of Arwen and really feeling the full power of the romantic keyboard music. I thought I was alone when an elderly couple pulled up in the lane beside me with their windows also rolled down. They gaped at me, angered by the volume and terrified I might be insane.

"Don't you just love *Starman*?" I yelled. "The most romantic movie music of all time! *E. T.* for grown-ups! *Starman*, baby! *Starman!*

Wooooooo!" I raised the volume to maximum.

The elderly duo's faces turned white. The light changed. They peeled away, doing seventy in a thirty-five-miles-per-hour-road.

"Ciao," I said happily to myself, and resumed driving at the speed limit level.

Since Mitchell had long since left my social orbit, I contented myself with hanging out with my coolest fellow 12th graders at Grace Coolidge High School. It was a three-star institution that represented a marked improvement over my zero-star middle school. I hung out with David Litvinov, Salty Margaritas, Kyle Ahearne, and their rotating batch of decorative, irritatingly taciturn girlfriends, all of whom were named Jennifer. Occasionally, Arwen and her too-cool-for-school boyfriend, Rolf Kaminsky, joined us. Nobody liked Rolf, but we invited them along because everybody wanted to fuck Arwen. ("I want to do terrible, terrible things to that bitch," Salty liked to tell me, just to make me clench my teeth and glare at him.) Unclean thoughts aside, Arwen was hilarious and ridiculously fun to hang out with. Hope sprang eternal that she would switch out Rolf for one of us other guys, but that never seemed to happen.

The guys and I wore trenchcoats and fedoras as a shared affectation, inspiring the Jennifers to refer to us as "The Trenchcoat Mafia." I could do without the nickname, myself, since I was never a fan of evoking the Mafia stereotype. When the same name was later applied to the social circle of the Columbine shooters, Eric Harris and Dylan Klebold, I found the nickname particularly unfortunate and stopped wearing trenchcoats altogether. I discarded such coats a little late, though. When I bumped into one of my favorite high school history teachers in the supermarket years later, I was delighted to see him. He was less delighted to see me, because he had made the connection between our group and the Columbine shooters and was not sure what violence I was capable of unleashing upon the world. This would not be the last time I would have an awkward and disheartening reunion with an old teacher.

I had little in common with anyone in our local chapter of the national Trenchcoat Mafia organization beyond David and Arwen, but their "Joe Sixpack" mannerisms taught me to loosen up a bit. Also, if it hadn't been for them, I may have never discovered more mainstream music, like Nirvana, Tom Petty, Green Day, Rush, Pearl Jam, Smashing Pumpkins, and R.E.M. Salty and Kyle were the leaders of our little entourage. When David was out with us, he was the bottom of our food chain and got teased the most. When he was not around, I was the one to be needled endlessly for being too sheltered, Catholic, allergy-prone, skittish around girls, and nerdy. I liked it when David was around to take the heat off me, but I never teased him, because I knew what it was like to be the "Jerry Gergich" of the group. On rare occasions, I spoke up in David's defense, but not often enough to brag about. The problem with being part of an entourage is it involved certain compromises, like having to see people you never wanted to hang out with on their best days all the time. The Jennifers were dull as dishwater, and painfully dainty. Spiders and small puddles on the road froze them in terror and indecision. The lameness of their, "Ooooh! A puddle!" drove me spare.

A puddle? Seriously? I guess I prefer tomboys after all.

Worst of all was Salty, who I avoided as much as I could. I tried to hang with the gang on days he wasn't around and stay home when he was. This meant I didn't see him as often as I might have, but I did see him far more often than I wanted to. One time, I asked Kyle if I could go over his house and play Nintendo with just him. We were both trying hard to defeat Soda Popinksi in *Mike Tyson's Punch-Out* and were eager to take turns facing off against our digital opponent. When I arrived at Kyle's house, Salty opened the door to let me in. "Howya doin', faggot?" he asked, then burped in my face. The three of us took turns and swapped partners while playing two-player games. When I got a moment alone with Kyle, I said, "What the hell?"

Kyle looked grave. "I had no choice. He arrived right before you did. I'm sorry."

"I'm sorry, too."

Experiencing this kind of nonsense time and again in the hermetically sealed culture of a Staten Island high school's student body is one of the reason's Jane Austen's *Emma* wound up becoming one of my favorite novels. Just as poor Emma Woodhouse couldn't do anything social in Highbury with her beloved Harriet, Mrs. Weston, and Mr. Knightley without being saddled with the company of Miss Bates, Mrs. Elton, and Jane Fairfax, I couldn't do anything fun with Kyle, David, or Arwen without being stuck with Salty, Rolf, or the Jennifers. Since there wasn't much to do on Staten Island, our little group most often hit Perkins for breakfast, hung out at the mall, smoked cigars at Clove Lakes Park, listened to Enya CDs laying on my basement floor with the lights out, visited chain restaurants like Applebee's for dinner, or went bowling and saw a movie on Friday at the UA Movies at Staten Island 14 on 145 E. Service Road, Travis-Chelsea. My favorite times out were when we played pool. Every time we did, I pretended I was Grandpa. I wasn't great at pool, but I wasn't abominable. Sadly, I didn't go whoring afterwards.

There was little to do in the afternoons right after school ended, so we sometimes stole political signs we didn't understand, especially if they were an eyesore and blanketed the borough. Why were there green "Mark Green: Public Advocate" signs on every block in the borough? What the fuck was a 'public advocate'? After Election Day, we made a mission of taking all of them down. The sign "No Loop!" was particularly puzzling. We were bolder with those signs and stole them well before the referendum vote in question. What the heck did these signs mean? Whatever! Throw them in the trunk! Of course, articles started appearing in the local news accusing the Pro-Loop contingent of launching a conspiracy against the No-Loop contingent by stealing their signs. We laughed hysterically at those articles, because it was just us, fucking around. It was only months later when David discovered, too late, that he himself was anti-loop. We should have been taking down the signs for the other side! When David revealed this, I wondered, vaguely, if I would have supported Mark Green if I had taken the time to research his platform. Deciding we were being too destructive taking down political signage, we stole a yellow flag with a red circle on it from a Mobile gas station and drove around waving it out the passenger window, like the rebels in *Less Miserables* and its sequel, *More Miserables*.

Sometimes the boys drove around catcalling pretty women of all ages. David invited them into the car to ride on his magic lap, Salty asked them in to sit on his face, and Kyle cheered, "You're workin' it!

I'm lovin' it!" The girls would yell at us to fuck off and we'd drive away. I couldn't bring myself to join in, because I noticed the end result was never positive. Not one woman actually got in the car and sat on anyone's face. Not one. I may have tried out a "hey, baby!" one time and gotten a middle finger before I announced my early retirement from catcalling and started drawing on my 401(k) plan.

As equal opportunity public nuisances, we also liked to annoy angry-looking middle-aged men. We would usually inform them they were ugly or throw water balloons at them as we screeched past. One time, while menacing a residential neighborhood, we pulled up beside a man standing in his own driveway, leaning under the open hood of his car, muttering. Salty shot the man in the coin slot with a massive NERF Super Soaker water gun for five seconds before he felt it and chased after us. Later, we passed another man in sandals reading a paperback on a park bench. Kyle yelled, "He dies at the end!" The guy waved an impotent fist at us. We added, "Nice sandals!" as we drove away. Good times.

Once every couple of months, we bought a Denino's cheese pizza or a Goodfellas vodka pie, drove up to house of a friend who said he was too busy to hang out that night, rang his doorbell, left the high-end pizza on his doorstep, ran to the car, and drove away as he opened the door. Each time, one of us would lean out the window and yell either, "Enjoy the pizza!" or "Tell your mom she's hot!" One time, I was the one who was home sick from school, but it wasn't a pizza I found when I opened the front door to the prank doorbell ring at 3:45 p.m. Instead of the vodka pie I adored, I was the lucky recipient of a pornographic greeting card from Spencer's Gifts. The card had a picture of Velma and Daphne from Scooby Doo lifting up their skirts on the front. Stuffed inside the card were two pairs of black panties, presumably stolen from someone's sister's dresser, with the inscription: "Sorry you're sick. We came to fuck you. Some other time, then. XOXO, Arwen and Marina." I heard peals of laughter, a honking horn, and saw Salty's car drive away. It was a funny note, in a *Ghost World*-sorta way, but I was upset by how predictable I'd become. The guys knew exactly how to sign the card. They knew the two girls I liked because I'd been stuck on the same two girls for years and had not moved on from either of them. It was beyond pathetic and boring. How was it, as a high-school student, that I still carried torches over two old junior high school crushes? Marina had even gone to a different high school: the Fiorello H. LaGuardia High School of Music & Art and Performing Arts. I was surprised that Marina's complete absence from my day-to-day life didn't help me forget her, but it sure didn't. I remained fixated upon her. Of course, Arwen had wound up in the same public school as me, so at least my continued proximity to her justified my obsession. As far as both girls were concerned, I found myself being tempted, once a month, to drive past their homes, wondering if there were any evildoers lurking outside that I could rescue them and their families from. The good and bad news was I was never called upon by fate to rescue either of them from burglars or serial killers. I would like to reassure you that I did not sing "On the Street Where You Live" as I made these borderline mentally ill drive-by trips, because I was well aware I cut a more pathetic and creepy figure than Freddy Eynsford-Hill from *My Fair Lady*. Yes: Idle hands do the devil's work. I needed new girls to pursue. I just had no idea where to look.

A few days after Election Day, I planted six Mark Green: Public Advocate signs on Kyle's front lawn. As I drove the final stake into the grass, I felt raindrops in my hair. It was time to get home. I managed to close the car door and turn over the engine before the sky broke open. Torrential rain bombarded my windshield. I was worried about driving in this downpour, but my wipers and lights made the road just clear enough that I chose to risk the twenty-minute trip home. I put on *John Denver's Greatest Hits* on CD and sang along to "Wild Montana Skies." At a red light, I pulled up in front of a bus stop with no inclement weather shelter attached to it. Drenched to the bone and shivering, an underdressed blonde woman stood there without an umbrella. How far was she going? How long would the bus take to arrive? *I should offer her a ride.* I lowered my window. "Hi, there! Would you–"

The woman's face contorted with rage and she bellowed "NO!" from somewhere deep in the recesses of her soul. She pointed down the road with a quaking hand. "GO! GO!"

"I'm sorry," I said quickly. "I just wanted to–"

"GET OUT OF HERE!" She reached into her purse for a concealed weapon.

The light turned green. My car hydroplaned. I floored the gas. The tires caught the ground. I sped away before she could produce the handgun, switchblade, or mace in her purse.

I broke into a cold sweat. My emotions were a tornado of guilt, fear, confusion, and moral outrage. I vented these bleak feelings by screaming at myself nonstop as I sped home. "That's what I get for trying to be a good Samaritan. Who the hell did she think I was? Buffalo Bill?" I glance at myself in the rearview mirror. "'It rubs the lotion on its skin or else it gets the hose again!'" I couldn't bring myself to laugh at my own joke. "That was totally uncalled for. What could possibly make her *that* angry? She looked ready to shoot me!"

I stopped talking to myself but kept thinking furiously. *Okay, fine. Fine! I get it! I'm on the lookout for a girlfriend. She was pretty. That means my motives were suspect. But once she got in my car, I wasn't about to put my hand on her thigh. If she wanted to grab my thigh, I'd welcome it, but I would not squeeze hers! She's a guest in my car, and vulnerable. That means I owe her my restraint and my protection. Guest-friendship demands I be a gentleman. Read your Homer. Read your Bible. Never violate the rules of hospitality. Ever. If, after I drop her off — and she is out of my power — she decides to volunteer her phone number, unasked? Fantastic! And if she doesn't offer up her digits? I've still done someone a good turn getting them out of the rain. Win-win. So why did she just assume, right off the bat that I'm some kind of sex predator and–*

Wait a minute. Wait a minute. Was I the fiftieth guy to pull up in front of her to offer her a ride in the past ten minutes? I looked at myself in the rearview mirror again. I said to myself, "Jesus H. Christ. I probably *was* the fiftieth guy to pull up and offer her a ride in the past ten minutes! Well, shit. If that's the world we all live in, then I guess I never will be able to pull a superhero and help a pretty stranger in need. It is just . . . not gonna happen. Ever."

I stopped speaking to my reflection and returned to raving via inner monologue.

Under what circumstances would a female stranger accept help from me? They would have to be extraordinary. After all, I'm a six-foot-tall dago. Nothing scarier than a big WOP. I need to live in a small town where everyone knows everyone so I can live my life like I live in an actual, functioning society with people who interact. Once the population gets too big, nobody trusts nobody. We all suspect one another of being secret members of the Red-Headed League.

The rain's deafening attack on my windshield built to a crescendo. Somehow, I found my way home despite the visibility growing exponentially worse. I pulled into our driveway, turned off the car, and sat inside. I watched the rain, listening to it fall against the car.

I'm never getting a girlfriend.

And what the hell is it like to be a woman these days? If a friendly offer causes a primal scream like that? What in hell is it like to be a woman? Wasn't it supposed to be better now?

I guess me and the guys need to stop catcalling chicks, at least. The shit those morons yell out is too gross and nobody thinks it's funny. But I'm not the one who catcalls. And I wasn't catcalling just now. I was just trying to be nice . . . I dunno . . . I give up...

As I entered the house, I found Mom waiting for me with a copy of today's *Chronicle*. "Listen, don't pull over to help any strange women on the side of the road with a flat tire."

Yeah, I'm retired. I ain't helping nobody no more. I'm done. Fuck that noise. "Why?"

"I've just read a terrifying local news story. There's a black widow running around loose on Staten Island."

"A black widow? Theresa Russell or the Russian chick who leads the Avengers?"

"She's lured three men to their deaths. They pull over to help her, she shoots them in the heads, and takes all their money. I'm reading this and I'm thinking, 'This is how my son is going to die. He's exactly the sort of person who'd pull my car over to help some strange woman he's never met before and get himself killed.'"

I gave Mom a wide-eyed innocent look and pointed to myself. "Do I look like the sort of person who'd pull over to offer help to a strange woman I don't know?"

"It seems like classic you, yes," Mom said. "Don't do it. Never, ever."

A black widow sounds pretty hot, though. If you gotta go . . .

Singing Billy Ocean's "Get Outta My Dreams, Get into My Car," I headed up to my room to put on some dry clothes.

CHAPTER TWENTY
Neutered Pepé Le Pew and the Stench of Desperate Need

November 6, 1993

Party at David Litvinov's house, when his parents are out of town
10:22 p.m.

Me: Why am I not seeing cartoon characters, David? I was promised cartoon characters.

David: That's LSD, Damien. This is weed.

Me: It has no effect on me. What's supposed to happen?

David: You get mellow, silly, and hungry.

Me: I'm like that usually.

David: Are you kidding? You're always tightly wound.

Me: My clothes stink. Why is this stuff banned? Why not ban elevator music?

David: Why'd you try it? I thought you didn't like breaking laws.

Me: I found the girl with the hairy arms rolling these things strangely attractive.

David: Her arms were way too hairy for me.

Me: This is the most boring drug of all time, David. I get higher from the Busch Gardens rollercoaster, penne alla vodka, and my pinup of Gillian Anderson. People do this all the time? For smelly clothes and zero Ralph Bakshi character hallucinations?

David: Yeah.

Me: I'm taking a shower and having an amaretto. This is the worst.

David: You seem pretty high to me, Damien.

Me: If I have any more of this, it will only be to talk to She-Wolf of London.

November 8, 1993

Dunkin' Donuts, 9:03 p.m.

I went to Dunkin' Donuts for a Dunkaccino and didn't expect to find a pretty twenty-something girl in a T-shirt and jeans sitting alone, reading a book, being publicly literate on Staten Island. *Dear Blessed*

Virgin Mary: Please let her be reading Flatland, The Thin Man, The Code of the Woosters, The Crucible, The Big Sleep, Leaves of Grass, 1984, Time and Again, Mystery and Manners, Lilies of the Field, Gulliver's Travels, The Good Times, Angel of the Revolution*, or anything else I've ever heard of or enjoyed.* "Hey, there. What're you readin'?"

Unperturbed by my nosy question, she held the book aloft. *The Electric Kool-Aid Acid Test.* Her hand covered the author's name. *Well, shit. I have no idea what the hell this book is.* "Cool," I said, pretending to know it. I hoped her T-shirt might offer me an alternative conversational opening: A somber man in a black hat under the caption: "What Would Billy Jack Do?" *God damn it! Who the fuck is Billy Jack?* I had no idea what this woman was all about, but she gave off good vibes. I strongly suspected: a) she was way too cool for me and b) it would do me a world of good to date her. I was also sure that: c) it was time to run away.

"Enjoy," I said.

"Thanks." She resumed her reading.

I turned and fled the Dunkin' Donuts.

When I got home, Dad was relaxing in his blue plaid pajamas, emerald green bath robe, and brown slippers, sipping tea in the wood-paneled living room of our semi-attached home. He wore simple brown glasses, had straight greying brown hair parted on the side, and had long-since shaved his 1970s moustache. A friendly, subdued smile flitted across his face. Since his father's death, he had grown more religious, quiet, and reclusive, transforming from a Peter Pan figure, sulking because his toys had been taken away from him, into Mr. Woodhouse from Jane Austen's *Emma*: nervous, depressed, terrified of death, and craving quiet and seclusion above all else. On the one recent occasion I had asked him to drive me to the comic book store Jim Hanley's Universe on New Dorp Lane, he dented the rear bumper of the car backing into an old, gnarled oak tree hanging low over his chosen parking spot on a nearby residential street. Spying the damage done to the car, he observed gravely, "This is what happens when you leave the safety of home."

Dad's new persona was as far removed from the one he had when I was growing up as I could imagine. He was more anti-profanity than ever, and championed humility and decorum as the most important character traits. He chided me for being flashy and profane, reminding me that quiet people are more emotionally authentic and loud people less sincere. He had a point that I could be a bit "extra" when nervous. Still, I've always tried to be emotionally authentic, even when engaging in showmanship, playing to my audience, or telling white lies.

Contributing to Dad's new persona was his embracing of the gentle artistic universe of Bob Ross and wet-on-wet landscape painting. After Dad had spent two years listlessly haunting our house, grieving for his austere, chess-master father, he stumbled across my old Bob Ross paints and instructional books and videotapes. I couldn't have been more surprised than when he used them. He hadn't done anything creative in years. When had he made his last Super 8 film? Ages ago. Now, it was only a matter of weeks before he had produced dozens of Bob Ross painting duplicates. He also taught himself to paint a portrait of Saint Therese of Lisieux.

The most surprising thing about Dad, given his lecherous streak, was just how religious he became, praying for the soul of his father, reading biographies of Saint Therese, and volunteering with a local order of nuns. The Daughters of Saint Paul had a convent on the north shore a few miles uphill from the Staten Island Ferry Terminal. Dad had heard them singing at a Christmas concert hosted by Chazz Palminteri at Our Lady of Pity Church, purchased their CDs, and listened to "Hail Holy Queen" on repeat for a month. I have to admit, I didn't give Dad the benefit of the doubt. I assumed that he had some sort of sleazy ulterior motive for hanging out with the nuns. Unlike the terrifying, stereotypical nuns of 1950s coming-of-age-stories, most of these sisters were young and attractive. Since the Daughters of Saint Paul were founded to bring Catholicism into the realm of the modern-day mass media, the order made a point of recruiting young novices. Consequently, when Dad volunteered to help them host a tag sale, decorate a concert venue, or cook a dinner, he was participating in his religion in honor of his deceased father, feeling selfless, and getting to hang out with a boatload of pretty celibate girls. It was this last part I found amusing. "Dad, you know that you can't have sex with any of them, right?"

"Damien!" Dad chastised me. "That's shallow of you. The nuns are my friends. There's nothing wrong with being friends with women. What you really don't want to do is hang out with gangs of boys all the time. I ran with this circle of Irish guys when I was a kid, and we sniffed glue, stole cars, got into fist fights in bars, and were just a total disaster area. Listen, don't ever hang out with groups of guys. Don't join street gangs, fraternities, or men's clubs. There's always one maniac who starts something thinking doing something evil will be fun, and he causes a huge disaster and makes everyone an accomplice or an accessory-after-the-fact. He's self-destructive and he drags everyone else down with him. 'Hey, let's try this pyramid scheme and get rich.' 'Hey, let's go to a meeting of the John Birch Society.' 'Hey, let's go into a pool hall in a Black neighborhood and start a brawl.' These were all terrible ideas. Every time I was ever arrested, or almost arrested, or made a choice I regretted for the rest of my life, I was with a bunch of jackass guys. On the other hand, no girl ever got me into trouble. Hanging out with a girl, you get to eat out at cool ethnic food restaurants and eat more than just burgers and fries and steak and potatoes. If you spend time with girls, you get to listen to all kinds of new music you never knew existed. Girls would take me out to the theater, take me clog dancing, and teach me how to do quilting and scrapbooking. Here's the thing: you won't get arrested going clog dancing. And sometimes girls let you feel them up. No girl ever got pregnant on me, or falsely accused me of rape, or ratted me out to the cops, or got me into life-threatening danger. Girls were just nice to be around. Boys? The opposite. Spend time with guys, you get hit in the head with a glass beer bottle, get into a knife fight, or become addicted to morphine. Whether you're looking for friends or lovers, chase around after women and you'll live a happy, safe, cultured, well-educated life. Run around with boys, and you'll wind up traumatized, dead, or in jail."

"This is why you hang out with nuns, now?" I asked. "They won't make you sniff glue, or kill someone and bury them by the side of the road and swear not to speak of it?"

"Exactly."

"Well, I agree with you completely, but you gave me the exact opposite advice as a kid. I thought you were always worried that men who were 'just friends' with women were all secretly gay. That's why you threw out my Wonder Woman toys."

Dad could not have looked more shocked and wounded. "I never said that! And I never threw out your toys! Why would you make those things up about me?"

I got surprisingly angry with Dad when he couldn't remember the incident with my Wonder Woman toys. His amnesia seemed a little too convenient. Then I remembered that, in my experience, very few people had the memory I did. Whenever I would say to my father or Mitchell or Kyle Ahearne: "Remember this hilarious thing you said to me three years ago?" they would invariably say, "No, I do not! How in the hell do you remember that so specifically? Anyway, the good news is, I guess I'm a funny guy if I said that!" People who could forget the past were fortunate. I often wish I could. If Dad was able to mentally block out his old parental misdeeds, more power to him. He could forgive himself and move on. Meanwhile, I still regretted failing to pass the salt to Aunt Beatrice one time in 1984, and always remembered the cutting remark she made afterwards. As much as a grudge-holder as Beatrice could be, I was certain she didn't remember the incident to this day, while it was burned in my brain for all eternity. I wouldn't wish that kind of memory on General Franco, let alone my father. Anyway, Dad was in the process of reinventing himself in the wake of his father's death, so what did he need me bringing up the errors that "old" Dad had made, now of all times? Had I insisted on his memories subordinating themselves to the authority of my recollections, I would have held the living-breathing Dad of today hostage to my static remembrance of him. Making matters worse, it would be a remembrance he didn't agree was legitimate. Anyway, I got along well with Dad during my high school years — aside from the time he read half a draft of my autobiography, declared it dull and profane, and suggested I burn it. The evening I returned home from my failed attempt to pick up a girl at a Dunkin Donuts, I plopped myself into the soft blue plush armchair facing Dad's plush brown armchair. "Dad, have you heard of Billy Jack?"

Dad sighed. "I knew it was only a matter of time before you discovered Billy Jack."

I spread my arms, gesturing animatedly, like a good Italian. "Who the hell is he?"

"He's a half-Indian, half-Mexican kung fu master. He defends a hippie commune in the desert from racist cops and Klansmen. When his hat comes off, prepare for kung fu. He's usually avenging the bullying of a midget or rape of a flower child. I think you'd like him. You're becoming the sort of person who would like Billy Jack. I root for the bad guys in those movies."

I laughed. "I think I just failed to meet my future wife. There was a woman in Dunkin' Donuts wearing a Billy Jack T-shirt and reading *The Electric Kool-Aid Acid Test*."

Dad shook his head. "Never heard of it. For all I know, it stars Billy Jack. But you need to go on a date or two before you start worrying about who your future wife is."

"A date or two with who?" I asked, helplessly.

November 12, 1993

Salty, David, Kyle, and I sat in the food court of the Staten Island Mall, eating Burger King, watching women go by and rating their level of attractiveness from 1–10 on scratch paper. Kyle took pride in never assigning tens, David rated everyone exactly one point below me each time, and Salty rated two points below me. Salty teased me for my beauty contest grade inflation. "If you become a college teacher, don't hand out As like candy, ya dirty Commie."

David was more conciliatory. "There's a part in *The Unbearable Lightness of Being* about the two different kinds of love. You guys are looking for the one, perfect beauty to love, and Damien sees the beauty in all things and all people. Both are legitimate loves."

Kyle rolled his eyes. "Whatever the fuck *The Unbearable Lightness of Being* is."

"Okay, Damien, who are the hottest James Bond women?" Salty asked mockingly, while removing the pickles from his Whopper. "Or are they all *equally* attractive?"

"I don't watch those stupid movies," Kyle scoffed. "Faggy British guy in a tux kills four hundred Russians with a handgun while drinking a martini as he goes down a ski jump."

I counted off my top three. "Tatiana Romanova, Fiona Volpe, and Doctor Goodhead."

David Litvinov applauded silently. "I approve."

"Just so you know, Kyle, he actually made surprisingly respectable choices," Salty observed. "Even if he left out Jane Seymour and Caroline Munro."

"Speaking of attractive older women . . . " I chose that moment to inform the boys I was about to begin a tireless quest to find a cougar of my own, as per my palm-reading instructions.

"No, you idiot!" Salty exclaimed. "We're all going to the prom together at the end of the year. We'll rent a limo together and go to Wildwood on a weekend getaway after. We *all* need to find senior girls to bring as dates! I don't suppose it crossed your mind that you could totally screw up our plans by wasting all your time chasing after cougars and college graduates?"

"It crossed my mind." I took a bite out of my Whopper and drank some Coke. "It doesn't matter who I ask to be my prom date, younger or older. It's a foregone conclusion I'm going to fail. I know I'm not going to the prom. I've known from the first day of freshman year."

"How can you be so certain?" asked David.

"I've seen it in my mind as if it has already happened. I'm not going."

Kyle shook his head. "I do not understand."

"I've always known...I'll be alone on prom night."

"So, you're not a 'the cup is half full' kinda guy then?" Salty was somber and teasing.

Kyle broke in, "That's a self-fulfilling prophecy. You shouldn't ever take a break from being on the prowl. Look at today. We're at the mall! Look at all these girls here! You should be doing everything in your power to get yourself some trim."

I ran a hand through my hair to check it. "I guess I do need a haircut."

Kyle crumpled up his burger wrapping and tossed it as trash in his Burger King paper bag. Then he pulled open the tab of his Hershey pie carton to unpack his dessert. "Listen, Eeyore: If you tried more often, there'd be less at stake for you when you do try. Instead, you wait 'til you've fallen head-over-heels in love with someone — not 'like' or 'lust,' freakin' 'love' — and then you ask them out. By then, the stakes are too high. Either that or you go to the opposite extreme and corner a random MILF you've never seen before in your life in the freezer section of Waldbaum's and are surprised when they're scared of you and want to call security. Just ask some chick you kinda know and kinda like a little. Not a total stranger. Not the love of your life. A nice girl to take on a low-stakes date. Stop being a crazy person for once."

"The real reason Damien scares the shit out of chicks he asks out to the movies is he gives off a stench of desperate neediness." Salty turned to me. "Dude, you're like a neutered Pepé Le Pew walking around looking for love, plaintively asking girls, 'Will *you* love me? How about you? How about *you?*' That's a major turn-off. Nobody wants to be asked out in a mealy-mouthed way by some clingy, teary-eyed bastard with a bouquet of flowers in his hands. You need to have a strut when you walk. A confidence. You need to let women know you can take them or leave them. Then they'll want you. The moment you look needy, all is lost."

"I definitely don't strut when I walk," I admitted. "I hunch."

"You shouldn't," advised Kyle.

David added way too much salt to his remaining French fries. "The problem is you need a girlfriend to get a girlfriend. It's like the ads for 'entry-level jobs' that 'require three-to-four-years of experience.' It makes no sense, but that's how it is. If you're single, nobody wants you. Why would any girl want a guy no other girl has claimed? If you're happily in a relationship, other girls see how nice you treat your girl, and they try to steal you away. You should ask out an ugly girl, get her, and see who shows up to swipe you away. Or buy a fake wedding ring and wear it. They'll line up around the block for you."

Kyle shook his head. "That's not the real problem. There's a woman for everybody, but Damien is stuck with a whole bunch of mouth-breathers on Staten Island. He's a genius. He needs to date another genius. He's Frasier Crane and he needs to find himself a Lilith."

"More like Niles Crane," Salty said, exasperated. "He's tense and sad and angry and humorless all the time. We need to get this guy laid or he'll have hypertension by twenty-two."

"No, he isn't always sad," Kyle said. "He's always calm and funny and easy to talk to."

"I never see Damien in a good mood!" Salty groused.

"That's because you show up and put him in a bad mood," Kyle laughed. "He's fine when you aren't around! Seriously, this guy only gets publicly angry once every two years, and it's always hilarious because he goes off like an atom bomb! Whoa, daddy! Stand back!"

"In case Kyle is right about me needing a smarter girl," I said, "I'm going to ask out someone who's already in college."

Kyle gestured to me as if I'd finally figured it all out. "Non-mouth-breathers! Find yourself a girl who is an honors student and a sophomore at Wagner College. They got an organization for English majors. Find a chick from that group."

Salty surprised everyone by banging his fist on the table. "For the love of God, just ask out a high school girl! One that might say, 'Yes!' Your problem is you ask out chicks would never go with you in a million years! Lesbians, virginity promise ring chicks, born-again Christians who think Catholics go to hell, Chinese Buddhists whose parents won't let them date white Christians, and feminists who are pissed off at you for having late-term abortion reservations. Why the fuck would you ask out any girls who fall into those categories?"

"You *do* do that," David agreed. "I guess you're worried you wouldn't know what to do with ass if you caught it, so you only chase unattainable ass? This way you never face the problem of not knowing what to do with an ass when it lands in your lap?"

"Who are you gonna ask out next week?" asked Salty. "A nun? A chick in a coma? A woman in a seventeenth-century painting?"

Oh, no. I hope that isn't true. Is that true? I blushed and laughed at myself. "I see. Okay. Look, I'm not sure if I'm sabotaging myself or not. I mean, it could be true. I don't think it is. But, you know, I'll admit, if I ever got a girl, I wouldn't have the first clue what to do with her."

David raised a dramatic finger. "If you want it, Damien, I have an instructional video called, 'How to Make Love to a Woman and Please Her Every Time.' I found it very useful."

Kyle and Salty collapsed into laughter.

"Can you give me the CliffsNotes version?" I asked.

David geared himself up to spend a great deal of time summarizing the video. "The most important thing to know is that women don't generally climax off of vaginal penetration."

Salty scoffed. "That's not true! I'm the living proof it's not true! You should see me in action, bitches!" Kyle laughed and they began a side conversation while I listened to David.

David added, "You need to pleasure the breasts, labia, and clitoris with your finger and tongue for as long as you can until they cum. The penis doesn't do it for women at all. Just pretend you don't have one. Penises are functionally useless in sex."

Salty and Kyle stopped talking to each other to turn and look at David. "Surprisingly," Salty said, "I find my penis useful. Maybe that's just me."

"Yeah," Kyle said. "What do you use when you clap cheeks, David?"

Defensive, David talked quickly. "Hey, I'm just repeating what the husband and wife doctors said on the video. Evolution is responsible. Humans had to mate fast in the prehistoric forests and grasslands, or they'd get eaten by a saber-toothed tiger in mid-coitus. That's why we men all turn on as fast as microwaves and cum fast. It is also why men evolved to dump their goo and run away as fast as possible — before they're eaten by apex predators. Women never liked hit-and-run sex to begin with, but now that humans are the apex predators and men *still* behave like they have to fuck-and-run or die, women *really, really* resent it. The saber-toothed tigers are gone and we *still* cum fast after all these centuries? Talk about slow adaptation! Meanwhile, women are ovens, not microwaves. They see the penis as a cyclopean sausage-knife that slaps at them and stabs into them unexpectedly, pulls out a second later, and then runs away and hides, never to be seen again. They really, really prefer gently lapping tongues and magic fingers to the cyclopean sausage-knife. If men can't adapt to that, they won't be allowed to have sex anymore. All sex will be lesbian sex because only women understand what pleasures women. And women hate how penises are tiny, limp chickens that peck at them."

"'Cyclopean sausage-knives?'" I felt goosebumps rise on my arm.

"'Tiny, limp chickens that peck at them?' I think someone just walked over my grave."

"We've all read *The Bell Jar's* penis scene," Kyle said. "Vaginas ain't beautiful, either."

David shook his head. "That's the wrong attitude, especially since women worry about what we think of how everything in their panties looks. We gotta reassure them it's wonderful."

"David may have a point," I said. "I've been wondering if the fact that women hate men for excellent reasons has negatively affected my success rate getting them to go out for coffee."

"Remember three rules:" — David ticked them off on three fingers — "*respect* the FUPA, *pleasure* the FUPA, and *love* the FUPA."

Kyle sighed. "I'm almost scared to ask. What the fuck is a FUPA?"

"Fat Upper Pussy Area," David declared. "The mons pubis or the mons Veneris."

"I think I may have to announce my retirement from dating." I removed the white handkerchief from my pocket and waived it in surrender. "Game over, man! Game over."

"How can you retire from something you've never done?" asked Salty.

"I'm just worried about premature ejaculation," David said. "The video helped me."

"*You're* worried?" Salty asked. "*He* should be worried! You're so screwed, Damien. You better start whoring ASAP so you can learn to keep from blowing your load too soon. Otherwise, you'll meet this true love you've been waiting for and she'll say, 'Your place or mine,' and you'll get so excited that you're about to feel a woman's touch for the first time that you'll cream your pants. Then she'll scream and vomit, and that will be the end of *that* relationship."

"I know! You think I don't? And I have no idea how to prevent that from happening!"

"Get thee to a brothel," Salty commanded. "I've got a phone number for a call girl service. The passphrase is, 'I'm a friend of a doctor.' Let me know if you want the number."

"Grandpa's cathouse addiction put my grandma in a mental hospital," I said. "That'll be a hard 'No' from me."

"Listen," Salty said, "Women are looking for men who project strength. Men who've been laid have a confidence. They have a swagger. You, my friend, have no swagger. You slouch your way through life, looking scared of other people. Once you get laid, you'll have a swagger. In the meantime, every girl who meets you for the first time will sense your nervousness, smell your virginity on you, and suspect you're the Son of Sam."

I cleared my throat loudly. "By the way, feel free to move onto a new topic any time."

Salty placed his hand over his heart. "Personally, I have a swagger. I come into a room, I have a sexual aura, like Casanova."

"Casanova?" I stared with disapproval at Salty. "Listen here: I knew Giacomo Casanova. Giacomo Casanova was a friend of mine. Salty . . . you're no Giacomo Casanova."

Kyle laughed and applauded. "Lloyd Bentsen!"

Salty nodded. "Very clever. I'll give you that one. I like political jokes."

"Anyway," David said, "I have the video if you want it, Damien. I found it empowering."

I returned the handkerchief to my pocket. "Okay, this conversation is going on too long. I promise I'll be more strategic about who I ask out, if you all promise to change the record."

"Just try to have a good attitude about it," Kyle said.

"Does hearing the *Mission: Impossible* theme in my head constitute a good attitude?"

"No!" said Salty.

"If you're shy, we can all go out as a group cruising for chicks," Kyle suggested.

"Nah," I said. "He who travels fastest travels alone." The last few times we went out cruising for girls together, I successfully struck up a conversation with someone cute, and one of these three humps swooped in, took over the conversation, and plucked the girl right out of my hands. If that's what a "wingman" is, I needed one like I needed irritable bowel syndrome.

"Fine, but you better find someone in time for the prom," said Salty.

"I still think I should skew older to get someone mature enough for me," I said. "Is a college sophomore old enough? Should I shoot for twenty? Twenty-five?"

Salty moaned. "Great plan! Why not cruise the nursing homes while you're at it? You ask out a twenty-five-year-old and she'll just say, 'Awwwwww' and squeeze both your cheeks. Mature or not, you'll only ever be a kid in a propeller beanie to a college graduate."

"You think so?" Kyle asked. "I'm pretty sure Damien is secretly forty-five."

"Don't help," Salty hushed. "Okay, you're just old enough she won't be prosecuted for statutory rape, but you're not gonna be able to do anything with some chick over twenty-five."

I massaged my jaw thoughtfully. "Be hard for her to respect me living with my parents."

"Go younger than you. Get a girl who's in awe of you that you can train, like a dog."

My anger flared. "I don't want a dog!"

"I'm just sayin' older women are less attractive and can't stand men. Too many years of too many shit boyfriends. Skew young. If she's old enough to bleed, she's old enough to breed."

I made a promise to myself not to react to anything Salty said, no matter how outrageous. I didn't want to give him the satisfaction.

"If she's old enough to pee, she's old enough to me," he added.

"Jesus H. Christ," I muttered.

Salty grinned. "Ha! You're so easy to bait."

"I want a woman," I shot back. "A grown-up with a mind of her own. Someone who's enjoyed arthouse films and written bleak death poetry. Who knows how to fucking spell!"

"I've met Salty's girlfriend," Kyle said. "I'm pretty sure she doesn't know how to spell."

Salty shook his head at the three of us. "I don't know why I'm wastin' my time with you people. I should be over at her place, givin' her the high hard one."

David wiped an invisible tear from his eye. "That was freakin' beautiful, man. Poetic."

"Who cares that she isn't a genius?" Salty yelled. "If I want to talk to someone in Greek, I'll talk to my barber. If I want to learn about science, I'll read my Carl Sagan."

I started opening my own Hershey pie. "Ever since I met you, Salty, you've been playing cool Jack Nicholson from *The Last Detail* to my simple-minded Randy Quaid. I'm sick of it."

"The truth hurts," declared Salty. "We're high-school seniors: I've fucked twenty girls and you haven't had pussy since pussy had you."

The whole table fell silent. We ate our food without speaking for the next three minutes.

"I might have crossed the line there," Salty finally acknowledged.

I grunted and ate another French fry.

David leaned forward and whispered to me. "Do you want to borrow my training video?"

"No, I don't want to borrow your fucking training video!" I bellowed.

David held up his hands in surrender. "Okay, okay. Just asking."

We ate another five minutes in silence.

I murmured, "You better bring it in tomorrow."

November 13, 1993

Kyle called me at seven p.m. on Saturday and asked me if I want to go bowling with the boys. I was tired of "the boys" and wracked my brains to come up with a plausible excuse for refusing. "You ever have cabin fever but don't really feel like going out?"

"Ha! No! What the fuck are you talking about?"

"I'm gonna have a night-in."

I didn't have a night-in. Even though my family had an-old-but-working-1970s-era washer-and-dryer pair in our basement, I took a load of dirty clothes to a public laundromat on Victory Boulevard, roll of quarters in tow, looking for an attractive woman to ask out. Recent magazine articles had made a lot of hay about coin-op laundry places being ideal locales for girlfriend hunting, so I thought I'd test the theory. I would come to this laundromat every other day for a month and see if I managed to accidentally meet a potential date for my senior prom. Thanks to being a compulsive collector of books and comic books, I had plenty of as-yet-unread reading material to ease me through a month of stakeouts.

A motley crew had assembled inside the claustrophobic laundromat interior under the flickering and burnt-out ceiling-mounted fluorescent tubes: a frumpy thirtysomething woman with four kids climbing all over her while waiting for a dryer load to finish, a dazed and elderly homeless man in a red plaid hunting cap and green Gore-Tex coat sitting in the corner on the wooden bench, and a twenty-year-old woman with a tasteful diamond nostril piercing angrily doing a crossword puzzle with the most closed body language in all of recorded Western history. Somehow, I didn't want to ask any of these folks out. Not wanting to give up immediately, I began my first-ever load of laundry, hoping I'd avoid staining all my white underclothes pink.

I sat down on the wooden bench and opened a copy of *A Confederacy of Dunces* by John Kennedy Toole, fastidiously trying not to crack the spine or add wear to the pristine cover. As I re-immersed myself in the story, I once again found myself relating too strongly to the protagonist, Ignatius Reilly. I was well into chapter seven — in which Ignatius landed a job selling hot dogs and wound up eating them all himself — when Annie Hall's identical twin sister entered the laundromat. She even had the hat. Annie chose an empty top-loading washer a yard away and set about transferring clothes into it from a military surplus olive drab laundry bag.

Excellent! She's the one. Wait a minute. Now what? How can I possibly speak to her without coming off as a creeper? Could I ask her if she needs any change? Show her my roll quarters? Be helpful? People respond to helpful, right? But what if she grunts 'thanks' or 'no thanks' and then stops talking? Do I take that as a firm 'no' and stop, or say one more thing?

Now finished loading her soiled clothes and adding detergent, Annie straightened. She shot me a sidelong glance. "I just want to do my laundry in peace."

I blushed. "I wasn't gonna say anything."

"Sure, you weren't." Annie produced quarters of her own, slotted them into the washer, and turned it on. She cast a second glance at me. "What are you? *Twelve*? Because I'm *thirty*."

I smiled pleasantly. "I'm *fine* with thirty!"

She rolled her eyes. "Mannaggia la miseria!"

I didn't know what that phrase meant, but her tone suggested I shouldn't get too excited.

Another half hour passed without incident. This laundromat scheme was a bust. Too bad, I was stuck waiting until the dryer cycle finished. Afterwards, I discovered the joys of walking home in the cool fall evening with a giant bag of clothes slung over my shoulder. My path home took me past my church, its façade illuminated by floodlights positioned over the name St. Luke's Roman Catholic Church. As I walked towards the entrance, I felt the weight of the laundry bag grow still more oppressive. I bucked myself up by starting to sing my current favorite song, Madonna's "Like a Prayer." I'd only gotten a few bars in when Miss O'Sullivan emerged from the rectory, slipping on a light brown coat as she walked. It had been six years since we first met and five-and-a-half years since we'd last seen one another. She'd known me as a pre-pubescent sixth grader. I was now a high school senior. I'd also worn glasses and was clean-shaven then. Now I wore contact lenses and a goatee. I didn't expect her to recognize me right away — or remember me *well* — but I was hopeful that I could jog her memory fairly quickly once she got a good look at me. "Is that you, Miss O'Sullivan?"

She stopped, half in and half out of her coat, eyes wide. "Who are you?"

I pitched my voice up half an octave and assumed a reassuring tone. "I'm Damien. You were my Confirmation teacher here a few years back."

The longer she looked me over, the less she believed I was who I said I was. "You're too old to have been one of my students."

"Not all that much time has passed, but blink and teenagers double in size."

Miss O'Sullivan finished putting her coat on. "You were in that class? If you were, I must be getting old. Very old. Am I getting that old?"

Sure, she looked older, but she still looked gorgeous. "Of course not! You look great!"

She swatted the compliment away. "Who are you supposed to be again?"

Ouch. This must be how Arwen felt when I didn't recognize her my first day in the library. "You taught us the importance of never doing anything evil, because our souls are pristine handkerchiefs that must remain spotless if we are to have a chance attaining paradise."

She stared at me. "I don't remember sharing those thoughts with the class."

"I have an unusually good memory." I assumed a comic heroic stance and placed my free hand on my hip. It was difficult flirting with an old teacher while holding a giant bag of laundry.

"I can see that." She sounded like she was beginning to remember some of the truth, but her posture remained defensive. Her eyes kept darting to the laundry bag slung over my shoulder, as if I were on the verge of scooping her up, forcing her inside, and carrying her off.

"I'm glad we bumped into each other." I smiled and stepped closer. "I don't suppose I could talk you into grabbing a coffee with me now, so we could catch up?"

Miss O'Sullivan clutched her coat to her neck and stepped backward. "What? No!"

"Okay! No worries!" I whirled around and walked briskly away from her. I trotted across the street so I could resume my path home while still giving her the widest berth possible. "Well, it was great to see you again, Miss O'Sullivan. God be with you!" Not listening for her reply, I broke into a sprint and fled home.

I returned home to find my mother asleep and father in his robe and pajamas, making tea, and preparing to watch an old movie on VHS. "Dad! Guess who I bumped into? My hot religion teacher. Remember her?"

"Who could forget her? Nice looking bitch. Is it too much to hope you made a pass?"

"You'll be proud of me. I did! But I got 'The Recoil.'"

Dad closed his eyes and frowned. "Oh. 'The Recoil.' That's rough."

I shrugged. "Whatever. I always get 'The Recoil.' I guess the moral of this story is don't ask out a mousey woman you've bumped into in the street in the dark of the night. This is true even if she's an old hero of yours. Still, I'm pretty mad she was scared of me."

"Why wouldn't she be scared? You're six-foot and larger than life. I'm scared of you!"

"Ha! Okay, I guess that's fair. What are you watching?"

"I can't decide between *The Body Snatcher* or Jeremy Brett in 'The Naval Treaty.'"

"I have a radical idea," I said. "I'll make myself some tea and we can watch both!"

"Good plan. And don't worry about finding a girl. The Virgin Mary will push the right one in your direction soon enough."

"Well, she better get cracking! The prom is coming up fast."

CHAPTER TWENTY-ONE
The Gooseberry

November 15, 1993

Cigarette smoke hung in the air over the Grace Coolidge High School cafeteria courtyard. To be social, I kept my Goth, chain-covered buddy Maureen ("Mo") Willis company as she puffed away. I listened with genuine interest as she described in detail her post-graduation cosmetology school plans. Afterwards, my reward for being a good listener was Mo regaling me with her favorite dirty joke:

"A newlywed couple moves into an old, broken-down house. The wife is more impatient and excited to get it all fixed up than her husband. On weekends, he's so burnt out by five days at work, he can only collapse in front of the TV. One Saturday, the wife says, 'Honey, can you fix a leak in the upstairs bathroom?'

"The husband says, 'Who do I look like, Mr. Plumber?'

"Another weekend, the wife says, 'Honey, will you please paint the house?'

"He says, 'Who do I look like, Sherwin Williams?'

"The next Saturday morning, she says, 'Honey, I know you're tired. Can you please at least mow the lawn for me?'

"He mutters, 'Who do I look like, John Deere?'"

"This sounds like every marriage," I remarked. "The husband complains about the Honeydew Weekend. 'Honey do this. Honey do that.'"

"No kidding," Mo said. "Then the husband ditches his wife to go fishing for the weekend. When he gets back from his trip, he's shocked to find the house painted, lawn cut, and bathroom leak fixed. He asked his wife how all this happened. She said, 'The teenage boy next door got it done. All he wanted in return was for me to either bake him a cake or give him a blowjob.' The husband asked, 'What kinda cake did you bake?' She said, 'Who do I look like, Betty Crocker?'"

I laughed loudly. "That's hilarious!"

"Isn't it?" Mo chuckled. "I wasn't sure if a guy would find it as funny as I did."

"That kid's a lucky bastard, isn't he? I wish I lived next door to her. *I* can mow a lawn!"

"The lawn alone is probably only worth a handjob."

"That's nothin' to sneeze at." We both laughed again.

We laughed a lot, spending lunch hour every weekday giggling and guffawing. Mo and I had been good friends for two years. I was only minimally attracted to her, so I thought that made her an ideal candidate to ask to the prom. We could sort of go as friends, and it would take so much of the pressure off us to have "The Most Romantic Weekend of Our Lives." Leaning against a pillar with my hands in my pockets, I asked Mo casually. "So, what's the story with you and the prom, Mo? You goin' with Luke Perry, or what?"

Mo shook her head of dyed black spiked hair. "I'm going with a group of girlfriends."

I made a circle in the air with my forefinger. "You'll form a circle and dance in it, and not let any guys in? Because once one gets in, he gets all puppyish and grabby and possessive?"

"Pretty much," said Mo, looking especially Goth in black eyeshadow and lipstick.

"Do the straight-girl on straight-girl grind?"

"Yup. Though I don't know why you assume we're all straight. Personally, I think all girls are at least a little bit lesbian. Don't you think?"

"You asking me what turns girls on?" I chuckled. "I'm the *last* person you should ask."

Mo gave me a sly look. "You gonna ask Arwen to the prom?"

"Nah! She's going with Fonzie. Besides, I was thinking about asking you."

"Me?" Mo Willis looked surprised, not threatened. "Oh, you don't want to go with me."

"Why not? You're cool."

"Well, thank you, but I'm pretty committed to dancing in a circle with the girls." There was no pity for me in her eyes, thank God.

I smirked. "Suit yourself."

Mo poked me in the shoulder with a long black fingernail. "Go talk to Arwen."

"No way, José."

Mo poked me again. "She wants to go to the prom with you, not her boyfriend."

"Wa'choo talkin' 'bout, Mo Willis?"

Mo smirked. "Seriously, what sane girl would rather date a Polish guy than an Italian?"

I laughed. "That's a little mean, but since you're trying to pump me up, I'll take it."

"You two would make *hot* lovers: C.S. Lewis and Joy Davidman reincarnated! If you two ever fucked, the Earth would crack open."

"You mistaking *Shadowlands* for *9 ½ Weeks* again?"

"I'm not really thinking of *Shadowlands*. I'm worried if you're not careful, you're gonna grow up to be like Jay Gatsby, or Pip from *Great Expectations*."

"It's too late. I'm already Pip."

Mo's black lips turned down into a frown. "Just ask Arwen to the prom, chicken shit!"

"Okay, okay! I'll talk to her. But I'm not even sure what to say to her anymore."

Mo cackled. "Here's what not to say: 'I could really use a handjob. Speaking of which, want to go to the prom with me?' Nice transition before, jackass!"

"Well, wait a minute. I didn't . . . "

Mo patted me on the shoulder. "I'm only teasing. You're a riot. You go get her."

"Okay. Hey, by the way . . . thanks for never treating me like I'm some sorta poor thing."

Mo smirked. "'Poor thing?' You? No way. You have the worst fucking luck of all time, but you ain't no poor thing."

I craned my neck and looked for Arwen. She was with Rolf by the water fountain. They were arguing. "I don't think now is the best moment."

"Go to the mall this afternoon, when she's working KFC," Mo suggested. "Ask her then."

I nodded. "Okay."

Mo took another puff of her cigarette. "'Just friends' for seven years? I swear to God, if you two don't bump uglies soon, I'm getting a gun and putting you both out of your misery."

"You're looking pretty sexy in your KFC outfit," I said.

Arwen stuck her tongue out at me. All kidding aside, her red polo shirt and red visor with the purple KFC lettering were cute on her. She stood behind the cash register at the KFC outlet in the Staten Island Mall food court, waiting for me to order so she wouldn't get yelled at by a sixty-year-old manager who had given up on life. "Welcome to KFC. May I take your order?"

I leaned over the counter. "I'll take two breasts, two legs, a muffin, and some chicken."

Arwen couldn't stop herself from laughing. She didn't notice her manager standing behind her, looking suspicious. When she recovered, she whispered back, "Sure. I'll let you eat my muffin, if you slip me some juicy Italian sausage when you're done."

"I'd like to slip you some sausage right now."

The manager stepped up beside Arwen. "Are you having trouble deciding your order?"

I stopped smiling. "I'll take a medium Pepsi. No ice."

"Will that be all?" Arwen asked.

"For now."

Taking my leave of Arwen before I got her fired, I meandered over to Blimpie and ordered a Blimpie Best. For the uninitiated, that was a ham, salami, capicola, prosciuttini, and provolone on wheat bread topped with tomatoes, lettuce, onion, vinegar, oil and oregano. I sat a few yards off to the side from the KFC, but not so far I couldn't watch Arwen work out of the corner of my eye as I ate. She caught sight of me a few minutes later and gave me a surreptitious, waist-level wave. She did seem to like me. And we flirted shamelessly. Don't ask me what was going on. Every time I feared I was harassing or hounding her, I'd stop flirting with her for a month, or keep her at a distance. She'd invariably track me down. "Where have you been, darling? I've missed you. I only had Rolf to entertain me. It's so boring without you."

"Gettin' me back on your hook?" I'd ask her. She'd nod, grin evilly, and mime hooking me on her fishing line. After three experiences like that, when I tried to leave her alone and she wouldn't let me, I figured I had every right to spy on her while she worked.

Rolf sat down across from me, blocking my view of his girlfriend. "How's my understudy doing?" He made it sound like a joke, but he wasn't being funny, and I wasn't laughing. I have a theory that there is no such thing as humor, in the end. There are only people who shock others into laughing by being surprisingly honest or startlingly insightful.

"Last I checked, we weren't in a play together," I said.

"Yeah, you know exactly what I mean."

I sucked my teeth in irritation. "If I was really gonna try to cut you out of the picture, I'd have told her parents you were a gentile years ago. Give me some credit for that, at least." I was gearing up to do some serious lying to Rolf, and I wasn't comfortable about it. I didn't like telling falsehoods. I would fly as close to the truth as possible, without owning up to my newfound determination to ask Arwen to the prom. I pretended that I hadn't just promised Mo to move in on Arwen and willed myself to recreate the mindset I'd been operating on for most of the past seven years of "unresolved sexual tension" sitcom friendship.

"Yeah, you're only making mealy-mouthed passes at my girl," Rolf said. "That makes you more of an annoyance than a threat, but I don't have to like you or your weasel bullshit."

"Weasel?" For half a second, I considered giving him the Dietrich Krebs treatment and attacking him with a pencil.

"Weasel. Vulture. Whatever."

"We haven't even held hands," I protested. "We haven't done anything."

"I know you love her."

I waved him off. "Everybody loves Arwen. She's a very loveable person."

"Yeah, but you want her more badly than anyone else," Rolf said evenly.

Of course, I knew I didn't have much of a leg to stand on. By all rights, I should respect Rolf's wishes, and their relationship, and make myself scarce. On the other hand, Arwen was one of the only people in my life who made me happy. I knew she and I could never really be a couple, but I didn't want him to take her away from me. *If I promised not to touch Arwen, could I stand close to her flame and warm my cold, dead heart just a teensy-weensy bit?* The good news was, I didn't resent our friendship, like your average, twenty-first century incel, who made sexist complaints like, "She put my ass in the Friend Zone." I liked her as a person and a friend way too much to allow my pent-up lust from congealing into nerd misogyny, thank God. I never wanted to become that sort of person: the fake "nice guy" who's secretly a serial killer in training. As these thoughts raced through my head in a manner of seconds, I concluded Rolf was overreacting, I was at least "not guilty," even if I wasn't "innocent."

I gestured at Rolf's leather jacket. "Dude, you look like Fonzie. You got nothing to worry about! Stop bustin' my chops."

Rolf crossed his arms in front of his chest. "I used to think you weren't a threat."

"So, what's changed?"

"You two talk too loudly in health class. People hear the shit you say to each other and then I gotta hear it from them. And they wanna know why I stand for your behavior."

"That's just health. They put condoms on bananas in that class. There's a lot of blue humor in the air because of shit like that. It don't mean nuthin'." I exaggerated my Brooklyn accent to sound more convincing.

"Oh, Come on, dude! Don't blow smoke. I'm tellin' you, I'm not sure I want you two hanging out anymore — especially not alone."

When the cat's not around, the mice dance. "Look, all I know is I've been a good friend to her for years, and I haven't laid a finger on her. That's all I know."

Rolf didn't want to break the tension he'd worked so hard to build, but he couldn't help but chuckle. "Yeah? Is that *all* you know?"

"That and my name and phone number."

That cracked Rolf up even more. "You are a charmer. I'll give you that, Damien." He eyed me again. This was the third time he had confronted me about the nature of my relationship with Arwen. The first time was a sort of a "Who the hell are you?" conversation, after which Rolf determined I represented no threat whatsoever because I wasn't half as masculine as he was. The second confrontation came during 1992, the year of Sweet Sixteens, when we all went to a catered Sweet Sixteen party a week. These parties were surprisingly opulent — as expensive as wedding receptions and held at similar venues, like restaurants and banquet halls. The dentist fathers and nurse mothers of the girls in our class put on a hell of a party for their little princesses. I got to do a lot of solo dancing, mostly by myself in my best blending of the styles of John Travolta, Michael Jackson, and Ed Norton. I loved the first five of these parties, because I adored music and dancing, but I made a mistake not taking Baby Bianca to some of those parties, so I could have someone to dance with.

At each of these Sweet Sixteen parties, circles of girls would form on the dance floor and they'd get down with their bad selves and refuse to dance with the boys. I'd occasionally try to get into these tightly formed circles, but they always seemed impenetrable. Then I'd give up and dance outside the French doors on the lawn or simply jump up and down on the dance floor and head bang like a Butabi brother. Only once did a straight guy penetrate the circle: Eric Indelicato. At least it was him. I liked him. When the girls got tired of dancing in a giant ring, they'd mix things up either by doing the Electric Slide or breaking up into pairs and grinding into each other. I didn't know how to do the Electric Slide, but I didn't mind watching the grinding from the sidelines as I drank a few Shirley Temples. If I thought too long about how I wasn't the one getting grinded against, I went back outside to dance some more on the lawn. At these Sweet Sixteens, the few times boys and girls danced together were when the long-established couples slow-danced, or the straight girls disco danced with the gay boys. On many evenings that year, I wished I were a gay man or in a committed relationship so I would be allowed to dance with someone other than myself. Since I was neither, I eventually concluded that I would not go to my senior prom unless I brought one date of my own. But I really, really liked dancing. I wanted to dance. My last remaining option was to dance as a friend with some other dude's girlfriend. It was a shitty option, but I could find no other alternative to dancing alone on a wet lawn at ten p.m. outside of a Chinese restaurant. What would you rather do: dance with someone else's girlfriend inside, or jump around on a lawn outside in total solitude?

The time of Arwen's stepsister's Sweet Sixteen came around. (I often forgot her name on purpose as a passive-aggressive form of revenge. She helped block me from dating Arwen, so I chose to block her name from my memory.) What's-her-name's party was especially great because Rolf had mono during it and I was able to dance with Arwen all evening without him cutting in. We danced for ninety minutes to a playlist that included L.A. Style's "James Brown is Dead," 2 Unlimited's "Twilight Zone," Kris Kross' "Jump," C+C Music Factory's "Gonna Make You Sweat," Roxette's "Spending My Time," and Young MC's "Bust A Move." It was a gloriously fun evening for us teenagers. The extended family members who were also invited to the shindig had less fun. The aunts, uncles, grandparents, and cousins were alarmed when the single straight guys got tired of dancing with each other and started moshing to Nirvana's "Smells Like Teen Spirit." The silver hairs also failed to see the humor when the boys and girls screamed the dialogue from Meatloaf's "Paradise by the Dashboard Light" to each other.

You know who else wasn't happy? Rolf. In the days that followed the party, Rolf heard reports that Arwen and I had slow danced to not one but four songs: Leonard Cohen's "A Thousand Kisses Deep," Chris de Burgh's "Lady in Red," The Cars' "Drive," and "Take My Breath Away" by Berlin. After he'd heard this, he kept Arwen away from me for a full eight months. Frequently, as they walked past me, he'd make a point of leading her around me by placing his hand on the small of her back or be sure to nuzzle her hair while I was watching. There must have been something in my expression that rewarded him for doing this, because he'd usually smile or wink at me right afterwards. Here we were again, sitting across from one another in the mall food court, having the same face-off again.

"Listen," I said, "I know why you're mad and I get it. I'll cool it with the on-the-line badinage if you agree to let me and Arwen stay friends."

"*On*-the-line? More like *over*-the-line."

"I'll cool it with the *over*-the-line badinage."

Rolf considered my word-choice carefully and decided I'd lost our little fencing match by surrendering too much power to him. "So, you admit it's my call?"

I shook my head. "No. It's Arwen's call. If she wants me to fuck off, I'll fuck off. But I'd feel better if I knew that you knew that I'm not here to make trouble for you. I mean, this may be hard to believe, but being a weasel has never been my lifelong ambition. It's not a good look for me. Neither is being a vulture."

"It isn't a good look, is it?"

"Being a decent guy has always been very important to me. I always try to be honest and above-board and a straight arrow in all my dealings."

Rolf looked skeptical. "I don't know. I have a really bad feeling I'm talking to the biggest bullshit artist of all time."

"What I've just said is the truth." *Unless I actually ask her to the prom. Then I'm lying.*

Rolf stared at me, looking completely unsatisfied. "I can't tell if you're telling the truth, lying to me, or lying to yourself, but how'd you like me to blow your case to smithereens?"

My fight or flight response had been on overdrive since he sat down but kicked up another notch still. "I don't think I would like that."

"If she asks you to go to bed with her, would you say 'no' on my account?"

I couldn't believe he asked me that. My jaw didn't drop literally, but metaphorically.

"Well?" he asked.

"'I refuse to answer that question on the grounds that I don't know the answer.'" I left the Douglas Adams attribution off because I didn't want Rolf to know I was quoting someone else.

Rolf slapped his palms down on his knees and made a loud smacking noise. "Well, I don't know if that resolved anything. All I know is that I've had enough of this fucking conversation." He stood to go.

"Is that really all you know?" I asked, trying to lighten the mood.

"Oh, go fuck yourself, Damien."

Three minutes after Rolf had gone, Arwen emerged from a door set into the food court wall I had never noticed before. She navigated her way through the dinner crowd, crept over to my table, and sat at the chair beside me, noticeably out of breath. "Rolf giving you grief?"

I smirked. "You noticed that?"

"No duh! I've only got five minutes, but I wanted to check on you. You okay?"

I took a sip of my soda to buy myself time to think of an answer. "I wish I had a girlfriend, so Rolf would chill out when we were together. I'm getting tired of his suspicion."

Arwen's expression changed into something I couldn't read anymore. "You think your having a girlfriend would put him at ease?"

"Wouldn't it? Maybe we could even go on double-dates together."

Arwen struggled not to smile. "It sounds idyllic. I'm not sure if you are operating in reality, my friend."

"Why?"

"For one thing, even if Rolf relaxed a bit, I'm not sure your girlfriend would be comfortable with me hovering around you."

I got a sinking feeling in my stomach. "Shit. I hadn't thought of that."

"No girlfriend of yours would ever be dumb enough to let you have female friends of any sort. Certainly not my sort!"

"What a terrible thought. That might make it difficult for me to have any friends at all. I don't usually click with dudes, after all. I'll have to stay home and watch *Doctor Who* 24/7."

Arwen tilted her head to the side and looked at me with genuine sympathy. "Sorry."

I felt hopeful. "But you've made it clear that Rolf has no control over who you pick to be friends with. Maybe I could make a similar demand of my girlfriend?"

Arwen snickered. "You are so adorable. You have no idea how women operate."

I was back to looking crestfallen. "No, I don't suppose I do."

Arwen patted my hand. "Cheer up, you. I have a present for you."

Once again, I was having trouble keeping up with the twists and turns of a conversation with Arwen. "Wait. You do? What? Why?"

She reached into her pants pocket and produced a folded piece of paper. "I remember you aren't big on math. Still, I know you've learned about the concept of the empty set."

The words "empty set" triggered instant anxiety. "I told you that story?"

"I was there when it happened," she said quietly.

"Oh, wonderful! I'm so glad you were there to witness my finest hour."

"Here." Arwen slid the paper across the table to me. "Read that."

Still disturbed, I picked up the paper and unfolded it. She had written "{Arwen}" on it in purple ink. I couldn't stop looking at it. "What's this?"

Arwen reached under my chin, tilted my head up, and forced me to look in her eyes. "That's the set of girls sitting at this table with you who find you sexually attractive."

Something odd was happening to the bustling food court. Everyone else was disappearing. It was just us at this table. "Oh," I said.

"Yeah," Arwen chuckled. "'Oh.'"

For the first time, I was able to keep my eyes fixed on Arwen's, and not feel that I needed to look away. Her eyes were silver. So, so silver.

"Still think Rolf will feel better if you dig up a girlfriend?" she asked.

"Um . . . no. Heh."

"Right?!"

"Yeah, I take all that back." I held up the piece of paper. "How do you know me so well? You knew exactly the right thing to say to me."

Arwen beamed.

I leaned forward. Our lips brushed together. My first kiss. I felt electricity coursing through my body. I lunged forward to embrace her.

Arwen placed both her hands on my chest and pushed me away. Her eyes showed desire. Her frown was an apology. "Down, boy," she whispered. "Down."

I'll bet I couldn't have looked more confused and disappointed. The exciting follow-up to my first kiss was a dog command. "I don't understand."

Arwen reached down and took my right hand in both of hers. "Not yet."

I made an unattractive bull sound with my nose and throat.

"Don't be angry with me," Arwen pleaded. I leaned forward again. She pulled her head back. "No. I told you. Be patient."

I found her silver eyes again. "When? I need to know when."

Arwen lifted my hand and placed it against her cheek. "I know. I'm working on it."

CHAPTER TWENTY-TWO
Arwen and Damien

November 15, 1993

Pouring over a thirty-page legal document, Arwen sat under a tree in the courtyard outside the cafeteria of Grace Coolidge High School. Eighteen senior girls and four senior guys milled around nearby, smoking as they did every lunch hour. Highly allergic to cigarette smoke, Arwen was there for the sunlight, last days of autumn leaves, and the comparative privacy. She soldiered on reading the document even as her eyes watered and nose ran amidst all the smoking.

Hoping that "Be patient" didn't mean "keep away," I walked up to her. "What's doin'?"

"I'm reading my mother's will," Arwen said distractedly. "I'm turning eighteen soon and wondering if that means anything of note."

"Is this your first time seeing it?" I asked. Out of the corner of my eye, I saw Mo Willis smoking nearby. She mouthed the words, "Fuck her hard!" I smiled and shook my head at her. Pressing the point, Mo made the "finger in hole gesture," and tossed her head back, mutely moaning. At least she was on our side. I returned my attention to Arwen, who was still absorbed in reading. She was about to snap at me to leave her in peace, but changed her mind abruptly, deciding instead to bring me up to speed. "I can't figure out how old I have to be to claim my inheritance money and share of Pokatny Confections. The legalese is incomprehensible."

Since she didn't invite me to sit on the grass next to her, I remained standing. "Pokatny Confections is your mom's company, but it's named after your dad?"

"If a couple co-founds a company, it sucks if it's only named after the husband, right?"

"Definitely!" I said with conviction.

Arwen smirked. "I'm glad I'm having a good influence on you, my friend. You've got a male chauvinist streak, there. Not sure if you're aware."

"Yeah, yeah, yeah." I pointed at the will. "You want me to have a look at that?"

Arwen smacked my hand away. "I don't want you to know how much money I'm getting. You'll go from just loving me for my big boobies to just loving me for my inheritance."

"I love everything about you," I said, without a trace of irony.

"Liar."

"No. I'm serious."

Arwen looked up. "You can't be. Come on. Tell me one thing you don't like about me."

I smiled crookedly. "The blue balls you give me."

"Gross." Arwen pulled a face and looked at the will again.

I tried to recover control of the conversation. "What are you gonna do about this will?"

"I have a big question, so I'm going to the law office tomorrow."

"What's that?"

"'An office maintained by a lawyer or a firm of lawyers for the practice of law.'"

I laughed. "Fine. Don't tell me."

"If I'm reading this right, I can start collecting enough money to move out of my dad's house, get away from my wicked stepmother and stepsister, and restart my life on my terms."

"And you can date whoever you want?" I would like to say I managed to keep the glee out of my voice, but I didn't.

Arwen arched an evil eyebrow. "I can fuck every guy in New York if I wanted to." Never before had I known how terrible and overpowering jealousy could feel. The redder my complexion got the wider Arwen's smile grew. "Something wrong?" she asked.

"Nothing. That sounds like a fantastic plan. You deserve to celebrate your freedom."

"Every guy in New York does sound like fun." She paused for effect. "Hey, Damien. I've just had a wild thought. You're a New Yorker, aren't you?"

"Why, yes." An image of Arwen roasting me over a spit with an apple shoved in my mouth popped into my head. "Yes, I am."

"Cool, cool. I might even fuck a few chicks, too. Try that out. I mean, scissoring sounds like such fun, doesn't it? Have you heard of scissoring?"

"You know me." I threw my hands up in the air. "Of course, I haven't!"

Arwen folded up the will, slipped it into her pocket, and stood. She stared at me with shining, silver eyes. "I know I've been needling you just now, but I'm deadly serious here. If I get my inheritance, I'm breaking up with Rolf. I want to be with you." She pointed a commanding finger at me. "But don't you dare get too excited! I almost didn't tell you. I wanted to be sure it was good news, first. But I can't keep secrets from you. You look so fucking miserable when I keep you in suspense, I just can't leave you hanging." She paused, debating whether or not to bring up a point that irritated her. "Of course, you need to . . . "

"What?" I asked.

Arwen poked me in the chest with her finger. "Listen, here, dummy. I'm gonna have to insist you stop asking random MILFs to the prom. It's bad enough I have to compete with your memory of St. Marina of Dazzo. Now I'm biting my nails worrying about you ogling cougars?"

"Wait a second—"

"Well, you gave me a kick in the pants. Forced me to look at this fakakta legal situation."

"The only reason I started looking elsewhere for prom dates is I had no idea there was any hope for us. You know. As a couple. I was okay with the friendship."

"Were you?" Arwen's eyes narrowed. "I wasn't."

I paused. "It'll be cool when I don't answer that question."

Arwen looked thoughtful. "Here's another difficult question for you."

"Uh-oh. Now what?"

"I realize this is putting the cart before the horse, but what are your feelings about wedding rings? I don't like them, myself. They're like a wolf peeing on a woman to mark his territory, don't you think?"

I grimaced. "If you want to be *negative* about it. I think they're romantic."

"I'd rather not feel peed on."

"I have no desire to pee on you."

"Cool." Arwen said. "Then don't ever buy me a ring."

I looked heavenwards. "If you insist."

Speaking of wolves marking their territory, Rolf chose that moment to come up behind Arwen and place his hand firmly on her ass. "Howya doin', honey?"

Arwen spun on her heels and kissed Rolf on the cheek. "Good. How are you?"

"Same shit, different day. What are you two conspiring about?"

November 21, 1993

"Greetings and salutations!"

I threw anaconda arms around Grandma Antje, squeezing the life out of her. "Okay, okay, I can't breathe!" she gasped. I released Grandma from the love-hold of death, murmuring, "Sorry! I'm just excited to see you!"

"He's been loud and demonstrative lately," Dad told his mother. "Unfortunately."

I pounded my chest with my fist, a boastful Klingon. "I'm good in small doses!"

Leo chuckled. "You and that Klingon chest punch you do!"

"Before I forget, these are for Gianna." Grandma fished some Weight Watchers coupons out of her purse handed them to Mom.

Mom thanked Grandma and hugged her. "Hi, Antje."

Grandma had arrived the Saturday before Thanksgiving to observe a small Thanksgiving "lunch" of coffee and cakes with us a few days early, since we would be celebrating the actual day at Uncle Carmine's. (Fortunately, things were going well between Mom and Carmine these days, their protracted argument over money long forgotten.) "Diet Thanksgiving" would only last about three hours before it was time for Dad to bring Grandma back to the Bronx. The welcome scene playing out in our living room by the front door was a low-rent re-enactment of the infamous Christmas visit that ended with the packing up of the Christmas tree, only Grandma was now doing a one-woman show.

Another major difference between now and then: my parents, brother, and I were all older, wiser, and happier. As different as Dad had become lately, a strong case could be made that my mother had undergone the most startling metamorphosis of all. This was the first fall of Mom's phased retirement. At the end of last spring's semester, she began an extended disability leave due to her now-pronounced hearing loss. The leave would take several years to run its course, finishing right when she reached sixty-five, when she could retire as planned without having to teach a single lesson again. Most importantly, Mom didn't have to sit in standstill traffic every day to get to "glorious downtown Brooklyn." Nor did she have to spend so much of her time at home grading unreadable freshman composition papers, and cooking and cleaning for the three agreeable-but-lazy male gadabouts taking up all the oxygen in her house. Indeed, she had taken to forgetting to cook dinner more and more of late, leaving the three of us humps to fend for ourselves, foraging for nuts and berries. These few-but-sweeping changes made Mom happier than I'd ever seen her. I was delighted for her.

With her college teaching career over, Mom could dedicate her newfound free time to her own hobbies. Unlike many other baby boomers — who dreaded the potential of existential angst and senility following retirement, and made blood vows to die at their desks rather than ever allowing themselves the luxury of retirement — Mom had no regrets leaving work behind with some years of life and moderately good health left to live. As Mom said, "Only boring people get bored." Mom was neither boring nor bored in retirement. A recent convert to the religion of genealogy, Mom had reconstructed her family tree going back as far as the late eighteenth century, to the family of Rocco Ambrogio Catorzia. While more recent ancestors had lived out their lives in and around Naples, we were surprised to discover that Rocco had been born in Armento, Italy, in 1788 and died in Paarl, South Africa, in 1858. Thanks to tracing her roots to Rocco Catorzia (a.k.a. Rocco Catoggio), Mom had found a cousin from a branch of our family currently in Namibia, also descended from Rocco. Retha-Louise Hofmeyr was a professional pianist, public radio music producer, Director of Arts in the Ministry of Education and the Ministry of Youth, Sport and Culture (MYNSSC) for Namibia, and the most wonderful newly discovered relative a person could ask for. Becoming pen pals with an overseas cousin who had a vibrant personality awakened in Mom an enthusiasm for a living extended family member — an enthusiasm that mitigated the pain she had felt mourning all the family members she had grown up with who had died over the years. Before long, Mom found several more extended family members located throughout America, and reached out to all of them by letter, since she could not hear well on the telephone. Still more surprising, Mom reigned in her mild, New-York-City-centric agoraphobia enough to travel to meet them in their homes in Virginia, Florida, and New Orleans. Sadly, she wasn't ready for Namibia or Armento yet, thanks to her collapsed arches. Health problems notwithstanding, Mom was traveling again. Like magic, new photos were appearing in her albums. These were the first trips since 1963 that she had taken solo or with friends, and not as a wife and mother on a family vacation. Thanks to this new lease on life, Mom had no trouble laughing off Grandma's Weight Watchers fliers. Mom held them up so I could take a gander at them. "Look what Grandma gave me!"

"What a lovely present!" I shouted. Then Mom and I gave each other a high five.

"A high five?" Dad tutted. "That was a bit uncouth."

Leo led Grandma into the kitchen from the family room. Cannolis, Napoleons, tiramisu, and panettone from Alfonso's Pastry Shoppe covered the kitchen table. We sat down to the sugary spread as Mom served us coffee and tea to accompany it. "You seem like you're in a good mood, Damien," Grandma mentioned. "That can't be because you have that terrible goatee. You need to shave. Beards are messy. And it has a red tint that doesn't match your brown hair."

I was expecting the complaint. Grandma never had a kind word to say about facial hair. "I'll shave it before my senior portrait. I wanted to look like the Master from *Doctor Who*."

Mom appeared over us brandishing an enormous knife, asking who wanted a slice of panettone. For a second, I worried she was about to saw off Grandma's tongue. I asked for the thinnest slice because I was planning on eating a little of everything.

"Be careful," Grandma warned. "Your metabolism may slow down soon. You'll get fat."

"Me?" I asked. "Fat? I'm as thin as Gumby! My metabolism will never slow that much."

"Just be careful." She looked at Leo, who was now a freshman in my high school. It had been a long time since we had been in the same school together, but we gave each other the room we needed to make our own friends. Our paths didn't cross much at all, even during breakfast and lunch periods. "You don't speak much, do you?"

"Not as much as some people," Leo said.

"What do you like to do with yourself? All the same things as Damien?"

"No. I have my own interests. LEGO. Computer games. Writing."

"What are these computer games you like?" Grandma had decided years ago that Leo simply didn't speak and had given up on him. This decision offended me on behalf of my brother, so I was relieved to see her give Leo another try today. Happily, Leo had been growing more outgoing and loquacious in recent years. This was the first time he responded to one of Grandma's overtures wholeheartedly. He shared his thoughts on *Warlords* and Sierra adventure games with her, and for an appropriate amount of time. Grandma listened for as long as she was capable before cutting him off. "Leo, I have a personal question to ask you."

"Sure."

"Have you ever heard the story of the death of Virginia Rappe?"

"No."

"She's the woman who was crushed to death by Fatty Arbuckle."

Somehow, Mom heard this entire exchange. Standing, fighting to keep her composure, Mom proceeded slowly downstairs to the basement. She placed her face against a decorative pillow on a couch in the downstairs study and laughed hysterically into it.

Meanwhile, upstairs, Leo fought to keep his own composure by committing himself wholeheartedly to Grandma's chosen topic. "Oh, yes! Of course. I remember now. I've been reading up on the scandal. There's some debate about what really happened. A lot of people say Arbuckle was innocent and was the victim of a smear campaign. Rappe died from a ruptured bladder. People assumed it ruptured because he crushed her to death, but she suffered from chronic cystitis, a condition that inflames the bladder."

Grandma produced a cigarette from her purse and lit it. "Fatty Arbuckle was guilty."

Leo shrugged. "I just thought you'd be interested that he might not have done it."

"Too bad Weight Watchers didn't exist back then. Virginia Rappe might still be alive. And you, Damien, better not eat so many pastries when your metabolism slows. You may get fat and crush a woman under your enormous girth during sex."

"That's true," said Leo. "We wouldn't want that."

I nodded sagely. "I can see it in my mind's eye as if it has already happened. Me flattening some poor girl to death. Pancaking her with my massive beer belly."

"Do you have a girlfriend, by the way?" Grandma asked me.

"If you'd asked me two days ago, I'd have said 'no,' but I might actually have a girlfriend. Her name is Arwen!"

Leo raised his eyebrows. "Which of her parents was way too into *Lord of the Rings*?"

"Her late mother."

"Is Arwen sexy?" Grandma asked. "You deserve a sexy woman because you have bedroom eyes. Don't go out with anyone morbidly obese. Get yourself a nice girl with a Body Mass Index of eighteen to twenty-five. She doesn't have a fat posterior, does she?"

Again, I was trying not to laugh at Grandma. "Her posterior is fine."

"Show us a picture of her culi," Leo demanded, facetiously.

Grandma was grave. "Her posterior is only going get bigger."

I coughed a half-laugh into my fist. "She has a normal-sized posterior."

"Okay. Good." Grandma punctuated the end of the exchange by exhaling more smoke.

This is all she wants to know about Arwen? "Can I tell you about her, now? Because her weight isn't interesting to me. She's been a friend of mine for years. It is really exciting and romantic — in a *When Harry Met Sally* kind of way — that we will be a couple after all this time."

"If she has the right Body Mass Index and a reasonable-sized posterior, then I think you two might be happy together."

Dad suddenly looked concerned and placed his hand gently on my wrist. "But her ass isn't too small, is it? If she doesn't have an ass, then there's nothing to cup in your hands."

I couldn't decide whether to be angry or laugh hysterically, so my emotions shorted out. "I can't believe this conversation. I'm only worried about religious differences."

"Who cares what her religion is if she's got a good ass?" Dad asked. "I wouldn't."

I sighed with relief. "Okay, then. No objections on your end."

"Just as long as Dad has no objections to her end," Leo joked.

"I have a surprise for you," Grandma said to me, unexpectedly.

"Oh?" I braced myself for anything. One never knew what Grandma would say or do next — unless, of course, she said exactly what you feared she would. Conversations with Grandma were among some of life's most surreal experiences. Grandma stood up and walked to the kitchen counter, where she had placed a soccer-ball sized paper bag without my noticing it. "Damien, since your dad only likes to see me once a year, I'm not sure if I'll be around when you graduate. So, I wanted to give you your 'Good luck in college' present early."

What can it be? A framed portrait of Fatty Arbuckle? Grandma never had much of a handle on my taste, so it can't possibly be a good present. She reached into the bag and produced a fully painted porcelain statuette of Wonder Woman soaring through the clouds. I jumped out of the chair and scooped the statue out of her hands. "Wow!"

Grandma sounded sad. "I didn't want to get it, but you still like comic books at your age, so I thought it was ideal. There was a magazine ad: Three payments of $29.99, plus shipping."

"Yes!" I put the statue down and gave Grandma anther bear hug.

"Ow! Ow! Stop it. Too tight. Can't breathe."

I let go. "Thank you! I'm taking it upstairs." I grabbed the statue and the shopping bag, sprinted out of the kitchen, up the stairs, and into my bedroom. The only other object I had like this was a similarly sized porcelain statue of the Joker, dressed in a formal purple suit and purple hat, laughing hysterically at the skull of Yorick, which he brandished over his head. Wonder Woman and the Joker: The two wolves inside me. I picked up the Joker statue from atop my dresser, placed it in the shopping bag, and placed the shopping bag on the floor of my closet. I then put the Wonder Woman statue prominently where the Joker statue once stood. I didn't need the Joker to help me deal with my rage and despair anymore. I needed Wonder Woman to help me hope for a better future than the dark present I'd been living in all these years, especially at school. Mom was happier since her retirement. Dad was mellower and easier to get along with. Leo and I were getting on better than ever. Grandma was suddenly funnier than she was offensive. I had a girlfriend. Now, my imaginary best friend was on my dresser: The comic book face of American Transcendentalism and ecofeminism. I wanted to be more like her, and less like the Joker. That seemed much more possible now. I looked down at the Diana of Themyscira, daughter of Hippolyta, soaring through the clouds, two doves flying through the clouds with her. I could fly with her, too. I called to mind my favorite words of Ralph Waldo Emerson. "Never mind the ridicule, never mind the defeat: up again, old heart! — it seems to say, — there is victory yet for all justice; and the true romance which the world exists to realize, will be the transformation of genius into practical power."

November 22, 1993

Arwen was absent on Monday. I was desperate to see her. The desperation was compounded by the realization that, since I'd only ever seen her at school, or in larger gatherings where I had not been the one to call to invite her, I didn't know her phone number. I considered looking it up in the white pages but wasn't sure if she had her own phone line in her room. If she didn't, I'd likely call the main line by mistake and get one of the folks who had been keeping us apart all these years. My not being able to see her or talk to her made me weird and obsessive. My imagination became alarmingly lurid, and I started having the kinds of graphic images in my mind I suspected Salty had when he fantasized about her. I wanted to do terrible things to her.

All day and all night since our first kiss, I fucked Arwen in my imagination. This was a strange fixation for me. I'd had my crushes before. I'd had my fixations before. I had never been as single-minded as *this* before. Of course, as Salty would be the first to point out, I knew virtually nothing about the sex act itself — what it looked like at its most basic, and what all the Masters and Johnson stages and positions were. Sure, I'd taken part in a hardcore double-feature at Kyle's house, when he, Salty, David, and I raided Kyle's evil step-father's porn collection and fast-forwarded to the good parts of *Candy Stripers* and *The Devil in Miss Jones*. The guys were beside themselves with laughter over my hypnotic fascination with all the extreme close-ups of fellatio, vaginal fisting, and anal penetration, accompanied by exactly the kind of 1970s porn film soundtrack I'd often been told to expect. *That's what it looks like?* I thought but dared not say aloud. *That isn't exactly romantic, is it? It seems a bit meaty? Like meat slapping meat?* I *said* none of these things, but my face said them all for me, which was why the guys started hooting and hollering at me. Despite this porn-centric crash-course — and David Litvinov's recently borrowed, clinical, New Age-instructional video about the joys of cunnilingus and fingerbanging — I was pretty sure I had no idea what sex was *actually* like. Still, I found myself stretching my knowledge and imagination to its breaking point picturing every kind of sex with Arwen in every possible location. Thanks to the unusually extended conversation I'd just had about her having just the right size ass, it featured more prominently than I expected it to in a couple of scenarios involving her and a pool table. When I ran out of positions and locations to imagine, I sampled a variety of role-playing scenarios. One of my favorites involved Arwen as a traffic cop who had pulled me over for speeding, drew her gun on me, and forced me to go down on her on the side of the road. I'd also imagined she was a librarian who had taken me into a rarely used records room on the pretext of showing me a valuable document, locked the door, and informed me there was no such document. Another scenario involved me arriving at a drive-up burger joint. Arwen was the carhop on roller skates who delivered my food, then joined me in the back seat of my bright red 1959 Cadillac Eldorado. In one of the more bizarre scenarios, Arwen and I found ourselves on a tropical beach after some sort of apocalypse, and the angel Gabriel was informing us that most of humanity had been killed off and it was our task as a couple to repopulate the planet. All this meant was, after two years of functional impotence and a dick so dead it could barely be coaxed into life in total privacy, I managed to masturbate over Arwen twenty-five times between the afternoon of November fifteenth and the morning of November 22. This was unheard of for me, and I was quite proud of myself. On that Monday at school, I was rock hard again and hoping to find Arwen. We could find our way into a bathroom stall or a utility closet somewhere and she could help me out with playing with my cock. Be nice to have her hand on me, instead of my own, for once. But no, she was absent. Where was she?

I ran the mile home that afternoon, made some excuses to my mom about needing the car, borrowed it, and drove right to the mall, hoping to find Arwen at Kentucky Fried Chicken in the food court. I blasted through a red light on Victory Boulevard with a newly installed motion camera and saw a flash of light out of the corner of my eye as I crossed the intersection. That ticket would be expensive, but there wouldn't be a moving violation on my driver's license, because the camera didn't identify the driver, just the offending car's plate. I almost got a second ticket driving slightly too quickly past a speed trap on Richmond Avenue, only someone else was going ten-miles-per-hour faster and they were the ones the police put their flashers and siren on for. I pulled into one of the parking lots surrounding the mall, and parked diagonally, taking up two spots with my one car. I knew someone would probably slash my tires or key the door in retaliation, but whatever. I sprinted into the second-floor entrance of the mall, pushed my way through the two sets of glass doors into the JC Penny wing, and almost bowled Arwen herself over. I skidded to a halt one yard behind her. Arwen whirled around and a "Whoa!" escaped from her mouth. She was in full KFC regalia, on her way to the food court for her shift.

"Arwen!" I cried, moving towards her to give her a romantic, crushing bear hug.

"No, no, no!" She closed her eyes, held up her hands "stop," and recoiled.

I paused in mid-air, my arms outstretched, frozen in time. *"The Recoil?" Oh, shit.*

She half-opened an eye, saw the hug wasn't going to happen, opened both eyes, and lowered her arms. "Hey, there."

Scoffing and pointing accusing fingers at me, three people brushed past, reminding me that Arwen and I stood in the JC Penny foyer, blocking the entrance doors. We were forcing a steady stream of disgruntled and scandalized people to skirt around us or shove their way through us. When a three-generation family of seven, complete with a double stroller appeared, Arwen and I sidestepped them and settled into the carpeted, lady's evening wear and undergarments department. Slipping my hands in my pockets to appear nonchalant, I summoned the courage to say, "I missed you in school."

Arwen remained tense and skittish. "I saw my lawyer today!" She said that oddly loud.

"Not a great conversation?" I asked quietly.

Tears escaped from her eyes and slid down her cheeks. "Not a stitch of good news."

"I'm sorry to hear that." I took a furtive look around at my surroundings and was once again annoyed that I was surrounded by headless, armless mannequins dressed in bras, panties, teddies, and sheer, see-through nightgowns. "Not just for what I'm losing, but for you."

"At least I still have a minimum wage job in food service," she said bitterly.

"Yeah."

She stared at me. "Is that it? Can I go now? I'm late."

I panicked. If I allowed the conversation to end, we would become strangers to each other. "Wait. What do we do now?"

Arwen gave a short, bitter laugh. "'We' don't do anything. I need to figure out what I must do now. There is no 'we.'"

"But couldn't we just—"

"Goodbye, Damien." This was Arwen's final farewell to me. Our relationship was over. It was Thanksgiving, and we wouldn't be graduating until next June, but we were done. We might see each other in the hallway, cafeteria, or gym, but we would no longer speak to one another beyond "good morning" or "how are you?" It would be professional and civil, but that would be all. Somehow, I held myself together. I wasn't sure why I hadn't melted into a small puddle of water on the floor next to the display of Cortland Intimates Open Bottom Girdles.

"I love you, Arwen." I always dreaded saying those words. For years, I'd avoided admitting to myself that I loved Arwen, but if this was going to be our final conversation, I had to say it now. The meteor was about to strike. I was being expelled. Moving to Paraguay. Dying. The words had barely been spoken when I feared I had made an awful mistake. Had I just done something profoundly cruel to her by telling her I loved her? Her reaction made me think my worst fears had been correct: her long, slow, sad exhale. I imagined her thinking: "I know. I've always known. Couldn't you have said it years ago when it might have meant more? Changed things? Why say this now, to make this terrible moment as hard on me as possible?"

"I know this isn't your decision," I added hastily, still looking at my shoes. "And I'm not saying this to make you sad. I just want you to know that, even if we can't be together, and we can't be friends, I'm so glad we met. I think you may have saved my life. You definitely saved my sanity, back in junior high, during all those library lunches. We had great times together."

"I liked when we danced," Arwen whispered. "At the Sweet Sixteen."

"Me, too. That was fun, wasn't it?"

"I got in so much trouble." Arwen smiled. "It was worth it."

"I think about that night all the time."

"Me, too. I think about it all the time, too."

We stood, two yards apart, both looking at the ground.

"I need to go," Arwen said.

"Okay."

"Bye."

"Okay."

Arwen turned, walked six steps away from me, towards the food court. Then stopped. Her shoulders hunched and her head bowed. She scuttled back in my direction, threw her arms around me and buried her face in my shoulder. "I love you, too." Then she hurried off and disappeared from my sight as hastily as she could, weeping quietly.

I looked down at the Cortland Intimates Open Bottom Girdles. They were $9.99, marked down from $14.99, but only if you had a JC Penny credit card. Wait. I'm confused. Aren't all girdles open bottomed? If so, why label this that, specifically?

"Can I help you, sir?" a saleswoman asked. She was sizing me up, trying to figure out if I was there to buy my girlfriend some lingerie as more of a present to myself than to her, or if I was single, and a pervert, and I was there to ogle and hump the headless mannequin in the teddy.

"Sorry," I said. "I was lost in thought. I'm headed to Waldenbooks." Even though I just told her I was heading into the mall proper, I turned around and left the building through the two sets of doors. I wondered if the saleswoman cared enough about my about-face to be befuddled.

November 23, 1993

In 1990, the classic Martin Scorsese gangster film *Goodfellas* dropped like a cultural atom bomb on Staten Island. Anecdotal evidence suggested to me that "everyone" on the island had seen this grotesque film multiple times in the theater, and "everyone" wanted to live inside it permanently. This idea was made particularly clear to me in the high school cafeteria during lunch period the day after my apocalyptic conversation with Arwen. I sat with Salty, David, and Kyle, not telling them anything about what had happened in the mall. Salty held aloft a small plastic cup of apple juice. "They're serving urine samples today! My favorite."

"Oh, God!" David moaned in ecstasy after taking a bite out of the obviously canned lumps of strawberry preserves on something resembling a pastry. "I love jelly ca-cas!"

Kyle stared down at his own pastry, which was covered in florescent blue icing. "I wish I'd gotten a jelly ca-ca. They ran out and gave me this. But what the hell is it?"

"I don't eat blue food that's not a berry," said David. "Who ever heard of blue icing?"

"I've seen it before," said Salty. "Your mother put that blue icing on my penis last night."

When I laughed until I cried, David got mad at me. "It wasn't *that* funny."

I laughed hysterically for another minute, holding my pained sides.

"Jesus Christ," Kyle murmured. "What the hell is up with you today, Damien?"

Tony emerged from the serving chamber holding a recyclable cardboard lunch tray and slid into the adjacent table with the Merry Men. They sat inches from each other but talked so loud during casual conversation, it was as if they were shouting to one another over a yawning chasm. "Mammolito! What's with this pastry, man?"

Bobby laughed. "It's good, Tony. Just what a growin' boy needs."

"But what's that shit they put on it?" Tony angrily yelled this out loud enough for the whole cafeteria to hear, in a thick Brooklyn accent. I couldn't help but burst out laughing hysterically again. Tony leaped out of his seat and ran up to me, crimson with rage. "What's so funny? What, do I amuse you, or something? Does something about me amuse you?"

"Sorry, Tony," I said. "I'm laughing in agreement. Don't worry, the icing may be blue, but its high in beta-carotene."

"Oh, you're laughing in agreement?" Tony asked. "Is that it?"

"You were just funny, just then, you know?" I offered, my laughter dying down.

"No, no, I don't know! You said it. How do I know? You said I'm funny. How the fuck am I funny? Am I a clown to you? What's so funny about me? Tell me! Tell me what's funny!"

I felt fear. Then it dawned on me. "Wait a minute! Are you quoting *Goodfellas* to me?"

Tony stepped back. "What?"

Kyle, Salty, and the assemblage of Scholars Academy students at our table who had been shrinking in their seats up until this point — not wanting to get involved or cause a rumble between the multiethnic gifted table and the Italian Merry Men table — suddenly sat upright.

"He is quoting *Goodfellas!*" David laughed. "He *is!*"

Tony looked more confused than caught out. He had

unintentionally quoted the scene. He held up a finger, declaring his emotional authenticity. "Not for nuthin', but I ain't quotin' *nobody*. I'm fuckin' angry ova here."

I grinned. "You're totally quoting Joe Pesci. Are we playing a scene here?"

"No, I'm serious, man," Tony insisted. "I'm mad at you."

"I tell you what: you wanna scare me, write your own dialogue. Don't bite off Martin Scorsese. I mean, I like to quote movies as much as anyone. More than most, even. But I know when I'm doing it! You're living Pesci's role by accident, or some weird voodoo shit right now."

Bobby guffawed, "You got wrecked, Tony! You're a mess! Egon just destroyed you!"

Tony flicked his chin at Bobby as he returned to his seat. "You're rooting for him? Didn't he kick your ass once?"

"Yeah, but I deserved it. Anyway, you got wrecked! By Egon! You're a mess!"

Thank you, Bobby, for the Italian solidarity. And you can call me Egon any time.

David grew thoughtful. "Don't you guys think HBO should produce a *Goodfellas* TV show? They should totally do that. I bet it would be the best weekly show of all time!"

"No!" I screamed. All conversation in the lunchroom ceased as people tried to figure out where the blood-curdling shriek came from. When they saw it was me and I appeared to be in neither pain nor danger, they shrugged and returned to their lunches. I looked at David. "No, I don't ever want to see a *Goodfellas* series. I'd strangle myself with dental floss."

"Surely as a devotee of serious cinema–"

"No!"

"How about a show that's a mashup of *Wall Street* and *Glengarry Glen Ross?*"

"No! I want a show about nice, decent human beings, not sociopathic white guys!"

"Maybe they can make the secretary a sympathetic viewpoint character, just for you."

"No! No, no, no, no, no!" I pounded my fist on the table to punctuate each "No!"

"You're getting weirder by the day, Damien," David declared.

During this unnaturally tense exchange, I almost missed it when Arwen and her stepsister, What's-her-name, walked by our table. "Hi, Arwen!" I called out. I couldn't tell you what my tone was. It wasn't high-pitched to make me sound non-threatening. It wasn't my normal baritone. It wasn't plaintive. It wasn't confident. It wasn't natural, or charming.

Arwen inclined her head in acknowledgement, said nothing, and kept moving. Whatshername threw me a dirty look and mouthed the words, "Don't talk to her!" After they were gone, my friends all looked at me with open curiosity, but didn't say anything. I tried to go back to eating but burst out laughing hysterically. I took two minutes to regain my composure.

"Damn, man," David breathed. "You laugh more than Jack Nicholson's Joker and Mark Hamill's Joker combined! And at the same kinds of totally inappropriate times."

"He laughs when he's in pain," Kyle said, looking at me sideways.

"I do," I admitted.

"You wanna tell us what's going on?" Kyle asked.

I regaled the boys with my interpretation of "O What a Beautiful Morning" from *Oklahoma!* and only stopped singing when they promised not to press me about Arwen.

November 24, 1993

I picked up the receiver of the rotary phone in my bedroom and called the number in the white pages under A. Pokatny. An answering machine recording came on that was a robot's voice repeating the phone number I had just dialed, pointedly failing to identify who lived at that residence, and asking callers to leave a message. I considered my options when it beeped. It was probably her number, but the robot voice was disconcerting. I also wasn't sure if she was sitting right next to the phone, screening all her calls. (Fun fact: In the days before cell phones, calls were only answered by people who were sitting within a few yards of the phone, which was attached to the wall by a cable.) Finally, both Salty and Kyle had recently teased me mercilessly for the general quality of my answering machine messages.

"I got your terrible message," Kyle said to me just last week.

"What was wrong with my message?" I had asked him.

"The better question is: what is wrong with you? You sound like a psychopath: Crispin Glover meets Jim Carrey. Learn how to leave a proper answering machine message!"

Salty had agreed, "They're bad in a different way each time, but they're always bad."

"Wait a minute," I gave Salty a skeptical look. "I never call you."

"Kyle plays me the ones you leave on his machine and we laugh at you together."

I glanced sheepishly Kyle. "Are my voice messages really *that* bad?"

"You need to stop leaving people answering machine messages. I'm not kidding."

I hung up at the beep. Then I worried that Arwen might have been in the kitchen downstairs and missed the call on her personal line. What if she ran upstairs to get the phone and just missed it? It was five p.m. Close to dinner. Did her family sit down together sometime between five and seven to eat, or was this one of those families that didn't eat together? Was she some sort of latchkey kid? I had no idea. I tried calling again. As the phone rang, I had a sudden terror that she'd pick up, have a neutral sounding voice that gave me no cues, and I'd have no idea what to say to her. As it turns out, I need not have worried. I got the answering machine again, felt an overwhelming temptation to leave a message, subdued the temptation, and hung up. The problem was, if I didn't leave a message, she'd never know I'd called. But I didn't want to leave a message. I should call again later. Or tomorrow.

Wait. I should just leave a dang message now *so I know that she knows that I called.* I dialed again. I heard the beep at the end of the robot voice salutation. Then I remembered Kyle's exhortation to stop leaving messages, so I hung up without leaving a message.

*

November 25, 1993

"What's your fucking problem?" Aunt Beatrice asked me.

"Nuthin'." Slouched posture and pale, hang-dog demeanor, I sat alone at the dining room table, staring glumly at my plate of turkey, cranberry sauce, stuffing, and peas, waiting for grace to be said so I could eat. Grumbling, Aunt Beatrice went to the adjoining kitchen to find my mother to complain about me. In the kitchen, fifteen relatives picked their way through a buffet of traditional and Italian-style Thanksgiving main and side dishes. Since several of my favorite family members, including the elder Bianca Natali, had passed away in the years since the pool party reunion, I felt disconnected from the Basile clan writ large. Baby Bianca and Cousin Gabriel were the exceptions since they were as fun and friendly as ever, as well as comparatively young and fit. Our deceased relatives were not the only ones missing this Thanksgiving: Emily Basile-Scrosciare and her husband Matt were both still vertical but had gradually phased out participation in any and all family gatherings. There was less mystery concerning the absence of Emily's leather-skirt-wearing sister Nicole: She had developed a series of physical and mental debilitations that had forced her into hermitage. Sadly, Dad wouldn't have Nicole's flat bottom to mock any more. I felt Uncle Skippy's absence keenly, as well, not because I saw him as a figure of fun, but because he was a lovely human being. In the wake of his wife's passing, and his own declining health, Skippy now came as a matched set with his unshaven, baseball-cap-wearing brother-in-law, Orlando, who did nothing but complain ad nauseum about immigrants and affirmative action. Mom and Carmine had nothing good to say about Orlando, but I have to admit, nothing could have prepared me for just how awful a person he was when I finally met him in the flesh the year before. Still, I would have put up with Orlando blaming Black people for his misbegotten life if it meant I got to see Skippy at least one more time before he died.

Replacing the deceased and missing in action were new extended-family recruits of questionable merit: Beatrice's daughter Concetta's agreeable new husband and the less agreeable members of his extended family, including his parents, sister, sister's husband, brother, and brother's wife. Thanksgiving was one of my favorite holidays, but *who the fuck were these people?* Admittedly, it occurred to me I should still be friendly and talk to everyone if I could get out of my funk long enough to do it. One of the new in-laws appeared to be the latest model aging divorcée in form-fitting clothing — spandex pants, a sports bra, and a headband. *I should ask* her *out*, I thought sadly, with almost no enthusiasm. I stared at her, trying to muster the will to take a mental picture of her to masturbate to later, but I was too damn sad to put in the effort.

Lorenzo ("Alexa Hente") Basile dropped into the chair beside me, sporting a John Franco New York Mets T-shirt. He caught me checking out his middle-aged sister-in-law and chuckled. "Sports bras don't do it for me. They're like Fort Knox." He grabbed a roll and bit right into it. His mom snapped at him from the kitchen sink, "Hey, Bluto! Wait for grace!"

Alexa Hente scowled and did what his mother ordered. He paused to stare at my skinny arms. "What's going on with these?" He squeezed my forearm and bicep, testing them. "You need some definition." These were the first four sentences he'd said to me in as many years.

I said, "Hey, yo, Alexa Hente. I got a question for you."

Alexa Hente turned his unenthusiastic eyes upon me.

I pressed on. "That Jewish girl you were in love with? You said she broke your heart?"

Alexa Hente blinked. "How do you know about Rachel?"

"You talked to Dad and Grandpa about her by the swimming pool at the reunion."

"You remember a conversation from ten years ago you heard about secondhand?"

I nodded.

Alexa Hente smirked. "I can't even remember what happened to me yesterday. Why are you asking me about Rachel Goodman?"

"I'm in love with a Jewish girl that I can't be with because her parents won't allow it. I was wondering how you got over Rachel. And how long it took."

Alexa Hente looked sad. "Who says I ever got over Rachel?"

"Oh."

"Yeah," Alexa Hente chuckled, "Nothing will fuck you up for life like falling head over heels for someone you can't be with."

Alexa Hente's more sensitive and loquacious twin brother Gabriel took the seat on the other side of me and said, "It'll get better. I fall in love with people who don't love me back every other week. It's a hobby of mine. And look at me! I'm fine. You will be, too."

"Yeah, you're fine," Alexa Hente scoffed.

"I am!" Gabriel smirked and returned his attention to me. "I love my brother to death, but don't listen to him. He's not the sharpest knife in the drawer." Once again, I was devastated, and Gabriel was here for me, restoring my faith that "This too shall pass." Gabriel had always been my Hope Doctor, giving me much needed medicine at just the right time. He had done me this favor many times during my years in junior high hell. Each time he came to Staten Island to visit my mom, or to see me on my birthday, he saw that I was looking pale and desolate, and did what he could to bolster my spirits. He told me tales of surviving his own difficult adolescence:

"When I was your age, I was the uncool, overweight twin brother of the coolest, manliest athlete in the school. Lorenzo was the football hero. I was his weakling opposite number. They teased me mercilessly. It was awful! But I got through it. I grew up, I lost weight, and I wound up making a ton of friends when I got older. Heck, these days, I'm more cut than Lorenzo. He's really let himself go since high school! So, things got better for me. They'll get better for you, too. I know that doesn't help you much now, but please try to hold onto that. Make it something to look forward to." Hearing this advice from Gabriel made me realize that I was not alone as I thought I was. Gabriel was instrumental in giving me the strength I needed to carry on — to make it to junior high graduation when I would have preferred to just give up on life.

And now, here I was in high school, damaged goods once again. And here was Gabriel, helping me pick up the pieces of my broken heart one more time. "You're basically the coolest cousin of all time," I told Gabriel at the Thanksgiving table. "You're my hero, man."

"Ah, I'm nothing to write home about." Gabriel flashed his infectious smile. He looked handsome, loving, and outgoing. How he ever had trouble making friends was beyond me.

To my enormous surprise, Mom's Uncle Skippy chose that moment to walk up to the long dining room table, accompanied by his dreadful brother-in-law, Orlando. I wanted to jump up to hug Skippy, but the room was suddenly filled to bursting. I felt pinned against the wall behind me. "Uncle Skippy!" I waved. "I missed you!"

I shouted too loud, even for Skippy's hearing problem. He flinched. "What? You missed me? Why did you miss me?" *Uh-oh. I'm getting the Recoil from Uncle Skippy.*

I blushed. "Not every day, of course. It has just been a while. It is good to see you."

Skippy had a deer in the headlights look, as if I'd asked him to prom. "I didn't miss you."

I waved him off. "That's fine. Fuggedaboutit! I'm not worth missing."

As Skippy and Orlando went as far from me as they could to find their seats, I heard Orlando grouse, "I coulda gone to college, but some Black athlete took my scholarship and failed out after one year, because he had natural sports talent but couldn't read!"

Alexa Hente sighed. "That guy does nothing but complain about his lost scholarship. I don't believe he even had a scholarship to lose. I think he pulled that grievance out of his ass."

I nodded. "Orlando sure spends plenty of time rummaging around in his own ass. He's got his head up it day and night."

Uncle Carmine sat across from me with his mountainous plate of spaghetti and no American Thanksgiving food in sight. "You talkin' to my sons?" he asked me. "I'm sorry about that. Well, I'm not sorry about Gabriel. He's got all the personality in the family. He's a great guy. I'm sorry about Alexa Hente, over here. He has no personality. And my daughter over there in the kitchen? Concetta? She's got the personality of an old shoe." I laughed a little too loud, then worried Alexa Hente would smack me upside the head over it. And yet, he sat motionless, proving his father correct. "How are you doin', there, Damien?" Uncle Carmine asked.

The question warmed my heart. I hadn't expected him to ask after me. "I'm so glad you asked, Uncle Carmine. Things have been a little crazy and I can really use someone to talk to."

Uncomfortable and impatient, Carmine held up a traffic-cop hand to stop me. "Listen, babe, when people ask you how you're doin', they don't really want you to go into an honest answer. They just want you to say 'Okay, can't complain.' I've got three adult kids, a son-in-law, and a wife with health problems. I lose way too much money each week at the races. I've got businesses losing money. Tax audits up the ass. I can't hear about new problems. I just wanted to say, 'hi' and 'happy Thanksgiving.' I didn't want to hear your life story."

I held my hands up in surrender. "I hear you."

Uncle Carmine visibly relaxed. "I tell you what, babe: let me give you the advice I give everyone every time they tell me their problems. It doesn't matter what the problems are. The same advice applies. Imagine you're at a long table with a buncha people you're jealous of. You're having a bad time of it. You think they're doing better than you. You take your bag o'problems and put it on the table. Everyone else does the same with their bag o'problems. Then everyone has a chance to swap out their bag o'problems with someone else's. Guess what? Everyone takes their own bag back. Every time."

"Yeah?"

"Everyone else's life looks better at first. Then you think about it and realize you don't appreciate what you got, and you don't want to trade places with them."

Solid bartender advice. He wasn't an intellectual, but Uncle Carmine had his moments. "That works for me."

"Yeah, well, good," Uncle Carmine said. "Let's try this again. 'How are you doin?'"

"'Can't complain, Uncle Carmine,'" I said.

"That is the correct answer. Anything new going on that isn't too deep or sad?"

"Mom still has a crush on Albert Finney from the first time she saw *Tom Jones*. I finally saw the movie and loved it, so I'm gonna read the Henry Fielding book."

Uncle Carmine brightened. "Ah! Tom Jones! What a fantastic singer. 'It's Not Unusual.' 'Delilah.' I saw him at the Garden State Arts Center back in '70. Best concert ever. He pals around with Albert Finney? I did not know that."

The mistake was so natural that it didn't catch me off guard. I smiled at it, and Uncle Carmine took my smile to be enthusiasm for Tom Jones. "Tom Jones is the man," I agreed.

"Isn't he?" my uncle asked. "I'm so glad you're into Tom Jones!"

Uncle Carmine, Cousin Gabriel, Alexa Hente, and I formed an impromptu barbershop quartet and began singing "It's Not Unusual." Our family members all turned to stare at us, blown away by our sudden decision to serenade them with Vegas showroom music.

When my parents, Leo, and I returned home, we found the day's issue of *The Staten Island Chronicle* rolled up in a rubber band, resting against our front door. As we went inside, I broke the rubber band and unfurled the paper. The headline read: *GOOD SAMARITAN KILLER STRIKES AGAIN, Roadside Seductress Claims Tenth Victim.* I was glad they changed the misnomer from Black Widow to Good Samaritan Killer. It had a good ring to it. I also liked the phrase "roadside seductress."

I laughed evilly. *If you gotta go, that's the way to go. Dead sexy.*

November 30, 1993

I kept getting Arwen's robot-voice answering machine and not leaving messages. If only she knew I was trying to reach her. Was she never in her room? Was she there, but assumed the hang-ups were all "you could be one of seven free Caribbean cruise contest winners" calls? I'd mailed her a love letter three days ago. It was four pages, heartfelt, and inspired by Elizabethan Love Lyric Poetry. I had written many beautiful sentiments into those pages, and one appallingly stupid one. Three days after mailing the letter, I had already forgotten all the beautiful sentiments and recalled only the stupid one. Somewhere at the end of page two, I promised to provide Arwen with regular oral sex if she accepted me. This asinine aside had been inspired by my nail-biting viewing of David Litvinov's sex-training video, "How to Make Love to a Woman and Please Her Every Time." The video had been so emphatic that oral sex was the only sex that mattered that I wanted to reassure Arwen I was in on this Big Womenfolk Secret. Of course, now that the letter was already in the mail and it was far too late to strike the sentence out, did I realize I had made a fatal error in including this line. Since Arwen had no idea I had seen such a video, she would have no context for the pledge, would not understand why I made it, and would be mortally offended, if not frightened and repulsed. I had thought I was making the best possible argument for myself as a boyfriend. Instead, I would most certainly come off as weird, overly explicit, and nauseatingly aggressive. Whatever. Whether or not that insane line single-handedly torpedoed my chances of a sympathetic response, Arwen should have the note in hand.

I'm a dead man and I refuse to admit it to myself. My time with Arwen is over. "My doom has come upon me; let me not then die ingloriously and without a struggle, but let me first do some great thing that shall be told among men hereafter."

I drove out to Arwen's home on Todt Hill with a big bouquet of flowers and a box of chocolates. The Victorian structure was impressive, surrounded by the largest yard I'd seen on Staten Island outside of the Conference House. Apparently, there was money in confectionary. I left Mom's car one block from the Pokatny Palace and crept under strategically placed security cameras mounted on the lampposts that illuminated the circular driveway. I scooted over the waist-high brick wall that cordoned off her front yard and driveway from the sidewalk. I snuck around the back of the house to locate Arwen's second-floor bedroom. I settled on the most likely candidate: the one with the pink curtains. Naturally, I would feel like a total horse's ass if I'd chosen What's-her-name's bedroom instead of hers, but my instincts told me it was Arwen's window. I tossed a small pebble. It plinked off the glass with a cracking sound that made me fear I'd broken a cobweb pattern into it. Looking again, I was relieved to see that the glass was undamaged. A light went on in the bedroom. A hand raised the window. Then it struck me: *Arwen is a tomboy. She probably wouldn't have pink curtains.* Arwen's stepsister poked her head out the window. Her face registered surprise, fear, annoyance, and derision all at once. "She isn't home, you idiot. Get off our property before I call the police."

"Can you tell her I was here?"

"Leave her alone. She's done with you."

"How do I know you're telling the truth?"

"I'm not a liar!" She couldn't have looked more affronted. "And what was with that dumbass letter you sent? What possessed you to offer to eat her out regularly, Crackhead?"

A feeling swept over me that was reminiscent of the worst stomach virus I'd ever had. *Is it too late to invent a time machine and go back in time to stop myself writing that note? Or, at the very least, omit the muff-diving paragraph?* "I was just kidding about that," I offered feebly.

She disappeared from the window, reappeared, and hurled four crumpled up pieces of paper out the window. They bounced a few times before settling into the grass near my feet. "Here! It was the kind of love letter a fascist would write. Arwen circled all the most patriarchal sentiments in red and corrected your most cringe-inducing sentences. There's also some marginalia that deconstructs your prose from a feminist perspective."

I plucked up the four pieces of paper but was too frightened to open them and smooth them out. "And will those be her thoughts and feelings in red ink, or yours? Wouldn't Arwen, of all people, have read it sympathetically? Given me the benefit of the doubt?"

"*Any woman* would have reacted to your shitty love letter the exact same way we did."

"Even a woman who really loved me?" If those red corrections were really from Arwen, I wasn't sure I could handle seeing them. I remembered how Mr. Darcy felt when Elizabeth Bennet ripped his marriage proposal to shreds and turned it against him, using it as proof positive that he was a heartless monster. If Elizabeth's litany of complaints almost broke Darcy's will to live, how would I hold up under a similar assault? Could I read Arwen's enraged, blood-red deconstruction of my pornographic profession of undying love without shattering into a billion glass fragments? No, I could not. I knew my limitations. Unsurprisingly, Darcy is the better man.

"Go!" Miriam yelled. "Make tracks now, or I'll set the Mastiff on you."

"But Lillian-"

"*Lillian*? My name is Miriam! How long have you known me?"

"Um . . . "

"I'm calling the police," she pulled her head back inside and slammed the window.

I dropped the flowers and chocolates on the grass, vaulted myself over the brick wall, and sprinted back to Mom's car.

I couldn't bring myself to look at the deconstructed love letter when I got home. What story would the corrections tell? That I'm a fucking idiot. I knew that already. I didn't need a spotlight shone on what I already knew. I tossed the letter into the kitchen trash. I spent the rest of the evening looking warily at the receptacle, wondering if the pieces of paper would leap out, unfurl themselves in front of me, and force me to face their contents.

Now that I had trespassed on her property, I realized the wise and considerate thing to do would be give Arwen a wide berth for at least a month. All I need do was listen to my head, and there would be plenty of time for us to cool off a little and discuss things as adults in four weeks.

The problem, of course, was I was no longer entirely sane.

December 1, 1993

I fit my clumsy index finger into the rotary dial, noticing my bitten-down fingernails. I'd only just dialed the last number when Arwen picked up so quickly that I hadn't heard it ring on my end. "Yes?" The ostensibly sweet single word left an angry, hurt, and impatient aftertaste.

I hadn't expected her to answer. "Oh, yes. Hi, Arwen. I wanted to tell you I was sorry."

"For what?"

"You know. Just sorry."

Pause. "The display on my nightstand phone reads: 'Damian Cavalieri: *57* missed calls.'"

A familiar chill swept over me. It came anytime I'd done something stupid to make her angry with me. "Your phone keeps track of who calls and how many times they called?"

"Yes, it does."

I looked down at my own, ancient, telecommunications device. "I didn't know that such technology existed. If I'd known, I would have only called one time and stopped." That *may* have been true. "Or called, waited a week, tried again." *Fifty-seven calls? That was villainous behavior. Hardly the actions of a gentleman. How could I consider myself a good person now?*

"Fifty-seven calls," she repeated. "This phone has been ringing off the hook and flashing your name for days. I've been sitting here next to it. I saw your name flash every time. I made a point of not picking up. And yet, the damn phone kept ringing." Arwen spoke without modulating her voice, in precise, Lauren Bacall tones. It was a voice I normally found sexy.

"And my love-letter writing skills leave something to be desired," I added miserably.

"Your communications skills can stand some improvement in general."

"That's a hard criticism for a literature and creative writing student to hear."

"You go from one extreme to the other. First you go way out on a limb, and then you run for the hills. It's maddening."

"I'm particularly sorry about that one part of my letter. You know."

Arwen harrumphed. "What the fuck was that all about? That was tacky and peculiar."

"There's a story there, but I won't bore you with it. Did your sister tell you I brought some flowers and chocolates by?"

"She may have mentioned it." Arwen paused, waiting for me to say more. When I couldn't think of anything to offer, she added, "I could have sworn we decided not to see each other anymore. Am I just imagining the conversation we had in JC Penny? We had it near all the bras if that helps jog your memory."

I took a moment to compose myself. "I wanted to honor your wishes, but I lost control of my feelings. I'm having a lot of trouble getting through all the stages of grief. I've gotten stuck in the mud of 'denial' and 'bargaining.' I don't want to believe that everything is different now."

"You've made this as hard on me as you possibly could," she said, flatly.

I didn't want to make it easy for you. I want it to be as hard for you as possible. But I didn't want revenge. I wanted you to change your mind. "I know I picked the worst time to tell you I loved you. I picked the wrong time to buy you flowers and write you a love letter. But I felt cheated. I was going to ask you to the prom. I'd always wanted to do these things, and I was robbed of the chance. In my heart, I knew there was no way I'd get you to change your mind about us, but I had to try. You're worth fighting for. And if I couldn't get you to change your mind, I at least wanted to show you, one last time, how I felt, as part of the goodbye."

Arwen's voice lost its neutrality. She was flustered. "That was selfish. The conversation we had in the mall should have been enough for you. It was enough for me. You spoilt it."

"Please don't say that."

She must have heard me sniffle since she allowed her tone to turn conciliatory. "Okay. I suppose you didn't *spoil* it."

"Thank you." I assumed she could hear each of my tears falling, though they were silent. "I took for granted we'd always be friends. I was biding my time for my chance to be with you when, suddenly, there wasn't any time left. I'm sorry I didn't respect your request to give you space. I accept that we can't be friends any more. I just wanted you to know before I went away how much you mean to me. And I overdid it." I paused. "I hope that was a real apology and not just a bunch of excuses and self-justifications. I know men aren't good at apologies and they give those 'I'm sorry if I offended you' bullshit apologies. I hope this is a real one and not that."

Her extended silence worried me. Just as my mounting panic was about to compel me to start speaking again, she replied, "I've never had a real apology from anyone before. Certainly not from a guy. Thank you. I appreciate this call. I really do."

I surprised myself by smiling. "Really? Call number fifty-eight wasn't awful?"

"Call fifty-eight was very nice. I'm glad I picked up."

CHAPTER TWENTY-THREE
Praying the Rosary on Prom Night

April 23, 1994

Lou Ferrigno's doppelganger, Eric Indelicato, stopped me for a hallway talk just before I entered my English classroom. "You get a prom date yet?"

I grit my teeth and shook my head. "I haven't heard the word 'No' so many times since the last time I listened to 'Nobody but Me' by the Human Beinz."

Eric frowned. "I thought you'd snatched Arwen away from that Polish beatnik guy."

"She dumped him, but not for me. None us are prom-bound now."

"Damn! I've been praying to Saint Jude for you to get laid for years. I thought the patron saint of lost causes was finally gonna come through. Anyway, what the hell is going on with this stupid prom? *You* can't get a prom date! *I* can't get a prom date."

No way! The sex god of junior high, Eric Indelicato, can't get a prom date? "You, too? I thought it was just me. I was starting to feel incurably unfuckable!"

Eric frowned the deepest frown I'd ever seen. "Check this out. The senior girls are all going to the prom, but they're not taking senior boys as their dates. As near as I can tell, the sexually active ones are taking their middle-aged sugar daddies with them, and the virgins are all bringing their first cousins! As of now, all the girls at this prom will be students from this school and all the guys will be from everywhere else *but* here. You know where that leaves you and me? Up shit's creek without a paddle! There ought to be a rule: Only students from here can attend!"

I massaged my jaw. "Middle-ages sugar daddies? I tried to bag me a cougar, but no dice."

"There's no precedent for a guy our age taking an older woman, but there's gonna be a shitload of girls taking hedge fund managers to this prom. I guess my best shot at going to a prom — any prom — is become a hedge fund manager and go with a teenage girl when I'm forty."

"I absolutely refuse to perpetuate this bullshit scenario. I won't screw a future version of me out of going to the prom by cradle robbing a high school girl when I'm forty."

Eric shrugged. "I don't know. Right now, that's the best plan I've got to go to the prom — twenty years from now."

"I don't remember the prom in *Back to the Future* being like this," I grumbled. "Of course, we both know what the cousins are all about. Parents are worried their daughters will have sex with their prom dates, so they send them with a relative. I guess they're so strict because they remember Woodstock well, and don't want any of us kids having that kinda fun."

"That might not work," Indelicato said. "I know I'd do *my* cousin. She's hot as shit."

Mr. Hopkins walked past us into the classroom and said, "We're starting soon."

I held up a finger to ask for a minute more. "So, what do we do, Eric? Take *our* cousins?"

"I'm at a total loss, dude." Eric admitted. "I just don't get it. I'm handsome. I should have a date already. You? Put you in a suit? You're diesel! What the hell?'"

I'm 'diesel?' I'm genuinely touched. A compliment from Eric! "That's nice of you to say, man. After twelve damn rejections, these girls got me thinking I look like Quasimodo."

"No, dude. You're, like, attractive and shit. No kidding."

"That's news to me. Interesting. Anyway, what the fuck are we supposed to do?"

"I got nothing," Eric said. "You're not going. I'm not. Cousins and dirty old men are."

"It'll be cool when we're shut out of the prom," I said breezily.

Eric patted me on the shoulder. "I know you're too Catholic for your own good, but we gotta make sure you and me don't spend prom night at home praying the rosary."

"Amen to that!" I exclaimed. "Hey, wait a minute. Why don't you ask Marina Dazzo?"

Eric laughed loudly. "Marina Dazzo? I haven't seen her in two years! You need to reset your brain clock and live in the present, not the past. This is 1994, not 1987!"

"You're right. I do tend to live in the past. Still, weren't you two good friends?"

Eric inclined his head, thinking. "Everyone else is asking out people who don't go to school here. I might as well, too! And Marina was just the sweetest, nicest Alpine ever. She'd probably say 'yes.'" Eric chucked me under the chin with his fist. "Rad idea, bro. I owe you."

This would be the first of two prom conversations that day. Improbably, the second conversation would be at a church, with a priest. That afternoon, I stepped into the rectory of St. Luke's and found Monsignor Tobin in his office. "I've heard whispers on the wind that you wanted to see me?"

Tobin rose from behind his desk to shake my hand. He gestured for me to sit in the chair across from him. "Speaking of whispers, I hear you wrote an excellent pro-life essay."

I was taken aback. "Who told you that?"

Tobin smiled enigmatically. "Rumor has it your pro-choice biology professor said it was the kindest, smartest pro-life essay she's ever read. Her husband liked it, too."

"Yeah, that's all true," I said. "Who told you that?"

"I have to be honest with you," he said. "I didn't just hear about it second-hand. I got a hold of a page and read it. I saw for myself that it was superb."

I snapped my fingers. "The draft page I forgot here the night I covered the phones."

Tobin looked at me over his steepled fingers. "Exactly."

I shifted in my seat. "Just so you know, I didn't want to write about that topic. I'm not comfortable writing about bleak, real-world themes. I prefer writing *Doctor Who* fan fiction."

Tobin shook his head in gentle disagreement. "You deal with harsh and important topics with intelligence and sensitivity. You should read your essay at World Youth Day, or on EWTN or Relevant Radio. If your writing is half as powerful as I suspect, you could wind up becoming an influential and well-paid member of the Legionaries of Christ. Or a Vatican press agent."

I looked down at my shoes. "It was only intended to be homework. Something private between me and my biology teacher. I never intended to make it a public, political thing."

Monsignor Tobin looked quizzically at me. "But it's great! When can I read it all?"

"I kinda don't have it anymore." I clamped my eyes shut and grimaced. "I lost it."

Tobin leaned back in his chair. "You must have it saved on your computer."

"The file got deleted."

"Passive voice sentence construction?" Monsignor Tobin finally understood. "'The file got deleted.' Who deleted it? You. Why would you destroy all print and electronic copies?"

"I'd rather not get into it," I said evasively.

"Why not?"

My dang throat was dry again. I cleared it too loudly. "I was worried I was wrong."

"But you weren't wrong."

"But I might be wrong."

"But you aren't."

"I don't want to be a villain in a dystopian science fiction story."

Monsignor Tobin snorted. "Like *The Handmaid's Tale*?"

I nodded. "I think so. I haven't seen the movie or read the book yet, but I've heard of it."

"*The Handmaid's Tale* is just well-written propaganda."

I raised both my eyebrows. "Like my biology essay?"

Monsignor Tobin snapped his fingers. "This has something to do with the prom!"

As a nervous tick, I ran my fingers back through my hair, like I was reapplying my morning hair gel. "I kept flipping through the essay during homeroom because I was proud of all the biology teacher's comments. I left it on my desk for a minute when I ran out to use the restroom. When I got back, my friend Nancy was reading it and crying."

Tobin's expression mixed sympathy with disappointment and paternalism. "You're unreliable when you're around women. They manipulate you too easily."

I held my head in my hands. "I hurt her. I think she's probably had an abortion."

"You moved her conscience!" Monsignor Tobin protested. "That's a good thing!"

"It didn't feel good." I shook my head. "I've known her since kindergarten. She's had a crush on me since sixth grade, when she saw my 'Music of the Night' solo. I've had a crush on her since ninth grade. I made her cry. A lot. I don't think she even likes me anymore."

"If Nancy can't handle the truth, then you shouldn't be friends with her. So, you made a mistake destroying the paper. No big deal. It is a mistake that can be rectified because you are still an excellent writer. Can you remember enough of it to reconstruct it from memory?"

In my mind's eye, I saw the photograph of the late-term abortion Miss O'Sullivan passed around the class. Then Arwen appeared in my head, wearing a T-shirt that read "PRO-CHOICE" with the image of a bloody coat hanger on it. Images followed of Nancy gushing over my solos, crying thanks to my essay, and quailing at my prom invitation. "I don't like it when girls cry. I cannot bring myself to reconstruct that essay. I shouldn't have written it in the first place."

Monsignor Tobin stared at me. "I can't believe it. You of all people. You're betraying your pro-life principals because you're sad you aren't going to the prom."

I sat bolt upright in my seat. "Now, that is a bit harsh."

"Are you really that weak? You'll do anything to please this girl?"

I grit my teeth together. "That isn't it, sir."

"I thought you had stronger willpower than this. I thought you had integrity and principle. Instead, you just let these girls wrap you around their little fingers."

I shook my head. "I'm a very stubborn person, sir. I do what I want to do when I want to do it and I think what I want to think. I am not a weathervane."

"From where I'm sitting, I have doubts about both your conviction and your credibility."

I scowled. "I have an overabundance of both conviction and credibility. They're my defining traits. To be honest, I could do with a lot less conviction, but whaddaya gonna do?"

"Are you sure about that?" asked the monsignor. "I feel like you've collapsed on me like a house of cards. I expected better of you."

I examined my chewed-down fingernails. "Let me see if I understand what you are saying to me, because I want to be clear on this. Are you saying my feelings of empathy and compassion for women suggests I have a lack of conviction as a practicing Catholic?"

"It does if your compassion is for perpetrators of maternal filicide. Empathy can be misguided and misplaced. There is such a thing as tough love, you know, just as there is a difference between right and wrong, and good and evil. You have to ask yourself where you stand: Are you a stalwart soldier of Christ, or will you falter in the presence of the devil?"

I crossed my arms in front of my chest and stared down Tobin. "I am a genuine Catholic, not a fake one. My compassion is for my sisters in Christ, who are fellow children of God. The problem we have here isn't that I have compassion for women. The problem is that you don't."

April 25, 1994

Art classes were informal affairs in which a human model or still life object was placed in the front of the room each lesson. Instead of remaining in the more traditional seats at their desks, students positioned themselves all around, finding the right vantage point to view the subject of the day — be it on the floor, desks, bookshelves, or windowsills. We worked in a variety of media throughout the school year, including pencil, colored pencils, pastels, charcoal, and watercolor. On that day, we were drawing a vase of flowers positioned tastefully on a tablecloth-covered end table using pastels on Canson Mi-Teintes paper.

Nancy, Christina, and I sat in front of the windows, on low-laying bookshelves. This was the same Nancy that the monsignor and I had quarreled about, and the same duo of Nancy and Christina who had heckled Miss O'Sullivan as she told us brothel zombie tales. While Nancy and I hadn't had a full conversation reconciling after she had stumbled upon my essay, she did needle me the following day by saying in a demonic voice, "I think we should kill *all* the babies!" It was genuinely funny, but I was so worried I had done irreparable damage to our friendship that I gave the joke less of a laugh than it was worth. That was a week ago. Things had been better between all three of us since, but a degree of heaviness had failed to dissipate from the air around us.

As usual, the CD player in the back of the room played music provided by an array of students with vastly different musical taste. Since September, we had made our way through my rockabilly collection, Christina's jazz catalogue, and Nancy's *fantastic* proto-"Lilith Fair" playlist (including Indigo Girls, Mazzy Star, Ani DiFranco, Sarah McLachlan, and Melissa Etheridge). Over the course of the last few days, we had gone through Fernando Estrella's metal archive: Iced Earth, Manowar, Iron Maiden, Blind Guardian, In Extremo, and Metallica. Today's selection was "Master of Puppets." The music was loud enough that, when Nancy and Christina spoke, their words went unheard by Mrs. Wasserman and the other students.

Mrs. Wasserman — a perky, pixie lady who could have played Tinker Bell on stage, or a Sandy-Duncan-style Peter Pan, or even Sandy Duncan herself — heaped praise upon our sketches before moving on to encourage all the artists' efforts. I adored Mrs. Wasserman. Honestly, it was so nice to finally have an art teacher who would offer encouragement for a change. All my previous art teachers would do is say to us, "I failed as an artist, as will you," and who needs that shit? What I needed, senior year of high school, was Mrs. Wasserman looking at my art and saying, "Beautiful! Keep going." Her instructional philosophy was an early version of Lynda Barry's: if the teacher makes teaching and learning seem like "play," then students will learn more, and become more spiritually and psychologically fulfilled. Students just need to keep making art, having fun, and meditating. They should not give themselves an ulcer measuring the artistic quality of their output against Jackson Pollock and Frida Kahlo. Nor should they pit the potential profitability of their work against Jeff Koons and Jasper Johns. In my experience, those who study under this educational model find that their talents improve naturally, and they complete a higher percentage of the works they begin. After studying with Mrs. Wasserman — and seeing my work improve steadily as my self-flagellating tendencies abated — I knew I wanted to be an educator like her.

My view of teaching was that the teacher's main role was to put widely respected, intellectually challenging, and potentially subversive materials in the hands of the students, help them understand what they might do with it, and stand back. The onus was on the student to improve and teach themselves based on the material provided. As a teacher, I would not worry much at all about establishing a meritocracy or holding students to the same uniform standards. If anything, I would evaluate each student based upon effort and progress, and that was all. If I made learning as much like play as possible, my students would learn to love education. They would choose to become lifelong learners of their own volition. Of course, I could opt to become the teaching equivalent of Gunnery Sergeant Hartman in *Full Metal Jacket*. I could make education into a Darwinian meritocracy and humiliate my own students. That would be an *excellent* way to ensure that my students would stop wanting to learn the instant they graduated. They would spend the rest of their lives leaving cable television on in their homes 24/7 as background noise, shut their brains down, and become exponentially dumber and angrier as they spent their declining years suckling the glass tit of fear. No thanks.

For their part, Christina and Nancy felt that teachers who abstained from pointing out their student's flaws left them rudderless, and without guidance. They were not fans of Mrs. Wasserman. When she called their work gorgeous, they'd roll their eyes. "What a surprise," Nancy grumbled to Christina. "Yours is beautiful! Mine is beautiful! Everyone's is beautiful!"

I smiled. "But yours is beautiful, and mine is beautiful, and everyone's is beautiful."

"If everything is beautiful, then nothing is," Christina replied.

I smirked. "I understand where you're coming from. I still say she rightly sees us as plants and gives us light, water, and love. She lets us grow on our own and in our own way."

"What about upholding standards?" Christina asked.

I made a face. "'Uphold standards!' The rallying cry of fascists. Fuck 'standards.'"

Christina had a mock-scandalized look. "Preaching egalitarianism again, you RINO? You know I'm not a fascist, but I believe in intervening when the train is about to go off the rails."

Nancy placed an affectionate hand on mine. "Damien is the nicest person in the world who listens to Rush Limbaugh every day."

I cleared my throat. I was doing that a lot lately. "He isn't hard on Catholics. I appreciate that. But I stopped listening to him when he kept peddling conspiracy theories about the Clintons murdering Vince Foster. That kinda crap isn't for me."

"That's a relief to hear, actually," Nancy said. "I was thunderstruck that you liked him."

"He was funny for a while. Then he got really mean. I do funny. I don't do mean."

"Yes," Christina nodded. "On a directly related front, there was something we wanted to talk to you about, Damien. Problem is, we know you have a lot of pride and we don't want to insult you. There's big potential for putting an asteroid-sized crater in your ego."

My spider-sense tingled. "Oh? Well, then, please feel free to not broach the subject."

Nancy added, "We would be trying to help, but I give it good odds you'll want to punch us in the face after we say what we plan to say. Please try to understand that we aren't teasing or attacking you. This is a loving, friendly, sisterly intervention. Cross our hearts."

"'Intervention?' Like for alcoholics?" I took the handkerchief out of my pocket and dabbed away sweat on my forehead. "How did this conversation get so alarming, so fast?"

Nancy patted my hand again. "We heard you're having trouble getting a prom date, and we're upset about it, because you deserve to go to the prom. Then we started thinking about *why* you're having so much trouble. There's really only one possible explanation."

"'On a directly related front?'" I snapped my fingers. "Aha! I'm too reactionary to date. Like the bumper sticker says: Just Say 'No' to Sex with Pro-Lifers! Very *Lysistrata*. I approve."

Christina avoided my eyes.

I spoke as low as I could and still be heard over the heavy metal. "Nancy, I'm really sorry you read my essay. I shouldn't have written it or left it out where you could find it."

Nancy bit her lower lip.

"I mean it," I said.

"I know," said Nancy. "Thank you."

Christina slipped me a phone number scrawled on a scrap of paper. "What's this?"

"I know a girl named Amanda," Christina said. "You'd like her."

"A blind date?" I arched an eyebrow. "You'll subject a friend to a crazy right-winger?"

"Oh, stop it," Nancy jumped in. "Anyway, she's gorgeous. Looks like Marisa Tomei."

"Yo! If she looks half as good as Marisa Tomei, fucking fuggedaboudit!"

"She's twenty-five," Christina added. "She's fantastic. So smart and nice and funny."

I exhaled sharply though my large nose. "What's the catch? What aren't you telling me?"

Nancy held up a finger to stop Christina from talking. "I've changed my mind. We can't do this." Nancy looked apologetically at me. "You don't want that phone number."

"We've come this far," Christina said. "We can't put the toothpaste back in the tube."

Nancy's voice became urgent. "We have to. He's not gonna take this in the right spirit."

"Hello?" I waved. "Remember me? This isn't a bloody call girl, is it?"

Christina adopted a more manic and enthusiastic tone to talk up the plan. "Here's the deal: Amanda is a big-hearted nymphomaniac with a crippling AIDS phobia."

"She's a what, what, and a *what*?" My eyes bulged. "I was not expecting that sentence."

"She loves having penises inside her but hates the way condoms feel. No matter what, she can't get off with latex. So, she's in a pickle."

"When she'd prefer that the pickle be in her?" I asked. "An unsheathed pickle?"

"Exactly!" Ridiculously, Christina gave me a thumbs up. "You see how it is? The only way she feels safe having sex bareback is if she knows for a fact that the person she's fucking has never been laid before. Also, if he's a virgin, he needs to be old enough to be of legal age so she doesn't get arrested for statutory rape. You fit the bill perfectly. You are of age, a virgin, and would appreciate her sex tutoring you. You even have a cougar fetish! Bonus! Meanwhile, she gets to have your penis inside her without a condom on it. Many times."

"Many times?" I asked.

"She's had flings that have lasted anywhere from a week to three months, so you could wind up pumping her for a good spell, if she sees your ability to please her improve steadily after what would understandably be rock-bottom performance early on."

Christina nodded vigorously. "Nancy and I have shown her a picture of you and she says you are way, way more attractive than the guy she's boning now. She's bored and ready for . . . "

" . . . a new penis?" I asked sarcastically.

Christina ignored me. "Listen, she is kind and discrete and she loves more than anything educating sensitive, inexperienced men how to be good lovers. She'd eat you up with a spoon."

One of the songs on the CD ended abruptly. Nobody noticed I was staring, ashen, at Nancy and Christina, and they were smiling nervously back at me. The next song began.

"I dunno," I grumbled. "I've already seen a training video. I may be good to go. I'll sit around waiting for someone who actually *loves me* to show up and . . . um . . . deflower me."

Nancy giggled nervously. "It was worth a try! Thanks for being a sport, Damien! See, Christina? Told ya he'd pass on the offer. Let's talk about something else before he throttles us."

Christina frowned. "We're trying to help him! He must see that."

I looked back and forth between them. "I guess you two cooked this scheme up together to fix me? Make me less uptight? You know . . . Amanda probably *would* fix me. Yep. She probably would." My eyes reddened. "Make me less stodgy. Reactionary. Male chauvinist."

Nancy reached out to touch my hand again but stopped herself, frightened to do the wrong thing. "Now I owe you the apology. I promise you, I meant well."

Mortified, I wiped the one tear away and tried to blink back any further ones.

Nancy said. "Please let me explain. We were there when Miss O'Sullivan showed you those abortion photos and batted her eyelashes at you. She did some serious psychological damage to you, man. We saw it with our own two fucking eyes. It's tough, because she had that banging figure and me and Nancy ain't nothin' to write home about, but we wanted to do something to get you out of her clutches. And then the way she snubbed you recently? And was *scared* of you? When you told us that story, we were so mad at her! So mad! And your bad luck getting a prom date? That's the worst! Why won't anyone go to a frickin' dance with you? *Nobody?* And you being jerked around like a puppet by Arwen with the 'she loves me, she loves me not' horseshit, because she's a greedy little whore who needs to crush you like a bug so she can have her chocolate factory? Fuck all that! So, now seemed like the time to approach you with this plan. You see, we see that you're lonely and suffering. We care about you, ya know!"

"I know. That's part of what makes this so hard for me." I was embarrassed that my voice quivered a little as I said this. "That you do care, and this is the best plan you could think of."

Nancy slapped Christina across the shoulder violently enough for a couple of students nearby to notice our conversation was going south fast. Leaning in, she whisper-hissed at Christina. "You are such an asshole, Christina."

"You're such a whole ass," Christina hissed back.

"How's about you French kiss my bunghole?" asked Nancy.

"How's about you eat my entire ass?" asked Christina.

"Fuck you and the horse you rode in on," said Nancy.

"Yo, you leave my horse outta this. My horse didn't do nothin' to you!"

Nancy returned her attention to me. "You okay over there, dude?"

I shrugged, looking drained and defeated. "I imagined my first time would be with someone I was in love with and who loved me. I guess that's a pretty quaint notion, huh? I can't help but think if you two really cared about me, at least one of you would be willing to go to the prom with me. Fool around after. But, no. Your master plan is to fob me off on some nympho I've never met instead of making a man out of me yourselves?"

"Oh, fuck you," Nancy whispered. "Why the fuck should I try to 'fix' you with sex? That's never a good plan for *any* woman. Too much risk, responsibility, and self-sacrifice is involved. And what's my incentive? Especially after I read your friggin' essay!"

"I suppose not much," I admitted.

Nancy crossed her arms in front of her chest. "If men want there to be fewer abortions, they shouldn't put more chains on women. We've got enough chains on us as it is. They should just get a reversible vasectomy, or wear a condom, or pull out when they say they're gonna pull out. Even better, maybe stop raping strangers, dates, and their own daughters. None of us are pumped to get abortions. We do it because men are assholes who put us in a predicament and vanish in a puff of smoke. Or men keep us prisoners in our own homes and rape us nightly. There's your solution to the abortion problem, right there. Stop blaming women for shit men do."

I felt dizzy and leaned back against the closed window. "I hadn't thought of it that way."

"And a fetus has rights that a woman doesn't? And corporations are considered people under the law and women aren't? To hell with the whole goddamn system, man! It reeks. And let's say you and me do go to pound town. How would that play out? Would you take Miss O'Sullivan's advice? Pray the rosary before you slide inside me? Whether you do or not, three minutes after we're done, you'll curse me for taking your purity and damning your soul!"

I couldn't bring myself to look at Nancy, so I cast my eyes down to the dirty, tiled floor. "That's not an unrealistic fear. Honestly, I have no idea how I'd feel afterwards. Since I've never had sex before, how could I possibly predict what the experience would do to me? I'd like to think it's not a foregone conclusion I'd treat you like shit afterwards."

Nancy sighed. "I'm not hopeful you'd react well. I'm sorry. I'd love to have sex with you. I really would. I think you're delectably nerdy. That's a real thing, you know: Geeky hot."

"Well, that's great!" I sat up straight. "Why didn't you tell me that before?"

She closed her eyes and held up her hand to silence me. "Just imagine if our condom broke and you knocked me up. That would be a tragedy of epic motherfucking proportions."

"But what if it didn't break?" I asked. "We can get the Consumer Reports condom issue."

Christina gave me a warning look. "Take the wax out of your ears, dude. She said 'no' and she meant 'no.' Listen up. You've got us all wrong. We're not jerks here. I'm not attracted to you, but I like you. Nancy wants your body, but you scare her shitless. So . . . we thought Amanda was the best of a bad buncha options. In case you didn't figure this out yourself, there's no easy way out of your particular problem."

"I wish you'd both had more faith in me." I handed Nancy the crumpled scrap of paper with Amanda's phone number on it. "And I wish this had been your phone number."

INTERLUDE I

April 2, 1994

> Honoria Buckingham Literary Agency, LTD
> Fulham, London SW6 1QR, United Kingdom

> Dear Mr. Damien Cavalieri,
> While we consider ourselves more of a Dr. Johnson than a Dr. Who literary agency, we will submit your manuscript, *Doctor Who: The Bringer of Darkness,* to Virgin Books.

> Honoria Buckingham, DBE

April 24, 1994

> Dear Mr. Damien Cavalieri,
> We regret to inform you that your manuscript, *The Bringer of Darkness*, is not an appropriate addition to the Virgin Missing Adventures line. Your stated goal of using your novel to resurrect Peri Brown bespeaks a fan endeavor and not serious art. Furthermore, your book's preponderance of legacy characters — two Doctors, Daleks, the Celestial Toymaker, Borusa, and other figures we do not have the rights to — earmarks your book as pastiche (a la *Dimensions in Time*). We will be publishing books that enlarge *Doctor Who*'s canvass, not dwell upon its past.

> Peter Darvill-Evans
> W.H. Allen & Co./Virgin Books

CHAPTER TWENTY-FOUR
Death by the Side of the Road

April 25, 1994

"As I see it," Mom explained, "you have a choice here. You can attend a college where you will learn how to say 'Jesus' in three different languages — Hebrew, Aramaic, and Greek — or you can go to a college where you will learn how to say 'Jesus' in three syllables: 'Jee-yah-zuzz!' I say you pick the school where you learn to say, 'Jesus' in three languages."

Monsignor Tobin had given me a brochure for Christendom College. It read: "We're not like other colleges. And that's a good thing. Founded in 1977 in response to the devastating blow inflicted on Catholic higher education by the cultural revolution which swept across America in the 1960s, Christendom's goal is to provide a truly Catholic education in fidelity to the Magisterium of the Catholic Church and thereby to prepare students for their role of restoring all things in Christ." Believe it or not, the purity of this school's mission spoke to me. I was still looking to be let inside a Green Door, and at least Tobin was promising to crack one open for me. It might have been a shitty Green Door, but beggars couldn't be choosers. It wasn't like anyone else was inviting me into their elite inner circle. I told Mom the upside of Christendom was it was not a Diet Catholic College for "Buffet Catholics" but a bona fide institution for "authentic" Catholics. Mom told me that under no circumstances would I be going there, especially since there were only forty or so undergraduates enrolled at the time. "What kind of college had such a small student body?" Mom asked. "I bet those people are pretty weird."

"I'm pretty weird!"

"Not that kinda weird, you aren't."

Mom had a brochure of her own: SUNY Geneseo. In the 1990s, there were two jewels in the crown of the State University of New York system: SUNY Binghamton, an urban and politically radical school with an activist, intellectually gifted student body, and SUNY Geneseo, a rural college filled to bursting with brilliant students who were more focused on studying and maintaining a 4.0 average than protesting injustice en masse. All the students I had spent K-12 with were going to Binghamton, and I'd had my fill of those people. I didn't want college to be High School II. I wanted to meet all new people and go somewhere unlike any place I'd ever been. A rural honors college seemed to fit the bill perfectly. I was sick of the blandness of the suburbs, felt a city might be too hectic and expensive for me, and had already learned to love rural areas from our frequent family trips to Pennsylvania. All this made Geneseo a no-brainer. Furthermore, sixty percent of the student body was female, and sixty percent of the students were Roman Catholic ethnic whites like me. As a bonus, there appeared to be an interdisciplinary history and English course in the catalogue called "Age of Dante" that would help me learn more about my Italian and Roman Catholic heritages. I could imagine both finding myself and meeting my future wife at Geneseo. I wasn't excited to go to any college, but this one seemed okay.

Mom read up on several campus cultures in a heavy tome filled to bursting with up-to-date student surveys and interviews. "They say Binghamton is where you go if you have a political ax to grind and an issue to fight for. I assume that's not you, right?"

I shook my head violently. "Hell no! How is it that everyone is so certain they have all the answers on politics and religion? Everybody's got the monopoly on truth!"

"You should go to Geneseo, I'm thinking," said Mom. "Oh! I hope there's good Italian food in western New York. I'm worried there won't be any Italians or Italian food anywhere near Geneseo. But Jerre Mangione's book *Mount Allegro* is about an Italian community in Rochester, and Rochester would only be a half-hour drive from Geneseo."

I shrugged. "I have no idea. I know nothing about upstate. Fingers crossed there's passably good gravy and tortellini." I knew what I really wanted. I wanted the ethnic and racial diversity of the city, the beautiful nature and wildlife of the rural area, the arts and food culture of the small college town, and the radically angry politics of none of the above. While I saw myself as a capital "R" Romantic, I had a confused political identity and could not imagine myself joining the far left or the far right. I was becoming a proudly militant moderate.

Dejected that I would be attending a public school as "liberal" as Geneseo, Tobin offered me, as a parting gift, a trilogy of science fiction books by C.S. Lewis that he described as being a jeremiad against secularist, morally relativist college education. I remember him pointing to the artwork on the cover of the third book, *That Hideous Strength* (1945), which featured a college academic building across the street from a laboratory. He said: "You see, the evil scientific ideas cooked up by the professors in the college lectures influence the students, who graduate and cross the street to work at the labs to make reality the dangerous thoughts that had been advanced by professors playing 'devil's advocate.' So, you see, the college professors and the scientists collude, indirectly, to aid the devil in his campaign against God." This was an instantly graspable allegory and pure propaganda, so I promised myself not to read the trilogy. I knew that not all college professors were evil. My Mom was a rather nice person, all told.

In a last-ditch effort to recruit me into Opus Dei — or whatever secret society he was working for — Monsignor Tobin took me to visit the Legionaries of Christ seminary in Thornwood, N.Y. When I looked about the seminary and saw all those men in black, playing pool in the rec room, walking across expansive lawns in prayer, and talking about Church politics in the cafeteria, I became aware of two things: 1) the complete absence of women and 2) that I was not that into sausage. After all, I spent my junior high and high school years loathing being an involuntary celibate, so why would I become a *voluntary* one?

As I wrestled with these questions during my senior year in high school, I suspected that Tobin was not necessarily a good influence on me — or the rest of the congregation. The alarm claxon finally rang when I heard his homily decrying the Church's decision to allow girls to be "altar boys." I was deeply offended by his wistful invocation of his childhood clubhouse with its harmless, charming "no girls allowed" sign. When I finally saw Tobin serve mass a year later with an adorable altar girl at his side, I remembered his words and fumed for the entire mass, not because there was an altar girl, but because I knew she was only there because his side had lost the debate. And she looked freakin' adorable in her little hood! What was the goddamn problem with her and her *adorable* hood?

The issue of gay rights rarely came up during homilies at St. Luke's in the early 1990s, so I was not often confronted by Catholic homophobia. This lack of discussion of homosexuality made me complacent and enabled me to pretend that the Church had no problem with gay people. Then there came the deeply troubling St. Patrick's Day Parade controversy. Irish gays petitioned to be allowed to march in the parade, but the Catholics involved in organizing banned their participation. In protest, the gays held their own parade, and Mayor David Dinkins joined the gays in solidarity instead of participating in the main parade. Conservative Catholic Staten Islander voters later had their revenge on Dinkins for choosing the side of the gays by being instrumental in sending Rudolph Giuliani to Gracie Mansion, thereby ensuring that New York City's first African American mayor served only one term. (Ironically, Mayor Giuliani ultimately choose to march with the gays, too.) I didn't follow the news closely and didn't know all the arguments, but the parade struck me as being more about the ethnic quality of "Irishness" then about Catholicism and homosexuality. Consequently, *all* Irish people should be allowed to march. Tobin did not agree. He told me that the Catholic Church could not be called anti-gay for not allowing gays to march in New York City's Saint Patrick's Day Parade because there was one gay group that the Church would approve of marching: Courage. Courage would pass muster because it promoted gay celibacy; its mission statement did not contravene Church teaching.

"Hmmm," I said. "If I were gay, I wouldn't think much of that argument. The members of Courage sound like gay people in denial."

"They aren't in denial," Tobin said. "They just aren't sexually active."

"That just doesn't sound right to me."

"It is a perfectly reasonable position."

"Does Jesus even care about sex?" I asked. "He seems more like he cares about feeding the hungry and healing the sick and not using violence against fellow men. He couldn't have had sex hang-ups. Many of his disciples were women. He was kind to prostitutes. And he opposed the stoning of the adulteress. He says not one word about homosexuality anywhere."

"But he told the adulteress to 'go and sin no more.' He did not give her license to continue to commit adultery. Jesus has rules about sexuality. He's against divorce and against lustful thoughts. He's quite clear on these points. You can't pin all the rules concerning sexuality on St. Paul the male-chauvinist pig and make Jesus a proponent of free love in the process."

"But I like pinning things on Paul," I muttered, clearly sulking now.

"Paul is misunderstood."

"Well . . . I don't know. You make some good points."

"Exactly."

"We sure spend a lot of time talking about what we're *against*. *Against* abortion. *Against* gays in the frickin' parade. Can we talk about what we're *for*? Be more positive? I don't want to be that guy who says 'no' to everything and is against everything."

Despite my reservations about Tobin and my faith, I still considered myself Catholic. I did not want to be a Catholic like Tobin or Miss O'Sullivan, but I did want to be a Catholic like Great Aunt Bianca and Father Jack Stańczyk. Mitchell had once described Liberation Theology to me. He told me of the heroism of Archbishop Oscar Romero of El Salvador, and of Dorothy Day and Thomas Merton. I could be that kind of Catholic. I recalled how Tobin tried to turn me on those very figures and ideas during my first real conversation with him. Opus Dei was good, and Dorothy Day was bad. He had it backwards.

Was I still Catholic? Probably? I knew that, at the very least, I had no trouble praying to St. Nicholas of Myra, the inspiration for Santa Claus. A bishop who lived in fourth-century Turkey, St. Nicholas was a secret gift-giver who would bestow money upon the poor. He was especially known for dropping bags of gold through the windows of poor women to help mitigate their suffering. Sometimes the gold was used to pay their dowries. He made these anonymous gifts, not because he expected romance from grateful women in return, but because he was a generous, holy man, and a proto-Marxist hoping to balance the scales a little in an unjust world. I didn't really have any wealth on hand to speak of that would enable me to leave secret, generous donations to the poor, but I loved the idea of gift giving, unexpected gift giving, secret gift giving, and making any kind gesture, however small, to add to a person's joy. Until the day I became rich enough to do the modern-day equivalent of dropping bags of gold through women's windows — without scaring the living shit out of them and getting arrested — I would confine myself to regifting items in good condition that I no longer valued, buying Whitman's samplers and leaving them in the mailboxes of friends of mine having an awful week at work, and generally striving to be as much like Santa Claus as I could without freaking people out with my behavior. Here again, was an attitude inspired in part by Mitchell's generous spirit, as well as by my mother's bursts of generosity, buying lots and lots of gifts for Leo and me on our birthdays and Christmas. Yes: if part of being Catholic meant mimicking Santa Claus, then that would not be hard for me. (This was my next step towards becoming a male Amélie Poulain.)

Still interested in attending a Catholic college, I applied for scholarships at Notre Dame, the University of Scranton, Loyola University Maryland, Fordham University, and St. Joseph College. Thanks in part to my underwhelming 1170 SAT score, whatever scholarships I did earn were between ten percent and seventy. Even with them, the tuitions were so high that Mom said the family couldn't afford to send me. She had raised similar objections when I had wanted to go to a private high school in Manhattan to study art. I resented her keeping me out of such specialty schools until the time I bumped into Marina Dazzo as a high school senior. Marina told me that taking the ferry into the city to attend LaGuardia every day made her grow up too fast and beat her love of music out of her. Marina had also put a lot of financial pressure on her parents to pay for private school. She told me Mom had been right to make me go to public high school and had saved me from her miserable fate. Was the debate about whether I should attend a private Catholic college essentially a retread of my School of Visual Arts clash with Mom? I didn't know. Maybe the prestige of a private college would be worth more than the prestige of a private high school? And yet, Geneseo was far more affordable and had prestige of its own. Mom did not want me to graduate college saddled with mountains of debt. She herself had gotten a full-ride scholarship with money left over to take her across Europe. She couldn't stomach the idea of going from that to my being burdened with thousands of dollars in debt that I might never pay off. Fortunately, Democrat Governor Mario Cuomo had kept the public college tuition low in New York State. SUNY Geneseo would only cost the family a few thousand per year, room and board included. Cuomo's successor, Republican Governor Pataki, would begin a years-long process of defunding SUNY, cutting its budget to ribbons, so that fantastic financial and educational deal was not long for this world. I made it in just under the wire before costs soared.

I'd wanted to go to a Catholic school, but I was okay with Geneseo. After all, with a sixty percent female student body, I was bound to meet *someone* to date, right? Supposedly, it was a great school that provided a first-rate education. Whatever. I was much more interested in the girls. I was already too smart for my own good. I wanted a chick of my very own. But what if I didn't find one? What if I went to school looking for a relationship with a strong, funny, independent woman and she had gone to school with one goal in mind: not getting saddled with a guy until her career was well on track and she had achieved financial independence? I suspected that I was going to college to date, and the women I'd be most interested in dating would be there exclusively to study and prepare for their careers.

The more I worried about this, the more I became convinced that my problem wasn't that I was a bad fit for Staten Island. My problem was I was a bad fit for America. Would I have to move to Italy to find love? Or maybe, the problem was just me. I was my own worst enemy, a nut-job who was a prisoner of his own God-awful personality. No matter where I went, no matter what I did, I would always be Ernest Borgnine in *Marty*: an eternally single *mammone*. I had hit on a terrible truth. College would not be a fresh start for me. It would be *Groundhog Day*. The setting and characters would change, yet my life would feel the same. I'd have all of the same problems. Nothing would ever fundamentally change for me. The Green Door would always be bolted shut with a chair leaned up against the doorknob on the other side. A taped-up note would always read, in a red ink scrawl: "Members only. Keep Out. This means you, Damien!"

I will never get in.

I will never play "Heart and Soul" on the piano with Marina Dazzo.

I will go through life as neutered Pepé Le Pew, giving off the stench of desperate need.

College was going to be more of the same, and a total waste of my time.

There was only one course of action left for me to take.

It was long past time I killed myself.

On the evening of April 25, 1994, I embarked on a quest to find "The Good Samaritan Killer" (a.k.a. the poorly named "Black Widow," a.k.a. the aptly named "Roadside Seductress"). Since I didn't have the guts to take my own life, I hoped that she would take my life for me. I would play the fool, pretend to fall for her trick, pull over, and let her do what she would. I froze. *My God! What if she spares me? What if the number of female serial killers who consider me worth murdering fill up an empty set?* No. I couldn't allow such fears to deter me. I had to be brave. I had to have faith that, if she did catch me, she would kill me. I could finally get some rest. I had earned a nice, peaceful dirt nap a thousand times over. Fingers crossed.

I do hope she's super hot. I wouldn't want to be murdered by a four out of ten. Just my luck, that's exactly what will happen. Nah. Be positive. I decided that she looked and dressed like Carmen Sandiego and started humming the song "Where in the World is Carmen Sandiego?"

According to the latest issue of *The Staten Island Chronicle*, the Good Samaritan Killer was still at large, and on her twentieth victim. It boggled my mind that a murderess who confined herself to the tristate area and focused on Staten Island was uncatchable. In any event, I was increasingly interested in meeting her in person. Of course, I had no idea *where* the Good Samaritan Killer would be tonight. How would my dad's father solve this mystery? Did I have enough of Grandpa's Mycroft Holmes intelligence to crack this case? Find the femme fatale!

I looked up where the bodies of all the Good Samaritan Killer's victims were found. I fished Mom's map of Staten Island out of the desk and marked it up, hoping to predict where the killer's next hunting ground would be. When I'd finished, I stared at the markings, disappointed that they didn't form some sort of obvious pentagram, like in police procedural television shows and in satires of police procedural television shows. *I have to use the Force.* I meditated like Yumi taught me. I reached out with my mind. *Where in Staten Island is "Carmen Sandiego?"*

Aha!

She's going to be near the Travis movie theater tonight at midnight. I can see her there in my mind's eye, as if she's there now. I'm going to join her. Because, if you've gotta go, there's no better way to go than be taken out by a hot vampire woman.

April 26, 1994

I woke up the next morning disgusted with my own impotence. I failed. I missed my hot date with Death. My appointment in Samarra. I couldn't find the fucking Good Samaritan Killer even after driving around the island for most of last night. I had hoped she would kill me, and I wouldn't have to take my own life. Sadly, if I really wanted to stop living, I was going to have to do the deed myself. I couldn't rely on someone else to save me the messy effort. The problem was, given how badly Mom's world had been rocked by her parent's deaths, I assumed my death might be something of a blow to her. I wasn't sure if there was a solution to that particular problem, because I really had had it up to here with being alive.

I went downstairs, in my robe and pajamas, too depressed to dress. Today's paper was waiting for me on the kitchen table. GOOD SAMARITAN KILLER ARRESTED IN TRAVIS: ROADSIDE SEDUCTRESS IN CUFFS. *What? She was in Travis last night!* I snatched up the paper, scanning the article. The police had caught her two hours before I set out to find her and half-a-mile away from the street I'd pinpointed to stakeout.

Well, shit.

I walked down the stairs to the basement and went to the back room with the LEGO, video games, action figures, posters of *Raise the Red Lantern* and *Star Trek VI: The Undiscovered Country*, the framed picture of the Sacred Heart of Jesus, and the statue of the Virgin Mary stepping on a snake. I stood before the statue of Mary with my hands clasped behind my back. "You had to save my life, didn't you? Like it was any of your business? If I can't even get intimate with the Roadside Seductress, then what hope is left for me?"

I sensed someone standing behind me and turned. Mom stood there, holding the same newspaper. She hadn't heard anything I said but looked shaken. "Did you see the news?"

"Yeah, I saw."

Mom was relieved that she didn't have to be the one to tell me. "I can't believe it."

"I know," I sighed, looking at the floor.

"Mitchell's dead."

I snapped my head back up. "What?"

"You didn't see?" Mom looked confused. "Mitchell died in a car accident in Texas."

I snatched the newspaper out of her hand. It was a front-page story, but below the fold, under the arrest of the Good Samaritan Killer: ISLAND YOUTHS KILLED IN TEXAS. I scanned the article, not quite taking in what I read. Mitchell and three friends were in a car that fishtailed on a highway and flipped over because of a freak accident involving a utility trailer and a tow hitch. They were returning from a spring break Grand Canyon trip, sight-seeing along the way back to the East Coast. He and one other had been killed. Two survived, including his girlfriend. There was a grayscale photo of a slim, handsome young man who must have been Mitchell. I kept looking at the picture. When we had played the *Honeymooners*, he was the chubby kid who played Ralph and I was the gawky kid who played Norton. The boy in this photo would never be cast as Ralph. Meanwhile, I'd gotten rounder since quitting Tae Kwon Do. These days, I only needed a little more padding to make a passable Ralph. How long had it been since we'd last seen each other? Long enough for him to look so different?

In the photo, Mitchell was with the girlfriend who had survived. Even in this still image, he seemed like a good person, as did she. I didn't know her at all. I was sad I didn't know her. But did I know him? I tried to remember all the times we spent together over the years. Why didn't I remember more about Mitchell? Wasn't my memory supposed to be great? Did I only remember bad things that happened to me? Maybe I didn't remember Mitchell well because he was the best part of my life? I forced myself to remember. I saw in my head: Both of us getting in trouble for forgetting to do homework; taking Tae Kwon Do together; buying issues of *Silent Invasion, Elfquest,* and *Saga of the Swamp Thing* at the comic book store next to the dojo; going to a sleepover party at William's house — me walking into the bathroom on Will's dad buck naked — telling Mitchell — Mitchell laughing 'til he cried; me spilling milk all over Mitchell's carpet as we watched the Hammer *Mummy*, his mom cleaning it up, getting me a new glass, and me spilling the second glass; playing duck-duck-goose in third grade and picking each other time and again just to mess with everyone else, and Mitchell reciting the comedy routine "My name is Friday, I work on Tuesday; Tuesday is my secretary." Was "You Got It" by Roy Orbison Mitchell's favorite song? I knew his celebrity crush was Jennifer Connelly — he called her "the most beautiful woman in the world." We went to see *The Rocketeer* four times in the theater just for her. Was that all I remembered? Was that enough? How was it possible he was dead?

Mom wasn't sure how much of the article I'd absorbed, so she said, "From what I can tell, they were in a car with a U-haul-type attachment. Two couples. One of his friends was driving. Mitchell was in the passenger seat. The driver fell asleep at the wheel and the car started drifting off the highway. Mitchell saw what was happening, grabbed the wheel, and tried to steer the car back into the middle of the lane. The sudden tug on the wheel caused the attachment to fishtail. The attachment flipped over and flipped the car after it. The driver was killed. Mitchell was thrown from the car and landed on the side of the road. His girlfriend was with him. She held him when he died."

Was I angry? Was I sad? Was I in shock? Why wasn't I crying? Why was I numb?

My only emotion was shame; shame that I had allowed us to grow apart.

I closed my eyes and handed the newspaper back. "That doesn't even look like him. Unreal. Newspapers will print anything these days. Damn liberal reporters, making things up."

Mom tucked the newspaper under her arm. "I'll keep this for you in case you want to look at it again." She saw I wasn't ready to talk and went back upstairs.

I returned my eyes to the statue of the Virgin Mary. I wanted to seize the statue in both hands and bring it smashing down on the table it rested on. "I was the one who was supposed to die on the side of the road yesterday. You took the good one and left the dud."

CHAPTER TWENTY-FIVE
Shabbos Goy

June 24, 1994

Grace Coolidge High School's graduation ceremony for the class of 1994 was most memorable for featuring a keynote speech from Chuck Schumer, representative of New York's 9th congressional district. Schumer told a moving story about how, when he was a teenager, he had an amazing career opportunity that he passed up on so he could stay close to his girlfriend. The audience gave out a collective sigh of approval. Tutting, Schumer held a finger aloft and hit us with the punchline: "Unfortunately for me, she broke up with me a few days later." *Funny rhetorical entrapment. Brilliant. I am going to have to remember that technique, Chuck.* It was an effective speech, and I didn't mind hearing it again a few years later at my college graduation. Still, when I saw him stand up to speak at Leo's college graduation three years later — by which time Schumer was a United States Senator — I left the ceremony early and got myself some coffee and three Boston Cream Donuts. After seeing Schumer those three times, I thought of him as a family friend, and enjoyed knowing that his graduation speech was so good he never updated it.

Class valedictorian Ari Zuckerman spoke right after Chuck. Since we had been friends since third grade, I was excited to hear his address. Unfortunately, by the time Ari took his place at the podium, my fellow graduates had become unruly. They were tired of sitting on white metal folding chairs on the football field, dressed in navy blue caps and gowns, baking in the blazing afternoon heat. Students were now openly talking with one another. Electronic hand fans appeared. A row of eight wise guys kept yelling, "Zuckerman's famous pig!" An inflatable beach ball magically appeared, was volleyed about for two minutes, and confiscated by security. (School Security! Always there to snatch the graduation beach ball and baseball caps off boy's heads, and to send girls home for showing too much leg. Never around any time I got jumped.)

By the time the valedictorian and community power brokers were done making speeches, and the names of all one thousand graduating seniors were read aloud, I was sweaty and stinky, and my perspiration-dampened boxer shorts were clinging to my thighs. Clutching my diploma, I was looking forward to going home and having a long, hot shower. It would be a challenge finding my parents in bleachers filled with three-thousand immediate family members of all the seniors. I cast my eyes about for my friends. Most of them had already sprinted to their famished parents and fled the scene of the crime to get lunch out at local staples like Perkins, Denny's, or the International House of Pancakes. I didn't mind their vanishing act. In the weeks leading up to graduation, I'd done a good job of getting my yearbook signed by everyone I liked and snapping photos with my friends with my KODAK disc 4000. Since I was not going to Binghamton, I would probably not be seeing most of them again. Many of these soon-to-be-absent friends were people I'd known for four years, seven years, or my entire K-12 educational career.

When it dawns upon you that you won't be seeing a certain set of people ever again, something funny happens that is true whether the occasion is an impending departure from a school or a job: you feel liberated to act towards them any way you want. Of course, the question becomes, do you treat them kindly or cruelly? As graduation had approached, I realized that I had several options: 1) business as usual for the high-functioning introvert (or omnivert) and keep mostly to myself, 2) burn as many bridges as possible and act like an angry tool, or 3) behave much as Mitchell would, and be extra kind and extra just to everyone around me. I chose to honor my late friend by following the third path. I would kill everyone with kindness. If I was never going to see these people again, I wanted to end all our relationships on as positive a note as possible — so positive as to befuddle any one of them who had written me off ages ago as angry, withdrawn, or reactionary. I would show them just how cool I was. It was also a funny sort of revenge: Make them realize they should have appreciated me more while I was around by adding to my air of mystery and likeability with only a few weeks to go. Ironically, what started out half as revenge and half as a tribute to my late best friend wound up being a deeply emotionally and spiritually rewarding experience. I internalized the "niceness," stopped "acting" more like Mitchell and wound up genuinely "becoming" more like Mitchell.

"The Path of the Righteous Mitchell" was a radical enough departure from my usual borderline-misanthropic behavior that I had to manufacture a new and more outgoing public persona for myself. I cultivated two slightly different personalities as part of my great fence-mending effort. When talking with the boys in my grade, I would be a loud, chummy Jimmy Stewart from *It's a Wonderful Life*, talking boldly about my globetrotting plans, clapping folks on the back to congratulate them for their good fortunes, and putting positive spins on all bad news with brazen, unrealistic good cheer, in imitation of Jimmy Stewart's gleeful exclamation, "Isn't it wonderful, I'm going to jail!"

I created a separate persona for interacting with girls that was heavily influenced by the fact that I had utterly failed to find a prom date and had vowed never to ask out any other girl ever again. As a high school graduate, I was officially retired from dating for the rest of my life. Consequently, I assumed an "avuncular gentleman" personality when talking to girls. I stepped up my efforts holding doors open for girls, picking up items they dropped, and soberly complimenting them on their appearance. I tried mightily to pass myself off as a low-rent American Jane Austen hero. I was able to assume this persona because, as deferential and complimentary as I was, I projected no intention whatsoever of pursuing any of the girls I aided or complimented. I was there simply to say emotionally uplifting things to the girls, help them if possible, and get out of their way. I did not follow anyone around like a puppy, I made no passes at anyone, and I was determined not to be a nuisance in any way, shape, or form. The effect was striking. Even knowing I was straight and single, the girls in the school felt as comfortable around me as if I had been a eunuch or a safely gay friend. If I said something nice, they were not afraid to accept the compliment and thank me for it. If I held open a door or carried heavy books for a girl, she would thank me, and we would go our separate ways. For the first time since hitting puberty and becoming a sex-obsessed teenager, I was not a neutered Pepé Le Pew figure! Astounding. Also, if any boy insulted or accosted a girl in my presence, I would step in, doing my best impression of Edward Hardwicke's Dr. John Watson from the

Jeremy Brett *Sherlock Holmes* series, and demand, quietly and firmly, that the "blackguard cease and desist his ungentlemanly treatment of this fine lady." Independent of my influence, Leo developed a similar personality, in which he acted gentlemanly while retaining working-class New York affectations. Leo referred to our pseudo-British mannerisms and speech patterns as "BBC WOP."

These two new "personalities" of mine — boisterous and demonstrative Jimmy Stewart for the boys and avuncular and gentlemanly Edward Hardwicke for the girls — were not insincere. If they had been insincere, they would not have elicited a positive response. The first few days I had adopted the new mannerisms, there had been a learning curve period and my speech and body language seemed forced. Once I got used to speaking and moving in new ways — and the other students became accustomed to my more cheery, confident, and carefree demeanor — I transitioned almost magically from playing the part of "a fun person to be around" to becoming a genuinely fun person to be around. It was only when I had a particularly appalling day or abominable bit of news that my attempts to put a brave face on things and bury my basest impulses backfired. During the moments when I was at my saddest and most nervous, I often came off as trying too hard. Under those circumstances, people who were well-inclined towards me were more likely to worry about me and ask me how I was really doing than castigate me for masking my true feelings. Those who were the best at seeing through my jokey demeanor during tough times — who could spot the tracks of my tears — always wound up being my favorite people.

I knew something in my heart was changing for the better when I walked through a department store and noted, absently, that two petite septuagenarians were reaching in vain for items on the top shelf that they would never reach in a million years. They stood on the tips of their toes. They extended their arms and swiped wildly. The items remained out of reach. *Someone should help them,* I thought. I walked to the next aisle, intent on finding whatever it was I was there to find, when I brought myself up short. *Wait a minute. I should help them. If those women had been young and gorgeous, I would have sprinted to help them. Every other guy in this store would have done the same. But they're old now, so to hell with them? No, way, no how. Those are people in trouble, and I'm going to help them.* And I did. I reached up, plucked what they wanted from the top shelf with ease, and lowered it into their waiting hands. They were more grateful for the gesture than I expected them to be. I needed to start being helpful to people, not because I expected something out of them in return — and not because they were *sexy* — but because people often need help. End of story. Why was coming to such a conclusion so hard?

My second opportunity to be a functioning member of society instead of a misanthropic recluse came on a Friday night when a neighbor knocked on our front door instead of using the doorbell. I opened it to our friendly-but-over-earnest neighbor, Anne Birnbaum, who looked even graver than usual. "I'm so sorry to bother you," she said quickly, "but my husband has a high fever. It is really worrying me. We have a prescription from the doctor, but we can't fill it because we aren't allowed to use or discuss money on Shabbos." She held a doctor's script aloft. "Would you be willing to use your money to pick up this prescription at the CVS on Victory? You can bring us the medicine tonight if you knock on our door and don't ring the doorbell. We can pay you back tomorrow night, after dark. Would you mind helping us?"

Oh, no! Larry is sick? Honestly, I thought Larry was the coolest guy on the block. I loved watching the badass truck driver tinker with his Triumph TR65 Thunderbird on his driveway in his white muscle shirt, faded jeans, glasses, goatee, and yarmulke. He was one of my models of masculinity growing up: a husband and father, working-man, religious Jew, and brawny biker all-in-one. Larry was the total package. Also, I was grateful to him for not stringing me up by my testicles when I dented the fender of his car backing out of my driveway while I was still learning to drive. Because no paint from his car transferred to mine and no paint from mine transferred to his, I had been briefly tempted to pretend I had nothing to do with the dent, and no knowledge of how it happened. *No, that would be a dick move.* I rang his doorbell and confessed to being responsible for the dent. He came out, looked it over, and shrugged fatalistically. "No big deal, really. Don't worry about it. That's what life is all about."

I laughed. "Well, I hope there's more to life than *that!*"

"Not really." He chuckled.

Thank you for being nice to me when I didn't deserve it. If somebody dents my car, I'll forgive them in your honor. Pay it forward.

I wanted to respond to Anne right away, but I had to figure out if I could get access to Mom's car and if I had enough cash on hand to lay out the money in advance. Fortunately, I'd just gotten my twenty-dollar weekly allowance and had yet to spend it all on books, VHS films, CDs, or comic books. "Would twenty dollars cover the cost?" I asked.

Anne tried to come up with a way of answering me without violating the rules of Shabbos. "My instinct is you shouldn't have trouble picking up the medicine for us."

After taking the script from Anne, I "forgot" to tell my parents I was making this CVS run. At times like these, they seemed a bit too nervous and reclusive by half. They probably wouldn't try to stop me helping Larry, but you never knew with them. They were weird. I snuck out, filled the prescription at CVS, and drove the medicine back home. I knocked on the Birnbaum's door, and Anne opened it. Over her shoulder, I saw a glass display case filled with die cast model cars, motorcycles, and trucks. It was an impressive home exhibit I hadn't seen before. It made perfect sense that Larry would have a cool collection of model vehicles.

"Thank you so much!" Anne exclaimed. "I'll pay you back tomorrow night."

"No rush. I'm only gonna spend it on French *Barbarella* comics."

Leo caught me sneaking back in the house. "Okay, what are you up to?"

Raising both eyebrows, I feigned an innocent expression. "What could I be up to?"

"Yeah, you look even more suspicious now that you're trying to look innocent."

I told him the full story. He looked sad when I finished. I asked him what was wrong. "You always have these heartwarming interactions with people. When do I get to have a heartwarming interaction with someone?"

"Do I?" I asked. "I thought most of my stories were pretty hair-raising."

"Well, they're more heartwarming than my stories, let me tell you!"

"Christ. I hope that isn't true, because my encounters with people are usually the pits. But I've always wanted my shot at being a 'Shabbos goy,' and help one of our neighbors out of a tight spot. It finally happened." I picked up the terminology reading Will Eisner's graphic novel *A Life Force,* about a wealthy Christian businessman who loses all his money in the Stock Market Crash of 1929 and is forced to move into a tenement building populated by Italian immigrants and Orthodox Jews. He is asked to do the same sorts of favors I was just asked to do and became affectionately known as the tenement's "Shabbos goy."

"Okay, but Larry better stop revving his motorcycle every morning at six," Leo declared.

The most promising consequence of my self-improvement campaign was that my number of friends at Grace Coolidge High School quadrupled in the final three months of my senior year. Acting more like Mitchell than myself was paying dividends. As much as I had felt ignored and put upon by so many of my fellow students ever since kindergarten, the lesson was that a great many of them were quite fine people, but I had been too introverted to get to know them. I had been angry at them for not reaching out to me, but I had not reached out to them, either. To this day, I have a yearbook filled with signatures and a photo album filled with photos of friends I had made the last semester of school, who I had missed out on knowing for all the years before. I had wanted to end high school on a positive note and had. Even though I was only truly friends with them for a few weeks, I was very grateful for those few weeks we had together.

The one person I did not try to interact with in any way, shape, or form was Arwen. I was cordial to her when seeing her was unavoidable. Luckily, we crossed paths on surprisingly few occasions in the final months of school. On graduation day, as the crowd broke up and I headed towards the football field seats in search of my parents, I almost walked right into Arwen, her stepsister, stepmother, and father. Keeping my head down, I looped around them in a wide arc. Arwen called out to me. I froze. She called me again. Nervous, I turned around and approached the Pokatny family. Arwen and her stepsister were dressed in their electric blue graduation gowns but had taken their caps off to liberate their long, wavy black hair. Their nondescript, suburban, middle-aged parents had the usual greying hair, khaki clothes, and excess weight about the midsection. They didn't look like candy factory moguls today, but typical, middle-class, Staten Island public school parents. *Spider-Man meets his archenemies, the Green Goblin and Doctor Octopus, in person, for the very first time, and finds them surprisingly innocuous. Maybe it is a good thing Tolkien kept Sauron in shadows, and Jane Austen never showed her readers Frank Churchill's aunt at Enscombe.*

"Congratulations," I said.

Arwen threw her arms around me and gave me a fierce hug. "You, too!"

"I didn't want to muscle in on your family celebration," I whispered, mid hug.

She smiled up at me. "You're not interrupting." Arwen released me and waved her dad over. "Dad! Can you get a picture of us?" Her father clearly had no idea who I was supposed to be. Her stepmother appeared in my line of vision. "Who's this, Arwen?"

Arwen slipped her arm into mine. "The nicest gentleman you'll ever meet. And I need a graduation photo with him."

"Really?" I was so surprised and moved it was all I could do not to burst into tears.

"Yes, really, dummy."

Without asking for more clarification about my identity, Arwen's father took a photo of the two of us. I hoped desperately it would not be blurry, that our heads wouldn't be chopped off, and that I didn't have sunken-looking allergy eyes, obvious pimples, or camera flash redeye.

Dear God, let this photo be good.

"I'll mail you a 5 x 7," Arwen assured me.

For some time, I had felt as if most of my life experiences had resulted in the weight of a new invisible boulder being placed upon my back — a back already weighed down under a dozen or so other invisible boulders. My insomnia and photographic memory would conspire to ensure that I would always remember these boulders were there, and that I would ever feel their full weight. Arwen's kind, affectionate gestures — giving me a positive introduction to her parents, asking for the photo, offering me a copy — had an instantaneous, nearly magical effect. One of the biggest boulders on my back — my collective regrets about my relationship with Arwen — disappeared, never to return. Feeling taller, I straightened my back. From now on, I'd sleep easier and walk with a more carefree step. I couldn't think of a better graduation present.

Arwen and I wished each other luck in college. She would be going to Binghamton.

"Give him his present, Mom," Arwen said.

"Oh? The gift is for him?" Looking more concerned, Arwen's stepmother fished a handmade, leather-bound travel journal out of her purse and handed it to me. She must have been holding it for Arwen because graduation gowns don't have pockets. Obviously, Arwen hadn't warned her that the graduation present was for a boy.

I opened the brass snap and flipped through the blank pages inside. "A diary?"

"It doesn't have to be a diary," Arwen said. "It could be. I could also see you using it for poems, prayers, plays, and Harvey-Pekar-style autobiographical comic strips."

I unzipped the pen pouch on the inside cover. It contained an elegant fountain pen. "I can imagine using this pen to fill these pages with all of the above," I said. "Not that I'm much of a poetry guy. I've never really understood why so much depends upon red wheelbarrows. There isn't much call to use them on Staten Island. And how an apology for eating plums is a poem is beyond me."

"I like the idea of you trying to write a poem." Arwen touched a finger to my chest, just above my cigarette-burn scar. "We need to get the pain out of the inside of you and put it here." She tapped the cover of the journal with the same finger.

I nodded. "'Each man hides a secret pain. It must be exposed and reckoned with. It must be dragged from the darkness and forced into the light.'"

Arwen laughed brightly. "Okay, Sybok! Stop quoting *Star Trek V* to make fun of me when you know I'm right." Her voice turned sad. "I just heard about Mitchell. And I'm sorry."

"Yeah. I don't believe it's real. I'm pretending it didn't happen."

"You're pretending you're not gutted, but you are. You need to bleed onto these pages."

I stared down at the blank pages of the journal. "I'm not ready to write about him yet."

"Mitchell deserves at least one short story or poem, right?" Arwen asked. "Failing that, you can badmouth me. I'd make a Golden-Globe-award-worthy villain!"

"I'd hope whatever I wrote about you would make you look good."

"Phew!" Arwen wiped invisible sweat from her brow. "I was afraid you hated me."

I flinched at the suggestion. "Hate you? Never! How could I possibly hate you?"

Arwen eased forward, slowly moving her arm around my waist. "Happy graduation."

I took a half-step back and lowered my arms, looking down into her silver eyes.

Arwen stood up on her tip toes and kissed me twice on the lips.

"Uh-oh," I heard Arwen's stepmother say.

"Happy graduation." I slipped my arms around her waist. Arwen reach up, grabbed me by the back of the head, and pulled me down towards her. She gave me another small peck on the lips. I opened my mouth to say something, and she slid her tongue into it.

CHAPTER TWENTY-SIX
The Cigarette-Ash Heart

You were the one
in the passenger seat
when the driver nodded off.

When you felt
the car veering, and
grabbed the wheel -

the trailer hitch
fishtailed and flipped,
taking your car with it.

You were the one
your girlfriend held
as you died.

I never met her,
though you'd been
together for years.

I'm the one who
let us grow apart.
I forgot how to be your friend.

I missed so much.
Different high schools.
Different college plans.

You were just headed home
from a cross-country trip.
You're supposed to be home now.

I missed your wake.
and your funeral.
I found out too late.

Had I been there, I'd have seen
all your friends — a more diverse cast
than a TV hospital drama.

You could make friends with
anyone, at any time, under
any circumstances.

You lived and breathed
solidarity, but you were no
bumper sticker.

I am a bumper sticker.
A burnt
right-wing one.

Now you're gone.
And who's still here?
Me.

The C.S. Lewis fan.
The Batman geek.
The kid in love with Enya.

Can anyone be duller?
More repressed Catholic,
suburban Republican?

But God took you.
If only He had taken me,
instead. I mean, look at me -

I'm just the sort of
old-fashioned jackass
who would call God "He."

The world needs way fewer
like me; way more like you,
but God took you and left me.

We all know the names
of the good people, the ones
shot trying to caulk a cracked world.

But David Duke will always be with us.
Pat Robertson will live forever,
and we will all sleep at the wheel.

God made a mistake
when He stole you from us.
The infallible one blew it.

I promise you,
I will fix it.
I have to.

People scare me.
I don't understand them.
I don't like them.

But that is the old me.
I need to make a new "me,"
more like you.

People scare me, but
I will bleed with them
when the bullies cut them.

I will speak up because you can't.
I will say what you would have said.
And I will silence my own cigarette-ash heart.

PART III: PASSEGGIATA

CHAPTER TWENTY-SEVEN
Where's Caligula?

August 28, 1994

They called her Emmeline. The bronze bear clung to the light pole at the center of the circular water-fountain smack dab in the middle of Main Street in the village of Geneseo. The sandstone-and-granite fountain was installed in 1888 as a memorial to the bear's namesake — Emmeline Austin Wadsworth — by her children, in recognition of her lifelong love of animals. According to my self-appointed tour guide, Sergio Savini, much folklore has sprung up around the fountain over the generations. One legend held that, should the statue be removed, the land grant both the village and university had been built on would revert to the Wadsworth heirs.

Sergio added, "Another legend goes: 'Should ever a virgin graduate from Geneseo, the Bear shall descend from her perch and flee down Main Street, never to be seen again.'"

I snorted. "If I were you, I wouldn't get too attached to that bear."

Sergio looked surprised. "Didn't you–? Wait, who kissed you at graduation?"

"That was a 'goodbye' kiss. It was very nice, but it was a one-, um, two-time thing. She caused her rich parents some consternation, and they caused us some consternation."

"I see. I haven't done the deed yet, myself, but I have all the training I need. Six years of tuba playing in marching band. Double-tonguing. Flutter-tonguing. I'm ready."

"Kudos." *Is it too late to call Nancy and Christina and get put in touch with that virgin-loving nymphomaniac who looks like Marisa Tomei? Probably. Me and my stupid pride!*

Sergio had already shown me Main Street, which had been designated a National Historic Landmark by the United States Department of the Interior three years before. It had a classic, Main Street USA charm undercut only slightly by the surprising number of law offices and psychics located on the main drag. "They love their lawyers and psychics, huh?" I observed. There was a VHS movie rental store that would provide me hours of entertainment during my freshman year

— introducing me to cult classics like *Withnail and I, Kind Hearts and Coronets, Candyman,* and *Get Carter* — before the FBI raided it and closed it down for peddling pirated films. There was also a local newspaper office that had been shuttered thanks to embezzlement, and another local restaurant shut down because of the owner's tax evasion. Still, my gothic-comic worldview was challenged by what was otherwise a thriving and culturally fulfilling mix of local businesses that provided non-chain restaurants, stores, and bed-and-breakfasts to all. Among these local fixtures were a handful of bars — quiet ones for the Townies and rave-like settings for the students — as well as a vintage movie theater called the Riviera, competing pizzerias Mama Mia's and Pizza Paul's, Aunt Cookie's Sub Shop, Main Moon takeout Chinese food, the Bronze Bear Restaurant, the Big Tree Inn, Sundance Books, and Sonny's Music. My favorite of all of these businesses was Sonny's, mainly because the eccentric Italian American owner, Sonny Verde, was the spitting image of Jerry Garcia and trapped patrons into the oddest imaginable conversations. Sergio and I had spent the afternoon touring Main Street's attractions, popping into the stores, poking around the parks, and taste-testing the Italian food at Pizza Paul's. Personally, I liked the Buffalo wings, French fries, and zeppole I ordered.

Afterwards, Sergio drove us out of town along the road leading into Letchworth State Park, "the Grand Canyon of the East," which was less than a half-hour away. The Village of Geneseo was in New York's Finger Lakes region thirty minutes south of Rochester. The land was once Iroquois Confederacy land, and the village's name was derived from the Iroquois for "beautiful valley": Gen-nis-he-yo. The gregarious Sergio explained all of this to me with gusto.

I met Sergio Joseph Savini a few hours before at freshman orientation. A short, barrel-chested Sicilian American boy with a well-manicured goatee and a blue-suit-and-tie, Sergio was a ringer for Mets catcher Mike Piazza. (Amusingly, Sergio saw me as a ringer for Giants quarterback Dave Brown, so he referred to me as "Dave Brown.") While I had fallen out of the practice of dressing in suits for school, I had picked Sergio out of the crowd because he was the only formally dressed freshman, and I presumed he was a fellow of taste and discrimination that I could relate to. Straightaway, I appreciated him both for his love of opera — he played a 1953 recording of *Tosca* featuring Maria Callas on our drive to Letchworth — and in food — he made me a fantastic penne alla vodka.

Still, the upper-middle-class graduate of Chaminade Roman Catholic High School grew up in financial security with a lawyer father and a primary school teacher mother that was a financial cut above my own upbringing. Mom never did buy that second house in Pennsylvania for Dad, but Sergio's family boasted a main home in Nassau County they lived in throughout the year, and a summer beach house in Suffolk County. I had the impression that Sergio and his parents could buy and sell my family three times over, which was why he was an ardent capitalist and could not help but express deeply libertarian sentiments once every three minutes. I'll admit that it probably doesn't take long for people to figure out I have an anarcho-socialist worldview, but this fellow never changed the record. His speech was also peppered with businessman and lawyer lingo and clichés. At some point, he must have gotten advice from a marketing maven that people love to hear their own names spoken aloud, so he called people by their names unnaturally frequently. He was, overall, a bit too "Anthony Scaramucci" for my taste. It also didn't help that his Catholicism was textbook Opus Dei. Monsignor Tobin would have wanted to adopt him. After three hours in his presence, I went from loving Sergio to deciding I could take him or leave him. After the fourth hour, I never wanted to see him again, but wasn't sure how to jettison him from my presence without being overwhelmingly rude.

Awkwardly for me, Sergio took to me far more than I took to him. As we drove back to campus, he started praising me for being a good Italian: "You seem cool, Dave Brown. You like a good calzone that doesn't drip grease, Fellini, and *Il Trovatore*. I just don't understand why you'd waste your time majoring in the humanities when you grew up eating, drinking, and breathing it. You live the humanities. You don't need a degree in it."

"And why would I waste my time majoring in business?" I asked. "I've already seen *Star Trek: Deep Space Nine* and learned all of Quark's

'Rules of Acquisition.' That's the whole major right there. And I'm not willing to take an oath swearing to dismantle the EPA. That's not my jam."

"I guess you're here to *find* yourself. I already know who I am. I don't need to find myself. I found out in high school. I'm here for a certificate to get a job. I'll be spending four years sleeping through the easiest classes in the world until they release me into the wilds."

"You sure you know who you are?" I asked. "I thought I knew what it meant to be Italian Catholic. Then my best friend died in a car accident. Now I'm not so sure how I feel about anything. Being an English major and a Medieval Studies minor will help me figure it all out."

"Be a business major! Italians are businessmen. The Medici invented capitalism."

"And Saint Francis invented anarcho-socialist Roman Catholicism. And Pasolini was some sort of iconoclastic Communist."

A freakishly wide rictus smile froze on Sergio's face. "Please, say it ain't so, Dave Brown! You're not a Liberation Theology Catholic, are you? That would be too much to bear. Do me a favor. Don't go to the Newman Community at Geneseo. They're all hippies there. I went to a mass there when I came to tour the place last spring. The priest talked about the importance of cutting funds to the military to underwrite better healthcare, education, and reparations for slavery. That's not a church I want any part of."

I frowned. "I remember that part of the Bible. Jesus considered paying for enough loaves and fishes to feed everyone who had come to hear him preach. Then he told Judas to keep the money in reserve so he could buy a bunch of intercontinental ballistic missiles instead."

Sergio took his eyes off the road to look at me. "You're a weird guy, Damien. Weird."

I arched my eyebrow at Sergio. "Seriously? You really think Jesus was a war hawk and social Darwinist who wanted to give gay people electro-shock therapy?"

Sergio sighed. "This isn't that complicated, Dave Brown. You should know all this by now. As Catholics, we should believe that the U.S. Constitution is not as important as the teachings of the Magisterium. What we need to do is, essentially, become politicians and judges and rewrite the laws of America to conform to Catholic doctrine. Our end game is to make illegal all forms of sodomy and birth control. We should be doing everything in our power to transform America from a democracy into a Roman Catholic theocracy. That, or we should promote libertarianism and the incremental dismantling of the federal government. Those are our two big strategies. Either way, that means voting Republican up-and-down ballot. As Catholics, we cannot vote Democrat, ever. Catholics who vote Democrat should be excommunicated."

I rolled my eyes. "Yeah, whatever, crazy man! Go back to smoking peyote. Talk like that validates the stereotypical liberal view that religious Catholics are enemies of the state. I don't want to see that kind of anti-Catholic bigotry validated."

"I'm serious. I'm part of a concerned Catholic citizens brigade. You should join!"

Oh, fuck. The liberals are right about us, aren't they? I grit my teeth as I spoke to keep myself from shouting at Sergio. "True religious people shouldn't be schemers in secret societies. We should have faith in God's plan for humanity, and not be creepy, cynical, and atheistic in our political maneuvering. Plotting a Christian takeover of America is, by nature, an unchristian enterprise. It makes no sense."

"There's nothing wrong with being practical and strategizing."

"Maybe, but you're assuming you're backing the right horse and that justifies your being sleazy. I'm becoming increasingly convinced the best way to promote old-fashioned family values is to vote for liberal Democrat candidates who make sure we all get the living wages and clean drinking water we need to keep a traditional family afloat."

"That's really counter-intuitive."

"Isn't it? And yet, the best way to get people to read is ban books. People are weird. If you want a conservative society, you should always vote liberal. Strange, but true. Install an all right-wing government, and you'll turn everyone — even my mom — into Huey P. Newton! Well, not everyone. My dad would probably love living in a totalitarian society."

Sergio laughed. "I think I would, too!"

I frowned. I was the one who made the joke, yet I didn't feel like laughing.

My last summer on Staten Island was dreadful, largely because Mom, who had chosen my college and my major, was miserable that I would soon be leaving home and going to a school six hours drive away. To deal with the coming separation anxiety, Mom suppressed her exploding emotions and spent the entire summer cleaning the house in quiet, existential despair. Red-faced, breathing heavily, carrying large baskets of laundry and vacuum cleaners up and down the stairs of our three-story house, she spent the whole summer looking within an exhalation of following in her mother's footsteps killing herself with excess housework. I tried to yell her into resting. I hid the broom. I attempted to sabotage the vacuum cleaner. These efforts all failed. Surrendering, I hid in my bedroom all summer reading comic books like *Batman vs. Predator, Batman vs. Judge Dredd,* and *Calvin and Hobbes.* I read *a lot* of Alan Davis' *Excalibur* comic books because of my Kitty Pryde crush. (Kitty Pryde was basically Arwen as a member of the X-Men.) Thankfully, Dad was better at dealing with his emotions than Mom. One evening, he visited me in my hiding place. He hugged me, told me he would miss me when I was gone, and cried. As for Leo, we had a perfectly fun summer, playing video games, making fake radio shows, reading comics together, taking walks locally, and hiding from Mom. During our funniest interaction, Leo joked about his plan to take over my bedroom the moment I was gone.

I exaggerated a pained expression. "You'd do that to me?"

Laughing, Leo replied, "You know how younger brothers are! We're all a bit like Loki!"

To help me plan my dorm room décor in advance, Dad took me on a special trip to Jerry Ohlinger's Movie Material Store on West 30th Street in Manhattan, where we picked up some cheesecake art. I grabbed two inoffensive posters — *The Umbrellas of Cherbourg* and *Silent Running* — and bought glossy glamour photos of the usual suspects: Emma Thompson, Gillian Anderson, Monica Bellucci, Gong Li, Veronica Carlson, and Ann-Margret. As a gift to me, Dad paid for all sexy artwork not featuring "washed-out blondes," which amounted to me paying $38 for my ten photos of Veronica Carlson.

At the end of the summer, Dad helped me load up my car with materials for college. It wasn't much, so it all fit in the small trunk and back seat. My entire wardrobe made it into two large suitcases. I packed up my desktop computer and printer, the usual toiletries, and bedsheets. I took a couple of boxes of comic books. I opted not to bring a television, VCR, or video game console. I would not have a cellphone (since regular people didn't have access to that kind of technology at the time). As a freshman, I would not be allowed a car on campus. On the day of our departure, Dad took out his huge road atlas, traced the driving route, and wrote the directions in blue pen on the back of a legal-sized envelope: I-278 W to I-80 W to I-380 N to I-81 N to NY-17 W to I-390 N. We would pass SUNY Binghamton at the halfway mark. As we drove by it, I planned to place my hand on the passenger side window, stare wistfully at the highway exit, and say, "Good luck in college, Arwen." Another three or four hours later, we would arrive. Dad would then help me unload the car, leave me in my unfurnished room, and depart. Leo and Mom would stay home so that there was enough room in the car for my belongings. That was the plan.

As I finished packing the car up, I saw my man Larry Birnbaum fiddling with his motorcycle on his driveway. I asked him how he was feeling. He looked up. "Much better. Thank you for getting me that medicine. I really appreciate it. Hope it wasn't too much trouble?"

"For you? You're the nicest dude on the block!" I was talking too loudly and waving my arms about too much, because this might be the last time I saw him for a while. If my over-the-top performance bothered Larry, he didn't show it. He waved his wrench vaguely at the houses up and down Kell Avenue. "I keep telling them they need to be friendlier to you guys. We all live on this block, right? I don't want to speak ill of my neighbors, but I do think they can be a little bit unfriendly to people who don't attend our synagogue. I try to do better than that."

"Some 'try.' You succeed." I meant what I said wholeheartedly but winced inwardly when I realized I had accidentally quoted Humphrey Bogart from *Casablanca*. Luckily, Larry hadn't noticed. Finished loading, I walked back inside to say my goodbyes to Mom and Leo. I found Leo waiting for me. "Did you just have another heartwarming talk with Larry?" he asked.

"I guess so," I said.

"Unbelievable," Leo muttered, exaggerating how upset he was for comic affect. "Some people have all the luck. All I get is woken up early by his motorcycle! Vroom vroom!"

Mom appeared, wearing her sunglasses indoors so I wouldn't see her tears.

"Sunglasses!" I exclaimed. "You're adorable! Little Mumu is adorable!" I threw my arms around her and gave her my anaconda hug.

"I promised myself I wouldn't cry," Mom whimpered.

"Too Cute for Words!" I bellowed, kissing Mom three times on each cheek. "TCFW!"

"You be good and have a great time in college," Mom said. "I think it is a good school."

"It should be good," I said softly. "If it isn't, don't worry. I MAKE MY OWN FUN!"

"That's good," said Mom. "I know you do."

"Because most people and places are BORING AND HOSTILE! HAHAHAHA!"

Leo laughed. "Cheeseball."

"Uh-oh." I looked about as if some sort of alarm had gone off, distracting me from hugging Mom. "The Cuteness Detector is going off. A second source of cuteness has registered." I let go of Mom, rushed over to Leo, scooped him up in my anaconda grip, and gave him four kisses on each cheek. "TOO CUTE FOR WORDS! TCFW!"

Eight hours later, including a commute, some pit stops at gas stations, and a dinner stop-off at a Cracker Barrel, Dad helped me finish unloading all my belongings from the car into a vacant, white-walled, ground-floor dormitory room. The room was eleven-feet by twelve-feet, with one set of bunk beds, an army cot propped up on four vertical cinder blocks, a closet, and one dresser. There was no décor anywhere. Even the floor was white-tiled and carpet-free. The room was set off from a suite in which a common living room of twelve-by-twelve linked two more rooms, identical to this one, only those contained two army cots and no bunkbed, because my suite was the only temporary triple. I would be sharing it with two fellow non-smokers, Tomo Ogata, a Japanese American student, and Mike

Zhōu, a Chinese American student. I had not met them yet and did not know their majors or what part of New York they grew up in. Arriving first meant that I did not get the leftover drawers and closet space after the room had been picked over by the others. On the other hand, with no one else around, the room was sparse and lifeless and terrifyingly silent. I feared I had been imprisoned in an empty army barracks.

Dad stood by the entrance to the room. "I guess I should head off."

I stuck my hands in my pockets. "Yeah."

"Your roommates will be along soon." Dad started to turn to go. Then he realized I didn't want to be the only soul left in the suite after he'd gone. Dad patted my shoulder, reassuringly. "You know how I know you'll be fine? Nobody alive has conversations the way you have conversations. The stories you tell me. Crazy stuff, really. More like lost scenes from *Pulp Fiction* and *Clerks* than any conversations I've ever had. If even half of the stories you've told me are true, it really blows my mind."

I chuckled. "My stories are all true."

"I can't deal with them *all* being true. I'm having trouble enough dealing with *half*."

I laughed. "Well, my stories are all between eighty-three and ninety-eight percent true."

Dad smiled thinly. "Worst comes to worse, even if you don't enjoy being here, I'll expect you to have many, many outrageous conversations with people. I'll want you to report them all back to me, but only after I've taken my blood-pressure medicine."

"I have a feeling you're right."

"I'm trying to figure out if I'm jealous of your nutty encounters or glad I've led a much more boring life than you. Since leaving the Bronx and my gang of criminal friends, anyway."

"Yeah, I'm the same. I'm not sure if I'm jealous of your boring life." *Or happy I keep bumping into characters straight outta Richard Russo, Shirley Jackson, and John Kennedy Toole.* "I think I can do well in college with the homework part and the learning to do my own laundry part, but I'm worried I really won't make any friends at all. My record is spotty."

Dad stopped himself once more from going. "I've made a lot of mistakes in my life. I've got a lot of demons. Still, I own my mistakes, and I'm on a first-name basis with all of my demons. I know I'm a screw-up. If I let someone I care about down, I'll be the first to admit it. Of course, if you enjoy throwing my faults in my face, like Beatrice used to, maybe I'll be in less of a hurry to own up to what I've done. As far as you're concerned? I know you. You know your own flaws better than anyone else does. You don't need them pointed out. You do the best you can. When you make a mistake, you apologize. Your record isn't spotty. It's good. You'll be behaving the same way here, so you should be okay. Nobody can ask any more of you than that."

After Dad left, I sat forlornly on the military cot, staring at the four blank, white walls. The room felt like a coffin. There was a window with white venetian blinds drawn down over it. I peered through the blinds onto an expansive parking lot. Did this window face the Genesee Valley, but I couldn't see it well with this parking lot between me and it? "I was promised a room with a view," I said out loud to myself, chuckling and pretending to be addressing Maggie Smith. "Perhaps we can switch rooms with Mr. Emerson and his son."

No, this place did not feel like home. I needed to do something to make me feel safe and welcome here, without another soul in sight, or I was about to crack up. How did I make myself feel better back home in Staten Island? In a lonely bedroom, in the dead of night? My Wonder Woman statue was back home. My equivalent of a "good luck" gargoyle designed to keep the evil spirits away was my Kelly Bundy cheesecake poster. That was back home, too. Who could protect me from the existential dread of loneliness and death if those two weren't here to save me? Then I remembered the manila envelope in my suitcase. I unzipped it, produced a glossy photo of Emma Thompson, and taped it up on the wall over my army cot.

"My dear, dear Emma. Oh, patron saint of English majors. I have come to university to study the great works of literature. Please give me your blessing and wish me luck for a happy and healthy four years of college. I want to do my best to become one of the greatest English majors in the history of New York State. I'm going to need your help to pull it off."

Unfortunately, Emma Thompson did not reply to my supplication.

"Oh, well. I'll assume you heard me, but you're a bit busy just now." Thinking I should at least unpack — but not manspread across a room I was sharing with two others — I emptied my suitcases on the army cot, singing Luis Bacalov's theme to the Franco Nero film *Django*.

Hours after meeting my roommates, decorating our room together, hitting freshman orientation, and touring Main Street with Sergio, I went to a TKE "Welcome to Geneseo" party with Tomo Ogata and Mike Zhōu. We stood in the backyard of the TKE house — an imposing Victorian home with red curtains covering each window and red floodlights bathing the lawns, making the building look like rural New York's answer to Castle Dracula. "Come on, Eileen" by Dexys Midnight Runners played on huge speakers behind me, blasting out my ear drums. The yard was filled to bursting with students — a testament to TKE's monopoly on partying at an isolated liberal arts college surrounded by farmland for at least twenty-minutes-drive in each direction. A couple of dozen junior and senior rubberheads and meat bags in sweat suits, t-shirts, and baseball caps bearing Greek letters and logos from a variety of sports franchises stood by a row of ten tapped beer kegs. They poured foamy beer into plastic cups and distributed them to a long line of freshman girls they hoped to get drunk enough to bring inside the house.

"Where's Caligula?" I asked.

"I don't hate this party," Mike said, adjusting his Lenny Kravitz t-shirt.

"I give this party two-and-a-half stars," I declared.

Tomo looked around in silent disapproval. Tomo was tall, slim, wore his long, straight black hair in a ponytail, and sported jeans and a *Final Fantasy IV* t-shirt. Despite my existential angst around quiet people, I already knew I felt more in sync with the quiet Tomo than I did the overly talkative Mike and his extensive 90s dance music CD collection.

I looked around again at the upperclassmen boys and the freshmen girls. "I feel like the frat guys are here for an orgy and the freshman girls are here for a party and that is a recipe for disaster. The girls didn't get the memo that this is a 'Save the Bear' party. I want to get out of here. And I don't think I want to come to any more of these parties."

"I agree," nodded Tomo.

"I'm stayin'," said Mike. "And you're being alarmist, and no fun. These girls can take care of themselves. They don't need you biting your nails on their behalf."

I shrugged. "Maybe these frat guys are fun and I'm just not. This isn't my scene."

Obviously, if the Greek organizations had a near monopoly on event planning in this college, choosing to boycott all their future shindigs would do incalculable damage to my social life. Still, I was never going to go for any gathering of this type. I had moral objections to fraternities. I didn't like hazing. After spending my entire sixth grade being bullied and tortured, I wasn't about to bring more torture upon myself for the glory and honor of joining an all-male organization of mostly athletes and business majors. And I would never eat an ookie cookie to earn the right to join any organization, no matter what it was. Fuck that! Besides, what would I have in common with the average fraternity boy? Probably less than nothing.

Tomo and I downed our one beer, tossed our plastic cups in the garbage, and walked back to our suite on the south side of campus in Nassau Hall, twenty-minutes away on foot. We returned to the suite we shared with Mike and four other freshmen. My desktop computer, a futon, a rocking chair, and a coffee table had materialized in the common room over the course of the several hours since my father's departure. In each corner of the suite was an adjoining room designed to accommodate two students. In addition to the room I was tripled in with Tomo and Mike, there was the room that housed Hernan Vallejo and Eladio Salazar and the room that held Hans Richter and Mike Gustafson. Tomo, Mike, and I joked that there was the White Room, the Hispanic Room, and the Asian Room, and I was the odd one out: the Italian shoehorned into the Asian room by mistake. I reassured them that it didn't bother me in the slightest, and it didn't. I took to them both quickly, even if I preferred Tomo's company. As Tomo and I entered the common room, Hans Richter and Mike Gustafson passed us, heading out into the hall, smelling of way too much Drakker Noir. "I'll be seeing you guys at the TKE party later, right?" Hans Richter asked, as he closed the door behind him.

"SEE YOU AT THE PAH-TY, RICHTER!" I yelled, doing my best Schwarzenegger.

"*Total Recall*," Tomo observed, stone-faced.

"I'm not really going back to the party, but that was too perfect a set-up to pass up."

"It was pretty funny," Tomo said, looking as if he didn't find it funny at all. Then the widest smile spread across his face. I loved it whenever he would do that: go from looking impassive to busting out the world's biggest grin. His smile-reveal made me happy to be alive.

Crossing the common room, we passed the wide-open door to Eladio and Hernan's room. Inside, Hernan and Eladio danced in front of a full-length mirror to Barry White's "You're the First, the Last, My Everything." The scene was so infectiously joyous that none of the four of us minded that the dancing men were combing their hair dressed only in their boxer shorts, tank tops, and gold neck chains. "Hey, guys!" Hernan yelled. "Me and Eladio are jazzing ourselves up to talk to the hot babes at TKE. You guys wanna come in and dance, too?" I was too shy to take him up on the offer. In retrospect, I wish I had. A few years after seeing this wonderful dance routine, I would do a spit-take watching an episode of *Ally McBeal* in which Peter MacNicol's lawyer character John Cage danced to the same song in front of a unisex bathroom mirror to get jazzed up to argue a tough case. Had Hernan become friends with the series creator, or what?

"Cool song," I said. "We just came back from TKE. There are a lot of pretty girls there."

"What are you doing back?" Eladio yelled.

"Not my scene. Reminded me of what Yogi Berra said: 'That place is so crowded, nobody goes there anymore.' It was also a real meat market."

"Sounds horrible!" Hernan laughed. "Let's get over there, fast, Eladio!"

The next song on Hernan's power mix came on: "Stayin' Alive" by the Bee Gees.

"So, seventies music, huh?" I asked. I was glad I wasn't the only one who liked oldies.

"You should talk!" Eladio yelled. "I heard you singing 'Blow the Man Down' three times today, while you were unpacking!"

"I'm not insulting you!" I said quickly. "I swear! I love *Saturday Night Fever!*" My taste in music would become a sticking point with the macho Eladio, who was in Geneseo's ROTC and was frequently offended by what he considered my feminine traits. Any time I listened to sad love songs by Roxette, he would slide a piece of paper under my door that read: "Roxette Sucks." That was when I knew it was time to lower the volume or change the CD. When he wasn't listening to seventies music with Hernan, Eladio was more of a New Age and World Music fan. He converted me to Deep Forest, Adiemus, and Enigma, but I never won him over to liking Marie Fredriksson and Per Gessle. "I came to college to chew gum and sing sea shanties, and 'Blow the Man Down' is the only sea shanty I know," I yelled over the music.

Eladio frowned. "Is this how you really talk, or is that your Deadpool impersonation?"

"Naw! Deadpool is a *murderer!* In my heart, I'm Spider-Man, with Doctor Who seasoning! Also, this is how I really talk."

In keeping with the day's nautical theme, Sergio called out, "Ahoy, there, Tomo Ogata and Dave Brown!" Sergio must have looked me up in the freshman directory because he didn't live in our suite or our building. We were supposed to meet at the TKE party I had only cameoed at, but he came here first. The dapper freshman strode into our suite holding his stomach in to appear slimmer. His posture and military gait gave him a Robocop-like appearance. *Clarence Boddicker, dead or alive, you're coming with me,* I thought. Then I recalled my Shakespeare. Sergio *"doth bestride the narrow world like Colossus, and we petty men walk under his huge legs and peep about."* Sergio flashed a perfect white smile and shook my hand and Tomo's. "I brought my roommate with me, Lance Faust."

Sergio's reptilian roommate slinked into our common room after him. The lanky Lance stood his ground behind Sergio, inclining his head at us. Sergio introduced me to Lance as a big movie fan, so Lance thought he'd gauge my taste: "You gotta just love *Top Gun, Animal House, Tango & Cash,* and *Road House!* You gotta! If you love movies, you gotta love *Top Gun!*"

I shuffled from one foot to the other, embarrassed. "I'm more of a *Quiz Show* and *Enchanted April* kinda guy, but the Berlin song from *Top Gun* is a favorite."

Lance laughed. "Are those movies even real? I've never heard of them!"

Sergio said to Tomo and me: "Tomo Ogata and Damien Cavalieri, you guys should rush TKE with us. Come to their Red Zone Party tonight and talk with the gentlemen in charge about the possibility of joining their esteemed organization."

Tomo laughed. "We just came from there. Didn't seem that cool."

Sergio raised both eyebrows. His perfect white teeth and perfect smile froze unnaturally on his face. "You went early? Gave up before ten? Things are probably just getting started now."

I exhaled sharply though my nose. "Bunch a guys in sweat pants and sports memorabilia? Blaring music. Beer. It all seems a little uncouth to me."

Lance scoffed. "What did you expect?"

I closed my eyes and pictured something more romantic. "I want a college party with four couples in a room listening to Dave Brubeck's 'Take Five,' drinking Bailey's Irish Crème, reading Andrew Marvell and Adrienne Rich poems to each other before making love until dawn. In the morning, we have waffles Florentine together and watch the sunrise over Conesus Lake. Then, we switch partners, go back to the bedroom, and fuck until noon. Now, *that's* a party."

Sergio frowned. "Is that a classier version of *Bob & Carol & Ted & Alice?*"

"I know I'm just a freshman, but I would really prefer visiting some nice senior or super senior girls in their homes, where they have home field advantage, and let them set the scene with incense, wine, and candles. And none of the guys go there with roofies, and the sex is consensual, and epic, and beautiful. That's what I want out of college."

Lance sucked his teeth. "You want 'nice' girls? Never met any 'nice' girls."

I pulled the key to the room I shared with Tomo and the absent Mike Zhōu out of my pocket. "I tell you what, Sergio. I'll definitely hang out when you go to Main Moon or Pizza Paul's for dinner. Play pool in the student center. Have a game of Texas Hold 'Em. Go see a movie at Cinema 4. But you can count me out of any Greek events from now on. Nothing against TKE per se. I'm sure I'll find all of them Greeks equally dull, stupid, and morally reprehensible."

"Dave Brown, this is our first night on campus as freshmen!" Sergio yelled. "Are you crazy? You give up on TKE, you give up on partying for the next four years."

"What are they, Ma Bell? I hate monopolies."

Sergio was like a dog with a bone. "I met a lot of cool TKE guys today, Damien. Did you see Chet Gorka at the party? He's damn cool. Damn cool! I talked to him for an hour today."

I couldn't recall what Chet Gorka looked like. I pictured sweatpants, a sweatshirt, and a baseball cap, and a nondescript Caucasian face. All these frat boys looked the same to me. "I talked to him for a minute. He was the one greeting people at the entrance. I think."

"Yes! Wasn't he awesome? Wouldn't you want to be in the same frat as him, Damien?"

"I suppose he'd make as good a fraternity brother as the next guy . . . if the next guy was a chimpanzee's asshole," I joked. Sergio was so shocked by what I said that his smile remained frozen, but his eyes moved back and forth between Tomo and I. I imagined Sergio spying through eyeholes poked out of an oil painting portrait concealing a mansion's secret passageway in a locked-door murder mystery.

Tomo pointed at me. "He's not going to join any Greek organization no matter what. I'm open to it. I'm just not joining TKE. Those guys were louts."

"Yeah," I said. "That's the operative word. 'Lout.'"

Lance frowned. "Dude, you seem to be making the girls at the party out to be innocent little lambs and the TKE guys are wolves feeding on them. But the girls should know what the guys are after. They've heard all their lives, 'Guys only want one thing.' So, they know! I'd argue the opposite, dude. The guys are the innocent ones. The girls are freakin' devious. They're laying traps for the guys. Don't you hate it whenever a girl goes home with you, you do the nasty, and then she just . . . *decides* . . . the next day that she was raped? So immature and crazy and dangerous. Destroying innocent guys' lives like that!"

I placed the key in my doorknob lock and was about to turn it when I stopped. I looked back over at Lance with undisguised revulsion. "If six was nine and up was down, what you just said might make sense."

Confused, Lance looked to Sergio for help. "You know what I'm saying, right?"

Sergio looked nervously back at me. "Yeah, girls do that all the time."

"Y'all sure 'bout dat?" I asked. "Cuz I ain't."

Lance patted Sergio on the shoulder. "I'm gonna wait outside for you." He huffed out.

Sergio pointed an accusing finger at me. "Listen up, Dave Brown. You weren't friendly to Lance just then."

I avoided Sergio's gaze. "Please don't bring that rapist fellow over here anymore. I'd rather not be subjected to his presence."

Sergio flinched. "You just met him! What makes you think the worst of him?"

"He's got the stench of brimstone about him. It offends my nostrils."

The part of Sergio that was the son of a lawyer came to the fore. "You're using your woman's intuition? In America, we're innocent until proven guilty."

"Last I checked, you're not Matlock and I'm not on the Ron Goldman-Nicole Brown Simpson murder trial jury. I'm an empath. I can sense evil. He's evil. And he paused around the word 'decides.' Dead giveaway. Might as well get a tattoo on his head that says, 'RAPIST.'"

Tomo spoke up. "His body language *was* all wrong. I'm with Damien on this."

"Don't trust Damien's instincts, Tomo Ogata! His taste and judgment are in question. Did you know, his favorite Pink Floyd album is *Momentary Lapse of Reason*!" Sergio sighed and put his hands in his pants pockets. "Besides, we men should stick together."

"Why?" I asked. "Most men blow dead moose. In my experience, if bad shit goes down, it's always the dude's fault, and the girl always gets the blame."

"Wow. Just the opposite is true. Women are wicked."

"Behind every wicked woman is a male oppressor who took away all her better options."

"Tomo Ogata and Damien Cavalieri. Two traitors to their gender."
Sergio waved dismissively at me and Tomo and left the suite.

"And what a magnificent gender it is," I muttered. Once the
interlopers had left, Tomo and I walked into our tiny dorm room,
still cramped but at least decorated by the three of us to reflect our
complimentary tastes and interests. After playing paper, scissor, rock,
I was saddled with the top bunk, but that wouldn't last more than a
week. I got up too often in the night to pee and kept waking the other
two up by leaping off the top bunk and taking too long to scramble
back up when I was done. In the end, I got the bottom bunk. This
meant that my Emma Thompson pin-up had to be moved three
times before she found her a permanent spot above my head to guard
me as I slept. In our three-way conversation about where to store all
our clothes, Mike and I settled on splitting the closet space. Tomo
claimed the dresser, primarily because he needed the top of it to place
his TV, VCR, SEGA Genesis, and Super Nintendo on. He had a ton
of video games for both stations I'd never played and an extensive
collection of anime films on VHS I'd never seen. In another bonus,
Tomo had sprung for cable television, which I'd never had growing
up. It took me less than a week to determine that cable television was
mostly rubbish except for MTV (I loved the *Oddities* and Beavis and
Butthead and Daria), Comedy Central (which broadcasted *Heathers*
thrice daily), Turner Classic Movies, and the SCI-FI Channel (which
showed repeats of *Dark Shadows* and a lot of Full Moon movies). For
broadcast television, I liked NBC for *Seinfeld, SNL,* and *NewsRadio*
and local networks for syndicated shows like *Babylon 5* and, in a year
or so, *Buffy* and *Xena.*

"Up for TV?" I asked. "Maybe the Science Fiction Channel is
showing *Bloodstone: Subspecies II*! Oh, and I'm sorry if I'm already
proving myself boring and militant."

Tomo shook his head. "Nah. There's got to be more to partying
around here than the Greek organizations. We'll figure it out. But we
can't spend four years watching the Science Fiction channel together
instead of going out on the weekends."

"We can't? I was going to really lean in on the Science Fiction
channel plan. Maybe I could play your copy of Super Mario World. I

need to see what Mario has been up to since the last time I saw him, back in Super Mario Brothers 2."

Tomo pursed his lips. "Mike says he's addicted to MUDs."

"Say what?"

"Multi-User Dungeons. Text-based games. Watch out you don't get addicted to video games and watching TV," Tomo warned. "Don't be like Mike."

I sighed. "It's an alternative to frat parties."

Tomo turned his television on to the Science Fiction channel. The picture came into focus halfway into the opening credits of an Italian horror film I'd neither seen before nor heard of. We had just missed the title but were in time for the names of Italian cast and crew members written in bone white letters in an elegant font, punctuated by a minimalist, music-box score. The ominous opening scene that followed involved a wholesome-looking ingénue walking out of a European airport into the driving rain and hailing a cab. "An Italian film *and* horror? If I watch this, I'll honor my mother *and* father," I said.

"I'm getting us a snack." Tomo went off to find the student study lounge down the hallway to cook us up some popcorn. The lounge in question included couches to loaf out in, a television, table-and-chairs, public microwave, toaster, vending machines, water fountain, and an empty fish tank with a bag of Pepperidge Farm Goldfish Crackers stuck inside it as a sight gag. While Tomo was off making the popcorn, it took me all of three minutes to become engrossed in the oddball foreign film. I was equally repulsed, terrified, and fascinated by its decadent beauty and claustrophobic atmosphere. "What is this? The greatest horror movie ever made?"

Tomo came back with the popcorn in time to see a blonde woman's head smashed through a bedroom window. A hairy, demonic hand clawed and stabbed her chest open, exposing her still-beating heart. The creature knifed her in the heart, wrapped her neck in a telephone-wire noose, and tossed her corpse through a brilliantly colored, stained-glass skylight. I covered my face, watching the violence through fanned fingers that obscured my view of the butchery.

Tomo laughed gleefully. "Those special effects aren't convincing at all!"

"Jesus!" I was scandalized. "That killing was sadistic! I'm good at willing suspension of disbelief, so the last thing I need is a *more* convincing still-beating heart getting stabbed."

Tomo sat down on his army cot, placing a ceramic bowl with his share of the popcorn in his lap. Once he was settled, he reached over and handed me the half-portion of popcorn remaining in the microwaveable bag. An equitable split. "Don't make yourself believe what you're seeing if it freaks you out. Keep yourself at a distance from it and pick it apart, like I do."

"Whoever made this movie is a maniac, a misogynist, and a genius."

"Aha!" Tomo declared. "This is *Suspiria*."

"Is this late Mario Bava?"

Tomo shook his head. "Dario Argento. I heard a crazy rumor that his mother ran off with her boyfriend on Christmas Eve when he was just a kid and he never forgave her. That's why he's got these violent murders of women who take forever to die."

"Damn," I said. "And I thought *my* mom ruined Christmas one time! If that's true, it sounds like Dario could use some *serious* therapy."

"I might be wrong. It might just be a plot point in the movie he made with Jennifer Connelly, *Creepers*. Or maybe it was another movie? *Deep Red* opens with an evil Christmas."

"Jennifer Connelly? Cool." *I wonder if Mitchell ever saw that one.* "Sounds to me like Argento hates Christmas more than Tim Burton does. And that's saying something!"

"Fair warning: Since this is an Italian horror movie, we are in for lots of gore and a plot that makes no sense whatsoever," said Tomo. "Still, I can stick with this film tonight."

"Cool. But here's hoping not too many more women get tortured slowly to death."

Tomo laughed. "I think you may be in for a rough movie night, Damien."

Less than an hour later, a ballet student fell into a pit of razor wire.

I covered my eyes again. "Mother of God! That poor girl! This is appalling!"

Tomo laughed and gave me some more popcorn to calm me.

CHAPTER TWENTY-EIGHT
Frenemy of the State

August 30, 1994

> To: KirbyAndDitko4ever@hotmail.com
>
> From: KAhearne@albany.edu
>
> August 30, 1994, 2:00 p.m.

I can't believe the story you just told me about your first college party. You stayed about twenty minutes and left after one tiny plastic cup of beer? I told Salty about it. He spent all day yesterday telling all of SUNY Cortland about what you did. You're now famous in SUNY Cortland. No one can believe someone like you exists. Now they all want to meet you to see you with their own eyes. If you visit Salty, you'll definitely get some play out of this.

I just had an email from David Litvinov. It was terrible. It was all about how he lost his virginity, had sex with three different women in one weekend to get a hat trick, and how he thought that going down on a girl would taste bad, but it was surprisingly sweet. He called me up an hour after I read it and said the same thing to me, verbatim. I found out from Salty he told the same story to him, word-for-word. Here's the problem with David: he's nice, but he prepares his stories in advance and tells them over and over the same way. He also gives himself head.

SUNY Albany is okay. You shoulda come here. This place is like a small city. More students means more girls for you to chase. Geneseo is a damn sandbox next to Albany. You're gonna run out of dating options over there fast. I have lots to tell you, but I want to keep this short. Your email to me was way too long. I only read about half of it. No. I read a quarter of it.

Try going to another party and staying for more than five minutes, will you, psychopath?

Kyle

P.S.–I know you're watching *My So-Called Life*.

*

To: KAhearne@albany.edu

    From: KirbyAndDitko4ever@hotmail.com

    August 30, 1994, 9:00 p.m.

    Hat trick? Must be tough to be David.

    What's *My So-Called Life*?

    Damien

    P.S.–That short enough for you?

    P.P.S.–You know, I just want someone to frickin' talk to!

To: KirbyAndDitko4ever@hotmail.com

    From: DLitvinov@humnet.ucla.edu

    August 30, 1994, 3:12 p.m.

    Damien–

This email business is great, isn't it? How did we survive so long in Staten Island without it? LA is overwhelming but great so far. I went to this bar in L.A. to see the Mighty Mighty Bosstones, and who did I see at the bar but Mark Hamill?!? I had to go up to him. I said, "I don't want to bother you, Mr. Hamill. I just wanted to say, you're my hero: The very best version of the Joker of all time in *Batman: The Animated Series*!" He smiled a little and he said to me, "That's not the one I usually get!" Get it? *Because he usually gets Luke Skywalker*!

    I can't remember if I told you, but I'm a film production major and theater minor. I haven't had too many exciting developments in film yet, but I've already got a great theater gig going working for the Royal Shakespeare Company. I'm a personal assistant to these two PBS types you probably know well: Ian McKellen and Olivia Williams. (I think Ian was the villain in the *Scarlet Pimpernel* miniseries you like.) They're touring the states doing a fascist-themed production of Richard III. I just taught Olivia how to use Hotmail, a day or two after I mastered it myself. She's trying out for a role in a Bill Murray movie called *Rushmore,* and we are reading lines together. I've attached a photo of us here. I kinda wish you had come to UCLA and you could've been in the picture with us!

So, I've only been in L.A. a couple of weeks, and — crazy of crazies — I had sex with 3 different women in 1 weekend. Hat trick! I didn't just lose my virginity, I killed it! Get this: I was worried going down on women would taste bad, but it was surprisingly sweet each time.

Gotta run. Olivia wants me to pick up her dry cleaning and Ian wants to do his "Winter of discontent" monologue for me.

Peace Out,

David

P.S.–Have you seen *My So-Called Life*? I've caught a few episodes. I think you'd dig it.

P.P.S.–You need to read the comic book *Hellboy*. I'm getting a B.P.R.D. tattoo tomorrow.

To: DLitvinov@humnet.ucla.edu

From: KirbyAndDitko4ever@hotmail.com

August 30, 1994, 9:11 p.m.

Please give Olivia Williams my name, address, phone number, and this photo of me.

Grazie,

Damien

P.S.–When's *Rushmore* coming out?

P.P.S.–I'll check out *My So-Called Life* soon. There's a comic called *Hellboy*?

P.P.P.S.–That Mark Hamill encounter? The greatest story ever told!

To: KirbyAndDitko4ever@hotmail.com

From: DMargaritis@cortland.edu

August 30, 1994, 5:57 p.m.

Fag boy!

I heard about your first frat party at Geneseo. You're a madman! You need to go out, get drunk, get laid, and stop being a raving lunatic. . . . On the other hand, you're hilarious. Never stop being you.

But please, for the love of God, have some sex already.

Salty

P.S.–If you get an email from David, don't read it. Unless you want to hear his deep thoughts about how good muff-diving tastes and read him bragging about meeting Luke Skywalker and teaching some kinda/sorta hot British stage actress how to use email.

P.P.S.–Me and Kyle are both convinced you're watching *My So-Called Life*.

To: DMargaritis@cortland.edu

From: KirbyAndDitko4ever@hotmail.com

August 30, 1994, 9:26 p.m.

Salty–I'm still getting the hang of this email business. I see there's a feature to block certain people from emailing you. I think I figured out how it works, but I'm not sure.

Can you email me back? If the email bounces, I got it to work. If it doesn't, let's try again.

Hugs and kisses,

Damien

August 29, 1994

My first college lesson was an upper-level course on the complete works of all the Brontës (Branwell included), which I had no business taking as a freshman. Of course, that's why I took it. I was a creature of habit and loved accelerated learning and hanging out with folks a tad older than me. I found myself among fifteen sophisticated juniors three years my senior, sitting at wood-tablet arm-desk folding chairs organized into a large circle, facing one-another. None of these upperclassmen had the callow freshman look found on my fellow first-year residents of Nassau Hall, nor were they afraid of "not getting an A" or "not graduating" or "not being able to afford" Geneseo's dirt-cheap tuition. Instead, these were majors with a passion for British literature and feminist empowerment that was a joy for me to behold. I'd seen this level of enthusiasm for learning among the STEM fanatics I was in ALEC grammar school classes with, but I had never seen so many humanists sitting in one room, driven to explore the same subject. I had finally found my tribe! I made it through the Green Door! Boom!

In fact, I felt so safe and at ease among fellow English majors that I missed the most glaringly obvious detail about the class.

Dr. Zachary McGovern, a white, Brillo-haired professor in tan dress pants and a powder blue, open-collared shirt walked into the room and sat at the empty silver chair in front of the blackboard, at the circle's twelve o'clock position. He looked me in the eyes. "Hi, Damien!"

"Um . . . hi?" I paused. "Have we met?"

Dr. McGovern chuckled. "No, but you're the only one here who could be Damien."

"Why?" The others had figured out what Dr. McGovern was getting at and all laughed. I didn't get the joke and was becoming frustrated. Was my fly unbuttoned? No. It was not.

Dr. McGovern's eyes widened. "You mean you really haven't noticed?"

I looked around again. "What?" There was some more laughter. I tried again. I saw a circle of female students sitting around me, with no other males in sight save for Dr. McGovern and myself. I slapped myself on the forehead. "Oh."

"You see it now?" the professor asked.

I blushed. "I honestly hadn't noticed." Looking again, I saw that the young women in the class were all roughly twenty, came in a wide variety of shapes, sizes, and ethnicities, and radiated intelligence and good humor. Of course, I felt safe and at home. These were my people.

"Do you feel overwhelmingly alone or overwhelmingly fortunate?" Dr. McGovern asked.

Great. Put the freshman and only dude on the spot, why don't you? This was the true no-win scenario. There was nothing I could say now that wouldn't come off as unnatural or immature. It would also determine my relationship with the rest of the English majors for the next three or four years. My best course of action was total honesty.

If I was gonna get in trouble, it should be for how I really felt. "Both. But I'm also disappointed in any male English major who wouldn't take this class. After all, the Brontës are kind of a big deal, right?"

"I think so." Dr. McGovern nodded. "Is this duty, or do you genuinely like the Brontës?"

"I grew up watching the Joan Fontaine and Orson Welles *Jane Eyre* film thirty times. I think that movie is awesome. I thought it was high time I read the book it was based on."

"A very reasonable position," the young woman sitting next to me chimed in. She had shoulder-length hair dyed royal purple and wore contact lenses and a matching dress the same color. She extended her hand. "I'm Sarah," the purple girl said. "Thank you for being here."

I shook Purple Sarah's hand. The more I tried not to blush, the redder I got. "Well, you know . . . Charlotte, right? Charlotte is the bomb!"

Sarah smiled. "Of course. And Anne and Emily."

Since all the literature courses were held in Welles Hall, I only had to walk two rooms down the hall to my next class, which was in a smaller room arranged in a more traditional rows-of-desks-facing-the-chalkboard style. The windows were all thrown open, letting in bright sunlight and the fresh air of the upper quadrangle, currently muddy and dotted with construction vehicles, as it was being renovated. The Beowulf and Old English course was taught by a bearded, frizzy-white-haired Italian man who had taken way too much LSD in the sixties. Dr. Russo introduced the class as being a study in the conflict between matriarchal and matrilineal cultures, represented by Grendel's mother, and the patriarchal, imperial cultures championed by Beowulf. Most of our readings would be in anthropology and archaeology, reinforcing this interpretation of Beowulf, and in linguistics and Old English. Our first assignment would be to memorize the first page of Beowulf in Old English, beginning with, "Hwæt! We Gardena in geardagum, þeod-cyninga þrym gefrunon, hu ða æþelingas ellen fremedon." The wild-haired professor addressed a class of ten male students who enrolled expecting the readings to be macho, blood-and-thunder tales in the vein of *Conan the Barbarian*. They were disappointed the class was going to be more about Grendel's mother than Shield Sheafson.

"Any questions?" asked Dr. Russo.

"Can we write a paper comparing Beowulf to Robert E. Howard's Conan mythos?" a portly young man asked.

"No," said Dr. Russo.

"Can we write a paper about Novalyne Price Ellis?" I joked.

"No," said Dr. Russo. "Though I appreciate your interest in female authors, even if they were associated with Robert E. Howard."

"That reminds me." I put my hands on my hips and regarded the class filled with only male students with mock disdain. "Why aren't you guys in the Brontës class? Too girly?"

"Real literature ended with Chaucer," one pallid-faced boy ventured.

"Why aren't the babes in the Brontë class *here*?" another boy asked, piqued.

"They should be!" I exclaimed. "This is *Beowulf.* How can you be an English major and not take *both* Beowulf and the Brontës? You need *both*, for the love of Dionysus. What is this 'girl literature' versus 'boy literature' baloney? Don't we all just like to read?"

"I don't like books written by women," the portly Conan fan said. "And most of us are history or linguistics majors or anthropologists, not English majors, so get off our backs."

Dr. Russo held a hand aloft and began reciting. "'There is, hidden or flaunted, a sword between the sexes. It is an arrogance in men to call frankness, fairness, and chivalry 'masculine' when we see them in a woman, it is arrogance in them, to describe a man's sensitiveness or tact or tenderness as 'feminine.' But also what poor warped fragments of humanity most mere men and women must be to make the implications of that arrogance plausible.' When the sexes interact as equals and read one another's literature, the sword is withdrawn."

The pallid guy was impressed despite himself. "Is that from Beowulf?"

"C.S. Lewis," Dr. Russo said. "*A Grief Observed.*"

"Lewis?" I asked. "I thought he was the ultimate conservative male."

"He's more complicated than that," Dr. Russo intoned.

After class ended, the pallid boy cornered me. He wasn't angry with me so much as miffed and amused. "Look at you, sounding all noble. I know the girls in that Victorian class you're taking. They're all hot. Must be tough to be you."

I shrugged. "I suppose that's one of the main perks of being an English major."

The pallid boy punched my shoulder. "Don't expect any of them to sleep with you."

"I suppose that's one of the main drawbacks of being an English major."

"Yes." The pallid boy sighed and looked down at his shoes. "Yes, it is."

I forced a smile. "That's okay. I've decided to spend my college career reading the great works of the Harold Bloom Western Canon. That won't leave time to waste chasing around chicks like a cat chases a flashlight. Down with dating! I've retired."

"You make it sound so easy," said the pallid boy. "Not trying to date. I don't think it is."

"Well, I don't know what I've been missing, which means I won't know what I'll be missing. Makes it easier! Booyah!"

The pallid boy decided I was a weirdo and didn't speak to me again. I didn't blame him. My father had joked around with me about all the unnatural conversations I'd had with people over the years. Today's Beowulf conversation was weird, but I was pretty sure that this time I was the loopy, over-the-top presence. I still needed to learn how to talk to new people and not sound like I'm putting on a post-modern vaudeville performance.

The Beowulf class, like the Brontës class, was designed for third- and fourth-year students, but I had sauntered into them both on day one. While most freshmen took core curriculum classes their first semester, I came into the school with eighteen advanced placement credits — which amounted to a semester and change worth of credit hours — that tested me out of Freshman Composition, Introduction to Literature, Basic Italian, Western Civilization I, and Art History I. I had been warned that survey classes were watered down and held in auditoriums filled with seventy-five to one-hundred students, so I wanted to take courses for upper classmen. I took two core requirement classes: The Bible as History, which fulfilled a Critical Thinking Core, and Geology, which served as a Natural Science Core class. The rest of my classes were for the English major. I enrolled in Age of Dante to fulfill a Major Author core requirement, Beowulf for my British Literature pre-Shakespeare requirement, and The Brontës to fulfill my British Literature post-Shakespeare requirement. My disinterest in general survey courses meant I had a deep, graduate school exposure to specific authors, but was not widely read in either British or American literature, and could be a bit stupid about not knowing basic English major texts like *As I Lay Dying* or *To the Lighthouse*. Geneseo education was also designed around teaching primary texts to education majors who were not likely to go on to get graduate degrees, so we did close readings of the traditional core texts of western literature. Thankfully, we were required to take a Multicultural course, and I chose African-American Drama, in which I read *Fences, A Raisin in the Sun, Blues for Mr. Charlie,* "Happy Endings" and "Day of Absence": *Two Plays, The Dutchman, The Colored Museum,* and *The River Niger.* One diversity course aside, the literature curriculum was somewhat old-fashioned in its privileging of New Criticism over both deconstruction and cultural studies, and its focus on the writings of dead, white, European males. I would have to wait for graduate school to catch up on literary theory, which I never mastered, and world and multicultural literature, which I embraced wholeheartedly. Strangest of all, I encountered cultural studies, my favorite approach to understanding narrative, for the first time several years after finishing my doctorate in literature in 2005 at Drew University.

My first day of classes wrapped by 3 p.m., but I felt sweaty and overdressed, so I stopped off in my dorm room to change into more comfortable clothing. On a lark, I put on a novelty t-shirt. Then I headed back to the center of campus to explore my new home more fully. I entered the atrium of the MacVittie College Union wearing a t-shirt that read "George 'The Animal' Steele Loves Miss Elizabeth" in flowery pink script. The lobby was encircled by information tables representing all the different student organizations, making me wish I had dressed differently for the occasion. Funny how these things always catch me flat-footed. I had no idea it was extracurricular group outreach day. I scanned the banners hanging from each table and approached the handful that spoke to me. I went to the Science Fiction club table first because it seemed to be the one least fraught with ideological peril. "Any of the folks in this club like *Doctor Who?*" I asked. The fellow sitting at the table stared at me, without saying a word. His T-shirt read "Ask Me About Cthulhu."

I asked. "I've always wanted to know: Is the 'C' silent, or do you say it?"

Dude kept staring at me, which I found irritating and disconcerting.

I tried again. "H.P. Lovecraft inspired *Ghostbusters?* Interdimensional rift opens and monsters invade our world? Good movie, but is it me, or is Lovecraft horror about the evils of immigrants, squid creatures, and vagina-shaped holes in the air? You know, I gotta say, as an immigrant who loves calamari and women, that stuff doesn't move me. I'll admit, I do like his evil, abandoned town stories, though. Very *Phantasm*. And Barbara Crampton is gorgeous."

Dude kept staring at me. I placed my fists on the table and leaned forward, putting my face an inch from his. "Are you doing recruitment because you're the club's biggest extrovert?"

Dude kept staring at me. "Okay, then," I said, and moved onto the Dungeons & Dragons table. That one was manned by a freckled fellow in a black suit and black goatee, reclining in a folding chair, sucking on the end of a sky-blue hookah. I greeted him cheerily and informed him that I always wanted to try the game, and maybe play a pretty, petite elf who is both an archer and uses a bola. He stopped smoking his hookah and sniffed. "I don't allow my players to play women. Not without giving them huge strikes against them for being physically weak and having to manage a menstrual cycle in the woods."

Taken aback, I placed my hands on my hips, angrily. "Why would I have to be weak? You ever hear of Bêlit, Boudica, Sadie the Goat, or Joan of Arc?"

"What are you gonna use to defeat a Beholder? Your 'Women's Intuition?' Just try it. Roll a d20 and add the appropriate modifiers." He returned to his Hookah.

"Wow." I snorted. "That was obnoxious. Fine. Make me a fasting vampire, like Barnabas Collins. I'm not sure if that makes me 'chaotic good,' or some form of 'neutral.'"

Mr. Goatee shook his head. "A self-denying vampire makes no sense. It is unintelligible."

"And *inconceivable!*" I joked.

"There's no such thing as a 'good vampire.' It is an oxymoron. If there's a Paladin in the band, he'll spend each turn trying to kill you. You would sow discord amongst the party by your very presence. Don't you want to play any useful characters?"

"Listen, I'm Italian and German. That's two-thirds of the Axis Powers. I'm a straight, white, middle-class guy. People like me have been the villains in every novel ever written. I either want to play myself — a vegetarian Great White — transplanted to a fantasy setting, or one of the oppressed: a woman or a Black man. See how the other half lives. Is that okay with you?"

"Are you the sort of guy who would rather flirt with the barmaid at the tavern than begin the quest to fight monsters, thereby miring the campaign in the mud before it even gets started?"

I chuckled. "That's a great idea! I'd love to try that. Think about it. Where is the real adventure? Killing an army of orcs is easy! Talking to the barmaid is hard!"

Mr. Goatee shook his head and resumed his hookah.

"Fine. I'll reread my old Endless Quest and Choose Your Own Adventure books."

I moved onto the InterVarsity Christian Fellowship table. Missy, a striking blonde, looked me over. "What are you, Jewish or Italian? With that nose, you have to be one of the two."

I wasn't sure where she was going with this but suspected it couldn't be good. "Italian."

Missy clasped her hands behind her back. She wore a white sweater, blue skirt, and a plain gold cross dangling over her chest. "I assumed you had to be either Jewish or Catholic. It made me wonder why you would be interested in IVCF."

Wow. So racist I want to kiss her, violently. "The sign says you're ecumenical."

"Members of all the Christian faiths are welcome," said Missy.

"Positively badass!" I gave Missy two enthusiastic thumbs up.

"Catholics aren't Christians," she said in clipped tones.

"Um . . . that's news to me! What are Catholics? Scientologists?"

"Have you taken Jesus into your heart and soul and mind? Have you been saved?"

"Who can know that? I won't know if I'm worthy of Heaven until I face judgement."

"But you *can* know that." She pointed at her heart. "Here. What's your go-to scripture?"

"*The Great Divorce.* Or *The Screwtape Letters.*"

Missy chuckled. "Those don't count. They aren't in the Bible. Pick a Bible book."

"I haven't read much of the Bible. Job? Matthew? Corinthians, Isaiah, and Exodus?"

Missy was still smirking at me, like I was some sort of talking monkey. "What do you think of all those fake branches of Christianity that elevate mythology, ritual, and holy relics, thereby deemphasizing the importance of true faith? Should fake Christian sects be abolished so they don't tempt people into following their sinful example?"

I spread my hands, confused. "I have no idea. I'm Catholic and we don't do that."

Missy laughed uproariously and slapped her knee. Yep. She's religiously intolerant. Probably racist, too. I was so enraged by her dogmatic beliefs that I was becoming insanely horny. I tried not to picture all kinds of angry sex with her. I needed to leave soon. "Are you sure you want to chase away a potential convert like this?" I asked, trying one last time to reach her.

"Goodbye," Missy said cheerfully, waving farewell in my face.

"'Don't say "Goodbye." Say "Good Journey." It is an old Eternian saying. Live the journey, for every destination is but a doorway to another.'"

Missy was confused. "Is that from the *Masters of the Universe* movie?"

"Yes!" I declared. "And that's *my* religion."

Missy rolled her eyes.

I bowed. "It has been a genuine pleasure, milady."

I went to the men's room to wash my face, then slap myself across the cheek three times. "Calm down, crazy man. Let go. Stop with the Miss O'Sullivan fetish bullshit. Stupid moron." I slapped myself a fourth time. "Stop wanting to nail sexy Nazi ladies." To finish up, I gave myself the sharpest slap across the face I could muster — just as another student walked into the restroom. He stopped at the entrance, half in and half out of the lavatory, his hand still on the door. He couldn't have looked more frightened and disgusted by the tableau if he had walked in on a naked Charles Manson singing "Jeepers Creepers" to himself. "Sorry to interrupt." He left.

I looked at myself in the mirror. "Well, that was embarrassing."

After five minutes of pacing around the men's room, I was sufficiently recovered to go back to the courtyard and see if any of the other organizations seemed any less god-awful than the first few I'd given a peak. The next table had a huge banner hanging over it that read: "SEX! Now that we have your attention, please join the GENESEO COLLEGE REPUBLICANS." The skinny fellow standing by the banner had an ineptly tended blonde beard and teeth pointing in every direction. He was the stereotype every liberal had of the nerdy right-winger who was conservative because he couldn't get any action. If he were in a movie, I wouldn't believe he was a realistically depicted character. It occurred to me that my two former art class compatriots probably saw me as a slightly handsomer version of this walking stereotype, and the realization made me angry. These days, I was six feet tall, wore contact lenses, had filled out to two-hundred pounds, and was well-tanned from all the walking I did for exercise that summer. Next to this dude, I was Franco Nero — even with the braces I found myself compelled to get two weeks before moving here. "What do Republicans actually stand for?" I asked him. "I've read two Rush Limbaugh books and listened to his show for a year, and I'm still not sure. He talks a lot about values and patriotism, which I dig. Still, it is poetic-but-empty rhetoric. He also talks a lot of smack about Black people, which I don't dig." The kid with the crooked teeth gave me a brochure that laid out the GOP platform surprisingly honestly and shamelessly: no taxes, strong military, pro-death penalty, anti-gun control, anti-environmentalist, anti-gay rights, anti-sexual harassment legislation, anti-immigration, anti-birth control, pro-ending public education, pro-selling off public lands to big oil, anti-affirmative action, anti-welfare, anti-healthcare, pro-NAFTA, anti-union. *Seeing it all written out here like this, without the distracting word 'abortion' included, and my parish priest breathing down my neck . . . I agree with . . . how many of these?* I started counting how many of the items on the list I instinctively agreed with.

"What do you think?" asked the snaggle-toothed fellow.

"Um . . . I'm not sure why my family votes Republican. We don't agree with too many of these. We like nature and education. We're pro-union, except we think they take us for granted a little. I guess we like low taxes and a strong defense. But some of these other stands . . . anti-immigration? We're Italians, so, we don't hold with anti-immigration laws." I looked up at the fellow. "And you guys want to defund public education while attending a public college?"

"That is correct."

"How's that work, exactly?"

"It isn't as counter-intuitive as it sounds."

"It isn't?" *There's no internal logic to these positions. This platform is as coherent as the plot to* Suspiria. *There's no thematic connective tissue between pro-death, pro-death, pro-death, pro-death, pro-life. At least the Catholic "consistent life ethic" is consistent . . . Wait. I got it.* "Aha! This is the 'What Would John Wayne Do?' platform."

"Correct," said the blonde fellow.

"I liked *Rio Bravo* and *The Cowboys,* but I've always preferred Jimmy Stewart and Robert Ryan. And Burt and Kirk and the Hepburns."

The blonde man gave me a pitying look. "You prefer the apron-wearing Jimmy Stewart to the man who actually shot Liberty Valance?"

"I never saw that movie, so I don't know what you're getting at."

"You're on the wrong side of history. In the end, Jimmy Stewart's womanish values will fall, and John Wayne's will return."

I considered this. "Since I'm Jimmy Stewart, that all sounds pretty awful to me. But thank you for your time." I returned the brochure and took a few steps back to take in the other tables. I didn't know what Amnesty International was. I wasn't the target audience for Habitat for Humanity, Bacchus, women's lacrosse, or the Womyn's Action Coalition. I was an environmentalist at heart but found environmental activism depressing and impossible to conceive of ever getting anywhere, so the Green Environmental Organization was out. Were there other options? I stopped briefly at the College Democrats table. Then I remembered Bill Clinton was president of the United States and how much I hated him. I never wanted to be a part of any organization he was a part of. So…no.

I found myself at the Gays, Lesbians, Bisexuals, and Friends table, wondering why I was there. Other than my awareness of the general handsomeness of Franco Nero, I wasn't gay. I guess, as a "friend," I could make myself useful as an ally? If the homophobes caused any kind of dustup, I could jump in and help these folks out in a fistfight? And they could hide out in my room if they ever felt threatened? I wasn't sure what else I could do to make myself useful. I was eager to help, especially given my affiliation with a church that had an organization like Courage built into it. A pleasantly plump junior with a cherubic face led outreach. He stood from his folding chair, shook my hand, and greeted me with far more genuine warmth and charm than anyone else had. "Hi! How are you, today? Are you interested in coming to a meeting?"

"I'm good. And, yes, I am. I would be a 'Friend,' if that's okay."

"Of course! You'd be very welcome! We're always looking for friends. I'm Victor."

Wow. Is this the nicest person I've ever met? I'm not worth such enthusiasm.

I cleared my throat and avoided Victor's friendly face. "I guess I'm not sure if this club is about dating, or . . . ? Because I'm not really dating *at all*, currently. Or ever, really . . . so I'm a bit of a stick-in-the-mud and not a lot of fun, in many ways. Bit of a downer, really."

Victor placed one hand over his heart, held another up to silence my self-depreciating comments. He nodded sagely with his eyes closed. "Listen, listen. A lot of us feel lonely and unloved. There are two things to remember. Firstly, this is a support group for anyone who feels lost and alone, no matter their sexual orientation. Secondly, there's something you should know: Even people who are not currently sexually active have sex lives. In fact, some of the most erotic people and the most erotic relationships are celibate. As Oscar Wilde said, 'Everything in the world is about sex except sex. Sex is about power.'"

"No shit?" I looked back up at Victor, who was astonishingly empathetic with me, a total stranger. "Oscar Wilde said that?"

"He sure did."

"I guess I need to do more Oscar Wilde homework. A lot of the jokes in *Importance of Being Earnest* just soared over my head. Anyway, the thing you said about celibacy sure is a nice sentiment. I'm not sure if I want it to be true in my case, or if I hope it isn't. I'm going to wind up living my life like Pierre Teilhard de Chardin. I think he had an interesting lady friend situation going." I caught sight of a sign on the table that asked: "How androgynous are YOU? Take our TEST!" I pointed at it. "What's all that about?"

Victor picked a pink triangle pen and a pre-printed sheet up off the table. "You're in luck, then." He asked me a series of introvert/extrovert questions, not unlike the sort I'd encountered taking the MBTI test. I answered instinctively. When we were done, Victor did some rapid calculations. "What do you think you are?" he asked me.

"I have a funny feeling I'm more female than male," I confessed. "I'm expecting 51% female and 49% male, or some such breakdown. I don't know what normal results look like?"

"'Normal'?" Victor winced. "Worst curse word of all time."

"I'm sorry. I'll try to remember to shelve it."

"Aha!" Victor smiled. "You think you might be *slightly* more female than male?"

"Yes."

He pointed to a graph paper chart divided up into four gender quadrants, and my dot appeared halfway up the sheet and pushed over to the extreme east. "This says you are 51% masculine and 90% female."

I didn't understand how the two numbers added up to more than 100%, but I was too embarrassed to ask why they did or exactly what they both signified. Once again, I was finding myself confused by math. "51% masculine and 90% female?" I asked.

"That's what I got for you."

I chuckled. "I wonder if those percentages explain everything about my life to me."

After having a nice conversation with Victor and promising to attend next week's bus trip to Rochester's Little Theater to see *The*

Adventures of Priscilla, Queen of the Desert, I headed back to my room. My triple was empty. Tomo had given me permission to play his video games when he was out, so I spent the afternoon playing *Road Rash 3* on the Sega Genesis. The easy level was too easy for me. I could win the races on my motorcycle with ease. I dialed the difficulty level up to medium and found that no matter how hard I tried, I could not win a single race. *Damn it. This happens when I play computer chess, too. I win one game, the computer figures me out, and I never win again.* I decided the best way to enjoy the game was to ride my motorcycle off road, draw my chain weapon, and kill random cows on the farmland I blasted through. Laughing like a hyaena, I spent the entire race driving on the grass, killing cows. Of course, since I wasn't even trying to win, I lost the race. I never had so much fun playing a video game. I must have murdered a dozen cows. I wiped tears of joy from my face and started a new race.

Sergio appeared at my door. "Yo! Dave Brown! What's all this laughing?"

I glanced up and nodded at him. It occurred to me that Sergio's calculated use of the direct address to curry favor with people didn't quite work when he deliberately got their names wrong as a joke. "Hey, Sergio. Take a seat on the lower bunk. I don't really know who Dave Brown is, so maybe we can lose that nickname?"

"I like it!" declared Sergio.

"Let's make a deal," I said. "You can call me Dave Brown if I can call you Ivo Shandor."

Sergio paused. "Okay, Damien. I won't call you Dave Brown anymore."

I grinned. "Thanks, Ivo."

"*Road Rash 3*!" Sergio exclaimed. "I have the top score in my family. Point of pride for me. I beat my dad, and I never beat him at anything." On screen, my biker avatar whipped his chain through the air and smacked a cow across the face. "What are you doing?" asked Sergio.

"Killing cows," I said gleefully.

"Yes, but that's not how the game is played."

"If the programmers let you do it, then you can do it," I said. I killed another cow.

"Maybe *once*," he complained. "The point of the game is to win races, not kill cows."

"Says you," I giggled. "For me, murdering innocent bovines is the *point* of this game."

A terrified smile spread across Sergio's face. "You're going to at least try to win, right?"

I killed another cow. "Where's the fun in trying to win and losing? More fun to *not* try to win and *kill me some motherfucking cows*."

"But Damien, why would you play a game if you're not going to try to win?" Sergio's terrified smile grew wider, faker, and more desperate.

"Why do anything?" I asked. "I'm convinced I'm never going to get anywhere in this game of life. No wife, no kids, no home, no career, no retirement. The writing is on the wall. I will lose every time. That being the case, I might as well be myself, play the game the way I want to, have as much fun as possible, and kill me some cows!" I killed another cow.

"Are you planning on being a loser and a drag on society?" Sergio asked.

"I'm not planning on it, but nobody is buying what I'm selling," I said. "They're too busy being mean. Have you noticed how *mean* people are? Everyone is convinced they're the only ones who work for a living. *Only they* deserve a cookie. They're so mad that other people expect cookies, too, that they're just assholes 24/7. Me? I know I work hard, but I know other people work hard, too. Frankly, I think we all deserve a cookie! Sadly, none of us will get any cookies, because Bill Gates, Sam Walton, and Donald Trump have eaten them all!" I killed a cow.

Sergio's smile melted away. "Listen, Damien, play the game right or turn it off."

"You're in a guest in my room. You don't get to call the shots here."

Sergio stood up to turn off the system just as the race ended. "Okay, it's over. Don't you dare play another race."

"Okay," I said, only because the game was now, mysteriously, no longer fun. "But I have to save my record." I saved my losses under my new character: *Prince Mamuwalde*. "Guess what my new email handle is? KirbyAndDitko4ever@hotmail.com. I love inventing stupid code names for myself. But what's the deal with the internet? Is it any good? Every time I look at it, all I find is the Internet Movie Database, Hotmail, Amazon, *Star Trek* fan sites censored by Paramount, and fake pictures of Gillian Anderson's head badly photoshopped on random nudes. Is that all there is to this internet business?"

"It's a work in progress," Sergio said. "There's plenty of porn to look up."

"Porn seems violent to me. I saw this website called *The Bang Bus*. It gave me nightmares. I don't want to spend all my time so worried about the women that I can't enjoy the sex, or I won't look up porn anymore. Though I do like being able to look up terms like 'cock ring' on the internet now. Before, I'd have to ask Salty what a cock ring was, and he wouldn't tell me." I spun around and straddled my chair to look at Sergio, who had returned to sitting on the lower bunk. "Now that you've spoiled all my fun, what do you want from my life?"

"Are you serious about not expecting to succeed?" Sergio asked. "Because I have a plan."

"Uh-oh," I chuckled. "I'm so not interested in your plan."

Sergio pressed on. "Our problem is we are middle-class. Women do not go for middle-class guys. Can we agree on that? Women are drawn to power. They like physically powerful working-class guys and financially powerful upper-class guys. Middle-class guys lack either physical or financial power, so they lack sexiness on any level."

"You're saying we're both Mr. Collins from *Pride and Prejudice*? Sounds plausible."

Sergio shrugged because he had no idea who Mr. Collins was. "We'd be better, more virile Italians if we were bricklayers like our grandparents, or if we became cool Italian investment bankers, like the Medici. We need to pick one of those."

"Or both, like Eric Indelicato plans to," I interjected. "He's a friend from grade school."

"Okay. Or both. But your stupid-ass plan is to choose a girl's major and adopt a girl's political and artistic values. For what? To condemn yourself to an unsexy middle-class intellectual life. Why? In the hopes of making yourself agreeable enough that some borderline cute English major might pity fuck you? Or maybe you can get yourself a pliant mail-order bride from Russia who will be your consort in exchange for a green card? This is your fantastic plan?"

I raised a hand. "Excuse me. No. I do not want a sex slave. I'm not Thomas Jefferson. And I do not want to turn some poor woman's life into a *Madame Butterfly* hellscape."

"But your options in life will be limited because of your awful plan to be some sort of underpaid teacher or artist! First off, you're surrendering yourself to liberal indoctrination, giving up on your conservative principals, for what? Unattractive feminists? I've seen the English majors here. Six out of ten, tops. And, since you started out Republican, you will never become liberal enough for these leftist English majors. Liberals eat each other, like piranha. They police each other and pick off the moderates. That's you, my friend: you're morphing into a moderate Democrat! Is there anything less respected or more hated than a centrist? Nobody likes John McCain and Joe Biden! Nobody! And yet, becoming them is your life's ambition!"

"Never heard of them." I snapped my fingers. "Hey! Can I ask you a question?"

"Shoot."

"If you killed someone with a handbag, would it be an accessory to murder?"

Ignoring my attempt to derail the conversation, Sergio looked about the room I shared with Tomo and Mike. Sergio instantly intuited which books and CDs were mine. "Women are your Achilles heel, aren't they? They'll be the cause of your downfall."

I laughed. "Thanks for the warning. You're a little late. They've caused my downfall five times already, yet here I stand. I'm a resilient sonofabitch, and harder to crush than a cockroach."

"Just so you know, these feminists you lust after will never respect you for liking John Denver more than Melissa Etheridge, preferring Dante to Alice Walker, or being a Paul VI Catholic instead of an atheist. That's the beginning and the end of the story. I don't care how many 'correct' opinions you allow these English professors and majors to force down your throat. No feminist you are hot for will ever fantasize about being tied up and raped by you."

"What?!?! I don't know what to be most offended by or complain about first. That—"

Sergio stomped his foot. "Let me finish!"

"Please don't."

"Guess what? You know who would hate you most of all if she ever met you? You know who would think you are just the biggest loser of all time?"

"I don't want to hear it," I warned.

"Emma Thompson." Sergio jerked a finger over his shoulder at the glossy photo on my wall. "I know she's your ideal. Your fantasy girlfriend. Guess what? If she ever meets you, she will have nothing but contempt for you and everything you stand for."

For all his years of teasing me for being square, berating me for being cowardly, and laughing at my eccentricities, Salty never made me so furious so quickly. For all the relentless bullying Tony Nocerino threw my way, there was a "comic book villain," ethnic-stereotype-street-tough quality to him that cracked me up, undercutting my ability to hate him. Also, in some ways, Tony and Salty never really saw into my soul. After knowing me for one day, Sergio had intuited exactly what to say to me to make me want to throttle him. I had never known such rage before. I was so angry, I frightened myself.

I did not know why I became so angry, so quickly. I've talked about this moment with friends since that day, trying to understand it. I like James Sheridan's theory best: "Sergio is like your evil double. He's to you what René Belloq is to Indiana Jones. He's 'but a shadowy reflection of you. It would take only a nudge to make you like' Sergio. 'To push you out of the light.'" I saw in Sergio what I hated in myself. I feared that, deep down, I agreed with all his most reprehensible opinions. If that sort of evil existed inside me, I needed to root it out. On top of that, I really, really, really wanted Emma Thompson to like me. Telling me that Emma Thompson would loathe me was one step removed from telling a six-year-old girl that she will never get another Christmas present because she was the one child Santa despised most. Sergio couldn't have come up with a meaner thing to say to me if he thought about it for a year.

In the meantime, I had no idea what to do with all this anger. It bubbled inside me like lava. The room swam. I knew if I jumped Sergio, I'd unleash something on him I could not control. I closed my eyes. I imagined myself in the dojo with Master Yumi Park. I was safe.

"Are you meditating?" Sergio asked incredulously.

I stayed with Yumi, in my mind, for an entire minute. I opened my eyes. "Women respond positively to men who don't treat them like brood mares. That's my cunning plan from now on. I suspect it will work. And that is why Emma Thompson would not hate me."

Sergio chuckled. "I say you are afraid of life and you are hiding from yourself."

I smiled. "'Americans fear new experiences more than they fear anything. They are the world's greatest dodgers because they dodge their own very selves.' D.H. Lawrence."

"Literature." Sergio chuckled. "You knowing that quote and having two dollars will get you a Häagen-Dazs ice cream cone. Let's face it: what are you even gonna read this year? What even passes for literature these days? *The Color Purple*? Some book written in Ebonics?"

I cleared my throat. "I haven't read Alice Walker, so I can't vouch for her skill-level as a writer, but that last thing you said was way too snooty about Black people, for my taste."

Sergio flashed an evil smile. "Maybe you'll at least read one legitimately great book before you graduate. I hope they assign you *American Psycho*."

"No thanks." I shuddered. "I read the decapitated head scene once by accident."

Sergio clapped his hands together, relishing the graphic memory. "Ha! I *love* that part!"

"You *would*. You may actually *be* Patrick Bateman." I paused. "In other news, if you're interested, I have a response to your question about why I like killing cows more than winning."

"Really?" Sergio leaned forward. "Do you? I just assumed you were defeatist."

"Oh, I *am* defeatist, but I have elevated defeatism to an art form. When society's definition of success is sick and diseased, being a loser becomes a sort of heroism, don't you think? I've never come across a successful person who looks truly happy. I rarely want what they have, if ever. It is just as well, because I never will get what they have, no matter how smart I am. What if I grow up to be funny, kind, religious, selfless, and brilliant? None of those traits translates into success in America because America is an evil country. I will never be successful. I've wanted very few things in life, and the answer has always been 'no.'"

I was only just warming up. Now I was going to unleash upon Sergio. He had asked for it, after all. "This 'no' is usually the result of some borderline arbitrary rule or regulation that has nothing to do with me, personally, but that seems designed by an evil wizard specifically to prevent me from getting what I want. 'Would you like to be in the gifted class and study Italian? Oh, I'm sorry, that's not allowed. If you want to take Italian, you have to leave the gifted program!' What a bizarre rule! What a massive impact it had on my life! What genius came up with that hot one? 'Would you like to go to art school? Sorry, it is only for rich people, and you're working class.' 'Do you like your martial arts instructor? Too bad, her father won't let her teach you anymore.' 'Is this your favorite priest? Would you like to be mentored by him? Sorry, he's only at this parish part-time for one hour a week.' 'Do you like your best friend Mitchell? Too bad. He's dead. God took him.' 'Do you like your father's aunt and cousin? So sorry, they're going into witness protection to hide from your crazy grandmother.' 'Would you like your fellow Italians to treat you as an equal? Sorry, they think you're a bit faggy and a bit intellectual, and they don't understand why you aren't more macho than you are. *Real* Italians are macho.' 'Would you like to date Arwen? Sorry! You can't! Because Hitler. And leukemia.' 'Are you trying to use vaudeville comedy routines to cheer up your clinically depressed family members? That might have worked if they weren't *clinically depressed*, you moron!' I'm always defeated before I even begin by circumstances completely out of my control."

Sergio's frozen smile looked even less natural and his eyes more panicked. "You're referencing events in your life you haven't told me about, but some of those things sound like problems everyone has. I don't think you've gone through anything particularly difficult. Maybe life isn't tough. Maybe you're just soft."

"Just so you know, I'm not crushed. I've never had more fun playing video games than when I killed cows. I was enjoying not playing to win. You're the one who spoiled my fun by asking me why I wasn't trying to 'win, win, win' like the athlete's dad from *The Breakfast Club*. I don't want to try to 'win, win, win.' Why bother? Knowing that the deck is stacked against me and I cannot win no matter what I do is, in fact, very liberating. Until society becomes more human — maybe more socialist, like in the Netherlands — I will fail. It is inevitable. I'm an INFP. Did you know the business community considers my Meyer's Briggs personality type unemployable? *Unemployable!* Why? Because I'm a fucking human being and not a cipher or a cog in the great capitalist machine. You'd think I'd be the *first* one hired by a boss with a real brain in his skull, not the *last*.

"Here's the problem. I'm only a kindhearted, religious, artistic genius in a world that rewards Philistines, warmongers and pirates. I'm Saint Francis of Assisi stationed in the trenches of World War I. On the one hand, I'm exactly where I'm needed most, if anyone needs me to comfort the frightened soldiers or help broker peace. On the other hand, I'm totally useless in the eyes of the generals who just want to press on with the lunatic plan of going over the top. Well, fuck the trenches and fuck going over the top. I'm gonna take a bath, light some candles, and listen to Enya. While America goes to hell in a handbasket, I'm gonna sit back, relax, and have a good conversation with a nice, smart, funny, beautiful woman. That's my goal in life. And I'm not going to treat her as a prize to be won: a bit of No Man's Land to take. I'll treat her as a human being it is my pleasure to spend time with. For an hour or so, I can be her Brother Son, and she can be my Sister Moon. Sitting with her, having cappuccino at an outdoor café discussing Leslie Marmon Silko, I can glean a few moments peace. My platonic friend and Sister Moon will help me steal a few precious seconds of happiness. And then, some asshole corporate suit will barge in on us. He'll berate me for not helping him steal the last remaining American Indian lands for his oil company to drill on. Why? Because that's what life is all about: stealing lands from Natives to drill on.

Anything else is a waste of resources."

Sergio had not listened to a word I said but sat waiting for his turn to talk. He had been on a debate team in school, and he did not want to understand me so much as defeat me in an argument. He was appalled that I could speak so quickly and so passionately, because it meant he had to wait longer before it was his turn to speak. The longer I talked, the more red-faced he got. When I finally said my peace, he leaped on the silence like a panther. "You want me to subsidize your laziness with my tax money? There's socialism for you. I'm not paying for your bath time and your Enya and your flirting with other men's women. Some of us work for a living."

"Oh, that's right," I said. "I forgot. I don't deserve a cookie. You're the only one who works hard, so you're the only one who deserves a cookie."

Sergio slapped his own knee. "Exactly!"

I snorted. "You want me to switch to your major, and you don't even like your major. You *know* its indoctrination with no real learning. You're just gonna mark time and waste four years of your life and thousands of dollars on bullshit. In fact, I guarantee you, the business major is so trivial, you could probably get all the information you learn here in four years in one four-hour human resources orientation on the first day at work. College is going to be transformative for me. You're gonna walk out of this school no different than you do walking in, except maybe you'll get even more conservative. I'm not the one telling you what to major in. You're making a stupid-ass decision and you're trying to get me to make the same one. The business major is a Ponzie scheme. Pick a real major or shut up about mine."

"My fake major is going to make me rich. Your real one will put you in the poorhouse."

I exhaled a long, slow breath. "Will no one rid me of this troublesome libertarian?"

"I'm operating in reality. You're trying to be the change that you wish to see in the world. I'm going to have a far happier life than you will."

I closed my eyes. "Dear God, send me a woman to talk to who understands me."

There was a light knock on my door. I heard the voice of Purple Sarah, my new friend from the Brontës class. "Damien! Me and the girls are going to dinner if you wanna come?"

I snapped my eyes open and looked at Sergio. "This is my friend, Sarah. She's a guest in my room. *My* guest, not yours."

Sarah stood in the doorway between the common area and my room, waving to Sergio.

Sergio stood and walked up to Sarah, examining her like a scientist scrutinizing a fungus. "Aha! Is this one of your new pro-choice, baby-killing English major friends? The ones you'd rather be with than cool business majors, who respect the unborn?" This was only the second day I'd known Sergio, and he was constantly offending my sensibilities, but the sledgehammer subtlety at work here seemed extreme, even for him. Was he speaking in radio-show villain dialogue now? Real people didn't talk like this. If I repeated what he'd just said to my dad, Dad wouldn't believe it. "Nobody actually talks like that," Dad would insist. Incredibly, he would be wrong. I jumped out of my seat and pointed an accusing finger at Sergio. "How dare you talk to my friend like that? Apologize!"

Sarah stepped back. "It's okay. I can go."

Sergio crossed his arms. "Apologize to a baby-killer? Never."

In one, swift, motion, I took three steps to close the gap between myself and Sergio, wrapped my arms about his waist, and lifted him up into the air. "Okay, that's it." I walked him to the suite exit and deposited him in the hallway. I pointed down the passage to the fire exit. "GET OUT! DON'T SPEAK! GET THE FUCK OUT, OR I'LL KILL YOU!"

Sergio was proud of himself for maintaining his cool as I raged. "You're just playing white knight to some purple chick."

"You're god damn right! This woman is under my protection! Get out!"

"You have no conviction and no credibility."

The same insult Tobin used? Weird. These lunatic, right-wing Catholics must have all had the same training in the Rhetoric of Tomás de Torquemada. "You want conviction?" I slammed the door in his face. I turned to Sarah. "He's just some asshole I met yesterday."

Sarah gestured towards the closed door. "I get shit like that from men at least once a day. I'm so used to that kind of treatment I convince myself I should expect it. Worse. I deserve it."

"You shouldn't expect it, and you sure as shit don't deserve it."

"The fact that you reacted that way, makes me realize how unacceptable that kind of treatment is. Also, I'm not used to men speaking up on my behalf. So . . . wow. Thank you, sir."

"I'm just upset I subjected you to him," I growled. "It was an accident. He had a nice suit on yesterday. I didn't think it would lead to this horseshit."

Sarah patted me reassuringly on the arm. "You look like you could use a drink. Let's skip the dining hall and go back to the apartment I share with some more friends from our *Jane Eyre* class. We have a big-ass liquor cabinet. Fun fact: My aunt owns her own bar and she taught me everything I know about mixing drinks."

I smiled with my lips closed to avoid revealing my braces. "Now that sounds like an excellent plan."

Purple Sarah turned thoughtful, which worried me.

I asked, "What is it?"

Sarah touched a finger to her lower lip and grinned mischievously. "Say it again."

I scratched the back of my neck, absently. "Say what again?"

"You know. Say it again." She attempted to imitate my baritone but couldn't pull it off. "'This woman is under my protection.' Say that!"

I blushed. "Oh, I can't. I'd feel weird. Did I really say that just now?"

Sarah laughed heartily. "You sure did. Say it again!"

"Please don't make me—"

She clasped her hands together and blinked Bambi eyes at me. "Please, please, please!"

I harrumphed. "Well . . . okay."

"Yay!" she pumped her fists in the air and jumped up and down once. Then she froze and waited for it, her eyes expectant.

I brought my baritone back out of hiding. "'This woman is under my protection.'"

Sarah laughed and clapped. "Whoo! There it is! Stupendous! I can't wait to tell the others you did this! Let's go have some booze with them."

"Yes, let's! I'm starving and I need alcohol."

Sarah smacked her hand to her forehead. "Oh, no! You're a freshman! Are you under twenty-one? You can't have booze! We should forgo the booze."

"I won't tell anyone if you won't," I said.

Sarah sighed. "I better not get you drunk. I'd wind up cradle-robbing a freshman."

I held my arms out to her, a baby waiting to be picked up. "Please, cradle-rob me!"

Sarah laughed. "Okay, let's go. Assuming that nut isn't lurking in the hallway."

"Now I'm scared to open the door." I poked her shoulder playfully. "Age before beauty."

"Ha! No, please. I insist. I'd like you to have the honor of meeting him first."

It was time to cast a Doctor Strange spell of protection. I formed the "hang loose" symbol with both hands and waved them in circles before the closed suite door. "In the name of Riall, scourge of demons, I command you to be gone!"

I opened the door.

The hallway was deserted.

"Thank Christ," I said, deliberately quoting Chief Brody.

CHAPTER TWENTY-NINE
STD Night

Purple Sarah led me on foot across campus, from my southside dormitory, past the gymnasium and student center, to the edge of campus. We crossed Court Street and arrived at Ambassador Apartments, a collection of long, two-story buildings. She unlocked the chalky periwinkle front door of the first brick-and-aluminum-siding building, then unlocked a second, interior apartment entrance. We stepped into the living room of a four-bedroom apartment she shared with three juniors — two English, one Geography — and at least one hanger-on boyfriend of the Geography major who sorta lived there, too. The four were seated on plush paisley furniture around a glass coffee table, engrossed in a game of Trivial Pursuit while eating bowls of freshly made spaghetti. The CD *ABBA Gold* played in the background. The walls, painted seafoam blue-green, were covered in tastefully arranged posters, vinyl album covers, and paintings, including a portrait of Kate Mulgrew as Captain Janeway from *Star Trek: Voyager*, a map of Middle Earth, a framed concert T-shirt for the Indigo Girls' 1993 *Rites of Passage* tour, a *Cranberries: No Need to Argue* (Coming Soon) advertisement, and a painting of Tonya Harding and Nancy Kerrigan on an Olympic ice rink, fencing with giant-ice-skate-blade-swords.

I did a slight bow at the knees, waved my arm hello at the assemblage, and said, in a voice pitched up two octaves to make me sound less threatening, "Heeeey, how's it going?"

"This is Damien," Sarah said. "I want you to be nice to him."

A saucy redhead with wild, curly hair on her third glass of Sutter Home Red Moscato giggled. "What is he, a Make-A-Wish kid?"

"No, but he's only a freshman, so don't scare him, Ashley," Sarah warned.

"Now you've done it," Ashley joked. "Now I'm gonna eat him alive. Howdy, Damien?" This was the first time I was meeting Ashley, but she would loom large in my sophomore year, when we were both on the staff of the school newspaper, *The Lamron*. In October of 1995, Ashley would write an anti-hazing editorial that related how she personally witnessed the ritualized humiliation of a sophomore outside the Phi Lambda Chi sorority house. Outraged at being singled out as being the worst hazing offenders, and terrified of seeing all their potential recruits for the year driven away, a group of Phi Lambs stole all the copies of *The Lamron* they could find and disposed of them in a dumpster outside of a Wegman's grocery store a few miles away. Ashley was persona non grata on campus that whole academic year, but she had nerves of steel and was happy to take a stand against hazing. To commemorate the incident, my friend James Sheridan, *The Lamron*'s editor, printed novelty t-shirts that read "Top 10 Reasons to Steal *The Lamron*," with #2 being "You are a brainless clod," and #1 "Your sister told you to."

Purple Sarah introduced the couple sitting on the couch, a girl with curly brown hair sitting with a possibly Sicilian American boyfriend: "That's Joe Ferrero, who lives here rent-free. He's a townie, likes to sing 'The Lion Sleeps Tonight,' and collects vintage cars. His girlfriend, Hazel, is the Geography major who *actually* lives here. That's her *Hobbit* map on the wall. She reminds me of Ripley from *Aliens*." I nodded hello. Then Purple Sarah pointed at a blonde girl with long, straight hair who wore jeans and a t-shirt dedicated to something called *"A Song of Ice and Fire" Book One: A Game of Thrones*. "She's Celeste. She talked way too long about how she thought Anne Brontë is criminally underrated."

"Oh, yeah," I said. "You piqued my interest."

Celeste pointed her chin out, defiantly. "*Tenant of Wildfell Hall* is great, if too long."

Ashley peered at me though a drunken haze. "Did I see you talking with that Missy bitch at the IVCF table?"

"She was a real sweetheart," I joked.

Sarah pointed inside her own mouth and mimed puking. "Sexy as she is mean. What were you doing wasting your time with evangelicals? When I think IVCF, I think the Venables."

I shrugged. "I think I'm too heterodox to join any of the clubs that were recruiting in the student union. There was a surfeit of gatekeepers, to boot. Even the Science Fiction Club guy thought I was a bad person for preferring *Doctor Who* to *At the Mountains of Madness*. I did like Victor at the GLBF table, though. He was the nicest person there."

"Victor is the absolute best person on campus!" Celeste proclaimed. "Bar none!"

"I'm thinking of checking out the Newman Community soon. Are those folks cool?"

"They're great," Hazel declared. "I'll introduce you to everyone anytime you want."

"And, if you want to learn sign language, I'm your man," Joe added. "I'm the president of GOHI: the Geneseo Organization for the Hearing Impaired."

"Oh, my mother could probably stand to learn sign language," I mused aloud. "But she doesn't know it . . . "

Sarah gestured dramatically towards me. "And here we have a fellow English major!"

Celeste said, "Speaking of gatekeeping, should we bestow active STD status upon him?"

I leaned closer to Sarah and whispered. "Can I get a translation on that?"

"STD is Sigma Tau Delta, the English major honor society," Sarah explained.

"It isn't really called STD, is it?" I asked.

"Believe it or not, it is," Sarah said.

Buzzed Ashley adopted a friendly teasing voice. "Boy English majors! Boo! They're all the same. They like Arthurian Romance, *A Confederacy of Dunces*, and Cormac McCarthy. They think *X-Men: Days of Future Past* is the best literary work of the last forty years, and always double-major in Film Studies or Philosophy. What's your senior project gonna be about: *April Fool's Day* as the ultimate post-modern slasher movie? And . . . you know . . . Damien, I bet the lion's share of your cultural literacy centers on movies and comic books. I bet you aren't even capable of making a joke based on a famous work of literature!"

Annoyed, I crossed my arms in front of my chest. "'To hell with you, Lady Ashley.'"

Ashley laughed so hard she almost fell over. She lifted her wine high in the air, both to salute me and to prevent it from spilling out all over the beige carpet. "Well played, sir!"

Sarah drew an armchair away from the dinner table and put it beside the coffee table, placing me within the Trivial Pursuit circle. As I sat, she asked me, "You a Hemingway man?"

"Nah," I said. "I didn't like that book. Hemingway seemed to poke fun at the Jewish fellow with the stuffed animal and I'm partial to Jews and stuffed animals. I also hate 'The Snows of Kilimanjaro.' And yet, I'm all about *Old Man and the Sea*, 'Hills Like White Elephants,' and 'A Clean, Well-Lighted Place.' I find him irksome. I love him. I hate him. I dunno."

Sarah eyed me suspiciously. "You don't like Hemingway's anti-Semitism, but you don't mention finding fault with his sexism."

"Why do you think I don't like 'Snows of Kilimanjaro'?"

"Ah," Sarah smiled. "Yes, of course."

Ashley had trouble getting the next question out without laughing wine out her nose. "Yeah, but what about *X-Men: Days of Future Past?*"

"Pretty much the best literary work of the last forty years!" When the round of giggles I was going for died down, I slyly added, "Along with *if on a winter's night a traveler . . .* and *Kindred.*"

"Ooooh," observed Hazel. "See what he did there?"

Celeste raised a hand. "Wait. We're not done. What's your favorite poem?"

I paused. "I have no — wait — I suppose 'Goblin Market.'"

"Why?"

"It's by an Italian, there's goblins in it, and there's a horny part."

This got me the laugh I was looking for.

"*Oranges Are Not the Only Fruit,*" Celeste said loudly, silencing the general chuckling.

"What's that?" I asked.

"*Oranges Are Not the Only Fruit,*" she repeated.

I was confused. This was some sort of code? "They aren't. I like them, but I prefer plums, mangoes, and fuji apples. I eat red, seedless grapes every day. Those are my favorites."

Celeste smirked. "Okay, then. We now know your preference in fruit."

"I only have red seedless grapes after sex," Ashley said dreamily. "I love it when my girlfriend feeds them to me! If it were up to me, everyone would only eat those grapes after sex."

Fare thee well, red, seedless grapes. We meet again in another life. "That was some sort of test? Did I pass?" I glanced over at Sarah for help.

"If you're here to find yourself a girlfriend, you're not gonna get anywhere until you do some more homework." Celeste reached into the bookbag tucked under the glass coffee table, withdrew a book from it, and tossed it to me. I barely managed to catch it without dropping it. "*Written on the Body* by Jeanette Winterson? I'm not sure I have enough estrogen to . . . wait. This looks awesome! We never find out the gender of the main character? How is that possible?"

Celeste nodded. "Technically, Damien, I'm not sure a man is capable of the range of emotions that character exhibits during the course of the book, but it is a pretty successful narrative experiment. To be brutally honest, I'm not sure if a man is capable of having the range of emotions required for him to enjoy *reading* that book."

"Celeste, he's only a freshman," Sarah pleaded. "This is you being nice to him?"

Celeste shushed Sarah.

"Challenge accepted," I said. "I am going to start reading this right away. But how does reading this help make me morally acceptable to Sigma Tau Delta?"

"It doesn't. You have to read it *and* like it."

I raised both my eyebrows, hopefully. "And if I like it?"

Celeste considered this. "I'll give you another book: *A Gathering of Old Men*. Know it?"

"I don't. Funny title."

"And the book is a real knee-slapper," Celeste said.

"Hmmm . . . I bet it isn't, though."

"Are you always this funny and agreeable, or only when you're being cross-examined?" Celeste asked.

"I'll admit I'm putting on a show for you. I want you all to like me. Usually, I'm moodier and as much fun to be around as Louis de Pointe du Lac."

Celeste looked over to Sarah. "I don't mind if he hangs around a little."

Hazel jumped back into the conversation. "Don't let them mislead you by accident. I've been doing a survey in my head and I don't think there *are* any single, straight girls left in STD."

"What about Bree?" Celeste asked.

Ashley yawned. "She's married to her 4.0 average. She'll never date. Boy or girl. Ever."

"Didn't she go on a date with that Déaglán person last night?" asked Celeste.

"'*He* wasn't worth shaving my legs for.' Direct quote from this morning," said Ashley. "I knew that wasn't going anywhere."

I couldn't conceal my disappointment. "There are *zero* single English majors right now?"

Everyone there shook their heads in unison.

I put on an operatically indignant expression to make the next remark into an obvious joke. "Then what good are you?"

"Yeah, we're all in committed relationships just to piss you off," Ashley said icily.

Oops. Maybe not that obvious a joke.

Celeste glanced at Sarah and jerked a finger at me. "This is the same guy who didn't notice he was among a whole class of girls? I thought he was deep."

I looked wounded because I felt wounded. "I *am* deep. I'm also a tad *lonely*, if that's okay with you all. But . . . you know . . . if nobody is looking, then nobody is looking."

"I'm pretty sure they're not," Hazel said apologetically.

I nodded and looked sideways at Ashley. "Sorry if that last joke was out of line."

Ashley stared at me over her wine glass. "Just so you know, I have a big pet peeve about dudes who say things like, 'Chicks won't date me cuz I'm too nice a guy for them, and they only date jerks!' Bitter, phony guy 'friends' will be first against the wall when the revolution comes."

The room fell silent. Everyone was staring at me. Again. *What the hell?* I nodded at Ashley, "I hear what you're saying."

"Climb out of his nose, Ashley," Hazel warned.

I smiled at Hazel but returned my attention to Ashley to do more damage control. "You're right. A wise woman once explained it takes a hundred days and a hundred nights to know a man's heart."

"Yes," said Ashley.

"I'm not looking for a girlfriend. I want to make good friends with good people."

Celeste jumped in. "You want to focus on your studies and get used to being away from home for the first time?"

"Yes."

"Are you telling us you're *not* on the prowl?" Ashley asked, incredulously. "Please. Tell me another one." She laughed at her own sarcastic remark.

I flashed my new braces and pointed at them. "I got saddled with these over the summer, and I'm not excited to ask anyone out while I'm wearing them. After all, I couldn't find anyone to go to the prom with me, and that was before I got these braces. So, heck with it." *And I'm still carrying a torch for someone I've loved since junior high when I shouldn't be, because there's no hope we'll ever get together in the future. So, I'm being a first-class idiot. Arwen kissed me at graduation and I've heard Robert Palmer's "Addicted to Love" and Leonard Cohen's "Hallelujah" in my head on repeat ever since. That kiss was meant to be a 'goodbye,' but I can't stop thinking about it. I keep pretending it was her signal to me that she will find her way back to me someday. All I need to do it wait. I'm transforming into Anne Elliot. "All the privilege I claim for' myself, 'is that of loving longest, when . . . hope is gone.'"*

Purple Sarah cleared her throat. "Before this conversation goes any further, there is something you should all know about Damien. He's the coolest guy on campus."

"What about Victor?" asked Celeste.

"Okay, fine. After Victor." Sarah then related the incident with Sergio that had happened less than an hour before. The story provoked many oaths and expressions of disgust when Sergio's actions were described, and some surprised and approving expressions when Sarah related my role in the encounter. When Sarah was finished, she concluded, "So, I already consider Damien a good friend of *mine*. I wouldn't have brought him here if I didn't think he was cool. I think he could be a good friend of *ours*."

"Are you intentionally using Mafia terminology?" I asked.

Sarah looked confused. "Mafia terminology? What Mafia terminology?"

"Never mind."

Celeste glanced at Ashley. "I know you're worried he's going to wind up being like Littlefinger or Tyrion Lannister, but — after hearing that story — he's exactly like Jon Snow."

Ashley looked at me through narrowed eyes for several seconds before she came to a decision. "Diogenes, put down your lantern! An honest man has arrived!" Ashley stood, placing her half-finished glass of wine on the table. "You're all jerks. Leaving it to the inebriated one to feed this man." Ashley gestured towards me. "You want spaghetti and some wine, or what?"

I beamed. I was hungry, and Italian food sounded particularly comforting and familiar. Also, the conversation had turned back in my favor, thank Christ. "Yes, please."

Ashley paused. "Did he really say, 'This woman is under my protection?'"

"He did, indeed," confirmed Sarah.

Ashley formed a Robert DeNiro inverted mouth and nodded in quiet approval. "I like it. Okay. I gotta get him his fucking food." Ashley stumbled off to the kitchen to fix me a plate of dinner, and Celeste followed to make sure she didn't drop anything.

Joe, Hazel's silent boyfriend, spoke for the first time. "You're doing way better than I did, first time they met me. I got all the interview questions wrong."

"I dunno," I said. "I think I missed a big one. Something about produce. I haven't the first clue why we were talking about oranges and grapes."

"You like theater, Damien?" Hazel asked. "STD organizes an annual trip to the Stratford Festival in Ontario every year. We went last year and got to see some great actors. I don't know if you know Brian Bedford, Geordie Johnson, or Megan Follows? Brian was the voice of Disney's *Robin Hood*, Geordie was Dracula in *Dracula: The Series*, and Megan Follows played *Anne of Green Gables*. We'll be going again to see *Amadeus* and *King Lear.*"

"Dude! I get to see Megan Follows live on stage?"

Hazel's eyes glinted sympathetically. We were copacetic. "Speaking as a big fan of the people of Avonlea, I was pretty pumped to see her myself."

"Sign me up!" I proclaimed.

"It's what college is all about," Hazel said. "Those kinds of trips."

Hazel's boyfriend, Joe, spoke up. "Are you Italian, Damien? What kind?"

"I have ancestors in Naples, Salerno, and Armento."

"Awesome. My people are from Palermo, Corleone, Cherda, and Naples. And County Cork Ireland." Joe proceeded to explain to me that he was a fourth-generation Italian, raised to speak only English. His great-grandparents had been processed through Ellis Island, were relocated to Rochester, and eventually settled in Geneseo on Court Street. Court Street was Geneseo's Little Italy, where grapes and vegetable gardens were grown on long, narrow properties. Over the years, his relatives worked as locksmiths, farmers in Livonia, and railroad workers on the Erie Railroad in Avon.

"And you collect vintage cars?" I asked.

"Oh, yeah!" Joe enthused.

"They're gorgeous," Hazel said. "He's still restoring a couple, but it is wonderful to watch them all coming together."

"What models?" I asked.

"A red, 1947 Oldsmobile Model 76 two-door fastback; a two-tone green 1948 Oldsmobile 4-door sedan; a baby-poop-green 1970 Chevy Nova, and a yellow 1976 Buick Electra Limited. The '48 was my first car. I got it when I was sixteen after saving up all summer working as a projectionist at the Riviera."

Distracted by his use of the phrase "baby-poop green color," I realized I was still getting a sense of Joe's easy charm and off-kilter sense of humor. "Where do you store them all? I have a hard-enough time housing my comic books and movies!"

"No kidding! My parents said, if I stay at home and saved on dorm fees at college, that I could build a four-car garage there for the hobby. And it happened! They just finished it!"

Celeste whispered behind her hand into my ear. "This is why he *unofficially* lives with us and won't go home."

"I heard that," Joe laughed, amiably.

What do you know? A nice Italian guy! I like him. "And you sing 'The Lion Sleeps Tonight' a lot? That was a very specific detail."

Joe beamed. "I sing lots of songs a lot. I like to cheer people up with jokes and songs. I know a lot of depressed people, so it is my way of bringing sunshine to the world. I most like to sing 'Lydia the Tattooed Lady,' by Groucho Marx." Unprompted, he began serenading the room, until Hazel patiently asked him to trail off before the end. As I suspected, if I sometimes blew people over with the force of my personality the way Winnie the Pooh did Rabbit, then Joe could easily have that effect on me, playing Tigger to my Pooh. This was not a bad thing, in any way. I liked it, in fact. I was also genuinely surprised by how much we appeared to have in common. "A Groucho Marx fan, too? I feel like we're the same guy, only you like cars more than I do."

"I think we may have been separated at birth," Joe agreed. He glanced at Hazel. "I like him because he reminds me of me. Does that mean you like him? It would stand to reason."

"Don't hog him," Hazel warned. "I want to show him my maps. You've already got all your car collector buddies!"

"Okay, fine. I'll let you hang with him. Sometimes."

"I was just going to ask you if you liked Tolkien," Hazel said to me.

"I'm all about Bilbo Baggins," I declared.

Purple Sarah moaned. "No! If you two are gonna start talking ad nauseum about Vala Yavanna, Beren and Lúthien, and the War of the Wrath, you can count my ass out."

I was mystified by everything Sarah said, because I hadn't read *The Silmarillion.* "I don't know about any of that. I just think Smaug and Gollum and the giant spiders are really cool."

"Tolkien helped me get into maps," Hazel said.

"That's cool. Makes total sense."

Ashley appeared with my plate of spaghetti and an enormous goblet of red wine.

"Whoa, that's a glass of wine!" I exclaimed.

"We're all hammered, and you have catching up to do," said Ashley.

I reached for the goblet and stopped. "I'm supposed to warn you I'm underage."

"Underage, schmunderage. Where I come from, this is called hospitality. And don't go getting any ideas. I'm not trying to get you drunk." Ashley displayed her Claddagh Ring after she handed me the glass. "You've met my girlfriend." She inclined her head towards Celeste.

Celeste stood, did a slight bow at the knees, waved her arm hello at me, and said, in a voice pitched up an octave to make her sound especially friendly, "Heeeey, how's it going?"

I looked at Sarah. "Is that really what I'm like? She made me look really cheesy."

Sarah chuckled. "Celeste is the queen of mimics. She has you cold already."

I threw my arm over my eyes, a stricken Greta Garbo. "Oh, no! I'm cheesy!"

Purple Sarah placed a reassuring hand on my shoulder. "Don't worry about it! Some of my best friends are cheesy."

I tipped the entire glass of wine down my throat. "Please, may I have some more?"

"Already?" Ashley chuckled. "Wow."

"Keep it coming. It's to help me grow a sense of humor about myself."

"That's the spirit," Ashley declared.

"I'm sorry you didn't like my impression," Celeste sulked.

"It was wonderful. That's why I need to grow a sense of humor. I blame sixth grade for making me boring."

Celeste sighed. "Whatever they did to you in sixth grade, I'm sorry."

"It wasn't you, but thank you all the same," I said.

Before heading back to the kitchen to bring out more wine, Ashley glanced at her roommates sitting about the coffee table. "Should I come back with my ceremonial knife?"

Purple Sarah raised a Black Power fist in the air. "I was going to suggest it."

"Bring it!" called out Celeste.

"I'm not Wiccan, but I'd like to participate," Hazel said. "I think Joe will, too."

"Are we doing sexy witch stuff?" Joe asked, wiggling his eyebrows like Groucho Marx.

Ashley left to get me my wine, plus this terrifying ceremonial knife thing. I looked again at Hazel. "You're participating in–?" I was really asking her what was about to happen, but Hazel answered a different implied question by saying, "I live to support my wonderful and eccentric friends." Hazel was soft-spoken, but when she said things, they carried a lot of weight.

"A rare, wise trait," I said. "You're like my friend Mitchell: A real mensch."

"She is also supportive of her wonderful and eccentric boyfriend!" Joe exclaimed.

"Yes," Hazel agreed.

"These Sigma Tau Deltans seem cool. How do the Newman folks compare?" I asked.

Hazel considered this. "You'll like them. Not *all* heterodox, but big-hearted people."

"Phat," I pronounced. "Who needs TKE with Hazel and her peeps around?"

Celeste punched the table in mock rage. "Down with TKE! Up with STD!"

Ashley arrived with my new glass of wine and an athame, a black-handled ceremonial blade. "I'm being a bit blasé about this, since I'm three sheets to the wind, but I'm thinking we should invite you into our STD circle with some cool pagan shit. If that isn't too weird for you."

I raised both my eyebrows. "But you just met me! I could be the new Son of Sam, for all you know." I slipped into an imitation of Dana Carvey imitating President George H.W. Bush. "Inviting me into your coven just wouldn't be prudent! Not gonna do it! Wouldn't be prudent!"

"Didn't you hear me call the question just now?" Ashley asked. "We all voted unanimously to initiate you. You did too well being super impressive just now."

"Wow," I breathed. I was not used to being treated this well.

Ashley dropped back into her old chair. "In all seriousness, Damien, I want to thank you for being a stand-up guy to my chum Sarah here. And I want to make a nice new freshman feel welcome in Geneseo and the English major. Besides, I am very against hazing freshmen and all other abusive, patriarchal bullshit, so, we're not going to make you jump through hoops for a whole year just to prove to us you're worth our time. That's not how we roll."

Joe wiggled his eyebrows again. "She's so hot when she talks feminazi, right, Damien?"

Ashley ignored Joe. "And aren't you far from home? You need a new family here, don't you? What's your accent? Brooklyn? That's six hours drive from here. You're alone out here."

"I'm from Staten Island."

Ashley nodded. "Long Island. Of course. I knew you were from New York City."

"Staten Island is the fifth borough," I corrected gently. "It's what Woody Guthrie meant by 'the New York Island.' He shouldn't have tweaked the lyric. 'Staten Island' is easier to sing."

Celeste looked confused. "Staten Island? Never heard of it. I know Long Island."

Hazel shook her head, smiling. "I'm from Long Island, knuckleheads. He's from Staten Island. They're two different places."

"Whatever. Welcome to the rest of New York. Are you willing to enter our circle?"

"I would love to join your cult," I beamed. "It has been my lifelong ambition to join a circle of cool people. I will finally get to see what's on the other side of the Green Door!"

"And here you are. I'm now going to call the quarters." Ashley pointed the knife to the four points of the compass, evoking the four elements and the guardian spirits, before returning her attention to me. "To quote Adriana Porter's 'Rede of the Wiccae,' 'Bide the Wiccan laws you must, in perfect love and perfect trust. Live and let live. Fairly take and fairly give.' If you are to join our circle, you must do so with an attitude of 'perfect love and perfect trust.'" Ashley raised the point of the blade to my chest. I drew back as if a cobra had leaped towards me. Ashley admonished me with her finger. "Ah! Ah! Come closer." I smiled nervously and allowed the blade to touch my shirt. Not for the first time that evening, I was glad that I had taken the time to change out of my George the Animal Steele shirt into a salmon-colored, button-down dress shirt over black slacks.

"I'm now going to quote the First-Degree Initiation passage from *The Gardnerian Book of Shadows*." A burp got caught in Ashley's throat. She punched herself in her chest and it popped out. "Excuse me."

"You *are* drunk!" Celeste barked a laugh. "That was gross."

"Shush! Don't spoil the mood. Okay, okay. Here we go. 'O thou, who standeth on the threshold between the world of men and the domains of the Vagina Americans' — I'm sure you can tell I made that part up because I like the sound of 'Vagina Americans' — 'hast thou the courage to make the assay? For I tell thee verily, it were better to rush on my weapon and perish miserably than to make the attempt with fear in thy heart.' So, now I'm going to ask you how you approach. You know what you have to say, right?"

Wow. She could do all that from memory? Drunk, to boot? I had no idea but ventured a guess. "'I am proud to pass through the threshold into the domain of the Vagina Americans'?"

"No, you idiot! 'I come to you with a heart filled with perfect love and perfect trust.'"

"Oh!" I exclaimed. "Of course. Excuse me. Well, that's a very nice sentiment, isn't it? I'd have no problem saying that. Jives quite well with good old Saint Francis of Assisi. You can all be my Sister Moons." Ashley nodded in agreement and gestured at me to stop jawing and get it over with. I adopted a more serious tone and said, "I come to you with a heart that was once made only of cigarette-ash but is now filled with perfect love and perfect trust."

Celeste pretended to be scandalized. "He ad-libbed ceremonial language!"

Ashley pursed her lips, thoughtfully. "I like it. I'll take it."

Joe chose that moment to whisper to Hazel. "We're not going to go to hell for participating in this, right?"

"Nah." Hazel shook her head confidently. "Don't worry about it."

"You may well ask," continued Ashley, "what our rules and regulations are."

"Uh-oh," I said.

"We have only one rule here, and that is that there are no rules. After all, we are all good people here, and good people are not inclined to be cruel to one another. We need no rules to keep us honest. As

Rabelias wrote, 'Do as thou wilt because we that are free, of gentle birth, well bred, and at home in civilized company possess a natural instinct that inclines us to virtue and saves us from vice. This instinct we name our honor.'"

"That is also why we are not into gatekeeping in quite the same way as other groups," Purple Sarah said. "All we want is nice people around us. The rest takes care of itself."

Ashley put the dagger down on the coffee table, next to the Trivial Pursuit board. "Welcome, Damien! Welcome!" she screamed, throwing her arms around me and giving me a wet, drunken, lipstick kiss on the cheek. "We are proud to have you among us."

"Thank you so much." I went from being startled at getting tackled without warning, to aroused by the hug and kiss, to deeply moved by the sentiments of sisterly affection, friendship, and bibliophile solidarity. I felt all these things in the span of a second. My eyes filled with tears.

"Listen, don't turn out to be a dick," Celeste joked. "Remember, we have that dagger, and we know where you sleep."

"Ha!" I laughed, wiping the tears from my eyes. "Nothing like a Lorena Bobbitt joke."

Celeste jumped on me next, giving me a lipstick-free kiss on my clean cheek after seeing the wet mess Ashley had left behind on my other cheek. Joe and Hazel took turns hugging me next. Then we all sat down again, and I realized I hadn't eaten my dinner yet.

"That was intensely cool," I said.

"I like watching them do that ceremony," Hazel said.

Ashley smiled. "I love Calling the Quarters. It makes me feel all witchy."

"Yeah, that was dope," I agreed.

Suddenly, no one knew what to say.

Purple Sarah cleared her throat. "I have a question. What do we do next? Once me and Damien finish our pasta, that is? Do we crash your Trivial Pursuit game . . . "

"You're welcome to join," Celeste said.

Sarah gave a thumbs up, adding, " . . . or do we move the furniture against the walls, and throw a mini rave in this apartment?"

"Dance to Technotronic, Erasure, Pet Shop Boys, and Depeche Mode?" asked Celeste.

"You can be the DJ," said Sarah. "I know you want to be."

All eyes turned to look at me.

"Do I get to dance in the circle with you?" *Will this be me, finally "going to the prom"?*

"Of course, silly," Ashley said. "And you can dance with us individually, too!"

"Yeah? Okay, then!" I downed my second full goblet of wine. "Let's have a rave!"

INTERLUDE II

On June 9, 1996, two notable wedding announcements appeared in *The Staten Island Chronicle*:

Dazzo-Indelicato

Marina Catherine Dazzo wedded Eric Salvatore Indelicato during a mass at Our Lady of Pity R.C. Church, Bulls Head, on June 8. The bride, a resident of Bulls Head, is a freelance flute player who has performed on Broadway for *Love! Valour! Compassion!*, *Blood Brothers*, *Smokey Joe's Café*, and *Show Boat*. She is a graduate of Fiorello H. LaGuardia High School of Music & Art and Performing Arts and is studying flute at Manhattan School of Music. The groom, a resident of Grasmere, is a day trader and a business major at Baruch College. He is a graduate of Grace Coolidge High School, Willowbrook.

Battaglia-Pokatny

Arwen Undómiel Pokatny married Sonny John Battaglia at the Unitarian Church of Staten Island, Stapleton, on June 8. The bride, who is keeping her surname, is a resident of Todt Hill, owner and operator of Pokatny Confections, Great Kills, a biology major at Wagner College, Silver Lake, and a graduate of Grace Coolidge High School, Willowbrook. The groom, a resident of Park Slope, Brooklyn, is a Senior Financial Analyst at Cantor Fitzgerald, and a graduate of Princeton University. The bride would like to honor the family members she has lost by offering remembrances for her mother, the former Margaret Walsh, who died in 1978, as well as her father, David Pokatny, step-mother, Eve (née Monash), and step-sister, Miriam, who died in American Airlines Flight 965 crash in Buga, Columbia, on Dec. 20, 1995 . . .

CHAPTER THIRTY
Lost in Siena

January 5, 1997

As the Alitalia flight made its final descent towards Leonardo da Vinci International Airport, I gazed through the airplane window down on a green vista that presented the illusion of a country untouched by industrialization. I had taken in lovely rural landscapes before: on one of my epic commutes between Staten Island and Geneseo, I was astonished to see a perfect rainbow cresting over farmland and livestock off the side of the highway after a heavy rainfall. I had thought rainbows only existed in Lucky Charms commercials, not in real life! Still, this was the grandest green tableau I'd ever witnessed. The contrast with the bird's-eye-view from the puddle jumper that took me from Newark Airport to Boston Logan International Airport on the first leg of my journey overseas could not have been greater. I had seen the usual factory smokestacks belching greenhouse gases into the air off the New Jersey Turnpike.

I took a photo of the gorgeous Italian landscape through the plane window, but the layers of plexiglass and the cloud covering that had crept into view meant I would likely be disappointed in the quality of the photo after I had the film roll developed. I lowered the camera and looked again, deciding to photograph the view with my memory instead of on film. I was surprised how moved I was by the scene. Perhaps I was experiencing the real-life equivalent of the wonder humans experienced taking their first trip through time and space in the TARDIS on *Doctor Who*. As the Doctor asked Ian Chesterton, "If you could touch the alien sand and hear the cries of strange birds . . . and watch them wheel in another sky — would that satisfy you?" *Yes. It would.* This was the trip I had been waiting to take all my life. I had finally escaped from the grime and endless class wars and racial strife of the tri-state area to see my homeland, beloved the world around for its beauty, food, and hospitality. I was a world-traveler, like my mother.

The plane landed smoothly. The long line to disembark was as boring as you would expect. I was relieved when I was able to retrieve my one large roller suitcase from the baggage claim without incident, and reunited it with my two carry-ons. The airport felt like any other airport I'd been in, but was granted an exotic quality by its liberal use of international languages on signage and the presence of machine-gun-toting uniformed security with bright red stripes running down their pants legs. I knew I was supposed to feel safer by their presence, but there's a reason pictures of these fellas tend not to make it onto "Italy is for Lovers" travel brochures. Somehow, without any of our passports being checked, the seven of us students and our two professor chaperones emerged from the airport onto a modern, urban-looking street that could have just as easily been in Baltimore or Boston. Where the lush greenery I'd seen from the sky went was anyone's guess.

"I'm not liking this," said my roommate, Byron Baldwin, who had never spent much time in cities of any kind, as he had grown up in the world's smallest village in western New York.

"Dr. Valancourt will get us all safely to Siena," I reassured him. "The man is as efficient as a well-oiled machine."

"The man looks like Admiral Ackbar," Byron grumbled. As I suspected, Valancourt had done something to annoy him when we had all met up at the departure gate of Boston Airport to take the same international flight together. Hopefully, it was nothing of consequence.

"Ha! Mean but funny. I always thought he looked like Don Knotts."

"Exactly. He looks like Don Knotts and Admiral Ackbar at the same time. Wait. Check that out." Byron pointed up at a ribbon-shaped flock of black birds soaring through the air in formation, cresting in the sky like a wave. An avid birder, Byron let enthusiasm creep into his deadpan voice. "Every October, a million starlings migrate from Northern Europe through Rome, in formations like this. That's an impressive sight, considering their droppings are a huge problem." I tapped my hair and shoulders, searching for bird poo I imagined feeling. Byron laughed and reassured me that I had not been strafed yet.

In many ways, Byron was my ideal fellow traveler. He was eager to see the world and expand his horizons well beyond the scope of his small-town childhood, and to cultivate a more polished and sophisticated taste. I may have been a suburban kid, but I had the same goals he did. Also, while he was a Business and Music Composition double-major in Air Force ROTC, he was a history buff who knew and liked the two humanities teachers in charge of our trip.

Our guides were the grey-haired, manic history professor Dr. Leland Valancourt and his sandy-haired assistant with the winning smile, Taran Prine. Prine was a former student of Valancourt's and had taken undergraduate courses with the medievalist the year I was born. Now middle-aged, Prine worked simultaneously as an adjunct (teaching Italian, Latin, and humanities classes) and director of Geneseo's Study Abroad Office, as well as lay minister assigned to the Newman Community. It struck me that, with an M.A. from St. Bonaventure, Taran was able to cobble together a full-time position doing everything he loved most at the college he adored without earning a doctoral degree or securing a traditional tenure-track job. I found his life path inspiring. I also never failed to be impressed by his appetite for living life to the fullest. The man was always laughing and smiling and outgoing, even as he enjoyed taking the piss out of everyone and everything. His charisma would even lead him to becoming Geneseo's Town Coordinator, a mayor in all but name, a few years after I graduated. I knew Taran through all his roles, since he was my hippie minister, Italian professor, and guide through Italy all-in-one. We were as much friends as anything. Byron had an equally friendly rapport with Taran, which he had developed while taking Taran's literature course, Arthurian Romance. We saw Taran as that rare breed: an adult male worth emulating. He was the Renaissance man — husband, father, teacher, and flower child shaman — we both wanted to grow up to be like.

The seven American undergraduates abroad, Byron and I included, were in Italy as students in "Medieval Italian City States," a one-month-long course in January's Winterim Term, sandwiched between the four-month Fall and Spring semesters. We were quite a motley crew. In addition to Byron and myself, there was "Bongo Guy," who spent each snow-filled winter at Geneseo living in an igloo of his construction behind Monroe Hall, playing the bongo on the grass all day and smoking weed inside the igloo all evening. (Someone once told me his name was Reed Poncemby, but to me, he would always be Bongo Guy.) The others members of our group included three familiar faces

— Purple Sarah, Bobby Mammolito, and Tuesday Phapant — and a mysterious blonde super senior laden with luggage. Bobby, Tuesday, and I were the only three people from Grace Coolidge High School who had chosen to go to Geneseo instead of the obvious alternatives: an Ivy League, any other SUNY, Rutgers, Wagner College, or the College of Staten Island. When I caught sight of them in the Red Jacket Dining Hall my first week as a freshman, I had been upset to see them. Their presence made it clear that one never could escape one's past, no matter how many miles one fled from it. And yet, they were nothing but nice to me these days, so I didn't find that spending copious amounts of time with them in Italy triggered as many bad memories as I expected.

Once we were gathered in a circle of nine across the street from the airport entrance, Dr. Valancourt was poised to launch us into our long journey to Siena. Taran managed to stop him by offering his old mentor a friendly reminder that we were nervous kids in a foreign country. "Would you like to say a few words to the troops, Dr. Valancourt?"

"Ah, yes, of course, of course." The little man, who Byron saw as Admiral Ackbar and I thought of as Don Knotts, recovered quickly from embarrassment. "We are going to be moving through a number of steps, on foot, by train, and by bus or cab to get to Siena. It will be intense. Thankfully, the most beautiful city in Italy lies waiting for us at the end of our journey."

Taran grinned. "The most beautiful city *in the world*."

Byron and I exchanged glances. *Taran's usually right about things, but . . . really?*

Without looking again at Taran, Valancourt cleared his throat. "Okay, let's get a move on." He huffed past me and walked with purpose, since he'd taken this route dozens of times.

Dr. Leland Valancourt was an aging gay Indianapolis native who had a penchant for fluorescent cowboy clothes and was never seen in public without an open can of Diet Pepsi clutched in his left hand. A medievalist who often co-taught interdisciplinary courses such as "Age of Dante" with my favorite literature professor, Dr. Herzman, Valancourt idolized St. Francis of Assisi and regularly attended mass at the Newman Community with his elderly mother. The pair sat with Dr. Herzman and his wife in the front row. Valancourt and Herzman were a reassuring presence at the Newman masses, proving that not all liberal college professors were "godless heathens filling young skulls with mush," as Rush Limbaugh proclaimed. I also thought it was cool that Valancourt and Herzman took Communion each week from Taran.

During the 1996 election season, Valancourt ran for Congress as a moderate Democrat, hoping to champion funding for infrastructure, healthcare, and education if he won. Since he was pro-life and had no interest in guns one way or the other, Valancourt ran as an anti-abortion Democrat with a grudging NRA endorsement. These political positions, which did not endear him to his feminist colleagues, helped me further nuance my blinkered view of Democrats as being part of a monolithic hive-mind, as Limbaugh had falsely claimed they were. As a moderate, Valancourt won me over, as well as a noteworthy percentage of the rural Republicans he courted. My support was mostly moral support, as I was not registered to vote in Geneseo. Unfortunately, Valancourt's awareness of my Republican Party affiliation was occasionally cause for friction between us. For example, when I took his Humanities course, I had a legitimate question about our homework that he was too skittish to answer because he didn't quite trust me. Perhaps it was because, over-the-top as he was, Valancourt could not, for the life of him, get a handle on my sense of humor, which vacillated between dry wit and loud, unsubtle hyperbole.

"Hey, Dr. Valancourt!" I yelled, bursting into the classroom as if storming Atlanta. "I just finished reading Thomas More's novel *Utopia* and I'm confused. Socialist science fiction? There's a shock! Are we sure this is the same dude from *A Man for All Seasons?* I don't remember him being a pinko in *A Man for All Seasons!*"

Valancourt's poker face was hard to read. "Are you a spy for my Republican opponent?"

"Aw, come on, Dr. Valancourt! I'm asking a real question, here. I just don't understand what he's going for with this book. Is it all about his opposing the enclosure movement?"

"Because you *sound* like a spy."

"Fine. Be too scared of me to teach me. I'm going back to my

FAKE ITALIAN • 457

dorm room to watch *A Man for All Seasons*. Robert Shaw is in it as Henry VIII. He was also Quint in *Jaws*."

Ultimately, Valancourt lost by six points instead of the usual forty-point trouncing Democrats took in the very Republican district. He should have won. His opponent was a tool.

None of our other talks were as awkward as the one about *Utopia*, but we never had an entirely smooth or casual conversation. Our exchanges were all business and no chit-chat. I would ask him specific questions about the homework for the lesson at hand, or to provide me with a post-mortem of one of my papers, which he invariably gave a B+ to no matter how much research I did or how many times I rewrote it. However, I did succeed in talking one quiz grade up to one hundred. In *The Bible as History*, Valancourt assigned a quiz on the two Creation stories in Genesis, asking us to read them as historians and individualist student-scholars, not as ideologically motivated members of oppositional faith communities. In other words, we were supposed to answer the questions using what the Bible actually said and not what our priests, ministers, or atheist buddies told us it said. For example, we couldn't refer to the serpent as Lucifer, since it was only identified in the text proper as a talking snake. This was a Genesis quiz, after all, not an exam on Milton's *Paradise Lost*. The first quiz question was: "According to Genesis, what part of Creation came first?" In a class of seventy-five, seventy-four students wrote "Light," and got the question right. I was the only one who wrote "Water" and got the question wrong. After class, I walked down the flight of steps to Valancourt's lecture-hall podium, armed with my quiz and Revised Standard Version Bible. "Dr. Valancourt, water existed before light. The very first lines of the Bible are: 'In the beginning when God created the heavens and the earth, the earth was a formless void and darkness covered the face of the deep, while a wind from God swept over the face of the waters. Then God said, "Let there be light"; and there was light.' Note the words 'deep' and 'waters.' God must have created the water *before* the first sentence of the Bible. Genesis begins with the work of Creation *in progress*. Ergo, my answer is correct." Valancourt changed the grade to 100 on both my paper and in his gradebook, muttering, "Fine. Never do that again." His tone somehow combined grudging respect, surprise, annoyance, and gentle teasing. I was proud of my victory but concerned about what Valancourt really thought of me. More than anything, I wanted his approval and respect, but I would settle for him liking me a little. I wagered I was giving off a whiff of skunk-stench neediness.

Our final, major disagreement over close readings of religious studies texts again came in The Bible as Literature, where I found myself objecting to Dr. Valancourt's embracing of "the historical Jesus." Valancourt told the class about the Jesus Seminar's conclusion that the sentence in the Bible that most epitomized the real Jesus' worldview was, of all things, "Render unto Caesar that which is Caesar's." He appeared to endorse the analysis. While taxes and tithes had far greater significance than I wanted to admit, the middle-class American male's never-ending whining about paying taxes had put me so off the subject that I never wanted to hear anyone talk about taxes ever again, even if Jesus himself supported my view that paying taxes was good for society. I was also irritated that members of the Jesus Seminar seemed keen to dismiss my favorite Jesus teachings — his protofeminist lessons and actions — as ahistorical myth-making by the author of John's Gospel. The Jesus Seminar scholars seemed united in the view that "John" was a less historically reliable writer than the crafters of the synoptic gospels, "Matthew," "Mark," and "Luke." These ideas were undeniably interesting, but they pushed my buttons. I expressed my displeasure in my paper on *Jesus: A New Vision,* and my immoderate tone earned me my usual B+ from Valancourt. After getting the grade back, I asked to talk to Valancourt about what I needed to do to finally get an A from him. His said I needed to adopt a more serious tone and a writing style fit for college. I should use less flowery English-major language, eschew humorous asides, and employ greater, more fastidious attention to historical detail. He was correct on all these counts, of course. Still, I wanted to reassure him that my slightly emotional reaction to the text was justified.

"I just don't get what Marcus Borg is going for, Dr. Valancourt!" I said too loudly, not out of anger, but a general Italian American loudness that didn't sit well with Valancourt's Midwestern temperament. "I'm used to people believing in *all* the miracles in the Bible or in *none* of them, or in the historical truth of *all* the Bible stories, or *none* of them. Why does Borg only believe the healing miracles and not the cooler ones, like the water into wine? Why does he only believe in the stories from the synoptic gospels? He's splitting hairs. What if John had access to sources or witnesses the others didn't?"

"You know, Damien, I think you're being a little hard on poor Marcus Borg. *Jesus: A New Vision* is a very respected text."

I nodded. "Sure. I'm taking to heart a lot of what he writes, even though it upsets me. I'm still processing the idea that Jesus is a hippie who would find me too stodgy if he met me. Still, I'm willing to go with that and do some serious self-reflection about my being kinda a Pharisee. Here's my problem: Borg says the scene in John's Gospel between Jesus and the woman by the well isn't factually true. Neither is the scene when Jesus prevents the stoning of the adulteress."

"Correct."

"But those are the two best Jesus stories, bar none!" I recalled the lines I liked so much in "the woman by the well" story: "Just then, Jesus' disciples came. They were astonished that he was speaking with a woman, but no one said, 'Why are you speaking with her?'" I did not remember the words verbatim, or that they appeared in John 4:27, but I recalled the gist of the passage accurately, and related it to Valancourt. "That is not an isolated passage or incident, Dr. Valancourt. In the Bible, Jesus exhorts his followers not to objectify women. From his words and deeds, readers learn that we should listen to women when they bring us news, even if we find that news hard to believe. Easter is an obvious example of that moral lesson. The woman-by-the-well conversation implicitly demonstrates that men should be able to talk to women in public without it being scandalous because she 'belongs' to another man, or because it is always assumed that the only reason a man would talk to a woman is to seduce her. What subversive, compassionate messaging! I want to treat women like that. As Jesus would treat them. But a historical reading of the Bible throws all that out the window. I guess I am a literature major after all, because I don't need a story to be *literally* true for it to be 'true.' Jane Eyre doesn't need to be a historical figure for me to love her. I feel the same about magical, proto-feminist Jesus. Both of them will always be more real to me than President James K. Polk. Lisa Simpson is more real to me than Polk, too, for that matter."

Valancourt had tuned out some of what I said because I spoke for too long and with too much emotion. He chose his words carefully, striving to be patient. "Borg didn't cast doubt on the historicity of John's Gospel merely to annoy you, Damien."

"That may be true, but it sure feels like he put his finger in my eye, going after my favorite Bible passages like that with his red magic marker."

"I still think you are being too hard on poor Marcus Borg."

I chuckled, finally developing the verbal irony I needed to hear myself and how ridiculously emotional I probably sounded. College textbooks were not assigned to students just to massage their egos and confirm all their pre-existing notions of life, the universe, and everything. Just the opposite. Valancourt assigned me a thoughtful, provocative book that would make the familiar strange and push me to consider seeing things in a new light. He assigned me the book to make me think. It made me emotional as well as made me think, proving how wise his choice of assigned text was. The paper I wrote condemning Borg's book wound up being, indirectly, its greatest vindication. "I *know* I'm being too hard on Borg. I'm sure I'll forgive him after I stew about this for a day. Don't worry. He's still on my Christmas card list."

"That's good to hear."

"By the way, have you ever seen *Star Trek: The Next Generation*?" I asked.

"No. Why?"

"Never mind."

As often as Valancourt and I disagreed, I found these exchanges intellectually stimulating and transformative. They are among the most important conversations of my life. And yet, I always feared that Dr. Valancourt found my manner and word-choice hyperbolic and off-putting, and misread my opinions as entrenched and immovable. In fact, Valancourt had done more than anyone to deepen and enrich my thinking on every political issue and religious teaching, from the most innocuous to the most controversial. Did he worry that I saw him as a leftist, secularist brainwasher of the American youth? I didn't, but since the Republican-owned-and-operated mass media depicted professors as Satanic traitors undermining America, it was no wonder he was scared. I was, after all, a loud, six-foot New Yorker who waved his arms about as he talked.

Eager to make my admiration for him clear, I dressed in fluorescent cowboy clothes one day. I thought my meaning was clear: imitation is the sincerest form of flattery. I may be Republican, but I dig Valancourt. Valancourt was mystified. "Why are you dressed like me?"

No! I got 'The Recoil' from Valancourt! "I want you to love me, Dr. Valancourt."

Valancourt looked even more confused and frightened.

This was the person I was going to Italy with instead of my mother.

Byron and I had been overwhelmed by our first sighting of Rome, but Valancourt knew exactly where he was going. He led our tour group across the street, into a building, down some stairs, and through a few large chambers filled with fellow travelers. I lost all track of time but couldn't stop wincing at the sound of my rolling suitcase's wheels screeching along cobblestone walkways. Next time, no wheeled luggage. It was loud, hard to steer, and was probably damaging the cobblestone. And where in hell were we? Valancourt wasn't about to update everyone. We just had to keep moving. Don Knotts' twin brother had worked things out with such speed, efficiency, and precision that all we had to do was keep the back of his head in our line of sight and chase after it. Still, the aging historian was fast and had little luggage, so it was tough keeping up. Staying within sight of Valancourt got still more difficult each time we hit the odd staircase, and I had to carry one suitcase and two carry-on bags up or down the stairs. This didn't bother me too much because it meant I dropped back to where the pretty Germanic blonde student was. She had the second most luggage of us all, and Byron and I would take turns helping her carry her stuff up and down those staircases. Byron had noticed her before I did, which was no surprise. He was always on the lookout. I had only recently begun "looking" again because I had not only outgrown my need for braces but my retainer as well. (I was no longer Trap Jaw from *Masters of the Universe*.) This was one of the rare instances where both Byron and I singled out the same girl. I usually went for women in sensible shoes and Byron tended to gravitate towards the more kittenish types who took some little time putting their faces on in the morning. This young woman carried herself with a regal air and had long, straight, blonde hair, sapphire blue eyes, skin as pale a Snow White's, a lightly freckled face, and a downturned mouth. She was dressed in a football Jersey, faded denim jeans, and a pair of brown cowboy boots under a long tan trench coat, and had not one stich of make-up on. There was enough in this young woman's ensemble to attract both of us. Byron liked the football jersey. I liked the lack of makeup. We both appreciated her hair and eyes. In retrospect, she looked remarkably like both Claudia Schiffer and Lena Headey's Cersei Lannister from *Game of Thrones*, except she was "regular person" pretty, not model or superstar pretty. I worried about what would happen if Byron and I both decided to throw down over who got to ask her out to dinner first.

Somehow, through some magic spell of Valancourt's, we all wound up on a train. We were shoved into the corridor of one of the train's cars, alternatively sitting on the floor or standing pressed against a wall or door, because the ticket seller had booked more passengers on the train than they had seats and standing room. I was confused. "Should we have waited for the next train? Why did they sell us tickets if there was no room for us?"

Taran flashed his infectious smile and began genially carpet-bombing his favorite country and people. "That's Italy for you. Beautiful countryside, majestic castles, delicious food, and the most stupidly, inefficiently operated government and public services in the world."

"That's exactly what America would be like if I ever became president," I said.

"However bad you would be as president, you couldn't be a worse choice for leader of a country than Silvio Berlusconi."

"Who's he when he's at home?" I asked.

"Knowing you? You would hate him with every fiber of your being. You'd be right to."

Aside from a handful of brief exchanges like this, no one packed into the train corridor was in much of a talking mood. We merely gazed at one another with bleary eyes. Bobby Mammolito caught sight of me looking down with half-closed eyes, on the verge of falling asleep on my feet. "Don't fall asleep, Egon!" he yelled.

Purple Sarah giggled. "Damien, you look like you've been bitten by a tsetse fly!"

I opened my eyes unnaturally wide to wake myself up.

"Dude!" Bobby yelled, startling the whole train. "Gotta ax you a question! You gonna be the world's biggest babe magnet here in Italy like you are in the States?"

I felt the eyes of Taran, Valancourt, Bobby, Byron, Purple Sarah, Tuesday, Bongo Guy, and the blonde girl on me. "I think you have me mistaken for someone else."

"No! You are a total babe magnet, Egon! Every time I see you, you've got like one, two, or six stone cold foxes sitting with you talkin' bout the meaning of life. I don't know how the hell you do it. You're amazing! Like James Bond!" This was a surprising sentiment coming from a guy who was, by all accounts, putting a sock over his dorm-room doorknob every night when Tuesday came to visit him. For my part, I had put a sock on my doorknob exactly zero times during my college career. I blushed. "Right. I'm exactly like James Bond, the most famous pacifist, Marxist-feminist celibate in film history!"

Byron laughed raucously and clapped his hands together.

Bobby nodded vigorously. "That's what I'm saying! Teach me, Egon! Tell me your secret! How do you get these groupies?"

Everyone was still watching my face for tell-tale signs of disconnect between what I was saying and what I was really thinking and feeling. "I don't know what to tell you. They're not groupies. They're my friends. We just talk."

Bobby mulled this over. "Let me get this straight. You control yourself? Never put a hand on their thighs?"

"I don't."

"That's a big part of it, I bet."

I cleared my throat, uncomfortably. "Possibly. I haven't given it any thought in years."

"That makes so much sense! No wonder I don't have as many groupies as you! I always go right for the thigh, and they bolt! I'm gonna try not grabbing me some thigh and see what happens, because the company you keep is mad impressive. I bow to your manly charisma!"

Tuesday smacked Bobby upside the head. "What are you going on and on about other girls for?"

Bobby cast a sheepish look at me. "Uh-oh. You got me in trouble, Egon."

"*I* got *you* in trouble?" I looked around again. *Yep. Everyone is still looking at me.*

I smiled sheepishly. "I have no idea who this guy is. Never seen him before in my life."

The Geneseo entourage took one train for about twenty minutes before getting a transfer. On the ride, Byron sat next to the blonde — whose name turned out to be Evelyn Krueger — and talked to her about music. He asked her if she liked Billy Joel and she said as far as she was concerned, the Beatles made the only rock music worth listening to. Byron's eyes grimaced when his mouth didn't. *Excellent. She's annoyed him with her elitist music taste. He takes his music personally. He may not pursue her now. If he stops chasing her, that leaves an opening for me. Assuming she would respond to my advances. But . . . no. That's absurd.*

Evelyn looked up at me unexpectedly. "You have a favorite band or song?"

I thought about it. "A tie, I guess. My favorite songs are 'Working-Class Hero' by John Lennon and 'Seven Spanish Angels' by Ray Charles and Willie Nelson."

Byron smirked. "You picked the Lennon song because she said she likes the Beatles."

"He's eager to please, is he?" Evelyn asked Byron.

"No! I picked the Lennon song because I'm an anarcho-socialist. I picked 'Seven Spanish Angels' because I'm incurably romantic. Meanwhile, the religious part of me likes Madonna's 'Like a Prayer.' And I suppose the evil side of my personality likes Alice Cooper's 'Poison.'"

Evelyn looked arch. "A favorite song for each side of your complicated personality?"

"They don't come more complicated than me, man!"

Byron laughed. "You're so cheesy."

It isn't fair to Byron, but I enjoy mentally associating him with beloved television sitcom character Ron Swanson. Aside from his gradual evolution into a Bernie Sanders supporter and Eurosocialist, my now lifelong friend Byron reminds me of the quiet, misanthropic, nature-loving jazz musician from *Parks and Recreation*. I first noticed the resemblance between Byron and Ron when Byron proudly declared that his athletic prowess and participation in multiple high school varsity sports won him six girlfriends named Tammy.

"You had *six* girlfriends named 'Tammy'?" I asked. "I don't even think of that as a common name. I only know Tammy Wynette and Tammy Faye Bakker."

"You don't think it's a common name? I do."

"Of course, *you* do! Where I come from, the only likely way to date six girls with the same name is if they're all named Jennifer."

Byron would refer to "the Tammys" by number, and I heard their names in the form of Roman numerals when he would say, "Tammy II loved hockey," or "I got Tammy V to like Barry Manilow." When I discovered that Ron Swanson's mother was named Tammy and he married three women named Tammy, I became convinced that Byron Baldwin and Ron Swanson were one and the same person. Ron even added the Roman numerals to Tammy I and Tammy II.

Byron disagreed quietly but firmly. "Ron Swanson's defining trait is he's a libertarian. Libertarians have laid waste to this country."

"Yeah, sure. But everything else about you is the same. If Ron Swanson was a socialist, he'd be you."

Byron scrunched his eyebrows together. "If Ron Swanson were nothing like Ron Swanson, he'd be exactly the same as me?"

"Fine, fine. You're nothing alike."

Byron laughed loudly. "I tell you what, if any of us is in *Parks and Recreation*, it's you! If you were any good at math and were a fiscal conservative, you'd be Ben Wyatt!"

"Oh, I noticed that once he stopped being a villain and fell in love with Leslie. Early Ben? Not me. Season Three and Four Ben? Me. Leslie Knope is my dream woman."

Of course, I made the connection between Byron and Ron in more recent years. While we were in college, I understood Byron Baldwin a different way: he had the romantic temperament of Lord Byron and the looks of Billy Baldwin, so his name was absurdly apt. My first sighting of him had been his playing moody Frédéric Chopin pieces at the upright piano in the student center. He played every day during the lunch hour specifically to attract the attention of admiring women. Frustratingly, when they flocked to listen to him, he would remain so engrossed in his music that they would eventually give up and move away. The first time I dared speak to this somber fellow, I joked, "What's with you, Schroeder? You have the looks and the piano playing. You could be more outgoing. I wish I had your looks and talent, and you had my verve. Together, we'd be almost as sexy as Franco Nero."

"He was great in *Camelot*." Byron gave me a small smile that seemed like a frown. "Sir Lancelot is my favorite. You sure you don't want my verve? Maybe I should take your looks?"

"Oh, Jesus Christ, no! What monstrous abominations would we become!"

Byron looked me up and down. "Are you always this big a wise-ass? I have to warn you, I prefer to make friends with serious-minded people."

I swept the mirth from my features. "I am the most serious-minded person who ever lived! My biggest secret of all? I have no sense of humor and I'm grumpy all the time."

"I find that hard to believe," Byron said, dispassionately.

"Can you teach me to play one sexy piano song so I can trick chicks into talking to me?"

"You want to 'vamp till she's ready?' No, I can't teach you that. I never advise lying to women. Just be yourself. I used to play 'Cristofori's Dream' by David Lanz — a song nobody really knows but me. I told one girl I composed it. That turned out to be a mistake."

I draped my arm over the top of the upright and leaned forward. "Oh! What happened?"

"It turned out to be a mistake."

As grim-faced as Byron was during this conversation, it was less than an hour before I saw him laugh until tears ran down his face. It happened when I discovered, much to my chagrin, that Byron was friends with Sergio Joseph Savini. This revelation convinced me that, if I were to start palling around with Byron, I would inevitably remain at least somewhat in Sergio's decaying orbit. When Byron and I bumped into Sergio in the courtyard outside the student center, the

Mike Piazza clone made no reference to my picking him up bodily and hurling him out of my room a week before. *Oh, the joys of going to a small college. You're never rid of any nuisance for long.* Byron considered Sergio annoying, too, but he also found Sergio as hysterically funny as I found Sergio infuriating. They had a painfully unhealthy dynamic where Sergio looked up to Byron and tried breathlessly to impress him with witty anecdotes and factoids about weapons and military history, none of which ever impressed Byron. The witty anecdotes were never actually witty but felt like jokes that petered out before the punchline. Also, Byron, who read a lot, soon cottoned on to the fact that Sergio didn't read at all, but had a photographic memory and gleaned all of his knowledge of science and society from cable television infotainment sources. Consequently, Byron found all sorts of errors in the information Sergio presented to impress him. The effect was excruciatingly embarrassing to witness, but oddly gratifying. Byron could twist Sergio into knots far more effectively than Sergio could push my buttons. On the day we bumped into Sergio in the student center courtyard, Sergio monologued non-stop for thirty minutes about the Chernobyl disaster. It was a topic that neither Byron nor I had broached with him, and one that I, at least, was utterly uninterested in. Large scale disasters bore and depress me because they are so epic in scope and fatalistic in outcome that all individual human agency of consequence is stripped from the narrative. The moral almost always boils down to either "shit happens" or "there is no God." At minute thirty of Sergio's monologue, Byron silenced the barrel-chested Italian and bellowed, "Sergio! I need to show you my impression of Gary Busey!"

"Gary Busey?" Sergio asked. "What a non sequitur! We were discussing Chernobyl."

Byron started preforming sections of Gary Busey's dialogue from the action movie *Under Siege*, beginning with, "You *think* you know Damien Cavalieri. 'You don't know Damien Cavalieri! He is an extreme psychopath. He hates officers. He hates America!...No one is to speak to him. No one is to let him out. If he tries to escape, shoot him right *here*!'" Byron pressed his thumb against Sergio's forehead.

"What's happening?" Sergio asked with his teeth clamped shut, a newbie ventriloquist not yet able to speak through a dummy without his lips moving. The grotesque expression proved too much for Byron and me. We collapsed onto the concrete floor, howling with laughter, and crying until Sergio walked away. For a split second, I felt bad for Sergio. Then, I went back to laughing uproariously, grabbing Byron's shoulder to steady myself.

"That guy *always* talks out of his ass!" Byron roared. "Always!"

Byron was a complicated fellow. That's why I could relate to him. His background fascinated me. Byron's parents practiced both Roman Catholicism and Buddhism simultaneously and lived in the village of South Stoddard, a rural community of twelve hundred residents that was a forty-minute drive south of Buffalo and known in the region for its annual strawberry festival. Members of his family gravitated towards military service, factory work, health care, and the service industries. His paternal grandfather, the village's first sheriff, was credited with brokering a peace between warring Italian and Irish immigrant communities. Byron was the smartest student in his very small grammar school and nobody knew what to do with him, because the curriculum was far too easy for him. In the end, he watched countless hours of nature videos, giving him an encyclopedic knowledge of animals and a keen environmentalist and animal rights sense. He saw his love of animals and nature as compatible with his hunting. He did not love good old boys who shot animals on snowbikes, whooped like drunken morons, and drove away, leaving the meat to rot in the snow. Byron was also not, in any way, a future militia member, survivalist, or white supremacist, though he knew some people from the region like that. Three months after we met, Byron took me back home and introduced me to his warm and welcoming family. He also introduced his mother to the twelve weeks of laundry he had been accumulating all semester and had no idea how to wash.

The next morning, he and his father took me out shooting. I still remember his father's safety lecture: "Rule number one: Act as if every gun is loaded. Don't point it at anything you don't want to shoot, and never point it at a human. It isn't a toy. It's a weapon. Rule number two: Since every gun is loaded, you better darn remember rule number one." We drove to their friend Clive Cussler's house to use his shooting range for the morning. As we drove up a dirt road to Clive Cussler's targets, I kept reminding myself that this Clive Cussler was not the famous novelist, but another person with the same name. At the range, I drew upon my vast knowledge of marksmanship culled from my archery lessons at various Pocono Mountain hotels and playing *Duck Hunt* and *Hogan's Alley* with the Nintendo Zapper Light Gun. I shot very well with the Ranch rifle and the double-barreled shotgun, but my aim was high and to the right when I fired Dirty Harry's handgun, the .45 Magnum, one-handed, against the advice of the Baldwins. During the time I held the weapons and fired them, I felt their raw power course through me. As each bullet struck its target, I felt with absolute certainty that my penis was eighteen inches long. When we were done, I surrendered my red, hearing-protecting earmuffs, and helped the men load the weapons back into the trunk of their car. As we drove up to Clive Cussler's house to thank him, the high of the shooting session wore off, and I remembered that my penis was below-average-size when erect, and nearly impossible to find when limp.

The Baldwins had talked Clive up and seemed happy to see him, but he struck me as a bit ornery, slouching about his house, unshaven, wearing a baseball cap indoors, a cigarette hanging from his mouth. Byron was excited to tell him how well I had done. "Clive, Damien's aim was really good, even though this was his first-time shooting."

Clive reacted as if he'd been stung in the neck by a yellowjacket. "What? You never been shooting before?" He had a gravelly, Tom Waits voice.

"No," I said.

I didn't appreciate it when he muttered, "Where'd you grow up? A septic tank?" Clive's posture suggested that: a) he knew at once that my dad didn't serve in Vietnam, and was not in a profession that involved the handling of guns, and b) that I had been raised to be a book-educated pacifist instead of a manly man who worked with his hands and knew how to defend himself with a gun. As a Vietnam vet, Clive took an instant dislike to me and my Letters to Cleo t-shirt. This dislike grew more intense when he offered to sell me a gun a few minutes later, and I refused. "That was fun, but I'm going to retire from my career as a marksman."

"Don't you want to protect yourself and your family?"

"From what? The Red Dawn?"

"Or crime. Or societal collapse." Clive held some sort of handgun out to me.

I held my hand up. "No thanks. I don't want to leave here with a gun. Still, if you happen to have any cannoli, I'll be happy to take them off your hands."

"You should really buy a gun."

"Maybe if I inherit a farm, I'll grab a rifle sometime to protect my chickens and pigs and cows from coyotes and rattlesnakes, or whatever. I don't think I'll ever want a handgun."

Byron guffawed. "I'm trying to picture you owning a farm!"

"Alright, alright," I said. "That's enough out of you."

"You're not going to want to be caught without this when the looting starts," Clive said.

"Nah. I'm just not that scared of Black people. I kinda like them." I didn't see any Confederate flags around, and South Stoddard was in New York, but I was becoming more and more convinced that Clive thought the wrong side had won the Civil War.

"Who said anything about Black people? Dangerous people come in all forms."

"I like Hispanics, too. And I'm too Catholic to own a gun."

Clive put the gun down on the table. "Whatever you say. I'm Catholic, too, you know."

"Anyway, thank you for your hospitality, and thank you for all the years of pleasure you gave me reading your Dirk Pitt novels. *Raise the Titanic* is a personal favorite."

When we left that day, I saw two different Byron Baldwin's assessing my behavior in Clive's house. One Byron was the Byron of South Stoddard, who thought Clive was cool, that his joke at my expense was funny, and that I wasn't a grateful guest. The other Byron was the Byron of SUNY Geneseo, who understood why I felt out of place in his home town, why I was offended by the septic tank joke, and why I was wary of the ideological sentiments responsible for Clive's gun collection, which was so massive it was stored in a second building.

Somewhere in Italy, our Geneseo entourage arrived at the next train station too late to catch the transfer Valancourt had planned for us to take. Delays we had hit during our flight were disrupting his finely tuned travel schedule. We stored our luggage in a large, dusty room, and went off in search of food. It would be my first time buying something in another language. I tried to prepare what to say as I scouted out a glass counter filled with cookies, pastries, and cold cuts. I was distracted in my efforts by my American comrades' orders, which all involved pointing a clumsy finger through the glass at the morsel they wanted, saying "uno," and adding "grazie" when the server handed them the item in question. Seeing that this worked, and not wanting to do anything to show up my friends, I fell back on "uno" and "grazie" myself. As I began eating my Napoleon, noting that Staten Island pastries did a respectable job measuring up to the real thing, I reflected on how disappointing it was that my first conversation with a local in Italy had been in Tarzan. I used the bathroom because I had been holding in pee for as long as I could remember. The dirty stall walls had Italian graffiti written on them. I knew enough of the language to recognize "for a good time call Tipi," "Death to fags," "AIDS is God's judgment," and "Dante was right." It was disappointing to see that Italy was a lot like America after all. A general shout from outside told me I better hustle because the train was here.

Several stopovers later, we reached the outskirts of Siena. We couldn't all fit in one cab, and the buses were just crowded enough that we couldn't smush into one, so we split up into one cab group and one bus group. Byron, Evelyn, and Valancourt opted to wait for a cab. I raced with Taran, Tuesday, Bobby, Purple Sarah, and Bongo Guy onto a bus. As I ran across the street to reach the bus, dodging speeding, careening cars, I heard Valancourt's voice in my head, warning us to pack light. I had ignored the warnings, hoping I wouldn't have to carry three bags for quite as long as this. The bus was crowded before I climbed aboard. My baggage didn't help.

"Remember to validate your ticket, or they'll behead you!" Taran called out.

We slid our tickets into a validating machine, which whirred and marked them. The bus tore away from the street corner, tossing me like a salad. I wrapped my arm around a support pole just in time to prevent myself bowling over enough passengers to get a spare. The bus made its way through the medieval walls of Siena while I was trying not to faceplant, so I missed what was probably a very nice view. A lot of careening about later, the bus slid to a stop, and Taran told us to jump off in front of the Basilica Cateriniana di San Domenico, an enormous, earth-tone building illuminated at dusk by bright yellow lights from the ground. It looked more like a castle than a church. Taran counted heads and saw we were all there. "Stay together. It's passegiata, so the streets are bustling. The Piazza del Campo is a nine-minute walk away. Our hotel, the Locanda Garibaldi is in the Onda neighborhood, on a street that winds downhill behind the tower."

He spoke quickly enough that I only half-heard the final, most important sentence. With that, Taran charged down the cobblestone streets into what looked like the fastest flowing river of people I had ever seen. Our group rushed against the grain, barely dodging locals and fellow tourists whose only concern was remaining on their own courses. Everyone in the student group was able to negotiate the crowd more skillfully than me because I had the most luggage. I cursed myself for not taking the cab with Evelyn of the Mammoth Luggage. How was I to know that passegiata — whatever the heck that was — would be going on? Or that the hilly, cobblestone streets would keep bouncing my luggage wheels, tipping my suitcase over every few yards if I moved too quickly? The people of Siena sailed past, not waiting for me to make way, laden as I was. None minded jostling my bags or smacking them to the ground. The fifth time my bag fell, I bent over to right it. Even before I straightened, I sensed I had lost my group. I was right. I stood at a busy intersection of steeply inclined roads, unable to see Taran or the others amidst the throng, and completely unsure which route they had taken. Tired and sweaty, I was still not yet ready to panic. I wanted to get to the hotel and go to bed. What was the hotel called? Lontano Garibaldi?

I stopped Ed Koch, or a bald man who resembled the former mayor of New York. "Mi scusi! Sono Americano. Dove Lontano Garibaldi?" Ed Koch gave me "The Recoil" and kept moving. A woman in a grey winter coat heard the question and gestured towards what looked like the way I had come. That couldn't be the right way, could it? Still, I was so disoriented by the waves of people that I assumed I had gotten myself more turned around than I realized. I trusted the advice enough to walk several blocks in that direction until I spotted a familiar statue. I had passed it not two minutes ago. Should I wait by the statue for rescue? That is what the Boy Scouts are taught: Stay in one place if you get lost. On the other hand, I wasn't a Boy Scout, I was tired of being a poor thing, and I wanted to find my own way to the Lontano Garibaldi.

I asked a teenage girl where the Lontano Garibaldi was. She didn't know. Two other people I stopped were German tourists. They didn't know. One man was visiting from Rome and didn't know Siena. Yet another directed me further along my present course, which was surely the wrong way. I asked another person, who again pointed back towards the bus depot. What the hell? Well, if three people in a row pointed me back towards the bus depot, maybe I had gotten separated from them earlier than I realized? Should I trust the advice of the three natives over my own instincts, which screamed not to proceed past the statue? I tried a follow-up sentence. "Lontano Garibaldi è il piccolo hotel." The man's eyes lit up. "Il Piccolo Hotel!" He again pointed past the statue, towards the bus depot, only more urgently. *But that's the wrong fucking way! Oh, fuck it. I must be wrong.* The man began to move away from me, but I called after him, "Cammina con me, per favore?" The man nodded and walked with me for fifteen minutes until we reached the correct street. The man pointed down the street, gesturing towards a small, white hotel, and went off, leaving me alone in an unexpectedly quiet and deserted area. Was passegiata over? Had I been led to Siena's equivalent of the middle of nowhere?

As I walked towards the hotel, I noticed with increasing alarm that it was called the Piccolo Hotel, and it was on Garibaldi Street. I moaned. What had I said to this fellow? "Lontano Garibaldi è il Piccolo Hotel." Did that mean something like, "Take me to The Small Hotel on Garibaldi Street?" I bolted into the reception area of the incorrect hotel and attempted to tell my sob story to the slightly round, grey-haired Italian woman at reception. This was not the time to be bashful about my command of the language, even if I mangled most of the sentences and peppered them with English words and botched cognates: "Buona sera. Sono studente. Ho andare a Italia con il professore. Desidero camminare a Lontano Garibaldi. Il professore in l'hotel e io sono ecco. Dove Lontano Garibaldi hotel? O posso telefono l'hotel Lontano Garibaldi? Il mio professore posso aiutarmi?"

The woman reached under the desk and withdrew a phone book. She leafed through it and found the hotel pages. She pointed to an ad for the Locanda Garibaldi and asked me if that was the hotel I meant. I nodded, not realizing until she put the phone book down to dial its number that I had gotten the hotel's name wrong. *Great Caesar's Ghost! There's no "Lontano" Garibaldi. There's only the "Locanda" Garibaldi!* The owner of the Piccolo Hotel spoke on the phone with the owner of the Locanda Garibaldi and related my situation. She was left waiting until another voice addressed her. After a few words, she handed me the phone. Taran's voice came through the receiver. "Ciao, Damien. Where are you?" I told Taran what happened and explained that I was too hopelessly lost to find my way back alone.

"I don't know where that hotel is," said Taran. "Can you put the lady back on?"

I gave the phone back to the receptionist and she offered Taran directions. After she hung up, she invited me to wait in the lobby. She had been so helpful that I felt guilty that I wasn't staying at this hotel after all. Naturally, from my perspective, it took Taran forever to arrive. I whistled the entire Henry Mancini theme to *The Pink Panther* and sang all of Paul Williams' "The Hell of It" from *Phantom of the Paradise* to myself, and still had twenty minutes to kill. (I would have kept whistling and singing, but I didn't want to drive the receptionist insane.) At last, Taran appeared in the lobby, unable to conceal his astonishment at how badly I had gotten lost.

"Valancourt, of course, is ready to give you a big speech when you get back."

"Cool."

"How in God's name did you wind up all the way out here? The last time I saw you, we were less than a block from the Campo!"

I smiled sheepishly. We thanked the receptionist and left. Since passegiata was over, we could walk at a reasonable pace. The wheels on my luggage were better able to roll over the cobblestone without bouncing up into the air and tipping the bag over. As we walked, I related everything that happened from when my bag fell over and I lost the group.

"If you hadn't misremembered the name of the hotel or if you'd waited by the statue, the evening would have gone better for you," Taran concluded.

"Yes," I said. "I did keep my head. I guess I don't know enough Italian to prevent myself from getting lost, but I know enough to get myself found."

CHAPTER THIRTY-ONE
There Are No Ossuaries on Staten Island . . . That I Know Of

January 6, 1997

Taran leaned forward as if sharing a secret with the handful of study abroad students gathered in the sitting room on the third floor of the Locanda Garibaldi. "If any of you ever get lost in Siena, there are three words I want you to use." He paused just long enough to make sure we were listening and perfectly enunciated the Italian phrase: "Dov'é il Campo?" At a gesture from Taran, the undergraduates half-heartedly repeated the phrase, preferring to botch the pronunciation completely rather than to get it partly wrong. Taran winced. "You're all just messing with me, right? How about actually trying to pronounce it now?" He made us repeat the phrase eight more times, until he heard everyone say it clearly and correctly.

"Very good," Taran nodded. "That means, 'Where is the Campo?' The Campo, in case you don't know, is the town square right up the street from this hotel. Once you find the square, finding the Locanda Garibaldi is easy. Right, Damien?"

I blushed. "Right." The sitting room had a lot of overstuffed couches and chairs with grandma-style floral patterns and tiny table lamps that barely illuminated the table when turned on at night. Taran explained that the Italians don't like bright illumination in the evenings because they got used to keeping things dark during World War II. Sounded plausible, anyway. One winding stairwell led upstairs, to the rooms where most of us were staying. A pine-green spiral staircase led down to the restaurant that doubled as the hotel lobby. The proprietors were named Sophia and Marcello, but were not, in fact, Sophia Loren or Marcello Mastroianni.

"Now, the only one of you who has ever been to Italy is Evelyn here. She went on this same trip with Valancourt and me two years ago." — Evelyn smiled and waved to the group. — "Evelyn is happy to help people who can't find their way around Siena. Like Damien."

I forced a "yes-I-know-getting-lost-is-funny-so-feel-free-to-laugh-at-me" smile.

Taran returned his attention to the others. "How many people here speak some Italian?"

I was one of the few to raise my hand. Despite my lack of any real mastery of the language, I wound up being the most proficient Italian speaker on the trip. I was worried people would look to me for leadership. I preferred solitude and had never been in a leadership role.

"I'm sure Damien wouldn't mind helping any of you with some difficult conversations, just as long as you don't use him as a dictionary," said Taran. "Or compass. He's a good man, but his moral compass is better than his physical one."

"That's right," I said.

"You're never gonna live this one down," Taran joked.

"I was just taking a butcher's hook 'round Siena." My first stab Cockney rhyming slang.

Purple Sarah smiled slyly, "But, Taran, if I follow Damien around, asking him for help speaking Italian, I might get mistaken for one of his stone-cold fox groupies."

I held my head in my hands as the entire room burst into laughter. When the laughter subsided, I said, "Thanks for this, Bobby. I really appreciate it."

Bobby spread his hands. "Hey! That's what I'm here for, Egon."

"Now everyone thinks I'm Bill Clinton," I grumbled.

Byron poked me in the shoulder. "You *are* both Leos. There's some similarities there."

"I don't want to hear it."

Purple Sarah's smile couldn't get bigger. "You really don't have a sense of humor about yourself, do you?"

"Listen, y'all. I'm just here to see Italy. Stop busting my chops."

Byron smiled at Sarah. "He takes needling so well, doesn't he?"

Sarah nodded. "Exceptionally!"

"Come on, with that crap!" I shot back.

Bongo Guy spoke for the first time. I forgot he was even with us. "How long do we have to wait for the horse race? I wanna see the horse race."

Taran looked quizzical. "The Palio? Six or seven months." We were only going to be there four weeks, so seeing a Palio would present a unique challenge.

"Bummer." Bongo Guy resumed not speaking.

"At least we didn't miss it by a nose," I said. "I went to New Orleans with Mom on Ash Wednesday. We were walking around Bourbon Street at eight a.m. and there was beads and empty alcohol bottles and food wrappers and people asleep in the gutter. We'd missed the world's biggest party by twelve hours, and it looked like it." Mom and I had gone to Louisiana to meet our newfound cousin, Retha-Louise from Namibia, for the first time in person. Retha-Louise was in New Orleans with the Namibian Youth Choir for an international music festival. Within fifteen minutes of our first conversation, Mom and I could tell that she was every bit as wonderful as we expected her to be. Still, we had missed Mardi Gras.

Byron slapped his knee and laughed. "You went to New Orleans the day after Mardi Gras? That's so typical of you!"

"Yeah, no kidding."

While I had been hopelessly lost in the city-state the night before, Byron picked out a room for us to share on the fourth floor, next door to Bobby and Tuesday's love nest. Sparsely furnished, with one floral design overstuffed chair, one small oak wardrobe, a tiny corner table and chair set, a mounted coat rack, and two army-cot-like beds with floral print bedsheets, the room was functional but not beautiful. Our quarters' biggest perk was it came with its own bathroom, unlike the third-floor room Evelyn and Purple Sarah opted to share, which had no amenities within, compelling them to use a hallway shower and bath. Outside our room was a modest sitting room with a sofa and coffee table, across from which was a third bedroom claimed by Bongo Guy. That accounted for all the students and their lodgings in the hotel. Valancourt was staying in the apartment he owned across town, which he lived in all summer and rented out during the school year. Meanwhile, Taran was rooming with local friends he had made during his years living in Siena, running its international study program.

"Evelyn and Purple Sarah are sharing a queen-sized bed downstairs?" Byron asked.

"That is correct."

"I bet you wish you could jump in between them and sleep there, too?"

"That is correct."

"You're goddam right, you do," Byron grinned. "Me, too."

"Of course."

"I'm really hoping to have sex in Italy."

"Sex? Is that when people press their orifices and/or genitals together in a surprising variety of combinations, producing a pleasurable effect? Word on the street is that this contact is designed to stave off awareness of the inevitability of death and/or generate offspring."

"Very funny."

"I've heard much talk of this 'sex' business. It sounds excessively diverting."

Speak of the devil and he doth appear. At just that moment, Bobby Mammolito's screaming orgasm sook the foundations of the hotel. It was so deafening it was as if he were getting blown right here in the room with us. *Of course.* The wall that separated our room from theirs did not rise all the way up to the ceiling, and the half-moon window cut into the dividing wall eleven feet off the ground didn't help, either. If a pin dropped in one room, the noise would startle the duo in the adjoining room. The extended roar that Bobby made when he came was just a taste of the moaning that awaited us each night, as Tuesday and Bobby took turns going down on one another. Byron gave me a deer-in-the-headlights look. I shrugged. "Whatever."

Face flushed red and hands clasped tight over her mouth to keep from laughing out loud, Sarah appeared at our doorway. Her eyes danced, telling that she and Evelyn could hear Bobby's bellowing flood tide through their ceiling. I guess she couldn't wait to race upstairs and catch the end of it. That the loud orgasm was still going on from the time she heard it downstairs to her arrival in our room was a testament to just how unnaturally long and loud Bobby's climax was. Sarah risked removing her hands and mouthed the words, "Holy shit."

Me and Byron mouthed back. "I know."

We huddled together. Sarah whispered, "Tuesday must be queen of the hummers."

"Wanna switch rooms?" Byron asked Sarah. "I can't listen to this shit every night."

"Love is in the air," I said. "I'm glad *somebody* is getting laid. Sure as shit ain't me."

Sarah said, "Evelyn has a whole bag of earplugs. I think I can talk her into sharing them."

Bobby howled again like a wolf baying at the moon.

"The Second Cumming!" Sarah whispered. "What's Tuesday's secret?"

"I think I may actually be in hell," Byron said. "I'm so jealous right now."

"So," I whispered, "who do you folks think Jack the Ripper was? Virginia Woolf's grandfather seems to be the in-vogue choice. Personally, I favor Montague Druitt."

"Walter Sickert," Sarah whispered. "One hundred percent. You seen his paintings?"

A deafening silence rose to fill the room.

"Is it over?" Sarah mouthed.

Byron nodded miserably.

"Are you two gonna spend the month chasing Italian ass, or what?" Sarah asked.

"Damn right," Byron confirmed.

"Nah," I said. "Fuck that. I'm just here to enjoy Italy."

"What's with you?" Sarah asked. "Have you asked out even one person the entire time you've been in college?"

"He hasn't!" Byron hissed. "Because he wore braces and thought the juniors he was attracted to found him too young for them! He's driving me nuts! He won't even try."

"I *did* make that one pass at a lady who worked in a rare bookstore," I offered feebly.

"When was that?" retorted Byron. "Thanksgiving, 1995?"

"I haven't heard this story," said Sarah.

I wasn't sure if I should smirk or frown. "I said to the rare books lady, 'Would you happen to have a *Ben Hur* (1860), 3rd edition, with a duplicated line on page one-sixteen?'"

Sarah laughed. "*The Big Sleep*! Fantastic! Did she get the reference?"

"She looked daggers at me and said the next line in the movie: "'Nobody would. There isn't one.'" I had a bad feeling I wasn't as clever as I thought I was. Then, she added, 'Men who want to flirt with me try that line from the *Big Sleep* on me ten times a week. I'm going to strangle the next person who quotes it to me!' I apologized, asked her out anyway, and she nearly tossed a book at my head. That's the extent of my college fornicating and debauchery."

"That's too bad," Sarah said. "That movie reference is fundamentally funny."

"It is a great joke with no audience," I said. "In the right place and at the right time, that joke should kill, but it's never the right place or time. In a rare bookstore, everyone has already heard it a dozen times. Outside a rare bookstore, nobody'd get it. I feel a great deal of empathy for that joke. I *am* that joke made flesh: cool dude never in the right place at the right time."

Sarah smiled sympathetically at me. "James Sheridan says you are exactly as funny as the person listening to you is culturally literate."

"Which is why I had six friends in Staten Island and sixty in Geneseo," I murmured.

"Why do you make so many cultural allusions in casual conversation, anyway?" asked Sarah. "You giving everyone you meet an I.Q. test to see who's worth hanging out with?"

"If you wanna be negative about it," I grumbled. "I'm just sending out signal flares to find bosom friends. It worked with you two, didn't it?"

"Just don't try it with any girls younger than us," Byron warned. "We're the last generation that has heard of *The Little Rascals*, Bobby Darin, and Mothra. You name-drop those things with someone born after *Star Wars*, they won't know what the hell you're talking about."

"I *have* tried it. They *don't*. And girls old enough to get my jokes are all married. Ergo, I have decided to retire from dating, because I am never with the right women at the right time."

Byron poked me in the shoulder. "So, fuck a married woman! Be Sir Lancelot!"

"I never liked him. He shoulda quit his job and fled the second he fell for the queen."

"And got another job where? Working for Meleagant? I hope to God one day you wind up in Lancelot's shoes. We'll see how you do in his place. Be a humbling experience for you. Maybe teach you some empathy and get that enormous stick out of your ass!"

I drew back as if stung. "Did you just place the Curse of the Cat People on me? You take that back this instant! I mean, that's just mean! Don't you know how Catholic I am?"

"Hold up!" Sarah exclaimed. "Damien, is that seriously the extent of your efforts to land a girlfriend? You meet a freshman, sing her the Mothra song, she doesn't recognize it, you bolt?"

"Um . . . ," I stared at my shoes. "If you put it that way, you make it sound pretty stupid. I admit it. I haven't really asked anyone out since I failed to land a prom date back in 1994."

"Was trying to get a prom date so traumatic for you that you've given up flirting?"

"I flirt with you two times a year," I said.

"Yeah, but we're just kidding around. I mean have you ever *really* tried to get even one person into bed while you've been at college? Even *one*?"

I shrugged. "Nah, but who cares? I always planned on having more of an *Educating Rita* college experience than an *Animal House* one."

Sarah looked melancholy. "What happened to you, to make you like this? I don't want to pry, but I worry something *awful* happened to you, and you need to talk to someone about it. Like, I worry you need serious psychological counseling."

"Speaking of awful," I said, "remember what a piece of shit Alcibiades was in *The History of the Peloponnesian War*? Thucydides blames him for the Sicilian Expedition."

"Don't change the subject on me," Sarah said. "It's me, your STD coven compadre!"

I shrugged. "I wouldn't even know where to begin. As much as I love and trust you, I dunno if I wanna subject you to eight hours' worth of my bad memories. You got better things to do with your time than listen to me bust out the violin. Let's just say I was humiliated trying to find a prom date. Keep it simple. But that's misleading cuz the prom is the tip of the iceberg."

Sarah grew pale. "Eight hours is a lot of bad memories." She noticed I was looking at my shoes again. "But if I'm your friend, you can trust me, and I'm willing to listen."

"Thank you." I paused. "No, its too humiliating. I don't want to open Pandora's Box."

Byron jerked a finger in my direction. "When he talks about failing to land a prom date, he gets that exact same haunted expression my dad's friend Clive gets talking about Vietnam."

I laughed loudly. "Okay, now that's funny. You can keep teasing me if you're always that funny about it."

Byron said, "Your braces are off. Arwen is married. Quit making excuses and get back on the horse. You can't waste your sexual prime reading all the Jeeves and Wooster books."

"Hey! I like the *Jeeves and Wooster* books. A lot."

"Don't read about Bertie Wooster's sex life. Explore your own!"

"I'm not sure he ever has sex. Over how many books with how many women?"

Sarah cut in. "If you're worried you're not attractive, don't be. I know of at least seven English majors currently in happy relationships who have confided in me that, if they ever break up with their boyfriend, you're their second-runner-up replacement option."

I felt flattered and insulted all at once. "I'm *everyone's third choice* for a boyfriend?"

"Yep! These seven girls love you to pieces. The second choice is usually the guy on campus who is the most cut and looks the best in jeans. Your David Hasselhoff types."

"*Knight Rider!*" Byron laughed. "Taran says that show is called *Supercar* here."

"David Hasselhoff is hot," I admitted. "He's as handsome as Franco Nero."

"Yes," Sarah purred. "Yes, he is. Anyway, after the hottest guy on campus at position two, you get the third position, which is guy with best personality. Bronze medal. So, if you're patient, at least *one* of the seven will call you up *sometime*...in the future . . . I think...maybe."

"After dating her current boyfriend for three more years, and Hasselhoff for seven, then I can go out dancing with her sometime around January of 2007? Sign me up!"

"I'm just trying to cheer you up."

"Are these seven English majors even cool?"

"I'm pretty sure you're aware that four are attractive, even if you try not to be."

"Yeah, I do try not to be aware. Just like I try not to know where Yale is located, since I'm never going there."

Sarah smirked. "Yale is in New—"

"Bah! I say, 'Bah!' I just burned ten years of my life waiting for Arwen. As Chief Brody said in *Jaws 2*, 'I'm not going through that hell again!' If you don't mind, I'll spend that time more productively, reading all the Jeeves and Wooster stories."

Sarah's face grew more resolved. "Now, you listen to me, Damien. You've got to do some serious flirting on this vacation, or you're gonna have to answer to me. I can't chase any ass this month. I'm in the middle of trying to convince my boyfriend of five years to ask me to marry him. So, I want to get you laid so I can get off on you getting off with someone else. It's called living vicariously. Capisce?"

I chuckled. "Living vicariously through me? You're going to be very bored and very disappointed. I wouldn't wish my sex life on Pol Pot."

That night, I made love to First Lady Hillary Rodham Clinton in the White House bedroom for the first time. I hadn't intended to do it, but she had been so inconsolable over her husband's philandering. I listened as she talked for hours about Gennifer Flowers and her husband's other sexual conquests. Hillary exhausted herself and clutched me to her, sobbing into my shoulder. After her crying died down, we sat on the edge of the bed, holding each other in silence. Before I understood what was happening, Hillary surprised me with a kiss. I found myself too drawn to her to resist. I fumbled with the buttons on her pale blue blouse. She tore at my belt. In moments, our clothes covered the floor. We were locked together, naked in each other's arms, on top of the covers.

The doors to the bedroom flew open, banging against the walls. Al Gore burst in on us, yelling, "Hillary! The Republicans are coming!"

"Shit!" Hillary scrambled to tuck herself under the covers, snatching up a paperback copy of *The Celestine Prophecy* from her nightstand. She pretended to read casually as she fought to gain control of her breathing. Hearing the sounds of two men racing towards the bedroom, I grabbed my clothes and hers, and dragged them with me under the bed, hoping no one would look there. Seconds after my head disappeared from view, Alan Keyes and Rush Limbaugh pushed past Al Gore and raced up to the foot of the bed. Red-faced and wheezing from running his enormous girth through the White House, Limbaugh puffed, "Where is she, FLOTUS? Where's the dyke strumpet you're sleeping with?"

Alan Keyes stomped his foot petulantly. "I tell you it's Damien Cavalieri! A young Republican. She's seducing one of our own to the other side. She's luring him to the dark side with her magically delicious pussy!"

Hillary smiled evilly behind her copy of *The Celestine Prophecy*. "It is, indeed, magically delicious."

My eyes snapped open in the middle of the night.

What the holy hell was that?

Someone stirred in the dark, in another bed across the room.

"Is that you, Hillary?" I whispered. "Or is it Alan Keyes?"

Byron Baldwin's voice came back. "It's me, Byron. What's going on?"

I breathed a sigh of relief. "Thank God. I was afraid you were Alan Keyes."

"What?" Byron reached over and turned on the small lamp that stood on a nightstand between us. "Okay, now I'm awake, and I need to hear about this dream."

I was embarrassed and excited to relate it to him, leaving no gory detail out.

"I should have gone right back to bed after you woke me," Byron declared. "If I had any idea . . . any at all . . . that you were going to tell me about a Hillary Clinton sex fantasy . . . "

"Pretty funny, huh?"

"Nobody likes Hillary Clinton! *Nobody*."

"The number of people worldwide who like Hillary Clinton is an empty set. That's why I like her. Somebody has to. All she said was she wasn't that into baking cookies and it was all over for her. But she's way cooler than her idiot husband, that's for damn sure."

"I'd heard Italian guys have terribly bad cases of the Oedipus Complex, but I had no idea just how true that was until you just told me this story."

"I wonder if I go right back to sleep now, will I be reunited with Hillary? Could we pick up where we left off?"

"Oh, my God," moaned Byron.

I dropped my head back down on the pillow, closed my eyes, and made a wish.

I'm coming, Hillary. I'm coming.

January 8, 1997

I lingered in the Locanda Garibaldi's empty ground floor restaurant, looking out through the windowed cherry-wood doors onto the wet street, wondering what Siena looked like when it wasn't storming or nighttime. Two days sprinting through heavy rains gave me the vague impression that the stone-walled medieval city-state was gorgeous but made me fear returning to America with twelve unused rolls of film. Since it was 9 a.m. and the restaurant opened at lunchtime, I took a seat at one of the empty tables. The table was set with a white table-runner over a red, floral tablecloth, an unlit candle, and a ceramic boat of spices and grated cheeses as garnishes and condiments. I glanced at the stack of assigned books I had brought down with me to read in the lobby, since I could never get comfortable reading in bed: *The Italian City Republics, Religious Poverty and the Profit Economy in Medieval Europe, The Life of Saint Francis of Assisi by Saint Bonaventure, The Cosmographia of Bernardus Silvestris,* and *Painting in Florence and Siena After the Black Death.* Valancourt had some nerve assigning so much reading for a four-week Italy trip. Sure, the class would provide the final three credits of my Medieval Studies minor, and I was fascinated by Italian history, but come on!

I did not notice Evelyn until she dropped into the seat across from me. I tried not to notice that I liked how she looked in her jeans and brown sweater. I was really in no mood to find anyone attractive any more ever again. I promised myself I would not make a pass at her.

Evelyn lightly tapped the cover. "Believe it or not, the best book is the one on the Black Death. It got me interested in art. I immediately added a second major to Psychology that spring. Of course, everyone else in the class last time hated it. They all found it more boring than watching fly fishing on television."

I picked it up. "I never agree with 'everyone else.' And the first pages of the book about the birth of capitalism were astonishingly riveting. It may be my new favorite nonfiction book."

"Lester K. Little is the man. Still, I'm glad I don't have to read all those books again."

I put the book down and pushed it a few inches away from me like a half-eaten meal I didn't want to finish. "Word on the street is you're a super senior, and twenty-five?"

"Why do you ask?"

"Just curious about you here among the young'uns. I'd love to hear what your story is."

Sizing me up, Evelyn regarded me with cautious interest. Her strong jaw and expressive eyes constantly betrayed her emotions, even when she thought she was looking calm or neutral. Mature and studious, she did not have the unseasoned look of an undergraduate. Born in 1971, she would be graduating with a class of students mostly born in 1975 because she had taken a few years off from school to tend to her father. In 1992, an industrial accident robbed Mr. Krueger of his fingers, and he was left with an insulting legal settlement and inadequate disability benefits. Compounding the problem, after these settlements were made, it gradually became clear that her father had lost most of his hearing working amongst loud machinery for decades. His body, ruined by factory work, made Evelyn a militant work-safety law champion and working-class rights advocate. She was also emotionally traumatized by his deafness, and wore protective pink earplugs day and night, even when the ambient noise was minimal.

Evelyn and her father were both only children, and Evelyn's mother had died giving birth to her. She had never moved out of the house she shared with her father. When she took an academic leave of absence, she exchanged her college courses for a series of part-time jobs she used to pay for his regular home care. After a few years, Evelyn eventually got him into a steady enough routine that she felt able to quit her jobs and return to Geneseo to finish her degree. Ever since her return, Evelyn worked with the librarians and Geneseo Student Health and Counseling office to locate an assisted living residence for her father. Having found three solid options, her remaining problem was talking her father into leaving behind the house both he and she had grown up in, and either selling it or passing it on to her before his death. Stubborn and independent, her father would not be easy to convince.

Of course, Evelyn had inherited both her father's stubbornness and independence, and was a loner to boot. She had grown up in Royville, a village of five-thousand residents, and had made not a single friend or encountered even one romantic prospect throughout her formative years. There was one little girl she played dolls with in first grade, a freckled boy named Harry who held her hand once in third grade, and her psychology teacher, Mrs. Perrine, who made her want to grow up to be a counselor. Those were her only sources of human contact outside of her sickly father. Evelyn's inquisitive mind served as an effective social wedge, preventing her from growing close to anyone in her rural community. By the time she was in high school, she had found her society in books alone, and shied away from males of all ages. Even enrolling in Geneseo, she did not live in the dormitory, because she could not countenance living in close proximity to so many strangers. Instead, Evelyn commuted the less than half-hour drive from her family home in Royville. Classroom discussions and overheard mealtime conversations made it clear to Evelyn that, as much as she thought herself the most cosmopolitan person in Royville, she was the proverbial intellectual big fish in a small pond. Next to the other Geneseo students from Buffalo, Rochester, Long Island, and New York City, she was just another Royville bumpkin. They would not take to her at all, even if she attempted to speak with them. Evelyn, Byron, and I made quite the trio. I thought I had too few friends growing up, and deeply resented my lingering virginity. Byron wished he had had more friends as a kid but was grateful for the romantic companionship of Tammy I through Tammy VI. Evelyn Krueger was, at twenty-five, the least socially adjusted of us all. Her choosing to sit across from me at the table that rainy morning in Siena was the friendliest and most socially aggressive move she had ever made.

"I have no story to tell," Evelyn said flatly. She pulled a pad out from her duffel bag, flipped it open, and placed alongside it a copy of *Let's Go Italy*. She then produced a map and unfolded it. "You're going to Rome this weekend, aren't you?"

"I don't know," I said. "I know I have to see the Vatican before we leave, but I was considering going to Venice this weekend."

Evelyn pulled a face. "Venice. I hate Venice. There's nothing to see there. No museums, no good paintings, no good sculptures. It's only scenery, seafood, and expensive blown glass." She tapped the side of her head with the eraser on her pencil. "No mental stimulation."

I frowned. This was not the first time I'd heard Venice slammed. In high school, Mike Bonavita complained that it smelled. Just last night, Taran monologued for five minutes during dinner accusing the Venetians of stealing everything good about their city from everywhere else, and proclaiming it a tourist trap of con artists and opportunists. Still, I had to see it. "My mother said that St. Marc's Cathedral was so beautiful that it made her cry."

Evelyn was clearly not impressed by the anecdote but didn't reiterate her dislike.

"I'm named after the Cathedral," I added. "Damien Marc Cavalieri."

Evelyn smiled. "Oh, now I see why you have to go." After a heartbeat she added, "But go next weekend. This weekend you have to come to Rome with me."

"With you?"

Evelyn paused. "Yeah. And Purple Sarah and Bongo Guy and Tuesday. We're all going."

I shrugged. "Okay."

Evelyn reached out and grasped my hand. "Don't worry! We will have a great time."

Bobby Mammolito paused halfway down the stairs. His face lit up when he saw Evelyn holding my hand. "Egon! My man! You're a fast worker! You are the mack daddy, Egon!"

I held up my copy of *Religious Poverty and the Profit Economy in Medieval Europe* by Lester K. Little. "I'm just here reading about usury, sin, and the birth of capitalism."

"I'm so jealous of you, man!" Bobby raced the rest of the way down the stairs, stood beside Evelyn and I and patted me on the head. "You're my hero." He glanced at Evelyn. "Nice sweater, Evelyn. You look delectable."

Evelyn shifted in her seat and looked down at her map.

"*You're* jealous of *me*?" I asked.

"Your animal magnetism is astounding!" Bobby pounded his chest in approval.

"Okay, please go away, now," I said.

Bobby sighed. "I will. I don't want to go out in the rain, but Tuesday is forcing me."

Tuesday came downstairs and walked up to Bobby's side. "I don't care how bad the rain is, I'm not staying cooped up a minute longer."

Bobby sighed. "The things you make me do for you, Tuesday."

I couldn't stop myself from laughing. Tuesday kicked me in the shin. "Shut the fuck up, Damien! For ten years now, you've been teasing me! Ten years! It gets old. Real old!"

"I'm sorry," I blushed. "I just wasn't expecting him to say that. I really am never trying to make fun of you. I promise. It is always an accident. I swear to God. I have no beef with you."

Tuesday glared daggers at me, daring me to say more. I didn't. Then they left.

"Do you really torment her?" Evelyn asked, once they were safely gone.

"She never sees me at my best," I insisted. "Something weird always happens."

"What's Bobby's deal? I can't tell if he likes you, hates you, or is secretly hot for you."

I leaned forward eagerly. "I know, right? I've been asking myself the same questions since 1987! I used to think people were complicated and deep, and that all the above was true about him. Now I think people are exactly what they appear to be: He just finds me funny."

"There is something funny about you, but I can't figure it out," Evelyn said. She was writing something the entire time I spoke but nodded as if she could pull off multitasking in a way I couldn't. She flipped back a page in her pad and turned it around so I could see what was written in it. "I've made up an itinerary." She ran the pencil past a list of names written in impeccable handwriting. "These are all the churches I have to see. They each have a work of art that's important to me. You know how Moses looked in *The Ten Commandments*, with the big, white beard? There's a church in Rome with the Michelangelo Moses statue that inspired the film. I missed it last time, and I can't miss it again."

"I hope you have Trajan's Column," I said. "I have to see it. From a certain point of view, it's the earliest graphic novel. Some comic book scholars think so, anyway."

"Oh, it's on the list, for sure."

I leaned forward. "Show me what else you got."

She leaned forward, too, and pointed at the next work of art on the agenda.

I liked her perfume.

January 9, 1997

Aside from the incidents related above, our first few days in Siena were uneventful because the time that was not spent indoors waiting for it to stop raining was taken up by Valancourt's lectures. A three-hour lecture in the morning in the hotel sitting room was followed by a three-hour break for lunch and personal time, and then another three-hour lecture on location in a random Sienese church or museum, where Dr. Valancourt would lead the students from fresco to fresco, using art to bring medieval Italy to life. Unlike Evelyn, I hated medieval art, finding a lot of the subject matters of the drawings difficult to relate to. I had a strong preference for later Italian art by Caravaggio, Raphael, and Artemisia Gentileschi. My first clue that Bobby Mammolito agreed with me came when he said, "How many of these fucking frescoes are we gonna have to look at, at length?"

Much of the art Valancourt showed us dealt with his personal hero, St. Francis. My favorite pieces of Francis-related art, and my all-time favorite St. Francis story, involved the Wolf of Gubbio. Unfortunately, another popular artistic theme was the Slaughter of the Innocents, the killing of all the children in Bethlehem following the birth of Christ. These pieces brought back bad memories of Miss O'Sullivan succeeding in scarring me for life with her blasted late-term abortion photos. Being particularly sensitive to the notion of dead children, I would have found these frescoes too hard to take if the artwork were not so arcane. It helped that Evelyn was flippant about it all. "Didn't I tell you that we'd be seeing it everywhere?" she laughed. "In this church, there are three different paintings of the Slaughter of the Innocents. In the church we're seeing tomorrow, there's another Slaughter of the Innocents. And there's more coming still. Pretty soon, you're going to be seeing the Slaughter of the Innocents in your soup. It'll be stuck in your head forever."

"That's about par for the course for me." I still saw Miss O'Sullivan's damn photos in my head from time to time. I guess Catholics have always gone for "dead baby art" in a big way. The next several times Valancourt led us past a Slaughter of the Innocents, Evelyn and I burst out laughing, clutching each other by the shoulder and pressing our foreheads together. By the end of the week, we had seen eight such portraits. On the ninth, I could barely contain my hysterics, much to Valancourt's chagrin. Perhaps, at long last, I was beginning to find Miss O'Sullivan a little ridiculous, too. The memory of her shrieking in terror at me, like the bride of Frankenstein, certainly helped me cement my new impression of her as a broadly comic figure, like a Nazi lady from the British World War II sitcom *'Allo 'Allo*.

Not every piece of medieval Italian art was fundamentally disturbing and triggered bad memories. The much more benevolently entertaining icon who appeared time and again on our tours of medieval Italian art was the Blessed Agostino Novello, an Augustinian monk who was born in 1240 in Termini and died in 1309. He loomed large in artwork found in more than one church, but most notably in the Blessed Agostino Novello Triptych (Trittico di Sant'Agostino) painting by Simone Martini — an altarpiece found in the collection of the Pinacoteca Nazionale Siena. The altarpiece illustrated the balding, robed monk performing a stunning array of miracles, which collectively inspired Pope Clement XIII to beatify him in 1761. The painting that most impressed our group of students depicted Agostino Novello swooping from the sky to catch a child before it was dashed upon the ground. The scene was featured in the lower left section of the altarpiece and called, appropriately enough, "Child Falling from a Balcony." Since I was "the comic book guy," I didn't want to say anything, but the image looked remarkably like Christopher Reeve swooping in to save Margot Kidder from falling to her death from the top of the Daily Planet building. As it turns out, I didn't have to be the one to bring up Jerry Siegel and Joe Shuster's comic book creation.

Bobby and Tuesday both raised their fists up in the air, imitating Superman in flight. "Superman!" they shouted, in unison. Then, Bobby added, in a bellowing Staten Island accent, "The Blessed Agostino Novello *was* Superman! The very first Kryptonian to arrive on Earth, years before Kal-El landed in Smallville, Kansas!" As Bobby yelled these words, Byron scatted the opening bars of the John Williams theme to *Superman*.

Valancourt cooled his troubled brow by placing his cold can of Diet Pepsi against his temple. "Oh, no! You *all* like superheroes? Not just Damien? That's truly unfortunate." He pointed an accusing finger at me. "I had to sit in the row behind him the entire flight across the ocean. You never heard somebody talk so much about Spider-Man. Never!"

Byron laughed and clapped his hands. "We had a great conversation, Dr. Valancourt! Sorry you didn't enjoy overhearing it."

"I remember every word!" Valancourt wailed. "About how there should be a *Spider-Man* movie, but it shouldn't be directed by James Cameron and star Leonardo DiCaprio. Nor should it feature Sandman and Electro as villains. Instead, Spider-Man should be played by an actor who is ugly by Hollywood standards, like Tobey Maguire, and the director should be someone who specializes in horror comedy films, like Barry Sonnenfeld or Tom Holland. Instead of Sandman, the villain should be the Green Goblin and the film should adapt both the Spider-Man origin story from *Amazing Fantasy* such-and-such-a-number, plus *The Death of Gwen Stacy* by Gerry Conway. However, the filmmakers should swap Gwen Stacy out for Mary Jane, who is the more complex character. Blonde actress Kirsten Dunst should dye her hair red to be able to play Mary Jane. The Goblin should throw Mary Jane off the Brooklyn Bridge instead of Gwen, only this time, Spider-Man should catch the girl and she should survive. After all, killing off Mary Jane is too sad for a first *Spider-Man* film marketed to families. I have to tell you, Damien, I've had this monologue in my head ever since we landed in Italy and I can't shake it. The worst part is, I have no idea who any of these actors or directors or characters are, but I remember every gosh darn word you spoke on that flight! I want the space back in my brain that you stole!"

Byron, Evelyn, Purple Sarah, Bobby, Tuesday, Taran, and Bongo Guy laughed uproariously at Valancourt's impeccable comic delivery, made increasingly hysterical each time my face turned a darker shade of crimson.

Byron pursed his lips. "You know, I really don't see what you've got against James Cameron and Leonardo DiCaprio."

I shouldn't have replied, but I couldn't let that pass. "I'm telling you, the first movie needs to have Tobey Maguire, Kirsten Dunst, and some scary middle-aged actor as the Green Goblin. I don't care which. Maybe John Glover. Di Caprio could play the Human Torch, Doctor Strange, Iron Man, or Captain America, but he is way, way, way too handsome to be Spider-Man. Maybe he could be a John Romita-era Peter Parker. Maybe. But only Tobey Maguire could play the Steve Ditko Peter Parker, and Ditko's is the version of Spider-Man that needs to be put on screen first, before John Romita's. I may be a bad Italian saying it, but I still love Romita."

This time, Valancourt laughed along with everyone else, and I was the only one standing there with a serious expression, hoping everyone was taking notes on my genius fan-casting.

Byron and I sat in the sitting-room outside our shared room, failing to come to a consensus on when to have our Roman holiday weekend. I was not making headway convincing him it was in our interest to tag along with Evelyn. "We need a guide in Rome. We need a long weekend. If we go tomorrow, we'll have both. If we wait another week, we'll have neither. Next weekend is short, and Venice is small. We can explore it on our own."

"I don't want to spend three days in Rome," he said. "It's a city. I hate cities."

"Isn't there anything you want to see there?"

"I told Taran I was bored with the same old crap," Byron complained. "Everywhere we go in Italy it's the usual parade of frescoes. He said if I wanted something truly different, I should try the Santa Maria della Concezione dei Cappuccini bone mosaic."

I massaged my jaw. "That's different? Sounds like more religious wall art."

"I don't know. It's a bone mosaic. Taran says it is an ossuary."

I scrunched my eyebrows together. "That makes everything a lot clearer, except I've never heard of either an ossuary or a bone mosaic, but if it'll keep you quiet, okay. What else?"

"That's it. I'm not interested in anything else."

I threw my arms up in the air. "So why did you come to Italy?"

Byron shrugged. "I should have gone to Scotland to get in touch with my heritage. I want to put on a kilt, visit a castle, and run across the battlements, pretending I'm William Wallace."

"But you're in Italy!"

"And I'm not Italian and none of this speaks to me."

"I was under the impression my culture was cool to those not in it, but I guess not!"

"Evelyn is visiting all these churches. I hate churches. And I'm not into art much either."

"We'll spend some time in the Vatican, too. See the Pope!"

"That's something you're interested in. I don't like being Catholic. You do."

"Jesus Christ, Byron! If you don't like art, you don't like cities, and you don't like Catholicism, then why the did you come? All Italy is, is one giant church filled with art!"

"Don't shout at me," Byron said quietly. "I don't deserve to be shouted at."

(Years later, when I saw *In Bruges*, the scenes in which Colin Farrell greeted most of Belgium with an indifference that enraged Brendan Gleeson filled me with nostalgic glee. Had writer-director Martin McDonagh overheard this conversation, and noticed that Byron looked even more like Colin Farrell than he did Billy Baldwin? Probably not, but I pretended he did.)

"Byron, all you've done from the first second we got here is complain and pick fights with people. How many times are you gonna bring up the nobility of hunting game for food when talking to a bunch of vegetarian girls? I can't take it anymore. I've wanted to come to this country all my life. If you ruin it for me, I'll never forgive you."

Byron didn't move, but it was clear I had shaken him with the force of my words. "Don't put that on me, Damien. It's not fair."

"You put it on yourself."

Evelyn chose that instant to appear at the top of the stairs. "How's Happy Boy?"

"Impossible," I growled, and stalked past her out of the room.

January 10, 1997

The next day was Friday. Valancourt gave us the day off from classes, so Evelyn led Byron and I to the Rome bus early in the morning. It would be a three-hour trip all told, and she knew the best subway stops to take to reach the hotel from our point of arrival. I had chosen the Hotel Fellini, on Via Rasella, because it was named for one of my favorite filmmakers. Finding a poster for my current favorite movie — *Le notti di Cabiria* — in the stairwell gave me exactly the thrill of recognition I was looking for. By happy coincidence, the hotel was mere yards away from Trevi Fountain, making me laugh at myself for picking the hotel for the gimmicky name "Fellini" and not for its proximity to Trevi. By Byron's standards, the hotel was in a filthy urban area and he was nervous, but he liked the buffet breakfast room, with the deli meats, cheeses, pastries, breads, yogurt, and cappuccinos. As for the accommodations, we all found bathrooms with toilets, sinks, showers, and bidets in each of our rooms, so we didn't have to play paper-scissor-rock anymore to determine who gets the rooms with facilities. I spent many a long minute staring down at the bidet, wondering what the hell I was looking at.

Armed with umbrellas, Byron and I braved the rain to poke around the city. Taran had warned us all to look out for pickpockets with pinched faces, children included, who glided like ghosts through the streets. We should shout to frighten them off, he said. Taran also warned the girls to be wary of Italian men on the make, who would follow them about with roses and try to pick them up. I never witnessed, first-hand, an aggressive Italian Lothario descending upon one of the girls in our group. However, on the first day out with Byron, we did see the pickpockets and scare them away. They wore grey clothes and dark blue rain ponchos. Taran and Valancourt had called them gypsies, but they looked nothing like Esméralda from *Hunchback of Notre Dame* or Maleva in *The Wolf Man*, so the appellation seemed inappropriate. I didn't want my pocket picked, but I was actually worried about the children, who looked undernourished and sickly. I've never understood why wealthy countries don't do better helping poor people.

To appease Byron, it was only Byron and me on the first leg of the Rome journey. We did not link up our expedition with Evelyn's. Sadly, two hopeless idiots with a map and no sense of direction meant we spent much of the day on a fruitless search for the Coliseum. You'd think the Coliseum would be easy to spot! It isn't tiny, after all. We did manage to stumble on some of the humbler exhibits, such as the Discus Thrower statue in the Roman Baths, but I was annoyed when we bumped into Tuesday, Bobby, Sarah, Evelyn, and Bongo Guy at the Pantheon. Naturally, Evelyn had seen about eleven major landmarks in the three hours that it took Byron and I to find that Discus motherfucker. I swore that, argument or no argument, we'd be traveling with the expert tomorrow. "Just as long as we see the bone mosaic tomorrow," Byron agreed.

"Why not? I don't know what the hell it is, but I'm curious."

What is a *bone* mosaic? A 'mosaic' is a kind of pattern or an art installation? And a 'bone' is . . . a bone. So, what is a 'bone mosaic?' Nope. No idea. Can't figure it out.

Evelyn overheard the bone mosaic discussion and found herself interested enough to want to join us. Byron didn't mind because she was joining his expedition and not the other way around. The next morning, we set out while the others still slept to find the site of the bone mosaic. I didn't like the mutual dislike that hung in the air between Byron and Evelyn, and I attempted to dispel it with the sheer force of my enthusiasm. "Right then troops! No, not troops, team, um . . . gang . . . no, peeps! We're off!" I hummed the theme to *The A-Team* to build up team spirit between us. This plan did not work.

The Santa Maria della Concezione dei Cappuccini was surprisingly close to Hotel Fellini — a six-minute walk to the Via Veneto along the Vias Boccaccio, Tritone, and Barberini — but it took us three times as long to find under Byron's direction, because he refused on two occasions to tell Evelyn its address. "I just want to take in the city, Evelyn. If you spend all your time making straight line journeys from point A to point B, you miss out on a lot."

"That's true," I agreed.

"If you spend all day lost, you miss out on more," Evelyn pouted.

"No doubt we will find it shortly." I offered the sparring partners my most reassuring smile. *Mia Madonna. Everyone I know is stubborn. I'd love to be stubborn, too, but then nobody would be reasonable. So, I guess I'm stuck being flexible.*

The church's distinctive white marble and red-brown brick entranceway featured a pair of stairways, two flights each, facing one another — leading to the same elevated entrance door — forming a horizontal, diamond-shaped design. On the one hand, it looked indistinguishable from any other ancient building in Rome. On the other, the façade gave a sense of foreboding: we were about to enter one of Dario Argento's lairs of black magic, with a relentless Goblin music score starting as we crossed the threshold. Byron went through the entrance first, returning a second later, embarrassed. "I need a translation."

I stepped past Byron into a dark, candle-lit room. A balding, bearded monk in a dark brown habit stood before me. I was half convinced we had gone back in time four hundred years until a car horn honked outside. Silently, the monk pointed to a basket by the side of the door, labeled "Donations" in English and Italian. I pulled a few bills from my wallet. Not feeling much like doing the math to figure out how many lire equaled a reasonable entry price in American dollars, I guessed and carelessly dropped a few of the smaller bills into the basket. I had no idea if I had just been generous, cheap, or about right. Sylvia Plath was right: Tipping *is* hard.

The monk gestured down a long, narrow corridor on the right. We three headed that way. Over the past few days, Byron had used the words "bone," "mosaic," "crypt," and "ossuary" to describe this place, but nothing could have prepared me for the view I was about to receive. Running along the ceiling of the corridor were patterns made from every bone in the human body. There were rows of diamonds made from sets of jaw bones, flower designs made from teeth, and lamps of bone hanging suspended from the ceiling by leg bones. I pointed over our heads at the art and light fixtures made from the pieces of thousands of dead humans. "What?"

The first of three chambers appeared on our left. The walls were covered in jawless human skulls stacked one on top of the other. Hundreds of pairs of empty eye sockets stared at us and through us. In the second chamber, three complete skeletons dressed in monks' robes stood before another three displays of skulls. In the third chamber was a throne made of pelvic bones. George R.R. Martin's Iron Throne was made of swords. Both were shocking, but this pelvic bone throne won the fear-inducing championship.

I didn't know enough about the human body to identify most of the body parts I was confronted with and was glad for it. I could pretend this tableau was a strange prank by a LEGO enthusiast, or something. None of this could be real, could it? Actual dead bodies turned into a madman's art installation? Indeed, on one level, what I was looking at didn't appear human at all. You don't mourn a dead thing that doesn't look human. The problem was, I knew it was human. These were real bones, pulled from real dead people, shaped by an artistic genius. But what kind of sick mind would make this? I tried not to think of the Holocaust or of dead relatives or my own mortality, but I thought of little else.

"'I make art when somebody dies,'" I murmured, paraphrasing the Joker.

On the ceiling of the final chamber, the skeleton of a five-year-old child hung suspended from the ceiling, clutching in its hand a giant scythe made of bone. I gaped up at it, trying not to think of abortion or crib death or any dead children of any kind.

"What the fuck is this?" Byron exclaimed. His eyes were wide. A smile of shock, horror and amusement spread across his face.

"This is the weirdest shit I've ever seen," I said.

"Talk about Slaughter of the Innocents," Evelyn whispered.

Byron pointed to a plaque on the wall beside us. "This says these murals are made from the bones of 3,700 Capuchin friars. When? The Black Death?"

"If these bones are from any other time period, I demand an explanation," I said.

"But who would make art from piles of Black Death casualties?" Byron asked.

I shrugged. "Speaking as someone who has no idea what in hell he's looking at right now, if I had to live through the Black Death, I'd be crazy, too."

"Crazy enough to build something like this?" asked Byron.

Evelyn flipped to the correct page in her tour book and read it aloud. "The monks came to this church in 1631, bringing with them 300 cartloads of the exhumed remains of their order's friars. Fr. Michael of Bergamo designed and arranged the bones into small, bone-mosaic chapels, using soil imported from Jerusalem."

"Oh, God!" Byron pointed excitedly at a sign held aloft by one of the skeletons: "What you are now, we once were. What we are now, you will be."

"Dude!" I exclaimed.

"That's the scariest thing I've ever read," Byron breathed.

"Yeah," whispered Evelyn.

I pointed at one of the complete skeletons and adopted my Arnold Schwarzenegger accent. "'Jim Hopper?' Byron, 'I know dis man! Green Beret out of Fort Bragg. But what is he doing here?'" The unbearable tension finally broken, Byron and I tossed our heads back and laughed. I felt guilty laughing hysterically in this charnel house, but something had to give.

Evelyn scowled. "Okay, Peter Parker, that's enough turning everything into a joke. Now is not an appropriate time to quote the movie *Predator*."

"Now's the perfect time to quote *Predator*!" Byron retorted.

"It would be a great pledge location," I observed. "Lock the new guy in here overnight and see if he gets through it without running off or killing himself."

"Too right," Byron said.

"Nothing is as bad as the ookie cookie, but this would come a close second."

We walked among the bones for another ten minutes, drinking in the sight of death, talking about how creepy it was, but not finding a way to get ourselves to leave.

"I've had enough," said Evelyn. "I'll meet you guys outside."

"No, no," I said. "We're coming."

Before we stepped out the door, Byron and I made sure to get postcards of the displays. We didn't know why they were paying to keep that sight with us, but we knew we wanted to remember how it looked in the years to come. As we left, we took one last look at the monk, wondering if his bones would be added to the display after he died. Was that mosaic still under construction? We wanted to know the answer, and we didn't.

Two days later, when Byron and I saw Taran again, we laughingly reproved him for suggesting it to us. "What the hell was that, Taran?" Byron needled.

"That crypt separates the real Catholics from the ones who are just kidding around," he said. "I know a lot of Catholics who walked out of that place as Quakers."

CHAPTER THIRTY-TWO
The Impenetrable Fortress of Montalcino

January 13, 1997

We were back in Siena following our weekend excursion to Rome. I was still operating on full sensory overload. In the span of a few days, I had seen some of the greatest masterpieces of western art — including a personal favorite, Raphael's "School of Athens" — explored two of the major cities of my homeland, and had immersed myself in the history and theology of my religion. I had even completed a pilgrimage to the Vatican and purchased two sets of rosary beads blessed by the pope. Overstimulated, I found myself bombarded by a slew of existential thoughts. I was like a dog with a bone, gnawing away at the same questions, over and over.

Why did I buy even one rosary, let alone two? Was I still Catholic? If so, what kind? Why was I born Italian and not something else? What does it mean to be Italian? The Italians I had known in Junior High School cursed or ignored me because I was too concerned with reading and joking around and wearing pinstripe suits and purple shirts. Meanwhile, as many friends as I had made in Geneseo, there were not a lot of Italians among the Newman Community members I befriended, and there weren't a lot of Catholic or centrist STD members. Did I have a people? Did I have a tribe? I had thought going to Italy would resolve this crisis for me in some manner or other. Had it?

My hopes were partly dashed by supremely weird sights such as the bone mosaic and the Slaughter of the Innocents. Still, having seen such sights, I understood better why Italian movie directors made such violent films. The culture was steeped in violent art. After the bone mosaic, the gory murders in *Suspiria* seemed like scenes out of *Toy Story*. No wonder Brian DePalma, Martin Scorsese, and Quentin Tarantino all made such violent films. Still, the omnipresent bloody imagery was a bit much to process.

The language barrier was a bigger problem than I expected. Also, the centuries of history, while making the country fascinating and far more delicious than the comparatively young United States, meant I had a lot of catch-up learning to do before I could begin to assimilate.

Were these Italians from Italy really my people? Or was Damien Cavalieri just an American after all? I thought of Superman, who probably never felt like a bona fide human being, but a disguised Kryptonian in permanent exile in Metropolis. He probably hoped one day he could go back in time to visit Krypton before it exploded. He would then immerse himself in his real heritage and discover his true self. But even if Superman could find a way to return to a thriving Krypton, what would he find? People dressed as aliens, while he wore Clark Kent's human clothing. People speaking Kryptonian, while he spoke English. Superman probably never felt more Kryptonian when he was on Earth and never felt more human than when he was back on Krypton. I felt the same way in Italy. I never felt more Italian than when I was in America, and never felt more American than when I was in Italy. I was sick to death of feeling alienated.

Of course, it wasn't all strangeness in Italy. The food, for one thing, made me eternally happy. If only all the fast-food burger joints in America could blink out of existence and be replaced by these Italian restaurants. Also, if anything made me feel safe and welcome in Italy, it was the reassuring presence of the Virgin Mary. Mary was a staple of front lawns in Italian Catholic neighborhoods of Staten Island and Brooklyn. Still, by and large, America's Puritanical obsession with the inherent evils of idolatry kept art depicting Mary hidden from view. This subtle censorship angered and bored me. Conservative Protestants hated Catholic art because it was the wrong kind of Christianity — and Catholics are all destined to go to hell — and too many liberals hated Catholic art because it wasn't secular. Yawn. It often seemed to me that the one truth that both Democrats and Republicans agreed on was that Catholics were Neanderthals. No wonder us Italian Americans had no idea how to vote. What was the good of having a multicultural nation if every culture was afraid of showing its true religious, political, and artistic colors? Yes, it made a nice change of pace seeing Mary frequently about town, always welcoming me with her open arms, offering a motherly embrace.

Perhaps the most moving moment of all served as both a cultural touchstone and the capstone to my three years of study as an English major and Medieval Studies minor at Geneseo. Valancourt took us on a day trip to Florence primarily to visit the Basilica di Santa Croce, a church filled with funerary monuments dedicated to great Italians I had taken entire courses about at Geneseo, including Galileo Galilei, Michelangelo Buonarroti, Niccolò Machiavelli, and Dante. I couldn't believe that monuments to these figures whose personal letters, writings, and works of art I had studied so deeply were all in the same place, along with Leonardo Da Vinci, who popped up in a variety of my classes. I placed my hand over each of their memorials, and silently thanked them for modeling for me what Italian greatness looked like. I didn't tear up, because there were some emotional disconnects: The Middle Ages was a very long time ago, and I was a Southern Italian studying a bunch of guys more from the north. Still, it was a moment I have always carried with me, and a happy one.

How many people did I know who could relate to me having such an experience? A handful? None? How many people value history, art, religion, science, literature, and politics enough to even begin to grasp how seeing those tombs made me feel? Perhaps the issue wasn't my being a real Italian or a real American. Perhaps the issue was my being a real humanist. Sergio was Italian, but he didn't talk like someone who would respect me for being this moved by Santa Croce. Arwen was Jewish, but she *would* understand my reaction. No, my alienation from other people was not necessarily caused by religion or ethnicity, but about my being a humanist over a capitalist. That was the dominant issue in my life. The question of my being a real Italian or not was a vitally important concern, but secondary to the humanist issue.

My friend James Sheridan had tried to explain this to me when Byron Baldwin first introduced us a couple of years ago. James was tall and slim, with a runner's physique, and handsome in a Farley-Granger-meets-Montgomery-Clift kinda way. He was a history major with a particular interest in the American Gilded Age and would become the editor of the Geneseo school newspaper, *The Lamron*. Byron met James while looking for a lab partner in a Chemistry general education course. They got to talking and the moment James mentioned he had grown up on Staten Island before moving to Syracuse when he was in sixth grade, Byron knew he had to put us together. It turned out, we had far more in common than Byron could have dreamed. James had been an ALEC student at the Alfred Dreyfus School and had Mr. Altman as a teacher one year before I did. Once we met, James' description of what the ALEC program meant to him and his life helped put my own experiences in some perspective. As he explained it, "If you want to know why I study so hard, and am such a perfectionist, it is because ALEC really affected me. There was so much one-upmanship. It was intense and hard to keep up."

I said, "I was under the impression I didn't fit in because I was Italian."

James pondered that idea. "I think it was because you weren't as competitive as the others, and because you were into art and the humanities. The other students had embraced Social Darwinist ideas and were almost all STEM students. The ethnic divide is a red-herring."

This new idea made me rethink my entire life, which flashed before my eyes as if I were a Looney Tunes character frozen in place, gaping up in the air at an anvil plummeting towards my head. "Wow," I said. "That makes so much sense. It also explains why I didn't instantly gel with all the Italians I met outside of the gifted program. They didn't value the arts or humanities either, not because they were ambitious STEM students, but the children of laborers who thought all that stuff wasn't manly enough. Man, does anybody appreciate art, music, or the humanities?"

James nodded, "Yeah. Women."

My life flashed before my eyes again. "Aha! That's why I don't like talking to men! Except for you and maybe five other dudes. James, I want to marry you and have your babies!"

After taking a moment to think what I'd just said over, James decided I was sane, and said what I hoped he would: "Thank you. I'll take that as a compliment."

"You two had the same fifth-grade teacher one year apart? That's nuts!" Byron looked like he was feeling a bit left out. I was sorry about that, since I was very grateful for him finding James for us to be friends with. Byron had placed me in the company of someone who solved the mystery of my educational identity, and the riddle of why I kept bouncing in and out of various gifted programs. It all came down to my relationship to the humanities, and the level of disrespect afforded the humanities in America. Before the end of this Italy trip, Byron would strike gold a second time. He would put me in the way of an old Italian man who would solve for me the riddle of my Italian heritage.

But first, I had to try to make out with Evelyn . . .

Another week of classes followed. While the other five students and I listened to Valancourt's lectures in the mornings, Evelyn explored Siena and made plans for her next weekend trip, which would *not* be Venice, but Ravenna. She kept urging me to change my mind and go with her. After all, Dante's real tomb was in Ravenna. That memorial in Santa Croce did not contain his actual corpse. Still, I had to see San Marco in Venice. Neither of us would budge for the sake of the other. For his part, Taran wouldn't stop lobbying me to go to Padua, and he had convinced Byron that was the way to go. I didn't understand why it was so confusing to the others why I wanted to go. It was Venice, after all. My church was there, the streets were made of water, and it was the setting of Henry James' novel *Wings of the Dove*. Venice was also the place where Indiana Jones made love to Elsa Schneider and the dwarf in the red coat stabbed Donald Sutherland to death. In the end, Byron and Purple Sarah accompanied me to Venice, and we all loved it, even if I didn't have a refined enough palette to enjoy eating an octopus in black-ink sauce. Since Evelyn had gone to Ravenna instead, I got to hum Charles Aznavour's "How Sad Venice Can Be" on the train ride down, but not really mean it. I was in too good a mood to be truly crushed. Even though it was touristy, we took a gondola ride and loved it. I took a huge ferry back and forth across Venice multiple times because it was awesome. In Saint Marc's Square, Byron stood like a scarecrow and let birds land on him. Purple Sarah photographed me in front of San Marco's, waving "Hello" to Mom.

Mother, I have come home!

That trip occurred on the weekend of the seventeenth. Between the thirteenth and seventeenth, Byron and I ate dinner with Sarah and Evelyn each night. Since the food at the Locanda Garibaldi was exceptional, we frequently ate there. Wherever we went, we tried a new meal. Each night Byron would wind up with a plate that looked twice as good as mine. Then, the next night, I'd get what he had the night before, and he would be blessed with something that looked better still. When I knew I would be going to Italy, part of me feared that the cooking there would be so good that it would make my mother's best dishes, especially her home-made lasagna, seem inadequate. I was thankful that lasagna from Siena tasted totally different from my mother's version. Since the two kinds were apples and oranges, her cooking could remain undefeated in my heart, even after I tasted the cuisine of the motherland. I could stop worrying.

Our palettes developed over the course of these meals. I had always been more of a tea drinker than a coffee drinker and, as a result, did not fully appreciate either cappuccino or tiramisu. Before long, I was drinking cappuccino and eating tiramisu with every meal and developing an insatiable hunger for them. They were so delicious. I had *no* idea! I was a full-on convert to both cappuccino and tiramisu now and would remain so for life. Also, while I had not been a huge olive fan, I started to really love them, cultivating my taste with the black olive — the gateway olive — before moving onto the green one. For all the food we ate, you would have thought that we put on a ton of weight while in Italy. The reverse was true. We ate a large lunch and light breakfasts and dinners, and did so much walking that, by the time we returned to America, we had all lost five to ten pounds.

Every night after dinner, I would walk around Siena with Evelyn. Sometimes Byron and Sarah walked with us, but not always. On a lark, the four of us saw an Italian-dubbed version of the Sylvester Stallone movie *Daylight* at a local theater. Since it was a disaster movie, dialogue was not important, and we all enjoyed it. We also went to see Madonna in *Evita* two nights in a row because we loved it. A few years had passed, but Madonna was still my old friend in the yummy teddy from the "Like a Prayer" music video, who had helped introduce me to the idea that women were "super purty." Taran went with us the first night and declared *Evita* the worst film he had ever seen. Amusingly, Taran could speak with perfect conviction about a subject, no matter how profound or how minor, and sway me almost every time, but I retained some of my enjoyment of *Evita*, even after Taran had put a huge dent in my enthusiasm.

"Own your reaction," Evelyn advised me. "There are no wrong responses to art. Even if there are, be proud of being wrong. Your experience of art is your experience of art. Embrace that and don't be influenced by anyone else. Respond to what you respond to."

I pointed to Taran. "I really want him to think I have good taste, but I kinda like *Evita*."

Taran nodded enthusiastically. "Evelyn is right. *Evita* is a pile of shit, but if you're the sort of person who likes immersing himself in shit, then by all means, take a deep dive into it."

"Madonna's my girl," I declared. "It's cool. I'm not too shy to tell people I actually like *Secret Wars*, Bon Jovi, and *Star Trek V*. Never fear: I hate *Maximum Carnage* and *Generations*."

Taran had never heard of *Secret Wars*, but closed his eyes and counted backwards from a hundred to stop himself from opining on Bon Jovi and William Shatner's opus, *Star Trek V*.

It was great spending all this time with Evelyn, but I desperately wanted to be alone with her on a date. What would it be like to have dinner with just her? There were too many people around us and it was too much of a habit for us all to get together every night for food to break off and do our own thing. For months prior to this trip, I had fantasized about having an affair in Italy. Would I meet a saucy Italian bar wench, or a bookish British tourist? Could I be the younger man one of the older British ladies from *Enchanted April* had a passionate affair with? Would a romance with such a woman — or with Evelyn — be a short fling, or would I be meeting my future wife? No. Let's not get carried away. This was me we were dealing with. And yet, could I take some concrete action to make a fantasy into a reality? What if I did, actually, ask Evelyn out? Could something happen between us? Or was sex only for Tuesday and Bobby Mammolito, who had been humping loudly the entire trip? Just as I settled on making a move, I felt my grandfather's reticence build within me. Failure was inevitable. Why even try? Also, I had such a nice friendship with her. Why would I want to ruin it? For the opportunity to make out? There would almost certainly not be sex, considering our personalities. Was a handful of kisses and maybe a quick breast squeeze worth the risk of blowing our friendship to smithereens?

I thought about it at length and concluded that I was prepared to destroy the friendship.

*

January 21, 1997

I returned to my room in the Locanda Garibaldi to greet Byron with a sullen face. "I don't know what to do about Evelyn."

"That makes two of us," Byron replied.

It was clear Byron was not overly interested in the conversation, but I needed to talk to him. "I think she knows I'm attracted to her."

"And?"

"She's pushing me away."

"So, don't hang out with her anymore."

"Weirdly, she may like me back. I think. I'm getting mixed signals."

"I don't know, Damien. She spends a lot of time following you around, but that might not mean anything. She might just want to be your friend, or some bullshit."

"I've just been talking to her for two hours in her room," I said. "For a while, it was a great conversation. She talked to me about why she loves medieval art and how her dream is to one day become a coach for the Mets."

"The Mets, huh? Not the Yankees?"

"She hates Steinbrenner," I confirmed. "Says he buys all his championships."

"That's great. You hate baseball and medieval art."

I smiled. "She's so enthusiastic about these things that it rubs off on me. I see the beauty of the art and the excitement of the sports through her. Anyway, we got to talking and I was so excited by her that I tried to move in closer. I wanted to kiss her. But I was scared I'd get the Recoil. I couldn't just plant one on her. But asking for permission is like negotiating a contract. Kills all the romance. I had to figure on something in between."

Byron was finally paying attention. "What did you do?"

"When the moment felt right, I brushed her cheek with my hand and told her she was beautiful."

"What happened?"

I dropped down onto my bed and stared up at the high, white ceiling. "I think it embarrassed her. I don't think she's used to that kind of attention."

Byron laughed. "That doesn't sound too good for you."

"She spent the last half hour telling me how she never wants to get married or have kids, and since the only purpose of dating is to find someone to marry, she's not interested." How had the conversation gone? I asked her if she wasn't worried about wasting her youth. She asked me what the upshot would be of enjoying her youth. From her perspective, the inevitable outcome would be one of two things: "So, I can be a divorced, thirty-year-old single mom saddled with a five-year-old kid? Or I could be a bitter, forty-year-old woman with two kids in high school and a mute, disengaged husband sleeping with his secretary? What price is paid for enjoying youth?"

I spread my hands in frustration. "Well, if you want to be *negative* about it."

I related all this to Byron and he clenched his hair in his fists. "That was her response to you telling her she's beautiful? That crap?"

"Yes. She does have a point."

"No, she doesn't. To hell with her."

I cleared my throat. "I think she's protecting me from falling for her because she knows we can't be together."

"She's right," Byron said. "You'll regret this down the line. She lives in Royville and you live on Staten Island."

"If I'm too scared to make a move in this situation, where there's little to lose and a lot to gain, then how can I hope to be brave when the stakes are higher?"

"You'll probably never see each other again after this trip is over."

"All the more reason to act quickly," I said.

"It's not worth it."

I sucked my teeth in irritation. "I thought you wanted me to act more like Lancelot!"

"I do."

"What's the deal? You want her for yourself?"

Byron was wounded. "No! Of course not. She doesn't like Billy Joel. You can have her. Still, I don't like the idea that she's the first person you're gonna ask out in three years, and she's frigid. What do you do when she breaks your heart? Take another vow of celibacy? You really are better off chasing some horny married broad than gambling on this 'available' ice queen."

I paused. "Speaking of Guinevere, is there anything I can do to convince you to take the curse of the Cat People off my head?"

"No, there isn't. It's for your own good."

I tried to sound indifferent to this news. "Good thing I'm not superstitious."

"But you *are* superstitious," Byron said.

I chuckled.

Tuesday's voice came through the wall. "Ask Evelyn out, Damien. If she says, 'No,' she says, 'No.' Shake off the rejection and try asking out someone else. That's how it works."

"Thanks, Tuesday!" I called back through the wall.

"There's no privacy in this damn hotel," Byron grumbled.

"Don't you think she's being slow to respond?" I called back to Tuesday.

Tuesday's voice broke back through the wall. "You were sitting on her bed talking for hours about the *Mets*? Maybe she thinks you're slow to respond. Maybe she's wondering why you haven't flipped her over and gently slid your dick into her asshole yet."

My jaw dropped. "What did she just say?" I mouthed to Byron.

"Come on," Byron said to the wall. "Evelyn's so damn repressed."

"All the more reason to fuck her ass good," Tuesday called back. "I'm quiet, and I love me some ass play, but only if enough lube is involved."

"Lube?" Don't auto mechanics use lube? Must be a different kind of lube...

Byron turned green and sat down on the edge of his bed. "I think I need to go downstairs and get me a mineral water."

"She's worried I'll get her pregnant, I think," I said to the wall.

"What have we been talking about?" Tuesday replied. "You are up on your biology, right? You won't get her pregnant if you give her a fierce ass ramming."

"She can probably hear all this through the ceiling," I whispered to Byron.

"Thanks for the advice," Byron called back to Tuesday.

"No problem," the wall replied in Tuesday's voice.

"Seems like great advice, if you want to get yourself arrested," Byron said quietly.

Byron and I laughed soundlessly until we cried. Once we recovered ourselves, I wanted to reassure Byron I wasn't ignoring his advice. "I'm not an idiot. I know I'm working against some kind of phobia of hers that's preventing her from giving in to her attraction to me. But I may manage to break down her defenses if I'm persistent."

"I'm a big believer in, 'If it don't come easy, you better let it go," Byron said.

"I'm just tired of being afraid of living," I said. "I'm going to do it. I don't care about the future. All I care about is right now."

Byron stared at me. "This doesn't sound like you. What changed?"

I smirked. "What you are now, we once were. What we are now, you will be."

Byron laughed. "Party now, before the next Black Death hits! Because, when it does, none of us will be allowed to fuck anyone without risking becoming lepers!"

January 22, 1997

The next afternoon, sitting on the great double-bed in Evelyn's room, with Evelyn beside me, I said, "How is it somebody as pretty as you has no boyfriend?"

Evelyn smiled and looked down on the bed. "I don't know. I just don't. I haven't even liked anyone since I was nineteen."

"*Six years?*"

Evelyn nodded. "I don't have much use for dating, anyway."

Okay, here goes. "Would you mind if I asked you to dinner? Just the two of us?"

"I'd like that very much," Evelyn said softly.

The dinner date happened that night. We were oddly formal with one another at the outset, typical of two people who had little experience with romance. Neither of us knew what we were doing, so we were forgiving of one another. After we got to the restaurant, it became clear that Evelyn was not the sort of person who responded well to gentlemanly gestures like opening doors or buying flowers. This put me on guard, because those traditions had helped me demonstrate my feelings in the past, and I was no longer able to use them as a crutch. Instead, I would be natural and talk to her as he had been all along. I made no romantic moves towards her the night before because she didn't seem ready for them, and the time wasn't right. I had wanted their relationship to evolve slowly and naturally. The evening was so enjoyable that I was only partly disappointed we didn't kiss. I still didn't know where I stood with her, because she was so eccentric, but I knew she wouldn't agree to the date if she didn't feel *something*.

January 23, 1997

The next major outing was to the Fortress Castle in Montalcino, designed by Mino Foresi and Domenico di Feo of Siena and built in 1361. Valancourt chartered a bus to take the students to the structure, which stood in the middle of the most beautiful scenery I had ever seen. Had I ever seen a horizon before that day in Montalcino? Growing up in the crowded suburbs, I rarely had an opportunity to see a clear sky, let alone the miles of beautiful land that cultivated the grapes used to make Brunello di Montalcino wine. The five-sided fortress was obviously man-made, but so old and grandiose that I imagined it had grown organically from the rocky ground — a stone plant that morphed into a fortress. An impressive tower sprouted from each angle of the pentagon, and all the students were eager to see the view of the hill town from the top of at least one of the towers. Thankfully, Valancourt gave us the time we needed to wander around the castle. As we explored, he sent Taran to buy and bring back lunch for us all, so we could picnic on the wooden tables in the courtyard.

I had hoped that the castle would be cool enough, and the walls high enough, that I could walk along the battlements atop the five walls without triggering my fear of heights. Sadly, that was not to be. When we reached the top of the main wall, Byron's face lit up like a kid at Christmas. He ran up and down the battlements whooping out with joy. As a fan of Drizzt Do'Urden of *Forgotten Realms* and worshipper of the move *Braveheart*, Byron had found the Italy he had been looking for. A startling contrast to Byron, I crept tentatively along the crumbling battlements, wondering how anyone could stand guard on such a precarious position, let alone defend it during a siege. One false move and you were a bloody pancake on the floor.

Byron stopped running around long enough to notice how unsteady I was on my feet. "Don't tell me you're scared."

I smiled sheepishly.

"You got to be kidding! This is the coolest thing ever, and you're scared?" He laughed and then continued running around, pretending to brandish a sword. "I am William Wallace! 'Every man dies, but not every man truly lives!' 'They may take our lives, but they will never take our freedom!' 'FREEDOM!'"

"Yeah, I'm not truly living," I grumbled, and felt myself teeter on the battlement edge.

Somehow, while I was trying to keep my balance, Evelyn and Sarah found their way up to this level. "You coming with us to see the tops of the towers?" Sarah asked.

"That's the plan." I swallowed the lump in my throat. *Towers, plural? One ain't enough?*

Evelyn made her way to the closest tower, and Sarah and I followed. Evelyn stopped at a long ladder made of sturdy pieces of wood. She stared up and saw that it was a long climb to the top. More than fifty feet? "Wow. That looks scary." She got halfway up the ladder before she felt a pang of fear, paused, and looked down at me.

"It's okay," I said. "Just head on up. Don't look down."

She nodded and crept her way up. She disappeared through the hole at the top of the tower. *If I dart up the ladder as quickly as I can, I can impress her by being extra brave. I can also be alone with her at the top of the tower. That would be a good time to kiss her. I can kiss a lady in a tower. Byron's Arthurian Romance high is becoming contagious.*

Without looking down, I raced up the ladder as quickly as I could. Reaching the top, I clambered up out of the gaping hole in the tower floor and stepped out onto what was probably the smallest elevated platform ever made. The half-ruined tower was missing large chunks of its wall, so there would be no barrier preventing anyone who wanted to from simply walking off the edge. Everywhere I looked, I saw a huge drop. In front of me, there was a sheer drop along the side of the castle. On my left and right were other drops where I could splatter all over the castle interior. Behind me was a plummet to my death down the long ladder.

Hail Mary, full of grace, the Lord is with thee . . .

Evelyn tossed her arms back and breathed in the open air. "What a wonderful view!"

"Oh, my God," I moaned. I didn't want to move my legs because any step would take me closer to the edge, but not moving my legs made me feel wobbly. Each time I wobbled, I saw the drop. *Uh-oh. Getting dizzy. I should just go back down the ladder. I got up it. I could go down.*

I peered down the ladder. The first rung was so far down I would have to lower myself waist-deep into the hole until my feet found support. What if I missed that first rung? My eyes fixed upon the plummet through space that awaited me if I slipped. I sat myself on the stone floor beside the hole, unwilling to try to lower myself onto the ladder. I hugged my knees to my chest, too afraid to do anything but stare off into nothingness. I wouldn't allow my eyes to register the sky around me. I had always been afraid of heights, but never had such an attack of vertigo before. Even during my most intense junior high school skirmishes with bullies, I never felt so close to my own death.

"Are you okay?" Evelyn asked. She rested a hand on my shoulder. "What's wrong?"

God, why does she have to see me like this? Why do I have to be so weak in front of a woman? I have to be strong. I have to impress her, so she loves me.

Purple Sarah popped her head up from the hole in the ground. "Ah, it's nice up here." She hoisted herself up off the ladder and out of the hole onto the tower. "What's wrong, Damien?"

"Nothing. I'm okay," I said. *Fuck. Fucko. Fucki. Fucka. Fuckiamo. Fuckate. Fuckano.*

Sarah must have adored the view from the tower because she faced each of the four main compass points and called the quarters, using the updated spell translation provided by the recent witchcraft movie, *The Craft*. "'Hail to the Guardians of the Watchtowers of the North! By the Powers of Mother and Earth, Hear us.'" She invoked the guardians for the other three points, too.

Bobby and Tuesday climbed up out of the ladder hole next. How could we all fit on such a small tower? As the students walked around the hole in the floor, they had to avoid bumping into one another. None of them seemed scared. *What's with these people?*

"What a beautiful view," said Tuesday.

"Egon!" Bobby yelled. "You look scared shitless! Are you okay?"

"I'm okay," I quivered.

Bobby punched my shoulder. "Shake it off, dude. You don't want to look bad in front of all these stone-cold foxes."

"I know, I know. I'm trying."

Impatient to see each of the towers in the time allotted by Valancourt, Bobby and Tuesday skittered back down the ladder, sprinted along the battlements below, and climbed at high speed up to the top of the next tower. I was half-aware they were bouncing around the castle top as easily as Spider-Man and I was amazed by their dexterity and bravery.

Byron's head appeared in the hole in the ground. "Hey! You're up here! Is it as awesome as it seems?" He pulled himself onto the tower, gushed at the scenery all around the castle, and proceeded to take as many photographs of it as he could. "This is a life-changing experience, dude. You should try to enjoy it."

"I wish I could," I said. I had clamped my eyes shut and had no access to any scenery.

Evelyn moved closer to me and said gently, "Want me to help you down the ladder?"

"Yes, please." *Oh, my God, I am heartily sorry for having offended thee . . .*

"Want me to go down first and you follow, or do you want me to help lower you down?"

"I don't know," I said, my voice wavering. As mortified as I was, I tried to be big and laugh at myself. I managed a smile and small laugh. *Glory be to the Father, and the Son . . .*

"You have to tell me, or I can't help you," said Evelyn.

"I'll go first." I moved slowly towards the hole in the ladder and then stopped abruptly. "Wait. No. I can't."

"Do you want me to go first?" Evelyn whispered.

"Yes, please, Miss Evelyn."

"Okay."

Evelyn walked over to the hole and tried to figure out how to lower herself onto the ladder. She sat on the edge of the hole, dangling her legs in the air over the first rung. She then planted her hands on either side of the hole and pushed her bottom over the edge. She hung in the air a moment, supported only by her locked arms. Then she bent her elbows and her feet found support. Once this was done, she had to do an awkward maneuver to turn herself around so she could back down the stairs. Then, she was ready and climbed quickly down the stairs.

What was that, a seventeen-step process to find the first ladder rung? Christ.

Several seconds went by.

"Damien!"

"Yes?"

"I made it down."

"Okay."

"Come and see."

I slowly leaned forward and peered into the hole. She was at the base of the ladder, looking up. She was so far below, she looked like an action figure. "You can do it, Damien."

Byron, who was still on the tower with me, agreed. "You can do it, man."

I exhaled sharply through my nose. "Okay."

I stood and tried to will myself to approach the ladder. I was posed as if I would start walking, but I wasn't in any danger of moving. Some time passed.

"What are you trying to do, use the Force?" asked Byron. "Go down the fucking ladder!"

I laughed. That joke was the inspiration I needed to get going. I'd had it with looking the fool in front of Evelyn. Focusing only on her face, I duplicated the same maneuver she used to find the first rung. I knew I was home free the moment my feet reached the rung. I went down the ladder as quickly as I could. Suddenly, I was at Evelyn's side again.

She gave me a thumbs up sign. "There you go. You made it."

"Thanks. That sucked."

She pointed up at the hole in the tower where Byron had appeared to make his descent. "You looked so cute when your head appeared up there, looking down on me. You had this adorable, frightened chipmunk face on."

I pictured it and laughed. "Good lord, I can imagine."

On the bus ride back to Siena, Evelyn was oddly cool to me. We sat next to one another, but she seemed to not want to speak to me at all. Saying she was not feeling well, she placed headphones over her ears and started listening to her Ringo Starr CD. She didn't speak a word the trip back. After reaching the hotel, I complained to Byron about her for twenty minutes. Byron agreed with everything I said, but no longer opposed my continued pursuit of her.

Shortly after nightfall at 6:30, I went to Evelyn's room. I sat on the bed beside her as she made up a list of all the Mets games of the current season and tried to calculate how many she'd be able to realistically see commuting from Royville. She spoke rapidly and nervously as she told me about it, again an odd mixture of standoffishness and eagerness. Part of her screamed out for me to kiss her while the other part just wanted to make me go away. For half a second, I thought that Evelyn was wordlessly signaling me to start unbuckling her belt, like Tuesday suggested. Then I realized that Tuesday was wrong. Evelyn wasn't signaling me. It was my dick asking me to reach for Evelyn's belt. This truth was surprisingly difficult for me to admit to myself, but it was the way things were. I couldn't grab her belt. Nope. Nope. Nope.

"Do you want to take a walk?" I asked. It was two hours earlier than we usually walked with Sarah and Byron, so the request was unusual.

Evelyn considered this before giving a slightly hesitant, "Yes."

It was a cold night out. We walked side by side to the D'Uomo, the main church of Siena. It was her favorite building in the city, and we would often include it on their walks, but she was particularly insistent that we head directly for the church. It was a none-too-subtle way of telling me she was still confused about our relationship. When we reached the church, she asked that we go to the other side of the main square and sit on a low wall across from its façade. I sat next to her on the cold stone, looking with her at the dozens of saints' statues on the Gothic structure. She considered saying something about the artistry of the church but didn't.

As I sat there with her, looking at the church, I knew there would never be a better time. She was ready and so was I. I reached down and gently placed my hand on hers. She lowered her head and smiled in muted disbelief. I laced my fingers through hers and moved closer.

"I don't understand," she whispered. "There must be so many things you'd rather be doing than sitting here with me."

"There are," I said, and leaned forward to kiss her.

She lifted her head to mine, letting my lips touch hers. I placed my arm around her waist and pulled her closer to me as I kissed her. I felt the warmth of her body through her coat. Once the kiss started, we abandoned all the inhibitions that had been holding us in check from the beginning. She put her arms tentatively around my neck and kept kissing me, not doing anything to push me away. As we kissed, I was aware of the D'Uomo beside us, standing there as it had always stood, every day for the past five hundred years.

How is this happening? How am I with this wonderful person? I shoved the unwanted thoughts aside. Even though I knew that we might never be together again after we returned to America, I felt happy and alive. For the first time in years, I wasn't afraid of living.

CHAPTER THIRTY-THREE
The Real Italian

January 23, 1997
    10:30 a.m.
    I was on my way back to the Locanda Garibaldi with a box of chocolates tucked under my left arm, a bouquet of yellow tulips in my left hand, and a bouquet of red roses in my right. I walked with a spring in my step while singing "Sugar, Sugar" by the Archies. I knew I was being cheesy, but I didn't care. I was too absurdly happy to concern myself with how ridiculous I must have looked to everyone I passed on the streets of Siena. Just as I reached the front entrance to our hotel, Taran emerged and almost walked into me. He looked me over and smiled at the spectacle I made, singing and bearing an armload of gifts into the hotel. "Are those for Evelyn?"

    I blushed. "Yeah."

    "Things are going well then?"

    "I think so. I don't want to jinx it."

    "Good." Taran rubbed his jaw, thoughtfully. "There's a lot of lonely, brilliant students in Geneseo with 4.0s. They've prepared all their lives for their careers. Romance? Not so much. I was worried you two would fail to mesh or push each other away. I'm so glad to be wrong!"

    "I'm glad you're wrong, too! Man, I was *super* lonely, and I only had a 3.34 GPA!"

    "You two had your first date already?" he asked.

    "We did. It went well!"

    "You're making me remember my first date with my wife. We went to see *Billy Jack Goes to Washington*. Awful movie. Wonderful date. You two enjoy yourselves." Taran beamed at me, waved goodbye, and headed off to run some errands.

    I stepped inside the Locanda Garibaldi and found Tuesday sitting alone at one of the restaurant tables, doing homework. Tuesday smiled at the flowers. "Evelyn will love those."

    "I hope she likes the roses." I held out the bouquet of yellow tulips. "These are for you."

    Tuesday looked up at the Tulips in muted surprise. "For me? Why?"

"Even though I never intended to tease or insult you, my intentions don't matter. What mattered is I hurt you. I'm genuinely sorry about that. I didn't mean it, but I still should have behaved better. That's why these flowers are for you. I swear they are a gesture of apology and not a romantic overture. Scout's honor. Nevertheless, I'll understand if you don't want them."

Tuesday reached up and accepted the flowers. "They're lovely."

"A couple of the other bouquets were a little wilted. I thought this one was fresh. I tried."

Tuesday became pensive. "I'm sorry about all that stuff you went through in the band room that time. You know, that whole scene with Marina and Eric carrying you around. I know Eric was trying to help you, and I wanted to help you, but it was so not good."

I waved the awkward scene from our past away. "Ah, fuhgeddaboudit. I wouldn't have known what to do in your shoes, either."

"I almost forgot that all that was about Bobby spreading stupid rumors about Marina. And now I'm dating him. Why? I have no idea. I shouldn't be with him after what he did to her."

"I guess that was a long time ago and some people grow and change?" I asked.

She looked the flowers over wistfully. "Bobby hasn't bought me any flowers yet."

The remark made me nervous. "I didn't buy these for you to cause Bobby problems. I just thought I owed you an apology. Maybe he hasn't had the opportunity yet?"

"You found one." Tuesday held aloft the flowers I just gave her.

"I'm just glad you like them. I didn't want to disturb you or your homework." I started towards the stairs.

Tuesday's voice stopped me. "Do you think Bongo Guy buys flowers for his girlfriends?"

I smiled, remembering him toking up inside his igloo. "He gives them weed, at any rate."

Tuesday turned grave. "Maybe I should go with Bongo Guy."

I held up my hands in surrender. "I'm gonna stay out of this one, if it's okay with you."

"It is," said Tuesday. "Hey, thanks for the flowers, Damien. They made my day."

We laughed together.

I stepped onto the third floor as Purple Sarah emerged from the room she shared with Evelyn. "Damien!" When she called out my name, I remembered I didn't like to hear it shouted. It made me think of all the times people shouted "Damien!" before being murdered by Satan in the *Omen* movies. One woman even yelled it before publicly hanging herself at a kid's birthday party. Sarah eyed my flowers and chocolates. "Those are for Evelyn?"

Her expression made me uneasy. "Oh, no. What's wrong?"

Sarah glanced back at the closed door of her room. Through the clouded window, we could see Evelyn dressing and putting make-up on. Sarah grabbed me by the elbow and led me towards the stairwell. Lowering her voice, she said, "Last night, Evelyn was so excited you kissed her, she couldn't sleep. So, we got dressed and took a walk really late at night to talk about you. And it was nice for a while. But now I'm so sorry we went out, because it screwed everything up for you."

I felt cold. "Oh?"

Sarah closed her eyes and kept speaking. "This Italian paratrooper saw us by the D'Uomo and came up to us. He was interested in both of us, but Evelyn looks like Claudia Schiffer, so he settled on her pretty quick. He was insanely handsome. Like . . . insane."

"Well, shit," I murmured.

"For a while, it was the three of us talking and joking, but I felt myself getting frozen out. I tried to get her away from him a few times, but she gave me this look like, 'I know you're friends with Damien, but stop messing this up for me.' So, I just came back here and left them there by the D'Uomo. I wasn't even two yards away when they started making out in front of it."

"That is an extremely cool place to make out. It has a powerful romantic ambiance."

"When I talked to her this morning, she said they stayed out late together. She's putting on her face now to go see him again. His name is Giuliano."

"Giuliani? There's gratitude for you! After Staten Island got him into Gracie Mansion?"

"Giuliano." Sarah looked at me pleadingly. "Listen, I know you just got her flowers and chocolates, but if I were you, I wouldn't go in there. I've been talking to her, and she's all into Giuliano now. And she's been saying weird stuff about you, like you reference movies too often, and used suspicious Cary Grant quotes when flirting with her."

"Oh, I never quote Cary Grant," I said. "A man's got to know his limitations. But I do reference movies too often. She's got me nailed to the wall."

"She says she thinks you're a seducer and your emotions aren't real. Don't take it too seriously. It's baloney she's using to justify running off with Giuliano because she feels guilty."

"She doesn't trust me? But this paratrooper dude is above suspicion?"

"And please don't feel bad about Giuliano. There's no shame in losing to him. He's dead sexy. Like, a ten out of ten. I mean, whoa. He's . . . *damn*! He's super hot. Super hot."

"Well, thank you for letting me know that," I said. "It puts things in perspective. Man, I tell you what, these military guys sure love putting me firmly in my place. Firmly. In my place."

"I'm only telling you this, so you know Evelyn wasn't out to hurt you. I mean, you shoulda seen this guy. Giuliano was Count Dracula sexy. He had this need to make love that you could feel crackling in the air around him. His Italian male sexual hunger was *overpowering*."

"Italian guys can be like that," I admitted. "Or so I've read."

"His godly handsomeness combined with that Italian hunger? No woman could resist it."

"I'll take your word for it. I mean, it sounds feasible."

"Just, please don't be too hard on her," Sarah said. "And don't allow her to walk all over you or talk crap about you being phony just to get herself off the hook."

"Okay, okay." I looked down at the roses and chocolates and had no idea what to do with them. "I better get this over with." I handed Sarah the chocolates. "I want you to have these. You're a good friend and a good person. Also, dropping truth bombs on a buddy is never fun."

Sarah took them and grimaced. "Are you sure?"

"Please. Enjoy the chocolates. You've earned them for doing everything you could to help me." I inclined my head towards Evelyn's room. "I'm going to go give her the roses now."

"I wish you wouldn't go in there."

"I have to try," I said. "If I don't even try, I'll make the same mistake my grandfather made. I'm going to go for the 'No.' Of course, that means making things extra hard for us both."

"If this ends badly, remember you still have friends."

"Thanks."

"Listen, when we get back to Geneseo for the spring term, me and the STD girls will take you out and toast your coolness. We'll go to Nick Tahou Hots to grab us some Garbage Plates, then hit the bars and see Spirit of the West play a set."

When she said this, I really did feel like smiling. "Now that's a date I'd be honored to go on with y'all! That sounds very, very fun."

"Then you better come out with us! Don't go back to hiding in your Hobbit hole."

"I won't. Don't worry. I'll go with you." I paused, then looked fearfully at the door to Evelyn's room. "I feel like Billy Martin about to walk into George Steinbrenner's office."

"Yeah."

"Little baseball joke." I cleared my throat. "So, this Giuliano guy is really mega hot?"

"Ten out of ten." Sarah was crying for me now. It wasn't every day someone cried for me. That meant a lot. It really did. I was still in shock, so I couldn't cry. I think she cried for me because I wasn't able to do it for myself.

"Oh, well. Thanks for worrying about me. You're a sweet kid." I chucked Sarah under the chin. Sighing, I walked up to the door to Evelyn's room with the bouquet of roses held up. I turned back to Sarah and mouthed, "This is gonna suck!" Then I knocked on the door.

Purple Sarah held her breath and closed her eyes as Evelyn let me in the room.

*

Byron nursed a pint of Guinness as I downed an amaretto on the rocks. We sat on the barstools in the Irish Pub in Siena, talking to the sandy-haired barkeep, Cormack. I had gotten off on the wrong foot with the man by toasting to the six counties under John Bull's tyranny, adding, "Twenty-six plus six equals one!" Cormack informed me, patiently, that seeing a Daniel Day-Lewis movie about the Troubles did not give me the right to make such toasts, so I apologized. I had already seen *In the Name of the Father*, and was one year away from seeing *The Boxer*, a painfully sexy "forbidden romance" movie about Daniel Day-Lewis' title character falling in love with Emily Watson, who plays the wife of a jailed IRA terrorist. Something about Daniel Day-Lewis' dilemma in that film spoke to the core of my being. Still, Cormack was right. I was no expert on the Troubles before or after seeing either *The Boxer* or *In the Name of the Father*.

Cormack said, "Ireland was the laboratory for imperialism. The British subjugated us first and learned how to be evil colonialists on Irish soil. They took that model and exported it around the world. As Ireland fell, so fell the globe, under the boot of the British Empire. Now, Britain's baton has been passed to America. That's why the world is the way it is. So, let's not be glib about the Troubles, my friend, because Ireland's chains are the chains we all wear."

"My friend here isn't totally hopeless," Byron said conspiratorially to Cormack. "He knows his Irish drinking songs, if you'd like to hear him regale us."

"We need a full pub for that kinda thing," Cormack said.

"He's not interested," I said.

Byron slapped me on the shoulder. "Come on! Give us 'Patriot Games.'"

I eyed Cormack warily. "No, anything but that one." I drank down my amaretto, gestured for another one, and launched into my best mimicry of the Clancy Brothers and Tommy Makem singing "Jug of Punch." After a verse, Byron joined in. Another verse later, Cormack surrendered and added his voice to what was now a trio. We finished loud and strong, and Cormack chuckled. "That's not a bad mimic job. I have the same vinyl. But you should sing from the heart and not just do impressions and Irish accents," he advised me.

"There's a lot of things I need to do from the heart," I admitted.

"That song rules with an iron fist!" yelled Byron.

"Alright, now," Cormack said. "I'm not surprised me and your friend know the lyrics to this song, but what's with Mr. Italian American knowing Irish drinking songs so well?"

"Dad loves them," I said. "And most of my best friends growing up have been Irish."

Byron thumped his chest. "Like me!"

I looked at him sideways. "I thought you were Scottish. Your whole *Braveheart* thing?"

"Half and half," Byron said. "Believe it or not, I'm a direct descendant of Brian Boru."

"You, too?" I asked. "I think James told me he's one, also."

Cormack raised his hand. "I, too, am a direct descendant of Brian Boru."

"No way!" I said. "Would you believe, I'm a direct descendant of Giuseppe Garibaldi?"

"You are?" asked Byron.

"No, I'm just kidding."

Cormack frowned. "Fine. Make fun. But I really am a direct descendant of Brian Boru."

"That Brian Boru guy must have been some playa."

Byron raised his Guinness to toast me. "Not half the playa you're gonna be in the nursing home when you get old."

I clinked my amaretto glass against his Guinness. "You said it. That's gonna be my prime. When I'm eighty-five, I'm doing all the Golden Girls in my retirement community in Ocala, Florida! I just have to spend all the years in-between now and then watching the same twenty-six seasons of *Doctor Who* serials on endless loop. Got a lot of time to kill!"

Cormack gestured to the Wonder Woman t-shirt I had on. "I'm not sure that attire bodes well for your future career as a geriatric philanderer."

I was very proud of my brand-new t-shirt, which featured a striking José Luis García-López portrait of Diana from the cover of last year's *Wonder Woman* #118. I had changed into it just after Evelyn gave me my walking papers and wore it in honor of Byron taking me out to the pub to cheer me up. "Wonder Woman is my buddy. Even if nobody else loves me, Diana does."

"I've got bad news for you," said Cormack. "She's a lesbian. No matter how much you may want her, you can't have her."

I shrugged. "So, what else is new?"

Byron interjected. "Just so you know, Cormack, Damien's level of affection for a woman is not limited by his estimation of the likelihood she'll go to bed with him."

"A damn good thing, too, *for obvious reasons*. Ha!" I looked sideways at Byron. "You're sounding like me."

"You're a bad influence," Byron grumbled, good-naturedly.

I smiled. "I love Diana. Now, you may ask, what percentage of each of C.S. Lewis' 'four loves' do I feel for her? Affection, Friendship, Romantic, or Charity? Do I draw a pie chart? Who cares? It's nobody's business but mine. 'Sides, I don't think much on it, or worry much about it. Neither should you, she, or anyone. That's my final word on the subject. Boom!"

Byron turned serious. "Okay, let's have it. What happened with Evelyn Krueger?"

I grunted. "I don't wanna talk about that in front of Cormack." Cormack laughed.

"Come on," Byron said. "Cormack doesn't care."

"He's right," said Cormack. "I don't care."

I laughed, despite myself. "Oh, you know how it is: I took a rowboat to China to see her, but she sent me away because she was too busy doing her laundry."

"I want to know what happened to you, not Matthew Wilder!" Byron yelled.

"She thinks I'm like Chauncey Gardner: a guy who grew up watching too much television who poses as being wise by quoting stuff he saw on VHS at an impressionable age. I'm deceptively charming because I borrow the charisma of better people, like Groucho Marx and Bill Murray, and quote them without attribution. Also, I am not really dating her because I love her, but because I'm a writer looking for material for a future book or screenplay."

Byron banged his fist on the table. "Where does she get all that shit from?"

I stared at my own fingernails. They were bitten down as far as they could go, so there was nothing left for me to gnaw on. "Insightful and unnerving. Still, I'd like to think she's being a little hard on me. I hope she's not God's prosecution attorney when I stand before the pearly gates, let me tell you. I'd have a hell of a time refuting any of that."

Byron growled. "I don't know how *anyone* could accuse you of being insincere or phony. What else did she say? You're not enough into Spider-Man? You're too into football and Tex-Mex? You don't take a strong enough stance against fraternities? You're soft on Bill Clinton?"

"Yeah, but it is possible she has some kind of point. I can't dismiss it all outright."

"You mean you aren't *really* living your life? You're doing research for a screenplay?"

"Of course, I'm living my life!" I chuckled. "Still, I understand why she's worried. I am a writer. I gave her a 'That's a great idea!' look, and she almost punched me. Then I said to her, 'If I ever write a story about us, I'll protect your identity by naming you after a villain from a horror movie. Or *Masters of the Universe*. Or both.' This did not reassure her. Of course, I've been in a lot of creative writing classes with short stories that are clearly just revenge hatchet jobs on a recent ex. I better be fairer to her than that, or my story will be just like any one of those. I'll just be writing: 'My girl kissed an Italian paratrooper and all I got was this dumb t-shirt' stories."

Byron blinked. "What was that about an Italian paratrooper?"

"Never mind about the paratrooper. The important thing is, I don't want to just mock her in print, you know? I gotta be fair. If I do decide to write my heart-wrenching memoirs."

Cormack chuckled. "Heart-wrenching memoirs? You look like someone who's had the easiest life ever! Has anything *ever* gone wrong for you? Big softie leading a charmed life!"

Byron laughed. "Oh, just mock her. Go ahead. Serves her right for messing with you. You really going to write this screenplay she's prophesized?"

I shook my head. "Be a boring fucking movie. Tobey Maguire wandering New York and Italy not getting laid in . . . drumroll . . . *The Forty-Year Old Virgin*! Just imagine a cinematic masterpiece produced by Harvey Weinstein, written by Richard Russo, and directed by Noah Baumbach. A celebration of First World Problems at their finest. Also, a slam dunk for the National Organization of Women's 2016 Film of the Year award for fostering much-needed sympathy for the underfucked straight white man."

"This is the world's smallest violin playing just for you," said Cormack.

I laughed. "Exactly! High-stakes drama. Who cares about the Armenian genocide, child-brides, and female genital mutilation when Damien doesn't have a widdle girl of his very own!"

"Could be a great art film," Byron said. "*Yakking in New Yawk.* Put John Turturro and Parker Posey in it!"

"You know who Jack Black is?" Cormack asked me. "He could be you."

Byron and I shook our heads.

"Never mind," said Cormack. "He hasn't made it big yet."

The fancasting reminded me of something disturbing. "Evelyn also said this: 'I bet that every time you meet someone new, you think of an actor they look like who could play them in a movie made about your life. I bet the first time you met Byron, you thought he looked like Billy Baldwin, and the first time you met me, you thought, "Oh, look! Dowdy Claudia Schiffer!"' That was frighteningly accurate. It made me feel like I'm a bad person."

Byron scratched his chin. "One: You're not the only one who does that. Two: The reason she was able to pin down who you'd cast for us so accurately is we actually do look a lot like Billy Baldwin and Claudia Schiffer. So, what she said isn't so much shocking, as true."

Cormack gave Byron a thumbs up. "You do have a Billy thing going on."

"More importantly, did you get any action before she bounced you?" Byron asked me.

"I suppose." I drank more amaretto.

"Which base?" Byron asked.

I waved him off. "I don't like sports."

Cormack chuckled. "First or second. Tops."

"The coolest part of our relationship was when she serenaded me with the theme to *Octopussy*," I said, lying brazenly, and not expecting to be believed.

Byron leaned towards Cormack. "I say second."

I punched the bar. "No, it was first! It was first. Let's move on, huh? Please?"

"Okay," said Byron.

My mood turned the bleakest it had been for many years. "Byron, what major historical milestone do you think will happen first? A) The polar ice caps melt. B) America gets a cool, Sidney-Poitier-reminiscent Black president. C) I finally get to have sex."

Byron didn't laugh. "That's some rough shit, man. I'm hoping those things happen in the opposite order you said them in, for all sorts of reasons."

"My money is on the cool Black guy," I said. "Mostly because social justice is important to me. And if Black people have to wait for me to get laid before they're allowed to have a Black man in the White House, they're looking to wait a hell of a long time. At this rate? 2037!"

"You just picked the wrong girl to chase. You need to ask out more people and pick better possible matches."

I sighed. "Evelyn really is a cool customer. I wonder if it's because she's German. I'm better off chasing after a passionate Italian girl, right?"

Cormack tutted. "Oh, no. That would be a colossal waste of time. Italian women are very difficult to get into bed. They want you to meet their families first."

I laughed. "Ironically, I'm difficult to get into bed! Just ask the girls in my art class. Ha!"

"What you boys need," Cormack continued, "is to go to the Netherlands. The liberalism there is fantastic. Women open their legs over there for nothing. You can't walk down the street at night without getting laid six ways from Sunday by total strangers. Here? Forget about it. I've had so little sex here these last few months, I'm chomping at the bit to go back to the Netherlands. And I thought I'd seen the last of Italy when I opened this place last year, but we had that emergency and I had to come racing back."

"What emergency?" Byron asked.

"I go around the world opening genuine Irish pubs in all sorts of countries. I opened this one and everything seemed fine. Then we found out Italians don't know how to drink. They look at alcohol like Americans look at soda: a drink at mealtime. They don't go to pubs. So, I have to come back to change the culture. And I get a great idea: I'll lower the price of the large beer to match the price of the medium. Trick them into drinking more. Guess what fucking happens?"

I said, "They ordered the medium drink."

Byron looked stricken, "They didn't!"

Cormack's frown couldn't get any deeper. "They order a *medium* drink! I tell them a large is the same price. *They stick with the medium!* What's wrong with Italians? No beer. No sex. Lotsa worshipping the Virgin Mary. Lotsa Saint Sebastian getting penetrated by arrows artwork. A whole country of repressed lunatics whose sexual frustration makes them violent!"

"You're not totally wrong," I said. "Though we did produce Casanova, so I just thought we were very physical people. Earthy. All about food, sex, and fisticuffs."

Cormack shook his head. "Italy. Who needs it? Go to the Netherlands. Free education. Free healthcare. Full employment. Pussy for everyone. Wages of socialism right there."

I handed my empty glass back for more amaretto. "Sign me up."

"I thought you were a Republican," Byron said.

"Free education? Free healthcare? Full employment? Pussy for everyone? I'm officially changing teams. I always suspected I was an anarcho-socialist. Now I know I am. The number one reason I'm unhappy is capitalism. I like to be a nice, educated, and peaceful person, and live in a beautiful, unpolluted environment. Capitalism encourages people to be cruel, stupid, warlike, and live in a polluted, impoverished hellscape. Well, fuck that noise."

Byron looked thoughtful. "You're officially all leftist now, huh?"

"I can't go back now. Last night, Pat Buchanan got footage of Hillary and me having sex on the steps of the Lincoln Memorial. The secret it out."

Byron groaned. "You and your weird dreams. That is so disgusting."

"Odd I'm dreaming about Hillary instead of Emma Thompson, but it makes some sense."

"You know who the first socialist was in history?" Cormack asked with a wry grin.

"Who?" Byron asked.

"Jesus Christ," Cormack and I said at the same time.

Byron raised his Guinness in the air, "Clothe the naked, feed the hungry, heal the sick, and turn the other cheek."

Cormack nodded in approval. "Now that's a real toast, right there."

"I do think I have two problems," I declared. "The first problem is America is too conservative. If it were a socialist country, I'd have a girlfriend by now. Capitalism is killing my sex life. Everyone is broke, everyone is angry, everyone is stupid, men and women hate each other, the races hate each other, the religions hate each other, and everyone has a gun, and no one is fucking any more. If America ever goes socialist, it'll be like heaven on Earth."

"Are you sure that's the problem?" Byron asked. "Because if you decide that, in your head, that lets you off the hook to even try, and you'll just give up. It is way simpler than that. Ask out more people. Stop cherry-picking, and picking rotten cherries, to boot."

"Well, you just put the curse of the Cat People on me! That's not gonna help. Making me fall for married broads! If anything happens to me remotely like what happened to Lancelot, I'm holding you personally responsible."

Byron took a sip from his Guinness. "You can't blame me for Arwen and Marina. They got married before I put the curse on you."

"How's about you take it off me anyway?"

Byron considered the option. "Nah."

"Well, fuck you, too. I bet my whole life, the same shit is going to happen to me over, and over, and over again. I'll be like John McClane in *Die Hard 2*. Every Christmas, I have to rescue Bonnie Bedelia from a new set of terrorists. Every year, I'll meet a new dream chick, and there will always be a new Rolf. Rolf is forever. Rolf is eternal. Rolf, Rolf, Rolf, Rolf, Rolf!"

Byron had an epiphany: "Hey! Remember who plays the main

villain in *Die Hard 2*?"

I raised my amaretto glass in the air. "Franco Nero!"

Byron pounded back the rest on his Guinness and slammed the empty pint glass down on the bar. "Fucking Franco Nero!"

"New Guinness?" asked Cormack.

"Hells, yeah!" Byron nodded. "Listen, dude, just try harder and go out on the town more instead of staying in and watching movies. It isn't rocket science."

"Who's gonna like me?" I asked, hopelessly. "My own people don't like me. I'm not a real Italian and all real Italians can smell that on me. That's the real stench. Italians can't stand the smell of me, and no other race wants to go near me because I'm not one of them. New Yorkers are segregated by race. The Chinese stay in Chinatown, the Blacks stay in Harlem, the Italians are in Little Italy, the Hispanics are in Jackson Heights, the Germans are in Wall Street, the Jews have their designated neighborhoods — like Willowbrook — and I'm not at home in any of them. The walls are up and I have no way in. I hate walls. I fucking hate them. But there's walls everywhere and they're all closing in on me. Now, I've heard rumors of people successfully intermarrying and dating outside their people, but I don't know if I've ever actually seen more than one or two mixed couples with my own eyes. I'm starting to doubt their existence. People seem to stay with their own people, and I have no people! I'm doomed to be alone, because I'm a fake Italian and I've never successfully asked anyone out from any other ethnicity."

A voice came from the corner of the bar behind Byron and me. "May I ask what a 'fake Italian' is?" The speaker was a kindly, wizened old man with unkempt white hair, wire-rimmed glasses, and a closed-lipped, smiling face.

How long had he been there? "I'm fake. I don't know the language. I live on Staten Island, which has more Italians on it than anywhere in the world but here, but I'm not like them and they don't like me. Is it because they're Sicilian and I'm Neapolitan? Am I too German? Too middle-class? We're all Catholic! All Southern Italians! We should feel more solidarity than division. Why is it that I feel so separated from them?"

"What separates you?" the old man asked himself. "A language, for one thing. Italy was never meant to be one country. Venetians are one people. Florentines another. Neapolitans. Sicilians. Each group has its own languages, histories, foods, and personalities."

"But what about efforts to unify Italy? What about Toscano?"

"Toscano?" the old man asked. "I guess we can give the Florentines credit for creating that common tongue because of the beauty of the literature of Dante. I'll give them that. Of course, I don't like to. I don't like the Florentines. But Toscano is more of a literary and political exercise than a real unifying language. The Italians are as divided as ever."

"Really?" I asked.

"You can't think in terms of Italians or Italian Americans. There's no such thing as Italians or Italian Americans. At best, you're Neapolitan American and the others you're talking about not relating to are Sicilian Americans. You can't expect to have the same cultural values and personality as them. You're not them. I'm not saying you're better than them or they're better than you. You're just not as similar as you think you are. You can't expect to feel an instant connection because you all like similar imported meats, cheeses, and pasta from Italy."

I rubbed my jaw, thinking furiously about what he was saying. "I think the one thing I have in common with Staten Island Italians is we all like salami."

"But that isn't enough, is it? In the end, it is just something you buy in a store. It tastes great. It's a product. It isn't your heart or their hearts. Which of you is the real Italian? Are only Neapolitans real Italians, and the rest fake Italians? Are only Sicilian Americans real Italian Americans and the rest fake Italian Americans? Who's 'real'? Who's 'fake'? Who's to say?"

I was at a loss. "I don't know."

The old man chuckled. "I just told you. There's no such thing as a 'real' Italian. And if there were, you would make as good a claim to being a 'real' Italian as any, if not a better one."

"That is very interesting," Byron interjected.

"I've got no horse in this race," Cormack said.

Byron gestured to the old man. "It is still a fundamentally interesting conversation."

I asked Cormack for a refill on my amaretto. When I got one, I turned around on my stool to better face the old man. "How can you know I have a better claim to being Italian than most?"

"You're an immigrant," the old man said. "Or you're descended from immigrants. You have the blood of immigrants in you. Their adventurous genes. Their thirst for a better life. Their drive to succeed. Their brazenness. Immigrants are always the best of their people because they are the ones with the guts to say, 'Enough is enough. I won't stand for this treatment anymore. I'm taking myself and my family out of this hell, and I'm going someplace new to build a fresh life for myself. I refuse to live under these circumstances for a minute longer.' Think of the bravery it takes to make a stand like that! Who has the guts to leave their homeland? Go someplace where they don't speak the language or have the same religion to forge a new life? To start a new family tree? Rewrite history? Only immigrants and refugees have those guts. Immigrants and refugees are more likely than anyone else to tell evil authority figures to go fuck themselves. That's you. Your genes. Your blood. Your legacy."

Outside of a couple of platitudes about heroism attached very specifically to Ellis Island immigrants in civics class or during a tour of Ellis Island itself, I had never once heard a kind word spoken about refugees or immigrants in my entire life. This old man's perspective was astonishing, refreshing, and inspiring. I felt a swell of pride for my immigrant ancestors. "In America, we are taught that immigrants are too pathetic to love. They're the dirty refuse from every other country. Uneducated, diseased welfare cases for the government to deal with. More mouths to feed that drain limited American resources. Terrorists and criminals from shithole countries. We are never, ever told they are brave, or honorable, or noble. And now we have a new 24-hour news channel dedicated solely to smearing Blacks and immigrants. It just debuted, and it is a God damn nightmare."

The old Italian man who spoke perfect English without an accent shook his head with disgust. "The people who say those things are evil racists. They aren't worth listening to. They have an agenda. White supremacy. Are you a white supremacist?"

"Absolutely not!"

"Then don't think in terms of 'real' and 'fake' people. People aren't 'fake.'"

I arched my eyebrow at Byron. "Check it out! I'm *not* 'fake.'"

"You're not a fake Italian," Byron said. "And your emotions aren't fake either. I don't know what Evelyn is smoking. Must have spent some time with Bongo Guy. Oh, yeah! I meant to ask you: since when is Bongo Guy going out with Tuesday? I just saw them together!"

"Are they? I think I know. I'll tell you later." I returned my attention to the old man. "That's reassuring. I suppose I just want to feel some sort of connection. Like, I wish I spoke the language better, at the very least."

"Oh, you don't speak the language? Oh, that is so sad." The old man mimicked crying and then stopped the mock tears abruptly. "Who cares?"

My eyes widened. "Who cares? Isn't the language all that matters? That's what separates the big time Italians from the people just messing around, right?"

The old man waved away the questions, disgusted. "You're still caught up in the Real Italian/Fake Italian dichotomy. It's nonsense. Let me tell you something. The average Italian who lives in Italy now and never left it — I don't care if they're Florentine, Milanese, or Venetian — does not have half the guts of the average Sicilian American, Neapolitan American or Friulian American. The average Italian didn't have the guts to leave when things got bad in Italy. They stayed and sweat it out because they were too scared to leave. The American branches of the Italian people did have those guts. They left. So even if they Americanized, and enculturated, and forgot how to speak Italian, they are still the boldest and best of us. You may not speak Italian, but you are the best of Italy in your blood, in your passion, in your creativity. All American immigrants are the bravest of their people. They should all be celebrated. You are the best of Italy and the best of America. Don't ever let anyone tell you that you are a fake American or fake Italian. There's no such thing. Anyone who tells you any different is a liar."

Cormack murmured to Byron, "Okay, I admit it. At some point, this got very interesting."

Byron nodded.

"Wow," I breathed.

"So," the old man said, "you may have just had a sad breakup, but you are not unlovable. You just haven't found the right girl. But finding someone to love is hard enough to do without putting on top of that pressure all these cultural anxieties that do not matter. 'How can I ask this Italian girl out since she speaks the language and I don't and she's a "real" Italian and I'm not?' Who needs nonsense like that rattling around in their heads? If that burden is holding you back, discard it. Purge it from your thoughts. And if you want to date someone who is not Italian — Black, Jewish, Russian, Inuit — don't worry if their people, their family, their friends think you are not worthy of them because you have the wrong religion, ethnicity, or political party. If you meet the right girl, you will click, and all that nonsense will go away. Because it is all nonsense."

Unless they stand to inherit a chocolate factory. But, yes. I drank down my next amaretto. "This is really refreshing."

The old man smiled because he wasn't sure if his words or the drink were refreshing. "In the end, we are all human and we are all going to die. We just need to be kind to one another and love one another while we are here. The rest is just noise and jingoism. Get it out of your head and don't let it screw you up. Yes, New York is segregated. That is particularly galling since it is supposed to be the seat of freedom and tolerance in the world. But that's not your fault. Be better than that and don't let it hold you back. Disregard the clannishness. Don't allow anyone to define you and circumscribe you. Be yourself. Don't worry about being a 'real' American or a 'real' Italian or a 'real' Catholic or a 'real' college student or a 'real' whatever. Just be you. Imposter syndrome is artificially inserted into working-class people to keep them in their place. Forget about imposter syndrome. It goes hand-in-hand with racism and class warfare. Evil imperials make everyone less wealthy than them experience imposter syndrome so they can feel superior and hold onto power."

"Fuhgeddaboudit," I murmured. "I hate evil imperialist rich people."

"Fucking pieces of shit!" Byron roared.

Cormack reached down and grabbed a fistful of his own crotch through his pants. "I got their imposter syndrome right here. Those rich fuckers can speak into the mic."

"And once you are comfortable in your own skin, you won't stink of need," continued the old man. "You will have a new confidence, and that is something that women find attractive. You be you. Love will follow. But if you hate yourself, if you really think you are a 'fake' Italian, you will never be happy and you will never be able to make anyone else happy."

I placed my glass on the counter and stood up. "That makes a whole lot of sense."

"I've been around a while," the old man said. "I've lived in Italy for twenty years, in America for twenty years, in Singapore for twenty years, and Antigua for twenty years. People are the same all the world over. The good people and the bad. There's always racists running around telling people they aren't human. Our job is to tell them to fuck off and die so the rest of us can live our lives in peace and love each other."

"That's some profound shit right there," Cormack proclaimed.

"Amen," said Byron.

I walked up to the old man with my hand outstretched. "I'm Damien."

The old man took my hand and shook it firmly. "I'm Pietro."

"It is a genuine pleasure to meet you," Byron said to Pietro.

"I'm really glad you came in tonight to meet these guys, Mr. Capaldi," Cormack said.

"Me, too," said Pietro.

"I think you may have just solved the defining problem of my life for me," I said.

"Only if you truly believe what I just told you and act on it," Pietro said.

"I intend to," I said with surprisingly firm, clear-eyed resolve — surprising considering how drunk I was by now.

"Good."

I looked at Pietro again. "You really mean it?"

"What?"

"There's no such thing as a 'fake Italian,' but if there were such a thing as a 'real Italian,' I'd be an ideal candidate? Because I'm from immigrant stock, and the immigrants represent the best of the people they come from?"

"Your ancestors left their homeland and struck out on their own. The rest were too chicken. They stayed behind. You have the DNA of adventurers in your veins."

I beamed at Byron. "I have the DNA of an adventurer."

"And I have the DNA of a Scottish swashbuckler!" Byron cried. "I knew I was descended from William Wallace!"

"You two are joking, but I meant every word I said," Pietro cut in.

"Oh, I'm not joking," Byron replied. "And neither is Damien." Byron nodded at Pietro. "Thank you for fixing Damien. He's been a nervous wreck for years."

"I've been a nervous wreck all my life," I replied.

Pietro smiled. "Non fa niente. I'm happy to help."

"I can't believe I bumped into you!" I whooped. "It feels like Jesus or Gandalf or Doctor Who sent you to me to fix me. You're my deus ex machina! If this were in a movie, I wouldn't believe it. On the other hand, I was due for some good luck, for God's sake. In coming to this bar tonight — thanks to Byron's annoying insistence — I got to meet you and have this huge, cathartic breakthrough! I was finally the right guy in the right place and at the right time!" I eyed Pietro suspiciously. "In all seriousness: Are you *actually* Doctor Who? Like, are you really a Time Lord from the planet Gallifrey in the flesh?"

"No," said Pietro. "But it's nice of you to think so. Besides, I don't think an Italian has ever played the Doctor."

"Hope springs eternal!" I laughed. "Anyway, more importantly, who needs counseling when you're around to talk to!"

Byron's amused concern for me was turning slowly into relief and pride. I was drunker than he had ever seen me, and yet I stood up straighter than I had before. I spoke more firmly and naturally in my baritone. I might have even been developing a confident strut. "Well? How do you feel, right now, Damien? You look like you're in a much better mood."

"How do I feel?" I flashed Byron the brightest, toothiest smile I had ever given. "Fantastic! Cormack! I need to celebrate! And I need to buy my friends Byron and Pietro some booze. You with me?"

"Alright!" cried Byron.

Pietro inclined his head in thanks. "I'd be honored to share a drink with you all."

"Sure, sure," Cormack laughed. "What would you like?"

I remembered that Evelyn had no time for my constant movie references. She thought that, each time I made them, I was hiding behind pop culture and undercutting the genuine emotional power of the experience. Still, at that moment, I found the perfect movie to quote to express the joy I was feeling: *Withnail and I.*

I stood heroically at the center of the bar and bellowed cheerfully at Cormack: "'We want the finest wines available to humanity! We want them here, and we want them now!'"

EPILOGUE
Thank you for my Freedom, Damien!
And Happy Graduation Day!

The following article appeared on the front page of *The Livingston County News* on May 25, 1997.

Beloved Bear Statue Feared Stolen
from Historic Geneseo Fountain

By Marsha Keller

Emmeline the bear has disappeared from her perch atop the light pole of the water fountain on Main Street.

Geneseo Police Chief Rick Bogosian said the statue disappeared sometime between 2 and 4 a.m. Police have made no suspects known to the press yet.

Residents of the village of Geneseo were distressed to wake up to the news that the beloved bear had gone missing. Eyes red with crying, Maude Montalbano, a lifelong resident of Geneseo, talked of how Emmeline had been a friend to her and her family all their lives. "That bear is Geneseo. We can't believe it's gone. I'm praying for her quick and safe return."

Built in 1888, the bear and the fountain have been the centerpiece of Geneseo village since the Grover Cleveland Administration. The bear is named after Emmeline Austin Wadsworth, honoring a beloved member of the Wadsworths, a prominent local family.

If the original Emmeline is not recovered, local historical societies have exact measurements of the bear and illustrations of its design. This means a replica may be constructed to replace the original. The police, however, say this will not be necessary. "We will find Emmeline, and we will find the one who stole her," Bogosian vowed.

According to Bogosian, the thief presumably used an acetylene torch to burn the bronze statuette free of the light pole it "clutched." Mysteriously, the torch left no visible scarring on the pole itself. Authorities remain unclear how the bear could have been removed while leaving behind a seemingly untouched pole surface. Bogosian refused to comment on this phenomenon.

The timing of the theft has inspired some to offer up supernatural explanations for Emmeline's disappearance last night, of all nights. Lifelong Geneseo resident and SUNY Genseo graduate Joe Ferrero said, "Yesterday was graduation. A virgin must have finally graduated from Geneseo. I can't believe the legend is true! I always thought it was just a joke."

According to Dr. Leland Valancourt, a history professor at SUNY Geneseo, local folklore contends that the bear will only leave its perch on the fountain and run away if an undergraduate earns a bachelor's degree without becoming sexually experienced first. "It's total nonsense, of course," said Valancourt. "An excuse for students to pressure one another into an intimacy they are not emotionally prepared to experience yet. While I do not, personally, believe Emmeline came to life, I do think there is some connection between graduation yesterday and the bear disappearing overnight. This legend is being slyly referenced for as-yet-unknown reasons. I believe this is either a fraternity prank, or the thief is an eccentric with a bizarre sense of humor."

Sonny Verde, proprietor of Sonny's Music, claims to have been the only eyewitness on Main Street at 2:37 am. According to Verde, he had just completed an inventory of his music and locked up his store, when he witnessed an incredible event: Emmeline shook herself awake, released her grip from the lamppost, and jumped down onto the street. Verde said, "It was the most amazing thing I ever saw! Then she opened her mouth and spoke. She said something like, 'Thank you for my Freedom! And Happy Graduation Day!' I think she thanked a specific student by name, but I didn't catch it. Then she ran straight past me, down the street, whooping and laughing. Right before she disappeared into the woods at the end of the street, she yelled, 'Freedom!' one more time, and she laughed joyously up at the stars."

ACKNOWLEDGEMENTS

I owe particular thanks to Jeanetta Calhoun Mish for her editing of the manuscript, as well as for her expertise, patience, and generosity.

I am also grateful to the following people for their feedback and moral support: Fred Alsberg, Umapagan Ampikaipakan, Tom Bierowski, Lauren Brown, Jim Buss, Erin Byrne, Stephen Burgess, Melinda Burgess, Bryan Cardinale-Powell, Joe Caputo, Steve Cerulli, Rick Coloccia, James Cooper, Keira DiPaolo, Quentin DiPaolo, Stacey DiPaolo, Kathy Downey, Gracie Eggleston, Jeremy Evert, Elyssa Faison, Michele Fazio, Jessica Femiani, Heather Hogarty Ferrero, Joe Ferrero, Jamie Feuerbach, Joanna DiPasquale Feuerbach, Tracy Floreani, Fred L. Gardaphe, Christopher González, Nicholas Grosso, Rachel Hall, Erik Heine, Brooke Hessler, Kate E Hirsch, Retha-Louise Malherbe Hofmeyr, Dennis Jowaisas, Heather Katz, Abigail Keegan, Marsha Keller, Conner Kirk, Jennifer Lapekas, Colleen LaVigne, Denise Landrum-Geyer, Anthony Lioi, Kelley Logan, Stephanie Lynch-Loscalzo, Diana Maltz, Elizabeth Matteo, Jessica Maucione, Nolan Meditz, Tom Molinaro, Jenna Moreci, John Kenneth Muir, Bill Murphy, Frederic Murray, Rebecca Wisor Muszynski, Taylor Orgeron, Samuele F. S. Pardini, Kristin Pitanza, Cherie Wibben Rankin, Allen H. Redmon, Marguerite Reed, Jill Rini, Rob Roensch, Abbie Rose, JoAnne Ruvoli, Jessica Salmans, Marlene A. Schiwy, Mitchell Sherry, Amanda Smith, Amy Soppet, James South, Wayne Stein, Brian Stevens, Janine Surmick, Brian Trent, Joe Varga, Jerry Vigna, Elwood Watson, Jamie Williams, Craig Wolf, Rob Wolf, Tom Wrobleski, and Karen DeMent Youmans.

ABOUT THE AUTHOR

MARC DiPAOLO has written three nonfiction books: *Fire and Snow: Climate Fiction from the Inklings to* Game of Thrones (2018), *War, Politics and Superheroes* (2011), and *Emma Adapted: Jane Austen's Heroine from Book to Film* (2007). He has appeared in the documentaries *Robert Kirkman's Secret History of Comics* (2017) and *Geek, and You Shall Find* (2019), and is Associate Professor of English at Southwestern Oklahoma State University.

VIA FOLIOS

A refereed book series dedicated to the culture of Italians and Italian Americans.

CPSIA information can be obtained
at www.ICGtesting.com
Printed in the USA
FSHW010151180421
80489FS